The INGOLDSBY LEGENDS OR MIRTH & MARVELS

BY THOMAS INGOLDSBY Esqre

ILLUSTRATATED BY ARTHUR RACKHAM A.R.W.S.

"Hey! up the chimney, lass! Hey after you!"

Prefatory Note
by the Illustrator

In 1898 Messrs. Dent and Co. first published the " Ingoldsby Legends," with about one hundred illustrations of mine. This book has met with a very satisfactory reception, but the publishers have felt with me that, with the addition of some new drawings, a careful overhauling would make it worthy of publication in a more important form, in which greater prominence could be given to the illustrations by better and larger reproductions, including a greater number of illustrations in colour.

To this end the following has been done :

The frontispiece and the coloured illustration facing page 508 have been specially drawn, and all the other illustrations in colour have been worked on to a considerable extent, and specially coloured for this edition. A few illustrations in the earlier edition have been omitted, and in their place have been added those facing page 254 and on pages vi, 25, 37, 316, 320 and 333.

Many of the pen drawings have been reconsidered and worked on again—those which have been worked on to any great extent being now signed with both dates, 1898 and 1907. Of the rest, reproductions on a larger scale have been made in all but a few cases, and the text has been revised and entirely reset for this edition.

ARTHUR RACKHAM.

HAMPSTEAD, 1907.

Publishers' Note

IT has been the desire of the Publishers to here present the " Ingoldsby Legends " in something like an " Edition Définitive de Luxe."

It has been carefully read with the edition finally corrected by the Author, and has been re-set in a fine type, while Mr. Arthur Rackham, in his hundred illustrations, has entered heartily into the wild humour and phantasy of this favourite old classic.

The coloured pictures, which owe so much to their delicacy of tint and fine line drawing, have all been reproduced by the Graphic Photo Engraving Co. in the latest and highest development of the three-colour work, and the Publishers owe them thanks for their great care in copying these originals and for their adequate and admirable results. The colour printing has been done by Messrs. McFarlane and Erskine of Edinburgh, and the text by the Ballantyne Press of London, to whom also the Publishers wish to acknowledge their obligations.

List of Contents

FIRST SERIES

SECOND SERIES

THIRD SERIES

MISCELLANEOUS POEMS

List of Illustrations

COLOURED DRAWINGS

xi

List of Illustrations

Preface to First Series

To Richard Bentley, Esq.

My Dear Sir,—

You wish me to collect into one single volume certain rambling extracts from our family memoranda, many of which have already appeared in the pages of your Miscellany. At the same time you tell me that doubts are entertained in certain quarters as to the authenticity of their details.

Now with respect to their genuineness, the old oak chest, in which the originals are deposited, is not more familiar to my eyes than it is to your own ; and if its contents have any value at all, it consists in the strict veracity of the facts they record.

To convince the most incredulous, I can only add, that should business—pleasure is out of the question—ever call them into the neighbourhood of Folkestone, let them take the high road from Canterbury to Dover till they reach the eastern extremity of Barham Downs. Here a beautiful green lane diverging abruptly to the right will carry them through the Oxenden plantations and the unpretending village of Denton, to the foot of a very respectable hill—as hills go in this part of Europe. On reaching its summit let them look straight before them —and if among the hanging woods which crown the opposite side of the valley, they cannot distinguish an antiquated Manor-house of Elizabethan architecture, with its gable ends, stone stanchions, and tortuous chimneys rising above the surrounding trees, why—the sooner they procure a pair of Dollond's patent spectacles the better.

If, on the contrary, they can manage to descry it, and, proceeding some five or six furlongs through the avenue, will ring at the Lodgegate—they cannot mistake the stone lion with the Ingoldsby escutcheon (Ermine, a saltire engrailed Gules) in his paws—they will be received with a hearty old English welcome.

The papers in question having been written by different parties, and at various periods, I have thought it advisable to reduce the more ancient of them into a comparatively modern phraseology, and to make my collateral ancestor, Father John, especially, " deliver himself like a man of this world " ; Mr. Maguire, indeed, is the only Gentleman who, in his account of the late Coronation, retains his own rich vernacular.

As to arrangement, I shall adopt the sentiment expressed by the Constable of Bourbon four centuries ago, *teste* Shakspeare, one which seems to become more fashionable every day,

> " The Devil take all order ! !—I'll to the throng ! "

Believe me to be,

My dear Sir,

Yours, most indubitably and immeasurably,

THOMAS INGOLDSBY.

l'Appington Everard,
Jan. 20*th*, 1840.

Preface to the Second Edition

To Richard Bentley, Esq.

MY DEAR SIR,—

I should have replied sooner to your letter, but that the last three days in January are, as you are aware, always dedicated, at the Hall, to an especial *battue*, and the old house is full of shooting-jackets, shot-belts, and " double Joes." Even the women wear percussion caps, and your favourite (?) Rover, who, you may remember, examined the calves of your legs with such suspicious curiosity at Christmas, is as pheasant-mad as if he were a biped, instead of being a genuine four-legged scion of the Blenheim breed. I have managed, however, to avail myself of a lucid interval in the general hallucination (how the rain *did* come down on Monday !), and as you tell me the excellent friend whom you are in the habit of styling " a Generous and Englightened Public " has emptied your shelves of the first edition, and " asks for more," why, I agree with you, it *would* be a want of *respect* to that very *respectable* personification, when furnishing him with a further supply, not to en-deavour at least to amend my faults, which are few, and your own, which are more numerous. I have, therefore, gone to work *con amore*, supplying occasionally on my own part a deficient note, or elucidatory stanza, and on yours knocking out, without remorse, your superfluous *i's*, and now and then eviscerating your *colon*.

My duty to our illustrious friend thus performed, I have a crow to pluck with him,—Why will he persist—as you tell me he does persist—in calling me by all sorts of names but those to which I am entitled by birth and baptism—my " Sponsorial and Patronymic appellations," as Dr. Pangloss has it ?—Mrs. Malaprop complains, and with justice, of an " assault upon her parts of speech : " but to attack one's very existence—to deny that one *is* a person *in esse*, and scarcely to admit that one *may be* a person *in posse*, is tenfold cruelty ;—" it is pressing to death, whipping, and hanging ! "—let me entreat all such likewise to remember that, as Shakspeare beautifully expresses himself elsewhere—

I give his words as quoted by a very worthy Baronet in a neighbouring county, when protesting against a defamatory placard at a general election—

> " Who steals my purse steals stuff !—
> 'Twas mine—'tisn't his—nor nobody elses !
> But he who runs away with my GOOD NAME,
> Robs me of what does not do him any good,
> And makes me deuced poor ! ! " *

In order utterly to squabash and demolish every gainsayer, I had thought, at one time, of asking my old and esteemed friend, Richard

Lane, to crush them at once with his magic pencil, and to transmit my features to posterity, where all his works are sure to be " delivered according to the direction ; " but somehow the noble-looking profiles which he has recently executed of the Kemble family put me a little out of conceit with my own, while the undisguised amusement which my " Mephistopheles Eyebrow," as he termed it, afforded him, in the " full face," induced me to lay aside the design. Besides, my dear Sir, since, as has well been observed, " there never was a married man yet who had not somebody remarkably like him walking about town," it is a thousand to one but my lineaments might, after all, out of sheer

* A reading which seems most unaccountably to have escaped the researches of all modern Shakspeareans, including the rival editors of the new and illustrated versions.

perverseness be ascribed to anybody rather than to the real owner. I have therefore sent you, instead thereof, a very fair sketch of Tappington, taken from the Folkestone road (I tore it last night out of Julia Simpkinson's *album*); get Gilks to make a wood-cut of it. And now, if any miscreant (I use the word only in its primary and " Pickwickian " sense of " Unbeliever,") ventures to throw any further doubt upon the matter, why, as Jack Cade's friend says in the play, " There are the chimneys in my father's house, and the bricks are alive at this day to testify it ! "

" Why, very well then—we hope here be truths ! "

Heaven be with you, my dear Sir !—I was getting a little excited ; but you, who are mild as the milk that dews the soft whisker of the new-weaned kitten, will forgive me when, wiping away the nascent moisture from my brow, I " pull in," and subscribe myself,

Yours quite as much as his own,

THOMAS INGOLDSBY.

' TAPPINGTON EVERARD,
    Feb. 2, 1843.

𝔉irst 𝔖eries

The Spectre of Tappington

"It is very odd, though; what can have become of them ? " said
Charles Seaforth, as he peeped under the valance of an old-fashioned
bedstead, in an old-fashioned apartment of a still more old-fashioned
manor-house; " 'tis confoundedly odd, and I can't make it out at all.
Why, Barney, where are they ?—and where the d—l are you ? "

No answer was returned to this appeal; and the Lieutenant, who was,
in the main, a reasonable person,—at least as reasonable a person as any
young gentleman of twenty-two in " the service " can fairly be expected
to be,—cooled when he reflected that his servant could scarcely reply
extempore to a summons which it was impossible he should hear.

An application to the bell was the considerate result; and the footsteps of as tight a lad as ever put pipe-clay to belt sounded along the
gallery.

"Come in ! " said his master.—An ineffectual attempt upon the
door reminded Mr. Seaforth that he had locked himself in.—" By
Heaven ! this is the oddest thing of all," said he, as he turned the key
and admitted Mr. Maguire into his dormitory.

" Barney, where are my pantaloons ? "

" Is it the breeches ? " asked the valet, casting an inquiring eye
round the apartment ;—" is it the breeches, sir ? "

" Yes ; what have you done with them ? "

" Sure then your honour had them on when you went to bed, and
it's hereabout they'll be, I'll be bail ; " and Barney lifted a fashionable
tunic from a cane-backed arm-chair, proceeding in his examination.
But the search was vain : there was the tunic aforesaid,—there was a
smart-looking kerseymere waistcoat ; but the most important article
of all in a gentleman's wardrobe was still wanting.

" Where *can* they be ? " asked the master, with a strong accent on
the auxiliary verb.

" Sorrow a know I knows," said the man.

" It *must* have been the Devil, then, after all, who has been here and
carried them off ! " cried Seaforth, staring full into Barney's face.

I

A

Mr. Maguire was not devoid of the superstition of his countrymen, still he looked as if he did not quite subscribe to the *sequitur*.

His master read incredulity in his countenance, "Why, I tell you, Barney, I put them there, on that arm-chair, when I got into bed ; and, by Heaven ! I distinctly saw the ghost of the old fellow they told me of, come in at midnight, put on my pantaloons, and walk away with them."

"May be so," was the cautious reply.

"I thought, of course, it was a dream ; but then,—where the d—l are the breeches ? "

The question was more easily asked than answered. Barney renewed his search, while the lieutenant folded his arms, and, leaning against the toilet, sunk into a reverie.

"After all, it must be some trick of my laughter-loving cousins," said Seaforth.

"Ah ! then, the ladies ! " chimed in Mr. Maguire, though the observation was not addressed to him ; " and will it be Miss Caroline, or Miss Fanny, that stole your honour's things ? "

"I hardly know what to think of it," pursued the bereaved lieutenant, still speaking in soliloquy, with his eye resting dubiously on the chamber-door. "I locked myself in, that's certain ; and—but there must be some other entrance to the room—pooh ! I remember—the private staircase ; how could I be such a fool ? " and he crossed the chamber to where a low oaken doorcase was dimly visible in a distant corner. He paused before it. Nothing now interfered to screen it from observation ; but it bore tokens of having been at some earlier period concealed by tapestry, remains of which yet clothed the walls on either side the portal.

"This way they must have come," said Seaforth ; "I wish with all my heart I had caught them ! "

"Och ! the kittens ! " sighed Mr. Barney Maguire.

But the mystery was yet as far from being solved as before. True, there *was* the " other door ; " but then that, too, on examination, was even more firmly secured than the one which opened on the gallery,— two heavy bolts on the inside effectually prevented any *coup de main* on the lieutenant's *bivouac* from that quarter. He was more puzzled than ever ; nor did the minutest inspection of the walls and floor throw any light upon the subject : one thing only was clear,—the breeches were gone ! "It is *very* singular," said the lieutenant.

    *   *   *   *   *   *   *

Tappington (generally called Tapton) Everard is an antiquated but commodious manor-house in the eastern division of the county of Kent. A former proprietor had been High-sheriff in the days of Elizabeth, and many a dark and dismal tradition was yet extant of the licentiousness of his life, and the enormity of his offences. The Glen, which the keeper's daughter was seen to enter, but never known to quit, still frowns darkly as of yore; while an ineradicable bloodstain on the oaken stair yet bids defiance to the united energies of soap and sand. But it is with one particular apartment that a deed of more especial atrocity is said to be connected. A stranger guest—so runs the legend—arrived unexpectedly at the mansion of the "Bad Sir Giles." They met in apparent friendship; but the ill-concealed scowl on their master's brow told the domestics that the visit was not a welcome one. The banquet, however, was not spared; the wine-cup circulated freely,—too freely, perhaps,—for sounds of discord at length reached the ears of even the excluded serving-men as they were doing their best to imitate their betters in the lower hall. Alarmed, some of them ventured to approach the parlour; one, an old and favoured retainer of the house, went so far as to break in upon his master's privacy. Sir Giles, already high in oath, fiercely enjoined his absence, and he retired; not, however, before he had distinctly heard from the stranger's lips a menace that "There was that within his pocket which could disprove the knight's right to issue that or any other command within the walls of Tapton."

The intrusion, though momentary, seemed to have produced a beneficial effect; the voices of the disputants fell, and the conversation was carried on thenceforth in a more subdued tone, till, as evening closed in, the domestics, when summoned to attend with lights, found not only cordiality restored, but that a still deeper carouse was meditated. Fresh stoups, and from the choicest bins, were produced; nor was it till at a late, or rather early hour, that the revellers sought their chambers.

The one allotted to the stranger occupied the first floor of the eastern angle of the building, and had once been the favourite apartment of Sir Giles himself. Scandal ascribed this preference to the facility which a private staircase, communicating with the grounds, had afforded him, in the old knight's time, of following his wicked courses unchecked by parental observation; a consideration which ceased to be of weight when the death of his father left him uncontrolled master of his estate and actions. From that period Sir Giles had established himself in what were called the "state apartments;" and the "oaken chamber" was rarely tenanted, save on occasions of extraordinary festivity, or when the yule log drew an unusually large accession of guests around the Christmas hearth.

On this eventful night it was prepared for the unknown visitor, who sought his couch heated and inflamed from his midnight orgies, and in the morning was found in his bed a swollen and blackened corpse. No marks of violence appeared upon the body; but the livid hue of the lips, and certain dark-coloured spots visible on the skin, aroused suspicions which those who entertained them were too timid to express. Apoplexy, induced by the excesses of the preceding night, Sir Giles's confidential leech pronounced to be the cause of his sudden dissolution; the body was buried in peace; and though some shook their heads as they witnessed the haste with which the funeral rites were hurried on, none ventured to murmur. Other events arose to distract the attention of the retainers; men's minds became occupied by the stirring politics of the day, while the near approach of that formidable armada, so vainly arrogating to itself a title which the very elements joined with human valour to disprove, soon interfered to weaken, if not obliterate, all remembrance of the nameless stranger who had died within the walls of Tapton Everard.

Years rolled on: the "Bad Sir Giles" had himself long since gone to his account, the last, as it was believed, of his immediate line; though a few of the older tenants were sometimes heard to speak of an elder brother, who had disappeared in early life, and never inherited the estate. Rumours, too, of his having left a son in foreign lands were at one time rife; but they died away, nothing occurring to support them: the property passed unchallenged to a collateral branch of the family, and the secret, if secret there were, was buried in Denton churchyard, in the lonely grave of the mysterious stranger. One circumstance alone occurred, after a long-intervening period, to revive the memory of these transactions. Some workmen employed in grubbing an old plantation, for the purpose of raising on its site a modern shrubbery, dug up, in the execution of their task, the mildewed remnants of what seemed to have been once a garment. On more minute inspection, enough remained of silken slashes and a coarse embroidery to identify the relics as having once formed part of a pair of trunk hose; while a few papers which fell from them, altogether illegible from damp and age, were by the unlearned rustics conveyed to the then owner of the estate.

Whether the squire was more successful in deciphering them was never known; he certainly never alluded to their contents; and little would have been thought of the matter but for the inconvenient memory of one old woman, who declared she heard her grandfather say that when the "stranger guest" was poisoned, though all the rest of his clothes were there, his breeches, the supposed repository of the supposed documents, could never be found. The master of Tapton Everard smiled when he heard Dame Jones's hint of deeds which might impeach the validity of his own title in favour of some unknown descendant of some unknown heir ; and the story was rarely alluded to, save by one or two miracle-mongers, who had heard that others had seen the ghost of old Sir Giles, in his night-cap, issue from the postern, enter the adjoining copse, and wring his shadowy hands in agony, as he seemed to search vainly for something hidden among the evergreens. The stranger's death-room had, of course, been occasionally haunted from the time of his decease ; but the periods of visitation had latterly become very rare,—even Mrs. Botherby, the housekeeper, being forced to admit that, during her long sojourn at the manor, she had never " met with anything worse than herself ; " though, as the old lady afterwards added upon more mature reflection, " I must say I think I saw the devil *once*."

Such was the legend attached to Tapton Everard, and such the story which the lively Caroline Ingoldsby detailed to her equally mercurial cousin Charles Seaforth, lieutenant in the Hon. East India Company's second regiment of Bombay Fencibles, as arm-in-arm they promenaded a gallery decked with some dozen grim-looking ancestral portraits, and, among others, with that of the redoubted Sir Giles himself. The gallant commander had that very morning paid his first visit to the house of his maternal uncle, after an absence of several years passed with his regiment on the arid plains of Hindostan, whence he was now returned on a three years' furlough. He had gone out a boy,— he returned a man ; but the impression made upon his youthful fancy by his favourite cousin remained unimpaired, and to Tapton he directed his steps, even before he sought the home of his widowed mother,— comforting himself in this breach of filial decorum by the reflection that, as the manor was so little out of his way, it would be unkind to pass, as it were, the door of his relatives without just looking in for a few hours.

But he found his uncle as hospitable and his cousin more charming than ever ; and the looks of one, and the requests of the other, soon precluded the possibility of refusing to lengthen the " few hours " into a few days, though the house was at the moment full of visitors.

The Peterses were there from Ramsgate ; and Mr., Mrs., and the two Miss Simpkinsons, from Bath, had come to pass a month with the family ; and Tom Ingoldsby had brought down his college friend the Honourable Augustus Sucklethumbkin, with his groom and pointers, to take a fortnight's shooting. And then there was Mrs. Ogleton, the rich young widow, with her large black eyes, who, people did say, was setting her cap at the young squire, though Mrs. Botherby did not believe it; and, above all, there was Mademoiselle Pauline, her *femme de chambre*, who "*mon-Dieu*'d" everything and everybody, and cried, "*Quel horreur!*" at Mrs. Botherby's cap. In short, to use the last-named and much respected lady's own expression, the house was "choke-full" to the very attics,—all, save the "oaken chamber," which, as the lieutenant expressed a most magnanimous disregard of ghosts, was forthwith appropriated to his particular accommodation. Mr. Maguire meanwhile was fain to share the apartment of Oliver Dobbs, the squire's

own man: a jocular proposal of joint occupancy having been first indignantly rejected by "Mademoiselle," though preferred with the "laste taste in life" of Mr. Barney's most insinuating brogue.

* * * * *

"Come, Charles, the urn is absolutely getting cold; your breakfast will be quite spoiled: what can have made you so idle?" Such was the morning salutation of Miss Ingoldsby to the *militaire* as he entered the breakfast-room half an hour after the latest of the party.

"A pretty gentleman, truly, to make an appointment with," chimed in Miss Frances. "What is become of our ramble to the rocks before breakfast?"

"Oh! the young men never think of keeping a promise now," said Mrs. Peters, a little ferret-faced woman with underdone eyes.

"When I was a young man," said Mr. Peters, "I remember I always made a point of——"

"Pray how long ago was that?" asked Mr. Simpkinson from Bath.

"Why, sir, when I married Mrs. Peters, I was—let me see—I was——"

"Do pray hold your tongue, P., and eat your breakfast!" interrupted his better half, who had a mortal horror of chronological references; it's very rude to tease people with your family affairs."

The lieutenant had by this time taken his seat in silence,—a good-humoured nod, and a glance, half-smiling, half-inquisitive, being the extent of his salutation. Smitten as he was, and in the immediate presence of her who had made so large a hole in his heart, his manner was evidently *distrait*, which the fair Caroline in her secret soul attributed to his being solely occupied by her *agrémens*,—how would she have bridled had she known that they only shared his meditations with a pair of breeches !

Charles drank his coffee and spiked some half-dozen eggs, darting occasionally a penetrating glance at the ladies, in hope of detecting the supposed waggery by the evidence of some furtive smile or conscious look. But in vain ; not a dimple moved indicative of roguery, nor did the slightest elevation of eyebrow rise confirmative of his suspicions. Hints and insinuations passed unheeded,—more particular inquiries were out of the question :—the subject was unapproachable.

In the meantime, " patent cords " were just the thing for a morning's ride ; and, breakfast ended, away cantered the party over the downs, till, every faculty absorbed by the beauties, animate and inanimate, which surrounded him, Lieutenant Seaforth of the Bombay Fencibles bestowed no more thought upon his breeches that if he had been born on the top of Ben Lomond.

      *   *   *   *   *   *   *

Another night had passed away ; the sun rose brilliantly, forming with his level beams a splendid rainbow in the far-off west, whither the heavy cloud, which for the last two hours had been pouring its waters on the earth, was now flying before him.

" Ah ! then, and it's little good it'll be the claning of ye," apostrophised Mr. Barney Maguire, as he deposited, in front of his master's toilet, a pair of " bran-new " jockey boots, one of Hoby's primest fits, which the lieutenant had purchased in his way through town. On that very morning had they come for the first time under the valet's depuriating hand, so little soiled, indeed, from the turfy ride of the preceding day, that a less scrupulous domestic might, perhaps, have considered the application of " Warren's Matchless," or oxalic acid, altogether superfluous. Not so Barney : with the nicest care had he removed the slightest impurity from each polished surface, and there they stood, rejoicing in their sable radiance. No wonder a pang shot across Mr. Maguire's breast, as he thought on the work now cut out for them, so different from the light labours of the day before ; no wonder he murmured with a sigh, as the scarce-dried window-panes disclosed a road now inch-deep in mud, " Ah ! then, it's little good the claning of ye ! "—for well had he learned in the hall below that eight miles of a stiff clay soil lay between the Manor and Bolsover Abbey, whose picturesque ruins,

    " Like ancient Rome, majestic in decay,"

the party had determined to explore. The master had already commenced dressing, and the man was fitting straps upon a light pair of crane-necked spurs, when his hand was arrested by the old question, " Barney, where are the breeches ? "

They were nowhere to be found !

*   *   *   *   *   *   *

Mr. Seaforth descended that morning, whip in hand, and equipped in a handsome green riding-frock, but no " breeches and boots to match " were there : loose jean trowsers, surmounting a pair of diminutive Wellingtons, embraced, somewhat incongruously, his nether man, *vice* the " patent cords," returned, like yesterday's pantaloons, absent without leave. The " top-boots " had a holiday.

" A fine morning after the rain," said Mr. Simpkinson from Bath.

" Just the thing for the 'ops," said Mr. Peters. " I remember when I was a boy——"

" Do hold your tongue, P.," said Mrs. Peters,—advice which that exemplary matron was in the constant habit of administering to " her P.," as she called him, whenever he prepared to vent his reminiscences. Her precise reason for this it would be difficult to determine, unless, indeed, the story be true which a little bird had whispered into Mrs. Botherby's ear,—Mr. Peters, though now a wealthy man, had received a liberal education at a charity school, and was apt to recur to the days of his muffin-cap and leathers. As usual, he took his wife's hint in good part, and " paused in his reply."

" A glorious day for the ruins ! " said young Ingoldsby. " But, Charles, what the deuce are you about ?—you don't mean to ride through our lanes in such toggery as that ? "

" Lassy me ! " said Miss Julia Simpkinson, " won't you be very wet ? "

" You had better take Tom's cab," quoth the squire.

But this proposition was at once overruled ; Mrs. Ogleton had already nailed the cab, a vehicle of all others the best adapted for a snug flirtation.

" Or drive Miss Julia in the phaeton ? " No; that was the post of Mr. Peters, who, indifferent as an equestrian, had acquired some fame as a whip while travelling through the midland counties for the firm of Bagshaw, Snivelby, and Ghrimes.

" Thank you, I shall ride with my cousins," said Charles, with as much *nonchalance* as he could assume,—and he did so ; Mr. Ingoldsby, Mrs. Peters, Mr. Simpkinson from Bath, and his eldest daughter, with her *album*, following in the family coach. The gentleman-commoner

" voted the affair d—d slow," and declined the party altogether in favour of the gamekeeper and a cigar. " There was 'no fun' in looking at old houses ! " Mrs. Simpkinson preferred a short *séjour* in the still-room with Mrs. Botherby, who had promised to initiate her in that grand *arcanum*, the transmutation of gooseberry jam into Guava jelly.

*   *   *   *   *   *   *

" Did you ever see an old abbey before, Mr. Peters ? "

" Yes, miss, a French one ; we have got one at Ramsgate ; he teaches the Miss Joneses to parley-voo, and is turned of sixty."

Miss Simpkinson closed her album with an air of ineffable disdain.

Mr. Simpkinson from Bath was a professed antiquary, and one of the first water ; he was master of Gwillim's Heraldry, and Milles's " History of the Crusades " ; knew every plate in the Monasticon ; had written an essay on the origin and dignity of the office of overseer, and settled the date of a Queen Anne's farthing. An influential member of the Antiquarian Society, to whose " Beauties of Bagnigge Wells " he had been a liberal subscriber, procured him a seat at the board of that learned body, since which happy epoch Sylvanus Urban had not a more indefatigable correspondent. His inaugural essay on the President's cocked hat was considered a miracle of erudition : and his account of the earliest application of gilding to gingerbread, a masterpiece of antiquarian research. His eldest daughter was of a kindred spirit : if her father's mantle had not fallen upon her, it was only because he had not thrown it off himself ; she had caught hold of its tail, however, while it yet hung upon his honoured shoulders. To souls so congenial, what a sight was the magnificent ruin of Bolsover ! its broken arches, its mouldering pinnacles, and the airy tracery of its half-demolished windows. The party were in raptures ; Mr. Simpkinson began to meditate an essay, and his daughter an ode : even Seaforth, as he gazed on these lonely relics of the olden time, was betrayed into a momentary forgetfulness of his love and losses ; the widow's eye-glass turned from her *cicisbeo's* whiskers to the mantling ivy : Mrs. Peters wiped her spectacles ; and " her P." supposed the central tower " had once been the county jail." The squire was a philosopher, and had been there often before ; so he ordered out the cold tongue and chickens.

" Bolsover Priory," said Mr. Simpkinson, with the air of a connoisseur,—" Bolsover Priory was founded in the reign of Henry the Sixth, about the beginning of the eleventh century. Hugh de Bolsover had accompanied that monarch to the Holy Land, in the expedition undertaken by way of penance for the murder of his young nephews in the Tower. Upon the dissolution of the monasteries, the veteran was enfeoffed in the lands and manor, to which he gave his own name of Bowlsover, or Bee-owls-over (by corruption Bolsover),—a Bee in chief, over three Owls, all proper, being the armorial ensigns borne by this distinguished crusader at the siege of Acre."

"Ah! that was Sir Sidney Smith," said Mr. Peters; "I've heard tell of him, and all about Mrs. Partington, and——"

"P., be quiet, and don't expose yourself!" sharply interrupted his lady. P. was silenced, and betook himself to the bottled stout.

"These lands," continued the antiquary, "were held in grand serjeantry by the presentation of three white owls and a pot of honey——"

"Lassy me! how nice!" said Miss Julia. Mr. Peters licked his lips.

"Pray give me leave, my dear—owls and honey, whenever the king should come a rat-catching into this part of the country."

"Rat-catching!" ejaculated the squire, pausing abruptly in the mastication of a drumstick.

"To be sure, my dear sir : don't you remember that rats once came under the forest laws—a minor species of venison ? 'Rats and mice, and such small deer,' eh ?—Shakspear, you know. Our ancestors ate rats; ("The nasty fellows!" shuddered Miss Julia in a parenthesis) and owls, you know, are capital mousers——"

"I've seen a howl," said Mr. Peters; "there's one in the Sohological Gardens,—a little hook-nosed chap in a wig,—only its feathers and——"

Poor P. was destined never to finish a speech.

"*Do* be quiet!" cried the authoritative voice, and the would-be naturalist shrank into his shell, like a snail in the "Sohological Gardens."

"You should read Blount's 'Jocular Tenures,' Mr. Ingoldsby," pursued Simpkinson. "A learned man was Blount! Why, sir, his Royal Highness the Duke of York once paid a silver horse-shoe to Lord Ferrers——"

"I've heard of him," broke in the incorrigible Peters; "he was hanged at the old Bailey in a silk rope for shooting Dr. Johnson."

The antiquary vouchsafed no notice of the interruption ; but, taking a pinch of snuff, continued his harangue.

"A silver hores-shoe, sir, which is due from every scion of royalty who rides across one of his manors ; and if you look into the penny county histories, now publishing by an eminent friend of mine, you will find that Langhale in Co. Norf. was held by one Baldwin *per saltum sufflatum, et pettum ;* that is, he was to come every Christmas into Westminster Hall, there to take a leap, cry hem! and——"

"Mr. Simpkinson, a glass of sherry?" cried Tom Ingoldsby, hastily.

"Not any, thank you, sir. This Baldwin, surnamed *Le——*"

"Mrs. Ogleton challenges you, sir; she insists upon it," said Tom, still more rapidly; at the same time filling a glass, and forcing it on the *sçavant*, who, thus arrested in the very crisis of his narrative, received and swallowed the potation as if it had been physic.

"What on earth has Miss Simpkinson discovered there?" continued Tom; "something of interest. See how fast she is writing."

The diversion was effectual; every one looked towards Miss Simpkinson, who, far too ethereal for "creature comforts," was seated apart on the dilapidated remains of an altar-tomb, committing eagerly to paper something that had strongly impressed her: the air,—the eye "in a fine frenzy rolling,"—all betokened that the divine *afflatus* was come. Her father rose, and stole silently towards her.

"What an old boar!" muttered young Ingoldsby; alluding, perhaps, to a slice of brawn which he had just begun to operate upon, but which, from the celerity with which it disappeared, did not seem so very difficult of mastication.

But what had become of Seaforth and his fair Caroline all this while? Why, it so happened that they had been simultaneously stricken with the picturesque appearance of one of those high and pointed arches, which that eminent antiquary, Mr. Horseley Curties, has described in his "Ancient Records" as "a *Gothic* window of the *Saxon* order;"—and then the ivy clustered so thickly and so beautifully on the other side, that they went round to look at that;—and then their proximity deprived it of half its effect, and so they walked across to a little knoll, a hundred yards off, and in crossing a small ravine, they came to what in Ireland they call a "bad step," and Charles had to carry his cousin over it;—and then, when they had to come back, she would not give him the trouble again for the world, so they followed a better but more circuitous route, and there were hedges and ditches in the way, and stiles to get over, and gates to get through; so that an hour or more had elapsed before they were able to rejoin the party.

"Lassy me!" said Miss Julia Simpkinson, "how long you have been gone!"

And so they had. The remark was a very just as well as a very natural one. They were gone a long while, and a nice cosey chat they had; and what do you think it was all about, my dear miss?

"O, lassy me! love, no doubt, and the moon, and eyes, and nightingales, and——"

Stay, stay, my sweet young lady; do not let the fervour of your feelings run away with you ! I do not pretend to say, indeed, that one or more of these pretty subjects might not have been introduced ; but the most important and leading topic of the conference was— Lieutenant Seaforth's breeches.

"Caroline," said Charles, " I have had some very odd dreams since I have been at Tappington."

"Dreams, have you ? " smiled the young lady, arching her taper neck like a swan in pluming. " Dreams, have you ? "

" Ay, dreams,—or dream, perhaps, I should say ; for, though repeated, it was still the same. And what do you imagine was its subject ? "

" It is impossible for me to divine," said the tongue ;—" I have not the least difficulty in guessing," said the eye, as plainly as ever eye spoke.

" I dreamt—of your great grandfather ! "

There was a change in the glance—" My great grandfather ? "

" Yes, the old Sir Giles, or Sir John, you told me about the other day : he walked into my bedroom in his short cloak of murrey-coloured velvet, his long rapier, and his Raleigh-looking hat and feather just as the picture represents him : but with one exception."

" And what was that ? "

" Why, his lower extremities, which were visible, were—those of a skeleton."

" Well."

" Well, after taking a turn or two about the room, and looking round him with a wistful air, he came to the bed's foot, stared at me in a manner impossible to describe,—and then he—he laid hold of my pantaloons ; whipped his long bony legs into them in a twinkling ; and strutting up to the glass, seemed to view himself in it with great complacency. I tried to speak, but in vain. The effort, however, seemed to excite his attention ; for, wheeling about, he showed me the grimmest-looking death's head you can well imagine, and with an indescribable grin strutted out of the room."

" Absurd ! Charles. How can you talk such nonsense ? "

" But, Caroline,—the breeches are really gone."

*   *   *   *   *   *   *

On the following morning, contrary to his usual custom, Seaforth was the first person in the breakfast parlour. As no one else was present, he did precisely what nine young men out of ten so situated would have done ; he walked up to the mantelpiece, established himself upon the rug, and subducting his coat-tails one under each arm, turned towards the fire that portion of the human frame which it is considered equally indecorous to present to a friend or an enemy. A serious, not to say anxious, expression was visible upon his good-humoured countenance, and his mouth was fast buttoning itself up for an incipient whistle, when little Flo, a tiny spaniel of the Blenheim breed,—the pet object of Miss Julia Simpkinson's affections,—bounced out from beneath a sofa, and began to bark at—his pantaloons.

They were cleverly "built," of a light grey mixture, a broad stripe, of the most vivid scarlet travers-ing each seam in a perpen-dicular direction from hip to ankle,—in short, the regi-mental costume of the Royal Bombay Fencibles. The animal, educated in the country, had never seen such a pair of breeches in her life —*Omne ignotum pro magnifico!* The scarlet streak, inflamed as it was by the reflection of the fire, seemed to act on Flora's nerves as the same colour does on those of bulls and turkeys; she advanced at the *pas de charge*, and her voci-feration, like her amazement, was unbounded. A sound kick from the disgusted officer changed its character, and induced a retreat at the very moment when the mistress of the pugnacious quadruped entered to the rescue.

"Lassy me! Flo! what *is* the matter?" cried the sympathising lady, with a scrutinising glance levelled at the gentleman.

It might as well have lighted on a feather bed.—His air of imper-turbable unconsciousness defied examination; and as he would not, and Flora could not, expound, that injured individual was compelled to pocket up her wrongs. Others of the household soon dropped in, and clustered round the board dedicated to the most sociable of meals; the urn was paraded "hissing hot," and the cups which "cheer, but not inebriate," steamed redolent of hyson and pekoe; muffins and marmalade, newspapers and Finnon haddies, left little room for observation on the character of Charles's warlike "turn-out." At length a look from Caroline, followed by a smile that nearly ripened to a titter, caused him to turn abruptly and address his neighbour. It was Miss Simpkinson, who, deeply engaged in sipping her tea and turning over her album, seemed, like a female Chrononotonthologos, "immersed in cogibundity of cogitation." An interrogatory on the subject of her studies drew from her the confession that she was at that moment employed in putting the finishing touches to a poem inspired by the romantic shades of Bolsover. The entreaties of the company were of course urgent. Mr. Peters. "who liked verses," was especially persevering, and Sappho at length compliant. After a preparatory hem! and a glance at the mirror to ascertain that her look was sufficiently sentimental, the poetess began :—

> " There is a calm, a holy feeling,
>   Vulgar minds can never know,
> O'er the bosom softly stealing—
>   Chasten'd grief, delicious woe !
> Oh ! how sweet at eve regaining
>   Yon lone tower's sequester'd shade,
> Sadly mute and uncomplaining—"

—Yow !—yeough !—yeough !—yow !—yow ! yelled a hapless sufferer from beneath the table.—It was an unlucky hour for quadrupeds ; and if " every dog will have his day," he could not have selected a more unpropitious one than this. Mrs. Ogleton, too, had a pet,—a favourite pug,—whose squab figure, black muzzle, and tortuosity of tail, that curled like a head of celery in a salad-bowl, bespoke his Dutch extraction. Yow ! yow ! yow ! continued the brute,—a chorus in which Flo instantly joined. Sooth to say, pug had more reason to express his dissatisfaction than was given him by the muse of Simpkinson ; the other only barked for company. Scarcely had the poetess got through her first stanza, when Tom Ingoldsby, in the enthusiasm of the moment, became so lost in the material world, that, in his abstraction, he unwarily laid his hand on the cock of the urn. Quivering with emotion, he gave it such an unlucky twist, that the full stream of its scalding contents descended on the gingerbread hide of the unlucky Cupid.—The confusion was complete ;—the whole economy of the table disarranged ;—the company broke up in most admired disorder ;—and " Vulgar minds will never know " anything more of Miss Simpkinson's ode till they peruse it in some forthcoming Annual.

Seaforth profited by the confusion to take the delinquent who had caused this " stramash " by the arm, and to lead him to the lawn, where he had a word or two for his private ear. The conference between the young gentlemen was neither brief in its duration nor unimportant in its result. The subject was what the lawyers call tripartite, embracing the information that Charles Seaforth was over head and ears in love with Tom Ingoldsby's sister; secondly, that the lady had referred him to " papa " for his sanction; thirdly and lastly, his nightly visitations, and consequent bereavement. At the two first items Tom smiled auspiciously; at the last he burst out into an absolute " guffaw."

" Steal your breeches!—Miss Bailey over again, by Jove," shouted Ingoldsby. " But a gentleman, you say,—and Sir Giles too.—I am not sure, Charles, whether I ought not to call you out for aspersing the honour of the family! "

" Laugh as you will, Tom,—be as incredulous as you please. One fact is incontestible,—the breeches are gone! Look here—I am reduced to my regimentals; and if these go, to-morrow I must borrow of you! "

Rochefoucault says, there is something in the misfortunes of our very best friends that does not displease us;—assuredly we can, most of us, laugh at their petty inconveniences, till called upon to supply them. Tom composed his features on the instant, and replied with more gravity, as well as with an expletive, which, if my Lord Mayor had been within hearing, might have cost him five shillings.

" There is something very queer in this, after all. The clothes, you say, have positively disappeared. Somebody is playing you a trick; and, ten to one, your servant has a hand in it. By the way, I heard something yesterday of his kicking up a bobbery in the kitchen, and seeing a ghost, or something of that kind, himself. Depend upon it, Barney is in the plot."

It now struck the lieutenant at once, that the usually buoyant spirits of his attendant had of late been materially sobered down, his loquacity obviously circumscribed, and that he, the said lieutenant, had actually rung his bell three several times that very morning before he could procure his attendance. Mr. Maguire was forthwith summoned, and underwent a close examination. The " bobbery " was easily explained. Mr. Oliver Dobbs had hinted his disapprobation of a flirtation carrying on between the gentleman from Munster and the lady from the Rue St. Honoré. Mademoiselle had boxed Mr. Maguire's ears, and Mr. Maguire had pulled Mademoiselle upon his knee, and the lady had *not* cried *Mon Dieu!* And Mr. Oliver Dobbs said it was very wrong; and Mrs. Botherby said it was " scandalous," and what ought not to be done in any moral kitchen; and Mr. Maguire had got hold of the Honourable Augustus Sucklethumbkin's powder-flask, and had put large pinches of the best double Dartford into Mr. Dobbs's tobacco-box ;— and Mr. Dobbs's pipe had exploded, and set fire to Mrs. Botherby's Sunday cap ;—and Mr. Maguire had put it out with the slop-basin, " barring the wig " ;—and then they were all so " cantankerous," that Barney had gone to take a walk in the garden ; and then—then Mr. Barney had seen a ghost ! !

"A what ? you blockhead ! " asked Tom Ingoldsby.

" Sure then, and it's meself will tell your honour the rights of it," said the ghost-seer. " Meself and Miss Pauline, sir,—or Miss Pauline and meself, for the ladies comes first anyhow,—we got tired of the hobstroppylous skrimmaging among the ould servants, that didn't know a joke when they seen one : and we went out to look at the comet, —that's the rory-bory-alehouse, they calls him in this country,—and we walked upon the lawn—and divil of any alehouse there was there at all ; and Miss Pauline said it was because of the shrubbery maybe, and why wouldn't we see it better beyonst the trees ?—and so we went to the trees, but sorrow a comet did meself see there, barring a big ghost instead of it."

" A ghost ?   And what sort of a ghost, Barney ? "

" Och, then, divil a lie I'll tell your honour.   A tall ould gentleman he was, all in white, with a shovel on the shoulder of him, and a big torch in his fist,—though what he wanted with that it's meself can't tell, for his eyes were like gig-lamps, let alone the moon and the comet, which wasn't there at all ;—and ' Barney,' says he to me,—'cause why he knew me,—' Barney,' says he, ' what is it you're doing with the *colleen* there, Barney ?'—Divil a word did I say.   Miss Pauline screeched, and cried murther in French, and ran off with herself ; and of course meself was in a mighty hurry after the lady, and had no time to stop palavering with him any way ; so I dispersed at once, and the ghost vanished in a flame of fire ! "

Mr. Maguire's account was received with avowed incredulity by both gentlemen ; but Barney stuck to his text with unflinching pertinacity.   A reference to Mademoiselle was suggested, but abandoned, as neither party had a taste for delicate investigations.

" I'll tell you what, Seaforth," said Ingoldsby, after Barney had received his dismissal, " that there is a trick here, is evident ; and Barney's vision may possibly be a part of it.   Whether he is most knave or fool, you best know.   At all events, I will sit up with you to-night and see if I can convert my ancestor into a visiting acquaintance.   Meanwhile your finger on your lip ! "

* * * * * * *

" 'Twas now the very witching time of night,
When churchyards yawn, and graves give up their dead."

Gladly would I grace my tale with decent horror, and therefore I do beseech the " gentle reader " to believe that if all the *succedanea* to this mysterious narrative are not in strict keeping, he will ascribe it only to the disgraceful innovations of modern degeneracy upon the sober and dignified habits of our ancestors. I can introduce him, it is true, into an old and high-roofed chamber, its walls covered on three sides with black oak wainscotting, adorned with carvings of fruit and flowers long anterior to those of Grinling Gibbons ; the fourth side is clothed with a curious remnant of dingy tapestry, once elucidatory of some Scriptural history, but of *which* not even Mrs. Botherby could determine. Mr. Simpkinson, who had examined it carefully, inclined to believe the principal figure to be either Bathsheba, or Daniel in the lions' den ; while Tom Ingoldsby decided in favour of the King of Bashan. All, however, was conjecture, tradition being silent on the subject.—A lofty arched portal led into, and a little arched portal led out of, this apartment ; they were opposite each other, and each possessed the security of massy bolts on its interior. The bedstead, too, was not one of yesterday, but manifestly coeval with days ere Seddons was, and when a good four-post " article " was deemed worthy of being a royal bequest. The bed itself, with all the appurtenances of palliasse, mattresses, &c., was of far later date, and looked most incongruously comfortable ; the casements, too, with their little diamond-shaped panes and iron binding had given way to the modern heterodoxy of the sash-window. Nor was this all that conspired to ruin the costume, and render the room a meet haunt for such " mixed spirits " only as could condescend to don at the same time an Elizabethan doublet and Bond Street inexpressibles.

With their green morocco slippers on a modern fender, in front of a disgracefully modern grate, sat two young gentlemen, clad in " shawl pattern " dressing gowns and black silk stocks, much at variance with the high cane-backed chairs which supported them. A bunch of abomination, called a cigar, reeked in the left-hand corner of the mouth of one, and in the right-hand corner of the mouth of the other ;—an arrangement happily adapted for the escape of the noxious fumes up the chimney without that unmerciful " funking " each other, which a less scientific disposition of the weed would have induced. A small pembroke table filled up the intervening space between them, sustaining at each extremity, an elbow and a glass of toddy ; —thus in " lonely pensive contemplation " were the two

B

worthies occupied, when the "iron tongue of midnight had tolled twelve."

"Ghost-time's come!" said Ingoldsby, taking from his waistcoat pocket a watch like a gold half-crown, and consulting it as though he suspected the turret-clock over the stables of mendacity.

"Hush!" said Charles; "did I not hear a footstep?"

There was a pause:—there *was* a footstep—it sounded distinctly—it reached the door—it hesitated, stopped, and—passed on.

Tom darted across the room, threw open the door, and became aware of Mrs. Botherby toddling to her chamber, at the other end of the gallery, after dosing one of the housemaids with an approved julep from the Countess of Kent's "Choice Manual."

"Good night, sir!" said Mrs. Botherby.

"Go to the d—l!" said the disappointed ghost-hunter.

An hour—two—rolled on, and still no spectral visitation; nor did aught intervene to make night hideous; and when the turret-clock sounded at length the hour of three, Ingoldsby, whose patience and grog were alike exhausted, sprang from his chair, saying,—

"This is all infernal nonsense, my good fellow. Deuce of any ghost shall we see to-night; it's long past the canonical hour. I'm off to bed; and as to your breeches, I'll insure them for the next twenty-four hours at least, at the price of the buckram."

"Certainly.—Oh! thankee;—to be sure!" stammered Charles, rousing himself from a reverie, which had degenerated into an absolute snooze.

"Good-night, my boy! Bolt the door behind me; and defy the Pope, the Devil, and the Pretender!——"

Seaforth followed his friend's advice, and the next morning came down to breakfast dressed in the habiliments of the preceding day. The charm was broken, the demon defeated; the light greys with the red stripe down the seams were yet *in rerum naturâ*, and adorned the person of their lawful prorpietor.

Tom felicitated himself and his partner of the watch on the result of their vigilance; but there is a rustic adage, which warns us against self-gratulation before we are quite "out of the wood."—Seaforth was yet within its verge.

*   *   *   *   *   *   *

A rap at Tom Ingoldsby's door the following morning startled him as he was shaving;—he cut his chin.

"Come in, and be d—d to you!" said the martyr, pressing his

thumb on the scarified epidermis.—The door opened, and exhibited Mr. Barney Maguire.

"Well, Barney, what is it?" quoth the sufferer, adopting the vernacular of his visitant.

"The master, sir——"

"Well, what does he want?"

"The loanst of a breeches, plase your honour."

"Why, you don't mean to tell me—By Heaven, this is too good!" shouted Tom, bursting into a fit of uncontrollable laughter. "Why, Barney, you don't mean to say the ghost has got them again?"

Mr. Maguire did not respond to the young squire's risibility; the cast of his countenance was decidedly serious.

"Faith, then, it's gone they are, sure enough! Hasn't meself been looking over the bed, and under the bed, and *in* the bed, for the matter of that, and divil a ha'p'orth of breeches is there to the fore at all:—I'm bothered entirely!"

"Hark'ee! Mr. Barney," said Tom, incautiously removing his thumb, and letting a crimson stream "incarnadine the multitudinous" lather that plastered his throat,—"this may be all very well with your master, but you don't humbug *me*, sir :—tell me instantly what have you done with the clothes?"

This abrupt transition from "lively to severe" certainly took Maguire by surprise, and he seemed for an instant as much disconcerted as it is possible to disconcert an Irish gentleman's gentleman.

"Me? is it meself, then, that's the ghost to your honour's thinking?" said he, after a moment's pause, and with a slight shade of indignation in his tones : "is it I would stale the master's things,—and what would I do with them?"

"That you best know :—what your purpose is I can't guess, for I don't think you mean to 'stale' them, as you call it; but that you are concerned in their disappearance, I am satisfied. Confound this blood! —give me a towel, Barney."

Maguire acquitted himself of the commission. "As I've a sowl, your honour," said he solemnly, "little it is meself knows of the matter : and after what I seen——"

"What you've seen! Why, what *have* you seen?—Barney, I don't want to enquire into your flirtations; but don't suppose you can palm off your saucer eyes and gig-lamps upon me!"

"Then, as sure as your honour's standing there I saw him : and why wouldn't I, when Miss *Pauline* was to the fore as well as meself, and——"

" Get along with your nonsense,—leave the room, sir ! "

" But the master ? " said Barney imploringly ; " and without a breeches ?—sure, he'll be catching cowld !——"

" Take that, rascal ! " replied Ingoldsby, throwing a pair of pantaloons at, rather than to, him : " but don't suppose, sir, you shall carry on your tricks here with impunity ; recollect there is such a thing as a tread-mill, and that my father is a county magistrate."

Barney's eye flashed fire,—he stood erect, and was about to speak ; but, mastering himself, not without an effort, he took up the garment, and left the room as perpendicular as a Quaker.

* * * * * * *

" Ingoldsby," said Charles Seaforth, after breakfast, " this is now past a joke ; to-day is the last of my stay ; for, notwithstanding the ties which detain me, common decency obliges me to visit home after so long an absence. I shall come to an immediate explanation with your father on the subject nearest my heart, and depart while I have a change of dress left. On his answer will my return depend ! In the meantime tell me candidly,—I ask it in all seriousness and as a friend,—am I not a dupe to your well-known propensity to hoaxing ? have you not a hand in——"

" No, by heaven ! Seaforth ; I see what you mean : on my honour, I am as much mystified as yourself : and if your servant——"

" Not he :—if there be a trick, he at least is not privy to it."

" If there *be* a trick ? Why, Charles, do you think——"

" I know not *what* to think, Tom. As surely as you are a living man, so surely did that spectral anatomy visit my room again last night, grin in my face, and walk away with my trousers ; nor was I able to spring from my bed, or break the chain which seemed to bind me to my pillow."

" Seaforth ! " said Ingoldsby, after a short pause, " I will— But hush ! here are the girls and my father.—I will carry off the females, and leave you a clear field with the governor : carry your point with him, and we will talk about your breeches afterwards."

Tom's diversion was successful ; he carried off the ladies *en masse* to look at a remarkable specimen of the class *Dodecandria Monogynia,*—which they could not find :—while Seaforth marched boldly up to the encounter, and carried " the Governor's " outworks by a *coup de main.* I shall not stop to describe the progress of the attack : suffice it that it was as successful as could have been wished, and that Seaforth was referred back again to the lady. The happy lover was off at a tangent ; the botanical party was soon overtaken ; and the arm of Caroline, whom a vain endeavour to spell out the Linnæan name of a daffy-down-dilly had detained a little in the rear of the others, was soon firmly locked in his own.

> " What was the world to them,
> Its noise, its nonsense, and its ' breeches ' all ? "

Seaforth was in the seventh heaven ; he retired to his room that night as happy as if no such thing as a goblin had ever been heard of, and personal chattels were as well fenced in by law as real property. Not so Tom Ingoldsby : the mystery,—for mystery there evidently was,—had not only piqued his curiosity, but ruffled his temper. The watch of the previous night had been unsuccessful, probably because it was undisguised. To-night he would " ensconce himself,"—not indeed " behind the arras,"—for the little that remained was, as we have seen, nailed to the wall,—but in a small closet which opened from one corner of the room, and, by leaving the door ajar, would give to its occupant a view of all that might pass in the apartment. Here did the young ghost-hunter take up a position, with a good stout sapling under his arm, a full half-hour before Seaforth retired for the night. Not even his friend did he let into his confidence, fully determined that if his plan did not succeed, the failure should be attributed to himself alone.

At the usual hour of separation for the night, Tom saw, from his concealment, the lieutenant enter his room, and, after taking a few turns in it, with an expression so joyous as to betoken that his thoughts were mainly occupied by his approaching happiness, proceed slowly to disrobe himself. The coat, the waistcoat, the black silk stock, were gradually discarded ; the green morocco slippers were kicked off, and then—ay, and then—his countenance grew grave ; it seemed to occur to him all at once that this was his last stake,—nay, that the very breeches he had on were not his own,—that to-morrow morning was his last and that if he lost *them*—— A glance showed that his mind was made up : he replaced the single button he had just subducted, and threw himself upon the bed in a state of transition—half chrysalis, half grub.

Wearily did Tom Ingoldsby watch the sleeper by the flickering light of the night-lamp, till the clock, striking one, induced him to increase the narrow opening which he had left for the purpose of observation. The motion, slight as it was, seemed to attract Charles's attention ; for he raised himself suddenly to a sitting posture, listened for a moment, and then stood upright upon the floor. Ingoldsby was on the point of discovering himself, when, the light, flashing full upon his friend's countenance, he perceived that, though his eyes were open, " their sense was shut,"—that he was yet under the influence of sleep. Seaforth advanced slowly to the toilet, lit his candle at the lamp that stood on it, then, going back to the bed's foot, appeared to search eagerly for something which he could not find. For a few moments he seemed restless and uneasy, walking round the apartment and examining the chairs, till, coming fully in front of a large swing-glass that flanked the dressing-table, he paused, as if contemplating his figure in it. He now returned towards the bed; put on his slippers, and, with cautious and stealthy steps, proceeded towards the little arched doorway that opened on the private staircase.

As he drew the bolt, Tom Ingoldsby emerged from his hiding-place; but the sleep-walker heard him not; he proceeded softly down stairs, followed at a due distance by his friend; opened the door which led out upon the gardens; and stood at once among the thickest of the scrubs, which there clustered round the base of a corner turret, and screened the postern from common observation. At this moment Ingoldsby had nearly spoiled all by making a false step: the sound attracted Seaforth's attention,—he paused and turned: and as the full moon shed her light directly upon his pale and troubled features, Tom marked, almost with dismay, the fixed and rayless appearance of his eyes:—

> "There was no speculation in those orbs
> That he did glare withal."

The perfect stillness preserved by his follower seemed to reassure him; he turned aside; and from the midst of a thickset laurustinus, drew forth a gardener's spade, shouldering which he proceeded with great rapidity into the midst of the shrubbery. Arrived at a certain point where the earth seemed to have been recently disturbed, he set himself heartily to the task of digging, till, having thrown up several shovelfuls of mould, he stopped, flung down his tool and very composedly began to disencumber himself of his pantaloons.

Up to this moment Tom had watched him with a wary eye: he now advanced cautiously, and, as his friend was busily engaged in disentangling himself from his garment, made himself master of the spade. Seaforth, meanwhile, had accomplished his purpose: he stood for a moment with

> "His streamers waving in the wind,"

occupied in carefully rolling up the small-clothes into as compact a form as possible, and all heedless of the breath of heaven, which might certainly be supposed, at such a moment, and in such a plight, to " visit his frame too roughly."

He was in the act of stooping low to deposit the pantaloons in the grave which he had been digging for them, when Tom Ingoldsby came close behind him, and with the flat side of the spade—

*   *   *

The shock was effectual; —never again was Lieutenant Seaforth known to act the part of a somnambulist. One by one, his breeches,—his trousers,—his pantaloons, — his silk-net tights,—his patent cords,— his showy greys with the broad red stripe of the Bombay Fencibles were brought to light,—rescued from the grave in which they had been buried, like the strata of a Christmas pie; and, after having been well aired by Mrs. Botherby, became once again effective.

The family, the ladies especially, laughed;—the Peterses laughed;—the Simpkinsons laughed; —Barney Maguire cried " Botheration ! " and *Ma'mselle Pauline,* " *Mon Dieu !* "

Charles Seaforth, unable to face the quizzing which awaited him on all sides, started off two hours earlier than he had proposed :—he soon returned, however; and having, at his father-in-law's request, given up the occupation of Rajah-hunting and shooting Nabobs, led his blushing bride to the altar.

Mr. Simpkinson from Bath did not attend the ceremony, being engaged at the Grand Junction Meeting of Sçavans, then congregating from all parts of the known world in the city of Dublin. His essay, demonstrating that the globe is a great custard, whipped into coagulation by whirlwinds, and cooked by electricity,—a little too much baked in the Isle of Portland, and a thought underdone about the Bog of Allen,—was highly spoken of, and narrowly escaped obtaining a Bridgewater prize.

Miss Simpkinson and her sister acted as bridesmaids on the occasion ; the former wrote an *epithalamium*, and the latter cried " Lassy me ! " at the clergyman's wig.—Some years have since rolled on ; the union has been crowned with two or three tidy little off-shoots from the family tree, of whom Master Neddy is " grandpapa's darling," and Mary-Anne mamma's particular " Sock." I shall only add, that Mr. and Mrs. Seaforth are living together quite as happily as two good-hearted, good-tempered bodies, very fond of each other, can possibly do : and, that since the day of his marriage Charles has shown no disposition to jump out of bed, or ramble out of doors o' nights,—though, from his entire devotion to every wish and whim of his young wife, Tom insinuates that the fair Caroline does still occasionally take advantage of it so far as to " slip on the Breeches."

It was not till some years after the events just recorded, that Miss Mary-Anne, the " pet Sock " before alluded to, was made acquainted with the following piece of family biography. It was communicated to her in strict confidence by Nurse Botherby, a maiden niece of the old lady's, then recently promoted from the ranks in the still-room, to be second in command in the Nursery department.

The story is connected with a dingy wizen-faced portrait in an oval frame, generally known by the name of " Uncle Stephen," though from the style of his cut-velvet, it is evident that some generations must have passed away since any living being could have stood towards him in that degree of consanguinity.

The Nurse's Story

The Hand of Glory

" Malefica quædam auguriatrix in Angliâ fuit, quam demones horribiliter extraxerunt, et imponentes super equum terribilem, per aera rapuerunt ; Clamoresque terribiles (ut ferunt) per quatuor fermè miliaria audiebantur."—*Nuremb. Chron.*

On the lone bleak moor,   At the midnight hour,
Beneath the Gallows Tree,
   Hand in hand   The Murderers stand
By one, by two, by three !
   And the Moon that night   With a grey, cold light
Each baleful object tips ;
   One half of her form   Is seen through the storm,
The other half's hid in Eclipse !
   And the cold Wind howls,   And the Thunder growls,

And the Lightning is broad and bright ;
  And altogether   It's very bad weather,
And an unpleasant sort of a night !
  " Now mount who list,   And close by the wrist
Sever me quickly the Dead Man's fist !—
  Now climb who dare   Where he swings in air,
And pluck me five locks of the Dead Man's hair ! "

* * * * *

There's an old woman dwells upon Tappington Moor,
She hath years on her back at the least fourscore,
And some people fancy a great many more ;
  Her nose it is hook'd,   Her back it is crook'd,
  Her eyes blear and red :   On the top of her head
  Is a mutch, and on that   A shocking bad hat,
Extinguisher-shaped, the brim narrow and flat !

Then,—My Gracious !—her beard !—it would sadly perplex
A spectator at first to distinguish her sex ;
Nor, I'll venture to say, without scrutiny could he
Pronounce her, off-handed, a Punch or a Judy.
Did you see her, in short, that mud-hovel within,
With her knees to her nose, and her nose to her chin,
Leering up with that queer indescribable grin,
You'd lift up your hands in amazement, and cry,
" —Well !—I never *did* see such a regular Guy ! "

        And now before   That old Woman's door,
    Where nought that's good may be,
        Hand in hand.   The Murderers stand
    By one, by two, by three !
Oh ! 'tis a horrible sight to view,
In that horrible hovel, that horrible crew,
By the pale blue glare of that flickering flame,
Doing the deed that hath never a name !
    'Tis awful to hear   Those words of fear !
The pray'r mutter'd backwards, and said with a sneer !
(Matthew Hopkins himself has assured us that when
A witch says her pray'rs, she begins with " Amen.")—
    —'Tis awful to see   On that Old Woman's knee
The dead, shrivell'd hand, as she clasps it with glee !—
    And now, with care,   The five locks of hair
From the skull of the Gentleman dangling up there,
    With the grease and the fat   Of a black Tom Cat
    She hastens to mix,   And to twist into wicks,
And one on the thumb, and each finger to fix.—
(For another receipt the same charm to prepare,
Consult Mr Ainsworth and *Petit Albert*.)

    " Now open lock   To the Dead Man's knock !
Fly bolt, and bar, and band !—
    Nor move, nor swerve   Joint, muscle, or nerve,
At the spell of the Dead Man's hand !
Sleep all who sleep !—Wake all who wake !—
But be as the Dead for the Dead Man's sake ! ! "

        *   *   *   *   *

There's an old woman dwells upon Tappington Moor

All is silent ! all is still,
Save the ceaseless moan of the bubbling rill
As it wells from the bosom of Tappington Hill ;
   And in Tappington Hall   Great and Small,
Gentle and Simple, Squire and Groom,
Each one hath sought his separate room,
And sleep her dark mantle hath o'er them cast,
For the midnight hour hath long been past !

All is darksome in earth and sky,
Save, from yon casement, narrow and high,
   A quivering beam   On the tiny stream
Plays, like some taper's fitful gleam
By one that is watching wearily.

Within that casement, narrow and high,
In his secret lair, where none may spy,
Sits one whose brow is wrinkled with care,
And the thin grey locks of his failing hair
Have left his little bald pate all bare ;
   For his full-bottom'd wig   Hangs bushy and big
On the top of his old-fashion'd, high-back'd chair.
   Unbraced are his clothes,   Ungarter'd his hose,
His gown is bedizened with tulip and rose,
Flowers of remarkable size and hue,
Flowers such as Eden never knew ;
—And there, by many a sparkling heap
   Of the good red gold,   The tale is told
What powerful spell avails to keep
That care-worn man from his needful sleep !

Haply, he deems no eye can see
As he gloats on his treasure greedily,—
   The shining store   Of glittering ore,
The fair Rose-Noble, the bright Moidore,
And the broad Double Joe from ayont the sea,—
But there's one that watches as well as he ;
   For, wakeful and sly,   In a closet hard by,

On his truckle-bed lieth a little Foot-page,
A boy who's uncommonly sharp of his age,
  Like young Master Horner,   Who erst in a corner
  Sat eating a Christmas pie :
And while that Old Gentleman's counting his hoards,
Little Hugh peeps through a crack in the boards !

*   *   *   *   *

  There's a voice in the air,   There's a step on the stair,
The old man starts in his cane-back'd chair ;
  At the first faint sound.   He gazes around,
And holds up his dip of sixteen to the pound.
  Then half arose   From beside his toes
His little pug-dog with his little pug nose,
But, ere he can vent one inquisitive sniff,
That little pug-dog stands stark and stiff,
  For low, yet clear,   Now fall on the ear,
—Where once pronounced for ever they dwell,—
The unholy words of the Dead Man's spell !
  " Open lock   To the Dead Man's knock !
  Fly bolt, and bar, and band !
  Nor move, nor swerve   Joint, muscle, or nerve,
At the spell of the Dead Man's hand !
Sleep all who sleep !—Wake all who wake !—
But be as the Dead for the Dead Man's sake ! "

Now lock, nor bolt, nor bar avails,
Nor stout oak panel thick-studded with nails.
Heavy and harsh the hinges creak,
Though they had been oil'd in the course of the week ;
The door opens wide as wide may be,
  And there they stand,   That murderous band,
    Lit by the light of the GLORIOUS HAND,
      By one !—by two !—by three !

They have pass'd through the porch, they have pass'd through
    the hall,
Where the Porter sat snoring against the wall ;
  The very snore froze   In his very snub nose,
You'd have verily deem'd he had snored his last
When the GLORIOUS HAND by the side of him past !

E'en the little wee mouse, as it ran o'er the mat
At the top of its speed to escape from the cat,
   Though half dead with affright,   Paused in its flight
And the cat that was chasing that little wee thing
Lay crouch'd as a statue in act to spring !
   And now they are there,   On the head of the stair,
And the long crooked whittle is gleaming and bare !
—I really don't think any money would bribe
Me the horrible scene that ensued to describe,
   Or the wild, wild glare   Of that old man's eye,
   His dumb despair,   And deep agony.

The kid from the pen, and the lamb from the fold,
Unmoved may the blade of the butcher behold ;
They dream not—ah, happier they !—that the knife,
Though uplifted, can menace their innocent life ;
It falls ;—the frail thread of their being is riven,
They dread not, suspect not, the blow till 'tis given.—
But, oh ! what a thing 'tis to see and to know
That the bare knife is raised in the hand of the foe,
Without hope to repel, or to ward off the blow !—
—Enough !—let's pass over as fast as we can
The fate of that grey, that unhappy old man !

   But fancy poor Hugh,   Aghast at the view
   Powerless alike to speak or to do !
   In vain doth he try   To open the eye
That is shut, or close that which is clapt to the chink,
Though he'd give all the world to be able to wink !—
No !—for all that this world can give or refuse,
I would not be now in that little boy's shoes,
Or indeed any garment at all that is Hugh's !
—'Tis lucky for him that the chink in the wall
He has peep'd through so long, is so narrow and small !
   Wailing voices, sounds of woe
     Such as follow departing friends,
   That fatal night round Tappington go,
     Its long-drawn roofs and its gable ends :
   Ethereal Spirits, gentle and good,
   Aye weep and lament o'er a deed of blood.

    *   *   *   *   *

'Tis early dawn—the morn is grey,
And the clouds and the tempest have pass'd away,
And all things betoken a very fine day ;
But, while the lark her carol is singing,
Shrieks and screams are through Tappington ringing !
    Upstarting all   Great and small,
Each one who's found within Tappington Hall,
Gentle and Simple, Squire or Groom,
All seek at once that old Gentleman's room ;
   And there on the floor,   Drench'd in its gore,
A ghastly corpse lies exposed to the view,
Carotid and jugular both cut through !
   And there, by its side,   'Mid the crimson tide,
Kneels a little Foot-page of tenderest years ;
Adown his pale cheeks the fast-falling tears
Are coursing each other round and big,
And he's staunching the blood with a full-bottomed wig !
Alas ! and alack for his staunching !—'tis plain,
As anatomists tell us, that never again
Shall life revisit the foully slain,
When once they've been cut through the jugular vein.

      *   *   *   *   *

There's a hue and a cry through the County of Kent,
And in chase of the cut-throats a Constable's sent,
But no one can tell the man which way they went,
There's a little Foot-page with that Constable goes,
And a little pug-dog with a little pug nose.

      *   *   *   *   *

    In Rochester town,   At the sign of the Crown,
Three shabby-genteel men are just sitting down
To a fat stubble-goose, with potatoes done brown ;
   When a little Foot-page   Rushes in, in a rage,
Upsetting the apple-sauce, onions, and sage.
That little Foot-page takes the first by the throat,
And a little pug-dog takes the next by the coat,
And a Constable seizes the one more remote ;
And fair rose-nobles and broad moidores,
The Waiter pulls out of their pockets by scores,
And the Boots and the Chambermaids run in and stare ;
And the Constable says, with a dignified air,

To Tappington mill-dam

" You're *wanted*, Gen'lemen, one and all,
For that ere precious lark at Tappington Hall ! "

There's a black gibbet frowns upon Tappington Moor,
Where a former black gibbet has frown'd before :
    It is as black as black may be,
       And murderers there   Are dangling in air,
    By one !—by two ! by three !

There's a horrid old hag in a steeple-crown'd hat,
Round her neck they have tied to a hempen cravat
A Dead Man's hand and a dead Tom Cat !
They have tied up her thumbs, they have tied up her toes,
    They have tied up her eyes, they have tied up her limbs !
Into Tappington mill-dam souse she goes,
    With a whoop and a halloo—" She swims !—She swims ! "
      They have dragg'd her to land,
      And every one's hand,
  Is grasping a faggot, a billet, or brand,
When a queer looking horseman, drest all in black,
Snatches up that old harridan just like a sack
To the crupper behind him, puts spurs to his hack,
Makes a dash through the crowd, and is off in a crack !—
    No one can tell,   Though they guess pretty well,
Which way that grim rider and old woman go,
For all see he's a sort of infernal Ducrow ;
    And she scream'd so, and cried, We may fairly decide
That the old woman did not much relish her ride !

Moral.

  This truest of stories confirms beyond doubt
  That truest of adages—" Murder will out ! "
  In vain may the blood-spiller " double " and fly,
  In vain even witchcraft and sorcery try :
  Although for a time he may 'scape by-and-by
  He'll be sure to be caught by a Hugh and a Cry !

One marvel follows another as naturally as one " shoulder of mutton " is said " to drive another down." A little Welsh girl, who sometimes makes her way from the kitchen into the nursery, after listening with intense interest to this tale, immediately started off at score with the sum and substance of what, in due reverence for such authority, I shall call—

Patty Morgan the Milkmaid's Story

" Look at the Clock ! "

" Look at the Clock ! " quoth Winifred Pryce,
  As she open'd the door to her husband's knock,
Then paus'd to give him a piece of advice,
  " You nasty Warmint, look at the Clock !
  Is this the way, you   Wretch, every day you
Treat her who vow'd to love and obey you ?—
  Out all night ! Me in a fright ;
Staggering home as it's just getting light !
You intoxified brute !—you insensible block !—
Look at the Clock !—Do !—Look at the Clock ! "

Winifred Price was tidy and clean,
Her gown was a flower'd one, her petticoat green,
Her buckles were bright as her milking cans,
And her hat was a beaver, and made like a man's ;
Her little red eyes were deep set in their socket-holes,
Her gown-tail was turn'd up, and tuck'd through the pocket-holes ;
  A face like a ferret   Betoken'd her spirit :
To conclude, Mrs. Pryce was not over young,
Had very short legs, and a very long tongue.

  Now David Pryce   Had one darling vice ;
Remarkably partial to anything nice,
Nought that was good to him came amiss,
Whether to eat, or to drink, or to kiss !
  Especially ale—   If it was not too stale
I really believe he'd have emptied a pail ;
  Not that in Wales   They talk of their Ales ;
To pronounce the word they make use of might trouble you,
Being spelt with a C, two Rs, and a W.

  That particular day,   As I've heard people say,
Mr. David Pryce had been soaking his clay,
And amusing himself with his pipe and cheroots,
The whole afternoon, at the Goat-in-Boots,

32

With a couple more soakers,   Thoroughbred smokers,
Both, like himself, prime singers and jokers ;
And long after day had drawn to a close,
And the rest of the world was wrapp'd in repose,
They were roaring out " Shenkin ! " and " Ar hydd y nos " ;
While David himself, to a Sassenach tune,
Sang, " We've drunk down the Sun, boys ! let's drink down the Moon !
    What have we with day to do ?
    Mrs. Winifred Pryce, 'twas made for you ! "
At length, when they couldn't well drink any more,
Old " Goat-in-Boots " showed them the door :
    And then came that knock,   And the sensible shock
David felt when his wife cried, " Look at the Clock ! "
For the hands stood as crooked as crooked might be,
The long at the Twelve, and the short at the Three !

That self-same clock had long been a bone
Of contention between this Darby and Joan ;
And often, among their pother and rout,
When this otherwise amiable couple fell out,
    Pryce would drop a cool hint,   With an ominous squint
At its case, of an " Uncle " of his, who'd a " Spout."
    That horrid word " Spout "   No sooner came out
Than Winifred Pryce would turn her about,
    And with scorn on her lip,   And a hand on each hip,
" Spout " herself till her nose grew red at the tip.
    " You thundering Willin,   I know you'd be killing
Your wife—ay, a dozen of wives—for a shilling !
    You may do what you please,   You may sell my chemise,
(Mrs. P. was too well-bred to mention her smock)
But I never will part with my Grandmother's Clock ! "

Mrs. Pryce's tongue ran long and ran fast ;
But patience is apt to wear out at last,
And David Pryce in temper was quick,
So he stretched out his hand, and caught hold of a stick ;
Perhaps in its use he might mean to be lenient,
But walking just then wasn't very convenient,
    So he threw it, instead,   Direct at her head ;
    It knock'd off her hat ;   Down she fell flat ;
Her case, perhaps, was not much mended by that :

c

But whatever it was,—whether rage and pain
Produced apoplexy, or burst a vein,
Or her tumble induced a concussion of brain,
I can't say for certain,—but *this* I can,
When, sober'd by fright, to assist her he ran,
Mrs. Winifred Pryce was as dead as Queen Anne !

The fearful catastrophe   Named in my last strophe
As adding to grim Death's exploits such a vast trophy,
Made a great noise ; and the shocking fatality,
Ran over, like wild-fire, the whole Principality,
And then came Mr. Ap Thomas, the Coroner,
With his jury to sit, some dozen or more, on her.
    Mr. Pryce to commence   His " ingenious defence,"
Made a " powerful appeal " to the jury's " good sense " :
    " The world he must defy   Ever to justify
Any presumption of ' Malice Prepense ; ' "—
    The unlucky lick   From the end of his stick
He " deplored,"—he was " apt to be rather too quick ; "—
    But, really, her prating   Was so aggravating :
Some trifling correction was just what he meant ;—all
The rest, he assured them, was " quite accidental ! "

    Then he calls Mr. Jones,   Who depones to her tones,
And her gestures, and hints about " breaking his bones."
While Mr. Ap Morgan, and Mr. Ap Rhys
    Declared the Deceased   Had styled him " a Beast,"
And swear they had witness'd, with grief and surprise,
The allusion she made to his limbs and his eyes.

The jury, in fine, having sat on the body
The whole day, discussing the case, and gin toddy,
Return'd about half-past eleven at night
The following verdict, " We find, *Sarve her right !* "

Mr. Pryce, Mrs. Winifred Pryce being dead,
Felt lonely, and moped ; and one evening he said
He would marry Miss Davis at once in her stead.

    Not far from his dwelling,
    From the vale proudly swelling,
Rose a mountain ; it's name you'll excuse me from telling,

For the vowels made use of in Welsh are so few
That the A and the E, the I, O, and the U,
 Have really but little or nothing to do ;
And the duty, of course, falls the heavier by far,
On the L, and the H, and the N, and the R.
 Its first syllable " PEN," Is pronounceable ;—then
Come two L Ls, and two H Hs, two F Fs, and an N,
About half a score Rs, and some Ws follow,
Beating all my best efforts at euphony hollow :
But we shan't have to mention it often, so when
We do, with your leave, we'll curtail it to " PEN."

 Well—the moon shone bright
 Upon " Pen " that night,
When Pryce, being quit of his fuss and his fright,
 Was scaling its side With that sort of stride
A man puts out when walking in search of a bride.
 Mounting higher and higher, He began to perspire,
Till, finding his legs were beginning to tire,
 And feeling opprest By a pain in his chest,
He paus'd, and turn'd round to take breath, and to rest :
A walk all up hill is apt, we know,
To make one, however robust, puff and blow,
So he stopp'd and look'd down on the valley below.

 O'er fell, and o'er fen, Over mountain and glen,
All bright in the moonshine, his eye roved, and then
All the Patriot rose in his soul, and he thought
Upon Wales, and her glories, and all he'd been taught
 Of her Heroes of old, So brave and so bold,—
Of her Bards with long beards, and harps mounted in gold ;
 Of King Edward the First, Of memory accurst ;
And the scandalous manner in which he behaved,
 Killing Poets by dozens,
 With their uncles and cousins,
Of whom not one in fifty had ever been shaved—
Of the Court Ball, at which by a lucky mishap,
Owen Tudor fell into Queen Katherine's lap ;
 And how Mr. Tudor Successfully woo'd her
Till the Dowager put on a new wedding-ring,
And so made him Father-in-law to the King.

He thought upon Arthur, and Merlin of yore,
On Gryffith ap Conan, and Owen Glendour ; ·
On Pendragon, and Heaven knows how many more.
He thought of all this, as he gazed, in a trice,
And on all things, in short, but the late Mrs. Pryce ;
When a lumbering noise from behind made him start,
And sent the blood back in full tide to his heart,
 Which went pit-a-pat
 As he cried out " What's that ? "—
 That very queer sound ?—
 Does it come from the ground ?
Or the air,—from above,—or below,—or around ?—
 It is not like Talking,   It is not like Walking,
It's not like the clattering of pot or of pan,
Or the tramp of a horse,—or the tread of a man,—
Or the hum of a crowd,—or the shouting of boys,—
It's really a deuced odd sort of a noise !
Not unlike a cart's,—but that can't be ; for when
Could " all the King's horses, and all the King's men,"
With Old Nick for a waggoner, drive one up " Pen " ?

Pryce, usually brimful of valour when drunk,
Now experienced what schoolboys denominate " funk."
 In vain he look'd back   On the whole of the track
He had traversed ; a thick cloud, uncommonly black,
At this moment obscured the broad disc of the moon,
And did not seem likely to pass away soon ;
 While clearer and clearer,   'Twas plain to the hearer,
Be the noise what it might, it drew nearer and nearer,
And sounded, as Pryce to this moment declares,
Very much " like a Coffin a-walking up stairs."

 Mr. Pryce had begun   To " make up " for a run,
As in such a companion he saw no great fun,
 When a single bright ray   Shone out on the way
He had passed, and he saw, with no little dismay,
Coming after him, bounding o'er crag and o'er rock,
The deceased Mrs. Winifred's " Grandmother's Clock ! ! "
'Twas so !—it had certainly moved from its place,
And come, lumbering on thus, to hold him in chase ;
'Twas the very same Head, and the very same Case,
And nothing was altered at all—but the Face !

In that he perceived, with no little surprise,
The two little winder-holes turned into eyes
    Blazing with ire,   Like two coals of fire ;
And the " Name of the Maker " was changed to a Lip,
And the Hands to a Nose with a very red tip.

No !—he could not mistake it,—'twas SHE to the life !
The identical face of his poor defunct Wife !

    One glance was enough   Completely " *Quant. suff.* "
As the doctors write down when they send you their " stuff,"—
Like a Weather-cock whirled by a vehement puff,
    David turned himself round ; Ten feet of ground
He cleared, in his start, at the very first bound !

I've seen people run at West-End Fair for cheeses—
I've seen Ladies run at Bow Fair for chemises—

At Greenwich Fair twenty men run for a hat,
And one from a Bailiff much faster than that—
At foot-ball I've seen lads run after the bladder—
I've seen Irish Bricklayers run up a ladder—
I've seen little boys run away from a cane—
And I've seen (that is, *read of*) good running in Spain ;*
   But I never did read   Of, or witness, such speed
As David exerted that evening.—Indeed
All I have ever heard of boys, women, or men,
Falls far short of Pryce, as he ran over " Pen ! "

He reaches its brow,—   He has past it,—and now
Having once gained the summit, and managed to cross it, he
Rolls down the side with uncommon velocity ;
   But, run as he will,   Or roll down the hill,
That bugbear behind him is after him still !
And close at his heels, not at all to his liking,
The terrible clock keeps on ticking and striking,
   Till, exhausted and sore,   He can't run any more,
But falls as he reaches Miss Davis's door,
And screams when they rush out, alarm'd at his knock,
" Oh ! Look at the Clock !—Do !—Look at the Clock ! ! "

Miss Davis look'd up, Miss Davis look'd down,
She saw nothing there to alarm her ;—a frown
   Came o'er her white forehead,   She said, " It was horrid
A man should come knocking at that time of night,
And give her Mamma and herself such a fright ;—
   To squall and to bawl   About nothing at all ! "
She begg'd " he'd not think of repeating his call :
   His late wife's disaster   By no means had past her,"
She'd " have him to know she was meat for his Master ! "
Then regardless alike of his love and his woes,
She turn'd on her heel and she turn'd up her nose.

Poor David in vain   Implored to remain,
He " dared not," he said, " cross the mountain again."
   Why the fair was obdurate
   None knows,—to be sure, it
Was said she was setting her cap at the Curate ;—

* I-run is a town said to have been so named from something of this sort.

"GENTLEMEN! LOOK AT THE CLOCK!!!"

Be that as it may, it is certain the sole hole
Pryce found to creep into that night was the Coal-hole !
   In that shady retreat   With nothing to eat,
And with very bruised limbs, and with very sore feet,
   All night close he kept ;   I can't say he slept ;
But he sigh'd, and he sobb'd, and he groan'd, and he wept ;
   Lamenting his sins,   And his two broken shins,
Bewailing his fate with contortions and grins,
And her he once thought a complete *Rara Avis*,
Consigning to Satan,—viz., cruel Miss Davis !

Mr. David has since had a " serious call,"
He never drinks ale, wine, or spirits, at all,
And they say he is going to Exeter Hall
   To make a grand speech,   And to preach and to teach
People that " they can't brew their malt liquor too small ! "
That an ancient Welsh Poet, one PYNDAR AP TUDOR,
Was right in proclaiming " ARISTON MEN UDOR ! "
   Which means " The pure Element
   Is for Man's belly meant ! "
And that *Gin's* but a *Snare* of Old Nick the deluder !

And " still on each evening when pleasure fills up,"
At the old Goat-in-Boots, with Metheglin, each cup,
   Mr. Pryce, if he's there,   Will get into " The Chair,"
And make all his *quondam* associates stare
By calling aloud to the Landlady's daughter,
" Patty, bring a cigar, and a glass of Spring Water ! "
The dial he constantly watches ; and when
The long hand's at the " XII.," and the short at the " X."
   He gets on his legs,   Drains his glass to the dregs,
Takes his hat and great-coat off their several pegs,
With his President's hammer bestows his last knock,
And says solemnly—" Gentlemen !
                    " LOOK AT THE CLOCK ! ! ! "

The succeeding Legend has long been an established favourite with all of us, as containing
much of the personal history of one of the greatest ornaments of the family tree.
   To the wedding between the sole heiress of this redoubted hero and· a direct ancestor is it
owing that the Lioncels of Shurland hang so lovingly parallel with the Saltire of the Ingoldsbys,
and now form as cherished a quartering in their escutcheon as the " dozen white lowses " in
the " old coat " of Shallow.

Grey Dolphin

A Legend of Sheppey

" He won't—won't he ?   Then bring me my boots ! " said the Baron.

Consternation was at its height in the castle of Shurland—a caitiff had dared to disobey the Baron ! and—the Baron had called for his boots !

A thunderbolt in the great hall had been a *bagatelle* to it.

A few days before, a notable miracle had been wrought in the neighbourhood ; and in those times miracles were not so common as they are now ;—no royal balloons, no steam, no railroads,—while the few Saints who took the trouble to walk with their heads under their arms, or to pull the Devil by the nose, scarcely appeared above once in a century ; so the affair made the greater sensation.

The clock had done striking twelve, and the Clerk of Chatham was untrussing his points preparatory to seeking his truckle-bed ; a half-emptied tankard of mild ale stood at his elbow, the roasted crab yet floating on its surface. Midnight had surprised the worthy functionary while occupied in discussing it, and with his task yet unaccomplished. He meditated a mighty draft : one hand was fumbling with his tags, while the other was extended in the act of grasping the jorum, when a knock on the portal, solemn and sonorous, arrested his fingers. It was repeated thrice ere Emmanuel Saddleton had presence of mind sufficient to inquire who sought admittance at that untimeous hour.

" Open ! open ! good Clerk of St. Bridget's," said a female voice, small, yet distinct and sweet,—an excellent thing in woman.

The Clerk arose, crossed to the doorway, and undid the latchet.

On the threshold stood a Lady of surpassing beauty : her robes were rich, and large, and full ; and a diadem, sparkling with gems that shed a halo around, crowned her brow : she beckoned the Clerk as he stood in astonishment before her.

" Emmanuel ! " said the Lady ; and her tones sounded like those of a silver flute. " Emmanuel Saddleton, truss up your points, and follow me ! "

The worthy Clerk stared aghast at the vision ; the purple robe, the cymar, the coronet,—above all, the smile ; no, there was no mistaking her ; it was the blessed St. Bridget herself !

41

And what could have brought the sainted lady out of her warm shrine at such a time of night ? and on such a night ? for it was as dark as pitch, and, metaphorically speaking, " rained cats and dogs."

Emmanuel could not speak, so he looked the question.

" No matter for that," said the Saint, answering to his thought. " No matter for that, Emmanuel Saddleton ; only follow me, and you'll see ! "

The Clerk turned a wistful eye at the corner-cupboard.

" Oh ! never mind the lantern, Emmanuel : you'll not want it : but you may bring a mattock and a shovel." As she spoke, the beautiful apparition held up her delicate hand. From the tip of each of her long taper fingers issued a lambent flame of such surpassing brilliancy as would have plunged a whole gas company into despair—it was a " Hand of Glory," * such a one as tradition tells us yet burns in Rochester Castle every St. Mark's Eve. Many are the daring individuals who have watched in Gundulph's Tower, hoping to find it, and the treasure it guards ;—but none of them ever did.

" This way, Emmanuel ! " and a flame of peculiar radiance streamed from her little finger as it pointed to the pathway leading to the churchyard.

Saddleton shouldered his tools, and . followed in silence.

The cemetery of St. Bridget's was some half-mile distant from the Clerk's domicile, and adjoined a chapel dedicated [to that illustrious lady, who, after leading but a so-so life, had died in the odour of sanctity. Emmanuel Saddleton was fat and scant of breath, the mattock was heavy, and the Saint walked too fast for him ; he paused to take second wind at the end of the first furlong.

" Emmanuel," said the holy lady good-humouredly, for she heard him puffing ; rest awhile, Emmanuel, and I'll tell you what I want with you."

Her auditor wiped his brow with the back of his hand, and looked all attention and obedience.

" Emmanuel," continued she, " what did you and Father Fothergill,

* One of the uses to which this mystic chandelier was put, was the protection of secreted treasure. Blow out all the fingers at one puff and you had the money.

and the rest of you, mean yesterday by burying that drowned man so close to me ? He died in mortal sin, Emmanuel ; no shrift, no unction, no absolution : why, he might as well have been excommunicated. He plagues me with his grinning, and I can't have any peace in my shrine. You must howk him up again, Emmanuel ! "

"To be sure, madam,—my lady,—that is, your holiness," stammered Saddleton, trembling at the thought of the task assigned to him. "To be sure, your ladyship ; only— that is——"

"Emmanuel," said the Saint, " you'll do my bidding ; or it would be better you had ! " and her eye changed from a dove's eye to that of a hawk, and a flash came from it as bright as the one from her little finger. The Clerk shook in his shoes ; and, again dashing the cold perspiration from his brow, followed the footsteps of his mysterious guide.

* * * *

The next morning all Chatham was in an uproar. The Clerk of St. Bridget's had found himself at home at daybreak, seated in his own arm-chair, the fire out, and—the tankard of ale out too ! Who had drunk it ?—where had he been ?—how had he got home ?—all was a mystery !—he remembered " a mass of things, but nothing distinctly ; " all was fog and fantasy. What he could clearly recollect was, that he had dug up the Grinning Sailor, and that the Saint had helped to throw him into the river again. All was thenceforth wonderment and devotion. Masses were sung, tapers were kindled, bells were tolled ; the monks of St. Romuald had a solemn procession, the abbot at their head, the sacristan at their tail, and the holy breeches of St. Thomas à Becket in the centre ;—Father Fothergill brewed a XXX puncheon of holy water. The Rood of Gillingham was deserted ; the chapel of Rainham forsaken ; every one who had a soul to be saved, flocked with his offering to St. Bridget's shrine, and Emmanuel Saddleton gathered more fees from the promiscuous piety of that one week than he had pocketed during the twelve preceding months.

Meanwhile the corpse of the ejected reprobate oscillated like a pendulum between Sheerness and Gillingham Reach. Now borne by the Medway into the Western Swale,—now carried by the refluent tide back to the vicinity of its old quarters,—it seemed as though the River god and Neptune were amusing themselves with a game of sub-aqueous battledore, and had chosen this unfortunate carcass as a marine shuttlecock. Fo some time the alternation was kept up with great spirit, till Boreas, interfering in the shape of a stiffish " Nor'-wester," drifted the bone (and flesh) of contention ashore on the Shurland domain, where it lay in all the majesty of mud. It was soon discovered by the retainers, and dragged from its oozy bed, grinning worse than ever. Tidings of the god-send were of course carried instantly to the castle ; for the Baron was a very great man ; and if a dun cow had flown across his property unannounced by the warder, the Baron would have kicked him, the said warder, from the topmost battlement into the bottommost ditch,—a descent of peril, and one which " Ludwig the leaper," or the illustrious Trenck himself might well have shrunk from encountering.

" An't please your lordship——" said Peter Periwinkle.

" No, villain ! it does not please me ! " roared the Baron.

His lordship was deeply engaged with a peck of Feversham oysters, —he doted on shellfish, hated interruption at meals, and had not yet despatched more than twenty dozen of the " natives."

" There's a body, my lord, washed ashore in the lower creek," said the Seneschal.

The Baron was going to throw the shells at his head ; but paused in the act, and said with much dignity,—

" Turn out the fellow's pockets ! "

But the defunct had before been subjected to the double scrutiny of Father Fothergill, and the Clerk of St. Bridget's. It was ill gleaning after such hands ; there was not a single maravedi.

We have already said that Sir Robert de Shurland, Lord of the Isle of Sheppey, and of many a fair manor on the mainland, was a man of worship. He had rights of free-warren, saccage and sockage, cuisage and jambage, fosse and fork, infang theofe and outfang theofe ; and all waifs and strays belonged to him in fee simple.

" Turn out his pockets ! " said the Knight.

" An't please you, my lord, I must say as how they was turned out afore, and the devil a rap's left."

" Then bury the blackguard ! "

" Please your lordship, he has been buried once."

" Then bury him again, and be——! " The Baron bestowed a benediction.

The Seneschal bowed low as he left the room, and the Baron went on with his oysters.

Scarcely ten dozen more had vanished when Periwinkle reappeared.

" An't please you, my lord, Father Fothergill says as how that it's the Grinning Sailor, and he won't bury him anyhow."

" Oh ! he won't—won't he ? " said the Baron. Can it be wondered at that he called for his boots ?

Sir Robert de Shurland, Lord of Shurland and Minster, Baron of Sheppey *in comitatu* Kent, was, as has been before hinted, a very great man. He was also a very little man ; that is, he was relatively great, and relatively little,—or physically little, and metaphorically great,— like Sir Sidney Smith and the late Mr. Bonaparte. To the frame of a dwarf he united the soul of a giant, and the valour of a gamecock. Then, for so small a man, his strength was prodigious ; his fist would fell an ox, and his kick—oh ! his kick was tremendous, and, when he had his boots on, would, to use an expression of his own, which he had picked up in the holy wars,—would " send a man from Jericho to June."—He was bull-necked and bandy-legged ; his chest was broad and deep, his head large, and uncommonly thick, his eyes a little bloodshot, and his nose *retroussé* with a remarkably red tip. Strictly speaking the Baron could not be called handsome, but his *tout ensemble* was singularly impressive : and when he called for his boots, everybody trembled and dreaded the worst.

" Periwinkle," said the Baron, as he encased his better leg, " let the grave be twenty feet deep ! "

" Your lordship's command is law."

" And, Periwinkle,"—Sir Robert stamped his left heel into its receptacle,—" and, Periwinkle, see that it be wide enough to hold not exceeding two ! "

" Ye—ye—yes, my lord."

" And, Periwinkle,—tell Father Fothergill I would fain speak with his Reverence."

" Ye—ye—yes, my lord."

The Baron's beard was peaked ; and his mustaches, stiff and stumpy, projected horizontally like those of a Tom Cat ; he twirled the one, he stroked the other, he drew the buckle of his surcingle a thought tighter, and strode down the great staircase three steps at a stride.

The vassals were assembled in the great hall of Shurland Castle ; every cheek was pale, every tongue was mute ; expectation and perplexity

were visible on every brow.   What would his lordship do ?—Were the
recusant anybody else, gyves to the heels and hemp to the throat were
but too good for him :—but it was Father Fothergill who had said " I
won't ; " and though the Baron was a very great man, the Pope was a
greater, and the Pope was Father Fothergill's great friend—some people
said he was his uncle.

Father Fothergill was busy in the refectory trying conclusions with a
venison pasty, when he received the summons of his patron to attend
him in the chapel cemetery.   Of course he lost no time in obeying it,
for obedience was the general rule in Shurland Castle.   If anybody
ever said " I won't," it was the exception ; and, like all other exceptions,
only proved the rule the stronger.   The Father was a friar of the Augustine persuasion ; a brotherhood which, having been planted in Kent
some few centuries earlier, had taken very kindly to the soil, and over-
spread the county much as hops did some few centuries later.   He was
plump and portly, a little thick-winded, especially after dinner,—stood
five feet four in his sandals, and weighed hard upon eighteen stone.
He was moreover a personage of singular piety ; and the iron girdle,
which, he said, he wore under his cassock to mortify withal, might
have been well mistaken for the tire of a cart-wheel.—When he arrived,
Sir Robert was pacing up and down by the side of a newly opened
grave.

" *Benedicite !* fair son,"—(the Baron was as brown as a cigar,)—
" *Benedicite !* " said the Chaplain.

The Baron was too angry to stand upon compliment.   " Bury me
that grinning caitiff there ! " quoth he, pointing to the defunct.

" It may not be, fair son," said the Friar ; " he hath perished
without absolution."

" Bury the body ! " roared Sir Robert.

" Water and earth alike reject him," returned the Chaplain ; " holy
St. Bridget herself——"

" Bridget me no Bridgets !—do me thine office quickly, Sir Shaveling ;
or, by the Piper that played before Moses——"   The oath was a fearful
one ; and whenever the Baron swore to do mischief, he was never known
to perjure himself.   He was playing with the hilt of his sword.—" Do
me thine office, I say.   Give him his passport to Heaven ! "

" He is already gone to Hell ! " stammered the Friar.

" Then do you go after him ! " thundered the Lord of Shurland.

His sword half leaped from its scabbard.   No !—the trenchant
blade, that had cut Suleiman Ben Malek Ben Buckskin from helmet to
chine, disdained to daub itself with the cerebellum of a miserable monk ;

One kick!—it was but one!—but such a one

—it leaped back again ;—and as the Chaplain, scared at its flash, turned him in terror, the Baron gave him a kick !—one kick !—it was but one !—but such a one ! Despite its obesity, up flew his holy body in an angle of forty-five degrees ; then, having reached its highest point of elevation, sunk headlong into the open grave that yawned to receive it. If the reverend gentleman had possessed such a thing as a neck, he had infallibly broken it ; as he did not, he only dislocated his vertebræ,—but that did quite as well. He was as dead as ditch-water !

"In with the other rascal !" said the Baron,—and he was obeyed ; for there he stood in his boots. Mattock and shovel made short work of it ; twenty feet of superincumbent mould pressed down alike the saint and the sinner. "Now sing a requiem who list !" said the Baron, and his lordship went back to his oysters.

The vassals at Castle Shurland were astounded, or, as the Seneschal Hugh better expressed it, "perfectly conglomerated," by this event. What ! murder a monk in the odour of sanctity,—and on consecrated ground too !—They trembled for the health of the Baron's soul. To the unsophisticated many it seemed that matters could not have been much worse had he shot a bishop's coach-horse ;—all looked for some signal judgment. The melancholy catastrophe of their neighbours at Canterbury was yet rife in their memories : not two centuries had elapsed since those miserable sinners had cut off the tail of the blessed St. Thomas's mule. The tail of the mule, it was well known, had been forthwith affixed to that of the Mayor ; and rumour said it had since been hereditary in the corporation. The least that could be expected was, that Sir Robert should have a friar tacked on to his for the term of his natural life ! Some bolder spirits there were, 'tis true, who viewed the matter in various lights, according to their different temperaments and dispositions ; for perfect unanimity existed not even in the good old times. The verderer, roistering Hob Roebuck, swore roundly, " 'Twere as good a deed as eat to kick down the chapel as well as the monk."—Hob had stood there in a white sheet for kissing Giles Miller's daughter.—On the other hand, Simpkin Agnew, the bell-ringer, doubted if the devil's cellar, which runs under the bottomless abyss, were quite deep enough for the delinquent, and speculated on the probability of a hole being dug in it for his especial accommodation. The philosophers and economists thought, with Saunders McBullock, the Baron's bag-piper, that "a feckless monk more or less was nae great subject for a clamjamphry," especially as "the supply considerably exceeded the demand ;" while Malthouse, the tapster, was arguing to Dame Martin that a murder now and then was a seasonable check to population, without which the Isle of Sheppey would in time be devoured, like a mouldy cheese, by inhabitants of its own producing.—Meanwhile, the Baron ate his oysters and thought no more of the matter.

But this tranquillity of his lordship was not to last. A couple of Saints had been seriously offended; and we have all of us read at school that celestial minds are by no means insensible to the provocations of anger. There were those who expected that St. Bridget would come in person, and have the friar up again, as she did the sailor; but perhaps her ladyship did not care to trust herself within the walls of Shurland Castle. To say the truth, it was scarcely a decent house for a female Saint to be seen in. The Baron's gallantries, since he became a widower, had been but too notorious; and her own reputation was a little blown upon in the earlier days of her earthly pilgrimage: then things were so apt to be misrepresented: in short, she would leave the whole affair to St. Austin, who, being a gentleman, could interfere with propriety, avenge her affront as well as his own, and leave no loophole for scandal. St. Austin himself seems to have had his scruples, though of their precise nature it would be difficult to determine, for it were idle to suppose him at all afraid of the Baron's boots. Be this as it may, the mode which he adopted was at once prudent and efficacious. As an ecclesiastic, he could not well call the Baron out,—had his boots been out of the question;—so he resolved to have recourse to the law. Instead of Shurland Castle, therefore, he repaired forthwith to his own magnificent monastery, situate just within the walls of Canterbury, and presented himself in a vision to its abbot. No one who has ever visited that ancient city, can fail to recollect the splendid gateway which terminates the vista of St. Paul's-street, and stands there yet in all its pristine beauty. The tiny train of miniature artillery which now adorns its battlements is, it is true, an ornament of a later date; and is said to have been added some centuries after by a learned but jealous proprietor, for the purpose of shooting any wiser man than himself who might chance to come that way. Tradition is silent as to any discharge having taken place, nor can the oldest inhabitant of modern days recollect any such occurrence.* Here it was, in a handsome chamber, immediately over the lofty archway, that the Superior of the monastery lay buried in a brief slumber snatched from his accustomed vigils. His mitre—for he was a Mitred Abbot, and had a seat in parliament—rested on a table beside him; near it stood a silver flagon of Gascony wine, ready, no doubt, for the pious uses of the morrow. Fasting and watching had made him more than

---

* Since the appearance of the first edition of this Legend " the guns " have been dismounted. Rumour hints at some alarm on the part of the Town Council.

usually somnolent, than which nothing could have been better for the purpose of the Saint, who now appeared to him radiant in all the colours of the rainbow.

"Anselm!"—said the beatific vision,—"Anselm! are you not a pretty fellow to lie snoring there, when your brethren are being knocked at head, and Mother Church herself is menaced?—It is a sin and a shame. Anselm!"

"What's the matter?—Who are you?" cried the Abbot, rubbing his eyes, which the celestial splendour of his visitor had set a-winking. "Ave Maria! St. Austin himself!—Speak, *Beatissime!* what would you with the humblest of your votaries?"

"Anselm!" said the Saint, "a brother of our order, whose soul Heaven assoilzie! hath been foully murdered. He hath been ignominiously kicked to the death, Anselm; and there he lieth cheek-by-jowl with a wretched carcass, which our sister Bridget has turned out of her cemetery for unseemly grinning.—Arouse thee, Anselm!"

"Ay, so please you, *Sanctissime!*" said the Abbot. "I will order forthwith that thirty masses be said, thirty *Paters*, and thirty *Aves*."

"Thirty fools' heads!" interrupted his patron, who was a little peppery.

"I will send for bell, book, and candle——"

"Send for an inkhorn, Anselm.—Write me now a letter to his Holiness the Pope in good round terms, and another to the Coroner, and another to the Sheriff, and seize me the never-enough-to-be-anathematised villain who hath done this deed! Hang him as high as Haman, Anselm!—up with him!—down with his dwelling-place, root and branch, hearthstone and roof-tree,—down with it all, and sow the site with salt and sawdust!"

St. Austin, it will be perceived, was a radical reformer.

"Marry will I," quoth the Abbot, warming with the Saint's eloquence: "ay, marry will I, and that *instanter*. But there is one thing you have forgotten, most Beatified—the name of the culprit."

"Robert de Shurland."

"The Lord of Sheppey! Bless me!" said the Abbot, crossing himself, "won't that be rather inconvenient? Sir Robert is a bold baron, and a powerful;—blows will come and go, and crowns will be cracked and——"

"What is that to you, since yours will not be of the number?"

"Very true, *Beatissime!*—I will don me with speed, and do your bidding."

"Do so, Anselm!—fail not to hang the baron, burn his castle, confiscate his estate, and buy me two large wax candles for my own particular shrine out of your share of the property."

With this solemn injunction the vision began to fade.

" One thing more ! " cried the Abbot, grasping his rosary.

" What is that ? " asked the Saint.

" *O Beate Augustine, ora pro nobis !* "

" Of course I shall," said St. Austin.   " *Pax vobiscum !* "—and Abbot Anselm was left alone.

Within an hour all Canterbury was in commotion. A friar had been murdered,—two friars—ten—twenty ; a whole convent had been assaulted,—sacked,—burnt,—all the monks had been killed, and all the nuns had been kissed !—Murder !—fire !—sacrilege ! Never was city in such an uproar. From St. George's gate to St. Dunstan's suburb, from the Donjon to the borough of Staplegate, all was noise and hub-bub. " Where was it ? "—" When was it ? "—" How was it ? " The Mayor caught up his chain, the Aldermen donned their furred gowns, the Town Clerk put on his spectacles. " Who was he ? "—" What was he ? "—" Where was he ? "—he should be hanged,—he should be burned,—he should be broiled,—he should be fried,—he should be scraped to death with red-hot oyster-shells ! " Who was he ? "—" What was his name ? "

The Abbot's Apparitor drew forth his roll and read aloud :—" Sir Robert de Shurland, Knight banneret, Baron of Shurland and Minster, and Lord of Sheppey."

The Mayor put his chain in his pocket, the Aldermen took off their gowns, the Town Clerk put his pen behind his ear.—It was a county business altogether :—the Sheriff had better call out the *posse comitatus.*

While saints and sinners were thus leaguing against him, the Baron de Shurland was quietly eating his breakfast. He had passed a tranquil night, undisturbed by dreams of cowl or capuchin ; nor was his appetite more affected than his conscience. On the contrary, he sat rather longer over his meal than usual : luncheon-time came, and he was ready as ever for his oysters : but scarcely had Dame Martin opened his first half-dozen when the warder's horn was heard from the barbican.

" Who the devil's that ? " said Sir Robert. " I'm not at home, Periwinkle. I hate to be disturbed at meals, and I won't be at home to anybody."

" An't please your lordship," answered the Seneschal, " Paul Prior hath given notice that there is a body——"

" Another body ! " roared the Baron. " Am I to be everlastingly plagued with bodies ? No time allowed me to swallow a morsel. Throw it into the moat ! "

" So please you, my lord, it is a body of horse,—and—and Paul says there is a still larger body of foot behind it ; and he thinks, my lord,—that is, he does not know, but he thinks—and we all think, my lord, that they are coming to—to besiege the castle ! "

" Besiege the castle ! Who ? What ? What for ? "

" Paul says, my lord, that he can see the banner of St. Austin, and the bleeding heart of Hamo de Crevecœur, the Abbot's chief vassal ; and there is John de Northwood, the sheriff, with his red-cross engrailed ; and Hever, and Leybourne, and Heaven knows how many more ; and they are all coming on as fast as ever they can."

" Periwinkle," said the Baron, " up with the drawbridge ; down with the portcullis ; bring me a cup of canary, and my nightcap. I won't be bothered with them. I shall go to bed."

" To bed, my lord ? " cried Periwinkle, with a look that seemed to say, " He's crazy ! "

At this moment the shrill tones of a trumpet were heard to sound thrice from the champaign. It was the signal for parley : the Baron changed his mind ; instead of going to bed, he went to the ramparts.

" Well, rapscallions ! and what now ? " said the Baron.

A herald, two pursuivants, and a trumpeter, occupied the foreground of the scene ; behind them, some three hundred paces off, upon a rising ground, was drawn up in battle array the main body of the ecclesiastical forces.

" Hear you, Robert de Shurland, Knight, Baron of Shurland and Minster, and Lord of Sheppey, and know all men, by these presents, that I do hereby attach you, the said Robert, of murder and sacrilege, now, or of late, done and committed by you, the said Robert, contrary to the peace of our Sovereign Lord the King, his crown and dignity : and I do hereby require and charge you, the said Robert, to forthwith surrender and give up your own proper person, together with the castle of Shurland aforesaid, in order that the same may be duly dealt with according to law. And here standeth John de Northwood, Esquire, good man and true, sheriff of this his Majesty's most loyal county of Kent, to enforce the same, if need be, with his *posse comitatus*——"

" His what ? " said the Baron.

" His *posse comitatus*, and——"

" Go to Bath ! " said the Baron.

A defiance so contemptuous roused the ire of the adverse commanders. A volley of missiles rattled about the Baron's ears.

Nightcaps avail little against contusions. He left the walls, and returned to the great hall.

"Let them pelt away," quoth the Baron; "there are no windows to break, and they can't get in."—So he took his afternoon nap, and the siege went on.

Towards evening his lordship awoke, and grew tired of the din. Guy Pearson, too, had got a black eye from a brick-bat, and the assailants were clambering over the outer wall. So the Baron called for his Sunday hauberk of Milan steel, and his great two-handed sword with the terrible name;—it was the fashion in feudal times to give names to swords: King Arthur's was christened Excalibar; the Baron called his Tickletoby, and whenever he took it in hand it was no joke.

"Up with the portcullis! down with the bridge!" said Sir Robert; and out he sallied, followed by the *élite* of his retainers. Then there was a pretty to-do. Heads flew one way—arms and legs another; round went Tickletoby; and, wherever it alighted, down came horse and man: the Baron excelled himself that day. All that he had done in Palestine faded in the comparison; he had fought for fun there, but now it was for life and lands. Away went John de Northwood; away went William of Hever, and Roger of Leybourne.—Hamo de Crevecœur, with the church vassals and the banner of St. Austin, had been gone some time.—The siege was raised, and the Lord of Sheppey was left alone in his glory.

But brave as the Baron undoubtedly was, and total as had been the defeat of his enemies, it cannot be supposed that *La Stoccata* would be allowed to carry it away thus. It has before been hinted that Abbot Anselm had written to the Pope, and Boniface the Eighth piqued himself on his punctuality as a correspondent in all matters connected with church discipline. He sent back an answer by return of post; and by it all Christian people were strictly enjoined to aid in exterminating the offender, on pain of the greater excommunication in this world and a million of years of purgatory in the next. But then, again, Boniface the Eighth was rather at a discount in England just then. He had affronted Longshanks, as the loyal lieges had nicknamed their monarch; and Longshanks had been rather sharp upon the clergy in consequence. If the Baron de Shurland could but get the King's pardon for what, in his cooler moments, he admitted to be a peccadillo, he might sniff at the Pope, and bid him "do his devilmost."

Fortune, who, as the poet says, delights to favour the bold, stood his friend on this occasion. Edward had been, for some time, collecting

Then there was a pretty to-do, heads flew one way—arms and legs another

a large force on the coast of Kent, to carry on his French wars for the recovery of Guienne; he was expected shortly to review it in person; but, then, the troops lay principally in cantonments about the mouth of the Thames, and his Majesty was to come down by water. What was to be done?—the royal barge was in sight, and John de Northwood and Hamo de Crevecœur had broken up all the boats to boil their camp-kettles.—A truly great mind is never without resources.

"Bring me my boots!" said the Baron.

They brought him his boots, and his dapple-grey steed along with them. Such a courser! all blood and bone, short-backed, broad-chested, and,—but that he was a little ewe-necked,—faultless in form and figure. The Baron sprang upon his back, and dashed at once into the river.

The barge which carried Edward Longshanks and his fortunes had by this time nearly reached the Nore: the stream was broad and the current strong, but Sir Robert and his steed were almost as broad, and a great deal stronger. After breasting the tide gallantly for a couple of miles, the Knight was near enough to hail the steersman.

"What have we got here?" said the King.—"It's a mermaid," said one.—"It's a grampus," said another.—"It's the devil," said a third.—But they were all wrong; it was only Robert de Shurland. "Grammercy," quoth the King, "that fellow was never born to be drowned!"

It has been said before that the Baron had fought in the Holy wars; in fact, he had accompanied Longshanks, when only heir apparent, in his expedition twenty-five years before, although his name is unaccountably omitted by Sir Harris Nicolas in his list of crusaders. He had been present at Acre when Amirand of Joppa stabbed the prince with a poisoned dagger, and had lent Princess Eleanor his own tooth-brush after she had sucked out the venom from the wound.—He had slain certain Saracens, contented himself with his own plunder, and never dunned the commissariat for arrears of pay.—Of course he ranked high in Edward's good graces, and had received the honour of knighthood at his hands on the field of battle.

In one so circumstanced it cannot be supposed that such a trifle as the killing of a frowzy friar would be much resented, even had he not taken so bold a measure to obtain his pardon. His petition was granted, of course, as soon as asked; and so it would have been had the indictment drawn up by the Canterbury Town Clerk, viz., "That he the said Robert de Shurland, &c., had then and there, with several, to wit, one thousands, pairs of boots, given sundry, to wit, two thousand, kicks, and therewith and thereby killed divers, to wit, ten thousand, Austin friars," been true to the letter.

Thrice did the gallant grey circumnavigate the barge, while Robert de Winchelsey, the chancellor, and archbishop to boot, was making out, albeit with great reluctance, the royal pardon. The interval was sufficiently long to enable His Majesty, who, gracious as he was, had always an eye to business, just to hint that the gratitude he felt towards the Baron was not unmixed with a lively sense of services, to come ; and that, if life were now spared him, common decency must oblige him to make himself useful. Before the archbishop, who had scalded his fingers with the wax in affixing the great seal, had time to take them out of his mouth, all was settled, and the Baron de Shurland had pledged himself to be forthwith in readiness, *cum suis*, to accompany his liege lord to Guienne.

With the royal pardon secured in his vest, boldly did his lordship turn again to the shore ; and as boldly did his courser oppose his breadth of chest to the stream. It was a work of no common difficulty or

danger ; a steed of less " mettle and bone " had long since sunk in the effort : as it was, the Baron's boots were full of water, and Grey Dolphin's chamfrain more than once dipped beneath the wave. The convulsive snorts of the noble animal showed his distress ; each instant they became more loud and frequent ; when his hoof touched the strand, and "the horse and his rider" stood once again in safety on the shore.

Rapidly dismounting, the Baron was loosening the girths of his demipique, to give the panting animal breath, when he was aware of as ugly an old woman as he had ever clapped eyes upon, peeping at him under the horse's belly.

"Make much of your steed, Robert Shurland! Make much of your steed!" cried the hag, shaking at him her long and bony finger. "Groom to the hide, and corn to the manger! He has saved your life, Robert Shurland, for the nonce; but he shall yet be the means of your losing it, for all that!"

The Baron started: "What's that you say, you old faggot?"—He ran round by his horse's tail;—the woman was gone!

The Baron paused; his great soul was not to be shaken by trifles; he looked around him, and solemnly ejaculated the word "Humbug!" —then slinging the bridle across his arm, walked slowly on in the direction of the castle.

The appearance, and still more the disappearance, of the crone, had however made an impression; every step he took he became more thoughtful. "'Twould be deuced provoking, though, if he *should* break my neck after all."—He turned and gazed at Dolphin with the scrutinizing eye of a veterinary surgeon.—"I'll be shot if he is not groggy!" said the Baron.

With his lordship, like another great Commander, "Once to be in doubt, was once to be resolved:" it would never do to go to the wars on a rickety prad. He dropped the rein, drew forth Tickletoby, and, as the enfranchised Dolphin, good easy horse, stretched out his ewe-neck to the herbage, struck off his head at a single blow. "There, you lying old beldame!" said the Baron; "now take him away to the knacker's."

* · * * * * * *

Three years were come and gone, King Edward's French wars were over; both parties, having fought till they came to a standstill, shook hands; and the quarrel, as usual, was patched up by a royal marriage. This happy event gave his Majesty leisure to turn his attention to Scotland, where things, through the intervention of William Wallace, were looking rather queerish. As his reconciliation with Philip now allowed of his fighting the Scotch in peace and quietness, the monarch lost no time in marching his long legs across the border, and the short ones of the Baron followed him of course. At Falkirk, Tickletoby was in great request; and in the year following, we find a contemporary poet hinting at his master's prowess under the walls of Caerlaverock,

Øbee eus fu achimineʒ
Li beau Robert de Shurland
Ki kant seoit sur le cheval
Ne sembloit home ke someille.

A quatrain which Mr. Simpkinson translates,

"With them was marching
The good Robert de Shurland,
Who, when seated on horseback,
Does not resemble a man asleep!"

So thoroughly awake, indeed, does he seem to have proved himself, that the bard subsequently exclaims, in an ecstasy of admiration,

Si ie estoie une pucelette
Je li donroie ceur et cors
Tant est de lu bons li recors.

"If I were a young maiden,
I would give my heart and person,
So great is his fame!"

Fortunately the poet was a tough old monk of Exeter; since such a present to a nobleman, now in his grand climacteric, would hardly have been worth the carriage. With the reduction of this stronghold of the Maxwells seem to have concluded the Baron's military services; as on the very first day of the fourteenth century we find him once more landed on his native shore, and marching, with such of his retainers as the wars had left him, towards the hospitable shelter of Shurland Castle. It was then, upon that very beach, some hundred yards distant from high-water mark, that his eye fell upon something like an ugly old woman in a red cloak! She was seated on what seemed to be a large stone, in an interesting attitude, with her elbows resting upon her knees, and her chin upon her thumbs. The Baron started : the remembrance of his interview with a similar personage in the same place some three years since, flashed upon his recollection. He rushed towards the spot, but the form was gone ;—nothing remained but the seat it had appeared to occupy. This, on examination, turned out to be no stone, but the whitened skull of a dead horse !—A tender remembrance of the deceased Grey Dolphin shot a momentary pang into the Baron's bosom ; he drew the back of his hand across his face ; the thought of the hag's prediction in an instant rose, and banished all softer emotions. In utter contempt of his own weakness, yet with a tremor that deprived his redoubtable kick of half its wonted force, he spurned the relic with his foot. One word alone issued from his lips, elucidatory of what was passing in his mind,—it long remained imprinted on the memory of his faithful followers,—that word was "Gammon!" The skull bounded across the beach till it reached the very margin of the stream ;—one instant more, and it would be engulfed for ever. At that moment a loud "Ha! ha! ha!" was distinctly heard by the whole train to issue from its bleached and toothless jaws ; it sank beneath the flood in a horse laugh !

Meanwhile Sir Robert de Shurland felt an odd sort of sensation in his right foot. His boots had suffered in the wars. Great pains had been taken for their preservation. They had been "soled" and "heeled" more than once;—had they been "goloshed," their owner might have defied Fate ! Well has it been said that "there is no such thing as a trifle." A nobleman's life depended upon a question of ninepence.

The Baron marched on; the uneasiness in his foot increased. He plucked off his boot;—a horse's tooth was sticking in his great toe !

The result may be anticipated. Lame as he was, his lordship, with characteristic decision, would hobble on to Shurland; his walk increased the inflammation ; a flagon of *aqua vitæ* did not mend matters. He was in a high fever; he took to his bed. Next morning the toe presented the appearance of a Bedfordshire carrot ; by dinner-time it had deepened to beet-root ; and when Bargrave, the leech, at last sliced it off, the gangrene was too confirmed to admit of remedy. Dame Martin thought it high time to send for Miss Margaret, who, ever since her mother's death, had been living with her maternal aunt, the abbess, in the Ursuline convent at Greenwich. The young lady came, and with her came one Master Ingoldsby, her cousin-german by the mother's side ; but the Baron was too far gone in the dead-thraw to recognise either. He died as he lived, unconquered and unconquerable. His last words were—"Tell the old hag she may go to——." Whither remains a secret. He expired without fully articulating the place of her destination.

But who and what *was* the crone who prophesied the catastrophe ? Ay, "that is the mystery of this wonderful history."—Some say it was Dame Fothergill, the late confessor's mamma ; others, St. Bridget herself ; others thought it was nobody at all, but only a phantom conjured up by conscience. As we do not know, we decline giving an opinion.

And what became of the Clerk of Chatham ?—Mr. Simpkinson avers that he lived to a good old age, and was at last hanged by Jack Cade, with his inkhorn about his neck, for "setting boys copies." In support of this he adduces his name "Emmanuel," and refers to the historian Shakspear. Mr. Peters, on the contrary, considers this to be what he calls one of Mr. Simpkinson's "Anacreonisms," inasmuch as, at the introduction of Mr. Cade's reform measure, the Clerk, if alive, would have been hard upon two hundred years old. The probability is, that the unfortunate alluded to was his great-grandson.

Margaret Shurland in due course became Margaret Ingoldsby, her portrait still hangs in the gallery at Tappington. The features are handsome, but shrewish, betraying, as it were, a touch of the old Baron's temperament; but we never could learn that she actually kicked her husband. She brought him a very pretty fortune in chains, owches, and Saracen ear-rings; the barony, being a male fief, reverted to the Crown.

In the abbey-church at Minster may yet be seen the tomb of a recumbent warrior, clad in the chain-mail of the 13th century.* His hands are clasped in prayer; his legs, crossed in that position so prized by Templars in ancient, and tailors in modern days, bespeak him a soldier of the faith in Palestine. Close behind his dexter calf lies sculptured in bold relief a horse's head; and a respectable elderly lady, as she shows the monument, fails not to read her auditors a fine moral lesson on the sin of ingratitude, or to claim a sympathising tear to the memory of poor " Grey Dolphin ! "

It is on my own personal reminiscences that I draw for the following story; the scene of its leading event was most familiar to me in early life. If the principal actor in it be yet living, he must have reached a very advanced age. He was often at the Hall, in my infancy, on professional visits. It is, however, only from those who " prated of his whereabouts " that I learned the history of his adventure with

The Ghost

THERE stands a City,—neither large nor small,
　　Its air and situation sweet and pretty;
It matters very little—if at all—
　　Whether its denizens are dull or witty,
Whether the ladies there are short or tall,
　　Brunettes or blondes, only, there stands a city !—
Perhaps 'tis also requisite to minute
That there's a Castle and a Cobbler in it.

---

* Subsequent to the first appearance of the foregoing narrative, the tomb alluded to has been opened during the course of certain repairs which the church has undergone. Mr. Simpkinson, who was present at the exhumation of the body within, and has enriched his collection with three of its grinders, says the bones of one of the great toes were wanting. He speaks in terms of great admiration at the thickness of the skull, and is of opinion that the skeleton is that of a great patriot much addicted to Lundy-foot.

A fair Cathedral, too, the story goes,
   And kings and heroes lie entomb'd within her ;
There pious saints, in marble pomp repose,
   Whose shrines are worn by knees of many a Sinner ;
There, too, full many an Aldermanic nose
   Roll'd its loud diapason after dinner ;
And there stood high the holy sconce of Becket,
—Till four assassins came from France to crack it.

The Castle was a huge and antique mound,
   Proof against all th' artillery of the quiver,
Ere those abominable guns were found,
   To send cold lead through gallant warriors' liver.
It stands upon a gently rising ground,
   Sloping down gradually to the river,
Resembling (to compare great things with smaller)
A well-scooped, mouldy Stilton cheese,—but taller.

The keep, I find, 's been sadly alter'd lately,
   And, 'stead of mail-clad knights, of honour jealous,
In martial panoply so grand and stately,
   Its walls are filled with money-making fellows,
And stuff'd, unless I'm misinformed greatly,
   With leaden pipes, and coke, and coals, and bellows ;
In short, so great a change has come to pass,
'Tis now a manufactory of Gas.

But to my tale.—Before this profanation,
   And ere its ancient glories were cut short all,
A poor hard-working Cobbler took his station
   In a small house, just opposite the portal ;
His birth, his parentage, and education,
   I know but little of—a strange, odd mortal ;
His aspect, air, and gait, were all ridiculous ;
His name was Mason—he'd been christened Nicholas.

Nick had a wife possessed of many a charm,
   And of the Lady Huntingdon persuasion ;
But, spite of all her piety, her arm
   She'd sometimes exercise when in a passion ;

And, being of a temper somewhat warm,
   Would now and then seize, upon small occasion,
A stick, or stool, or anything that round did lie ,
And baste her lord and master most confoundedly.

No matter !—'tis a thing that's not uncommon,
   'Tis what we all have heard, and most have read of,—
I mean, a bruizing, pugilistic woman,
   Such as I own I entertain a dread of,
—And so did Nick,—whom sometimes there would come on
   A sort of fear his Spouse might knock his head off,
Demolish half his teeth, or drive a rib in,
She shone so much in " facers " and in " fibbing."

" There's time and place for all things," said a sage,
   (King Solomon, I think,) and this I can say,
Within· a well-roped ring, or on a stage,
   Boxing may be a very pretty *Fancy*,
When Messrs. Burke or Bendigo engage ;
   —'Tis not so well in Susan, Jane, or Nancy :—
To get well mill'd by any one's an evil,
But by a lady—'tis the very Devil.

And so thought Nicholas, whose only trouble,
   (At least his worst,) was this his rib's propensity,
For sometimes from the alehouse he would hobble,
   His senses lost in a sublime immensity
Of cogitation—then he couldn't cobble—
   And then his wife would often try the density
Of his poor skull, and strike with all her might,
As fast as kitchen-wenches strike a light.

Mason, meek soul, who ever hated strife,
   Of this same striking had a morbid dread,
He hated it like poison—or his wife—
   A vast antipathy !—but so he said—
And very often, for a quiet life,
   On these occasions he'd sneak up to bed,
Grope darkling in, and, soon as at the door
He heard his lady—he'd pretend to snore.

One night, then, ever partial to society,
   Nick, with a friend (another jovial fellow,)
Went to a Club—I should have said Society—
   At the " City Arms," once call'd the Porto Bello ;
A Spouting party, which, though some decry it, I
   Consider no bad lounge when one is mellow ;
There they discuss the tax on salt, and leather,
And change of ministers and change of weather.

In short, it was a kind of British Forum,
   Like John Gale Jones's, erst in Piccadilly,
Only they managed things with more decorum,
   And the Orations were not *quite* so silly ;
Far different questions, too, would come before 'em,
   Not always Politics, which, will ye nill ye,
Their London prototypes were always willing,
To give one *quantum suff*. of—for a shilling.

It more resembled one of later date,
   And tenfold talent, as I'm told in Bow Street,
Where kindlier natured souls do congregate,
    And, though there are who deem that same a low street,
Yet, I'm assured, for frolicsome debate
    And genuine humour it's surpassed by no street,
When the " Chief Baron " enters, and assumes
To " rule " o'er mimic " Thesigers " and " Broughams."

Here they would oft forget their Ruler's faults,
    And waste in ancient lore the midnight taper,
Inquire if Orpheus first produced the Waltz,
    How Gas-lights differ from the Delphic Vapour,
Whether Hippocrates gave Glauber's Salts,
    And what the Romans wrote on ere they'd paper ;—
This night the subject of their disquisitions
Was Ghosts, Hobgoblins, Sprites, and Apparitions.

One learned gentleman, a " sage grave man,"
    Talk'd of the Ghost in Hamlet, " sheath'd in steel ; "—
His well-read friend, who next to speak began,
    Said, " That was Poetry, and nothing real ; "
A third, of more extensive learning, ran
    To Sir George Villiers' Ghost, and Mrs. Veal ;
Of sheeted spectres spoke with shorten'd breath,
And thrice he quoted " Drelincourt on Death."

Nick smoked, and smoked, and trembled as he heard
    The point discuss'd, and all they said upon it,
How, frequently, some murder'd man appear'd,
    To tell his wife and children who had done it ;
Or how a Miser's ghost, with grisly beard,
    And pale lean visage, in an old Scotch bonnet,
Wander'd about to watch his buried money !
When all at once Nick heard the clock strike One,—he

Sprang from his seat, not doubting but a lecture
    Impended from his fond and faithful She ;
Nor could he well to pardon him expect her,
    For he had promised to " be home to tea ; "

If Orpheus first produced the waltz

But having luckily the key o' the back door,
   He fondly hoped that, unperceived, he
Might creep up stairs again, pretend to doze,
And hoax his spouse with music from his nose.

Vain, fruitless hope !—The wearied sentinel
   At eve may overlook the crouching foe,
Till, ere his hand can sound the alarum-bell
   He sinks beneath the unexpected blow ;
Before the whispers of Grimalkin fell,
   When slumb'ring on her post, the mouse may go ;—
But woman, wakeful woman, 's never weary,
—Above all, when she waits to thump her deary.

Soon Mrs. Mason heard the well-known tread ;
   She heard the key slow creaking in the door,
Spied, through the gloom obscure, towards the bed
   Nick creeping soft, as oft he had crept before ;
When, bang, she threw a something at his head,
   And Nick at once lay prostrate on the floor ;
While she exclaim'd with her indignant face on,—
" How dare you use your wife so, Mr. Mason ? "

Spare we to tell how fiercely she debated,
   Especially the length of her oration,—
Spare we to tell how Nick expostulated,
   Roused by the bump into a good set passion,
So great, that more than once he execrated,
   Ere he crawl'd into bed in his usual fashion ;
—The Muses hate brawls ; suffice it then to say,
He duck'd below the clothes—and there he lay !

'Twas now the very witching time of night,
   When churchyards groan, and graves give up their dead,
And many a mischievous, enfranchised Sprite
   Had long since burst his bonds of stone or lead,
And hurried off, with schoolboy-like delight,
   To play his pranks near some poor wretch's bed,
Sleeping perhaps serenely as a porpoise,
Nor dreaming of this fiendish Habeas Corpus.

Not so our Nicholas, his meditations
  Still to the same tremendous theme recurred,
The same dread subject of the dark narrations,
  Which, back'd with such authority, he'd heard ;
Lost in his own horrific contemplations,
    He ponder'd o'er each well-remember'd word ;
When at the bed's foot, close beside the post,
He verily believed he saw—a Ghost !

Plain and more plain the unsubstantial Sprite
  To his astonish'd gaze each moment grew ;
Ghastly and gaunt, it rear'd its shadowy height,
  Of more than mortal seeming to the view,
And round its long, thin, bony fingers drew
    A tatter'd winding sheet, of course *all white ;*
The moon that moment peeping through a cloud,
Nick very plainly saw it *through the shroud !*

And now those matted locks, which never yet
  Had yielded to the comb's unkind divorce,
Their long-contracted amity forget,
  And spring asunder with elastic force ;
Nay, e'en the very cap, of texture coarse,
    Whose ruby cincture crown'd that brow of jet,
Uprose in agony—the Gorgon's head
Was but a type of Nick's up-squatting in the bed.

From every pore distill'd a clammy dew,
  Quaked every limb,—the candle too no doubt,
En règle, would have burnt extremely blue,
  But Nick unluckily had put it out ;
And he, though naturally bold and stout,
    In short, was in a most tremendous stew ;—
The room was fill'd with a sulphureous smell,
But where that came from Mason could not tell.

All motionless the Spectre stood,—and now
  Its rev'rend form more clearly shone confest ;
From the pale cheek a beard of purest snow
  Descended o'er its venerable breast ;

The thin grey hairs, that crown'd its furrow'd brow,
Told of years long gone by.—An awful guest
It stood, and with an action of command,
Beckon'd the Cobbler with its wan right hand.

"Whence, and what art thou,
　　Execrable Shape?"
　Nick *might* have cried,
　　could he have found a
　　tongue,
But his distended jaws could
　　only gape,
　And not a sound upon the
　　welkin rung:
His gooseberry orbs seem'd
　　as they would have
　　sprung
　Forth from their sockets,—
　　like a frightened Ape
He sat upon his haunches,
　　bolt upright,
And shook, and grinn'd, and
　　chatter'd with affright.

And still the shadowy finger,
　　long and lean,
　Now beckon'd Nick, now
　　pointed to the door;
And many an ireful glance,
　　and frown, between,
The angry visage of the
　　Phantom wore,
As if quite vex'd that Nick
　　would do no more
Than stare, without e'en ask-
　　ing, "What d'ye mean?"
Because, as we are told,—a
　　sad old joke too,—
Ghosts, like the ladies, "never speak till spoke to."

Cowards, 'tis said, in certain situations,
　Derive a sort of courage from despair.

E

And then perform, from downright desperation,
  Much more than many a bolder man would dare,
Nick saw the Ghost was getting in a passion,
  And therefore, gróping till he found the chair,
Seized on his awl, crept softly out of bed,
And follow'd quaking where the Spectre led.

And down the winding stair, with noiseless tread,
  The tenant of the tomb pass'd slowly on,
Each mazy turning of the humble shed
  Seem'd to his step at once familiar grown,
So safe and sure the labyrinth did he tread
  As though the domicile had been his own,
Though Nick himself, in passing through the shop,
Had almost broke his nose against the mop.

Despite its wooden bolt, with jarring sound,
  The door upon its hinges open flew ;
And forth the Spirit issued,—yet around
  It turn'd as if its follower's fears it knew,
And, once more beckoning, pointed to the mound,
  The antique Keep, on which the bright moon threw
With such effulgence her mild silvery gleam,
The visionary form seem'd melting in her beam.

Beneath a pond'rous archway's sombre shade,
  Where once the huge portcullis swung sublime,
'Mid ivied battlements in ruin laid,
  Sole, sad memorials of the olden time,
The Phantom held its way,—and though afraid
  Even of the owls that sung their vesper chime,
Pale Nicholas pursued, its steps attending,
And wondering what on earth it all would end in.

Within the mouldering fabric's deep recess
  At length they reach a court obscure and lone ;—
It seem'd a drear and desolate wilderness,
  The blacken'd walls with ivy all o'ergrown ;
The night-bird shriek'd her note of wild distress,
  Disturb'd upon her solitary throne,
As though indignant mortal step should dare,
So led, at such an hour, to venture there !

—The Apparition paused, and would have spoke,
  Pointing to what Nick thought an iron ring,
But then a neighbouring chanticleer awoke,
  And loudly 'gan his early matins sing ;
And then " it started like a guilty thing,"
  As that shrill clarion the silence broke.
—We know how much dead gentlefolks eschew
The appalling sound of " Cock-a-doodle-do ! "

The vision was no more—and Nick alone—
  " His streamers waving " in the midnight wind,
Which through the ruins ceased not to groan ;
  —His garment, too, was somewhat short behind,—
And, worst of all, he knew not where to find
  The ring,—which made him most his fate bemoan ;—
The iron ring,—no doubt of some trap door,
'Neath which the old dead Miser kept his store.

" What's to be done ? " he cried, " 'Twere vain to stay
  Here in the dark without a single clue—
Oh, for a candle now, or moonlight ray !
  'Fore George, I'm vastly puzzled what to do,"
(Then clapped his hand behind)—" 'Tis chilly too—
  I'll mark the spot, and come again by day.
What can I mark it by ?—Oh, here's the wall—
The mortar's yielding—here I'll stick my awl ! "

Then rose from earth to sky a withering shriek,
  A loud, a long protracted note of woe,
Such as when tempests roar, and timbers creak,
  And o'er the side the masts in thunder go ;
While on the deck resistless billows break,
  And drag their victims to the gulfs below ;—
Such was the scream when, for the want of candle,
Nick Mason drove his awl in up to the handle.

Scared by his Lady's heart-appalling cry,
  Vanished at once poor Mason's golden dream—
For dream it was ;—and all his visions high,
  Of wealth and grandeur, fled before that scream—

And still he listens with averted eye,
  When gibing neighbours make " the Ghost " their theme ;
While ever from that hour they all declare
That Mrs. Mason used a cushion in her chair !

Confound not, I beseech thee, reader, the subject of the following monody with the hapless hero of the tea-urn, Cupid, of " Yow-Yow "-ing memory. Tray was an attached favourite of many years' standing. Most people worth loving have had a friend of this kind ; Lord Byron says he " never had but one, and here he (the dog, not the nobleman) lies ! "

THE CYNOTAPH

Poor Tray charmant !
Poor Tray de mon Ami !
  Dog-bury and Vergers.

Oh ! where shall I bury my poor dog Tray,
Now his fleeting breath has passed away ?—
Seventeen years, I can venture to say,
Have I seen him gambol, and frolic, and play,
Evermore happy, and frisky, and gay,
As though every one of his months was May,
And the whole of his life one long holiday—
Now he's a lifeless lump of clay,
Oh ! where shall I bury my faithful Tray ?

I am almost tempted to think it hard
That it may not be there, in yon sunny churchyard,
  Where the green willows wave
    O'er the peaceful grave,
Which holds all that once was honest and brave,
Kind, and courteous, and faithful, and true ;
Qualities, Tray, that were found in you.

But it may not be—yon sacred ground,
By holiest feelings fenced around,
May ne'er within its hallow'd bound
Receive the dust of a soul-less hound.

I would not place him in yonder fane,
Where the mid-day sun through the storied pane
Throws on the pavement a crimson stain ;
Where the banners of chivalry heavily swing
O'er the pinnacled tomb of the Warrior King,
With helmet and shield, and all that sort of thing.
   No !—come what may.   My gentle Tray
Shan't be an intruder on bluff Harry Tudor,
Or panoplied monarchs yet earlier and ruder;
   Whom you see on their backs,   In stone or in wax,
Though the Sacristans now are " forbidden to ax "
For what Mister Hume calls " a scandalous tax ; "
While the Chartists insist they've a right to go snacks.—
No !—Tray's humble tomb would look but shabby
'Mid the sculptured shrines of that gorgeous Abbey.
   Besides, in the place   They say there's no space
To bury what wet-nurses call " a Babby."
Even " Rare Ben Jonson," that famous wight,
I am told, is interr'd there bolt upright,
In just such a posture, beneath his bust,
As Tray used to sit in to beg for a crust.
   The epitaph, too,   Would scarcely do ;
For what could it say, but, " Here lies Tray,
A very good kind of a dog in his day ? "
And satirical folks might be apt to imagine it
Meant as a quiz on the House of Plantagenet.

No ! no !—The Abbey may do very well
For a feudal " Nob," or poetical " Swell,"
" Crusaders," or " Poets," or " Knights of St. John,"
Or Knights of St. John's Wood, who once went on
   To the Castle of Goode Lorde Eglintonne,
Count Fiddle-fumkin, and Lord Fiddle-faddle,
" Sir Craven," " Sir Gael," and " Sir Campbell of Saddell,"
(Who, as poor Hook said, when he heard of the feat,
" Was somehow knock'd out of his family-seat : ")

The Esquires of the body   To my Lord Tomnoddy ;
" Sir Fairlie," " Sir Lamb,"
And the " Knight of the Ram,"
The " Knight of the Rose," and the " Knight of the Dragon,"
   Who, save at the flagon,   And prog in the wagon,
The newspapers tell us did little " to brag on ; "
And more, though the Muse knows but little concerning 'em,
" Sir Hopkins," " Sir Popkins," " Sir Gage," and " Sir Jerningham,"
All *Preux Chevaliers*, in friendly rivalry
Who should best bring back the glory of Chi-valry.—
—(Pray be so good, for the sake of my song,
To pronounce here the ante-penultimate long ;
Or some hyper-critic will certainly cry,
" The word ' Chivalry ' is but a ' rhyme to the eye.' "
   And I own it is clear   A fastidious ear
Will be, more or less, always annoy'd with you when you in-
sert any rhyme that's not perfectly genuine.
   As to pleasing the " eye,"   'Tisn't worth while to try,
Since Moore and Tom Campbell themselves admit " Spinach "
Is perfectly antiphonetic to " Greenwich.")—
But stay !—I say !   Let me pause while I may—
This digression is leading me sadly astray
From my object—A grave for my poor dog Tray !

I would not place him beneath thy walls,
And proud o'ershadowing dome, St. Paul's !
Though I've always consider'd Sir Christopher Wren,
As an architect, one of the greatest of men ;
And,—talking of Epitaphs,—much I admire his,
" *Circumspice, si Monumentum requiris ;* "
Which an erudite Verger translated to me,
" If you ask for his monument, *Sir-come-spy-see !* "—
   No !—I should not know where   To place him there ;
I would not have him by surly Johnson be ;—
Or that queer-looking horse that is rolling on Ponsonby ;—
   Or those ugly minxes   The sister Sphynxes,
Mix'd creatures, half lady, half lioness, *ergo*,
(Denon says), the emblems of *Leo* and *Virgo ;*
On one of the backs of which singular jumble,
Sir Ralph Abercrombie is going to tumble,

With a thump which alone were enough to despatch him,
If the Scotchman in front shouldn't happen to catch him.

No ! I'd not have him there,—nor nearer the door,
Where the man and the Angel have got Sir John Moore,*
And are quietly letting him down through the floor,
By Gillespie, the one who escaped, at Vellore,
   Alone from the row ;—Neither he, nor Lord Howe
Would like to be plagued with a little Bow-wow.
   No, Tray, we must yield,   And go further a-field ;
To lay you by Nelson were downright effront'ry ;—
—We'll be off from the City, and look at the country.

   It shall not be there,   In that sepulchred square,
Where folks are interr'd for the sake of the air,
(Though, pay but the dues, they could hardly refuse
To Tray what they grant to Thuggs, and Hindoos,
Turks, Infidels, Heretics, Jumpers, and Jews,)
   Where the tombstones are placed   In the very *best taste*
   At the feet and the head   Of the elegant Dead,
And no one's received who's not " buried in lead : "
For, there lie the bones   Of Deputy Jones,
Whom the Widow's tears, and the orphan's groans
Affected as much as they do the stones
His executors laid on the Deputy's bones ;
   Little rest, poor knave !   Would Tray have in his grave ;
   Since Spirits, 'tis plain,   Are sent back again,
To roam round their bodies,—the bad ones in pain,—
Dragging after them sometimes a heavy jack-chain ;
Whenever they met, alarm'd by its groans, his
Ghost all night long would be barking at Jones's.

   Nor shall he be laid   By that cross Old Maid,
Miss Penelope Bird,—of whom it is said
All the dogs in the parish were ever afraid.
   He must not be placed   By one so strait-laced
   In her temper, her taste,   And her morals, and waist.
For, 'tis said, when she went up to heaven, and St. Peter,
   Who happened to meet her,   Came forward to greet her,

* See note at end of " The Cynotaph."

She pursed up with scorn every vinegar feature,
And bade him " Get out for a horrid Male Creature ! "
So, the Saint, after looking as if he could eat her,
Not knowing, perhaps, very well how to treat her,
And not being willing,—or able,—to beat her,
Sent her back to her grave till her temper grew sweeter,
With an epithet—which I decline to repeat here.
   No,—if Tray were interr'd   By Penelope Bird,
No dog would be e'er so be-" whelp " 'd and be-" cur " r'd.—
All the night long her cantankerous Sprite
Would be running about in the pale moon-light,
Chasing him round, and attempting to lick
The ghost of poor Tray with the ghost of a stick.

   Stay !—let me see !—   Ay—here it shall be
At the root of this gnarled and time-worn tree,
   Where Tray and I   Would often lie,
And watch the bright clouds as they floated by
In the broad expanse of the clear blue sky,
When the sun was bidding the world good b'ye ;
And the plaintive Nightingale, warbling nigh,
Pour'd forth her mournful melody ;
While the tender Wood-pigeon's cooing cry
Has made me to say to myself, with a sigh,
" How nice you would eat with a steak in a pie ! "

Ay, here it shall be !—far, far from the view
Of the noisy world and its maddening crew.
   Simple and few,   Tender and true
The lines o'er his grave.—They have, some of them, too,
The advantage of being remarkably new.

Epitaph.

   Affliction sore   Long time he bore,
Physicians were in vain !—
   Grown blind, alas ! he'd   Some Prussic Acid,
And that put him out of his pain !

NOTE, PAGE 71.

In the autumn of 1824, Captain Medwin having hinted that certain beautiful lines on the burial of this gallant officer might have been the production of Lord Byron's Muse, the late Mr. Sydney Taylor, somewhat indignantly, claimed them for their rightful owner, the late Rev. Charles Wolfe. During the controversy a third claimant started up in the person of a *soi-disant* " Doctor Marshall," who turned out to be a Durham blacksmith, and his pretensions a hoax. It was then that a certain " Doctor Peppercorn " put forth *his* pretensions, to what he averred was the only " true and original " version, viz. :

Not a *sous* had he got,—not a guinea or note,
  And he look'd confoundedly flurried,
As he bolted away without paying his shot,
  And the Landlady after him hurried.

We saw him again at dead of night,
  When home from the Club returning ;
We twigg'd the Doctor beneath the light
  Of the gas-lamp brilliantly burning.

All bare, and exposed to the midnight dews,
  Reclined in the gutter we found him ;
And he look'd like a gentl man taking a snooze,
  With his *Marshall* cloak around him.

" The Doctor's as drunk as the d——," we said,
  And we managed a shutter to borrow ;
We raised him, and sigh'd at the thought that his head
  Would " consumedly ache " on the morrow.

We bore him home, and we put him to bed,
  And we told his wife and his daughter
To give him, next morning, a couple of red
  Herrings, with soda-water.—

Loudly they talk'd of his money that's gone,
  And his Lady began to upbraid him ;
But little he reck'd, so they let him snore on
  'Neath the counterpane just as we laid him.

We tuck'd him in, and had hardly done
  When, beneath the window calling,
We heard the rough voice of a son of a gun
  Of a watchman " One o'clock ! " bawling.

Slowly and sadly we all walk'd down
  From his room in the uppermost story ;
A rushlight we placed on the cold hearth-stone,
  And we left him alone in his glory ! !

———————————

Hos ego versiculos feci, tulit alter honores.—VIRGIL.
I wrote the lines—* * owned them—he told stories !
                              THOMAS INGOLDSBY.

Mrs. Botherby's Story

The Leech of Folkestone

READER, were you ever bewitched?—I do not mean by a "white wench's black eye," or by love potions, imbibed from a ruby lip;—but, were you ever really and *bonâ fide* bewitched, in the true Matthew Hopkins sense of the word? Did you ever, for instance, find yourself from head to heel one vast complication of cramps?—or burst out into sudorific exudation like a cold thaw, with the thermometer at zero?— Were your eyes ever turned upside down, exhibiting nothing but their whites?—Did you ever vomit a paper of crooked pins? or expectorate Whitechapel needles?—These are genuine and undoubted marks of possession; and if you never experienced any of them,—why, " happy man be his dole!"

Yet such things have been: yea, we are assured, and that on no mean authority, still are.

The World, according to the best geographers, is divided into Europe, Asia, Africa, America, and Romney Marsh. In this last-named, and fifth quarter of the globe, a Witch may still be occasionally discovered in favourable, *i.e.*, stormy, seasons, weathering Dungeness Point in an egg-shell, or careering on her broomstick over Dymchurch wall. A cow may yet be sometimes seen galloping like mad, with tail erect, and an old pair of breeches on her horns, an unerring guide to the door of the crone whose magic arts have drained her udder.—I do not, however, remember to have heard that any Conjuror has of late been detected in the district.

Not many miles removed from the verge of this recondite region, stands a collection of houses, which its maligners call a fishing-town, and its well-wishers a Watering-place. A limb of one of the Cinque Ports, it has (or lately had) a corporation of its own, and has been thought considerable enough to give a second title to a noble family. Rome stood on seven hills ; Folkestone seems to have been built upon seventy. Its streets, lanes, and alleys,—fanciful distinctions without much real difference,—are agreeable enough to persons who do not mind running up and down stairs ; and the only inconvenience, at all felt by such of its inhabitants as are not asthmatic, is when some heedless urchin tumbles down a chimney, or an impertinent pedestrian peeps into a garret window.

At the eastern extremity of the town, on the sea-beach, and scarcely above high-water mark, stood, in the good old times, a row of houses then denominated " Frog-hole." Modern refinement subsequently euphonized the name into " East-street ; " but " what's in a name ? "— the encroachments of Ocean have long since levelled all in one common ruin.

Here, in the early part of the seventeenth century, flourished in somewhat doubtful reputation, but comparative opulence, a compounder of medicines, one Master Erasmus Buckthorne ; the effluvia of whose drugs from within mingling agreeably with the " ancient and fish-like smells " from without, wafted a delicious perfume throughout the neighbourhood.

At seven of the clock, on the morning when Mrs. Botherby's narrative commences, a stout Suffolk " punch," about thirteen hands and a half in height, was slowly led up and down before the door of the pharma-copolist by a lean and withered lad, whose appearance warranted an opinion, pretty generally expressed, that his master found him as useful in experimentalizing as in household drudgery ; and that, for every pound avoirdupois of solid meat, he swallowed, at least, two pounds troy-weight of chemicals and galenicals. As the town clock struck the quarter, Master Buckthorne emerged from his laboratory, and, putting the key carefully in to his pocket, mounted the surefooted cob aforesaid, and proceeded up and down the acclivities and declivities of the town with the gravity due to his station and profession. When he reached the open country, his pace was increased to a sedate canter, which, in somewhat more than half an hour, brought " the horse and his rider " in front of a handsome and substantial mansion, the numerous gable-ends and bayed windows of which bespoke the owner a man of worship, and one well to do in the world.

"How now, Hodge Gardener ? " quoth the Leech, scarcely drawing bit ; for Punch seemed to be aware that he had reached his destination and paused of his own accord ; "How now, man ? How fares thine employer, worthy Master Marsh ? How hath he done ? How hath he slept ?—My potion hath done its office ? Ha ! "

"Alack ! ill at ease, worthy sir—ill at ease," returned the hind ; "his honour is up and stirring ; but he hath rested none, and complaineth that the same gnawing pain devoureth, as it were, his very vitals : in sooth he is ill at ease."

"Morrow, doctor ! " interrupted a voice from a casement opening on the lawn. "Good morrow ! I have looked for, longed for, thy coming, this hour and more ; enter at once ; the pasty and tankard are impatient for thine attack ! "

"Marry, Heaven forbid that I should baulk their fancy ! " quoth the Leech *sotto voce*, as, abandoning the bridle to honest Hodge, he dismounted, and followed a buxom-looking handmaiden into the breakfast parlour.

There, at the head of his well-furnished board, sat Master Thomas Marsh, of Marston Hall, a Yeoman well respected in his degree : one of that sturdy and sterling class which, taking rank immediately below the Esquire (a title in its origin purely military,) occupied, in the wealthier counties, the position in society now filled by the Country Gentleman. He was one of those of whom the proverb ran :

> "A Knight of Cales,
>> A Gentleman of Wales,
>>> And a Laird of the North Countree ;
>> A Yeoman of Kent,
>> With his yearly rent,
>>> Will buy them out all three ! "

A cold sirloin, big enough to frighten a Frenchman, filled the place of honour, counter-checked by a game-pie of no stinted dimensions ;

while a silver flagon of " humming-bub,"—viz., ale strong enough to blow a man's beaver off,—smiled opposite in treacherous amenity. The sideboard groaned beneath sundry massive cups and waiters of the purest silver ; while the huge skull of a fallow deer, with its branching horns, frowned majestically above. All spoke of affluence, of comfort,—all save the master, whose restless eye and feverish look hinted but too plainly the severest mental or bodily disorder. By the side of the proprietor of the mansion sat his consort, a lady now past the bloom of youth, yet still retaining many of its charms. The clear olive of her complexion, and " the darkness of her Andalusian eye," at once betrayed her foreign origin ; in fact, her " lord and master," as husbands were even then, by a legal fiction, denominated, had taken her to his bosom in a foreign country. The cadet of his family, Master Thomas Marsh, had early in life been engaged in commerce. In the pursuit of his vocation he had visited Antwerp, Hamburg, and most of the Hanse Towns ; and had already formed a tender connection with the orphan offspring of one of old Alva's officers, when the unexpected deaths of one immediate, and two presumptive, heirs placed him next in succession to the family acres. He married, and brought home his bride ; who, by the decease of the venerable possessor, heart-broken at the loss of his elder children, became eventually lady of Marston Hall. It has been said that she was beautiful, yet was her beauty of a character that operates on the fancy more than the affections ; she was one to be admired rather than loved. The proud curl of her lip, the firmness of her tread, her arched brow and stately carriage, showed the decision, not to say haughtiness, of her soul ; while her glances, whether lightening with anger, or melting in extreme softness, betrayed the existence of passions as intense in kind as opposite in quality. She rose as Erasmus entered the parlour, and, bestowing on him a look fraught with meaning, quitted the room, leaving him in unrestrained communication with his patient.

" 'Fore George, Master Buckthorne ! " exclaimed the latter, as the Leech drew near, " I will no more of your pharmacy ;—burn, burn,—gnaw, gnaw,—I had as lief the foul fiend were in my gizzard as one of your drugs. Tell me, in the devil's name, what is the matter with me ! "

Thus conjured, the practitioner paused, and even turned somewhat pale. There was a perceptible faltering in his voice, as, evading the question, he asked, " What say your other physicians ? "

" Doctor Phiz says it is wind,—Doctor Fuz says it is water,—and Doctor Buz says it is something between wind and water."

" They are all of them wrong," said Erasmus Buckthorne.

"Truly, I think so," returned the patient. "They are manifest asses; but you, good Leech, you are a horse of another colour. The world talks loudly of your learning, your skill, and cunning in arts the most abstruse; nay, sooth to say, some look coldly on you therefore, and stickle not to aver that you are cater-cousin with Beelzebub himself."

"It is ever the fate of science," murmured the professor, "to be maligned by the ignorant and superstitious. But a truce with such folly; let me examine your palate."

Master Marsh thrust out a tongue long, clear, and red as beetroot. "There is nothing wrong there," said the Leech. "Your wrist :— no;—the pulse is firm and regular, the skin cool and temperate. Sir, there is nothing the matter with you!"

"Nothing the matter with me, Sir 'Potecary?—But I tell you there is the matter with me,—much the matter with me. Why is it that something seems ever gnawing at my heart-strings?—Whence this pain in the region of the liver?—Why is it that I sleep not o' nights,—rest not o' days? Why?"

"You are fidgety, Master Marsh," said the doctor.

Master Marsh's brow grew dark; he half rose from his seat, supported himself by both hands on the arms of his elbow-chair, and in accents of mingled anger and astonishment repeated the word "Fidgety!"

"Ay, fidgety," returned the doctor calmly. "Tut, man, there is nought ails thee save thine own overweening fancies. Take less of food, more air, put aside thy flagon, call for thy horse; be boot and saddle the word! Why,—hast thou not youth?"——

"I have," said the patient.

"Wealth and a fair domain?"

"Granted," quoth Marsh cheerily.

"And a fair wife?"

"Yea," was the response, but in a tone something less satisfied.

"Then arouse thee, man, shake off this fantasy, betake thyself to thy lawful occasions,—use thy good hap,—follow thy pleasures, and think no more of these fancied ailments."

"But I tell you, master mine, these ailments are not fancied. I lose my rest, I loathe my food, my doublet sits loosely on me,—these racking pains. My wife, too,—when I meet her gaze, the cold sweat stands on my forehead, and I could almost think——" Marsh paused abruptly, mused awhile, then added, looking steadily at his visitor, "These things are not right; they pass the common, Master Erasmus Buckthorne."

A slight shade crossed the brow of the Leech, but its passage was momentary; his features softened to a smile, in which pity seemed slightly blended with contempt. " Have done with such follies, Master Marsh. You are well, an you would but think so. Ride, I say, hunt, shoot, do anything,—disperse these melancholic humours, and become yourself again."

"Well, I will do your bidding," said Marsh thoughtfully. " It may be so; and yet,—but I will do your bidding. Master Cobbe of Brenzet writes me that he hath a score or two of fat ewes to be sold a pennyworth; I had thought to have sent Ralph Looker, but I will essay to go myself. Ho, there !—saddle me the brown mare, and bid Ralph be ready to attend me on the gelding."

An expression of pain contracted the features of Master Marsh as he rose and slowly quitted the apartment to prepare for his journey; while the Leech, having bidden him farewell, vanished through an opposite door, and betook himself to the private boudoir of the fair mistress of Marston, muttering as he went a quotation from a then newly published play,

> " Not poppy, nor mandragora,
> Nor all the drowsy syrups of the world,
> Shall ever medicine thee to that sweet sleep
> Which thou own'dst yesterday."

*   *   *   *   *   *   *

Of what passed at this interview between the Folkestone doctor and the fair Spaniard, Mrs. Botherby declares she could never obtain any satisfactory elucidation. Not that tradition is silent on the subject, —quite the contrary; it is the abundance, not paucity, of the materials she supplies, and the consequent embarrassment of selection, that makes the difficulty. Some have averred that the Leech, whose character, as has been before hinted, was more than threadbare, employed his time in teaching her the mode of administering certain noxious compounds, the unconscious partaker whereof would pine and die so slowly and gradually as to defy suspicion. Others there were who affirmed that Lucifer himself was then and there raised *in propriâ personâ*, with all his terrible attributes of horn and hoof. In support of this assertion, they adduce the testimony of the aforesaid buxom housemaid, who protested that the hall smelt that evening like a manufactory of matches. All, however, seemed to agree that the confabulation, whether human or infernal, was conducted with profound secrecy, and protracted to a considerable length; that its object, as far as could be divined, meant anything but good to the head of the family : that the lady, moreover, was heartily tired of her husband ; and that, in the event of his removal by disease or casualty, Master Erasmus Buckthorne, albeit a great philosophist, would have no violent objection to " throw physic to the dogs," and exchange his laboratory for the estate of Marston, its live stock included. Some, too, have inferred that to him did Madame Isabel seriously incline ; while others have thought, induced perhaps by subsequent events, that she was merely using him for her purposes ; that one José, a tall, bright-eyed, hook-nosed stripling from her native land, was a personage not unlikely to put a spoke in the doctor's wheel ; and that, should such a chance arise, the Sage, wise as he was, would, after all, run no slight risk of being " bamboozled."

Master José was a youth well-favoured, and comely to look upon. His office was that of page to the dame ; an office which, after long remaining in abeyance, has been of late years revived, as may well be seen in the persons of sundry smart hobbledehoys, now constantly to be met with on staircases and in boudoirs, clad, for the most part, in garments fitted tightly to the shape, the lower moiety adorned with a broad stripe of crimson or silver lace, and the upper with what the first Wit of our times has described as " a favourable eruption of buttons." The precise duties of this employment have never, as far as we have heard, been accurately defined. The perfuming a handkerchief, the combing a lap-dog, and the occasional presentation of a sippet-shaped *billet doux*, are, and always have been, among them ; but these a young gentleman standing five foot ten, and aged nineteen " last grass," might well be supposed to have outgrown. José, however, kept his place, perhaps because he was not fit for any other. To the conference between his mistress and the physician he had not been admitted ; his post was to keep watch and ward in the ante-room ; and, when the interview was concluded, he attended the lady and her visitor as far as the court-yard, where he held, with all due respect, the stirrup for the latter, as he once more resumed his position on the back of Punch.

Who is it that says " little pitchers have large ears ? " Some deep metaphysician of the potteries, who might have added that they have also quick eyes, and sometimes silent tongues. There was a little metaphorical piece of crockery of this class, who, screened by a huge elbow-chair, had sat a quiet and unobserved spectator of the whole proceedings between her mamma and Master Erasmus Buckthorne. This was Miss Marian Marsh, a rosy-cheeked laughter-loving imp of some six years old ; but one who could be mute as a mouse when the fit was on her. A handsome and highly polished cabinet of the darkest ebony occupied a recess at one end of the apartment ; this had long been a great subject of speculation to little Miss. Her curiosity, however, had always been repelled ; nor had all her coaxing ever won her an inspection of the thousand and one pretty things which its recesses no doubt contained. On this occasion it was unlocked, and Marian was about to rush forward in eager anticipation of a peep at its interior, when, child as she was, the reflection struck her that she would stand a better chance of carrying her point by remaining *perdue*. Fortune for once favoured her : she crouched closer than before, and saw her mother take something from one of the drawers, which she handed over to the Leech. Strange mutterings followed, and words whose sound was foreign to her youthful ears. Had she been older, their import, perhaps, might have been equally unknown.—After a while there was a pause ; and then the lady, as in answer to a requisition from the gentleman, placed in his hand a something which she took from her toilet. The transaction, whatever its nature, seemed now to be complete, and the article was carefully replaced in the drawer from which it had been taken. A long, and apparently interesting, conversation than took place between the parties, carried on in a low tone. At its termination, Mistress Marsh and Master Erasmus Buckthorne quitted the boudoir together. But the cabinet !—ay, that was left unfastened ; the folding-doors still remained invitingly expanded, the bunch of keys dangling from the lock. In an instant the spoiled child was in a chair ; the drawer, so recently closed, yielded at once to her hand, and her hurried researches were rewarded by the prettiest little waxen doll imaginable. It was a first-rate prize, and Miss lost no time in appropriating it to herself. Long before Madame Marsh had returned to her *Sanctum*, Marian was seated under a laurestinus in the garden, nursing her new baby with the most affectionate solicitude.

* ‑ ‑ * * * * *

"Susan, look here ; see what a nasty scratch I have got upon my hand," said the young lady, when routed out at length from her hiding-place to her noontide meal.

"Yes, Miss, this is always the way with you ! mend, mend, mend,— nothing but mend ! Scrambling about among the bushes, and tearing your clothes to rags. What with you, and with madam's farthingales and kirtles, a poor bower-maiden has a fine time of it !"

"But I have not torn my clothes, Susan, and it was not the bushes ; it was the doll : only see what a great ugly pin I have pulled out of it ! and look, here is another !" As she spoke, Marian drew forth one of those extended pieces of black pointed wire, with which, in the days of

F

toupees and pompoons, our foremothers were wont to secure their fly-caps and head-gear from the impertinent assaults of " Zephyrus and the Little Breezes."

" And pray, Miss, where did you get this pretty doll as you call it ? " asked Susan, turning over the puppet, and viewing it with a scrutinising eye.

' Mamma gave it me," said the child.—This was a fib !

" Indeed ! " quoth the girl thoughtfully ; and then, in half soliloquy, and a lower key, " Well ! I wish I may die if it doesn't look like master !— But come to your dinner, Miss !   Hark ! the *bell is striking One !* "

Meanwhile Master Thomas Marsh, and his man Ralph, were threading the devious paths, then, as now, most pseudonymously dignified with the name of roads, that wound between Marston Hall and the frontier of Romney Marsh.   Their progress was comparatively slow ; for though the brown mare was as good a roadster as man might back, and the gelding no mean nag of his hands, yet the tracts, rarely traversed save by the rude wains of the day, miry in the " bottoms," and covered with loose and rolling stones on the higher grounds, rendered barely passable the perpetual alternation of hill and valley.

The master rode on in pain, and the man in listlessness ; although the intercourse between two individuals so situated was much less restrained in those days than might suit the refinement of a later age, little passed approximating to conversation beyond an occasional and half-stifled groan from the one, or a vacant whistle from the other.   An hour's riding had brought them among the woods of Acryse ; and they were about to descend one of those green and leafy lanes, rendered by matted and over-arching branches alike impervious to shower or sunbeam, when a sudden and violent spasm seized on Master Marsh, and nearly caused him to fall from his horse.   With some difficulty he succeeded in dismounting, and seating himself by the road side.   Here he remained for a full half-hour in great apparent agony ; the cold sweat rolled in large round drops adown his clammy forehead, a universal shivering palsied every limb, his eye-balls appeared to be starting from their sockets, and to his attached, though dull and heavy serving-man, he seemed as one struggling in the pangs of impending dissolution.   His groans rose thick and frequent ; and the alarmed Ralph was hesitating between his disinclination to leave him, and his desire to procure such assistance as one of the few cottages, rarely sprinkled in that wild country, might afford, when, after a long-drawn sigh, his master's features as suddenly relaxed ; he declared himself better, the pang had passed away, and, to use his own expression, he " felt as if a knife had been drawn from out his very heart."   With Ralph's assistance, after a while, he again reached his saddle; and though still ill at ease, from a deep-seated and gnawing pain, which ceased not, as he averred, to torment him, the violence of the paroxysm was spent, and it returned no more.

Master and man pursued their way with increased speed, as, emerging from the wooded defiles, they at length neared the coast; then, leaving the romantic castle of Saltwood, with its neighbouring town of Hithe, a little on their left, they proceeded along the ancient paved causeway, and, crossing the old Roman road, or Watling, plunged again into the woods that stretched between Lympne and Ostenhanger.

The sun rose high in the heavens, and its meridian blaze was power-fully felt by man and horse, when, again quitting their leafy covert, the travellers debouched on the open plain of Aldington Frith, a wide tract of unenclosed country stretching down to the very borders of "the Marsh" itself.

Here it was, in the neighbouring chapelry, the site of which may yet be traced by the curious antiquary, that Elizabeth Barton, the "Holy Maid of Kent," had, something less than a hundred years previous to the period of our narrative, commenced that series of supernatural pranks which eventually procured for her head an unenvied elevation upon London Bridge; and though the parish had since enjoyed the benefit of the incumbency of Master Erasmus's illustrious and en-lightened Namesake, still, truth to tell, some of the old leaven was even yet supposed to be at work. The place had, in fact, an ill name; and, though Popish miracles had ceased to electrify its denizens, spells and charms, operating by a no less wondrous agency, were said to have taken their place. Warlocks, and other unholy subjects of Satan, were reported to make its wild recesses their favourite rendezvous, and that to an extent which eventually attracted the notice of no less a personage than the sagacious Matthew Hopkins himself, Witchfinder-General to the British government.

A great portion of the Frith, or Fright, as the name was then, and is still, pronounced, had formerly been a Chase, with rights of Free-warren, &c., appertaining to the Archbishops of the province. Since the Reformation, however, it had been disparked; and when Master Thomas Marsh, and his man Ralph, entered upon its confines, the open greensward exhibited a lively scene, sufficiently explanatory of certain sounds that had already reached their ears while yet within the sylvan screen which concealed their origin.

It was Fair-day: booths, stalls, and all the rude *paraphernalia* of an assembly that then met as much for the purposes of traffic as festivity, were scattered irregularly over the turf; pedlars, with their packs, horse-coupers, pig-merchants, itinerant vendors of crockery and cutlery, wandered promiscuously among the mingled groups, exposing their several wares and commodities, and soliciting custom. On one side was the gaudy riband, making its mute appeal to rustic gallantry; on the other, the delicious brandy-ball and alluring lollipop, compounded after the most approved receipt in the "True Gentlewoman's Garland," and "raising the waters" in the mouth of many an expectant urchin.

Nor were rural sports wanting to those whom pleasure, rather than business, had drawn from their humble homes. Here was the tall and slippery pole, glittering in its grease, and crowned with the ample cheese, that mocked the hopes of the discomfited climber. There the fugitive pippin, swimming in water not of the purest, and bobbing from the expanded lips of the juvenile Tantalus. In this quarter the ear was pierced by squeaks from some beleagured porker, whisking his well-soaped tail from the grasp of one already in fancy his captor. In that, the eye rested, with undisguised delight, upon the grimaces of grinning candidates for the honours of the horse-collar. All was fun, frolic, courtship, junketing, and jollity.

Maid Marian, indeed, with her lieges, Robin Hood, Scarlet, and Little John, was wanting; Friar Tuck was absent; even the Hobby-horse had disappeared: but the agile Maurice-dancers yet were there, and jingled their bells merrily among stalls well stored with gingerbread, tops, whips, whistles, and all those noisy instruments of domestic torture in which scenes like these are even now so fertile.—Had I a foe whom I held at deadliest feud, I would entice his favourite child to a Fair, and buy him a Whistle and a Penny-trumpet.

In one corner of the green, a little apart from the thickest of the throng, stood a small square stage, nearly level with the chins of the spectators, whose repeated bursts of laughter seemed to intimate the presence of something more than usually amusing. The platform was divided into two unequal portions; the smaller of which, surrounded by curtains of a coarse canvass, veiled from the eyes of the profane the *penetralia* of this moveable temple of Esculapius, for such it was. Within its interior, and secure from vulgar curiosity, the Quack-salver had hitherto kept himself ensconced; occupied, no doubt, in the preparation and arrangement of that wonderful *panacea* which was hereafter to shed the blessings of health among the admiring crowd. Meanwhile his attendant Jack-pudding was busily employed on the *proscenium*, doing his best to attract attention by a practical facetiousness which took wonderfully with the spectators, interspersing it with the melodious notes of a huge cow's horn. The fellow's costume varied but little in character from that in which the late (alas! that we should have to write the word—late!) Mr. Joseph Grimaldi was accustomed to present himself before " a generous and enlightened public : " the principal difference consisted in this, that the upper garment was a long white tunic of a coarse linen, surmounted by a caricature of the ruff then fast falling into disuse, and was secured from the throat downwards by a single row of broad white metal buttons ; and his legs were cased in loose wide trowsers of the same material ; while his sleeves, prolonged to a most disproportionate extent, descended far below the fingers, and acted as flappers in the somersets and caracoles, with which he diversified and enlivened his antics. Consummate impudence, not altogether unmixed with a certain sly humour, sparkled in his eye through the chalk and ochre with which his features were plentifully bedaubed ; and especially displayed itself in a succession of jokes, the coarseness of which did not seem to detract from their merit in the eyes of his applauding audience.

He was in the midst of a long and animated harangue explanatory of his master's high pretensions ; he had informed his gaping auditors that the latter was the seventh son of a seventh son, and of course, as they very well knew, an Unborn Doctor ; that to this happy accident of birth he added the advantage of most extensive travel ; that in his search after science he had not only perambulated the whole of this world, but had trespassed on the boundaries of the next : that the depths of the Ocean and the bowels of the Earth were alike familiar to him ; that besides salves and cataplasms of sovereign virtue, by combining sundry mosses, gathered many thousand fathom below the surface of the sea, with certain unknown drugs found in an undiscovered island, and boiling the whole in the lava of Vesuvius, he had succeeded in producing his celebrated balsam of Crackapanoko, the never-failing remedy for all human disorders, and which, a proper trial allowed, would go near to reanimate the dead. " Draw near ! " continued the worthy, " draw near, my masters ! and you, my good mistresses, draw near, every one of you. Fear not high and haughty carriage : though greater than King or Kaiser, yet is the mighty Aldrovando milder than mother's milk ; flint to the proud, to the humble he is as melting wax ; he asks not your disorders, he sees them himself at a glance—nay, without a glance ; he tells your ailments with his eyes shut !—Draw near ! draw near ! the more incurable the better ! List to the illustrious Doctor Aldrovando, first physician to Prester John, Leech to the Grand Llama, and Hakim in Ordinary to Mustapha Muley Bey ! "

" Hath your master ever a charm for the toothache, an't please you ? " asked an elderly countryman, whose swollen cheek bespoke his interest in the question.

"A charm !—a thousand, and every one of them infallible. Tooth-ache, quotha ! I had hoped you had come with every bone in your body fractured or out of joint. A toothache ! propound a tester, master o' mine—we ask not more for such trifles : do my bidding, and thy jaws, even with the word, shall cease to trouble thee ! "

The clown, fumbling a while in a deep leathern purse, at length produced a sixpence, which he tendered to the jester. "Now to thy master, and bring me the charm forthwith."

"Nay, honest man ; to disturb the mighty Aldrovando on such slight occasion were pity of my life : areed my counsel aright, and I warrant thee for the nonce. Hie thee home, friend ; infuse this powder in cold spring-water, fill thy mouth with the mixture, and sit upon thy fire till it boils ! "

"Out on thee for a pestilent knave ! " cried the cozened country-man ; but the roar of merriment around bespoke the bystanders well pleased with the jape put upon him. He retired, venting his spleen in audible murmurs ; and the mountebank, finding the feelings of the mob enlisted on his side, waxed more impudent every instant, filling up the intervals between his fooleries with sundry capers and contortions, and discordant notes from the cow's horn.

"Draw near, draw near, my masters ! Here have ye a remedy for every evil under the sun, moral, physical, natural, and supernatural ! Hath any man a termagant wife ?—here is that will tame her presently ! Hath any one a smoky chimney ?—here is an incontinent cure ! "

To the first infliction no man ventured to plead guilty, though there were those standing by who thought their neighbours might have profited withal. For the last-named recipe started forth at least a dozen candidates. With the greatest gravity imaginable, Pierrot, having pocketed their groats, delivered to each a small packet curiously folded and closely sealed, containing, as he averred, directions which, if truly observed, would preclude any chimney from smoking for a whole year. They whose curiosity led them to dive into the mystery, found that a sprig of mountain ash culled by moonlight was the charm recom-mended, coupled, however, with the proviso that no fire should be lighted on the hearth during its exercise.

The frequent bursts of merriment proceeding from this quarter at length attracted the attention of Master Marsh, whose line of road necessarily brought him near this end of the fair ; he drew bit in front of the stage just as its noisy occupant, having laid aside his formidable horn, was drawing still more largely on the amazement of " the public " by a feat of especial wonder,—he was eating fire ! Curiosity mingled with astonishment was at its height ; and feelings not unallied to alarm were beginning to manifest themselves, among the softer sex especially, as they gazed on the flames that issued from the mouth of the living volcano. All eyes, indeed, were fixed upon the fire-eater with an intentness that left no room for observing another worthy who had now emerged upon the scene. This was, however, no less a personage than the *Deus ex machinâ*,—the illustrious Aldrovando himself.

Short in stature and spare in form, the sage had somewhat increased the former by a steeple-crowned hat adorned with a cock's feather ; while the thick shoulder-padding of a quilted doublet, surmounted by a falling band, added a little to his personal importance in point of breadth. His habit was composed throughout of black serge, relieved with scarlet slashes in the sleeves and trunks ; red was the feather in his hat, red were the roses in his shoes, which rejoiced moreover in a pair of red heels. The lining of a short cloak of faded velvet, that hung transversely over his left shoulder, was also red. Indeed, from all that we could ever see or hear, this agreeable alternation of red and black appears to be the mixture of colours most approved at the court of Beelzebub, and the one most generally adopted by his friends and favourites. His features were sharp and shrewd, and a fire sparkled in his keen grey eye, much at variance with the wrinkles that ran their irregular furrows above his prominent and bushy brows. He had advanced slowly from behind the screen while the attention of the multitude was absorbed by the pyrotechnics of Mr. Merryman, and, stationing himself at the extreme corner of the stage, stood quietly leaning on a crutch-handle walking-staff of blackest ebony, his glance steadily fixed on the face of Marsh, from whose countenance the amusement he had insensibly begun to derive had not succeeded in removing all traces of bodily pain.

For a while the latter was unobservant of the inquisitorial survey with which he was regarded ; the eyes of the parties, however, at length met. The brown mare had a fine shoulder ; she stood pretty nearly sixteen hands. Marsh himself, though slightly bowed by ill health, and the " coming autumn " of life, was full six feet in height. His elevation giving him an unobstructed view over the heads of the pedestrians, he had naturally fallen into the rear of the assembly, which brought him close to the diminutive Doctor, with whose face, despite the red heels, his own was about upon a level.

" And what makes Master Marsh here ?—what sees he in the

mummeries of a miserable buffoon to divert him when his life is in jeopardy ? " said a shrill cracked voice that sounded as in his very ear. It was the Doctor who spoke.

" Knowest thou me, friend ? " said Marsh, scanning with awakened interest the figure of his questioner : " I call thee not to mind ; and yet—stay, where have we met ? "

" It skills not to declare," was the answer ; " suffice it we *have* met, —in other climes perchance,—and now meet happily again—happily at least for thee."

" Why truly the trick of thy countenance reminds me of somewhat I have seen before ; where or when I know not : but what wouldst thou with me ? "

" Nay, rather what wouldst thou here, Thomas Marsh ? What wouldst thou on the Frith of Aldington ?—is it a score or two of paltry sheep ? or is it something *nearer to thy heart ?* "

Marsh started as the last words were pronounced with more than common significance : a pang shot through him at the moment, and the vinegar aspect of the charlatan seemed to relax into a smile half compassionate, half sardonic.

" Grammercy," quoth Marsh, after a long-drawn breath, " what knowest thou of me, fellow, or of my concerns ? What knowest thou——"

" This know I, Master Thomas Marsh," said the stranger gravely, " that thy life is even now perilled, evil practices are against thee ; but no matter, thou art quit for the nonce—other hands than mine have saved thee ! Thy pains are over. Hark ! *the clock strikes One !* " As he spoke a single toll from the bell-tower of Bilsington came, wafted by the western breeze, over the thick-set and lofty oaks which intervened between the Frith and what had been once a priory. Doctor Aldro-vando turned as the sound came floating on the wind, and was moving, as if half in anger, towards the other side of the stage, where the mounte-bank, his fires extinct, was now disgorging to the admiring crowd yard after yard of gaudy-coloured riband.

" Stay ! Nay, prithee stay ! " cried Marsh eagerly, " I was wrong ; in faith I was. A change, and that a sudden and most marvellous, hath indeed come over me ; I am free ; I breathe again ; I feel as though a load of years had been removed ; and—is it possible ?—hast thou done this ? "

" Thomas Marsh ! " said the doctor, pausing, and turning for the moment on his heel, " I have *not* : I repeat that other and more inno-cent hands than mine have done this deed. Nevertheless, heed my counsel well ! Thou art parlously encompassed ; I, and I only, have the means of relieving thee. Follow thy courses ; pursue thy journey ; but as thou valuest life and more than life, be at the foot of yonder woody knoll what time the rising moon throws her first beam upon the bare and blighted summit that towers above its trees."

He crossed abruptly to the opposite quarter of the scaffolding, and was in an instant deeply engaged in listening to those whom the cow's horn had attracted, and in prescribing for their real or fancied ailments. Vain were all Marsh's efforts again to attract his notice ; it was evident that he studiously avoided him ; and when, after an hour or more spent in useless endeavour, he saw the object of his anxiety seclude himself once more within his canvass screen, he rode slowly and thoughtfully off the field.

What should he do ? Was the man a mere quack ? an imposter ?— His name thus obtained ?—that might be easily done. But then, his secret griefs ; the doctor's knowledge of them ; their cure ; for he felt that his pains were gone, his healthful feelings restored !

True, Aldrovando, if that were his name, had disclaimed all co-operation in his recovery ; but he knew, or he at least announced it. Nay, more, he had hinted that he was yet in jeopardy ; that practices— and the chord sounded strangely in unison with one that had before vibrated within him—that practices were in operation against his life ! It was enough ! He would keep tryst with the Conjuror, if conjuror he were ; and, at least, ascertain who and what he was, and how he had become acquainted with his own person and secret afflictions.

When the late Mr. Pitt was determined to keep out Bonaparte, and prevent his gaining a settlement in the county of Kent, among other ingenious devices adopted for that purpose, he caused to be constructed what was then, and has ever since been conventionally termed a " Military Canal." This is a not very practicable ditch, some thirty feet wide, and nearly nine feet deep—in the middle,— extending from the town and port of Hithe to within a mile of the town and port of Rye, a distance of about twenty miles, and forming, as it were, the cord of a bow, the arc of which constitutes that remote fifth quarter of the globe spoken of by travellers. Trivial objections to the plan were made at the time by cavillers ; and an old gentleman of the neighbour-hood, who proposed as a cheap substitute, to put down his own cocked-hat upon a pole, was deservedly pooh-pooh'd down ; in fact, the job, though rather an expensive one, was found to answer remarkably well. The French managed indeed to scramble over the Rhine and the Rhone, and other insignificant currents, but they never did, or could, pass Mr. Pitt's " Military Canal." At no great distance from the centre of this cord rises abruptly a sort of woody promontory, in shape almost conical; its sides covered with thick underwood, above which is seen a bare and brown summit rising like an Alp in miniature. The " defence of the nation " not being then in existence, Master Marsh met with no obstruction in reaching this place of appointment long before the time prescribed.

So much, indeed, was his mind occupied by his adventure and extraordinary cure, that his original design had been abandoned, and Master Cobbe remained unvisited. A rude hostel in the neighbourhood furnished entertainment for man and horse; and here, a full hour before the rising of the moon, he left Ralph and the other beasts, proceeding to his rendezvous on foot and alone.

" You are punctual, Master Marsh," squeaked the shrill voice of the Doctor, issuing from the thicket as the first silvery gleam trembled on the aspens above. " 'Tis well: now follow me and in silence."

The first part of the command Marsh hesitated not to obey, the second was more difficult of observance.

" Who and what are you ? Whither are you leading me ? " burst not unnaturally from his lips; but all question was at once cut short by the peremptory tones of his guide.

" Hush ! I say; your finger on your lip, there be hawks abroad: follow me, and that silently and quickly." The little man turned as he spoke, and led the way through a scarcely perceptible path or track, which wound among the underwood. The lapse of a few minutes brought them to the door of a low building, so hidden by the surrounding trees that few would have suspected its existence. It was a cottage of rather extraordinary dimensions, but consisting of only one floor. No smoke rose from its solitary chimney; no cheering ray streamed from its single window, which was, however, secured by a shutter of such thickness as to preclude the possibility of any stray beam issuing from within. The exact size of the building it was, in that uncertain light, difficult to distinguish, a portion of it seeming buried in the wood behind. The door gave way on the application of a key, and Marsh followed his conductor resolutely but cautiously along a narrow passage, feebly lighted by a small taper that winked and twinkled at its farther extremity. The Doctor, as he approached, raised it from the ground, and, opening an adjoining door, ushered his guest into the room beyond.

It was a large and oddly furnished apartment, insufficiently lighted by an iron lamp that hung from the roof, and scarcely illuminated the walls and angles, which seemed to be composed of some dark-coloured wood. On one side, however, Master Marsh could discover an article bearing strong resemblance to a coffin ; on the other was a large oval mirror in an ebony frame, and in the midst of the floor was described in red chalk a double circle about six feet in diameter, its inner verge inscribed with sundry hieroglyphics, agreeably relieved at intervals with an alternation of skulls and cross bones. In the very centre was deposited one skull of such surpassing size and thickness as would have filled the soul of a Spurzheim or De Ville with wonderment. A large book, a naked sword, an hour glass, a chafing dish, and a black cat, completed the list of moveables ; with the exception of a couple of tapers which stood on each side of the mirror, and which the strange gentleman now proceeded to light from the one in his hand. As they flared up with what Marsh thought a most unnatural brilliancy, he perceived reflected in the glass behind a dial suspended over the coffin-like article already mentioned : the hand was fast verging towards the hour of nine. The eyes of the little Doctor seemed riveted on the horologe.

" Now strip thee, Master Marsh, and that quickly : untruss, I say ! discard thy boots, doff doublet and hose, and place thyself incontinent in yonder bath."

The visitor cast his eyes again upon the formidable-looking article, and perceived that it was nearly filled with water. A cold bath, at such an hour and under such auspices, was anything but inviting : he hesitated, and turned his eyes alternately on the Doctor and the Black Cat.

" Trifle not the time, man, an you be wise," said the former : " Passion of my heart ! let but yon minute-hand reach the hour, and thou not immersed, thy life were not worth a pin's fee ! "

The Black Cat gave vent to a single Mew,—a most unnatural sound for a mouser,—it seemed as it were mewed through a cow's horn.

" Quick, Master Marsh ! uncase, or you perish ! " repeated his strange host, throwing as he spoke a handful of some dingy-looking powders into the brazier. " Behold the attack has begun ! " A thick cloud rose from the embers ; a cold shivering shook the astonished Yeoman ; sharp pricking pains penetrated his ankles and the palms of his hands, and, as the smoke cleared away, he distinctly saw and recognised in the mirror the boudoir of Marston Hall.

The doors of the well-known ebony cabinet were closed ; but fixed against them, and standing out in strong relief from the contrast afforded by the sable background, was a waxen image—of himself ! It appeared to be secured, and sustained in an upright posture, by large black pins driven through the feet and palms, the latter of which were extended in a cruciform position. To the right and left stood his wife and José ; in the middle, with his back towards him, was a figure which he had no

difficulty in recognising as that of the Leech of Folkestone.   The latter
had just succeeded in fastening the dexter hand of the image, and was now
in the act of drawing a broad and keen-edged sabre from its sheath.   The
Black Cat mewed again.   " Haste or you die ! " said the Doctor,—Marsh
looked at the dial ; it wanted but
four minutes of nine : he felt that the ·
crisis of his fate was come.   Off went
his heavy boots ; doublet to the right,

galligaskins to the left ;   never was man more
swiftly disrobed : in two minutes, to use an
Indian expression, " he was all face ! " in another he was on
his back, and up to his chin, in a bath which smelt strongly
as of brimstone and garlic.

"Heed well the clock ! " cried the Conjuror : " with the first
stroke of Nine plunge thy head beneath the water, suffer not a hair
above the surface : plunge deeply, or thou art lost ! "

The little man had seated himself in the centre of the circle upon
the large skull, elevating his legs at an angle of forty-five degrees.   In
this position he spun round with a velocity to be equalled only by that
of a tee-totum, the red roses on his insteps seeming to describe a circle
of fire.   The best buckskins that ever mounted at Melton had soon
yielded to such rotatory friction—but he spun on—the Cat mewed,
bats and obscene birds fluttered over-head ; Erasmus was seen to raise
his weapon, the clock struck !—and Marsh, who had " ducked " at the
instant, popped up his head again, spitting and sputtering, half-choked
with the infernal solution, which had insinuated itself into his mouth,
and ears, and nose.   All disgust at his nauseous dip, was, however, at
once removed, when, casting his eyes on the glass, he saw the consternation of the party whose persons it exhibited.   Erasmus had evidently

made his blow and failed; the figure was unmutilated; the hilt remained in the hand of the striker, while the shivered blade lay in shining fragments on the floor.

The Conjuror ceased his spinning, and brought himself to an anchor; the Black Cat purred,—its purring seemed strangely mixed with the self-satisfied chuckle of a human being.—Where had Marsh heard something like it before?

He was rising from his unsavoury couch, when a motion from the little man checked him. "Rest where you are, Thomas Marsh; so far all goes well, but the danger is not yet over!" He looked again, and perceived that the shadowy triumvirate were in deep and eager consultation; the fragments of the shattered weapon appeared to undergo a close scrutiny. The result was clearly unsatisfactory; the lips of the parties moved rapidly, and much gesticulation might be observed, but no sound fell upon the ear. The hand of the dial had nearly reached the quarter; at once the parties separated: and Buckthorne stood again before the figure, his hand armed with a long and sharp-pointed *misericorde*, a dagger little in use of late, but such as, a century before, often performed the part of a modern oyster-knife, in tickling the osteology of a dismounted cavalier through the shelly defences of his plate armour. Again he raised his arm. "Duck!" roared the Doctor, spinning away upon his cephalic pivot :—the Black Cat cocked his tail, and seemed to mew the word "Duck!" Down went Master Marsh's head;—one of his hands had unluckily been resting on the edge of the bath: he drew it hastily in, but not altogether scatheless; the stump of a rusty nail, projecting from the margin of the bath, had caught and slightly grazed it. The pain was more acute than is usually produced by such trivial accidents; and Marsh, on once more raising his head, beheld the dagger of the Leech sticking in the little finger of the wax figure, which it had seemingly nailed to the cabinet door.

"By my truly, a scape o' the narrowest!" quoth the Conjuror: "the next course, dive you not the readier, there is no more life in you than in a pickled herring.—What! courage, Master Marsh; but be heedful; an they miss again, let them bide the issue!"

He drew his hand athwart his brow as he spoke, and dashed off the perspiration which the violence of his exercise had drawn from every pore. Black Tom sprang upon the edge of the bath, and stared full in the face of the bather: his sea-green eyes were lambent with unholy fire, but their marvellous obliquity of vision was not to be mistaken ;— the very countenance, too!—Could it be?—the features were feline, but their expression was that of the Jack Pudding! Was the Mounte-bank a Cat?—or the Cat a Mountebank?—it was [all a mystery;—and Heaven knows how long Marsh might] have continued staring at Grimalkin, had not his attention been again called by Aldrovando to the magic mirror.

Great dissatisfaction, not to say dismay, seemed now to pervade the conspirators; Dame Isabel was closely inspecting the figure's wounded hand, while José was aiding the pharmacopolist to charge a huge petronel with powder and bullets. The load was a heavy one; but Erasmus seemed determined this time to make sure of his object. Somewhat of trepidation might be observed in his manner as he rammed down the balls, and his withered cheek appeared to have acquired an increase of paleness; but amazement rather than fear was the prevailing symptom, and his countenance betrayed no jot of irresolution. As the clock was about to chime half-past nine, he planted himself with a firm foot in front of the image, waved his unoccupied hand with a cautionary gesture to his companions, and, as they hastily retired on either side, brought the muzzle of his weapon within half a foot of his mark. As the shadowy form was about to draw the trigger, Marsh again plunged his head beneath the surface; and the sound of an explosion, as of fire-arms, mingled with the rush of water that poured into his ears. His immersion was but momentary, yet did he feel as though half suffocated: he sprang from the bath, and, as his eye fell on the mirror, he saw,—or thought he saw,—the Leech of Folkestone lying dead on the floor of his wife's boudoir, his head shattered to pieces, and his hand still grasping the stock of a bursten petronel.

He saw no more; his head swam; his senses reeled, the whole room was turning round, and, as he fell to the ground, the last impressions to which he was conscious were the chucklings of a hoarse laughter, and the mewings of a Tom Cat!

Master Marsh was found the next morning by his bewildered serving-man, stretched before the door of the humble hostel at which he sojourned. His clothes were somewhat torn and much bemired! and deeply did honest Ralph marvel that one so staid and grave as Master Marsh of Marston should thus have played the roisterer, missing, perchance, a profitable bargain for the drunken orgies of midnight wassail, or the endearments of some rustic light-o'-love. Tenfold was his astonishment increased when, after retracing in silence their journey of the preceding day, the Hall, on their arrival about noon, was found in a state of uttermost confusion.—No wife stood there to greet with the smile of bland affection her returning spouse; no page to hold

The little man had seated himself in the centre of the circle upon the large skull

his stirrup, or receive his gloves, his hat, and riding-rod.—The doors were open, the rooms in most admired disorder ; men and maidens peeping, hurrying hither and thither, and popping in and out, like rabbits in a warren.—The lady of the mansion was nowhere to be found.

José, too, had disappeared ; the latter had been last seen riding furiously towards Folkestone early in the preceding afternoon ; to a question from Hodge Gardener he had hastily answered, that he bore a missive of moment from his mistress. The lean apprentice of Erasmus Buckthorne declared that the page had summoned his master, in haste, about six of the clock, and that they had rode forth together, as he verily believed, on their way back to the Hall, where he had supposed Master Buckthorne's services to be suddenly required on some pressing emergency. Since that time he had seen nought of either of them : the grey cob, however, had returned late at night, masterless, with his girths loose, and the saddle turned upside down.

Nor was Master Erasmus Buckthorne ever seen again. Strict search was made through the neighbourhood, but without success ; and it was at length presumed that he must, for reasons which nobody could divine, have absconded, together with José and his faithless mistress. The latter had carried off with her the strong box, divers articles of valuable plate, and jewels of price. Her boudoir appeared to have been completely ransacked ; the cabinet and drawers stood open and empty ; the very carpet, a luxury then newly introduced into England, was gone. Marsh, however, could trace no vestige of the visionary scene which he affirmed to have been last night presented to his eyes.

Much did the neighbours marvel at his story :—some thought him mad ; others, that he was merely indulging in that privilege to which, as a traveller, he had a right indefeasible. Trusty Ralph said nothing, but shrugged his shoulders ; and, falling into the rear, imitated the action of raising a wine-cup to his lips. An opinion, indeed, soon prevailed, that Master Thomas Marsh had gotten, in common parlance, exceedingly drunk on the preceding evening, and had dreamt all that he so circumstantially related. This belief acquired additional credit when they, whom curiosity induced to visit the woody knoll of Aldington Mount, declared that they could find no building such as that described, nor any cottage near ; save one, indeed, a low-roofed hovel, once a house of public entertainment, but now half in ruins. The " Old Cat and Fiddle "—so was the tenement called—had been long uninhabited ; yet still exhibited the remains of a broken sign, on which the keen observer might decipher something like a rude portrait of the animal from which it derived its name. It was also supposed still to afford an occasional asylum to the smugglers of the coast, but no trace of any visit from sage or mountebank could be detected; nor was the wise Aldrovando, whom many remembered to have seen at the fair, ever found again on all that country-side.

. Of the runaways nothing was ever certainly known. A boat, the property of an old fisherman who plied his trade on the outskirts of the town, had been seen to quit the bay that night; and there were those who declared that she had more hands on board than Carden and his son, her usual complement; but, as the gale came on, and the frail bark was eventually found keel upwards on the Goodwin Sands, it was presumed that she had struck on that fatal quicksand in the dark, and that all on board had perished.

Little Marian, whom her profligate mother had abandoned, grew up to be a fine girl, and a handsome. She became, moreover, heiress to Marston Hall, and brought the estate into the Ingoldsby family by her marriage with one of its scions.

Thus far Mrs. Botherby.

It is a little singular that, on pulling down the old Hall in my grandfather's time, a human skeleton was discovered among the rubbish; under what particular part of the building I could never with any accuracy ascertain; but it was found enveloped in a tattered cloth that seemed to have been once a carpet, and which fell to pieces almost immediately on being exposed to the air. The bones were perfect, but those of one hand were wanting; and the skull, perhaps from the labourer's pick-axe, had received considerable injury; the worm-eaten stock of an old-fashioned pistol lay near, together with a rusty piece of iron which a workman, more sagacious than his fellows, pronounced a portion of the lock, but nothing was found which the utmost stretch of human ingenuity could twist into a barrel.

The portrait of the fair Marian hangs yet in the Gallery of Tappington; and near it is another, of a young man in the prime of life, whom Mrs. Botherby affirms to be that of her father. It exhibits a mild and rather melancholy countenance, with a high forehead, and the peaked beard and mustaches of the seventeenth century. The signet-finger of the left hand is gone, and appears, on close inspection, to have been painted out by some later artist: possibly in compliment to the tradition, which, *teste Botherby*, records that of Mr. Marsh to have gangrened, and to have undergone amputation at the knuckle-joint. If really the resemblance of the gentleman alluded to, it must have been taken at some period antecedent to his marriage. There is neither date nor painter's name ; but, a little above the head, on the dexter side of the picture, is an escutcheon, bearing " Quarterly, Gules and Argent, in the first quarter a horse's head of the second ; " beneath it are the words " *Ætatis suæ* 26." On the opposite side is the following mark, which Mr. Simpkinson declares to be that of a Merchant of the Staple, and pretends to discover, in the monogram comprised in it, all the characters which compose the name of THOMAS MARSH, of MARSTON.

Respect for the feelings of an honourable family—nearly connected with the Ingoldsbys,—has induced me to veil the real "sponsorial and patronymic appellations" of my next hero under a *sobriquet* interfering neither with rhyme nor rhythm.* I shall merely add that every incident in the story bears, on the face of it, the stamp of veracity, and that many "persons of honour" in the county of Berks, who well recollected Sir George Rooke's expedition against Gibraltar, would, if they were now alive, gladly bear testimony to the truth of every syllable.

* Pack o' nonsense !—Everybody as belongs to him is dead and gone—and everybody knows that the poor young gentleman's real name wasn't *Sobriquet* at all, but Hampden Pye, Esq., and that one of his uncles—or cousins—used to make verses about the king and the queen, and had a sack of money for doing it every year ;—and that's his picture in the blue coat and little gold-laced cocked hat, that hangs on the stairs over the door of the passage that leads to the blue room.—*Sobriquet !*—but there !—The Squire wrote it after dinner !

ELIZABETH BOTHERBY.

G

Legend of Hamilton Tighe

THE Captain is walking his quarter-deck,
With a troubled brow and a bended neck
One eye is down through the hatchway cast,
The other turns up to the truck on the mast
Yet none of the crew may venture to hint
" Our Skipper hath gotten a sinister squint ! "

The Captain again the letter hath read
Which the bum-boat woman brought out to Spithead—
Still, since the good ship sail'd away,
He reads that letter three times a day
Yet the writing is broad and fair to see
As a Skipper may read in his degree,
And the seal is as black, and as broad, and as flat,
As his own cockade in his own cock'd hat :
He reads, and he says, as he walks to and fro,
" Curse the old woman—she bothers me so ! "

He pauses now, for the topmen hail—
" On the larboard quarter a sail ! a sail ! "
That grim old Captain he turns him quick,
And bawls through his trumpet for Hairy-faced Dick.
" The breeze is blowing—huzza ! huzza !
The breeze is blowing—away ! away !

The breeze is blowing—a race ! a race !
The breeze is blowing—we near the chase !
Blood will flow, and bullets will fly,—
Oh where will be then young Hamilton Tighe ? "

—" On the foeman's deck, where a man should be,
With his sword in his hand, and his foe at his knee.
Cockswain, or boatswain, or reefer may try,
But the first man on board will be Hamilton Tighe ! "

     *   *   *   *   *

Hairy-faced Dick hath a swarthy hue,
Between a gingerbread-nut and a Jew,
And his pigtail is long, and bushy, and thick,
Like a pump-handle stuck on the end of a stick.
Hairy-faced Dick understands his trade ;
He stands by the breech of a long carronade,
The linstock glows in his bony hand,
Waiting that grim old Skipper's command.

" The bullets are flying—huzza ! huzza !
The bullets are flying—away ! away ! "—
The brawny boarders mount by the chains,
And are over their buckles in blood and in brains.
On the foeman's deck, where a man should be,
   Young Hamilton Tighe   Waves his cutlass high,
And *Capitaine Crapaud* bends low at his knee.

Hairy-face Dick, linstock in hand,
Is waiting that grim-looking Skipper's command :—
   A wink comes sly   From that sinister eye—
Hairy-face Dick at once lets fly,
And knocks off the head of young Hamilton Tighe !

There's a lady sits lonely in bower and hall,
Her pages and handmaidens come at her call :
" Now, haste ye, my handmaidens, haste and see
How he sits there and glow'rs with his head on his knee ! "
The maidens smile, and, her thought to destroy,
They bring her a little, pale, mealy-faced boy ;

And the mealy-faced boy says, " Mother dear,
Now Hamilton's dead, I've a thousand a year ! "

The lady has donn'd her mantle and hood,
She is bound for shrift at St. Mary's Rood :—
" Oh ! the taper shall burn, and the bell shall toll,
And the mass shall be said for my step-son's soul,
And the tablet fair shall be hung on high,
Orate pro animâ Hamilton Tighe ? "

     Her coach and four Draws up to the door,
With her groom, and her footman, and half a score more ;
The lady steps into her coach alone,
And they hear her sigh, and they hear her groan ;
They close the door, and they turn the pin,
But there's One rides with her that never stept in !
All the way there, and all the way back,
The harness strains, and the coach-springs crack,
The horses snort, and plunge, and kick,
Till the coachman thinks he is driving Old Nick ;
And the grooms and the footmen wonder, and say
" What makes the old coach so heavy to-day ? "
But the mealy-faced boy peeps in, and sees
A man sitting there with his head on his knees !

'Tis ever the same,—in hall or in bower,
Wherever the place, whatever the hour,
That Lady mutters, and talks to the air,
And her eye is fix'd on an empty chair ;
But the mealy-faced boy still whispers with dread,
" She talks to a man with never a head ! "
     *   *   *   *   *

There's an old Yellow Admiral living at Bath,
As grey as a badger, as thin as a lath ;
And his very queer eyes have such very queer leers,
They seem to be trying to peep at his ears ;
That old Yellow Admiral goes to the Rooms,
And he plays long whist, but he frets and he fumes,
For all his Knaves stand upside down,
And the Jack of Clubs does nothing but frown ;

And the Kings, and the Aces, and all the best trumps
Get into the hands of the other old frumps ;
While, close to his partner, a man he sees
Counting the tricks with his head on his knees.

In Ratcliffe Highway there's an old marine store,
And a great black doll hangs out of the door ;
There are rusty locks, and dusty bags,
And musty phials, and fusty rags,
And a lusty old woman, call'd Thirsty Nan,
And her crusty old husband's a Hairy-faced man !

That Hairy-faced man is sallow and wan,
And his great thick pigtail is wither'd and gone ;
And he cries, " Take away that lubberly chap
That sits there and grins with his head in his lap ! "
And the neighbours say, as they see him look sick,
" What a rum old covey is Hairy-faced Dick ! "

That Admiral, Lady, and Hairy-faced man
May say what they please, and may do what they can ;
But one thing seems remarkably clear,—
They may die to-morrow, or live till next year,—
But wherever they live, or whenever they die,
They'll never get quit of young Hamilton Tighe !

The When,—the Where,—and the How,—of the succeeding narrative speak for themselves. It may be proper, however, to observe, that the ruins here alluded to, and improperly termed " the Abbey," are not those of Bolsover, described in a preceding page, but the remains of a Preceptory once belonging to the Knights Templars, situate near Swynfield, Swinkefield, or, as it is now generally spelt and pronounced, Swingfield Minnis, a rough tract of common land now undergoing the process of enclosure, and adjoining the woods and arable lands of Tappington, at the distance of some two miles from the Hall, to the south-eastern windows of which the time-worn walls in question, as seen over the intervening coppices, present a picturesque and striking object.

The Witches' Frolic

[Scene, the " Snuggery " at Tappington.—Grandpapa in a high-backed, cane-bottomed elbow-chair of carved walnut-tree, dozing; his nose at an angle of forty-five degrees,—his thumbs slowly perform the rotatory motion described by lexicographers as " twiddling." —The " Hope of the family " astride on a walking-stick, with burnt-cork mustaches, and a pheasant's tail pinned in his cap, solaceth himself with martial music.—Roused by a strain of surpassing dissonance, Grandpapa *loquitur.*]

COME hither, come hither, my little boy Ned !
  Come hither unto my knee—
I cannot away with that horrible din,
That sixpenny drum, and that trumpet of tin.
Oh, better to wander frank and free
Through the Fair of good Saint Bartlemy,
Than listen to such awful minstrelsie.
Now lay, little Ned, those nuisances by,
And I'll rede ye a lay of Grammarye.

[Grandpapa riseth, yawneth like the crater of an extinct volcano, proceedeth slowly to the window, and apostrophiseth the Abbey in the distance.]

I love thy tower, Grey Ruin,
  I joy thy form to see,
  Though reft of all, Cell, cloister, and hall,
Nothing is left save a tottering wall
That, awfully grand and darkly dull,
Threaten'd to fall and demolish my skull,
As, ages ago, I wander'd along
Careless thy grass-grown courts among,
In sky-blue jacket, and trousers laced,
The latter uncommonly short in the waist.
Thou art dearer to me, thou Ruin grey,
Than the Squire's verandah over the way ;
  And fairer, I ween, The ivy sheen
  That thy mouldering turret binds,
Than the Alderman's house about half a mile off,
  With the green Venetian blinds.

Full many a tale would my Grandam tell,
  In many a bygone day,
Of darksome deeds, which of old befell
  In thee, thou Ruin grey !

And I the readiest ear would lend,
  And stare like frighten'd pig !
While my Grandfather's hair would have stood up on end,
  Had he not worn a wig.

One tale I remember of mickle dread—
Now lithe and listen, my little boy Ned !
      *   *   *   *   *
Thou mayest have read, my little boy Ned,
  Though thy mother thine idlesse blames,
In Doctor Goldsmith's history book,
  Of a gentleman called King James,
In quilted doublet, and great trunk breeches,
Who held in abhorrence Tobacco and Witches.

Well,—in King James's golden days,—
  For the days were golden then,—
They could not be less, for good Queen Bess
  Had died, aged threescore and ten,
    And her days we know,   Were all of them so ;
While the Court poets sung, and the Court gallants swore
That the days were as golden still as before.

Some people, 'tis true, a troublesome few,
  Who historical points would unsettle,
Have lately thrown out a sort of a doubt
  Of the genuine ring of the metal ;
But who can believe to a monarch so wise
People would dare tell a parcel of lies !

—Well then, in good King James's days,—
Golden or not does not matter a jot,—
Yon Ruin a sort of a roof had got ;
For though, repairs lacking, its walls had been cracking
Since Harry the Eighth sent its people a-packing,
  Though joists, and floors,   And windows, and doors
Had all disappear'd, yet pillars by scores
Remain'd, and still propp'd up a ceiling or two,
While the belfry was almost as good as new ;
You are not to suppose matters look'd just so
In the Ruin some two hundred years ago.

Just in that farthermost angle, where
There are still the remains of a winding-stair,
One turret especially high in air
    Uprear'd its tall gaunt form ;
As if defying the power of Fate, or
The hand of " Time the Innovator ; "
    And though to the pitiless storm
Its weaker brethren all around
Bowing, in ruin had strew'd the ground,
Alone it stood, while its fellows lay strew'd,
Like a four-bottle man in a company " screw'd,"
Not firm on his legs, but by no means subdued.

One night—'twas in Sixteen hundred and six,—
I like when I can, Ned, the date to fix,—
    The month was May,   Though I can't well say
At this distance of time the particular day—
But oh ! that night, that horrible night !
—Folks ever afterwards said with affright
That they never had seen such a terrible sight.

The Sun had gone down fiery red ;
And if, that evening, he laid his head
In Thetis's lap beneath the seas,
He must have scalded the goddess's knees.
He left behind him a lurid track
Of blood-red light upon clouds so black,
That Warren and Hunt with the whole of their crew,
Could scarcely have given them a darker hue.

There came a shrill and a whistling sound,
Above, beneath, beside, and around,
    Yet leaf ne'er moved on tree !
So that some people thought old Beelzebub must
Have been lock'd out of doors, and was blowing the dust
From the pipe of his street-door key.
And then a hollow moaning blast
Came, sounding more dismally still than the last,
And the lightning flash'd, and the thunder growl'd,
And louder and louder the tempest howl'd,
And the rain came down in such sheets as would stagger a
Bard for a simile short of Niagara.

Rob Gilpin "was a citizen;"
　But, though of some " renown,"
Of no great " credit " in his own,
　Or any other town.

He was a wild and roving lad,
　For ever in the alehouse boozing;
Or romping,—which is quite as bad,—
　With female friends of his own choosing.

And Rob this very day had made,
　Not dreaming such a storm was brewing,
An assignation with Miss Slade,—
　Their trysting-place that same grey Ruin.

But Gertrude Slade become afraid,
　And to keep her appointment unwilling,
When she spied the rain on her window-pane
　In drops as big as a shilling;
She put off her hat and her mantle again,
" He'll never expect me in all this rain ! "

But little he recks of the fears of the sex,
　Or that maiden false to her tryst could be,
He had stood there a good half hour
Ere yet had commenced that perilous shower,
　Alone by the trysting-tree !

Robin looks east, Robin looks west,
But he sees not her whom he loves the best ;
Robin looks up, and Robin looks down,
But no one comes from the nighbouring town.

The storm came at last,—loud roar'd the blast,
And the shades of evening fell thick and fast ;
The tempest grew ; and the straggling yew,
His leafy umbrella, was wet through and through ;
Rob was half dead with cold and with fright,
When he spies in the Ruins a twinkling light—
A hop, two skips, and a jump, and straight
Rob stands within that postern gate.

And there were gossips sitting there,
  By one, by two, by three :
  Two were an old ill-favour'd pair ;
  But the third was young, and passing fair,
With laughing eyes, and with coal-black hair ;
  A daintie quean was she !
Rob would have given his ears to sip
But a single salute from her cherry lip.

As they sat in that old and haunted room,
In each one's hand was a huge birch broom,
On each one's head was a steeple-crown'd hat,
On each one's knee was a coal-black cat ;
Each had a kirtle of Lincoln green—
It was, I trow, a fearsome scene.

" Now riddle me, riddle me right, Madge Gray,
What foot unhallow'd wends this way ?
Goody Price, Goody Price, now areed me aright,
Who roams the old Ruins this drearysome night ? "
Then up and spake that sonsie quean,
  And she spake both loud and clear :
" Oh, be it for weal, or be it for woe,
Enter friend, or enter foe,
  Rob Gilpin is welcome here ! "—

" Now tread we a measure ! a hall ! a hall !
Now tread we a measure," quoth she—
  The heart of Robin
  Beat thick and throbbing—
" Roving Rob, tread a measure with me ! "
" Ay, lassie ! " quoth Rob, as her hand he gripes,
" Though Satan himself were blowing the pipes ! "

Now around they go, and around, and around,
With hop-skip-and-jump, and frolicsome bound,
  Such sailing and gliding,
  Such sinking and sliding,
  Such lofty curvetting,   And grand pirouetting ;
Ned, you would swear that Monsieur Gilbert
And Miss Taglioni were capering there !

And there were gossips sitting there,   By one, by two, by three

And oh ! such awful music ! ne'er
Fell sounds so uncanny on mortal ear,
There were the tones of a dying man's groans
Mix'd with the rattling of dead men's bones :
Had you heard the shrieks, and the squeals, and the squeaks,
You'd not have forgotten the sound for weeks.

And around, and around, and around they go,
Heel to heel, and toe to toe,
Prance and caper, curvet and wheel,
Toe to toe, and heel to heel.
" 'Tis merry, 'tis merry, Cummers, I trow,
To dance thus beneath the nightshade bough ! "—

" Goody Price, Goody Price, now riddle me right,
Where may we sup this frolicsome night ? "

" Mine host of the Dragon hath mutton and veal !
The Squire hath partridge, and widgeon, and teal ;
But old Sir Thopas hath daintier cheer,
A pasty made of the good, red deer,
A huge grouse pie, and a fine Florentine,
A fat roast goose, and a turkey and chine."
—" Madge Gray, Madge Gray,
Now tell me, I pray,
Where's the best wassail bowl to our roundelay ? "

—" There is ale in the cellars of Tappington Hall,
But the Squire * is a churl, and his drink is small ;
    Mine host of the Dragon   Hath many a flagon
Of double ale, lamb's wool, and *eau de vie*,
    But Sir Thopas, the Vicar,   Hath costlier liquor,—
A butt of the choicest *Malvoisie*.
    He doth not lack   Canary or sack ;
And a good pint stoup of Clary wine
Smacks merrily off with a Turkey and Chine ! "

---

* Stephen Ingoldsby, surnamed " The Niggard," second cousin and successor to " The Bad Sir Giles." (Visitation of Kent, 1666.) For an account of his murder by burglars, and their subsequent execution, see Dodsley's " Remarkable Trials," &c., Lond., 1776, vol. ii. p. 264, ex the present volume, Art. " Hand of Glory."

" Now away ! and away ! without delay,
Hey *Cockalorum !* my Broomstick gay !
We must be back ere the dawn of the day :
Hey up the chimney ! away ! away ! "—
   Old Goody Price   Mounts in a trice,
In showing her legs she is not over nice ;
   Old Goody Jones,   All skin and bones,
Follows " like winking."—Away go the crones,
Knees and nose in a line with the toes.
Sitting their brooms like so many Ducrows ;
   Latest and last   The damsel pass'd,
One glance of her coal-black eye she cast ;
She laugh'd with glee loud laughters three,
" Dost fear, Rob Gilpin, to ride with me ? "—
Oh, never might man unscath'd espy
One single glance from that coal-black eye.
   —Away she flew !—   Without more ado
Rob seizes and mounts on a broomstick too.
" Hey ! up the chimney, lass !   Hey after you ! "

It's a very fine thing, on a fine day in June,
To ride through the air in a Nassau Balloon ;
But you'll find very soon, if you aim at the Moon
In a carriage like that, you're a bit of a " Spoon,"
   For the largest can't fly   Above twenty miles high,
And you're not half way then on your journey, nor nigh :
   While no man alive   Could ever contrive,
Mr. Green has declared, to get higher than five.
And the soundest Philosophers hold that, perhaps,
If you reach'd twenty miles your balloon would collapse,
   Or pass by such action   The sphere of attraction,
Getting into the track   Of some comet—Good-lack !
'Tis a thousand to one that you'd never come back ;
And the boldest of mortals a danger like that must fear,
Rashly protruding beyond our own atmosphere.
   No, no ; when I try   A trip to the sky,
I shan't go in that thing of yours, Mr. Gye,
Though Messieurs Monk Mason, and Spencer, and Beazly,
All join in saying it travels so easily.
   No ; there's nothing so good   As a pony of wood—
Not like that which of late,   They stuck up on the gate

At the end of the Park, which caused so much debate,
And gave so much trouble to make it stand straight,—
But a regular Broomstick—you'll find that the favourite—
Above all, when, like Robin, you haven't to pay for it.
   —Stay—really I dread—   I am losing the thread
Of my tale ; and it's time you should be in your bed,
So lithe now, and listen, my little boy Ned !

    *   *   *   *   *

The Vicarage walls are lofty and thick,
And the copings are stone, and the sides are brick,
The casements are narrow, and bolted and barr'd,
And the stout oak door is heavy and hard ;
Moreover, by way of additional guard,
A great big dog runs loose in the yard,
And a horse-shoe is nailed on the threshold sill,—
To keep out aught that savours of ill,—
But, alack ! the chimney-pot's open still !
—That great big dog begins to quail,
Between his hind-legs he drops his tail,
Crouch'd on the ground, the terrified hound
Gives vent to a very odd sort of a sound ;
It is not a bark, loud, open and free,
As an honest old watch-dog's bark should be ;
It is not a yelp, it is not a growl,
But a something between a whine and a howl ;
And, hark !—a sound from the window high
Responds to the watch-dog's pitiful cry :
   It is not a moan,   It is not a groan ;
It comes from a nose,—but is not what a nose
Produces in healthy and sound repose.
Yet Sir Thopas the Vicar is fast asleep,
And his respirations are heavy and deep !

He snores, 'tis true, but he snores no more
As he's aye been accustom'd to snore before,
And as men of his kidney are wont to snore ;—
(Sir Thopas's weight is sixteen stone four ;)
He draws his breath like a man distress'd
By pain or grief, or like one oppress'd
By some ugly old Incubus perch'd on his breast.
   A something seems   To disturb his dreams,

And thrice on his ear, distinct and clear,
Falls a voice as of somebody whispering near
In still small accents, faint and few,
" Hey down the chimney-pot !—Hey after you ! "

Throughout the Vicarage, near and far,
There is no lack of bolt or of bar ;
   There are plenty of locks   To closet and box,
Yet the pantry wicket is standing ajar !
And the little low door, through which you must go,
Down some half-dozen steps, to the cellar below,
Is also unfastened, though no one may know
By so much as a guess, how it comes to be so ;
   For wicket and door,   The evening before,
Were both of them lock'd, and the key safely placed
On the bunch that hangs down from the Housekeeper's waist.

Oh ! 'twas a jovial sight to view
In that snug little cellar that frolicsome crew !
   Old Goody Price   Had got something nice,
A turkey-poult larded with bacon and spice ;—
   Old Goody Jones
Would touch nought that had bones,
She might just as well mumble a parcel of stones.
Goody Jones, in sooth, hath got never a tooth,
And a New-College pudding of marrow and plums
Is the dish of all others that suiteth her gums.

   Madge Gray was picking   The breast of a chicken,
Her coal-black eye, with its glance so sly,
Was fixed on Rob Gilpin himself, sitting by
With his heart full of love, and his mouth full of pie ;
   Grouse pie, with hare   In the middle, is fare
Which, duly concocted with science and care,
Doctor Kitchener says, is beyond all compare ;
   And a tenderer leveret   Robin had never ate ;
So, in after times, oft he was wont to asseverate.

" Now pledge we the wine-cup !—a health ! a health !
Sweet are the pleasures obtain'd by stealth !

Fill up ! fill up !—the brim of the cup
Is the part that aye holdeth the toothsomest sup !
Here's to thee, Goody Price !—Goody Jones, to thee !—
To thee, Roving Rob ! and again to me !
Many a sip, never a slip
Come to us four 'twixt the cup and the lip ! "

The cups pass quick,   The toasts fly thick,
Rob tries in vain out their meaning to pick,
But hears the words " Scratch," and " Old Bogey," and " Nick."
    More familiar grown,   Now he stands up alone,
Volunteering to give them a toast of his own.
    " A bumper of wine !   Fill thine !   Fill mine !
Here's a health to old Noah who planted the Vine ! "
    Oh then what sneezing,
    What coughing and wheezing,
Ensued in a way that was not over pleasing !
Goody Price, Goody Jones, and the pretty Madge Gray,
All seem'd as their liquor had gone the wrong way.

But the best of the joke was, the moment he spoke
Those words which the party seem'd almost to choke,
As by mentioning Noah some spell had been broke,
Every soul in the house at that instant awoke !
And, hearing the din from barrel and binn,
Drew at once the conclusion that thieves had got in,
Up jump'd the Cook and caught hold of her spit ;
Up jump'd the Groom and took birdle and bit ;
Up jump'd the Gardener and shoulder'd his spade ;
Up jump'd the Scullion,—the Footman,—the Maid ;
(The two last, by the way, occasioned some scandal,
By appearing together with only one candle,
Which gave for unpleasant surmises some handle ;)
Up jump'd the Swineherd,—and up jump'd the big boy,
A nondescript under him, acting as Pig-boy ;
Butler, Housekeeper, Coachman—from bottom to top
Everybody jump'd up without parley or stop,
With the weapon which first in their way chanced to drop—
Whip, warming-pan, wig-block, mug, musket, and mop.

    Last of all doth appear,
    With some symptoms of fear,

Sir Thopas in person to bring up the rear,
In a mix'd kind of costume half *Pontificalibus*,
Half what scholars denominate pure *Naturalibus*;
   Nay, the truth to express,   As you'll easily guess,
They have none of them time to attend much to dress;
   But He, or She,   As the case may be,
He or She seizes what He or She pleases,
Trunk-hosen or kirtles, and shirts or chemises,
And thus one and all, great and small, short and tall,
Muster at once in the Vicarage-hall,
With upstanding locks, startling eyes, shorten'd breath,
Like the folks in the Gallery Scene in Macbeth,
When Macduff is announcing their Sovereign's death.
And hark!—what accents clear and strong,
To the listening throng came floating along!
'Tis Robin encoring himself in a song—
   " Very good song! very well sung!
   Jolly companions every one! "

On, on to the cellar! away! away!
On, on to the cellar without more delay!
The whole *posse* rush onwards in battle array—
Conceive the dismay of the party so gay,
Old Goody Jones, Goody Price, and Madge Gray,
When the door bursting wide, they descried the allied
Troops, prepared for the onslaught, roll in like a tide,
And the spits, and the tongs, and the pokers beside!
" Boot and saddle's the word! mount, Cummers, and ride! "—
Alarm was ne'er caused more strong and indigenous
By cats among rats, or a hawk in a pigeon-house;
   Quick from the view   Away they all flew,
With a yell and a screech, and a halliballoo,
" Hey up the chimney!   Hey after you! "—
The Volscians themselves made an exit less speedy
From Corioli, " flutter'd like doves " by Macready.

   They are gone,—save one,   Robin alone!
Robin whose high state of civilisation
Precludes all idea of aerostation,
   And who now has no notion   Of more locomotion
Than suffices to kick, with much zeal and devotion,

Right and left at the party, who pounced on their victim,
And maul'd him, and kick'd him, And lick'd him, and prick'd him,
As they bore him away scarce aware what was done,
And believing it all but a part of the fun,
Hic—hiccoughing out the same strain he'd begun,
" Jol—jolly companions every one ! "

*　　*　　*　　*　　*

　　Morning grey　Scarce burst into day
Ere at Tappington Hall there's the deuce to pay ;
The tables and chairs are all placed in array
In the old oak-parlour, and in and out
Domestics and neighbours, a motley rout,
Are walking, and whispering, and standing about ;
　　And the Squire is there　In his large arm-chair,
Leaning back with a grave magisterial air ;
　　In the front of a seat a　Huge volume, called Fleta,
And Bracton, a tome of an old-fashion'd look,
And Coke upon Lyttelton, then a new book ;
　　And he moistens his lips　With occasional sips
From a luscious sack-posset that smiles in a tankard
Close by on a side-table—not that he drank hard,
　　But because at that day,　I hardly need say,
The Hong Merchants had not yet invented How Qua,
Nor as yet would you see Souchong or Bohea
At the tables of persons of any degree :
How our ancestors managed to do without tea
I must fairly confess is a mystery to me ;
　　Yet your Lydgates and Chaucers
　　Had no cups and saucers ;
Their breakfast, in fact, and the best they could get,
Was a sort of a *déjeûner à la fourchette ;*
　　Instead of our slops　They had cutlets and chops,
And sack-possets, and ale in stoups, tankards, and pots ;
And they wound up the meal with rumpsteaks and 'schalots.

　　Now the Squire lifts his hand
　　With an air of command,
And gives them a sign, which they all understand,
To bring in the culprit ; and straightway the carter

And huntsman drag in that unfortunate martyr,
Still kicking, and crying, " Come,—what are you arter ? "
The charge is prepared, and the evidence clear,
" He was caught in the cellar a-drinking the beer !
And came there, there's very great reason to fear,
With companions,—to say but the least of them,—queer ;
   Such as Witches, and creatures
   With horrible features,
   And horrible grins, And hook'd noses and chins,
Who'd been playing the deuce with his Reverence's binns."

The face of his worship grows graver and graver,
As the parties detail Robin's shameful behaviour;
Mister Buzzard, the clerk, while the tale is reciting,
Sits down to reduce the affair into writing,
   With all proper diction, And due " legal fiction ; "
Viz. : " That he, the said prisoner, as clearly was shown,
Conspiring with folks to deponents unknown,
With divers, that is to say, two thousand people,
In two thousand hats, each hat peak'd like a steeple,
   With force and with arms,
   And with sorcery and charms,
   Upon two thousand brooms ;
   Enter'd four thousand rooms,
To wit, two thousand pantries, and two thousand cellars,
Put in bodily fear twenty thousand in-dwellers,
And with sundry,—that is to say, two thousand,—forks,
Drew divers,—that is to say, ten thousand—corks,
And, with malice prepense, down their two thousand throttles,
Emptied various,—that is to say, ten thousand—bottles ;
All in breach of the peace,—moved by Satan's malignity—
And in spite of King James, and his Crown, and his Dignity."

   At words so profound Rob gazes around,
But no glance sympathetic to cheer him is found.
   —No glance, did I say ? Yes, one !—Madge Gray !—
She is there in the midst of the crowd standing by,
And she gives him one glance from her coal-black eye,
One touch to his hand, and one word to his ear,—
(That's a line which I've stolen from Sir Walter, I fear,)—
   While nobody near Seems to see her or hear ;

As his worship takes up, and surveys, with a strict eye,
The broom now produced as the *corpus delicti*,
Ere his fingers can clasp, It is snatch'd from his grasp,
The end poked in his chest with a force makes him gasp,
And, despite the decorum so due to the *Quorum*,
His worship's upset, and so too is his jorum,
And Madge is astride on the broomstick before 'em.
" *Hocus Pocus !* Quick, *Presto !* and *Hey Cockalorum !*
Mount, mount for your life, Rob !—Sir Justice, adieu !—
—Hey up the chimney-pot ! hey after you ! "

Through the mystified group,
With a halloo and a whoop,
Madge on the pommel, and Robin *en croupe*,
The pair through the air ride as if in a chair,
While the party below stand mouth open, and stare !
" Clean bumbaized " and amazed, and fix'd, all the room stick,
" Oh ! what's gone with Robin,—and Madge,—and the broomstick ?
Ay, " what's gone " indeed, Ned ?—of what befell
Madge Gray, and the broomstick, I never heard tell :
But Robin was found, that morn, on the ground,
In yon old grey Ruin again, safe and sound,
Except that at first he complained much of thirst,
And a shocking bad headache, of all ills the worst,
And close by his knee A flask you might see,
But an empty one, smelling of *eau-de-vie.*

Rob from this hour is an alter'd man ;
He runs home to his lodgings, as fast as he can,
Sticks to his trade, Marries Miss Slade,
Becomes a Te-totaller—that is the same
As Te-totallers now, one in all but the name ;
Grows fond of Small-beer, which is always a steady sign,
Never drinks spirits except as a medicine ;
Learns to despise Coal-black eyes,
Minds pretty girls no more than so many Guys ;
Has a family, lives to be sixty, and dies !

Now, my little boy Ned Brush off to your bed,
Tie your night-cap on safe, or a napkin instead,[3]
Or these terrible nights you'll catch cold in your head ;

And remember my tale, and the moral it teaches,
Which you'll find much the same as what Solomon preaches :
Don't flirt with young ladies, don't practise soft speeches ;
Avoid waltzes, quadrilles, pumps, silk hose, and knee-breeches ;—
Frequent not grey Ruins,—shun riot and revelry,
Hocus Pocus, and Conjuring, and all sorts of devilry ;—
Don't meddle with broomsticks,—they're Beelzebub's switches ;
Of cellars keep clear,—they're the devil's own ditches ;
And beware of balls, banquetings, brandy, and—witches !
Above all ! don't run after black eyes !—if you do,—
Depend on't you'll find what I say will come true,—
Old Nick, some fine morning, will " hey after you ! "

Strange as the events detailed in the succeeding narrative may appear, they are, I have
not the slightest doubt, true to the letter. Whatever impression they may make upon the
Reader, that produced by them on the narrator, I can aver, was neither light nor transient.

SINGULAR PASSAGE

IN THE LIFE
OF
THE LATE HENRY HARRIS
DOCTOR IN DIVINITY

AS RELATED BY THE REV. JASPER INGOLDSBY, M.A.,
HIS FRIEND AND EXECUTOR.

IN order that the extraordinary circumstance which I am about to relate may meet with the credit it deserves, I think it necessary to premise, that my reverend friend, among whose papers I find it recorded, was, in his lifetime, ever esteemed as a man of good plain understanding, strict veracity, and unimpeached morals,—by no means of a nervous temperament, or one likely to attach undue weight to any occurrence out of the common course of events, merely because his reflections might not, at that moment, afford him a ready solution of its difficulties.

On the truth of this narrative, as far as he was personally concerned, no one who knew him would hesitate to place the most implicit reliance. His history is briefly this :—He had married early in life, and was a widower at the age of thirty-nine, with an only daughter, who had then arrived at puberty, and was just married to a near connection of our own family. The sudden death of her husband, occasioned by a fall from his horse, only three days after her confinement, was abruptly communicated to Mrs. S—— by a thoughtless girl, who saw her master brought lifeless into the house, and, with all that inexplicable anxiety to be the first to tell bad news, so common among the lower orders, rushed at once into the sick-room with her intelligence. The shock was too severe ; and though the young widow survived the fatal event several months, yet she gradually sunk under the blow, and expired, leaving a boy, not a twelvemonth old, to the care of his maternal grandfather.

My poor friend was sadly shaken by this melancholy catastrophe ; time, however, and a strong religious feeling succeeded at length in moderating the poignancy of his grief—a consummation much advanced by his infant charge, who now succeeded, as it were by inheritance, to the place in his affections left vacant by his daughter's decease. Frederick S—— grew up to be a fine lad ; his person and features were decidedly handsome ; still there was, as I remember, an unpleasant expression in his countenance, and an air of reserve, attributed, by the few persons who called occasionally at the vicarage, to the retired life led by his grandfather, and the little opportunity he had, in consequence, of mixing in the society of his equals in age and intellect. Brought up entirely at home, his progress in the common branches of education was, without any great display of precocity, rather in advance of the generality of boys of his own standing ; partly owing, perhaps, to the turn which even his amusements took from the first. His sole associate was the son of the village apothecary, a boy about two years older than himself, whose father, being really clever in his profession, and a good operative chemist, had constructed for himself a small laboratory, in which, as he was fond of children, the two boys spent a great portion of their leisure time, witnessing many of those little experiments so attractive to youth, and in time aspiring to imitate what they admired.

In such society, it is not surprising that Frederick S—— should imbibe a strong taste for the sciences which formed his principal amusement ; or that, when, in process of time, it became necessary to choose his walk in life, a profession so intimately connected with his favourite pursuit, as that of medicine, should be eagerly selected. No opposition was offered by my friend, who, knowing that the greater part of his own income would expire with his life, and that the remainder would prove an insufficient resource to his grandchild, was only anxious that he should follow such a path as would secure him that moderate and respectable competency which is, perhaps, more conducive to real happiness than a more elevated or wealthy station. Frederick was, accordingly, at the proper age, matriculated at Oxford, with the view of studying the higher branches of medicine, a few months after his friend, John W——, had proceeded to Leyden, for the purpose of making himself acquainted with the practice of surgery in the hospitals and lecture-rooms attached to that university. The boyish intimacy of their younger days did not, as is frequently the case, yield to separation; on the contrary, a close correspondence was kept up between them. Dr. Harris was even prevailed upon to allow Frederick to take a trip to Holland to see his friend; and John returned the visit to Frederick at Oxford.

Satisfactory as, for some time, were the accounts of the general course of Frederick S——'s studies, by degrees rumours of a less pleasant nature reached the ears of some of his friends; to the vicarage, however, I have reason to believe they never penetrated. The good old Doctor was too well beloved in his parish for any one voluntarily to give him pain; and, after all, nothing beyond whispers and surmises had reached X——, when the worthy Vicar was surprised on a sudden by a request from his grandchild that he might be permitted to take his name off the books of the university, and proceed to finish his education in conjunction with his friend W—— at Leyden. Such a proposal, made, too, at a time when the period for his graduating could not be far distant, both surprised and grieved the Doctor; he combated the design with more perseverance than he had ever been known to exert in opposition to any declared wish of his darling boy before, but, as usual, gave way, when more strongly pressed, from sheer inability to persist in a refusal which seemed to give so much pain to Frederick, especially when the latter, with more energy than was quite becoming their relative situations, expressed his positive determination of not returning to Oxford, whatever might be the result of his grandfather's decision. My friend, his mind, perhaps, a little weakened by a short but severe nervous attack which he had scarcely recovered from, at length yielded a reluctant consent, and Frederick quitted England.

It was not till some months had elapsed after his departure, that I had reason to suspect, that the eager desire of availing himself of opportunities for study abroad, not afforded him at home, was not the sole or even the principal, reason which had drawn Frederick so abruptly from his *Alma Mater*. A chance visit to the university, and a conversation with a senior fellow belonging to his late college, convinced me of this; still I found it impossible to extract from the latter the precise nature of his offence. That he had given way to most culpable indulgences, I had before heard hinted; and when I recollected how he had been at once launched, from a state of what might be well called seclusion, into a world where so many enticements were lying in wait to allure,— with liberty, example, everything to tempt him from the straight road,— regret, I frankly own, was more the predominant feeling in my mind than either surprise or condemnation. But here was evidently something more than mere ordinary excess—some act of profligacy, perhaps of a deeper stain, which had induced his superiors, who, at first, had been loud in his praises, to desire him to withdraw himself quietly, but for ever; and such an intimation, I found, had in fact been conveyed to him from an authority which it was impossible to resist. Seeing that my informant was determined not to be explicit, I did not press for a disclosure, which, if made, would, in all probability, only have given me pain, and that the rather, as my old friend the Doctor had recently obtained a valuable living from Lord M——, only a few miles distant from the market town in which I resided, where he now was, amusing himself in putting his grounds into order, ornamenting his house, and getting everything ready against his grandson's expected visit in the following autumn. October came, and with it came Frederick: he rode over more than once to see me, sometimes accompanied by the Doctor, between whom and myself the recent loss of my poor daughter Louisa had drawn the cords of sympathy still closer.

More than two years had flown on in this way, in which Frederick S—— had as many times made temporary visits to his native country. The time was fast approaching when he was expected to return and finally take up his residence in England, when the sudden illness of my wife's father obliged us to take a journey into Lancashire, my old friend, who had himself a curate, kindly offering to fix his quarters at my parsonage, and superintend the concerns of my parish till my return.—Alas! when I saw him next he was on the bed of death!

My absence was necessarily prolonged much beyond what I had anticipated. A letter, with a foreign postmark, had, as I afterwards found, been brought over from his own house to my venerable substitute in the interval, and barely giving himself time to transfer the charge he had undertaken to a neighbouring clergyman, he had hurried off at once to Leyden. His arrival there was, however, too late. Frederick *was dead!*—killed in a duel, occasioned, it was said, by no ordinary provocation on his part, although the flight of his antagonist had added to the mystery which enveloped its origin. The long journey, its melancholy termination, and the complete overthrow of all my poor friend's earthly hopes, were too much for him. He appeared too,—as I was informed by the proprietor of the house in which I found him, when his summons at length had brought me to his bed-side,—to have received some sudden and unaccountable shock, which even the death of his grandson was inadequate to explain. There was, indeed, a wildness in his fast glazing eye, which mingled strangely with the glance of satisfaction thrown upon me as he pressed my hand ;—he endeavoured to raise himself, and would have spoken, but fell back in the effort, and closed his eyes for ever.—I buried him there, by the side of the object of his more than parental affection,—in a foreign land.

It is from the papers that I discovered in his travelling-case that I submit the following extracts, without, however, presuming to advance an opinion on the strange circumstances which they detail, or even as to the connection which some may fancy they discover between different parts of them.

The first was evidently written at my own house, and bears date August the 15th, 18—, about three weeks after my own departure from Preston.

It begins thus :—

" Tuesday, August 15th.—Poor girl !—I forget who it is that says, ' the real ills of life are light in comparison with fancied evils ' ; and certainly the scene I have just witnessed goes some way towards establishing the truth of the hypothesis.—Among the afflictions which flesh is heir to, a diseased imagination is far from being the lightest, even when considered separately, and without taking into the account those bodily pains and sufferings which,—so close is the connection between mind and matter,—are but too frequently attendant upon any disorder of the fancy. Seldom has my interest been more powerfully excited than by poor Mary Graham. Her age, her appearance, her pale, melancholy features, the very contour of her countenance, all conspired to remind me, but too forcibly, of one who, waking or sleeping, is never long absent from my thoughts ;—but enough of this.

" A fine morning had succeeded one of the most tempestuous nights I ever remember, and I was just sitting down to a substantial breakfast, which the care of my friend Ingoldsby's housekeeper, kind-hearted Mrs. Wilson, had prepared for me, when I was interrupted by a summons, to the sick-bed of a young parishioner whom I had frequently seen in my walks, and had remarked for the regularity of her attendance at Divine worship.—Mary Graham is the elder of two daughters, residing with their mother, the widow of an attorney, who, dying suddenly in the prime of life, left his family but slenderly provided for. A strict though not parsimonious economy has, however, enabled them to live with an appearance of respectability and comfort ; and from the personal attractions which both the girls possess, their mother is evidently not without hopes of seeing one, at least, of them advantageously settled in life. As far as poor Mary is concerned, I fear she is doomed to inevitable disappointment, as I am much mistaken if consumption has not laid its wasting finger upon her ; while this last recurrence, of what I cannot but believe to be a most formidable epileptic attack, threatens to shake out with even added velocity, the little sand that may yet remain within the hour-glass of time. Her very delusion, too, is of such a nature as, by adding to bodily illness the agitation of superstitious terror, can scarcely fail to accelerate the catastrophe, which I think I see fast approaching.

" Before I was introduced into the sick-room, her sister, who had been watching my arrival from the window, took me into their little parlour, and, after the usual civilities, began to prepare me for the visit I was about to pay. Her countenance was marked at once with trouble and alarm, and in a low tone 'of voice, which some internal emotion, rather than the fear of disturbing the invalid in a distant room, had subdued almost to a whisper, informed me that my presence was become necessary, not more as a clergyman than a magistrate ;—that the disorder, with which her sister had, during the night, been so suddenly and unaccountably seized, was one of no common kind, but attended with circumstances which, coupled with the declarations of the sufferer, took it out of all ordinary calculations, and, to use her own expression, that ' malice was at the bottom of it.'

" Naturally supposing that these insinuations were intended to intimate the partaking of some deleterious substance on the part of the invalid, I inquired what reason she had for imagining, in the first place, that anything of a poisonous nature had been administered at all ; and secondly, what possible incitement any human being could have for the perpetration of so foul a deed towards so innocent and unoffending an individual ? Her answer considerably relieved the apprehensions I had begun to entertain lest the poor girl should, from some unknown cause, have herself been attempting to rush uncalled into the presence of her Creator ; at the same time, it surprised me not a little by its apparent want of rationality and common sense. She had no reason to believe, she said, that her sister had taken poison, or that any attempt upon her life had been made, or was, perhaps, contemplated, but that

' still malice was at work,—the malice of villains or fiends, or of both combined ; that no causes purely natural would suffice to account for the state in which her sister had been now twice placed, or for the dreadful sufferings she had undergone while in that state,' and that she was determined the whole affair should undergo a thorough investigation. Seeing that the poor girl was now herself labouring under a great degree of excitement, I did not think it necessary to enter at that moment into a discussion upon the absurdity of her opinion, but applied myself to the tranquillising her mind by assurances of a proper inquiry, and then drew her attention to the symptoms of the indisposition, and the way in which it had first made its appearance.

"The violence of the storm last night had, I found, induced the whole family to sit up far beyond their usual hour, till, wearied out at length, and, as their mother observed, ' tired of burning fire and candle to no purpose,' they repaired to their several chambers.

"The sisters occupied the same room ; Elizabeth was already at their humble toilet, and had commenced the arrangement of her hair for the night, when her attention was at once drawn from her employment by a half-smothered shriek and exclamation from her sister, who, in her delicate state of health, had found walking up two flights of stairs, perhaps a little more quickly than usual, an exertion, to recover from which she had seated herself in a large arm-chair.

"Turning hastily at the sound, she perceived Mary deadly pale, grasping, as it were convulsively, each arm of the chair which supported her, and bending forward in the attitude of listening ; her lips were trembling and bloodless, cold drops of perspiration stood upon her forehead, and in an instant after exclaiming in a piercing tone. ' Hark ! they are calling me again ! it is—*it is the same voice ;*—Oh no ! no !—Oh my God ! save me, Betsy,—hold me—save me ! ' she fell forward upon the floor. Elizabeth flew to her assistance, raised her, and by her cries brought both her mother, who had not yet got into bed, and their only servant girl to her aid. The latter was despatched at once for medical help ; but from the appearance of the sufferer it was much to be feared that she would soon be beyond the reach of art. Her agonised parent and sister succeeded in bearing her between them and placing her on a bed : a faint and intermittent pulsation was for a while perceptible ; but in a few moments a general shudder shook the whole body ; the pulse ceased, the eyes became fixed and glassy, the jaw dropped, a cold clamminess usurped the place of the genial warmth of life. Before Mr. I—— arrived everything announced that dissolution had taken place, and that the freed spirit had quitted its mortal tenement.

" The appearance of the surgeon confirmed their worst apprehensions ; a vein was opened, but the blood refused to flow, and Mr. I—— pronounced that the vital spark was indeed extinguished.

" The poor mother, whose attachment to her children was perhaps the more powerful as they were the sole relatives or connections she had in the world, was overwhelmed with a grief amounting almost to frenzy ; it was with difficulty that she was removed to her own room by the united strength of her daughter and medical adviser. Nearly an hour had elapsed during the endeavour at calming her transports ; they had succeeded, however, to a certain extent, and Mr. I—— had taken his leave, when Elizabeth, re-entering the bedchamber in which her sister lay, in order to pay the last sad duties to her corpse, was horror-struck at seeing a crimson stream of blood running down the side of the counterpane to the floor. Her exclamation brought the girl again to her side, when it was perceived, to their astonishment, that the sanguine stream proceeded from the arm of the body, which was now manifesting signs of returning life. The half-frantic mother flew to the room, and it was with difficulty that they could prevent her in her agitation from so acting as to extinguish for ever the hope which had begun to rise in their bosoms. A long-drawn sigh, amounting almost to a groan, followed by several convulsive gaspings, was the prelude to the restoration of the animal functions in poor Mary : a shriek, almost preternaturally loud, considering her state of exhaustion, succeeded ; but she did recover, and with the help of restoratives was well enough towards morning to express a strong desire that I should be sent for,—a desire the more readily complied with, inasmuch as the strange expressions and declarations she had made since her restoration to consciousness had filled her sister with the most horrible suspicions. The nature of these suspicions was such as would at any other time, perhaps, have raised a smile upon my lips ; but the distress, and even agony of the poor girl, as she half hinted and half expressed them, were such as entirely to preclude every sensation at all approaching to mirth. Without endeavouring, therefore, to combat ideas, evidently too strongly impressed upon her mind at the moment to admit of present refutation, I merely used a few encouraging words, and requested her to precede me to the sick-chamber.

" The invalid was lying on the outside of the bed partly dressed, and wearing a white dimity wrapping-gown, the colour of which corresponded but too well with the deadly paleness of her complexion. Her cheek was wan and sunken, giving an extraordinary prominence to her eye, which gleamed with a lustrous brilliancy not unfrequently characteristic of the aberration of intellect. I took her hand ; it was chill and clammy, the pulse feeble and intermittent, and the general debility of her frame was such that I would fain have persuaded her to defer any conversation which, in her present state, she might not be able to support. Her positive assurance that until she had disburdened herself of what she called her ' dreadful secret,' she could know no rest either of mind or body, at length induced me to comply with her wish, opposition to which in her then frame of mind might perhaps be attended with even worse effects than its indulgence. I bowed acquiescence, and in a low and faltering voice, with frequent interruptions occasioned by her weakness, she gave me the following singular account of the sensations which, she averred, had been experienced by her during her trance :—

" ' This, sir,' she began, ' is not the first time that the cruelty of others has, for what purpose I am unable to conjecture, put me to a degree of torture which I can compare to no suffering, either of body or mind, which I have ever before experienced. On a former occasion I was willing to believe it the mere effect of a hideous dream, or what is vulgarly termed the nightmare ; but this repetition, and the circumstances under which I was last *summoned*, at a time, too, when I had not even composed myself to rest, fatally convince me of the reality of what I have seen and suffered.

" ' This is no time for concealment of any kind. It is now more than a twelvemonth since I was in the habit of occasionally encountering in my walks a young man of prepossessing appearance and gentlemanly deportment. He was always alone, and generally reading : but I could not be long in doubt that these rencounters, which became every week more frequent, were not the effect of accident, or that his attention, when we did meet, was less directed to his book than to my sister and myself. He even seemed to wish to address us, and I have no doubt would have taken some other opportunity of doing so, had not one been afforded him by a strange dog attacking us one Sunday morning in our way to church, which he beat off, and made use of this little service to promote an acquaintance. His name, he said, was Francis Somers, and added that he was on a visit to a relation of the same name, resident a few miles from X———. He gave us to understand that he was himself studying surgery with the view to a medical appointment in one of the colonies. You are not to suppose, sir, that he had entered thus into his concerns at the first interview ; it was not till our acquaintance had ripened, and he had visited our house more than once with my mother's sanction, that these particulars were elicited. He never disguised from the first that an attachment to myself was his object originally in introducing himself to our notice ; as his prospects were comparatively flattering, my mother did not raise any impediment to his attentions, and I own I received them with pleasure.

" ' Days and weeks elapsed ; and although the distance at which his relation resided prevented the possibility of an uninterrupted intercourse, yet neither was it so great as to preclude his frequent visits. The interval of a day, or at most of two, was all that intervened, and these temporary absences certainly did not decrease the pleasure of the meetings with which they terminated. At length a pensive expression began to exhibit itself upon his countenance, and I could not but remark that at every visit he became more abstracted and reserved. The eye of affection is not slow to detect any symptom of uneasiness in a quarter dear to it. I spoke to him, questioned him on the subject ; his answer was evasive, and I said no more. My mother too, however, had marked the same appearance of melancholy, and pressed him more strongly. He at length admitted that his spirits were depressed, and that their depression was caused by the necessity of an early, though but a temporary, separation. His uncle and only friend, he said, had long insisted on his spending some months on the Continent with the view of completing his professional education, and that the time was now fast approaching when it would be necessary for him to commence his journey. A look made the inquiry which my tongue refused to utter. " Yes, dearest Mary," was his reply, " I have communicated our attachment to him, partially at least ; and though I dare not say that the intimation was received as I could have wished, yet I have, perhaps, on the whole, no fair reason to be dissatisfied with his reply.

" ' " ' The completion of my studies, and my settlement in the world, must, my uncle told me, be the first consideration ; when these material points were achieved, he should not interfere with any arrangement that might be found essential to my happiness ; at the same time he has positively refused to sanction any engagement at present, which may, he says, have a tendency to divert my attention from those pursuits, on the due prosecution of which my future situation in life must depend. A compromise between love and duty was eventually wrung from me, though reluctantly ; I have pledged myself to proceed immediately to my destination abroad, with a full understanding that on my return, a twelvemonth hence, no obstacle shall be thrown in the way of what are, I trust, our mutual wishes."

" ' I will not attempt to describe the feelings with which I received this communication, nor will it be necessary to say anything of what passed at the few interviews which took place before Francis quitted

X——. The evening immediately previous to that of his departure he passed in this house, and, before we separated, renewed his protestations of an unchangeable affection, requiring a similar assurance from me in return. I did not hesitate to make it. "Be satisfied, my dear Francis," said I, "that no diminution in the regard I have avowed can ever take place, and though absent in body, my heart and soul will still be with you."—"Swear this," he cried, with a suddenness and energy which surprised, and rather startled me ; "promise that you will be with me *in spirit*, at least, when I am far away." I gave him my hand, but that was not sufficient. "One of these dark shining ringlets, my dear Mary," said he, "as a pledge that you will not forget your vow!" I suffered him to take the scissors from my work-box and to sever a lock of my hair, which he placed in his bosom.—The next day he was pursuing his journey, and the waves were already bearing] him from England.

"'I had letters from him repeatedly during the first three months of his absence ; they spoke of his health, his prospects, and of his love, but by degrees the intervals between each arrival became longer, and I fancied I perceived some falling off from that warmth of expression which had at first characterised his communications.

"'One night I had retired to rest rather later than usual, having sat by the bed-side, comparing his last brief note with some of his earlier letters, and was endeavouring to convince myself that my apprehensions of his fickleness were unfounded, when an undefinable sensation of restlessness and anxiety seized upon me. I cannot compare it to anything I had ever experienced before ; my pulse fluttered, my heart beat with a quickness and violence which alarmed me, and a strange tremour shook my whole frame. I retired hastily to bed, in hopes of getting rid of so unpleasant a sensation, but in vain ; a vague apprehension of I knew not what occupied my mind, and vainly did I endeavour to shake it off. I can compare my feelings to nothing but those which we sometimes experience when about to undertake a long and unpleasant journey, leaving those we love behind us. More than once did I raise myself in my bed and listen, fancying that I heard myself called, and on each of those occasions the fluttering of my heart increased. Twice I was on the point of calling to my sister, who then slept in an adjoining room, but she had gone to bed indisposed, and an unwillingness to disturb either her or my mother checked me ; the large clock in the room below at this moment began to strike the hour of twelve. I distinctly heard its vibrations, but ere its sounds had ceased, a burning heat, as if a hot iron had been applied to my temple, was succeeded by a dizziness,—a swoon,—a total loss of consciousness as to where or in what situation I was.

" ' A pain, violent, sharp, and piercing, as though my whole frame were lacerated by some keen-edged weapon, roused me from this stupor, —but where was I ? Everything was strange around me—a shadowy dimness rendered every object indistinct and uncertain ; methought, however, that I was seated in a large, antique, high-backed chair, several of which were near, their tall black carved frames and seats inter-woven with a lattice-work of cane. The apartment in which I sat was one of moderate dimensions, and from its sloping roof, seemed to be the upper story of the edifice, a fact confirmed by the moon shining without, in full effulgence, on a huge round tower, which its light rendered plainly visible through the open casement, and the summit of which appeared but little superior in elevation to the room I occupied. Rather to the right, and in the distance, the spire of some cathedral or lofty church was visible, while sundry gable-ends, and tops of houses told me I was in the midst of a populous but unknown city.

" ' The apartment itself had something strange in its appearance ; and, in the character of its furniture and appurtenances, bore little or no resemblance to any I had ever seen before. The fireplace was large and wide, with a pair of what are sometimes called andirons, betokening that wood was the principal, if not the only fuel consumed within its recess ; a fierce fire was now blazing in it, the light from which rendered visible the remotest parts of the chamber. Over a lofty old-fashioned mantelpiece, carved heavily in imitation of fruits and flowers, hung the half-length portrait of a gentleman in a dark-coloured foreign habit, with a peaked beard and mustaches, one hand resting upon a table, the other supporting a sort of a *baton*, or short military staff, the summit of which was surmounted by a silver falcon. Several antique chairs, similar in appearance to those already mentioned, surrounded a massive oaken table, the length of which much exceeded its width. At the lower end of this piece of furniture stood the chair I occupied ; on the upper, was placed a small chafing-dish filled with burning coals, and darting forth occasionally long flashes of various-coloured fire, the brilliance of which made itself visible, even above the strong illumina-tion emitted from the chimney. Two huge, black, japanned cabinets, with clawed feet, reflecting from their polished surfaces the effulgence of the flame, were placed one on each side the casement-window to which I have alluded, and with a few shelves loaded with books, many of which were also strewed in disorder on the floor, completed the list of the furniture in the apartment.   Some strange-looking instruments, of unknown form and purpose, lay on the table near the chafing-dish, on the other side of which a miniature portrait of myself hung, reflected by a small oval mirror in a dark-coloured frame, while a large open volume, traced with strange characters of the colour of blood, lay in front ; a goblet, containing a few drops of liquid of the same ensanguined hue, was by its side.

" ' But of the objects which I have endeavoured to describe, none arrested my attention so forcibly as two others.   These were the figures of two young men, in the prime of life, only separated from me by the table.   They were dressed alike, each in a long flowing gown, made of some sad-coloured stuff, and confined at the waist by a crimson girdle ; one of them, the shorter of the two, was occupied in feeding the embers of the chafing-dish with a resinous powder, which produced and maintained a brilliant but flickering blaze, to the action of which his companion was exposing a long lock of dark chestnut hair, that shrank and shrivelled as it approached the flame.   But, O God !—that hair !— and the form of him who held it ! that face ! those features !—not for one instant could I entertain a doubt—it was He ! Francis !—the lock he grasped was mine, the very pledge of affection I had given him, and still, as it partially encountered the fire, a burning heat seemed to scorch the temple from which it had been taken, conveying a torturing sensation that affected my very brain.

" ' How shall I proceed ?—but no, it is impossible,—not even to you, sir, can I—dare I—recount the proceedings of that unhallowed night of horror and of shame.   Were my life extended to a term commensurate with that of the Patriarchs of old, never could its detestable, its damning pollutions be effaced from my remembrance ; and oh ! above all, never could I forget the diabolical glee which sparkled in the eyes of my fiendish tormentors, as they witnessed the worse than useless struggles of their miserable victim.   Oh ! why was it not permitted me to take refuge in unconsciousness—nay, in death itself, from the abominations of which I was compelled to be, not only a witness—but a partaker !   But it is enough, sir ; I will not further shock your nature by dwelling longer on a scene, the full horrors of which, words, if I even dared employ any, would be inadequate to express ; suffice it to say, that after being subjected to it, how long I knew not, but certainly for more than an hour, a noise from below seemed to alarm my persecutors ; a pause ensued,—the lights were extinguished,—and, as the sound of a footstep ascending a staircase became more distinct, my forehead felt again the excruciating sensation of heat, while the embers, kindling into a momentary flame, betrayed another portion of the ringlet consuming in the blaze. Fresh agonies succeeded, not less severe, and of a similar description to those which had seized upon me at first ; oblivion again· followed, and on being at length restored to consciousness, I found myself as you see me now, faint and exhausted, weakened in every limb, and every fibre quivering with agitation.—·My groans soon brought my sister to my aid ; it was long before I could summon resolution to confide, even to her, the dreadful secret, and when I had done so, her strongest efforts were not wanting to persuade me that I had been labouring under a severe attack of night-mare. I ceased to argue, but I was not convinced : the whole scene was then too present, too awfully real, to permit me to doubt the character of the transaction ; and if, when a few days had elapsed, the hopelessness of imparting to others the conviction I entertained myself, produced in me. an apparent acquiescence with their opinion, I have never been the less satisfied that no cause reducible to the known laws of nature occasioned my sufferings on that hellish evening. Whether that firm belief might have eventually yielded to time, whether I might at length have been brought to consider all that had passed, and the circumstances which I could never cease to remember, as a mere phantasm, the offspring of a heated imagination, acting upon an enfeebled body, I know not—last night, however, would in any case have dispelled the flattering illusion—last night—last night was the whole horrible scene acted over again. The place—the. actors—the whole infernal apparatus were the same ;—the same insults, the same torments, the same brutalities—all were renewed, save that the period of my agony was not so prolonged. I became sensible to an incision in my arm, though the hand that made it was not visible ; at the same moment my persecutors paused ; they were manifestly disconcerted, and the companion of him, whose name shall never more pass my lips, muttered something to his abettor in evident agitation ; the formula of an oath of horrible import was dictated to me in terms fearfully distinct. I refused it unhesitatingly ; again and again was it proposed, with menaces I tremble to think on—but I refused ; the same sound was heard—interruption was evidently apprehended,—the same ceremony was hastily repeated, and I again found myself released, lying on my own bed, with my mother and my sister weeping over me.—O God ! O God ! when and how is this to end !—When will my spirit be left in peace ?—Where, or with whom shall I find refuge ? '

"It is impossible to convey any adequate idea of the emotions with which this unhappy girl's narrative affected me. It must not be

I

supposed that her story was delivered in the same continuous and un-interrupted strain in which I have transcribed its substance. On the contrary, it was not without frequent intervals, of longer or shorter duration, that her account was brought to a conclusion : indeed, many passages of her strange dream were not without the greatest difficulty and reluctance communicated at all.—My task was no easy one ; never, in the course of a long life spent in the active duties of my Christian calling,—never had I been summoned to such a conference before !

"To the half-avowed, and palliated, confession of committed guilt, I had often listened, and pointed out the only road to secure its forgive-ness. I had succeeded in cheering the spirit of despondency, and some-times even in calming the ravings of despair ; but here I had a different enemy to combat, an ineradicable prejudice to encounter, evidently backed by no common share of superstition, and confirmed by the mental weakness attendant upon severe bodily pain. To argue the sufferer out of an opinion so rooted was a hopeless attempt. I did, however, essay it ; I spoke to her of the strong and mysterious con-nection maintained between our waking images and those which haunt us in our dreams, and more especially during that morbid oppression commonly called nightmare. I was even enabled to adduce myself as a strong, and living, instance of the excess to which fancy sometimes carries her freaks on these occasions ; while by an odd coincidence, the impression made upon my own mind, which I adduced as an example, bore no slight resemblance to her own. I stated to her, that on my recovery from the fit of epilepsy, which had attacked me about two years since, just before my grandson Frederick left Oxford, it was with the greatest difficulty I could persuade myself that I had not visited him, during the interval, in his rooms at Brazenose, and even conversed both with himself and his friend W——, seated in his arm-chair, and gazing through the window full upon the statue of Cain, as it stands in the centre of the quadrangle. I told her of the pain I underwent both at the commencement and termination of my attack,—of the extreme lassi-tude that succeeded ; but my efforts were all in vain ; she listened to me, indeed, with an interest almost breathless, especially when I informed her of my having actually experienced the very burning sensation in the brain alluded to, no doubt a strong attendant symptom of this peculiar affection, and a proof of the identity of the complaint ; but I could plainly perceive that I failed entirely in shaking the rooted opinion which possessed her, that her spirit had, by some nefarious and unhallowed means, been actually subtracted for a time from its earthly tenement."

*   *   *   *   *   *   *

The next extract which I shall give from my old friend's memoranda is dated August 24th, more than a week subsequent to his first visit at Mrs. Graham's. He appears, from his papers, to have visited the poor young woman more than once during the interval, and to have afforded her those spiritual consolations which no one was more capable of communicating. His patient, for so in a religious sense she may well be termed, had been sinking under the agitation she had experienced; and the constant dread she was under, of similar sufferings, operated so strongly on a frame already enervated, that life at length seemed to hang only by a thread. His papers go on to say:

" I have just seen poor Mary Graham,—I fear for the last time. Nature is evidently quite worn out; she is aware that she is dying, and looks forward to the termination of her existence here, not only with resignation but with joy. It is clear that her dream, or what she persists in calling her ' subtraction,' has much to do with this. For the last three days her behaviour has been altered; she has avoided conversing on the subject of her delusion, and seems to wish that I should consider her as a convert to my view of her case. This may, perhaps, be partly owing to the flippances of her medical attendant upon the subject, for Mr. I—— has, somehow or other, got an inkling that she has been much agitated by a dream, and thinks to laugh off the impression,—in my opinion injudiciously; but though a skilful, and a kind-hearted, he is a young man, and of a disposition, perhaps, rather too mercurial for the chamber of a nervous invalid. Her manner has since been much more reserved to both of us: in my case, probably because she suspects me of betraying her secret."

*   *   *   *   *   *   *

" August 26th.—Mary Graham is yet alive, but sinking fast; her cordiality towards me has returned since her sister confessed yesterday, that she had herself told Mr. I—— that his patient's mind ' had been affected by a terrible vision.' I am evidently restored to her confidence. —She asked me this morning, with much earnestness, ' What I believed to be the state of departed spirits during the interval between dissolution and the final day of account?—And whether I thought they would be safe, in another world, from the influence of wicked persons employing an agency more than human?'—Poor child!—One cannot mistake the prevailing bias of her mind.—Poor child!"

*   *   *   *   *   *   *

" August 27th.—It is nearly over; she is sinking rapidly, but quietly and without pain. I have just administered to her the sacred elements, of which her mother partook. Elizabeth declined doing the same;

she cannot, she says, yet bring herself to forgive the villain who has destroyed her sister. It is singular that she, a young woman of good plain sense in ordinary matters, should so easily adopt, and so pertinaciously retain a superstition so puerile and ridiculous. This must be matter of a future conversation between us; at present, with the form of the dying girl before her eyes, it were vain to argue with her. The mother, I find, has written to young Somers, stating the dangerous situation of his affianced wife; indignant, as she justly is, at his long silence, it is fortunate that she has no knowledge of the suspicions entertained by her daughter. I have seen her letter, it is addressed to Mr. Francis Somers, in the Hogewoert, at Leyden,—a fellow student then of Frederick's. I must remember to inquire if he is acquainted with this young man."

    *   *   *   *   *   *   *

Mary Graham, it appears, died the same night. Before her departure she repeated to my friend the singular story she had before told him, without any material variation from the detail she had formerly given. To the last she persisted in believing that her unworthy lover had practised upon her by forbidden arts. She once more described the apartment with great minuteness, and even the person of Francis's alleged companion, who was, she said, about the middle height, hardfeatured, with a rather remarkable scar upon his left cheek, extending in a transverse direction from below the eye to the nose. Several pages of my reverend friend's manuscript are filled with reflections upon this extraordinary confession, which, joined with its melancholy termination, seems to have produced no common effect upon him. He alludes to more than one subsequent discussion with the surviving sister, and piques himself on having made some progress in convincing her of the folly of her theory respecting the origin and nature of the illness itself.

His memoranda on this and other subjects are continued till about the middle of September, when a break ensues, occasioned, no doubt, by the unwelcome news of his grandson's dangerous state, which induced him to set out forthwith for Holland. His arrival at Leyden was, as I have already said, too late. Frederick S—— had expired, after thirty hours' intense suffering, from a wound received in a duel with a brother student. The cause of quarrel was variously related; but according to his landlord's version it had originated in some silly dispute about a dream of his antagonist's, who had been the challenger. Such, at least, was the account given to him, as he said, by Frederick's friend and fellow lodger, W——, who had acted as second on the occasion, thus acquitting himself of an obligation of the same kind due to the deceased, whose services he had put in requisition about a year before on a similar occasion, when he had himself been severely wounded. in the face.

From the same authority I learned that my poor friend was much affected on finding that his arrival had been deferred too long. Every attention was shown him by the proprietor of the house, a respectable tradesman, and a chamber was prepared for his accommodation; the books and few effects of his deceased grandson were delivered over to him duly inventoried, and, late as it was in the evening when he reached Leyden, he insisted on being conducted immediately to the apartments which Frederick had occupied, there to indulge the first ebullitions of his sorrow before he retired to his own. Madame Müller accordingly led the way to an upper room, which, being situated at the top of the house, had been, from its privacy and distance from the street, selected by Frederick as his study. The Doctor entered, and taking the lamp from his conductress, motioned to be left alone. His implied wish was of course complied with; and nearly two hours had elapsed before his kind-hearted hostess reascended, in the hope of prevailing upon him to return with her and partake of that refreshment which he had in the first instance peremptorily declined. Her application for admission was unnoticed; she repeated it more than once without success; then, becoming somewhat alarmed at the continued silence, opened the door and perceived her new inmate stretched on the floor in a fainting fit. Restoratives were instantly administered, and prompt medical aid succeeded at length in restoring him to consciousness. But his mind had received a shock from which, during the few weeks he survived, it never entirely recovered. His thoughts wandered perpetually; and though, from the very slight acquaintance which his hosts had with the English language, the greater part of what fell from him remained unknown, yet enough was understood to induce them to believe that something more than the mere death of his grandson had contributed thus to paralyse his faculties.

When his situation was first discovered, a small miniature was found tightly grasped in his right hand. It had been the property of Frederick, and had more than once been seen by the Müllers in his possession. To this the patient made continued reference, and would not suffer it one moment from his sight. It was in his hand when he expired. At my request it was produced to me. The portrait was that of a young woman in an English morning dress, whose pleasing and regular features, with their mild and somewhat pensive expression were not, I thought, altogether unknown to me. Her age was apparently about twenty.

A profusion of dark chestnut hair was arranged in the Madonna style above a brow of unsullied whiteness, a single ringlet depending on the left side. A glossy lock of the same colour, and evidently belonging to the original, appeared beneath a small crystal, inlaid in the back of the picture, which was plainly set in gold, and bore in a cipher the letters M. G. with the date 18—. From the inspection of this portrait I could at the time collect nothing, nor from that of the Doctor himself, which also I found the next morning in Frederick's desk, accompanied by two separate portions of hair. One of them was a lock, short, and deeply tinged with grey, and had been taken, I have little doubt, from the head of my old friend himself; the other corresponded in colour and appearance with that at the back of the miniature. It was not till a few days had elapsed, and I had seen the worthy Doctor's remains quietly consigned to the narrow house, that while arranging his papers previous to my intended return upon the morrow, I encountered the narrative I have already transcribed. The name of the unfortunate young woman connected with it forcibly arrested my attention. I recollected it immediately as one belonging to a parishioner of my own, and at once recognised the original of the female portrait as its owner.

I rose not from the perusal of his very singular statement till I had gone through the whole of it. It was late, and the rays of the single lamp by which I was reading did but very faintly illumine the remoter parts of the room in which I sat. The brilliancy of an unclouded November moon, then some twelve nights old, and shining full into the apartment, did much towards remedying the defect. My thoughts filled with the melancholy details I had read, I rose and walked to the window. The beautiful planet rode high in the firmament, and gave to the snowy roofs of the houses and pendant icicles, all the sparkling radiance of clustering gems. The stillness of the scene harmonised well with the state of my feelings. I threw open the casement and looked abroad. Far below me the waters of the principal canal shone like a broad mirror in the moonlight. To the left rose the Burght, a huge round tower of remarkable appearance, pierced with embrasures at its summit; while a little to the right and in the distance, the spire and pinnacles of the Cathedral of Leyden rose in all their majesty, presenting a *coup d'œil* of surpassing though simple beauty. To a spectator of calm, unoccupied mind the scene would have been delightful. On me it acted with an electric effect. I turned hastily to survey the apartment in which I had been sitting. It was the one designated as the study of the late Frederick S——. The sides of the room were covered with dark wainscot; the spacious fire-place opposite to me, with its polished andirons, was surmounted by a large old-fashioned mantelpiece, heavily carved in the Dutch style with fruits and flowers ; above it frowned a portrait, in a Vandyke dress, with a peaked beard and mustaches ; one hand of the figure rested on a table, whilst the other bore a marshal's staff, surmounted with a silver falcon ; and— either my imagination, already heated by the scene, deceived me,—or a smile as of malicious triumph curled the lip and glared in the cold leaden eye that seemed fixed upon my own. The heavy, antique, cane-backed chairs,—the large oaken table,—the book-shelves, the scattered volumes—all, all were there ; while, to complete the picture, to my right and left, as half breathless I leaned my back against the casement, rose on each side a tall, dark, ebony cabinet, in whose polished sides the single lamp upon the table shone reflected as in a mirror.

    *   *   *   *   *   *   *

What am I to think ? Can it be that the story I've been reading was written by my poor friend here, and under the influence of delirium ? Impossible ! Besides they all assure me that from the fatal night of his arrival he never left his bed—never put pen to paper. His very directions to have me summoned from England were verbally given during one of those few and brief intervals in which reason seemed partially to resume her sway. Can it then be possible that—— ? W—— ? where is he who alone may be able to throw light on this horrible mystery ?—No one knows. He absconded, it seems, immediately after the duel. No trace of him exists, nor, after repeated and anxious inquiries, can I find that any student has ever been known in the University of Leyden by the name of Francis Somers.

> " There are more things in heaven and earth
> Than are dreamt of in your philosophy ! ! "

Father John Ingoldsby, to whose papers I am largely indebted for the Saintly records which follow, was brought up by his father, a cadet of the family, in the Romish faith, and was educated at Douai for the church. Besides the manuscripts now at Tappington, he was the author of two controversial treatises on the connection between the Papal Hierarchy and the Nine of Diamonds.

From his well-known loyalty, evinced by secret services to the Royal cause during the Protectorate, he was excepted by name out of the acts against the Papists, became superintendent of the Queen Dowager's chapel at Somerset House, and enjoyed a small pension until his death, which took place in the third year of Queen Anne (1704), at the mature age of ninety-six. He was an ecclesiastic of great learning and piety, but from the stiff and antiquated phraseology which he adopted, I have thought it necessary to modernise it a little : this will account for certain anachronisms that have unavoidably crept in ; the substance of his narratives, has, however, throughout been strictly adhered to.

His hair-shirt, almost as good as new, is still preserved at Tappington,—but nobody ever wears it.

The Jackdaw of Rheims

"Tunc miser Corvus adeo conscientiæ stimulis compunctus fuit, et execratio eum tantopere excarneficavit, ut exinde tabescere inciperet, maciem contraheret, omnem cibum aversaretur, nec ampliùs crocitaret : pennæ præterea ei defluebant, et alis pendulis omnes facetias intermisit, et tam macer apparuit ut omnes ejus miserescent."

"Tunc abbas sacerdotibus mandavit ut rursus furem absolverent ; quo facto, Corvus, omnibus mirantibus, propediem convaluit, et pristinam sanitatem recuperavit."

De Illust. Ord. Cisterc

THE Jackdaw sat on the Cardinal's chair !
Bishop and abbot, and prior were there ;
   Many a monk, and many a friar,
   Many a knight, and many a squire,
With a great many more of lesser degree,—
In sooth a goodly company ;
And they served the Lord Primate on bended knee.
   Never, I ween, Was a prouder seen,
Read of in books, or dreamt of in dreams,
Than the Cardinal Lord Archbishop of Rheims !

   In and out Through the motley rout
That little Jackdaw kept hopping about ;
   Here and there, Like a dog in a fair,
   Over comfits and cates, And dishes and plates,
Cowl and cope, and rochet and pall,
Mitre and crosier ! he hopp'd upon all !
   With a saucy air, He perch'd on the chair
Where, in state, the great Lord Cardinal sat
In the great Lord Cardinal's great red hat ;

Heedless of grammar they all cried, "That's him"

And he peer'd in the face   Of his Lordship's Grace,
With a satisfied look, as if he would say,
" We Two are the greatest folks here to-day ! "
    And the priests, with awe,   As such freaks they saw,
Said, " The Devil must be in that little Jackdaw ! ! "

The feast was over, the board was clear'd,
The flawns and the custards had all disappear'd,
And six little Singing-boys,—dear little souls !
In nice clean faces, and nice white stoles,
    Came, in order due.   Two by two,
Marching that grand refectory through !
A nice little boy held a golden ewer,
Emboss'd and fill'd with water, as pure
As any that flows between Rheims and Namur,
Which a nice little boy stood ready to catch
In a fine golden hand-basin made to match.
Two nice little boys, rather more grown,
Carried lavender-water, and eau de Cologne ;
And a nice little boy had a nice cake of soap,
Worthy of washing the hands of the Pope.
    One little boy more   A napkin bore,
Of the best white diaper, fringed with pink,
And a Cardinal's Hat mark'd in " permanent ink."

The great Lord Cardinal turns at the sight
Of these nice little boys dress'd all in white :
    From his finger he draws   His costly turquoise :
And, not thinking at all about little Jackdaws,
    Deposits it straight   By the side of his plate,
While the nice little boys on his Eminence wait ;
Till, when nobody's dreaming of any such thing,
That little Jackdaw hops off with the ring !

There's a cry and a shout, And a deuce of a rout,
And nobody seems to know what they're about,
But the monks have their pockets all turn'd inside out ;
   The friars are kneeling, And hunting, and feeling
The carpet, the floor, and the walls, and the ceiling.
   The Cardinal drew Off each plum-colour'd shoe,
And left his red stockings exposed to the view ;
   He peeps, and he feels In the toes and the heels ;
They turn up the dishes,—they turn up the plates,—
They take up the poker and poke out the grates,
   —They turn up the rugs, They examine the mugs :—
   But, no !—no such thing ;— They can't find THE RING !
And the Abbot declared that, " when nobody twigg'd it,
Some rascal or other had popp'd in, and prigg'd it ! "

The Cardinal rose with a dignified look,
He call'd for his candle, his bell, and his book !
   In holy anger, and pious grief,
   He solemnly cursed that rascally thief !
   He cursed him at board, he cursed him in bed ;
   From the sole of his foot to the crown of his head ;
   He cursed him in sleeping, that every night
   He should dream of the devil, and wake in a fright ;
   He cursed him in eating, he cursed him in drinking,
   He cursed him in coughing, in sneezing, in winking ;
   He cursed him in sitting, in standing, in lying ;
   He cursed him in walking, in riding, in flying,
   He cursed him in living, he cursed him dying !—
Never was heard such a terrible curse ! !
   But what gave rise To no little surprise,
Nobody seem'd one penny the worse !

   The day was gone, The night came on,
The Monks and the Friars they search'd till dawn ; .
   When the sacristan saw, On crumpled claw,
Come limping a poor little lame Jackdaw !
   No longer gay, As on yesterday ;
His feathers all seem'd to be turn'd the wrong way ;—
His pinions droop'd—he could hardly stand,—
His head was as bald as the palm of your hand ;
   His eye so dim, So wasted each limb,
That, heedless of grammar, they all cried, " THAT'S HIM —

That's the scamp that has done this scandalous thing !
That's the thief that has got my Lord Cardinal's Ring ! "
   The poor little Jackdaw,   When the monks he saw,
Feebly gave vent to the ghost of a caw ;
And turn'd his bald head, as much as to say,
" Pray, be so good as to walk this way ! "
   Slower and slower   He limp'd on before,
Till they came to the back of the belfry door,
   Where the first thing they saw,
   Midst the sticks and the straw,
Was the RING, in the nest of that little Jackdaw !

Then the great Lord Cardinal call'd for his book,
And off that terrible curse he took ;
   The mute expression   Served in lieu of confession
And, being thus coupled with full restitution,
The Jackdaw got plenary absolution !
   —When those words were heard,
   That poor little bird
Was so changed in a moment, 'twas really absurd,
   He grew sleek, and fat ;   In addition to that,
A fresh crop of feathers came thick as a mat !
   His tail waggled more   Even than before ;
But no longer it wagg'd with an impudent air,
No longer he perched on the Cardinal's chair.
   He hopp'd now about   With a gait devout ;
At Matins, at Vespers, he never was out ;
And, so far from any more pilfering deeds,
He always seem'd telling the Confessor's beads.
If any one lied,—or if any one swore,—
Or slumber'd in pray'r-time and happen'd to snore,
   That good Jackdaw   Would give a great " Caw ! "
As much as to say, " Don't do so any more ! "
While many remark'd, as his manners they saw,
That they " never had known such a pious Jackdaw ! "
   He long lived the pride   Of that country side,
And at last in the odour of sanctity died ;
   When, as words were too faint   His merits to paint
The Conclave determined to make him a Saint ;
And on newly-made Saints and Popes, as you know,
It's the custom, at Rome, new names to bestow,
So they canonized him by the name of Jem Crow !

If any one lied,—or if any one swore

A Lay of St. Dunstan

"This holy childe Dunstan was borne in ye yere of our Lorde ix. hondred & xxb. that tyme regnynge in this londe Kinge Athelston. * * *
"Whan it so was that Saynt Dunstan was wery of prayer than used he to werke in goldsmythes werke with his owne handes for to eschewe ydelnes."

Golden Legend.

ST. DUNSTAN stood in his ivied tower,
   Alembic, crucible, all were there ;
When in came Nick to play him a trick,
   In guise of a damsel passing fair.
     Every one knows   How the story goes :
He took up the tongs and caught hold of his nose.
But I beg that you won't for a moment suppose
That I mean to go through, in detail, to you
A story at least as trite as it's true ;
   Nor do I intend   An instant to spend
On the tale, how he treated his monarch and friend,
When, bolting away to a chamber remote,
Inconceivably bored by his Witen-gemote
   Edwy left them all joking,   And drinking, and smoking
So tipsily grand, they'd stand nonsense from no King,
   But sent the Archbishop   Their Sovereign to fish up,
With a hint that perchance on his crown he might feel taps,
Unless he came back straight and took off his heel-taps.
You must not be plagued with the same story twice,
And perhaps have seen this one, by W. DYCE,
At the Royal Academy, very well done,
And mark'd in the catalogue, Four, seven, one.

You might there view the Saint, who in sable array'd is,
Coercing the Monarch away from the Ladies ;
His right hand has hold of his Majesty's jerkin,
His left shows the door, and he seems to say, " Sir King,
Your most faithful Commons won't hear of your shirking !
Quit your tea, and return to your Barclai and Perkyn,
Or, by Jingo,* ere morning, no longer alive, a
Sad victim you'll lie to your love for Elgiva ! "

* St. Jingo, or Gengo (Gengulphus), sometimes styled "The Living Jingo," from the great tenaciousness of vitality exhibited by his severed members. See his Legend, as recorded hereafter in the present volume.

No farther to treat   Of his ungallant feat,
What I mean to do now is succinctly to paint
One particular fact in the life of the Saint,
Which somehow, for want of due care, I presume
Has escaped the researches of Rapin and Hume,
In recounting a miracle, both of them men, who a
Great deal fell short of Jaques Bishop of Genoa,
An Historian who likes deeds like these to record—
See his *Aurea Legenda*, by 𝔚𝔶𝔫𝔨𝔶𝔫 𝔡𝔢 𝔚𝔬𝔯𝔡𝔢.

St. Dunstan stood again in his tower,
   Alembic, crucible, all complete ;
He had been standing a good half hour,
And now he utter'd the words of power,
   And call'd to his broomstick to bring him a seat

The words of power !—and what be they
To which e'en Broomsticks bow and obey ?—
Why,—'twere uncommonly hard to say,
As the prelate I name has recorded none of them,
   What they may be,   But I know they are three,
And ABRACADABRA, I take it, is one of them :
For I'm told that most Cabalists use that identical
Word, written thus in what they call " a Pentacle."

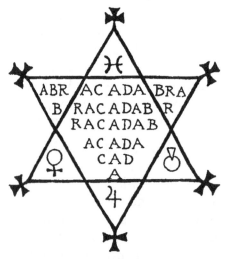

However that be,   You'll doubtless agree
It signifies little to you or to me,
As not being dabblers in Grammarye ;

Still, it must be confess'd, for a Saint to repeat
Such language aloud is scarcely discreet ;
For, as Solomon hints to folks given to chatter,
" A bird of the air may carry the matter ; "
   And in sooth,   From my youth   I remember a truth
Insisted on much in my earlier years,
To wit, " Little Pitchers have very long ears ! "
Now, just such a " Pitcher " as those I allude to
Was outside the door, which his " ears " appeared glued to.

   Peter, the Lay-brother, meagre and thin,
     Five feet one in his sandal-shoon,
  While the saint thought him sleeping,
  Was listening and peeping,
     And watching his master the whole afternoon.

This Peter the Saint had pick'd out from his fellows,
To look to his fire, and to blow with the bellows,
To put on the Wall's-Ends and Lambtons whenever he
Chose to indulge in a little *orfèvrerie ;*
   —Of course you have read,
   That St. Dunstan was bred
A Goldsmith, and never quite gave up the trade !
The Company—richest in London, 'tis said—
Acknowledge him still as their Patron and Head ;
  Nor is it so long   Since a capital song
In his praise—now recorded their archives among—
Delighted the noble and dignified throng   ·
Of their guests, who, the newspapers told the whole town,
With cheers " pledged the wine-cup to Dunstan's renown,"
When Lord Lyndhurst, THE DUKE, and Sir Robert, were dining
At the Hall some time since with the Prime Warden Twining.
—I am sadly digressing—a fault which sometimes
One can hardly avoid in these gossiping rhymes—
A slight deviation's forgiven ! but then this is
Too long, I fear, for a decent parenthesis,
So I'll rein up my Pegasus sharp, and retreat, or
You'll think I've forgotten the Lay-brother Peter,
  Whom the Saint, as I said,   Kept to turn down his bed,
  Dress his palfreys and cobs,   And do other odd jobs,—
  As reducing to writing   Whatever he might, in

The course of the day or the night, be inditing,
And cleaning the plate of his mitre with whiting ;
Performing, in short, all those duties and offices
Abbots exact from Lay-brothers and Novices.

It occurs to me here   You'll perhaps think it queer
That St. Dunstan should have such a personage near,
   When he'd only to say   Those words,—be what they may,—
And his Broomstick at once his commands would obey.—
   That's true—but the fact is 'Twas rarely his practice
Such aid to resort to, or such means apply,
Unless he'd some " dignified knot " to untie,
Adopting, though sometimes, as now, he'd reverse it,
Old Horace's Maxim " *nec Broomstick intersit.*"—
—Peter, the Lay-brother, meagre and thin,
Heard all the Saint was saying within ;
Peter, the Lay-brother, sallow and spare,
Peep'd through the key-hole, and—what saw he there ?—
Why,—A BROOMSTICK BRINGING A RUSH-BOTTOM'D CHAIR.

What Shakspeare observes, in his play of King John,
   Is undoubtedly right,   That " ofttimes the sight
Of means to do ill deeds will make ill deeds done."
Here's Peter, the Lay-brother, pale-faced and meagre,
A good sort of man, only rather too eager
To listen to what other people are saying,
When he ought to be minding his business or praying,
Gets into a scrape,—and an awkward one too,—
As you'll find, if you've patience enough to go through
   The whole of the story   I'm laying before ye,—
Entirely from having " the means " in his view
Of doing a thing which he ought not to do !

   Still rings in his ear,   Distinct and clear,
Abracadabra ! that word of fear !
And the two which I never yet happen'd to hear.
   Still doth he spy,   With Fancy's eye,
The Broomstick at work, and the Saint standing by ;
And he chuckles, and says to himself with glee,
" Aha ! that Broomstick shall work for *me !* "

Peep'd through the key-hole, and—what saw he there?

Hark ! that swell   O'er flood and o'er fell,
Mountain, and dingle, and moss-cover'd dell !
List !—'tis the sound of the Compline bell,
And St. Dunstan is quitting his ivied cell ;
    Peter, I wot,   Is off like a shot,
Or a little dog scalded by something that's hot.
For he hears his Master approaching the spot
Where he'd listened so long, though he knew he ought not :
Peter remember'd his Master's frown—
He trembled—he'd not have been caught for a crown ;
    Howe'er you may laugh,   He had rather by half,
Have run up to the top of the tower and jump'd down.

     *   *   *   *   *

The Compline hour is past and gone,
Evening service is over and done ;
    The monks repair   To their frugal fare,
A snug little supper of something light
And digestible, ere they retire for the night.
For, in Saxon times, in respect to their cheer,
St. Austin's Rule was by no means severe,
But allowed from the Beverley Roll 'twould appear,
Bread and cheese, and spring onions, and sound table beer,
And even green peas, when they were not too dear ;
Not like the rule of La Trappe, whose chief merit is
Said to consist in its greater austerities ;
And whose monks, if I rightly remember their laws,
    Ne'er are suffer'd to speak,   Think only in Greek,
And subsist, as the Bears do, by sucking their paws.
    Astonish'd I am   The gay Baron Geramb,
With his head sav'ring more of the Lion than Lamb,
Could e'er be persuaded to join such a set—I
Extend the remark to Signor Ambrogetti.—
For a monk of La Trappe is as thin as a rat,
While an Austin Friar was jolly and fat ;
Though, of course, the fare to which I allude,
With as good table-beer as ever was brew'd,
Was all " caviare to the multitude,"
Extending alone to the clergy, together in
Hall assembled,—and not to Lay-brethren.
St. Dunstan himself sits there at his post,
    On what they say is   Called a Daïs,

K

O'erlooking the whole of his clerical host,
And eating poached eggs with spinach and toast ;
Five Lay-brothers stand behind his chair,
But where is the sixth ?—Where's Peter !—Ay, WHERE ?

'Tis an evening in June,   And a little half moon,
A brighter no fond lover ever set eyes on,
  Gleaming and beaming,   And dancing the stream in,
Has made her appearance above the horizon ;
Just such a half moon as you see, in a play,
On the turban of Mustapha Muley Bey,
Or the fair Turk who weds with the " Noble Lord Bateman ; "
—*Vide* plate in George Cruickshank's memoirs of that great man.

She shines on a turret remote and lone,   .
A turret with ivy and moss overgrown,
And lichens that thrive on the cold dank stone ;
Such a tower as a poet of no mean *calibre*
I once knew and loved, poor, dear Reginald Heber,
Assigns to oblivion *—a den for a She bear ;
  Within it are found,   Strew'd above and around,
On the hearth, on the table, the shelves, and the ground,
All sorts of instruments, all sorts of tools,
To name which, and their uses, would puzzle the Schools,
And make very wise people look very like fools ;
  Pincers and hooks,   And black-letter books,
All sorts of pokers, and all sorts of tongs,
And all sorts of hammers, and all that belongs
To Goldsmith's work, chemistry, alchymy,—all,
  In short, that a Sage, In that erudite age,
Could require, was at hand, or at least within call.
In the midst of the room lies a Broomstick !—and there
A Lay-brother sits in a rush-bottom'd chair !

Abracadabra, that fearful word,
And the two which, I said, I have never yet heard,
  Are utter'd.—'Tis done !   Peter, full of his fun,

* And cold oblivion, midst the ruin laid,
  Folds her dank wing beneath the ivy shade.
                                        PALESTINE.

Cries, " Broomstick ! you lubberly son of a gun !
Bring ale !—bring a flagon—a hogshead—a tun !
  'Tis the same thing to you ; I have nothing to do ;
And, 'fore George, I'll sit here, and I'll drink till all's blue ! "

No doubt you've remark'd how uncommonly quick
A Newfoundland puppy runs after a stick,
Brings it back to his master, and gives it him—Well,
  So potent the spell,
The Broomstick perceived it was vain to rebel,
So ran off like that puppy ;—some cellar was near,
For in less than ten seconds 'twas back with the beer !
Peter seizes the flagon ; but ere he can suck
Its contents, or enjoy what he thinks his good luck,
The Broomstick comes in with a tub in a truck ;
  Continues to run   At the rate it begun,
And, *au pied de lettre*, next brings in a tun !
A fresh one succeeds, then a third, then another,
Discomfiting much the astounded Lay-brother ;
Who, had he possess'd fifty pitchers or stoups,
They had all been too few : for, arranging in groups
The barrels, the Broomstick next *started the hoops ;*
  The ale deluged the floor,
  But, still, through the door,
Said Broomstick kept bolting, and bringing in more.
  E'en Macbeth to Macduff
  Would have cried " Hold ! enough ! "
If half as well drench'd with such " perilous stuff,"
And Peter, who did not expect such a rough visit,
Cried lustily, " Stop !—That will do, Broomstick !—*Sufficit !* "

  But ah, well-a-day ! The Devil they say,
'Tis easier at all times to raise than to lay.
Again and again Peter roar'd out in vain
His Abracadabra, and t'other words twain :—
  As well might one try   A pack in full cry
To check, and call off from their headlong career
By bawling out, " Yoicks ! " with one's hand at one's ear.
The longer he roar'd, and the louder and quicker,
The faster the Broomstick was bringing in liquor.

The poor Lay-brother knew　Not on earth what to do—
He caught hold of the Broomstick and snapt it in two.—
　Worse and Worse !—Like a dart　Each part made a start,
And he found he'd been adding more fuel to fire,
For *both* now came loaded with Meux's entire ;
Combe's, Delafield's, Hanbury's, Truman's—no stopping—
Goding's, Charenton's, Whitbread's continued to drop in,
With Hodson's pale ale, from the Sun Brewhouse, Wapping.
The firms differ'd then, but I can't put a tax on
My memory to say what their names were in Saxon.
　To be sure the best beer　Of all did not appear ;
For I've said 'twas in June, and so late in the year
The " Trinity Audit Ale " is not come-at-able,
—As I've found to my great grief when dining at that table.

Now extremely alarm'd, Peter scream'd without ceasing,
For a flood of Brown-stout he was up to his knees in,
Which, thanks to the Broomstick, continued increasing ;
　He fear'd he'd be drown'd,
　And he yell'd till the sound
Of his voice, wing'd by terror, at last reach'd the ear
Of St. Dunstan himself, who had finish'd *his* beer,
And had put off his mitre, dalmatic, and shoes,
And was just stepping into his bed for a snooze.

His Holiness paused when he heard such a clatter ;
He could not conceive what on earth was the matter.
Slipping on a few things, for the sake of decorum,
He issued forthwith from his *Sanctum sanctorum*,
And calling a few of the Lay-brothers near him,
Who were not yet in bed, and who happen'd to hear him,
　At once led the way　Without further delay,
To the tower where he'd been in the course of the day.
Poor Peter !—alas !—though St. Dunstan was quick,
There were two there before him—Grim Death, and Old Nick !—
When they open'd the door out the malt-liquor flow'd,
Just as when the great Vat burst in Tot'n'am Court Road ;
The Lay-brothers nearest were up to their necks
In an instant, and swimming in strong double X ;
While Peter, who, spite of himself now had drank hard,
After floating awhile, like a toast in a tankard,

A flood of brown-stout he was up to his knees in

To the bottom had sunk,   And was spied by a monk,
Stone-dead, like poor Clarence, half drown'd and half drunk.

In vain did St. Dunstan exclaim, " *Vade retro*
Strongbeerum !—discede a Lay-fratre Petro ! "—
   Queer Latin, you'll say,   That præfix of " *Lay,*"
And *Strongbeerum !*—I own they'd have call'd me a blockhead if
At school I had ventured to use such a Vocative ;
'Tis a barbarous word, and to me it's a query
If you'll find it in Patrick, Morell, or Moreri ;
But, the fact is, the Saint was uncommonly flurried,
And apt to be loose in his Latin when hurried ;
The Brown-stout, however, obeys to the letter,
Quite as well as if talk'd to, in Latin much better,
   By a grave Cambridge Johnian,   Or graver Oxonian
Whose language, we all know, is quite Ciceronian.
It retires from the corpse, which is left high and dry ;
But, in vain do they snuff and hot towels apply,
And other means used by the faculty try.
   When once a man's dead   There's no more to be said ;
Peter's " Beer with an *e* " was his " Bier with an *i ! !* "

Moral.

By way of a moral, permit me to pop in
The following maxims :—Beware of eaves-dropping !—
Don't make use of language that isn't well scann'd !—
Don't meddle with matters you don't understand !—
Above all, what I'd wish to impress on both sexes
Is,—Keep clear of Broomsticks, Old Nick, and three XXXs.

L'Envoye.

In Goldsmiths' Hall there's a handsome glass case,
And in it a stone figure, found on the place,
When, thinking the old Hall no longer a pleasant one,
They pull'd it all down, and erected the present one.
If you look, you'll perceive that this stone figure twists
A thing like a broomstick in one of its fists.
It's so injured by time, you can't make out a feature ;
But it is not St. Dunstan,—so doubtless it's Peter.

Gengulphus, or, as he is usually styled in this country, " Jingo," was perhaps more in the mouths of the " general " than any other Saint, on occasions of adjuration (see note, page 141). Mr. Simpkinson from Bath had kindly transmitted me a portion of a primitive ballad, which has escaped the researches of Ritson and Ellis, but is yet replete with beauties of no common order. I am happy to say that, since these Legends first appeared, I have recovered the whole of it.—*Vide infra.*

> " A Franklyn's dogge leped ober a style,
>   And hys name was littel Byngo.
> B wyth a Y—Y wyth an N,—
> N with a G—G with an O,—
> They call'd hym littel Byngo !
>
> Thys Franklyn, Syrs, he brewed goode ayle,
>   And he called it Rare goode Styngo !
> S, T, Y, N, G, O !
> He call'd it Rare goode Styngo !
>
> Nowe is notte thys a prettie song ?
> I thinke it is bye Jyngo !
> J wythe a Y—N, G, O—
> I sweare yt is, by Jyngo ! "

A Lay of St. Gengulphus

"Non multò post, Gengulphus, in domo suâ dormiens, occisus est à quodam clerico qui cum uxore suâ adulterare solebat. Cujus corpus dum, in fereto, in sepulturam portaretur, multi infirmi de tactu sanati sunt."

*   *   *   *   *   *

" Cum hoc illius uxori referretur ab ancilla suâ, scilicet dominum suum, quam martyrem sanctum, miracula facere, irridens illa, et subsurrans, ait, ' Ita Gengulphus miracula facitat ut pulvinarium meum cantat,' " &c. &c.   WOLFII MEMORAB.

GENGULPHUS comes from the Holy Land,
  With his scrip, and his bottle, and sandal shoon,
Full many a day hath he been away,
  Yet his lady deems him return'd full soon.

Full many a day hath he been away,
  Yet scarce had he crossed ayont the sea,
Ere a spruce young spark of a Learned Clerk
  Had called on his Lady, and stopp'd to tea.

This spruce young guest, so trimly drest,
  Stay'd with that Lady, her revels to crown ;
They laugh'd, and they ate and they drank of the best,
  And they turn'd the old castle quite upside down.

They would walk in the park, that spruce young Clerk,
  With that frolicsome Lady so frank and free,
Trying balls and plays, and all manner of ways,
  To get rid of what French people called *Ennui*.

*   *   *   *   *

Now the festive board with viands is stored,
  Savoury dishes be there, I ween,
Rich puddings and big, and a barbecued pig,
  And oxtail soup in a China tureen.

There's a flagon of ale as large as a pail—
  When, cockle on hat, and staff in hand,
While on nought they are thinking save eating and drinking,
  Gengulphus walks in from the Holy Land !

" You must be pretty deep to catch weasels asleep,"
  Says the proverb ; that is " take the Fair unawares ; "
A maid o'er the banisters chancing to peep,
  Whispers, " Ma'am, here's Gengulphus a-coming upstairs."

Pig, pudding, and soup, the electrified group,
  With the flagon, pop under the sofa in haste,
And contrive to deposit the Clerk in the closet,
  As the dish least of all to Gengulphus's taste.

Then oh ! what rapture, what joy was exprest,
  When " poor dear Gengulphus " at last appear'd !
She kiss'd and she press'd " the dear man " to her breast,
  In spite of his great, long, frizzly beard.

Such hugging and squeezing ! 'twas almost unpleasing,
  A smile on her lips, and a tear in her eye ; *
She was so very glad, that she seem'd half mad,
  And did not know whether to laugh or to cry

  * Ενι δακρυσι γελασασα.—Hom.

Then she calls up the maid and the table-cloth's laid,
    And she sends for a pint of the best Brown Stout ;
On the fire, too, she pops some nice mutton-chops,
    And she mixes a stiff glass of " Cold Without."

Then again she began at the " poor dear " man ;
    She press'd him to drink, and she press'd him to eat,
And she brought a foot-pan, with hot water and bran,
    To comfort his " poor dear " travel-worn feet.

" Nor night nor day since he'd been away,
    Had she had any rest," she " vow'd and declared."
She " never could eat one morsel of meat,
    For thinking how ' poor dear ' Gengulphus fared."

She " really did think she had not slept a wink
    Since he left her, although he'd been absent so long ; "
He here shook his head,—right little he said,
    But he thought she was " coming it rather too strong."

Now his palate she tickles with the chops and the pickles,
    Till, so great the effect of that stiff gin grog,
His weaken'd body, subdued by the toddy,
    Falls out of his chair, and he lies like a log.

Then out comes the Clerk from his secret lair ;
    He lifts up the legs, and she lifts up the head,
And, between them, this most reprehensible pair
    Undress poor Gengulphus and put him to bed.

Then the bolster they place athwart his face,
    And his night-cap into his mouth they cram ;
And she pinches his nose underneath the clothes,
    Till the " poor dear soul " goes off like a lamb.

        *   ·   *   *   *   *

And now they tried the deed to hide ;
    For a little bird whisper'd, " Perchance you may swing ;
Here's a corpse in the case with a sad swell'd face,
    And a Medical Crowner's a queer sort of thing ! "

So the Clerk and his wife, they each took a knife,
    And the nippers that nipp'd the loaf-sugar for tea ;
With the edges and points they sever'd the joints
    At the clavicle, elbow, hip, ankle, and knee.

Thus, limb from limb, they dismember'd him
    So entirely, that e'en when they came to his wrists,
With those great sugar-nippers they nipped off his " flippers,"
    As the Clerk, very flippantly, termed his fists.

When they'd cut off his head, entertaining a dread
    Lest folks should remember Gengulphus's face,
They determined to throw it where no one could know it,
    Down the well,—and the limbs in some different place.

But first the long beard from the chin they shear'd,
    And managed to stuff that sanctified hair,
With a good deal of pushing, all into the cushion
    That filled up the seat of a large arm-chair.

They contriv'd to pack up the trunk in a sack,
    Which they hid in an osier-bed outside the town,
The Clerk bearing arms, legs, and all on his back,
    As that vile Mr. Greenacre served Mrs. Brown.

But to see now how strangely things sometimes turn out,
　And that in a manner the least expected !
Who could surmise a man ever could rise
　Who'd been thus carbonado'd, cut up, and dissected ?

No doubt 'twould surprise the pupils at Guy's ;
　I am no unbeliever—no man can say that o' me—
But St. Thomas himself would scarce trust his own eyes
　If he saw such a thing in his School of Anatomy.

You may deal as you please with Hindoos and Chinese,
　Or a Mussulman making his heathen *salaam*, or
A Jew or a Turk ; but it's other guess work
　When a man has to do with a Pilgrim or Palmer.

　　　*　　　*　　　*　　　*　　　*

By chance the Prince Bishop, a Royal Divine,
　Sends his cards round the neighbourhood next day, and urges his
Wish to receive a snug party to dine,
　Of the resident clergy, the gentry, and burgesses

At a quarter past five they are all alive,
　At the palace, for coaches are fast rolling in ;
And to every guest his card had express'd
　" Half-past " as the hour for " a greasy chin."

Some thirty are seated, and handsomely treated
　With the choicest Rhine wines in his Highness's stock ;
When a Count of the Empire, who felt himself heated,
　Requested some water to mix with his Hock.

The Butler, who saw it, sent a maid out to draw it,
　But scarce had she given the windlass a twirl,
Ere Gengulphus's head, from the well's bottom, said
　In mild accents, " Do help us out, that's a good girl ! "

Only fancy her dread when she saw a great head
　In her bucket ;—with fright she was ready to drop :—
Conceive, if you can, how she roar'd and she ran,
　With the head rolling after her, bawling out " Stop ! "

She ran and she roar'd till she came to the board
   Where the Prince Bishop sat with his party around,
When Gengulphus's poll, which continued to roll
   At her heels, on the table bounced up with a bound.

Never touching the cates, or the dishes or plates,
   The decanters or glasses, the sweetmeats or fruits,
The head smiles, and begs them to bring him his legs,
   As a well-spoken gentleman asks for his boots.

Kicking open the casement, to each one's amazement,
   Straight a right leg steps in, all impediment scorns,
And near the head stopping, a left follows hopping
   Behind,—for the left leg was troubled with corns.

Next, before the beholders, two great brawny shoulders,
   And arms on their bent elbows dance through the throng,
While two hands assist, though nipp'd off at the wrist,
   The said shoulders in bearing a body along.

They march up to the head, not one syllable said,
   For the thirty guests all stare in wonder and doubt,
As the limbs in their sight arrange and unite,
   Till Gengulphus, though dead, looks as sound as a trout.

I will venture to say, from that hour to this day,
   Ne'er did such an assembly behold such a scene ;
Or a table divide fifteen guests of a side
   With a dead body placed in the centre between.

Yes, they stared,—well they might, at so novel a sight :
   No one utter'd a whisper, a sneeze, or a hem,
But sat all bolt upright, and pale with affright ;
   And they gazed at the dead man, the dead man at them.

The Prince Bishop's Jester, on punning intent,
   As he view'd the whole thirty, in jocular terms
Said, " They put him in mind of a Council of *Trente*
   Engaged in reviewing the Diet of Worms."

But what should they do ?—Oh ! nobody knew
  What was best to be done, either stranger or resident ;
The Chancellor's self read his Puffendorf through,
  In·vain, for his books could not furnish a precedent.

The Prince Bishop mutter'd a curse, and a prayer,
  Which his double capacity hit to a nicety :
His Princely, or Lay, half induced him to swear,
  His Episcopal moiety said " *Benedicite !* "

The Coroner sat on the body that night,
  And the jury agreed,—not a doubt could they harbour,—
" That the chin of the corpse—the sole thing brought to light—
  Had been recently shaved by a very bad barber."

They sent out Von Taûnsend, Von Bûrnie, Von Roe,
  Von Maine, and Von Rowantz—through châlets and châteaux,
Towns, villages, hamlets, they told them to go,
  And they stuck up placards on the walls of the Stadthaus.

" Murder ! !

" Whereas, a dead gentleman, surname unknown,
  Has been recently found at his Highness's banquet,
Rather shabbily dressed in an Amice or gown,
  In appearance resembling a second-hand blanket ;

" And Whereas, there's great reason indeed to suspect
  That some ill-disposed person, or persons, with malice
Aforethought, have kill'd, and begun to dissect
  The said Gentleman, not very far from the palace ;

" This is to give Notice !—Whoever shall seize,
  And such person or persons, to justice surrender,
Shall receive—such Reward—as his Highness shall please,
  On conviction of him, the aforesaid offender.

" And, in order the matter more clearly to trace
  To the bottom, his Highness, the Prince Bishop further,
Of his clemency, offers free Pardon and Grace
  To all such as have *not* been concern'd in the murther.

" Done this day, at our palace,—July twenty-five,—
  By Command,
              (Signed)
                  Johann Von Rüssell,
                                  N.B.
Deceased rather in years—had a squint when alive :
  And smells slightly of gin—linen mark'd with a ' G.' "

The Newspapers, too, made no little ado,
  Though a different version each managed to dish up ;
Some said " The Prince Bishop had run a man through,"
  Others said " an assassin had kill'd the Prince Bishop."

The " Ghent Herald " fell foul of the " Bruxelles Gazette,"
  The " Bruxelles Gazette " with much sneering ironical,
Scorned to remain in the " Ghent Herald's " debt,
  And the " Amsterdam Times " quizz'd the " Nuremberg
    Chronicle."

In one thing, indeed, all the journals agreed,
  Spite of " politics," " bias," or " party collision ; "
Viz. : to " give," when they'd " further accounts " of the deed,
  " Full particulars " soon, in " a later Edition."

But now, while on all sides they rode and they ran,
  Trying all sorts of means to discover the caitiffs,
Losing patience, the holy Gengulphus began
  To think it high time to " astonish the natives."

First, a Rittmeister's Frau, who was weak in both eyes,
  And supposed the most short-sighted woman in Holland,
Found greater relief, to her joy and surprise,
  From one glimpse of his " squint " than from glasses by Dollond.

By the slightest approach to the tip of his Nose,
  Megrims, headache, and vapours were put to the rout ;
And one single touch of his precious Great Toes
  Was a certain specific of chilblains and gout.

Rheumatics,—sciatica,—tic-doloureux !
  Apply to his shin-bones—not one of them lingers ;—
All bilious complaints in an instant withdrew,
  If the patient was tickled with one of his fingers.

Much virtue was found to reside in his thumbs ;
　　When applied to the chest, they cured scantness of breathing,
Sea-sickness, and cholic ; or, rubb'd on the gums,
　　Were " A blessing to Mothers," for infants in teething.

Whoever saluted the nape of his neck,
　　Where the mark remain'd visible still of the knife,
Notwithstanding east winds perspiration might check,
　　Was safe from sore throat for the rest of his life.

Thus, while each acute and each chronic complaint
　　Giving way, proved an influence clearly divine,
They perceived the dead Gentleman must be a Saint,
　　So they lock'd him up, body and bones, in a shrine.

Through country and town his new Saintship's renown
　　As a first-rate physician kept daily increasing,
Till, as Alderman Curtis told Alderman Brown,
　　It seem'd as if " Wonders had never *done ceasing.*"

The Three Kings of Cologne began, it was known,
　　A sad falling off in their off'rings to find,
His feats were so many—still the greatest of any,—
　　In every sense of the word, was—behind ;

For the German Police were beginning to cease
　　From exertions which each day more fruitless appear'd,
When Gengulphus himself, his fame still to increase,
　　Unravell'd the whole by the help of—his beard !

If you look back you'll see the aforesaid *barbe gris,*
　　When divorced from the chin of its murder'd proprietor,
Had been stuff'd in the seat of a kind of settee,
　　Or double-arm'd chair, to keep the thing quieter.

It may seem rather strange, that it did not arrange
　　Itself in its place when the limbs join'd together ;
P'rhaps it could not get out, for the cushion was stout
　　And constructed of good, strong, maroon-colour'd leather.

Or, what is more likely, Gengulphus might choose,
    For Saints, e'en when dead, still retain their volition,
It should rest there, to aid some particular views,
    Produced by his very peculiar position.

Be that as it may, on the very first day
    That the widow Gengulphus sat down on that settee,
What occurr'd almost frighten'd her senses away,
    Beside scaring her hand-maidens, Gertrude and Betty.

They were telling their mistress the wonderful deeds
    Of the new Saint, to whom all the Town said their orisons :
And especially how as regards invalids,
    His miraculous cures far outrivall'd Von Morison's.

" The cripples," said they, " fling their crutches away,
    And people born blind now can easily see us ! "—
But she, (we presume, a disciple of Hume,)
    Shook her head, and said angrily, " *Credat Judæus !* "

" Those rascally liars, the Monks and the Friars,
    To bring grist to their mill, these devices have hit on.—
He works miracles !—pooh !—I'd believe it of you
    Just as soon, you great Geese,—or the Chair that I sit on ! "

The Chair !—at that word—it seems really absurd,
    But the truth must be told,—what contortions and grins
Distorted her face !—She sprang up from her place
    Just as though she'd been sitting on needles and pins !

For, as if the Saint's beard the rash challenge had heard
    Which she utter'd, of what was beneath her forgetful,
Each particular hair stood on end in the chair,
    Like a porcupine's quills when the animal's fretful.

That stout maroon leather, they pierced altogether,
    Like tenter-hooks holding when clench'd from within,
And the maids cried " Good gracious ! how very tenacious ! "
    —They as well might endeavour to pull off her skin !—

She shriek'd with the pain, but all efforts were vain ;
  In vain did they strain every sinew and muscle,—
The cushion stuck fast !—From that hour to her last
  She could never get rid of that comfortless " Bustle ! "

And e'en as Macbeth, when devising the death
  Of his King, heard " the very stones prate of his whereabouts ; "
So this shocking bad wife heard a voice all her life,
  Crying " Murder ! " resound from the cushion,—or thereabouts.

With regard to the Clerk, we are left in the dark
  As to what his fate was ; but I cannot imagine he
Got off scot-free, though unnoticed it be
  Both by Ribadaneira and Jacques de Voragine :

For cut-throats, we're sure, can be never secure,
  And " History's Muse " still to prove it her pen holds,
As you'll see, if you look in a rather scarce book,
  " *God's Revenge against Murder*," by one Mr. Reynolds.

MORAL.

Now, you grave married Pilgrims, who wander away,
  Like Ulysses of old,* (*vide* Homer and Naso,)
Don't lengthen your stay to three years and a day,
  And when you *are* coming home, just write and say so !

And you, learned Clerks, who're *not* given to roam,
  Stick close to your books, nor lose sight of decorum ;
Don't visit a house when the master's from home !
  Shun drinking,—and study the " *Vitæ Sanctorum !* "

Above all, you gay ladies, who fancy neglect
  In your spouses, allow not your patience to fail ;
But remember Gengulphus's wife !—and reflect
  On the moral enforced by her terrible tale !

        * Qui mores hominum multorum vidit et urbes.

And the maids cried "Good gracious, how very tenacious!"

Mr. Barney Maguire has laid claim to the next Saint as a countrywoman; and "Why wouldn't he?" when all the world knows the O'Dells were a fine ould, ancient family, sated in Tipperary

> "Ere the Lord Mayor stole his collar of gowld,
> And sowld it away to a trader!" *

He is manifestly wrong; but, as he very rationally observes, "No matter for that,—she's a Saint any way!"

The Lay of St. Odille

ODILLE was a maid of a dignified race;
Her father, Count Otto, was lord of Alsace;
  Such an air, such a grace, Such a form, such a face,
All agreed, 'twere a fruitless endeavour to trace
In the Court, or within fifty miles of the place.
Many ladies in Strasburg were beautiful, still
They were beat all to sticks by the lovely Odille.

But Odille was devout, and, before she was nine,
Had "experienced a call" she consider'd divine,
To put on the veil at St. Ermengarde's shrine.—
Lords, Dukes, and Electors, and Counts Palatine
Came to seek her in marriage from both sides the Rhine;
  But vain their design, They are all left to pine,
Their oglings and smiles are all useless; in fine,
Not one of these gentlefolks, try as they will,
Can draw "Ask my papa" from the cruel Odille.

At length one of her suitors, a certain Count Herman,
A highly respectable man as a German,
Who smoked like a chimney, and drank like a Merman,
Paid his court to her father, conceiving his firman
  Would soon make her bend, And induce her to lend
An ear to a love-tale in lieu of a sermon.
He gain'd the old Count, who said, "Come, Mynheer, fill!—
Here's luck to yourself and my daughter Odille!"

---

* The "Inglorious Memory" of this ould ancient transaction is still, we understand, kept up in Dublin by an annual proclamation at one of the city gates. The jewel, which has replaced the abstracted ornament, is said to have been presented by King William, and worn by Daniel O'Connell, Esq.

The Lady Odille was quite nervous with fear,
When a little bird whisper'd that toast in her ear ;
   She murmur'd " O, dear ! My Papa has got queer,
I am sadly afraid, with that nasty strong beer !
He's so very austere, and severe, that it's clear,
If he gets in his ' tantrums,' I can't remain here ;
But St. Ermengarde's convent is luckily near ;
   It were folly to stay *Pour prendre congé,*
I shall put on my bonnet, and e'en run away ! "
—She unlock'd the back door and descended the hill,
On whose crest stood the towers of the sire of Odille.

—When he found she'd levanted, the Count of Alsace
At first turn'd remarkably red in the face ;
He anathematised, with much unction and grace,
Every soul who came near, and consign'd the whole race
Of runaway girls to a very warm place ;
   With a frightful grimace He gave orders for chase ;
His vassals set off at a deuce of a pace,
And of all whom they met, high or low, Jack or Jill,
Ask'd, " Pray have you seen anything of Lady Odille ? "

Now I think I've been told,—for I'm no sporting man,—
That the " Knowing ones " call this by far the best plan,
" Take the lead and then keep it ! "—that is, if you can.—
Odille thought so too, so she set off and ran,
   Put her best leg before, Starting at score,
As I said some lines since, from that little back door,
And not being miss'd until half after four,
Had what hunters call " law " for a good hour and more ;
   Doing her best, Without stopping to rest,
Like " young Lochinvar who came out of the West."
" 'Tis done !—I am gone !—over briar, brook, and rill !
They'll be sharp lads who catch me ! " said young Miss Odille.

But you've all read in Æsop, or Phædrus, or Gay,
How a tortoise and hare ran together one day ;
   How the hare, making play,
   " Progress'd right slick away,"
As " them tarnation chaps " the Americans say ;
While the tortoise, whose figure is rather *outré*

These stiles sadly bothered Odille

For racing, crawl'd straight on, without let or stay,
Having no post-horse duty or turnpikes to pay,
   Till, ere noon's ruddy ray
   Changed to eve's sober grey,
Though her form and obesity caused some delay,
Perseverance and patience brought up her lee-way,
And she chased her fleet-footed " praycursor " until
She o'ertook her at last ;—so it fared with Odille !

For although, as I said, she ran gaily at first,
And show'd no inclination to pause, if she durst ;
She at length felt opprest with the heat and with thirst,
Its usual attendant ; nor was that the worst,
Her shoes went down at heel ; at last one of them burst.
   Now a gentleman smiles At a trot of ten miles ;
But not so the Fair ; then consider the stiles,
And as then ladies seldom wore things with a frill
Round the ankle, these stiles sadly bother'd Odille.

Still, despite all the obstacles placed in her track,
She kept steadily on, though the terrible crack
In her shoe made of course her progression more slack,
Till she reach'd the Swartz Forest (in English the Black) ;
   I cannot divine How the boundary line
Was pass'd which is somewhere there form'd by the Rhine—
   Perhaps she'd the knack To float o'er on her back—
Or, perhaps, cross'd the old bridge of boats at Brisach,
(Which Vauban, some years after, secured from attack
By a bastion of stone which the Germans call " Wacke,")
All I know is, she took not so much as a snack,
Till, hungry and worn, feeling wretchedly ill,
On a mountain's brow sank down the weary Odille.

I said on its " brow," but I should have said " crown,"
For 'twas quite on the summit, bleak, barren, and brown,
And so high that 'twas frightful indeed to look down
Upon Friburg, a place of some little renown,
That lay at its foot ; but imagine the frown
That contracted her brow, when full many a clown
She perceived coming up from that horrid post-town.

They had follow'd her trail,
And now thought without fail,
As little boys say, to " lay salt on her tail ; "
While the Count, who knew no other law but his will,
Swore that Herman that evening should marry Odille.

Alas, for Odille ! poor dear ! what could she do ?
Her father's retainers now had her in view,
As she found from their raising a joyous halloo ;
While the Count, riding on at the head of his crew,
In their snuff-colour'd doublets and breeches of blue,
Was huzzaing and urging them on to pursue.—
　　What, indeed, *could* she do ?　She very well knew
If they caught her how much she should have to go through ;
But then—she'd so shocking a hole in her shoe !
And to go further on was impossible ;—true,
She might jump o'er the precipice ;—still there are few
In her place, who could manage their courage to screw
Up to bidding the world such a sudden adieu :—
Alack ! how she envied the birds as they flew ;
No Nassau balloon, with its wicker canoe,
Came to bear her from him she loath'd worse than a Jew ;
So she fell on her knees in a terrible stew,
　　Crying " Holy St. Ermengarde !
　　Oh, from these vermin guard
Her whose last hope rests entirely on you ;—
Don't let papa catch me, dear Saint !—rather kill
At once, *sur-le-champ,* your devoted Odille ! "

It's delightful to see those who strive to oppress
Get baulk'd when they think themselves sure of success.
The Saint came to the rescue !—I fairly confess
I don't see, as a Saint, how she well could do less
Than to get such a votary out of her mess.
Odille had scarce closed her pathetic address,
When the rock, gaping wide as the Thames at Sheerness,
Closed again, and secured her within its recess,　.
　　In a natural grotto,　Which puzzled Count Otto,
Who could not conceive where the deuce she had got to
'Twas her voice !—but 'twas *Vox et præterea Nil !*
Nor could any one guess what was gone with Odille !

What, indeed, *could* she do?

Then burst from the mountain a splendour that quite
Eclipsed, in its brilliance, the finest Bude light,
And there stood St. Ermengarde, drest all in white,
A palm-branch in her left hand, her beads in her right ;
While, with faces fresh gilt, and with wings burnish'd bright,
A great many little boys' heads took their flight
Above and around to a very great height,
And seem'd pretty lively considering their plight,
   Since every one saw,   With amazement and awe,
They could never sit down, for they hadn't *de quoi*.—
   All at the sight,   From the knave to the knight,
Felt a very unpleasant sensation, call'd fright ;
   While the Saint, looking down,
   With a terrible frown,
Said, " My Lords, you are done most remarkably brown !—
I am really ashamed of you both ;—my nerves thrill
At your scandalous conduct to poor, dear Odille !

" Come, make yourselves scarce !—it is useless to stay,
You will gain nothing here by a longer delay.
' Quick ! Presto ! Begone ! ' as the conjurors say ;
For as to the Lady, I've stow'd her away
In this hill, in a stratum of London blue clay ;
And I shan't, I assure you, restore her to-day
Till you faithfully promise no more to say ' Nay.'
But declare, ' If she will be a nun, why, she may.'
For this you've my word, and I never yet broke it,
So put that in your pipe, my Lord Otto, and smoke it !—
One hint to your vassals,—a month at the ' Mill '
Shall be nuts to what they'll get who worry Odille ! "

The Saint disappear'd as she ended, and so
Did the little boys' heads, which, above and below,
As I told you a very few stanzas ago,
Had been flying about her, and jumping Jem Crow ;
Though, without any body, or leg, foot, or toe,
How they managed such antics, I really don't know ;
Be that as it may, they all " melted like snow
Off a dyke," as the Scotch say in sweet Edinbro'.
   And there stood the Count,
   With his men on the mount,
Just like " twenty-four jackasses all on a row."

What was best to be done ?—'twas a sad bitter pill—
But gulp it he must, or else lose his Odille.

The lord of Alsace therefore alter'd his plan,
And said to himself, like a sensible man,
" I can't do as I would,—I must do as I can ;
It will not do to lie under any Saint's ban,
For your hide, when you do, they all manage to tan ;
So Count Herman must pick up some Betsy or Nan,
Instead of my girl,—some Sue, Polly, or Fan ;—
If he can't get the corn he must do with the bran,
And make shift with the pot if he can't have the pan."
    With such proverbs as these
    He went down on his knees,
And said, " Blessed St. Ermengarde, just as you please—
They shall build a new convent,—I'll pay the whole bill,
(Taking discount,) its Abbess shall be my Odille ! "

There are some of my readers, I'll venture to say,
Who have never seen Friburg, though some of them may,
And others, 'tis likely may go there some day.
Now, if ever you happen to travel that way,
I do beg and pray, 'twill your pains well repay,—
That you'll take what the Cockney folks call a " po-shay,"
(Though in Germany these things are more like a dray,)
You may reach this same hill with a single relay,—
    And do look how the rock,
    Through the whole of its block,
Is split open, as though by some violent shock
From an earthquake, or lightning, or horrid hard knock
From the club-bearing fist of some jolly old cock
Of a germanised giant, Thor, Woden, or Lok :
    And see how it rears   Its two monstrous great ears,
For when once you're between them such each side appears ;
And list to the sound of the water one hears
Drip, drip, from the fissures, like rain-drops or tears,
—Odille's, I believe,—which have flowed all these years ;
—I think they account for them so ;—but the rill
I am sure is connected some way with Odille.

MORAL.

Now then, for a moral, which always arrives
At the end, like the honey bees take to their hives,
And the more one observes it the better one thrives,—
We have all heard it said in the course of our lives,
" Needs must when a certain old gentleman drives ; "
'Tis the same with a lady,—if once she contrives
To get hold of the ribands, how vainly one strives
To escape from her lash, or to shake off her gyves !
Then let's act like Count Otto, and while one survives,
Succumb to *our* She-Saints—videlicet wives !
(*Aside.*)
That is if one has not a " good bunch of fives."—
(I can't think how that last line escaped from my quill,
For I am sure it has nothing to do with Odille.)
   Now, young ladies, to you !—
   Don't put on the shrew !
And don't be surprised if your father looks blue
When you're pert, and won't act as he wants you to do !
Be sure that you never elope ;—there are few,—
Believe me, you'll find what I say to be true,—
Who run restive, but find as they bake they must brew,
And come off at last with " a hole in their shoe ; "
Since not even Clapham, that sanctified ville,
Can produce enough saints to save *every* Odille.

" Nycolas, cytezyn of ye cyte * of Pancracs, was borne of ryche and holye kynne,
And hys fader was named Epiphanus, and hys moder Johane."

He was born on a cold frosty morning, on the 6th of December, (upon which day his feast is still observed,) but in what *anno Domini* is not so clear ; his baptismal register, together with that of his friend and colleague, St. Thomas at Hill, having been " lost in the great fire of London."

St. Nicholas was a great patron of Mariners, and, saving your presence—of Thieves also, which honourable fraternity have long rejoiced in the appellation of his " Clerks."   Cervantes's story of Sancho's detecting a sum of money in a swindler's walking-stick is merely the Spanish version of a " Lay of St. Nicholas," extant " in choice Italian " a century before honest Miguel was born.

* Parish.

A Lay of St. Nicholas

" Statim sacerdoti apparuit diabolus in specie puellæ pulchritudinis miræ, et ecce Divus, fide catholicâ, et cruce, et aquâ benedicta armatus venit, et aspersit aquam in nomine Sanctæ et Individuæ Trinitatis, quam, quasi ardentem, diabolus, nequaquam sustinere valens, mugitibus fugit." ·   ROGER HOVEDEN.

" LORD ABBOT ! Lord Abbot ! I'd fain confess ;
 I am a-weary, and worn with woe ;
Many a grief doth my heart oppress,
 And haunt me whithersoever I go ! "

On bended kneé spake the beautiful Maid ;
 " Now lithe and listen, Lord Abbot, to me ! "—
" Now naye, Fair Daughter," the Lord Abbot said,
 " Now naye, in sooth it may hardly be ;

" There is Mess Michael, and holy Mess John,
 Sage Penitauncers I ween be they !
And hard by doth dwell, in St. Catherine's cell,
 Ambrose, the anchorite old and grey ! "

" —Oh, I will have none of Ambrose or John,
 Though sage Penitauncers I trow they be ;
Shrive me may none save the Abbot alone,
 Now listen, Lord Abbot, I speak to thee.

" Nor think foul scorn, though mitre adorn
 Thy brow, to listen to shrift of mine !
I am a Maiden royally born,
 And I come of old Plantagenet's line.

" Though hither I stray, in lowly array,
 I am a damsel of high degree ;
And the Compte of Eu, and the Lord of Ponthieu,
 They serve my father on bended knee !

" Counts a many, and Dukes a few,
 A-suitoring came to my father's Hall ;
But the Duke of Lorraine, with his large domain,
 He pleased my father beyond them all.

" Dukes a many, and Counts a few,
　　I would have wedded right cheerfullie ;
But the Duke of Lorraine was uncommonly plain,
　　And I vow'd that he ne'er should my bridegroom be !

" So hither I fly, in lowly guise,
　　From their gilded domes and their princely halls ;
Fain would I dwell in some holy cell,
　　Or within some Convent's peaceful walls ! "

—Then out and spake that proud Lord Abbot,
　　" Now rest thee, Fair Daughter, withouten fear ;
Nor Count nor Duke but shall meet the rebuke
　　Of Holy Church an he seek thee here :

" Holy Church denieth all search
　　'Midst her sanctified ewes and her saintly rams ;
And the wolves doth mock who would scathe her flock,
　　Or, especially, worry her little pet lambs.

" Then lay, Fair Daughter, thy fears aside,
　　For here this day shalt thou dine with me ! "—
" Now naye, now naye," the fair maiden cried ;
　　" In sooth, Lord Abbot, that scarce may be.

" Friends would whisper, and foes would frown,
　　Sith thou art a Churchman of high degree,
And ill mote it match with thy fair renown
　　That a wandering damsel dine with thee !

" There is Simon the Deacon hath pulse in store,
　　With beans and lettuces fair to see ;
His lenten fare now let me share,
　　I pray thee, Lord Abbot, in charitie ! "

—" Though Simon the Deacon hath pulse in store,
　　To our patron Saint foul shame it were
Should wayworn guest, with toil oppress'd,
　　Meet in his Abbey such churlish fare.

" There is Peter the Prior, and Francis the Friar,
   And Roger the Monk shall our convives be ;
Small scandal I ween shall then be seen ;
   They are a goodly companie ! "

The Abbot hath donn'd his mitre and ring,
   His rich dalmatic, and maniple fine ;
And the choristers sing, as the lay-brothers bring
   To the board a magnificent turkey and chine.

The turkey and chine, they are done to a nicety ;
   Liver, and gizzard, and all are there ;
Ne'er mote Lord Abbot pronounce *Benedicite*
   Over more luscious or delicate fare.

But no pious stave he, no *Pater* or *Ave*
   Pronounced, as he gazed on that maiden's face :
She ask'd him for stuffing, she ask'd him for gravy,
   She asked him for gizzard :—but not for Grace !

Yet gaily the Lord Abbot smiled, and press'd,
   And the blood-red wine in the wine-cup fill'd ;
And he help'd his guest to a bit of the breast,
   And he sent the drumsticks down to be grill'd.

There was no lack of old Sherris sack,
   Of Hippocras fine, or of Malmsey bright ;
And aye, as he drain'd off his cup with a smack,
   He grew less pious and more polite.

She pledged him once, and she pledged him twice,
   And she drank as Lady ought not to drink ;
And he press'd her hand 'neath the table thrice,
   And he wink'd as Abbot ought not to wink.

And Peter the Prior, and Francis the Friar,
   Sat each with a napkin under his chin ;
But Roger the Monk got excessively drunk,
   So they put him to bed, and they tuck'd him in !

The lay-brothers gazed on each other, amazed ;
And Simon the Deacon, with grief and surprise,
As he peep'd through the key-hole, could scarce fancy real
The scene he beheld, or believe his own eyes.

In his ear was ringing the Lord Abbot singing,—
He could not distinguish the words very plain,
But 'twas all about " Cole," and " jolly old Soul,"
And " Fiddlers," and " Punch," and things quite as profane.

Even Porter Paul, at the sound of such revelling,
With fervour himself began to bless ;
For he thought he must somehow have let the devil in,—
And perhaps was not very much out in his guess.

The Accusing Buyers * " flew up to Heaven's Chancery,"
Blushing like scarlet with shame and concern ;
The Archangel took down his tale, and in answer he
Wept—(See the works of the late Mr. Sterne).

* The Prince of Peripatetic Informers, and terror of Stage Coachmen when such things
were.   Alack ! alack ! the Railroads have ruined his " vested interest."

Indeed, it is said, a less taking both were in
    When, after a lapse of a great many years,
They book'd Uncle Toby five shillings for swearing,
    And blotted the fine out again with their tears !

But St. Nicholas' agony who may paint ?
    His senses at first were well-nigh gone ;
The beautiful saint was ready to faint
    When he saw in his Abbey such sad goings on !

For never, I ween, had such doings been seen
    There before, from the time that most excellent Prince
Earl Baldwin of Flanders, and other Commanders,
    Had built and endowed it some centuries since.

—But hark !—'tis a sound from the outermost gate !
    A startling sound from a powerful blow.—
Who knocks so late ?—it is half after eight
    By the clock,—and the clock's five minutes too slow.

Never, perhaps, had such loud double raps
    Been heard in St. Nicholas' Abbey before ;
All agreed " it was shocking to keep people knocking,"
    But none seem'd inclined to " answer the door."

Now a louder bang through the cloisters rang,
    And the gate on its hinges wide open flew ;
And all were aware of a Palmer there,
    With his cockle, hat, staff, and his sandal shoe.

Many a furrow, and many a frown,
    By toil and time on his brow were traced ;
And his long loose gown was of ginger brown,
    And his rosary dangled below his waist.

Now seldom, I ween, in such costume seen,
    Except at a stage-play or masquerade ;
But who doth not know it was rather the go
    With Pilgrims and Saints in the second Crusade ?

With noiseless stride did that Palmer glide
   Across that oaken floor ;
And he made them all jump, he gave such a thump
   Against the Refectory door !

Wide open it flew, and plain to the view
   The Lord Abbot they all mote see ;
In his hands was a cup, and he lifted it up,
   " Here's the Pope's good health with three ! ! "

Rang in their ears three deafening cheers,
   " Huzza ! huzza ! huzza ! "
And one of the party said, " Go it, my hearty ! "—
   When outspake that Pilgrim grey—

" A boon, Lord Abbot ! a boon ! a boon !
   Worn is my foot, and empty my scrip ;
And nothing to speak of since yesterday noon
   Of food, Lord Abbot, hath pass'd my lip.

" And I am come from a far countree,
   And have visited many a holy shrine ;
And long have I trod the sacred sod
   Where the Saints do rest in Palestine ! "—

" An thou art come from a far countree,
   And if thou in Paynim lands hast been,
Now rede me aright the most wonderful sight
   Thou Palmer grey, that thine eyes have seen

" Arede me aright the most wonderful sight,
   Grey Palmer, that ever thine eyes did see,
And a manchette of bread, and a good warm bed,
   And a cup o' the best shall thy guerdon be ! "

" Oh ! I have been east, and I have been west,
   And I have seen many a wonderful sight ;
But never to me did it happen to see
   A wonder like that which I see this night !

" To see a Lord Abbot, in rochet and stole,
   With Prior and Friar,—a strange mar-velle !—
O'er a jolly full bowl, sitting cheek by jowl,
   And hob-nobbing away with a Devil from Hell ! "

He felt in his gown of ginger-brown,
   And he pull'd out a flask from beneath ;
It was rather tough work to get out the cork,
   But he drew it at last with his teeth.

O'er a pint and a quarter of holy water
   He made the sacred sign ;
And he dashed the whole on the *soi-disant* daughter
   Of old Plantagenet's line !

Oh ! then did she reek, and squeak, and shriek,
   With a wild, unearthly scream ;
And fizzl'd, and hiss'd, and produced such a mist,
   They were all half-choked by the steam.

Her dove-like eyes turn'd to coals of fire,
   Her beautiful nose to a horrible snout,
Her hands to paws, with nasty great claws,
   And her bosom went in, and her tail came out.

On her chin there appear'd a long Nanny-goat's beard,
   And her tusks and her teeth no man mote tell ;
And her horns and her hoofs gave infallible proofs
   'Twas a frightful Fiend from the nethermost Hell !

The Palmer threw down his ginger gown,
   His hat and his cockle ; and, plain to sight,
Stood St. Nicholas' self, and his shaven crown
   Had a glow-worm halo of heavenly light.

The Fiend made a grasp, the Abbot to clasp ;
   But St. Nicholas lifted his holy toe,
And, just in the nick, let fly such a kick
   On his elderly Namesake, he made him let go.

Into the bottomless pit he fell slap

And out of the window he flew like a shot,
  For the foot flew up with a terrible thwack,
And caught the foul demon about the spot
  Where his tail joins on to the small of his back.

And he bounded away, like a foot-ball at play,
  Till into the bottomless pit he fell slap,
Knocking Mammon the meagre o'er pursy Belphegor,
  And Lucifer into Beelzebub's lap.

Oh! happy the slip from his Succubine grip,
  That saved the Lord Abbot,—though breathless with fright
In escaping he tumbled and fractured his hip,
  And his left leg was shorter thenceforth than his right!

        *   *   *   *   *

On the banks of the Rhine, as he's stopping to dine,
  From a certain Inn-window the traveller is shown
Most picturesque ruins, the scene of these doings,
  Some miles up the river, south-east of Cologne.

And, while "*sour-kraut*" she sells you, the Landlady tells you
  That there, in those walls, now all roofless and bare,
One Simon, a Deacon, from a lean grew a sleek one,
  On filling a *ci-devant* Abbot's state chair.

How a *ci-devant* Abbot, all clothed in drab, but
  Of texture the coarsest, hair shirt, and no shoes,
(His mitre and ring, and all that sort of thing
  Laid aside,) in yon Cave lived a pious recluse;

How he rose with the sun, limping "dot and go one,"
  To yon rill of the mountain, in all sorts of weather,
Where a Prior and a Friar, who lived somewhat higher
  Up the rock, used to come and eat cresses together;

How a thirsty old codger, the neighbours called Roger,
  With them drank cold water in lieu of old wine!
What its quality wanted he made up in quantity,
  Swigging as though he would empty the Rhine!

And how, as their bodily strength fail'd, the mental man
  Gain'd tenfold vigour and force in all four ;
And how, to the day of their death, the " Old Gentleman "
  Never attempted to kidnap them more.

And how, when at length, in the odour of sanctity,
  All of them died without grief or complaint ;
The Monks of St. Nicholas said 'twas ridiculous
  Not to suppose every one was a Saint.

· And how, in the Abbey, no one was so shabby
  As not to say yearly four masses a head,
On the eve of that supper, and kick on the crupper
  Which Satan received, for the souls of the dead !

How folks long held in reverence their reliques and memories,
  How the *ci-devant* Abbot's obtain'd greater still,
When some cripples, on touching his fractured *os femoris*,
  Threw down their crutches, and danced a quadrille !

And how Abbot Simon, (who turn'd out a prime one,)
  These words, which grew into a proverb full soon,
O'er the late Abbot's grotto, stuck up as a motto,
  " 𝔚𝔥𝔬 𝔰𝔲𝔭𝔭𝔢𝔰 𝔴𝔦𝔱𝔥 𝔱𝔥𝔢 𝔇𝔢𝔟𝔦𝔩𝔩𝔢 𝔰𝔥𝔬𝔩𝔡𝔢 𝔥𝔞𝔟𝔢 𝔞 𝔩𝔬𝔫𝔤 𝔰𝔭𝔬𝔬𝔫𝔢 ! ! "

Rohesia, daughter of Ambrose, and sister to Sir Everard Ingoldsby, was born about the beginning of the 16th century, and was married in 1526, at St. Giles's, Cripplegate, in the City of London.   The following narrative contains all else that is known of

The Lady Rohesia

THE Lady Rohesia lay on her death-bed !
  So said the doctor,—and doctors are generally allowed to be judges in these matters ;—besides, Dr. Butts was the Court Physician : he carried a crutch-handled staff, with its cross of the blackest ebony,— *raison de plus !*
  " Is there no hope, Doctor ? " said Beatrice Grey.

"Is there no hope?" said Everard Ingoldsby.

"Is there no hope?" said Sir Guy de Montgomeri.—He was the Lady Rohesia's husband;—he spoke the last.

The doctor shook his head: he looked at the disconsolate widower *in posse*, then at the hour-glass;—its waning sand seemed sadly to shadow forth the sinking pulse of his patient. Dr. Butts was a very learned man. "*Ars longa, vita brevis!*" said Doctor Butts.

"I am very sorry to hear it," quoth Sir Guy de Montgomeri.

Sir Guy was a brave knight, and a tall; but he was no scholar.

"Alas! my poor Sister!" sighed Ingoldsby.

"Alas! my poor Mistress!" sobbed Beatrice.

Sir Guy neither sighed nor sobbed;—his grief was too deep-seated for outward manifestation.

"And how long, Doctor——?" The afflicted husband could not finish the sentence.

Doctor Butts withdrew his hand from the wrist of the dying lady; he pointed to the horologe; scarcely a quarter of its sand remained in the upper moiety. Again he shook his head; the eye of the patient waxed dimmer, the rattling in the throat increased.

"What's become of Father Francis?" whimpered Beatrice.

"The last consolations of the church——" suggested Everard.

A darker shade came over the brow of Sir Guy.

"Where *is* the Confessor?" continued his grieving brother-in-law.

"In the pantry," cried Marion Hacket pertly, as she tripped down stairs in search of that venerable ecclesiastic;—"in the pantry, I warrant me."—The bower-woman was not wont to be in the wrong;—in the pantry was the holy man discovered,—at his devotions.

"*Pax vobiscum!*" said Father Francis, as he entered the chamber of death.

"*Vita brevis!*" retorted Doctor Butts:—he was not a man to be browbeat out of his Latin,—and by a paltry Friar Minim, too. Had it been a Bishop, indeed, or even a mitred Abbot;—but a miserable Franciscan!

"*Benedicite!*" said the friar.

"*Ars longa!*" returned the Leech.

M

Doctor Butts adjusted the tassels of his falling band; drew his short sad-coloured cloak closer around him; and, grasping his cross-handled walking-staff, stalked majestically out of the apartment.—Father Francis had the field to himself.

The worthy chaplain hastened to administer the last rites of the church. To all appearance he had little time to lose; as he concluded, the dismal toll of the passing-bell sounded from the belfry tower; little Hubert, the bandy-legged sacristan, was pulling with all his might.—It was a capital contrivance that same passing-bell:—which of the Urbans or Innocents invented it is a query; but, whoever he was, he deserved well of his country and of Christendom.

Ah! our ancestors were not such fools, after all, as we, their degenerate children, conceit them to have been. The passing-bell! a most solemn warning to imps of every description, is not to be regarded with impunity: the most impudent *Succubus* of them all dare as well dip his claws in holy water, as come within the verge of its sound. Old Nick himself, if he sets any value at all upon his tail, had best convey himself clean out of hearing, and leave the way open to Paradise. Little Hubert continued pulling with all his might, and St. Peter began to look out for a customer.

The knell seemed to have some effect even upon the Lady Rohesia; she raised her head slightly; inarticulate sounds issued from her lips,—inarticulate, that is, to the profane ears of the laity. Those of Father Francis, indeed, were sharper; nothing, as he averred, could be more distinct than the words, "A thousand marks to the priory of St. Mary Rouncival."

Now the Lady Rohesia Ingoldsby had brought her husband broad lands and large possessions; much of her ample dowry, too, was at her own disposal; and nuncupative wills had not yet been abolished by Act of Parliament.

"Pious soul!" ejaculated Father Francis. "A thousand marks, she said——"

"If she did, I'll be shot!" said Guy de Montgomeri.

"—A thousand marks!" continued the Confessor, fixing his cold grey eye upon the knight, as he went on heedless of the interruption;—"a thousand marks! and as many *Aves* and *Paters* shall be duly said—as soon as the money is paid down."

Sir Guy shrank from the monk's gaze; he turned to the window, and muttered to himself something that sounded like "Don't you wish you may get it?"

*   *   *   *   *   *   *

The bell continued to toll. Father Francis had quitted the room, taking with him the remains of the holy oil he had been using for Extreme Unction. Everard Ingoldsby waited on him down stairs.

" A thousand thanks ! " said the latter.

" A thousand marks ! " said the friar.

" A thousand devils ! " growled Sir Guy de Montgomeri, from the top of the landing-place.

But his accents fell unheeded; his brother-in-law and the friar were gone; he was left alone with his departing lady and Beatrice Grey.

Sir Guy de Montgomeri stood pensively at the foot of the bed : his arms were crossed upon his bosom, his chin was sunk upon his breast; his eyes were filled with tears; the dim rays of the fading watch-light gave a darker shade to the furrows on his brow, and a brighter tint to the little bald patch on the top of his head,—for Sir Guy was a middle-aged gentleman, tall and portly withal, with a slight bend in his shoulders, but that not much : his complexion was somewhat florid,—especially about the nose; but his lady was *in extremis,* and at this particular moment he was paler than usual.

" Bim ! bome ! " went the bell. The knight groaned audibly; Beatrice Grey wiped her eye with her little square apron of lace de Malines; there was a moment's pause,—a moment of intense affliction; she let it fall,—all but one corner, which remained between her finger and thumb.—She looked at Sir Guy; drew the thumb and forefinger of her other hand slowly along its border, till they reached the opposite extremity. She sobbed aloud : " So kind a lady ! " said Beatrice Grey. —" So excellent a wife ! " responded Sir Guy. " So good ! " said the damsel.—" So dear ! " said the knight.—" So pious ! " said she.—" So humble ! " said he.—" So good to the poor ! "—" So capital a manager ! " —" So punctual at matins ! "—" Dinner dished to a moment ! "— " So devout ! " said Beatrice.—" So fond of me ! " said Sir Guy.—" And of Father Francis ! "—" What the devil do you mean by that ? " said Sir Guy de Montgomeri.

* * * * * * *

The knight and the maiden had rung their antiphonic changes on the fine qualities of the departing Lady, like the *Strophe* and *Antistrophe* of a Greek play. The cardinal virtues once disposed of, her minor excellences came under review :—She would drown a witch, drink lambs'-wool at Christmas, beg Dominie Dumps's boys a holiday, and dine upon sprats on Good Friday !—A low moan from the subject of these eulogies seemed to intimate that the enumeration of her good deeds was not altogether lost on her,—that the parting spirit felt and rejoiced in the testimony.

"She was too good for earth!" continued Sir Guy.

"Ye-ye-yes!" sobbed Beatrice.

"I did not deserve her!" said the knight.

"No-o-o-o!" cried the damsel.

"Not, but that I made her an excellent husband, and a kind; but she is going, and—and—where, or when, or how—shall I get such another?"

"Not in broad England—not in the whole wide world!" responded Beatrice Grey; "that is, not *just* such another!"—Her voice still faltered, but her accents on the whole were more articulate; she dropped the corner of her apron, and had recourse to her handkerchief; in fact, her eyes were getting red,—and so was the tip of her nose.

Sir Guy was silent; he gazed for a few moments steadfastly on the face of his lady. The single word "Another!" fell from his lips like a distant echo;—it is not often that the viewless nymph repeats more than is necessary.

"Bim! bome!" went the bell.—Bandy-legged Hubert had been tolling for half an hour;—he began to grow tired, and St. Peter fidgety.

"Beatrice Grey!" said Sir Guy de Montgomeri, "what's to be done? What's to become of Montgomeri Hall?—and the buttery,—and the servants? And what—what's to become of *me*, Beatrice Grey?" There was pathos in his tones, and a solemn pause succeeded. "I'll turn monk myself!" said Sir Guy.

"Monk?" said Beatrice.

"I'll be a Carthusian!" repeated the knight, but in a tone less assured: he relapsed into a reverie.—Shave his head!—he did not so much mind that,—he was getting rather bald already;—but, beans for dinner,—and those without butter—and then a horse-hair shirt!

The knight seemed undecided: his eye roamed gloomily around the apartment; it paused upon different objects, but as if it saw them not; its sense was shut, and there was no speculation in its glance: it rested at last upon the fair face of the sympathising damsel at his side, beautiful in her grief.

Her tears had ceased; but her eyes were cast down, and mournfully fixed upon her delicate little foot, which was beating the devil's tattoo.

There is no talking to a female when she does not look at you. Sir Guy turned round,—he seated himself on the edge of the bed; and, placing his hand beneath the chin of the lady, turned up her face in an angle of fifteen degrees.

"I don't think I shall take the vows, Beatrice; but what's to become of me ? Poor, miserable, old—that is, poor, miserable, middle-aged man that I am!—No one to comfort, no one to care for me!"— Beatrice's tears flowed afresh, but she opened not her lips.—"'Pon my life!" continued he, " I don't believe there is a creature now would care a button if I were hanged to-morrow!"

" Oh! don't say so, Sir Guy!" sighed Beatrice; " you know there's —there's Master Everard, and—and Father Francis——"

" Pish!" cried Sir Guy testily.

" And—there's your favourite old bitch."

" I am not thinking of old bitches!" quoth Sir Guy de Montgomeri.

Another pause ensued : the knight had released her chin, and taken her hand;—it was a pretty little hand, with long taper fingers and filbert-formed nails, and the softness of the palm said little for its owner's industry.

" Sit down, my dear Beatrice," said the knight, thoughtfully; " you must be fatigued with your long watching. Take a seat, my child."— Sir Guy did not relinquish her hand; but he sidled along the counter-pane, and made room for his companion between himself and the bed-post.

Now this is a very awkward position for two people to be placed in, especially when the right hand of the one holds the right hand of the other :—in such an attitude, what the deuce can the gentleman do with his left ? Sir Guy closed his till it became an absolute fist, and his knuckles rested on the bed a little in the rear of his companion.

" Another!" repeated . Sir Guy, musing;—" if, indeed, I could find such another!"—He was talking to his thought, but Beatrice Grey answered him.

" There's Madam Fitzfoozle."

" A frump!" said Sir Guy.

" Or the Lady Bumbarton."

" With her hump!" muttered he.

" There's the Dowager——"

" Stop—stop!" said the knight, " stop one moment!"—He paused; he was all on the tremble; something seemed rising in his throat, but he gave a great gulp, and swallowed it. " Beatrice," said he, " what think you of—" his voice sank into a most seductive softness, —" what think you of Beatrice Grey ?"

The murder was out :—the knight felt infinitely relieved; the knuckles of his left hand unclosed spontaneously; and the arm he had felt such a difficulty in disposing of, found itself,—nobody knows how,— all at once, encircling the gimp waist of the pretty Beatrice. The

young lady's reply was expressed in three syllables. They were,—
" O, Sir Guy ! " The words might be somewhat indefinite, but there
was no mistaking the look. Their eyes met ; Sir Guy's left arm contracted itself spasmodically : when the eyes meet,—at least, as theirs
met,—the lips are very apt to follow the example. The knight had
taken one long, loving kiss—nectar and ambrosia ! He thought on
Doctor Butts and his *repetatur haustus,*—a prescription Father Francis
had taken infinite pains to translate for him :—he was about to repeat
it, but the dose was interrupted *in transitu.*—Doubtless the adage,

> " There is many a slip
> 'Twixt the cup and the lip,"

hath reference to medicine. Sir Guy's lip was again all but in conjunction with that of his bride elect.

It has been hinted already that there was a little round polished
patch on the summit of the knight's *pericranium,* from which his locks
had gradually receded ; a sort of *oasis,*—or rather a *Mont Blanc* in
miniature, rising above the highest point of vegetation. It was on
this little spot, undefended alike by Art and Nature, that at this interesting moment a blow descended, such as we must borrow a term from
the Sister Island adequately to describe,—it was a " Whack ! "

Sir Guy started upon his feet ; Beatrice Grey started upon hers ;
but a single glance to the rear reversed her position,—she fell upon her
knees and screamed.

The knight, too, wheeled about, and beheld a sight which might
have turned a bolder man to stone.—It was She !—the all but defunct
Rohesia—there she sat, bolt upright !—her eyes no longer glazed with
the film of impending dissolution, but scintillating like flint and steel ;
while in her hand she grasped the bed-staff,—a weapon of mickle might,
as her husband's bloody coxcomb could now well testify. Words were
yet wanting, for the quinsy, which her rage had broken, still impeded
her utterance ; but the strength and rapidity of her guttural intonation
augured well for her future eloquence.

Sir Guy de Montgomeri stood for a while like a man distraught ;
this resurrection—for such it seemed—had quite overpowered him.
" A husband ofttimes makes the best physician," says the proverb ; he
was a living personification of its truth. Still it was whispered he had
been content with Doctor Butts ; but his lady was restored to bless
him for many years.—Heavens, what a life he led !

The Lady Rohesia mended apace ; her quinsy was cured ; the bell
was stopped ; and little Hubert, the sacristan, kicked out of the chapelry.

St. Peter opened his wicket, and looked out ;—there was nobody there so he flung-to the gate in a passion, and went back to his lodge, grumbling at being hoaxed by a runaway ring.

"WHACK!"

Years rolled on.—The improvement of Lady Rohesia's temper did not keep pace with that of her health ; and one fine morning Sir Guy de Montgomeri was seen to enter the *porte-cochère* of Durham House, at that time the town residence of Sir Walter Raleigh. Nothing more was ever heard of him ; but a boat full of adventurers was known to have dropped down with the tide that evening to Deptford Hope, where lay the good ship the Darling, commanded by Captain Keymis, who sailed next morning on the Virginia voyage.

A brass plate, some eighteen inches long, may yet be seen in Denton chancel, let into a broad slab of Bethersden marble ; it represents a lady kneeling, in her wimple and hood ; her hands are clasped in prayer, and beneath is an inscription in the characters of the age—

"𝔓raie for ye sowle of ye 𝕷ady 𝕽ouse,
𝔄nd for alle 𝕮hristen sowles !"

The date is illegible ; but it appears that she survived King Henry the Eighth, and that the dissolution of monasteries had lost St. Mary Rouncival her thousand marks.—As for Beatrice Grey, it is well known that she was alive in 1559, and then had virginity enough left to be a maid of Honour to " good Queen Bess."

It was during the " Honey (or, as it is sometimes termed, the " Treacle,) Moon," that Mr. and Mrs. Seaforth passed through London. A " good-natured friend," who dropped in to dinner, forced them in the evening to go to the theatre for the purpose of getting rid of him. I give Charles's account of the Tragedy, just as it was written, without altering even the last couplet—for there would be no making " Egerton " rhyme with " Story."

The Tragedy

Quæque ipse miserrima vidi.—VIRGIL.

CATHERINE of Cleves was a Lady of rank,
She had lands and fine houses, and cash in the Bank;
    She had jewels and rings,
    And a thousand smart things ;
    Was lovely and young,   With a *rather* sharp tongue,
And she wedded a Noble of high degree
With the star of the order of *St. Esprit ;*
    But the Duke de Guise   Was, by many degrees,
Her senior, and not very easy to please ;
He'd a sneer on his lip, and a scowl with his eye,
And a frown on his brow,—and he look'd like a Guy,—

The Duchess shed tears large as marrow-fat peas

So she took to intriguing   With Monsieur St. Megrin,
A young man of fashion, and figure, and worth,
But with no great pretensions to fortune or birth ;
  He would sing, fence, and dance
  With the best man in France,
And took his rappee with genteel *nonchalance ;*
He smiled, and he flatter'd, and flirted with ease,
And was very superior to Monseigneur de Guise.

Now Monsieur St. Megrin was curious to know
If the Lady approved of his passion or no ;
  So without more ado,
  He put on his *surtout,*
And went to a man with a beard like a Jew,
  One Signor Ruggieri,
  A Cunning-man near, he
Could conjure, tell fortunes, and calculate tides,
Perform tricks on the cards, and Heaven knows what besides,
Bring back a stray'd cow, silver ladle, or spoon,
And was thought to be thick with the Man in the Moon.
  The Sage took his stand
  With his wand in his hand,
Drew a circle, then gave the dread word of command,
Saying solemnly—" *Presto !—Hey, quick !—Cock-a-lorum ! !* "
When the Duchess immediately popp'd up before 'em.

Just then a Conjunction of Venus and Mars,
Or something peculiar above in the stars,
Attracted the notice of Signor Ruggieri,
Who " bolted," and left him alone with his deary.—
Monsieur St. Megrin went down on his knees,
And the Duchess shed tears large as marrow-fat peas,
  When,—fancy the shock,—   A loud double knock,
Made the Lady cry " Get up, you fool !—there's De Guise ! "—
  'Twas his Grace, sure enough ;
  So Monsieur, looking bluff,
Strutted by, with his hat on, and fingering his ruff,
While, unseen by either, away flew the Dame
Through the opposite key-hole, the same way she came ;
  But, alack ! and alas !   A mishap came to pass,

In her hurry she, some how or other, let fall
A new silk *Bandana* she'd worn as a shawl ;
   She used it for drying   Her bright eyes while crying,
And blowing her nose, as her Beau talk'd of dying !

Now the Duke, who had seen it so lately adorn her,
And he knew the great C with the Crown in the corner,
The instant he spied it, smoked something amiss,
And said, with some energy, " D—— it ! what's this ? "
 He went home in a fume,   And bounced into her room,
Crying, " So, Ma'am, I find I've some cause to be jealous !
Look here !—here's a proof you run after the fellows !
—Now take up that pen,—if it's bad choose a better,—
And write, as I dictate, this moment a letter
   To Monsieur,—you know who ! "
   The Lady look'd blue ;
But replied with much firmness—" Hang me if I do ! "
   De Guise grasped her wrist   With his great bony fist,
And pinched it, and gave it so painful a twist,
That his hard, iron gauntlet the flesh went an inch in,—
She did not mind death, but she could not stand pinching,
   So she sat down and wrote   This polite little note :—

" Dear Mister St. Megrin,   The Chiefs of the League in
Our house mean to dine   This evening at nine ;
   I shall, soon after ten,   Slip away from the men,
And you'll find me upstairs in the drawing-room then ;
Come up the back way, or those impudent thieves
Of Servants will see you ;   Yours
                        CATHERINE OF CLEVES."

She directed and sealed it, all pale as a ghost,
And De Guise put it into the Twopenny Post.

St. Megrin had almost jumped out of his skin
For joy that day when the post came in ;
   He read the note through,   Then began it anew,
And thought it almost too good news to be true.—
   He clapp'd on his hat,   And a hood over that,
With a cloak to disguise him, and make him look fat ;

SHE DID NOT MIND DEATH, BUT SHE COULD NOT STAND PINCHING

So great his impatience, from half after Four
He was waiting till Ten at De Guise's back-door.
When he heard the great clock of St. Genevieve chime,
He ran up the back staircase six steps at a time.
   He had scarce made his bow,   He hardly knew how,
   When alas ! and alack !   There was no getting back,
For the drawing-room door was bang'd to with a whack ;—
   In vain he applied To the handle and tried,
Somebody or other had locked it outside !
And the Duchess in agony mourn'd her mishap,
" We are caught like a couple of rats in a trap."

   Now the Duchess's Page,   About twelve years of age,
For so little a boy was remarkably sage ;
And, just in the nick, to their joy and amazement,
Popp'd the Gas-lighter's ladder close under the casement.
   But all would not do,—
   Though St. Megrin got through
The window,—below stood De Guise and his crew.
And though never a man was more brave than St. Megrin,
Yet fighting a score is extremely fatiguing ;
   He thrust *carte* and *tierce*   Uncommonly fierce,
But not Beelzebub's self could their cuirasses pierce ;
   While his doublet and hose,   Being holiday clothes,
Were soon cut through and through from his knees to his nose.
Still an old crooked sixpence the Conjuror gave him
From pistol and sword was sufficient to save him,
   But, when beat on his knees,
   That confounded De Guise
Came behind with the " fogle " that caused all this breeze,
Whipp'd it tight round his neck, and, when backward he'd
    jerk'd him,
The rest of the rascals jump'd on him and Burked him.
The poor little Page, too, himself got no quarter, but
   Was served the same way,
   And was found the next day .
With his heels in the air, and his head in the water-butt ;
   Catherine of Cleves
   Roar'd " Murder ! " and " Thieves ! "
   From the window above
   While they murder'd her love ;

Till, finding the rogues had accomplish'd his slaughter,
She drank Prussic acid without any water,
And died like a Duke-and-a-Duchess's daughter !

MORAL.

Take warning, ye Fair, from this tale of the Bard's,
And don't go where fortunes are told on the cards,

But steer clear of Conjurors,—never put query
To " Wise Mrs. Williams," or folks like Ruggieri.
When alone in your room, shut the door close, and lock it ;
Above all,—KEEP YOUR HANDKERCHIEF SAFE IN YOUR POCKET !
Lest you too should stumble, and Lord Leveson Gower, he
Be call'd on,—sad poet !—to tell your sad story !

It was in the summer of 1838 that a party from Tappington reached the metropolis with a view of witnessing the coronation of their youthful Queen, whom God long preserve !—This purpose they were fortunate enough to accomplish by the purchase of a peer's ticket, from a stationer in the Strand, who was enabled so to dispose of some, greatly to the indignation of the hereditary Earl Marshal. How Mr. Barney managed to insinuate himself into the Abbey remains a mystery : his characteristic modesty and address doubtless assisted him, for there he unquestionably was. The result of his observations were thus communicated to his associates in the Servants' Hall upon his return, to the infinite delectation of *Mademoiselle Pauline* over a *Cruiskeen* of his own concocting.

MR BARNEY MAGUIRE'S ACCOUNT of the CORONATION

AIR—"The Groves of Blarney."

Och ! the Coronation ! what celebration
    For emulation can with it compare ?
When to Westminster the Royal Spinster,
    And the Duke of Leinster, all in order did repair !
'Twas there you'd see the new Polishemen,
    Making a skrimmage at half after four,
And the Lords and Ladies, and the Miss O'Gradys,
    All standing round before the Abbey door.

Their pillows scorning, that self-same morning
    Themselves adorning, all by the candle-light,
With roses and lilies, and daffy-down-dillies,
    And gould, and jewels, and rich di'monds bright.
And then approaches five hundred coaches,
    With Gineral Dullbeak.—Och ! 'twas mighty fine
To see how asy bould Corporal Casey,
    With his sword drawn, prancing, made them kape the line.

191

Then the Guns' alarums, and the King of Arums,
    All in his Garters and his Clarence shoes,
Opening·the massy doors to the bould Ambassydors,
    The Prince of Potboys, and great haythen Jews ;
'Twould have made you crazy to see Esterhazy
    All joo'ls from his jasey to his di'mond boots,
With Alderman Harmer, and that swate charmer,
    The famale heiress, Miss Anjā-ly Coutts.

And Wellington, walking with his swoord drawn, talking
    To Hill and Hardinge, haroes of great fame ;
And Sir De Lacy, and the Duke Dalmasey,
    (They call'd him Sowlt afore he changed his name,)
Themselves presading Lord Melbourne, lading
    The Queen, the darling, to her royal chair,
And that fine ould fellow, the Duke of Pell-Mello,
    The Queen of Portingal's Chargy-de-fair.

Then the Noble Prussians, likewise the Russians,
    In fine laced jackets with their goulden cuffs,
And the Bavarians, and the proud Hungarians,
    And Everythingarians all in furs and muffs.
Then Misthur Spaker, with Misthur Pays the Quaker,
    All in the Gallery you might persave ;
But Lord Brougham was missing, and gone a-fishing,
    Ounly crass Lord Essex would not give him lave.

There was Baron Alten himself exalting,
    And Prince Von Swartzenburg, and many more,
Och ! I'd be bother'd, and entirely smother'd
    To tell the half of 'em was to the fore ;
With the swate Peeresses, in their crowns and dresses,
    And Aldermanesses, and the Boord of Works ;
But Mehemet Ali said, quite gintaly,
    " I'd be proud to see the likes among the Turks ! "

Then the Queen, Heaven bless her ! och ! they did dress her
    In her purple garments and her goulden Crown ;
Like Venus or Hebe, or the Queen of Sheby,
    With eight young Ladies houlding up her gown,

Sure 'twas grand to see her also for to he-ar
   The big drums bating, and the trumpets blow,
And Sir George Smart ! Oh ! he play'd a Consarto,
   With his four-and-twenty fiddlers all on a row !

Then the Lord Archbishop held a goulden dish up,
   For to resave her bounty and great wealth,
Saying, " Plase your Glory, great Queen Vic-tory !
   Ye'll give the Clargy lave to dhrink your health ! "
Then his Riverence, retrating, discoorsed the mating ;
   " Boys ! Here's your Queen ! deny it if you can !
And if any bould traitour, or infarior craythur,
   Sneezes at that, I'd like to see the man ! "

Then the Nobles kneeling to the Pow'rs appealing,
   " Heaven send your Majesty a glorious reign ! "
And Sir Claudius Hunter he did confront her,
   All in his scarlet gown and goulden chain.
The great Lord May'r, too, sat in his chair, too,
   But mighty sarious, looking fit to cry,
For the Earl of Surrey, all in his hurry,
   Throwing the thirteens, hit him in his eye.

Then there was preaching, and good store of speeching,
   With Dukes and Marquises on bended knee :
And they did splash her with raal Macasshur,
   And the Queen said, " Ah ! then thank ye all for me ! "—
Then the trumpets braying, and the organ playing,
   And sweet trombones with their silver tones ;
But Lord Rolle was rolling ;—'twas mighty consoling
   To think his Lordship did not break his bones !

Then the crames and custard, and the beef and mustard,
   All on the tombstones like a poultherer's shop ;
With lobsters and white-bait, and other swate-meats,
   And wine and nagus, and Imparial Pop !
There was cakes and apples in all the Chapels,
   With fine polonies, and rich mellow pears,—
Och ! the Count Von Strogonoff, sure he got prog enough,
   The sly ould Divil, undernathe the stairs.

Then the cannons thunder'd, and th: people wonder'd,
   Crying, " God save Victoria, our .oyal Queen ! "—
Och ! if myself should live to be a hndred
   Sure it's the proudest day that I'l have seen !
And now, I've ended, what I preteried,
   This narration splendid in swate pe-thry,
Ye dear bewitcher, just hand the pizher,
   Faith, it's myself that's getting mzhty dhry !

As a *pendant* to the foregoing, I shall venture to insert Ir. Simpkinson's lucubrations on a subject to him, as a *Savant* of the first class, scarcely less inter ting. The aerial voyage to which it alludes took place about a year and a half previously to ie august event already recorded, and the excitement manifested in the learned Antiquary's ffusion may give some faint idea of that which prevailed generally among the Sons of Scienc at that memorable epoch.

The " Monstre " Blloon

Oh ! the balloon, the great balloon,
It left Vauxhall one Monday at noon,
And every one said we should hear of it)on
With news from Aleppo or Scanderoon.
But very soon after folks changed their tne :
" The netting had burst —the silk—the halloon ;—
It had met with a trade-wind—a deucec monsoon—
It was blown out to sea—it was blown t the moon—
They ought to have put off their journe till June ;
Sure none but a donkey, a goose, or babon,
Would go up in November in any balloo ! "

Then they talk'd about Green—" Oh ! here's Mister Green ?
And where's Mister Holland who hired he machine ?
And where is Monk Mason, the man tha has been
Up so often before—twelve times or thiteen—
And who writes such nice letters describg the scene ?
And where's the cold fowl, and the ham and poteen ?
The press'd·beef, with the fat cut off—nthing but lean,

And the portable sop in the patent tureen ?
Have they got to Gind Cairo, or reach'd Aberdeen ?
Or Jerusalem—Hamurg—or Ballyporeen ?
No ! they have not ben seen !   Oh ! they haven't been seen ! "

Stay ! here's Mister Gye—Mr. Frederick Gye—
" At Paris," says he, ' I've been up very high,
A couple of hundred of toises, or nigh,
A cockstride the Tuieries' pantiles, to spy,
With Dollond's best elescope stuck at my eye,
And my umbrella uner my arm like Paul Pry,
But I could see notlng at all but the sky ;
So I thought with mself 'twas of no use to try
Any longer : and, feeing remarkably dry
From sitting all day tuck up there, like a Guy,
I came down again, nd—you see—here am I ! "

But here's Mr. Hughs !—What says young Mr. Hughes ?—
" Why, I'm sorry to ay we've not got any news
Since the letter they hrew down in one of their shoes,
Which gave the mayc's nose such a deuce of a bruise,
As he popp'd up his ye-glass to look at their cruise
Over Dover ; and wlch the folks flock'd to peruse
At Squiers's bazaar, ne same evening, in crews—
Politicians, news-mogers, town-council, and blues,
Turks, Heretics, Infiels, Jumpers, and Jews,
Scorning Bachelor's ppers, and Warren's reviews ;
But the wind was tha blowing towards Helvoetsluys,
And my father and hre in terrible stews,
For so large a ballooiis a sad thing to lose ! "—

Here's news come at ist !—Here's news come at last !
A vessel's come in, wich has sail'd very fast ;
And a gentleman sering before the mast—
Mister Nokes—has declared that " the party has past
Safe across to The Hgue, where their grapnel they cast,
As a fat burgomaster vas staring aghast
To see such a monste come borne on the blast,
And it caught in his aistband, and there it stuck fast ! "—
Oh ! fie ! Mister Noke,—for shame, Mr. Nokes !
To be poking your fu at us plain-dealing folks—

Sir, this isn't a time to be cracking your jokes,
And such jesting your malice but scurvily cloaks ;
Such a trumpery tale every one of us smokes,
And we know very well your whole story's a hoax !—

" Oh ! what shall we do ?—Oh ! where will it end ?—
Can nobody go ?—Can nobody send
To Calais—or Bergen-op-zoom—or Ostend ?
Can't you go there yourself ?—Can't you write to a friend,
For news upon which we may safely depend ? "—

Huzza ! huzza ! one and eight-pence to pay
For a letter from Hamborough, just come to say
They descended at Weilburg, about break of day ;
And they've lent them the palace there, during their stay,
And the town is becoming uncommonly gay ;
And they're feasting the party, and soaking their clay
With Johannisberg, Rudesheim, Moselle, and Tokay !
And the Landgraves, and Margraves, and Counts beg and pray
That they won't think, as yet, about going away ;
Notwithstanding, they don't mean to make much delay,
But pack up the balloon in a waggon, or dray,
And pop themselves into a German " *po-shay*,"
And get on to Paris by Lisle and Tournay ;
Where they boldly declare, any wager they'll lay,
If the gas people there do not ask them to pay,
Such a sum as must force them at once to say " Nay,"
They'll inflate the balloon in the Champs-Elysées,
And be back again here the beginning of May.—
Dear me ! what a treat for a juvenile *fête*
What thousands will flock their arrival to greet !
There'll be hardly a soul to be seen in the street,
For at Vauxhall the whole population will meet,
And you'll scarcely get standing-room, much less a seat,
For this all preceding attraction must beat :
Since, they'll unfold, what we want to be told,
How they cough'd,—how they sneez'd,—how they shiver'd with
      cold,—
How they tippled the " cordial " as racy and old
As Hodges, or Deady, or Smith ever sold,
And how they all then felt remarkably bold :

How they thought the boil'd beef worth its own weight in gold ;
And how Mr. Green was beginning to scold
Because Mr. Mason would try to lay hold
Of the moon, and had very near overboard roll'd !

And there they'll be seen—they'll be all to be seen !
The great-coats, the coffee-pot, mugs, and tureen !
With the tight rope, and fire-works, and dancing between,
If the weather should only prove fair and serene,
And there, on a beautiful transparent screen,
In the middle you'll see a large picture of Green,
Mr. Hollond on one side, who hired the machine,
Mr. Mason on t'other, describing the scene ;
And Fame, on one leg, in the air, like a queen,
With three wreaths and a trumpet, will over them lean ;
While Envy, in serpents and black bombazin,
Looks on from below with an air of chagrin !
Then they'll play up a tune in the Royal Saloon,
And the people will dance by the light of the moon,
And keep up the ball till the next day at noon ;
And the peer and the peasant, the lord and the loon,
The haughty grandee, and the low picaroon,
The six-foot life-guardsman, and little gossoon,
Will all join in three cheers for the " Monstre " Balloon.

It is much to be regretted that I have not as yet been able to discover more than a single specimen of my friend " Sucklethumbkin's " Muse. The event it alludes to, probably the *euthanasia* of the late Mr. Greenacre, will scarcely have yet faded from the recollection of an admiring public. Although, with the usual diffidence of a man of fashion, Augustus has " sunk " the fact of his own presence on that interesting occasion, I have every reason to believe that, in describing the party at the *auberge* hereafter mentioned, he might have said, with a brother Exquisite, " *Quorum pars magna fui.*"

Hon. Mr. Sucklethumbkin's Story

The Execution

A SPORTING ANECDOTE

My Lord Tomnoddy got up one day;
  It was half after two, He had nothing to do,
So his Lordship rang for his cabriolet.

  Tiger Tim Was clean of limb,
His boots were polish'd, his jacket was trim;
With a very smart tie in his smart cravat,
And a smart cockade on the top of his hat;
Tallest of boys, or shortest of men,
He stood in his stockings just four foot ten:
And he ask'd, as he held the door on the swing,
" Pray, did your Lordship please to ring ? "

My Lord Tomnoddy he raised his head,
And thus to Tiger Tim he said,
  " Malibran's dead, Duvernay's fled,
Taglioni has not yet arrived in her stead;
Tiger Tim, come tell me true,
What may a Nobleman find to do ? "—

Tim look'd up, and Tim look'd down,
He paused, and he put on a thoughtful frown,
And he held up his hat, and he peep'd in the crown;
He bit his lip, and he scratch'd his head,
He let go the handle, and thus he said,
As the door, released, behind him bang'd :
" An't please you, my Lord, there's a man to be hang'd."

My Lord Tomnoddy jump'd up at the news,
  " Run to M'Fuze, And Lieutenant Tregooze,
And run to Sir Carnaby Jenks, of the Blues.
  Rope-dancers a score I've seen before—
Madame Sacchi, Antonio, and Master Black-more;
  But to see a man swing At the end of a string
With his neck in a noose, will be quite a new thing ! "

My Lord Tomnoddy stept into his cab—
Dark rifle green, with a lining of drab ;
  Through street, and through square,
  His high-trotting mare,
Like one of Ducrow's, goes pawing the air.
Adown Piccadilly and Waterloo Place
Went the high-trotting mare at a very quick
    pace ;
  She produced some alarm, But did no
  great harm,
Save frightening a nurse with a child on her
  arm,
  Spattering with clay Two urchins at play,
Knocking down—very much to the sweeper's
  dismay—
An old woman who wouldn't get out of the
  way,
  And upsetting a stall Near Exeter Hall,
Which made all the pious Church-Mission
  folks squall.
  But eastward afar, Through Temple Bar,
My Lord Tomnoddy directs his car ;
  Never heeding their squalls,
  Or their calls, or their bawls,
He passes by Waithman's Emporium for
  shawls,
And, merely just catching a glimpse of St.
  Paul's,
  Turns down the Old Bailey,
  Where in front of the gaol, he

Pulls up at the door of the gin-shop, and gaily
Cries, " What must I fork out to-night, my trump,
For the whole first-floor of the Magpie and Stump ? "

     *   *   *   *   *

The clock strikes twelve—it is dark midnight—
Yet the Magpie and Stump is one blaze of light.
  The parties are met ; The tables are set ;
There is " punch," " cold *without*," " hot *with*," " heavy wet,"
  Ale-glasses and jugs, And rummers and mugs,
And sand on the floor, without carpets or rugs,

Cold fowl and cigars,   Pickled onions in jars,
Welsh rabbits and kidneys—rare work for the jaws !—
And very large lobsters, with very large claws ;
    And there is M'Fuze,   And Lieutenant Tregooze,
And there is Sir Carnaby Jenks, of the Blues,
    All come to see a man " die in his shoes ! "

The clock strikes One !   Supper is done,
And Sir Carnaby Jenks is full of his fun,
Singing " Jolly companions every one ! "
    My Lord Tomnoddy   Is drinking gin-toddy,
And laughing at ev'ry thing, and ev'ry body,—
The clock strikes Two ! and the clock strikes Three !
—" Who so merry, so merry as we ? "
    Save Captain M'Fuze,   Who is taking a snooze,
While Sir Carnaby Jenks is busy at work,
Blacking his nose with a piece of burnt cork.

The clock strikes Four !—   Round the debtors' door
Are gather'd a couple of thousand or more ;
    As many await   At the press-yard gate,
Till slowly its folding doors open, and straight
The mob divides, and between their ranks
A waggon comes loaded with posts and with planks.

The clock strikes Five !   The Sheriffs arrive,
And the crowd is so great that the street seems alive ;
    But Sir Carnaby Jenks   Blinks, and winks,
A candle burns down in the socket, and stinks.
    Lieutenant Tregooze   Is dreaming of Jews,
And acceptances all the bill-brokers refuse ;
    My Lord Tomnoddy   Has drunk all his toddy,
And just as the dawn is beginning to peep,
The whole of the party are fast asleep.

Sweetly, oh ! sweetly, the morning breaks,
    With roseate streaks,
Like the first faint blush on a maiden's cheeks ;
Seem'd as that mild and clear blue sky
Smiled upon all things far and nigh,
On all—save the wretch condemn'd to die !

Alack ! that ever so fair a Sun
As that which its course has now begun,
Should rise on such a scene of misery !—
Should gild with rays so light and free
That dismal, dark-frowning Gallows-tree !

And hark !—a sound comes, big with fate ;
The clock from St. Sepulchre's tower strikes—Eight !—
List to that low funereal bell :
It is tolling, alas ! a living man's knell !—
And see !—from forth that opening door
They come—HE steps that threshold o'er
Who never shall tread upon threshold more !
—God ! 'tis a fearsome thing to see
That pale wan man's mute agony,—
The glare of that wild, despairing eye,
Now bent on the crowd, now turn'd to the sky,
As though 'twere scanning, in doubt and in fear,
The path of the Spirit's unknown career ;
Those pinion'd arms, those hands that ne'er
Shall be lifted again—not even in prayer ;
That heaving chest !—Enough—'tis done !
The bolt has fallen !—the spirit is gone—
For weal or for woe is known but to One !
—Oh ! 'twas a fearsome sight !—Ah me !
A deed to shudder at,—not to see.

Again that clock ! 'tis time, 'tis time !
The hour is past :—with its earliest chime
The cord is severed, the lifeless clay
By " dungeon villains " is borne away :
Nine !—'twas the last concluding stroke !
And then—my Lord Tomnoddy awoke !
And Tregooze and Sir Carnaby Jenks arose,
And Captain M'Fuze, with the black on his nose :
And they stared at each other, as much as to say,
  " Hullo ! Hullo ! Here's a rum Go !
Why, Captain !—my Lord !—Here's the devil to pay !
The fellow's been cut down and taken away !—
  What's to be done ? We've miss'd all the fun !—
Why, they'll laugh at and quiz us all over the town,
We are all of us done so uncommonly brown !"

What *was* to be done ?—'twas perfectly plain
That they could not well hang the man over again :
What *was* to be done ?—The man was dead !
Nought *could* be done—nought could be said ;
So—my Lord Tomnoddy went home to bed !

The following communication will speak for itself :—

"On their own actions modest men are dumb ! "

Some Account of a New Play

In a Familiar Epistle to my brother-in-law, Lieut. Seaforth,
   H.P., late of the Hon. E.I.C.'s 2nd Regt. of Bombay
   Fencibles

"The play's the thing ! "—*Hamlet.*

Tavistock Hotel, Nov. 1839.

DEAR CHARLES,
               —In reply to your letter, and Fanny's,
Lord Brougham, it appears, isn't dead,—though Queen Anne is ;
'Twas a " plot " and a " farce "—you hate farces, you say—
Take another " plot," then, viz., the plot of the Play.

        *   *   *   *   *

The Countess of Arundel, high in degree,
As a lady possess'd of an earldom in fee,
Was imprudent enough, at fifteen years of age,
—A period of life when we're not over sage,—
To form a *liaison*—in fact, to engage
Her hand to a Hop-o'-my-thumb of a Page.
  This put her Papa— She had no Mamma—
As may well be supposed, in a deuce of a rage.

Mr. Benjamin Franklin was wont to repeat,
In his budget of proverbs, " Stol'n kisses are sweet ! "

He bounced up and down

But they have their alloy— ˙Fate assumed, to annoy
Miss Arundel's peace, and embitter her joy,
The equivocal shape of a fine little Boy.

When, through " the young Stranger," her secret took wind,
The old Lord was neither " to haud nor to bind."
　He bounced up and down,　And so fearful a frown
Contracted his brow, you'd have thought he'd been blind.
　The young lady, they say,　Having fainted away
Was confin'd to her room for the whole of that day¯;
While her beau—no rare thing in the old feudal system—
Disappear'd the next morning, and nobody miss'd him.

The fact is, his Lordship, who hadn't, it seems,
Form'd the slightest idea, not ev'n in his dreams,
That the pair had been wedded according to law,
Conceived that his daughter had made a *faux pas ;*
　So he bribed at a high rate
　A sort of a Pirate
To knock out the poor dear young Gentleman's brains,
And gave him a handsome *douceur* for his pains.
The Page thus disposed of, his Lordship now turns
His attention at once to the Lady's concerns ;
　And, alarm'd for the future,
　Looks out for a suitor,
One not fond of raking, nor giv'n to " the pewter,"
But adapted to act both the husband and tutor—
Finds a highly respectable, middle-aged widower,
Marries her off, and thanks Heaven that he's rid of her.
　Relieved from his cares,　The old Peer now prepares
To arrange in good earnest his worldly affairs ;
Has his will made anew by a Special Attorney,
Sickens,—takes to his bed,—and sets out on his journey.
　Which way he travell'd　Has not been unravell'd ;
To speculate much on the point were too curious,
If the climate he reach'd were serene or sulphureous.
To be sure in his balance-sheet all must declare
One item—the Page—was an awkward affair ;
But *per contra*, he'd lately endow'd a new Chantry
For Priests, with ten marks, and the run of the pantry.

Be that as it may,   It's sufficient to say
That his tomb in the chancel stands there to this day,
Built of Bethersden marble—a dark bluish grey.
The figure, a fine one of pure alabaster,
Some cleanly churchwarden has covered with plaster ;
    While some Vandal or Jew,   With a taste for *virtu*,
Has knock'd off his toes, to place, I suppose,
In some Pickwick Museum, with part of his nose ;
    From his belt and his sword   And his *misericorde*
The enamel's been chipp'd out, and never restored ;
His *ci-gît* in old French is inscribed all around,
And his head's in his helm, and his heel's on his hound,
The palms of his hands, as if going to pray,
Are joined and upraised o'er his bosom—But stay !
I forgot that his tomb's not described in the Play !

    *   *   *   *   *

Lady Arundel, now in her own right a Peeress,
Perplexes her noddle with no such nice queries,
But produces in time, to her husband's great joy,
Another remarkably " fine little boy."
    As novel connections   Oft change the affections,
And turn all one's love into different directions,
Now to young " Johnny Newcome " she seems to confine hers,
Neglecting the poor little dear out at dry-nurse ;
    Nay, far worse than that,
    She considers " the brat "
As a bore—fears her husband may smell out a rat.
    For her legal adviser   She takes an old Miser,
A sort of " poor cousin."   She might have been wiser ;
    For this arrant deceiver,   By name Maurice Beevor,
A shocking old scamp, should her own issue fail,
By the law of the land stands the next in entail ;
So, as soon as she ask'd him to hit on some plan
To provide for her eldest, away the rogue ran
To that self-same unprincipled sea-faring man ;
In his ear whisper'd low . . .—" Bully Gaussen " said " Done !—
I Burked the papa, now I'll Bishop the son ! "
    'Twas agreed ;· and, with speed
    To accomplish the deed,
He adopted a scheme he was sure would succeed.

By long cock-and-bull stories   Of Candish and Noreys,
Of Drake, and bold Raleigh, (then fresh in his glories,
Acquired 'mongst the Indians, and Rapparee Tories,)
  He so work'd on the lad,   That he left, which was bad,
The only true friend in the world that he had,
Father Onslow, a priest, though to quit him most loth,
Who in childhood had furnish'd his pap and his broth,
At no small risk of scandal, indeed to his cloth.

  The kidnapping crimp   Took the foolish young imp
On board of his cutter so trim and so jimp,
Then, seizing him just as you'd handle a shrimp,
Twirl'd him thrice in the air with a whirligig motion,
And soused him at once neck and heels in the ocean ;
  This was off Plymouth Sound,
  And he must have been drown'd,
For 'twas nonsense to think he could swim to dry ground,
  If " A very great Warman,   Call'd Billy the Norman,"
Had not just at that moment sail'd by, outward bound.
  A shark of great size,   With his great glassy eyes,
Sheer'd off as he came, and relinquish'd the prize ;
So he pick'd up the lad,* swabb'd, and dry-rubb'd, and mopp'd
    him,
And, having no children, resolv'd to adopt him.

  Full many a year   Did he hand, reef, and steer,
And by no means consider'd himself as small beer,
When old Norman at length died and left him his frigate,
With lots of pistoles in his coffer to rig it.
  A sailor ne'er moans ;   So, consigning the bones
Of his friend to the locker of one Mr. Jones,
  For England he steers.—On the voyage it appears
That he rescued a maid from the Dey of Algiers ;

  * An incident very like one in Jack Sheppard—
    A work some have lauded, and others have pepper'd—
    Where a Dutch pirate kidnaps, and tosses Thames Darrel
    Just so in the sea, and he's saved by a barrel,—
    On the coast, if I recollect rightly, it's flung whole,
    And the hero, half-drown'd, scrambles out of the bung-hole.
[It aint no sich thing !—the hero aint bung'd in no barrel at all.—He's picked up by a
Captain, just as Norman was afterwards.—Print. Dev.]

And at length reached the Sussex coast, where, in a bay,
Not a great way from Brighton, most cosey-ly lay
His vessel at anchor, the very same day
That the Poet begins,—thus commencing his play :

Act I.

Giles Gaussen accosts old Sir Maurice de Beevor,
And puts the poor Knight in a deuce of a fever,
By saying the boy, whom he took out to please him,
Is come back a Captain on purpose to tease him.—
Sir Maurice, who gladly would see Mr. Gaussen
Breaking stones on the highway, or sweeping a crossing,
Dissembles—observes, It's of no use to fret,—
And hints he may find some more work for him yet ;
Then calls at the castle, and tells Lady A.
That the boy they had ten years ago sent away
Is return'd a grown man, and, to come to the point,
Will put her son Percy's nose clean out of joint ;
But adds, that herself she no longer need vex,
If she'll buy him (Sir Maurice) a farm near the Ex.
" Oh ! take it," she cries ; " but secure every document."—
" A bargain," says Maurice,—" including the stock you meant ? "

The Captain, meanwhile,   With a lover-like smile,
And a fine cambric handkerchief, wipes off the tears
From Miss Violet's eyelash, and hushes her fears.
(That's the Lady he saved from the Dey of Algiers.)
Now arises a delicate point, and this is it—
The young Lady herself is but down on a visit.
   She's perplexed ; and in fact,
   Does not know how to act.
It's her very first visit—and then to begin
By asking a stranger—a gentleman, in—
One with mustaches too—and a tuft on his chin—
   She " really don't know—   He had much better go,"—
Here the Countess steps in from behind, and says " No !—
Fair sir, you are welcome.   Do, pray, stop and dine—
You will take our pot-luck—and we've decentish wine."
He bows, looks at Miss,—and he does not decline.

He rescued a maid from the Dey of Algiers

Act II.

After dinner, the Captain recounts, with much glee,
All he's heard, seen, and done since he first went to sea,
   All his perils and scrapes,
   And his hair-breadth escapes,
Talks of boa-constrictors, and lions, and apes,
And fierce " Bengal Tigers," like that which, you know,
If you've ever seen any respectable " Show,"
" Carried off the unfortunate Mr. Munro."
Then, diverging a while, he adverts to the mystery
Which hangs, like a cloud, o'er his own private history—
How he ran off to sea—how they set him afloat
(Not a word, though, of barrel or bung-hole—*See Note*)
   —How he happen'd to meet
   With the Algerine fleet,
And forced them, by sheer dint of arms to retreat,
Thus saving his Violet—(One of his feet
Here just touch'd her toe, and she moved on her seat,)—
   How his vessel was batter'd—
   In short, he so chatter'd,
Now lively, now serious, so ogled and flatter'd,
That the ladies much marvell'd a person should be able
To " make himself," both said, " so very agreeable."

Captain Norman's adventures were scarcely half done,
When Percy Lord Ashdale, her ladyship's son,
   In a terrible fume,   Bounces into the room,
And talks to his guest as you'd talk to your groom,
Claps his hand on his rapier, and swears he'll be through him—
The Captain does nothing at all but " pooh ! pooh ! " him.
   Unable to smother   His hate of his brother,
He rails at his cousin, and blows up his mother.—
" Fie ! fie ! " says the first.—Says the latter, " In sooth,
This is sharper by far than a keen serpent's tooth ! "
(A remark, by the way, which King Lear had made years ago,
When he ask'd for his Knights, and his Daughter said " Here's a go ")
   This made Ashdale ashamed ;
   But he must not be blamed
Too much for his warmth, for, like many young fellows, he
Was apt to lose temper when tortur'd by jealousy.

Still speaking quite gruff,   He goes off in a huff ;
Lady A., who is now what some call " up to snuff,"
     Straight determines to patch
     Up a clandestine match
Between the Sea-Captain she dreads like Old Scratch,
And Miss,—whom she does not think any great catch
For Ashdale ; besides, he won't kick up such shindies
Were she once fairly married and off to the Indies.

Act III.

Miss Violet takes from the Countess her tone ;
She agrees to meet Norman " by moonlight alone,"
     And slip off to his bark,   " The night being dark,"
Though " the moon," the Sea-Captain says, rises in Heaven
" One hour before midnight," *i.e.*, at eleven.
     From which speech I infer,—
     Though perhaps I may err—
That, though weatherwise, doubtless, 'midst surges and surf, he
When " capering on shore " was by no means a Murphy.

He starts off, however, at sunset, to reach
An old chapel in ruins, that stands on the beach,
Where the Priest is to bring, as he's promised by letter, a
Paper to prove his name, " birthright," &c.
     Being rather too late,   Gaussen, lying in wait,
Gives poor Father Onslow a knock on the pate,
But bolts, seeing Norman, before he has wrested
From the hand of the Priest, as Sir Maurice requested,
The marriage certificate duly attested.—
Norman kneels by the clergyman fainting and gory,
And begs he won't die till he's told him his story ;
     The Father complies,   Re-opens his eyes,
And tells him all how and about it—and dies !

Act IV.

Norman, now call'd Le Mesnil, instructed of all,
Goes back, though it's getting quite late for a call,
Hangs his hat and his cloak on a peg in the hall,
And tells the proud Countess it's useless to smother
The fact any longer—he knows she's his Mother !

His Pa's wedded Spouse,— She questions his *vous*,
And threatens to have him turn'd out of the house.—
    He still perseveres, Till, in spite of her fears,
She admits he's the son she had cast off for years,
And he gives her the papers " all blister'd with tears,"
When Ashdale, who chances his nose in to poke,
    Takes his hat and his cloak, Just as if in a joke,
Determined to put in his wheel a new spoke,
And slips off thus disguis'd, when he sees by the dial it
's time for the rendezvous fixed with Miss Violet.—
—Captain Norman, who, after all, feels rather sore
At his mother's reserve, vows to see her no more,
Rings the bell for the servant to open the door,
And leaves his Mamma in a fit on the floor.

Act V.

Now comes the catastrophe !—Ashdale, who's wrapt in
The cloak with the hat and the plume of the Captain,
Leads Violet down through the grounds to the chapel
Where Gaussen's conceal'd—he springs forward to grapple
The man he's erroneously led to suppose
Captain Norman himself by the cut of his clothes.
    In the midst of their strife, And just as the knife
Of the Pirate is raised to deprive him of life, ·
The Captain comes forward, drawn there by the squeals
Of the Lady, and, knocking Giles head over heels,
    Fractures his " nob," Saves the hangman a job,
And executes justice most strictly, the rather,
'Twas the spot where that rascal had murder'd his father.
    Then in comes the mother, Who, finding one brother
Had the instant before saved the life of the other,
    Explains the whole case. Ashdale puts a good face
On the matter ; and, since he's obliged to give place,
Yields his coronet up with a pretty good grace ;
Norman vows he won't have it—the kinsmen embrace,—
And the Captain, the first in this generous race,
    To remove every handle For gossip and scandal,
Sets the whole of the papers alight with the candle ;
An arrangement takes place—on the very same night, all
Is settled and done, and the points the most vital

o

Are, N. takes the personals ;—A., in requital,
Keeps the whole real property, Mansion, and Title.—
V. falls to the share of the Captain, and tries a
Sea-voyage, as a Bride, in the " Royal Eliza."—
Both are pleased with the part they acquire as joint heirs,
And old Maurice Beevor is bundled down stairs !

MORAL.

The public, perhaps, with the drama might quarrel
If deprived of all epilogue, prologue, and moral ;
This may serve for all three then :—

            " Young Ladies of property,
Let Lady A.'s history serve as a stopper t'ye ;
Don't wed with low people beneath your degree,
And if you've a baby, don't send it to sea !

" Young Noblemen ! shun every thing like a brawl ;
And be sure when you dine out, or go to a ball,
Don't take the best hat that you find in the hall,
And leave one in its stead that worth's nothing at all !

" Old Knights, don't give bribes !—above all, never urge a man
To steal people's things, or to stick an old Clergyman !

" And you, ye Sea-Captains ! who've nothing to do
But to run round the world, fight, and drink till all's blue,
And tell us tough yarns, and then swear they are true,
Reflect, notwithstanding your sea-faring life,
That you can't get on well long, without you've a wife ;
So get one at once, treat her kindly and gently,
Write a nautical novel,—and send it to Bentley ! "

It has been already hinted that Mr..Peters had been a " traveller " in his day. The only
story which his lady would ever allow " her P." to finish—he began as many as would furnish
an additional volume to the " Thousand and One Nights "—is the last I shall offer. The
subject, I fear me, is not over new, but will remind my friends

        " Of something better they have seen before."

Mr. Peters's Story

The Bagman's Dog

Stant littore Puppies !—Virgil.

It was a litter, a litter of five,
Four are drown'd and one left alive,
He was thought worthy alone to survive ;
And the Bagman resolved upon bringing him up,
To eat of his bread, and to drink of his cup,
He was such a dear little cock-tail'd pup !

The Bagman taught him many a trick ;
He would carry, and fetch, and run after a stick,
   Could well understand   The word of command,
   And appear to doze   With a crust on his nose
Till the Bagman permissively waved his hand :
Then to throw up and catch it he never would fail,
As he sat up on end, on his little cock-tail.
Never was puppy so *bien instruit*,
Or possess'd of such natural talent as he ;
   And as he grew older,   Every beholder
Agreed he grew handsomer, sleeker, and bolder.—

Time, however his wheels we may clog,
Wends steadily still with onward jog,
And the cock-tail'd puppy's a curly-tail'd dog !
   When, just at the time   He was reaching his prime,
And all thought he'd be turning out something sublime,
   One unlucky day,   How, no one could say,
Whether soft *liaison* induced him to stray,
Or some kidnapping vagabond coax'd him away,

211

He was lost to the view,   Like the morning dew ;—
He had been, and was not—that's all that they knew !
And the Bagman storm'd, and the Bagman swore
As never a Bagman had sworn before ;
But storming or swearing but little avails
To recover lost dogs with great curly tails.—

In a large paved court, close by Billiter Square,
Stands a mansion, old, but in thorough repair,
The only thing strange, from the general air
Of its size and appearance, is how it got there ;
In front is a short semicircular stair
    Of stone steps,—some half score,—
    Then you reach the ground floor,
With a shell-pattern'd architrave over the door.
It is spacious, and seems to be built on the plan
Of a Gentleman's house in the reign of Queen Anne ;
    Which is odd, for, although,   As we very well know,
Under Tudors and Stuarts the City could show
Many Noblemen's seats above Bridge and below,
Yet that fashion soon after induced them to go
From St. Michael, Cornhill, and St. Mary-le-Bow,
To St. James, and St. George, and St. Anne in Soho.—
Be this as it may,—at the date I assign
To my tale,—that's about Seventeen Sixty Nine,—
This mansion, now rather upon the decline,
Had less dignified owners,—belonging, in fine,
To Turner, Dry, Weipersyde, Rogers, and Pyne—
A respectable House in the Manchester line.

    There were a score   Of Bagmen, and more,
Who had travell'd full oft for the firm before ;
But just at this period they wanted to send
Some person on whom they could safely depend—
A trustworthy body, half agent, half friend—
On some mercantile matter, as far as Ostend ;
And the person they pitch'd on was Anthony Blogg,
A grave, steady man, not addicted to grog,—
The Bagman, in short, who had lost this great dog.

                *   *   *   *   *

"The Sea ! the Sea ! the open Sea !
That is the place where we all wish to be,
Rolling about on it merrily ! "—
  So all sing and say   By night and by day,
In the *boudoir*, the street, at the concert, and play,
In a sort of coxcombical roundelay ;—
You may roam through the City, transversely or straight,
From Whitechapel turnpike to Cumberland gate,
And every young Lady who thrums a guitar,
Ev'ry mustachio'd Shopman who smokes a cigar,
  With affected devotion,   Promulgates his notion,
Of being a " Rover " and " child of the Ocean "—
Whate'er their age, sex, or condition may be,
They all of them long for the " Wide, Wide Sea ! "
  But, however they dote,   Only send them afloat
In any craft bigger at all than a boat,
  Take them down to the Nore,
  And you'll see that before
The " Wessel " they " Woyage " in has made half her way
Between Shell-Ness Point and the pier at Herne Bay,
Let the wind meet the tide in the slightest degree,
They'll be all of them heartily sick of " the Sea ! "

       *   *   *   *   *

I've stood in Margate, on a bridge of size
  Inferior far to that described by Byron,
Where " palaces and pris'ns on each hand rise."—
  —That too's a stone one, this is made of iron—
  And little donkey-boys your steps environ,
Each proffering for your choice his tiny hack,
  Vaunting its excellence ; and, should you hire one,
For sixpence, will he urge, with frequent thwack,
The much-enduring beast to Buenos Ayres—and back

And there, on many a raw and gusty day,
  I've stood, and turn'd my gaze upon the pier,
And seen the crews, that did embark so gay
  That self-same morn, now disembark so queer ;
  Then to myself I've sigh'd and said, " Oh dear !
Who would believe yon sickly-looking man's a
  London Jack Tar,—a Cheapside Buccaneer ! "—

But hold, my Muse !—for this terrific stanza
Is all too stiffly grand for our Extravaganza.

　　　*　　　　*　　　　*　　　　*

" So now we'll go up, up, up,
　And now we'll go down, down, down,
And now we'll go backwards and forwards,
　And now we'll go roun', roun,' roun'."—
—I hope you've sufficient discernment to see,
Gentle Reader, that here the discarding the *d*
Is a fault which you must not attribute to me ;
Thus my Nurse cut it off when, " with counterfeit glee,"
She sung, as she danced me about on her knee,
In the year of our Lord eighteen hundred and three :—
All I mean to say is, that the Muse is now free
From the self-imposed trammels put on by her betters,
And no longer like Filch, midst the felons and debtors
At Drury Lane, dances her hornpipe in fetters.
　Resuming her track,　At once she goes back
To our hero, the Bagman—Alas ! and Alack !
　Poor Anthony Blogg　Is as sick as a dog,
Spite of sundry unwonted potations of grog,
By the time the Dutch packet is fairly at sea,
With the sands called the Goodwins a league on her lee.

And now, my good friends, I've a fine opportunity
To obfuscate you all by sea terms with impunity,
　And talking of " caulking,"　And " quarter deck walking,"
　" Fore and aft,"　And " abaft,"·
" Hookers," " barkeys," and " craft,"
(At which Mr. Poole has so wickedly laught),
Of binnacles,—bilboes,—the boom call'd the spanker,
The best bower cable,—the jib,—and sheet anchor ;
Of lower-deck guns,—and of broadsides and chases,
Of taffrails and topsails, and splicing main-braces,
And " Shiver my timbers ! " and other odd phrases
Employ'd by old pilots with hard-featured faces ;
Of the expletives sea-faring Gentlemen use,
The allusions they make to the eyes of their crews ;—
　How the Sailors, too, swear,
　How they cherish their hair,
And what very long pigtails a great many wear.—

But, Reader, I scorn it—the fact is, I fear,
To be candid, I can't make these matters so clear
As Marryat, or Cooper, or Captain Chamier,
Or Sir E. Lytton Bulwer, who brought up the rear
Of the " Nauticals," just at the end of the year
Eighteen thirty-nine—(how Time flies !—Oh dear !)—
With a well-written preface, to make it appear
That his play, the " Sea Captain," 's by no means small beer ;
There !—" brought up the rear "—you see there's a mistake,
Which none of the authors I've mentioned would make,
I ought to have said, that he " sail'd in their wake."—
So I'll merely observe, as the water grew rougher,
The more my poor hero continued to suffer,
Till the Sailors themselves cried in pity, " Poor Buffer ! "

　　Still rougher it grew,　And still harder it blew,
And the thunder kick'd up such a halliballoo,
That even the Skipper began to look blue ;
　　While the crew, who were few,　Look'd very queer, too,
And seem'd not to know what exactly to do,
And they who'd charge of them wrote in the logs
" Wind N.E.—blows a hurricane—rains cats and dogs."
In short it soon grew to a tempest as rude as
That Shakspeare describes near the " still vext Bermudas," *
　　When the winds, in their sport,
　　Drove aside from its port
The King's ship, with the whole Neapolitan Court,
And swamp'd it to give " the King's Son, Ferdinand," a
Soft moment or two with the Lady Miranda,
While her Pa met the rest, and severely rebuked 'em
For unhandsomely doing him out of his Dukedom.
You don't want me, however, to paint you a Storm,
As so many have done, and in colours so warm ;
Lord Byron, for instance, in manner facetious,
Mr. Ainsworth more gravely,—see also Lucretius,
—A writer who gave me no trifling vexation
When a youngster at school on Dean Colet's foundation.—
　　Suffice it to say　That the whole of that day,
And the next, and the next, they were scudding away
　　Quite out of their course,　Propell'd by the force

* See Appendix, page 226.

Of those flatulent folks known in Classical story as
Aquilo, Libs, Notus, Auster, and Boreas,
   Driven quite at their mercy
   'Twixt Guernsey and Jersey,
Till at length they came bump on the rocks and the shallows,
In West longitude, One, fifty-seven, near St. Maloes :
   There you'll not be surprised]
   That the vessel capsized,
Or that Blogg, who had made, from intestine commotions,
His specifical gravity less than the Ocean's,
   Should go floating away,   Midst the surges and spray,
Like a cork in the gutter, which, swoln by a shower,
Runs down Holborn-hill about nine knots an hour.

You've seen, I've no doubt, at Bartholomew fair,
Gentle Reader,—that is, if you've ever been there,—
With their hands tied behind them, some two or three pair
Of boys round a bucket set up on a chair,
   Skipping, and dipping   Eyes, nose, chin, and lip in,
Their faces and hair with the water all dripping,
In an anxious attempt to catch hold of a pippin,
That bobs up and down in the water whenever
They touch it, as mocking the fruitless endeavour ;
Exactly as Poets say,—how, though, they can't tell us,—
Old Nick's Nonpareils play at bob with poor Tantalus.
   Stay !—I'm not clear,   But I'm rather out here ;
'Twas the water itself that slipp'd from him, I fear ;
Faith, I can't recollect—and I haven't Lempriere.—
No matter,—poor Blogg went on ducking and bobbing,
Sneezing out the salt water, and gulping and sobbing,
Just as Clarence, in Shakspeare, describes all the qualms he
Experienced while dreaming they'd drown'd him in Malmsey.

" O Lord," he thought, " what pain it was to drown ! "
   And saw great fishes with great goggling eyes,
Glaring as he was bobbing up and down,
   And looking as they thought him quite a prize ;
When as he sank, and all was growing dark,
A something seized him with its jaws !—A shark ?—

No such thing, Reader ;—most opportunely for Blogg,
'Twas a very large, web-footed, curly-tail'd Dog !
        *   *   *   *   *

Poor Blogg went on bobbing and ducking

I'm not much of a trav'ler, and really can't boast
That I know a great deal of the Brittany coast,
   But I've often heard say That e'en to this day,
The people of Granville, St. Maloes, and thereabout
Are a class that society doesn't much care about ;
Men who gain their subsistence by contraband dealing,
And a mode of abstraction strict people call " stealing ; "
Notwithstanding all which, they are civil of speech,
Above all to a stranger who comes within reach ;
   And they were so to Blogg, When the curly-tail'd dog
At last dragg'd him out, high and dry on the beach.
   But we all have been told, By the proverb of old,
By no means to think " all that glitters is gold ; "
   And, in fact, some advance That most people in France
Join the manners and airs of a *Maître de Danse*
To the morals—(as Johnson of Chesterfield said)—
Of an elderly Lady, in Babylon bred,
Much addicted to flirting, and dressing in red.—
   Be this as it might, It embarrass'd Blogg quite
To find those about him so very polite.

A suspicious observer perhaps might have traced
The *petites soins*, tendered with so much good taste,
To the sight of an old-fashion'd pocket-book, placed
In a black leather belt well secured round his waist,
And a ring set with diamonds, his finger that graced,
So brilliant, no one could have guess'd they were paste.
   The group on the shore Consisted of four ;
You will wonder, perhaps, there were not a few more ;
But the fact is they've not, in that part of the nation,
What Malthus would term a " too dense population,"
Indeed the sole sign there of man's habitation
   Was merely a single Rude hut, in a dingle
That led away inland direct from the shingle,
Its sides clothed with underwood, gloomy and dark,
Some two hundred yards above high-water mark ;
   And thither the party, So cordial and hearty,
Viz., an old man, his wife, and two lads, made a start, he,
   The Bagman, proceeding, With equal good breeding,
To express in indifferent French, all he feels,
The great curly-tail'd Dog keeping close to his heels.—

They soon reach'd the hut, which seem'd partly in ruin,
All the way bowing, chattering, shrugging, *Mon-Dieu*-ing,
Grimacing, and what sailors call *parley-vooing*.

*   *   *   *   *

Is it Paris, or Kitchener, Reader, exhorts
You, whenever your stomach's at all out of sorts,
To try, if you find richer viands won't stop in it,
A basin of good mutton broth with a chop in it ?
(Such a basin and chop as I once heard a witty one
Call, at the Garrick, " a c—d Committee one,"
An expression, I own, I do not think a pretty one.)
   However, it's clear   That, with sound table beer,
Such a mess as I speak of is very good cheer ;
   Especially too   When a person's wet through,
And is hungry, and tired, and don't know what to do.
Now just such a mess of delicious hot pottage
Was smoking away when they enter'd the cottage,
And casting a truly delicious perfume
Through the whole of an ugly, old, ill-furnish'd room ;
   " Hot, smoking hot,"   On the fire was a pot
Well replenish'd, but really I can't say with what ;
For, famed as the French always are for ragouts,
No creature can tell what they put in their stews,
Whether bull-frogs, old gloves, or old wigs, or old shoes ;
Notwithstanding, when offer'd I rarely refuse,
Any more than poor Blogg did, when, seeing the reeky
Repast placed before him, scarce able to speak, he
In ecstasy mutter'd " By Jove, Cockey-leeky ! "
   In an instant, as soon   As they gave him a spoon,
Every feeling and faculty bent on the gruel, he
No more blamed Fortune for treating him cruelly,
But fell tooth and nail on the soup and the *bouilli*.

*   *   *   *   *

Meanwhile that old man standing by,
Subducted his long coat-tails on high,
With his back to the fire, as if to dry
A part of his dress which the watery sky
Had visited rather inclemently.—
Blandly he smil'd, but still he look'd sly,
And a something sinister lurk'd in his eye.

Indeed, had you seen him his maritime dress in,
You'd have own'd his appearance was not prepossessing ;
He'd a " dreadnought " coat, and heavy *sabots*
With thick wooden soles turn'd up at the toes,
His nether man cased in a striped *quelque chose*,
And a hump on his back, and a great hook'd nose,
So that nine out of ten would be led to suppose
That the person before them was Punch in plain clothes.

Yet still, as I told you, he smiled on all present,
And did all that lay in his power to look pleasant.
    The old woman, too,   Made a mighty ado,
Helping her guest to a deal of the stew ;
She fish'd up the meat, and she help'd him to that,
She help'd him to lean, and she help'd him to fat,
And it look'd like Hare—but it might have been Cat.
The little *garçons* too strove to express
Their sympathy towards the " Child of distress "
With a great deal of juvenile French *politesse ;*
    But the Bagman bluff   Continued to " stuff "
Of the fat, and the lean, and the tender and tough,
Till they thought he would never cry " Hold, enough ! "
And the old woman's tones became far less agreeable,
Sounding like *peste !* and *sacré !* and *diable !*

I've seen an old saw, which is well worth repeating,
That says,
            " 𝕮𝖔𝖔𝖉 𝕰𝖆𝖙𝖞𝖓𝖌𝖊
𝕯𝖊𝖘𝖊𝖗𝖛𝖊𝖙𝖍 𝖌𝖔𝖔𝖉 𝕯𝖗𝖞𝖓𝖐𝖞𝖓𝖌𝖊."
You'll find it so printed by 𝕮𝖆𝖝𝖙𝖔𝖓 or 𝖂𝖞𝖓𝖐𝖞𝖓,
And a very good proverb it is to my thinking.
    Blogg thought so too ;—   As he finish'd his stew,
His ear caught the sound of the word " *Morbleu !* "
Pronounced by the old woman under her breath.
Now, not knowing what she could mean by " Blue Death ! "
He conceiv'd she referr'd to a delicate brewing
Which is almost synonymous,—namely, " Blue Ruin."
So he pursed up his lip to a smile, and with glee,
In his cockneyfy'd accent, responded, " Oh, *Vee !* "
    Which made her understand he
    Was asking for brandy ;
So she turn'd to the cupboard, and having some handy,

Produced, rightly deeming he would not object to it,
An orbicular bulb with a very long neck to it ;
In fact you perceive her mistake was the same as his,
Each of them " reasoning right from wrong premises ; "—
      —And here by the way,   Allow me to say,
Kind Reader, you sometimes permit me to stray—
'Tis strange the French prove, when they take to aspersing,
So inferior to us in the science of cursing :
      Kick a Frenchman down stairs,
      How absurdly he swears !
And how odd 'tis to hear him when beat to a jelly,
Roar out, in a passion, " Blue Death ! " and " Blue Belly ! "

" To return to our sheep," from this little digression :—
Blogg's features assumed a complacent expression
As he emptied his glass, and she gave him a fresh one ;
      Too little he heeded   How fast they succeeded.
Perhaps you or I might have done, though, as he did ;
For when once Madame Fortune deals out her hard raps,
      It's amazing to think   How one " cottons " to Drink !
At such times, of all things, in nature, perhaps,
There's not one that is half so seducing as *Schnaps*.

Mr. Blogg, besides being uncommonly dry,
Was, like most other Bagmen, remarkably shy,
      —" Did not like to deny "—
      " Felt obliged to comply "
Every time that she ask'd him to " wet t'other eye ; "
For 'twas worthy remark that she spared not the stoup,
Though before she had seem'd so to grudge him the soup.
      At length the fumes rose ₐ To his brain ; and his nose
Gave hints of a strong disposition to doze,
And a yearning to seek " horizontal repose."—
      His queer-looking host,   Who, firm at his post,
During all the long meal had continued to toast
      That garment 'twere rude to   Do more than allude to,
Perceived, from his breathing and nodding, the views
Of his guest were directed to " taking a snooze : "
So he caught up a lamp in his huge dirty paw,
With (as Blogg used to tell it) " *Mounseer, swivvy maw !* "
      And " marshall'd " him so   " The way he should go,"
Upstairs to an attic, large, gloomy, and low,

Without table or chair,   Or a moveable there,
Save an old-fashion'd bedstead, much out of repair,
That stood at the end most remov'd from the stair.—
    With a grin and a shrug   The host points to the rug,
Just as much as to say " There !—I think you'll be snug ! "
    Puts the light on the floor,   Walks to the door,
Makes a formal *Salaam*, and is then seen no more ;
When just as the ear lost the sound of his tread,
To the Bagman's surprise, and, at first, to his dread,
The great curly-tail'd Dog crept from under the bed !—

It's a very nice thing when a man's in a fright,
And thinks matters all wrong, to find matters all right ;
As, for instance, when going home late-ish at night
Through a Churchyard, and seeing a thing all in white,
Which, of course, one is led to consider a Sprite,
    To find that the Ghost   Is merely a post,
Or a miller, or chalky-faced donkey at most ;
Or, when taking a walk as the evenings begin
To close, or, as some people call it, " draw in,"
And some undefined form, " looming large " through the haze,
Presents itself, right in your path, to your gaze,
    Inducing a dread   Of a knock on the head,
Or a sever'd carotid, to find that instead
Of one of those ruffians who murder and fleece men,
It's your uncle, or one of the " Rural Policemen ; "—
Then the blood flows again   Through artery and vein ;
You're delighted with what just before gave you pain ;
You laugh at your fears—and your friend in the fog
Meets a welcome as cordial as Anthony Blogg
Now bestow'd on *his* friend—the great curly-tail'd Dog.

For the Dog leap'd up, and his paws found a place
On each side his neck in a canine embrace,
And he lick'd Blogg's hands, and he lick'd his face,
And he waggled his tail as much as to say,
" Mr. Blogg, we've foregather'd before to-day ! "
And the Bagman saw, as he now sprang up,
    What, beyond all doubt,   He might have found out
Before, had he not been so eager to sup,
'Twas Sancho !—the Dog he had rear'd from a pup !—

The Dog who when sinking had seized his hair,—
The Dog who had saved and conducted him there,—
The Dog he had lost out of Billiter Square ! !

It's passing sweet,   An absolute treat
When friends, long sever'd by distance, meet,—
With what warmth and affection each other they greet .
Especially too, as we very well know,
If there seems any chance of a little *cadeau*,
A " Present from Brighton," or " Token," to show,
In the shape of a work-box, ring, bracelet, or so,
That our friends don't forget us, although they may go
To Ramsgate, or Rome, or Fernando Po.
If some little advantage seems likely to start
From a fifty-pound note to a two-penny tart,
It's surprising to see how it softens the heart,
And you'll find those whose hopes from the other are strongest,
Use, in common, endearments the thickest and longest.
    But it was not so here ;   For, although it is clear,
When abroad, and we have not a single friend near,
E'en a cur that will love us becomes very dear,
And the balance of interest 'twixt him and the Dog
Of course was inclining to Anthony Blogg,
    Yet he, first of all, ceased   To encourage the beast,
Perhaps thinking " Enough is as good as a feast ; "
And besides, as we've said, being sleepy and mellow,
He grew tired of patting, and crying " Poor fellow ! "
So his smile by degrees harden'd into a frown,
And his " That's a good dog ! " into " Down, Sancho, down ! "

But nothing could stop his mute fav'rite's caressing,
Who, in fact, seem'd resolv'd to prevent his undressing,
Using paws, tail, and head,   As if he had said,
" Most beloved of masters, pray, don't go to bed ;
You had much better sit up, and pat me instead ! "
Nay, at last, when determined to take some repose,
Blogg threw himself down on the outside the clothes,
    Spite of all he could do,   The Dog jump'd up too,
And kept him awake with his very cold nose ;
    Scratching and whining,   And moaning and pining,
Till Blogg really believed he must have some design in

Thus breaking his rest ; above all, when at length
The Dog scratch'd him off from the bed by sheer strength.

Extremely annoy'd by the " tarnation whop," as it
's call'd in Kentuck, on his head and its opposite,
   Blogg show'd fight ; When he saw, by the light
Of the flickering candle, that had not yet quite
Burnt down in the socket, though not over bright,
Certain dark-colour'd stains, as of blood newly spilt,
Reveal'd by the dog's having scratch'd off the quilt,—
Which hinted a story of horror and guilt !—
   'Twas " no mistake,"— He was " wide awake "
In an instant ; for, when only decently drunk,
Nothing sobers a man so completely as " funk."

   And hark !—what's that ?— They have got into chat
In the kitchen below—what the deuce are they at ?—
There's the ugly old Fisherman scolding his wife—
And she !—by the Pope ! she's whetting a knife !—
   At each twist Of her wrist,
   And her great mutton fist,
The edge of the weapon sounds shriller and louder !—
   The fierce kitchen fire Had not made Blogg perspire
Half so much, or a dose of the best James's powder.—
It ceases—all's silent !—and now, I declare
There's somebody crawls up that rickety stair.
     *   *   *   *   *
The horrid old ruffian comes, cat-like, creeping ;—
He opens the door just sufficient to peep in,
And sees, as he fancies, the Bagman sleeping !
For Blogg, when he'd once ascertain'd that there was some
" Precious mischief " on foot, had resolv'd to play " 'Possum ; "—
   Down he went, legs and head, Flat on the bed,
Apparently sleeping as sound as the dead ;
While, though none who look'd at him would think such a thing
Every nerve in his frame was braced up for a spring.
   Then, just as the villain Crept, stealthily still, in,
And you'd not have insur'd his guest's life for a shilling,
As the knife gleam'd on high, bright and sharp as a razor,
Blogg, starting upright, " tipped " the fellow " a facer ; "—
—Down went man and weapon—Of all sorts of blows,

From what Mr. Jackson reports, I suppose
There are few that surpass a flush hit on the nose

Now, had I the pen of old Ossian or Homer,
(Though each of these names some pronounce a misnomer,
  And say the first person
  Was call'd James M'Pherson,
While, as to the second, they stoutly declare
He was no one knows who, and born no one knows where,)
Or had I the quill of Pierce Egan, a writer
Acknowledged the best theoretical fighter
  For the last twenty years, By the lively young Peers,
Who, doffing their coronets, collars, and ermine, treat
Boxers to " Max," at the One Tun in Jermyn Street ;—
—I say, could I borrow these Gentlemen's Muses,
More skill'd than my meek one in " fibbings " and bruises,
  I'd describe now to you As " prime a Set-to,"
And " regular turn-up," as ever you knew ;
Not inferior in " bottom " to aught you have read of,
Since Cribb, years ago, half knock'd Molyneux' head off.
But my dainty Urania says, " Such things are shocking ! "
  Lace mittens She loves, Detesting " The Gloves ; "
And turning, with air most disdainfully mocking,
From Melpomene's buskin, adopts the silk stocking.
  So, as far as I can see, I must leave you to " fancy "
The thumps, and the bumps, and the ups and the downs,
And the taps, and the slaps, and the raps on the crowns,
That pass'd 'twixt the Husband, Wife, Bagman, and Dog,
As Blogg roll'd over them, and they roll'd over Blogg ;
  While what's called " The Claret "
  Flew over the garret :
  Merely stating the fact, As each other they whack'd,
The Dog his old master most gallantly back'd ;
Making both the *garçons*, who came running in, sheer off,
With " Hippolyte's " thumb, and " Alphonse's " left ear off
  Next, making a stoop on The buffeting group on
The floor, rent in tatters the old woman's *jupon ;*
Then the old man turn'd up, and a fresh bite of Sancho's
Tore out the whole seat of his striped Calimancoes.—
  Really, which way This desperate fray
Might have ended at last, I'm not able to say,

The dog keeping thus the assassins at bay :
But a few fresh arrivals decided the day ;
　For bounce went the door,　In came half a score
Of the passengers, sailors, and one or two more
Who had aided the party in gaining the shore !

It's a great many years ago—mine then were few—
Since I spent a short time in the old *Courageux* ;　·
　I think that they say　She had been, in her day,
A First-rate,—but was then what they term a *Rasée*,—
And they took me on board in the Downs where she lay.
(Captain Wilkinson held the command, by the way.)
In her I pick'd up, on that single occasion,
The little I know that concerns Navigation,
And obtained, *inter alia*, some vague information
Of a practice which often, in cases of robbing,
Is adopted on shipboard—I think it's called " Cobbing."
How it's managed exactly I really can't say,
But I think that a Boot-jack is brought into play—
That is, if I'm right :—it exceeds my ability
　To tell how 'tis done ;　But the system is one
Of which Sancho's exploit would increase the facility.
And, from all I can learn, I'd much rather be robb'd
Of the little I have in my purse, than be " cobb'd ; "—
　That's mere matter of taste :
　But the Frenchman was placed—
I mean the old scoundrel whose actions we've traced—
In such a position, that, on this unmasking,
His consent was the last thing the men thought of asking.
　The old woman, too,　Was obliged to go through,
With her boys, the rough discipline used by the crew,
Who, before they let one of the set see the back of them,
" Cobb'd " the whole party,—ay, " every man Jack of tham."

Moral.

And now, Gentle Reader, before that I say
Farewell for the present, and wish you good day,
Attend to the moral I draw from my lay !

If ever you travel, like Anthony Blogg,　　‘
Be wary of strangers !—don't take too much grog !—

And don't fall asleep, if you should, like a hog !—
Above all—carry with you a curly-tail'd Dog !

Lastly, don't act like Blogg, who, I say it with blushing,
Sold Sancho next month for two guineas at Flushing ;
But still on these words of the Bard keep a fix'd eye,
    Ingratum si dixeris, omnia dixti ! ! !

L'Envoye.

I felt so disgusted with Blogg, from sheer shame of him,
I never once thought to inquire what became of him
If *you* want to know, Reader, the way, I opine,
    To achieve your design,—
    —Mind, it's no wish of mine,—
Is,—(a penny will do't,)—by addressing a line
To Turner, Dry, Weipersyde, Rogers, and Pyne.

APPENDIX.*

Since penning this stanza, a learn'd Antiquary
Has put my poor Muse in no trifling quandary,
By writing an essay to prove that he knows a
    Spot which, in truth, is   The *real* " Bermoothes,"
In the Mediterranean,—now called Lampedosa ;
—For proofs, having made, as he farther alleges, stir,
An entry was found in the old Parish Register,
The which at his instance the excellent Vicar ex-
tracted : viz., " Caliban, base son of Sycorax."
    —He had rather, by half,
    Have found Prospero's " Staff ; "
But 'twas useless to dig, for the want of a pick or axe
Colonel Pasley, however, 'tis everywhere said,
Now he's blown up the old Royal George at Spithead,
And the great cliff at Dover, of which we've all read,
Takes his whole apparatus, and goes out to look
And see if he can't try and blow up " the Book."
—Gentle Reader, farewell !—If I add one more line,
" He'll be, in all likelihood, blowing up *mine !* "

       * See page 215.

𝔖econd 𝔖eries

To Richard Bentley, Esq.

My DEAR SIR,

You tell me that a " generous and enlightened Public " has given a favourable reception to those extracts from our family papers, which, at your suggestion, were laid before it some two years since ;—and you hint, with all possible delicacy, that a second volume might not be altogether unacceptable at a period of the year when " auld warld stories " are more especially in request. With all my heart,—the old oak chest is not yet empty ; in addition to which, I have recently laid my hand upon a long MS. correspondence of my great-uncle, Sir Peregrine Ingoldsby, a cadet of the family, who somehow contrived to attract the notice of George the Second, and received from his " honour-giving hand " the *accolade* of knighthood. To this last-named source I am indebted for several of the accompanying histories, while my inestimable friend Simpkinson has bent all the powers of his mighty mind to the task. From Father John's stores I have drawn largely. Our " Honourable " friend Sucklethumbkin—by the way, he has been beating our covers lately, when he shot a woodcock, and one of the Governor's pointers—gives a graphic account of the Operatic " row " in which he was heretofore so conspicuous ; while even Mrs. Barney Maguire (*née Mademoiselle Pauline*), whose horror of Mrs. Botherby's cap has no jot diminished, furnishes me with the opening Legend of the series from the *historiettes* of her own *belle France*.

Why will you not run down to Tappington this Christmas ?—We have been rather busy of late in carrying into execution the enclosure of Swingfield Minnis under the auspices of my Lord Radnor, and Her Majesty's visit to the neighbourhood has kept us quite alive : the Prince in one of his rides pulled up at the end of the avenue, and, as A—— told Sucklethumbkin, was much taken with the picturesque appearance of our old gable-ends. Unluckily we were all at Canterbury that morning, or proud indeed should we have been to offer his Royal Highness the humble hospitalities of the Hall—and then—fancy Mrs. Botherby's —" My Gracious ! " By the way, the old lady tells me you left your

227

night-cap here on your last visit ; it is laid up in lavender for you ;—
come and reclaim it. The Yule log will burn bright as ever in the
cedar room. Bin No. 6 is still one liquid ruby—the old October yet
smiles like mantling amber, in utter disdain of that vile concoction
of camomile which you so pseudonymously dignify with the title of
" Bitter Ale." Make a start, then :—pitch printers'-ink to old Harry,—
and come and spend a fortnight with

Yours, till the crack of doom,
THOMAS INGOLDSBY.

Tappington Everard,
Dec. 16th, 1842.

The Black Mousquetaire

A Legend of France

FRANÇOIS XAVIER AUGUSTE was a gay Mousquetaire,
The Pride of the Camp, the delight of the Fair :
He'd a mien so *distingué*, and so *débonnaire*,
And shrugg'd with a grace so *recherché* and rare,
And he twirl'd his mustache with so charming an air,
—His mustaches I should say, because he'd a pair,—
And, in short, show'd so much of the true *sçavoir faire*,
All the ladies in Paris were wont to declare,
    That could any one draw
    Them from Dian's strict law,
Into what Mrs. Ramsbottom calls a " Fox Paw,"
It would be François Xavier Auguste de St. Foix.

    Now, I'm sorry to say,   At that time of day,
The Court of Versailles was a little too gay ;
The Courtiers were all much addicted to Play,
To Bordeaux, Chambertin, Frontignac, St. Peray,
    Lafitte, Château Margaux,   And Sillery (a cargo
On which John Bull sensibly (?) lays an embargo),
    While Louis Quatorze   Kept about him, in scores,
What the Noblesse, in courtesy, term'd his " Jane Shores "
—They were call'd by a much coarser name out of doors—
    This, we all must admit, in   A King's not befitting !

For such courses, when followed by persons of quality,
Are apt to detract on the score of morality. ·

François Xavier Auguste acted much like the rest of them,
Dress'd, drank, and fought, and *chassée*'d with the best of them ;

HE WOULD THEN SALLY OUT IN THE STREETS FOR "A SPREE"

Took his *œil de perdrix*   Till he scarcely could see,
He would then sally out in the streets for " a spree ; "
   His rapier he'd draw,   Pink a *Bourgeois*,
(A word which the English translate " Johnny Raw,")
For your thorough French Courtier, whenever the fit he's in
Thinks it prime fun to astonish a citizen ;

And, perhaps it's no wonder that this kind of scrapes,
In a nation which Voltaire, in one of his japes,
Defines " an amalgam of Tigers and Apes,"
Should be merely considered as " Little Escapes."
   But I'm sorry to add,   Things are almost as bad
A great deal nearer home, and that similar pranks
Amongst young men who move in the very first ranks,
Are by no means confined to the land of the Franks.

Be this as it will,   In the general, still,
   Though blame him we must,   It is really but just
To our lively young friend, François Xavier Auguste,
   To say, that howe'er   Well known his faults were,
At his Bacchanal parties he always drank fair,
And, when gambling his worst, always play'd on the square,
So that, being much more of pigeon than rook, he
Lost large sums at faro (a game like " Blind Hookey "),
   And continued to lose,   And to give I O U's,
Till he lost e'en the credit he had with the Jews ;
And, a parallel if I may venture to draw
Between François Xavier Auguste de St. Foix,
And his namesake, a still more distinguished François,
   Who wrote to his " *sœur* " *   From Pavia, " *Mon cœur,*
I have lost all I had in the world *fors l'honneur.*"
   So St. Foix might have wrote   No dissimilar note,
" *Vive la bagatelle !—toujours gai—idem semper—*
I've lost all I had in the world but—my temper ! "
   From the very beginning,   Indeed, of his sinning,
His air was so cheerful, his manners so winning,
That once he prevailed—or his friends coin the tale for him—
On the bailiff who " nabbed " him, himself to " go bail " for him.

Well—we know in these cases
   Your " Crabs " and " Deuce Aces "
Are wont to promote frequent changes of places ;

---

* Mrs. Ingoldsby, who is deeply read in Robertson, informs me that this is a mistake ; that the lady to whom this memorable *billet* was delivered by the hands of Pennalosa, was the unfortunate monarch's mamma, and not his sister. I would gladly rectify the error, but then,—what am I to do for a rhyme ?—On the whole, I fear I must content myself, like Talleyrand, with admitting that " it is worse than a fault—it's a blunder ! " for which enormity—as honest old Pepys says when he records having kissed his cookmaid—" I humbly beg pardon of Heaven, and Mrs. Ingoldsby ! "

Town doctors, indeed, are most apt to declare
That there's nothing so good as the pure " country air,"
Whenever exhaustion of person, or purse, in
An invalid cramps him, and sets him a-cursing :
A habit, I'm very much grieved at divulging,
François Xavier Auguste was too prone to indulge in.
   But what could be done ? It's clear as the sun,
That, though nothing's more easy than say " Cut and run ! "
Yet a Guardsman can't live without some sort of fun—
   E'en I or you, If we'd nothing to do,
Should soon find ourselves looking remarkably blue.
   And, since no one denies What's so plain to all eyes,
It won't, I am sure, create any surprise
That reflections like these half reduced to despair
François Xavier Auguste, the gay Black Mousquetaire.

Patience par force ! He *considered*, of course,
But in vain—he could hit on no sort of resource—
   Love ?—Liquor ?—Law ?—Loo ?
   They would each of them do.
There's excitement enough in all four, but in none he
Could hope to get on *sans l'argent—i.e.,* money.
Love ?—no ;—ladies like little *cadeaux* from a suitor.
Liquor ?—no,—that won't do, when reduced to " the Pewter."—
   Then Law ?—'tis the same ; It's a very fine game,
But the fees and delays of " the Courts " are a shame,
As Lord Brougham says himself—who's a very great name,
Though the TIMES made it clear he was perfectly lost in his
Classic attempt at translating Demosthenes,
   And don't know his " particles."
  Who wrote the articles,
Showing his Greek up so, is not known very well ;
Many thought Barnes, others Mitchell,—some Merivale ;
   But it's scarce worth debate, Because from the date
Of my tale one conclusion we safely may draw,
Viz. : 'twas not François Xavier Auguste de St. Foix !

   Loo ?—no ;—that he had tried ;
  'Twas, in fact, his weak side,
But required more than any a purse well supplied

" Love ?—Liquor ?—Law ?—Loo ?   No ! 'tis all the same
    story.
Stay ! I have it—*Ma foi !* (that's ' Odd's Bobs ! ') there is
    Glory !
    Away with dull care ! *Vive le Roi !   Vive la Guerre !*
Peste ! I'd almost forgot I'm a Black Mousquetaire !
    When a man is like me,   *Sans six sous, sans souci,*
    A bankrupt in purse,   And in character worse,
With a shocking bad hat, and his credit at Zero,
What on earth can he hope to become,—but a Hero ?
    What a famous thought this is !   I'll go as Ulysses
Of old did—like him I'll see manners, and know countries ; *
Cut Paris,—and gaming,—and throats in the Low Countries."

So said, and so done—he arranged his affairs,
And was off like a shot to his Black Mousquetaires.

    Now it happen'd just then   That Field-Marshal Turenne
Was a good deal in want of " some active young men,"
    To fill up the gaps   Which, through sundry mishaps,
Had been made in his ranks by a certain " Great Condé,"
A General unrivall'd—at least in his own day—
    Whose valour was such,   That he did not care much
If he fought with the French,—or the Spaniards,—or Dutch,—
A fact which has stamped him a rather " Cool hand,"
Being nearly related to *Louis le Grand.*
It had been all the same had that King been his brother ;
He fought sometimes with one, and sometimes with another ;
    For war, so exciting,   He took such delight in,
He did not care whom he fought, so he *was* fighting.
And, as I've just said, had amused himself then
By tickling the tail of Field-Marshal Turenne ;
Since which, the Field-Marshal's most pressing concern
Was to tickle some other Chief's tail in his turn.

What a fine thing a battle is !—not one of those
Which one saw at the late Mr. Andrew Ducrow's,
Where a dozen of scene-shifters, drawn up in rows,
Would a dozen more scene-shifters boldly oppose,

---

    * Qui mores hominum multorum vidit et urbes.
      Who viewed men's manners, Londons, Yorks, and Derbys.

Taking great care their blows
Did not injure their foes,
And alike, save in colour and cut of their clothes,
Which were varied, to give more effect to " *Tableaux*,"
  While Stickney the Great
  Flung the gauntlet to Fate,
And made us all tremble, so gallantly did he come
On to encounter bold General Widdicombe—
But a real, good fight, like Pultowa, or Lützen,
(Which Gustavus the great ended all his disputes in,)
Or that which Suwarrow engaged without boots in,
Or Dettingen, Fontenoy, Blenheim, or Minden,.
Or the one Mr. Campbell describes, Hohenlinden,
  Where " the sun was low,"
  The ground all over snow,
And dark as mid-winter the swift Iser's flow,—
Till its colour was alter'd by General Moreau ;
While the big drum was heard in the dead of the night,
Which rattled the Bard out of bed in a fright,
And he ran up the steeple to look at the fight.
  'Twas in just such another one,
  (Names only bother one—
Dutch ones, indeed, are sufficient to smother one—)
In the Netherlands somewhere—I cannot say where—
  Suffice it that there *La Fortune de guerre*
Gave a cast of her calling to our Mousquetaire.
One fine morning, in short, François Xavier Auguste,
After making some scores of his foes " bite the dust,"
Got a mouthful himself of the very same crust ;
And though, as the Bard says, " No law is more just
Than for *Necis artifices*,"—so they call'd fiery
Soldados at Rome,—" *arte suâ perire*,"
  Yet Fate did not draw This poetical law
To its fullest extent in the case of St. Foix.
His Good Genius most probably found out some flaw,
  And diverted the shot From some deadlier spot
To a bone which, I think, to the best of my memory, 's
Call'd by Professional men the " *os femoris* ; "
And the ball being one of those named from its shape,
And some fancied resemblance it bears to the grape,
  St. Foix went down, With a groan and a frown,
And a hole in his small-clothes the size of a crown.—

—Stagger'd a bit　By this " palpable hit,"
He turn'd on his face, and went off in a fit !

Yes !—a Battle's a very fine thing while you're fighting,
These same Ups-and-Downs are so very exciting.

But a sombre sight is a Battle-field
　To the sad survivor's sorrowing eye,
Where those, who scorn'd to fly or yield
　In one promiscuous carnage lie ;
　　When the cannon's roar　Is heard no more,
And the thick dun smoke has roll'd away,
And the victor comes for a last survey
Of the well-fought field of yesterday !

No triumphs flush that haughty brow,—
　No proud exulting look is there,—
His eagle glance is humbled now,
　As, earth-ward bent, in anxious care
It seeks the form whose stalwart pride
But yester-morn was by his side !

And there it lies !—on yonder bank
　Of corses, which themselves had breath
But yester-morn—now cold and dank,
　With other dews than those of death !
Powerless as it had ne'er been born
The hand that clasp'd his—yester-morn !

And there are widows wand'ring there,
　That roam the blood-besprinkled plain,
And listen in their dumb despair
　For sounds they ne'er may hear again !
One word, however faint and low,—
Ay, e'en a groan,—were music now !

And this is Glory !—Fame !—
　　　　　　　　　　But, pshaw !
　Miss Muse, you're growing sentimental ;
Besides, such things *we* never saw ;
　In fact, they're merely Continental.

And then your Ladyship forgets
Some widows came for epaulettes.

So go back to your canter ; for one, I declare,
Is now fumbling about our capsized Mousquetaire,
  A beetle-brow'd hag, With a knife and a bag,
And an old tatter'd bonnet which, thrown back, discloses
The ginger complexion, and one of those noses
Peculiar to females named Levy and Moses,
Such as nervous folks still, when they come in their way, shun
Old vixen-faced tramps of the Hebrew persuasion.

  You remember, I trust, François Xavier Auguste,
Had uncommon fine limbs, and a very fine bust.
Now there's something—I cannot tell what it may be—
About good-looking gentlemen turn'd twenty-three,
Above all when laid up with a wound in the knee,
Which affects female hearts, in no common degree,
With emotions in which many feelings combine,
Very easy to fancy, though hard to define ;
  Ugly or pretty, Stupid or witty,
Young or old, they experience, in country or city,
What's clearly not Love—yet it's warmer than Pity—
And some such a feeling, no doubt, 'tis that stays
The hand you may see that old Jezebel raise,
  Arm'd with the blade, So oft used in her trade,
The horrible calling e'en now she is plying,
Despoiling the dead, and despatching the dying !
For these " nimble Conveyancers," after such battles,
Regarding as *treasure trouvé* all goods and chattels,
Think nought, in " perusing and settling " the titles,
So safe as six inches of steel in the vitals.

  Now don't make a joke of That feeling I spoke of ;
For, as sure as you're born, that same feeling,—whate'er
It may be,—saves the life of the young Mousquetaire !—
The knife, that was levell'd erewhile at his throat,
Is employ'd now in ripping the lace from his coat,
And from what, I suppose, I must call his *culotte ;*
  And his pockets, no doubt, Being turned inside out,
That his *mouchoir* and gloves may be put " up the spout

(For of coin, you may well conceive, all she can do
Fails to ferret out even a single *écu ;*)
As a muscular Giant would handle an elf,
The virago at last lifts the soldier himself,
And, like a She-Samson, at length lays him down
In a hospital form'd in the neighbouring town !
　　I am not very sure,　But I think 'twas Namur ;
And there she now leaves him, expecting a cure.

Canto II.

I ABOMINATE physic—I care not who knows
That there's nothing on earth I detest like " a dose "—
That yellowish-green-looking fluid, whose hue
I consider extremely unpleasant to view,
With its sickly appearance, that trenches so near
On what Homer defines the complexion of Fear ;
　Χλωρον δεος, I mean,　A nasty pale green,
Though for want of some word that may better avail,
I presume, our translators have rendered it " pale ; "
　　For consider the cheeks
　　Of those " well-booted Greeks,"
Their Egyptian descent was a question of weeks ;
Their complexion, of course, like a half-decayed leek's ;
And you'll see in an instant the thing that I mean in it,
A Greek face in a funk had a good deal of green in it.

I repeat, I abominate physic ; but then,
If folks *will* go campaigning about with such men
As the Great Prince de Condé, and Marshal Turenne,
　　They may fairly expect　To be now and then check'd
By a bullet, or sabre cut.　Then their best solace is
Found, I admit, in green potions, and boluses ;
　　So, of course, I don't blame
　　St. Foix, wounded and lame,
If he swallowed a decent *quant. suff.* of the same ;
Though I'm told, in such cases, it's not the French plan
To pour in their drastics as fast as they can,
The practice of many an English *Savan,*
　　But to let off a man　With a little *ptisanne,*
And gently to chafe the *patella* (knee-pan).

" Oh, woman ! " Sir Walter observes, " when the brow
's wrung with pain, what a minist'ring Angel art thou ! "
Thou'rt a " minist'ring Angel " in no less degree,
I can boldly assert, when the pain's in the knee ;
  And medical friction   Is, past contradiction,
Much better performed by a She than a He.
A fact which, indeed, comes within my own knowledge,
For I well recollect, when a youngster at College,
  And, therefore, can quote A surgeon of note,
Mr. Grosvenor of Oxford, who not only wrote
On the subject a very fine treatise, but, still as his
Patients came in, certain soft-handed Phyllises
Were at once set to work on their legs, arms, and backs,
And rubbed out their complaints in a couple of cracks.—
  Now, they say, To this day,
  When sick people can't pay
On the Continent, many of this kind of nurses
Attend, without any demand on their purses ;
And these females, some old, others still in their teens,
Some call " Sisters of Charity," others " Beguines."
They don't take the vows ; but, half-Nun and half-Lay,
Attend you ; and when you've got better, they say,
" You're exceedingly welcome ! There's nothing to pay.
  Our task is now done. You are able to run.
We never take money ; we cure you for fun ! "
  Then they drop you a curt'sy, and wish you good day,
And go off to cure somebody else the same way.
—A great many of these, at the date of my tale,
In Namur walked the hospitals, workhouse, and jail.

  Among them was one, A most sweet Demi-nun.
Her cheek pensive and pale ; tresses bright as the Sun,—
Not carroty—no ; though you'd fancy you saw burn
Such locks as the Greeks lov'd, which moderns call auburn.
These were partially seen through the veil which they wore all ;
Her teeth were of pearl, and her lips were of coral ;
Her eyelashes silken ; her eyes, fine large blue ones,
Were sapphires (I don't call these similes new ones ;
But, in metaphors, freely confess I've a leaning
To such, new or old, as convey best one's meaning).—

Then, for figure ? In faith it was downright barbarity
    To muffle a form   Might an anchorite warm
In the fusty stuff gown of a *Sœur de la Charité ;*
And no poet could fancy, no painter could draw
One more perfect in all points, more free from a flaw,
Than her's who now sits by the couch of St. Foix,
    Chafing there,   With such care,
    And so dove-like an air,
His leg, till her delicate fingers are charr'd
With the Steer's opodeldoc, joint-oil, and goulard ;
—Their Dutch appellations are really too hard
To be brought into verse by a transmarine Bard.—

    Now you'll see,   And agree,   I am certain, with me,
When a young man's laid up with a wound in his knee :
    And a Lady sits there,   On a rush-bottom'd chair,
To hand him the mixtures his doctors prepare,
And a bit of lump-sugar to make matters square ;
Above all, when the Lady's remarkably fair,
And the wounded young man is a gay Mousquetaire,
It's a ticklish affair, you may swear, for the pair,
And may lead on to mischief before they're aware.

I really don't think, spite of what friends would call his
" *Penchant* for *liaisons,*" and graver men " follies,"
(For my own part, I think planting thorns on their pillows,
And leaving poor maidens to weep and wear willows,
Is not to be classed among mere peccadilloes),
His " *faults,*" I should say—I don't think François Xavier
Entertain'd any thoughts of improper behaviour
Tow'rds his nurse, or that once to induce her to sin he meant
While superintending his draughts and his liniment.
    But, as he grew stout,   And was getting about
Thoughts came into his head that had better been out ;
    While Cupid's an urchin   We know deserves birching,
He's so prone to delude folks, and leave them the lurch in.
    'Twas doubtless his doing   That absolute ruin
Was the end of all poor dear Thérèse's shampooing.—
'Tis a subject I don't like to dwell on : but such
Things will happen—ay, e'en 'mongst the phlegmatic Dutch.

" When Woman," as Goldsmith declares, " stoops to folly,
   And finds out too late that false man can betray,"
She is apt to look dismal, and grow " melan-choly,"
   And, in short, to be anything rather than gay.

He goes on to remark that " to punish her lover,
   Wring his bosom, and draw the tear into his eye,
There is but one method " which he can discover
   That's likely to answer—that one is " to die ! "

He's wrong—the wan and withering cheek ;
   The thin lips, pale, and drawn apart ;
The dim yet tearless eyes that speak
   The misery of the breaking heart ;

The wasted form, th' enfeebled tone
   That whispering mocks the pitying ear ;
Th' imploring glances heaven-ward thrown,
   As heedless, helpless, hopeless here ;

These wring the false one's heart enough,
If " made of penetrable stuff."
   And poor Thérèse Thus pines and decays,
Till, stung with remorse, St. Foix takes a post-chaise,
   With, for " wheelers," two bays,
   And, for " leaders," two greys,
And soon reaches France, by the help of relays,
Flying shabbily off from the sight of his victim,
And driving as fast as if Old Nick had kick'd him.

   She, poor sinner Grows thinner and thinner,
Leaves off eating breakfast, and luncheon, and dinner,
Till you'd really suppose she could have nothing in her.—
One evening—'twas just as the clock struck eleven—
They saw she'd been sinking fast ever since seven,—
She breath'd one deep sigh, threw one look up to Heaven,
   And all was o'er !— Poor Thérèse was no more—
She was gone !—the last breath that she managed to draw
Escaped in one half-utter'd word—'twas " St. Foix ! "

      *   *   *   *   *

Who can fly from himself ?   Bitter cares, when you feel 'em,
Are not cured by travel—as Horace says, " *Cœlum*
Non animum mutant qui currunt trans mare ! "
It's climate, not mind, that by roaming men vary—
Remorse for temptation to which you have yielded, is
A shadow you can't sell as Peter Schlemil did his ;
It haunts you for ever—in bed and at board,—
    Ay, e'en in your dreams.
  And you can't find, it seems,
Any proof that a guilty man ever yet snored !
It is much if he slumbers at all, which but few,
—François Xavier Auguste was an instance—can do.
    Indeed, from the time   He committed the crime
Which cut off poor Sister Thérèse in her prime,
He was not the same man that he had been—his plan
Was quite changed—in wild freaks he no more led the van ;
    He'd scarce sleep a wink in
    A week ; but sit thinking,
    From company shrinking—
    He quite gave up drinking.
At the mess-table, too, where now seldom he came,
Fish, *fricassée, fricandeau, potage,* or game,
Dindon aux truffes, or *turbot à la crême,*
No !—he still shook his head,—it was always the same,
Still he never complained that the cook was to blame !
'Twas his appetite fail'd him—no matter how rare
And *recherché* the dish, how delicious the fare,—
What he used to like best he no longer could bear ;
    But he'd there sit and stare   With an air of despair :
    Took no care, but would wear
    Boots that wanted repair
Such a shirt too ! you'd think he'd no linen to spare.
He omitted to shave ;—he neglected his hair,
And looked more like a Guy than a gay Mousquetaire.

One thing, above all, most excited remark :
In the evening he seldom sat long after dark.
Not that then, as of yore, he'd go out for " a lark "
    With his friends ; but when they,
    After taking *café*

Would have broiled bones and kidneys brought in on a tray.
—Which I own I consider a very good way,
If a man's not dyspeptic, to wind up the day—
No persuasion on earth could induce him to stay ;
But he'd take up his candlestick, just nod his head
By way of " Good evening ! " and walk off to bed.
Yet even when there he seem'd no better off,
For he'd wheeze, and he'd sneeze, and he'd hem ! and he'd cough ;
   And they'd hear him all night,
   Sometimes, sobbing outright,
While his valet, who often endeavour'd to peep,
Declared that " his master was never asleep !
But would sigh, and would groan, slap his forehead, and weep ;
   That about ten o'clock   His door he would lock,
And then never would open it, let who would knock !—
   He had heard him," he said,
   " Sometimes jump out of bed,
And talk as if speaking to one who was dead !
   He'd groan and he'd moan   In so piteous a tone,
Begging some one or other to let him alone,
That it really would soften the heart of a stone
To hear him exclaim so, and call upon Heaven ;
Then—The bother began always *just at eleven !* "

François Xavier Auguste, as I've told you before,
I believe, was a popular man in his *corps,*
   And his comrades, not one   Of whom knew of the Nun
Now began to consult what was best to be done.
   Count Cordon Bleu   And the Sieur de la Roue
Confess'd they did *not* know at all what to do :
But the Chevalier Hippolyte Hector Achille
Alphonso Stanislaus Émile de Grandville
   Made a fervent appeal   To the zeal they must feel
For their friend, so distinguished an officer, 's weal.
" The first thing," he said, " was to find out the matter
That bored their poor friend so, and caused all this clatter—
   Mort de ma vie ! "   —Here he took some rapee—
" Be the cause what it may, he shall tell it to me ! "—
He was right, sure enough—in a couple of days
He worms out the whole story of Sister Thérèse,
Now entomb'd, poor dear soul ! in some Dutch *Père la Chaise.*

Q

—" But the worst thing of all," François Xavier declares,
" Is, whenever I've taken my candle up-stairs,
There's Thérèse sitting there—upon one of those chairs !
　Such a frown, too, she wears,　And so frightfully glares
That I'm really prevented from saying my pray'rs,
While an odour,—the very reverse of perfume,—
More like rhubarb or senna,—pervades the whole room!"

　　Hector Achille　Stanislaus Emile,
When he heard him talk so felt an odd sort of feel ;
Not that *he* cared for Ghosts—he was far too genteel ;
Still a queerish sensation came on when he saw
　Him, whom, for fun,　They'd, by way of a pun
On his person and principles, nick-named *Sans Foi*,
　—A man whom they had, you see,
　Mark'd as a Sadducee,—
In his horns, all at once, so completely to draw,
And to talk of a Ghost with such manifest awe !—
It excited the Chevalier Grandville's surprise ;
He shrugg'd up his shoulders, he turn'd up his eyes,
And he thought with himself that he could not do less
Than lay the whole matter before the whole Mess.

　　Repetition's detestable ;—　So, as you're best able,
Paint to yourself the effect at the Mess-table—
　How the bold Brigadiers　Prick'd up their ears,
And received the account, some with fears, some with sneers ;
　How the Sieur de la Roue　Said to Count Cordon Bleu,
" *Ma foi—c'est bien drôle*—Monseigneur, what say you ? "—
　How Count Cordon Bleu
　Declared he " thought so too " ;—
How the Colonel affirmed that " the case was quite new " ;—
　How the Captains and Majors　Began to lay wagers
How far the Ghost part of the story was true ;—
How, at last, when asked, " What was the best thing to do ? "
Everybody was silent,—for nobody knew !—
And how, in the end, they said, " No one could deal
With the matter so well, from his prudence and zeal,
As the Gentleman who was the first to reveal
This strange story—viz., Hippolyte Hector Achille
Alphonse Stanislaus Emile de Grandville ! "

I need scarcely relate   The plans, little and great,
Which came into the Chevalier Hippolyte's pate
To rescue his friend from his terrible foes,
Those mischievous Imps, whom the world, I suppose,
From extravagant notions respecting their hue
Has strangely agreed to denominate " Blue,"
Inasmuch as his schemes were of no more avail
Than those he had, early in life, found to fail,
When he strove to lay salt on some little bird's tail.
   In vain did he try   With strong waters to ply
His friend, on the ground that he never could spy
Such a thing as a Ghost, with a drop in his eye ;
St. Foix never would drink now unless he was dry ;
Besides, what the vulgar call " sucking the monkey "
Has much less effect on a man when he's funky.
In vain did he strive to detain him at table
Till his " dark hour " was over—he never was able,
   Save once, when at Mess,   With that sort of address
Which the British call " Humbug," and Frenchmen " *Finesse*,"
(It's " Blarney " in Irish—I don't know the Scotch,)
He fell to admiring his friend's English watch.*
   He examined the face,   And the back of the case,
And the young Lady's portrait there, done on enamel, he
" Saw by the likeness was one of the family ; "
   Cried " *Superbe !—Magnifique !* "
(With his tongue in his cheek)—
Then he open'd the case, just to take a peep in it, and
Seized the occasion to pop back the minute-hand.
With a demi-*congé*, and a shrug, and grin, he
Returns the *bijou* and—*c'est une affaire finie*—
" I've done him," thinks he, " now I'll wager a guinea ! "

   It happen'd that day   They were all very gay,
'Twas the *Grand Monarque's* birthday—that is, 'twas St.
   Louis's,
Which in Catholic countries, of course, they would view as his—
   So when Hippolyte saw   Him about to withdraw,
He cried, " Come—that won't do, my fine fellow, St. Foix,—
Give us five minutes longer and drink *Vive le Roi*."

   * " Tompion's, I presume ? "—Farquhar.

François Xavier Auguste,   Without any mistrust
Of the trick that was play'd, drew his watch from his fob,
Just glanced at the hour, then agreed to " hob-nob,"
  Fill'd a bumper, and rose
  With " *Messieurs*, I propose "—
He paused—his blanch'd lips fail'd to utter the toast !
'Twas *eleven !*—he thought it half-past ten at most—
Ev'ry limb, nerve, and muscle grew stiff as a post,—
  His jaw dropp'd—his eyes
  Swell'd to twice their own size—
And he stood as a pointer would stand—at a Ghost !
—Then shriek'd, as he fell on the floor like a stone.
" Ah ! Sister Thérèse ! now—do let me alone ! "

*   *   *   *   *

It's amazing by sheer perseverance what men do,—
As waters wear stone by the " *Sæpe cadendo*,"
If they stick to Lord Somebody's motto, " *Agendo !* "
Was it not Robert Bruce ?—I declare I've forgot,
But I think it was Robert—you'll find it in Scott—
Who, when cursing Dame Fortune, was taught by a spider,
" She's sure to come round, if you will but abide her."
  Then another great Rob,
  Called " White-headed Bob,"
Whom I once saw receive such a thump on the " nob "
From a fist which might almost an elephant brain,
That I really believed, at the first, he was slain,
For he lay like a log on his back on the plain,
Till a gentleman present, accustomed to *train*,
Drew out a small lancet, and open'd a vein
Just below his left eye, which relieving the pain,
He stood up, like a trump, with an air of disdain,
  While his " backer " was fain,
  —For he could not refrain—
(He was dress'd in pea-green, with a pin and gold chain,
And I think I heard somebody call him " Squire Hayne,")
To whisper *ten words* one should always retain,
—" TAKE A SUCK AT THE LEMON, AND AT HIM AGAIN ! ! ! "—
A hint ne'er surpassed, though thus spoken at random,
Since Teucer's apostrophe—*Nil desperandum !*
—Grandville acted on it, and order'd his Tandem.

He had heard St. Foix say,   That no very great way
From Namur was a snug little town call'd Grandpré,
Near which, a few miles from the banks of the Maese,
Dwelt a pretty twin-sister of poor dear Thérèse,
Of the same age, of course, the same father, same mother,
And as like to Thérèse as one pea to another ;
    She liv'd with her Mamma,   Having lost her Papa,
Late of contraband *schnaps* an unlicensed distiller,
And her name was Des Moulins (in English, Miss Miller).

    Now, though Hippolyte Hector
    Could hardly expect her
To feel much regard for her sister's " protector,"
When she'd seen him so shamefully leave and neglect her ;
    Still, he very well knew   In this world there are few
But are ready much Christian forgiveness to shew,
For other folk's wrongs—if well paid so to do—
And he'd seen to what acts " *Res angustæ* " compel *beaux*
And *belles*, whose affairs have once got out at elbows,
With the magic effect of a handful of crowns
Upon people whose pockets boast nothing but " browns ;"
    A few *francs* well applied
    He'd no doubt would decide
Miss Agnes Des Moulins to jump up and ride
As far as head-quarters, next day, by his side ;
For the distance was nothing, to speak by comparison,
To the town where the Mousquetaires now lay in garrison ;
    Then he thought, by the aid
    Of a veil, and gown made

Like those worn by the lady his friend had betray'd,
They might dress up Miss Agnes so like to the Shade,
Which he fancied he saw, of that poor injured maid,
Come each night, with her pale face, his guilt to upbraid ;
That if once introduced to his room thus array'd,
And then unmask'd as soon as she'd long enough stay'd,
'Twould be no very difficult task to persuade
Him the whole was a scurvy trick, cleverly play'd,
Out of spite and revenge, by a mischievous jade !

With respect to the scheme—though I do not call that a gem—
Still I've known soldiers adopt a worse stratagem,
And that, too, among the decided approvers
Of General Sir David Dundas's " Manœuvres."
    There's a proverb, however,
    I've always thought clever,
Which my Grandmother never was tired of repeating,
" The proof of the Pudding is found in the eating ! "
We shall see, in the sequel, how Hector Achille
Had mix'd up the suet and plums for *his* meal.

The night had set in ;—'twas a dark and a gloomy one ;—
Off went St. Foix to his chamber ; a roomy one,
    Five stories high,   The first floor from the sky,
And lofty enough to afford great facility
For playing a game, with the youthful nobility
    Of " crack *corps* " a deal in
    Request, when they're feeling,
In dull country quarters, *ennui* on them stealing ;
    A wet wafer's applied   To a sixpence's side,
Then it's spun with the thumb up to stick on the ceiling ;
Intellectual amusement, which custom allows old troops,—
I've seen it here practised at home by our Household troops.
    He'd a table, and bed,
    And three chairs ; and all's said.—
A bachelor's barrack, where'er you discern it, you're
Sure to find not overburthen'd with furniture.

François Xavier Auguste lock'd and bolted his door
With just the same caution he'd practised before ;

Little he knew   That the Count Cordon Bleu,
With Hector Achille, and the Sieur de la Roue,
Had been up there before him, and drawn ev'ry screw !

And now comes the moment—the watches and clocks
All point to *eleven !*—the bolts and the locks
Give way—and the party turn out their bag-fox !—
  With step noiseless and light,   Though half in a fright,
" A cup in her left hand, a draught in her right,"
In her robe long and black, and her veil long and white,
Ma'amselle Agnes des Moulins walks in as a sprite !—
  She approaches the bed   With the same silent tread
Just as though she had been at least half a year dead !
Then seating herself on the " rush-bottom'd chair,"
Throws a cold stony glance on the Black Mousquetaire.

If you're one of the " play-going public," kind reader,
And not a Moravian or rigid Seceder,
  You've seen Mr. Kean,   I mean in that scene
Of Macbeth,—by some thought the crack one of the piece,
Which has been so well painted by Mr. M'Clise,—
When he wants, after having stood up to say grace,*
To sit down to his haggis, and can't find a place ;
  You remember his stare
  At the high-back'd arm-chair,
Where the Ghost sits that nobody else knows is there,
And how, after saying " What man dares I dare ! "
  He proceeds to declare   He should not so much care
If it came in the shape of a " tiger " or " bear,"
But he don't like its shaking its long gory hair !
While the obstinate Ghost, as determined to brave him,
  With a horrible grin,   Sits, and cocks up his chin,
Just as though he was asking the tyrant to shave him.
  And Lenox and Rosse   Seem quite at a loss
If they ought to go on with their sheep's head and sauce ;
And Lady Macbeth looks uncommonly cross,
  And says in a huff   It's all " Proper stuff ! "—
All this you'll have seen, Reader, often enough ;

* May good digestion wait on appetite,
  And health on both.—*Macbeth.*

So, perhaps 'twill assist you in forming some notion
Of what must have been François Xavier's emotion,
 If you fancy what troubled Macbeth to be *doubled*
And, instead of *one* Banquo to stare in his face
Without " speculation," suppose he'd *a brace !*

I wish I'd poor Fuseli's pencil, who ne'er I bel-
ieve was exceeded in painting the terrible,
 Or that of Sir Joshua Reynolds, who was so a-
droit in depicting it—*vide* his piece
Descriptive of Cardinal Beaufort's decease,
 Where that prelate is lying Decidedly dying,
 With the King and his *suite*,
 Standing just at his feet,
And his hands, as Dame Quickly says, fumbling the sheet ;
While, close at his ear, with the air of a scorner,
" Busy, meddling," Old Nick's grinning up in the corner.
But painting's an art I confess I am raw in,
The fact is, I never took lessons in drawing :
 Had I done so, instead Of the lines you have read,
I'd have giv'n you a sketch should have fill'd you with dread ;
François Xavier Auguste squatting up in his bed,
 His hands widely spread, His complexion like lead,
Ev'ry hair that he has standing up on his head,
As when, Agnes des Moulins first catching his view,
Now right, and now left, rapid glances he threw,
Then shriek'd with a wild and unearthly halloo,
   " *Mon Dieu ! v'la deux ! !*
   By the Pope there are two ! ! ! "

He fell back—one long aspiration he drew.
 In flew De la Roue, And Count Cordon Bleu,
Pommade, Pomme-de-terre, and the rest of their crew.
He stirr'd not,—he spoke not,—he none of them knew !
 And Achille cried " Odzooks ! I fear by his looks,
Our friend, François Xavier, has popp'd off the hooks ! "

 'Twas too true ! *Malheureux ! !*
It was done !—he had ended his earthly career,—
He had gone off at once with a flea in his ear ;
—The Black Mousquetaire was as dead as Small-beer ! !

L'Enboye.

A moral more in point I scarce could hope
Than this, from Mr. Alexander Pope.

If ever chance should bring some Cornet gay,
And pious Maid,—as, possibly, it may,—
From Knightsbridge Barracks, and the shades serene
Of Clapham Rise, as far as Kensal Green ;
O'er some pale marble when they join their heads
To kiss the falling tears each other sheds ;
Oh ! may they pause !—and think, in silent awe,
He, that he reads the words, " *Ci git St. Foix !* "—
She, that the tombstone which her eye surveys
Bears this sad line,—" *Hic jacet Sœur Thérèse !* "—
Then shall they sigh, and weep, and murmuring say,
" Oh ! may we never play such tricks as they ! "—
And if at such a time some Bard there be,
Some sober Bard, addicted much to tea
And sentimental song—like Ingoldsby—
If such there be—who sings and sips so well,
Let him this sad, this tender story tell !
Warn'd by the tale, the gentle pair shall boast,
" I've 'scaped the Broken Heart ! "—" and I the Ghost ! "

The next in order of these " lays of many lands " refers to a period far earlier in point of date, and has for its scene the banks of what our Teutonic friends are wont to call their " own imperial River ! " The incidents which it records afford sufficient proof (and these are days of demonstration), that a propensity to flirtation is not confined to age or country, and that its consequences were not less disastrous to the mail-clad *Ritter* of the dark ages than to the silken courtier of the seventeenth century. The whole narrative bears about it the stamp of truth, and from the papers among which it was discovered I am inclined to think it must have been picked up by Sir Peregrine in the course of one of his valetudinary visits to " The German Spa."

Sir Rupert the Fearless

A Legend of Germany

SIR RUPERT THE FEARLESS, a gallant young knight,
Was equally ready to tipple or fight,
 Crack a crown, or a bottle, Cut sirloin, or throttle ;·
In brief, or as Hume says, " to sum up the tottle,"
Unstain'd by dishonour, unsullied by fear,
All his neighbours pronounced him a *preux chevalier*.

Despite these perfections, corporeal and mental,
He had one slight defect, viz., a rather lean rental ;
Besides, as 'tis own'd there are spots in the sun,
So it must be confessed that Sir Rupert had one ;
 Being rather unthinking, He'd scarce sleep a wink in
A night, but addict himself sadly to drinking,
 And, what moralists say Is as naughty—to play,
To *Rouge et Noir*, Hazard, Short Whist, *Ecarté ;*
Till these and a few less defensible fancies
Brought the Knight to the end of his slender finances.

 When at length through his boozing,
 And tenants refusing
Their rents, swearing " times were so bad they were losing,"
 His steward said, " O, sir, It's some time ago, sir,
Since aught through my hands reach'd the baker or grocer,
And the tradesmen in general are grown great complainers."
Sir Rupert the brave thus addressed his retainers :

 " My friends, since the stock Of my father's old hock
Is out, with the Kürchwasser, Barsac, Moselle,
And we're fairly reduced to the pump and the well,
 I presume to suggest, We shall all find it best
For each to shake hands with his friends ere he goes,
Mount his horse, if he has one, and—follow his nose ;
 As to me, I opine, Left *sans* money or wine,
My best way is to throw myself into the Rhine,
Where pitying travellers may sigh, as they cross over,
' Though he lived a *roué*, yet he died a philosopher.' "

They'd such very odd heads and such very odd tails

The Knight, having bow'd out his friends thus politely,
Got into his skiff, the full moon shining brightly,
   By the light of whose beam,
   He soon spied on the stream
A dame, whose complexion was fair as new cream,
   Pretty pink silken hose   Cover'd ankles and toes,
In other respects she was scanty of clothes ;
For, so says tradition, both written and oral,
Her *one* garment was loop'd up with bunches of coral.

Full sweetly she sang to a sparkling guitar,
With silver cords stretch'd over Derbyshire spar, .
   And she smiled on the Knight,
   Who, amazed at the sight,
Soon found his astonishment merged in delight ;
   But the stream by degrees
   Now rose up to her knees,
Till at length it invaded her very chemise,
While the heavenly strain, as the wave seemed to swallow her,
And slowly she sank, sounded fainter and hollower ;
   —Jumping up in his boat,   And discarding his coat,
" Here goes," cried Sir Rupert, " by jingo I'll follow her ! "
Then into the water he plunged with a souse
That was heard quite distinctly by those in the house.

Down, down, forty fathom and more from the brink,
Sir Rupert the Fearless continues to sink,
   And, as downward he goes,
   Still the cold water flows
Through his ears, and his eyes, and his mouth, and his nose,
Till the rum and the brandy he'd swallow'd since lunch
Wanted nothing but lemon to fill him with punch ;
Some minutes elapsed since he enter'd the flood,
Ere his heels touch'd the bottom, and stuck in the mud.

   But oh ! what a sight   Met the eyes of the Knight,
When he stood in the depth of the stream bolt upright !—
   A grand stalactite hall,   Like the cave of Fingal,
Rose above and about him ;—great fishes and small
Came thronging around him, regardless of danger,
And seemed all agog for a peep at the stranger.

Their figures and forms to describe, language fails—
They'd such very odd heads, and such very odd tails ;
Of their genus or species a sample to gain,
You would ransack all Hungerford market in vain ;
   E'en the famed Mr. Myers
   Would scarcely find buyers,
Though hundreds of passengers doubtless would stop
To stare, were such monsters exposed in his shop.

But little reck'd Rupert these queer-looking brutes,
   Or the efts and the newts   That crawled up his boots,
For a sight, beyond any of which I've made mention,
In a moment completely absorb'd his attention.
A huge crystal bath, which, with water far clearer
Than George Robins' filters, or Thorpe's (which are dearer),
   Have ever distill'd,   To the summit was fill'd,
Lay stretch'd out before him,—and every nerve thrill'd
   As scores of young women
   Were diving and swimming,
Till the vision a perfect quandary put him in ;—
All slightly accoutred in gauzes and lawns,
They came floating about him like so many prawns.

Sir Rupert, who (barring the few peccadilloes
Alluded to,) ere he lept into the billows
Possess'd irreproachable morals, began
To feel rather queer, as a modest young man ;
When forth stepp'd a dame, whom he recognised soon
As the one he had seen by the light of the moon,
And lisp'd, while a soft smile attended each sentence,
" Sir Rupert, I'm happy to make your acquaintance ;
   My name is Lurline,   And the ladies you've seen,
All do me the honour to call me their Queen ;
I'm delighted to see you, sir, down in the Rhine here,
And hope you can make it convenient to dine here."

   The Knight blush'd, and bowed,
   As he ogled the crowd
Of subaqueous beauties, then answer'd aloud :
" Ma'am, you do me much honour,—I cannot express
The delight I shall feel—if you'll pardon my dress—

May I venture to say, when a gentleman jumps
In the river at midnight for want of ' the dumps,'
He rarely puts on his knee-breeches and pumps ;
If I could but have guess'd—what I sensibly feel—
Your politeness—I'd not have come *en dishabille*,
But have put on my *silk* tights in lieu of my *steel*."
Quoth the lady, " Dear sir, no apologies, pray,
You will take our ' pot-luck ' in the family way ;
  We can give you a dish   Of some decentish fish,
And our water's thought fairish ; but here in the Rhine,
I can't say we pique ourselves much on our wine."

The Knight made a bow more profound than before,
When a Dory-faced page oped the dining-room door,
  And said, bending his knee,   " *Madame, on a servi !* "
Rupert tender'd his arm, led Lurline to her place,
And a fat little Mer-man stood up and said grace.

What boots it to tell of the viands, or how she
Apologiz'd much for their plain water-souchy,
  Want of Harvey's, and Cross's,
  And Burgess's sauces ?
Or how Rupert, on his side, protested, by Jove, he
Preferr'd his fish plain, without soy or anchovy.
  Suffice it the meal   Boasted trout, perch, and eel,
Besides some remarkably fine salmon peel.
The Knight, sooth to say, thought much less of the fishes
Than of what they were served on, the massive gold dishes ;
While his eye, as it glanced now and then on the girls,
Was caught by their persons much less than their pearls,
And a thought came across him and caused him to muse,
  " If I could but get hold   Of some of that gold,
I might manage to pay off my rascally Jews ! "

When dinner was done, at a sign to the lasses,
The table was clear'd, and they put on fresh glasses ;
  Then the lady addrest   Her redoubtable guest
Much as Dido, of old, did the pious Eneas,
" Dear sir, what induced you to come down and see us ? "—
Rupert gave her a glance most bewitchingly tender,
Loll'd back in his chair, put his toes on the fender,

And told her outright How that he, a young Knight,
Had never been last at a feast or a fight ;
   But that keeping good cheer Every day in the year,
And drinking neat wines all the same as small-beer,
   Had exhausted his rent, And, his money all spent,
How he borrow'd large sums at two hundred per cent. ;
   How they follow'd—and then,
   The once civillest of men,
Messrs. Howard and Gibbs, made him bitterly rue it he
'd ever raised money by way of annuity ;
And, his mortgages being about to foreclose,
How he jump'd in the river to finish his woes !

Lurline was affected, and own'd, with a tear,
That a story so mournful had ne'er met her ear ;
   Rupert, hearing her sigh, Look'd uncommonly sly,
And said, with some emphasis, " Ah ! miss, had I
   A few pounds of those metals
   You waste here on kettles,
   Then, Lord once again Of my spacious domain,
A free Count of the Empire once more I might reign,
   With Lurline at my side, My adorable bride,
(For the parson should come, and the knot should be tied ;)
No couple so happy on earth should be seen
As Sir Rupert the brave and his charming Lurline ;
Not that money's my object—No, hang it ! I scorn it—
And as for my rank—but that *you'd* so adorn it—
   I'd abandon it all To remain your true thrall,
And, instead of ' the *Great*,' be call'd ' Rupert the *Small* ; '
—To gain but your smiles, were I Sardanapalus,*
I'd descend from my throne, and be boots at an ale-house."

   Lurline hung her head, Turn'd pale, and then red,
Growing faint at this sudden proposal to wed,
As though his abruptness, in " popping the question "
So soon after dinner, disturb'd her digestion.
   Then, averting her eye, With a lover-like sigh,
" You are welcome," she murmur'd, in tones most bewitching,
" To every utensil I have in my kitchen ! "

* " Sardanapalus " and " Boots," the *Zenith* and *Nadir* of human society.

They came floating about him like so many prawns

Upstarted the Knight,   Half mad with delight,
Round her finely-form'd waist
He immediately placed
One arm, which the lady most closely embraced,
Of her lily-white fingers the other made capture,
And he press'd his adored to his bosom with rapture.
" And, oh ! " he exclaim'd, " let them go catch my skiff, I
'll be home in a twinkling, and back in a jiffy,
Nor one moment procrastinate longer my journey
Than to put up the banns and kick out the attorney."

One kiss to her lip, and one squeeze to her hand,
And Sir Rupert already was half-way to land,
   For a sour-visaged Triton,
   With features would frighten
Old Nick, caught him up in one hand, though no light one,
Sprang up through the waves, popp'd him into his funny,
Which some others already had half-fill'd with money ;
In fact, 'twas so heavily laden with ore
And pearls, 'twas a mercy he got it to shore ;
   But Sir Rupert was strong,   And, while pulling along,
Still he heard, faintly sounding, the water-nymphs' song.

LAY OF THE NAIADS.

" Away ! away ! to the mountain's brow,
   Where the castle is darkly frowning ;
And the vassals, all in goodly row,
   Weep for their lord a-drowning !
Away ! away ! to the steward's room,
   Where law with its wig and robe is ;
Throw us out John Doe and Richard Roe,
   And sweetly we'll tickle their tobies ! "

The unearthly voices had ceased their yelling,
When Rupert reach'd his old baronial dwelling.

   What rejoicing was there !
   How the vassals did stare !
The old housekeeper put a clean shirt down to air,

For she saw by her lamp
That her master's was damp,
And she fear'd he'd catch cold, and lumbago and cramp ;
But, scorning what she did,   The Knight never heeded
Wet jacket or trowsers, nor thought of repining,
Since their pockets had got such a delicate lining.
   But oh ! what dismay   Fill'd the tribe of *Ca Sa*,
When they found he'd the cash, and intended to pay !
Away went " *cognovits*," " bills," " bonds," and " escheats,"—
Rupert clear'd off all scores, and took proper receipts.

   Now no more he sends out
   For pots of brown stout
Or *schnaps*, but resolves to do henceforth without,
Abjure from this hour all excess and ebriety,
Enrol himself one of a Temp'rance Society,
   All riot eschew,   Begin life anew,
And new-cushion and hassock the family pew !
Nay, to strengthen him more in his new mode of life,
He boldly determines to take him a wife.

Now, many would think that the Knight, from a nice sense
Of honour, should put Lurline's name in the licence,
And that, for a man of his breeding and quality,
   To break faith and troth,   Confirm'd by an oath,
Is not quite consistent with rigid morality ;
But whether the nymph was forgot, or he thought her
From her essence scarce wife, but at best wife-and-water,
   And declined as unsuited,   A bride so diluted—
   Be this as it may,   He, I'm sorry to say,
(For, all things considered, I own 'twas a rum thing,)
Made proposals in form to Miss *Una Von*—something,
(Her name has escaped me,) sole heiress, and niece
To a highly respectable Justice of Peace.

   " Thrice happy's the wooing   That's not long a-doing ! "
So much time is saved in the billing and cooing—
The ring is now bought, the white favours, and gloves,
And all the *et cetera* which crown people's loves ;
A magnificent bride-cake comes home from the baker,
And lastly appears, from the German Long Acre,

That shaft which the sharpest in all Cupid's quiver is,
A plum colour'd coach, and rich Pompadour liveries.

'Twas a comely sight   To behold the Knight,
With his beautiful bride, dress'd all in white,
And the bridesmaids fair with their long lace veils,
As they all walk'd up to the altar rails,
While nice little boys, the incense dispensers,
March'd in front with white surplices, bands, and gilt censers.

With a gracious air, and a smiling look,
Mess John had open'd his awful book,
And had read so far as to ask if to wed he meant?
And if " he knew any just cause or impediment?"
When from base to turret the castle shook ! ! !
Then came a sound of a mighty rain
Dashing against each storied pane,
The wind blew loud,   And a coal-black cloud
O'ershadowed the church, and the party, and
    crowd ;
How it could happen they could not divine
The morning had been so remarkably fine !

Still the darkness increased, till it reach'd such a
    pass
That the sextoness hasten'd to turn on the gas ;
  But harder it pour'd,   And the thunder roar'd,
As if heaven and earth were coming together ;
None ever had witness'd such terrible weather.
  Now louder it crash'd,   And the lightning flash'd,
  Exciting the fears   Of the sweet little dears
In the veils, as it danced on the brass chandeliers ;
The parson ran off, though a stout-hearted Saxon,
When he found that a flash had set fire to his caxon.

Though all the rest trembled, as might be expected,
Sir Rupert was perfectly cool and collected,
  And endeavoured to cheer   His bride, in her ear
Whisp'ring tenderly, " Pray don't be frighten'd, my dear,
Should it even set fire to the castle, and burn it, you're
Amply insured, both for buildings and furniture."

R

But now, from without   A trustworthy scout
Rush'd hurriedly in,   Wet through to the skin,
Informing his master " the river was rising,
And flooding the grounds in a way quite surprising."

He'd no time to say more,   For already the roar
Of the waters was heard as they reach'd the church door,
While, high on the first wave that roll'd in, was seen,
Riding proudly, the form of the angry Lurline ;
And all might observe, by her glance fierce and stormy,
She was stung by the *spretæ injuriâ formæ.*

What she said to the Knight, what she said to the bride,
What she said to the ladies who stood by her side,
What she said to the nice little boys in white clothes,
Oh, nobody mentions,—for nobody knows ;
For the roof tumbled in, and the walls tumbled out,
And the folks tumbled down, all confusion and rout,
    The rain kept on pouring,
    The flood kept on roaring,
The billows and water-nymphs roll'd more and more in ;
    Ere the close of the day
    All was clean washed away—
One only survived who could hand down the news,
A little old woman that open'd the pews ;
    She was borne off, but stuck,
    By the greatest good luck,
In an oak-tree, and there she hung, crying and screaming,
And saw all the rest swallow'd up the wild stream in ;
    In vain all the week,   Did the fishermen seek
For the bodies, and poke in each cranny and creek ;
    In vain was their search
    After aught in the church,
They caught nothing but weeds, and perhaps a few perch ;
    The Humane Society   Tried a variety
Of methods, and brought down, to drag for the wreck, tackles
But they only fish'd up the clerk's tortoise-shell spectacles.

MORAL.

This tale has a moral.   Ye youths, oh, beware
Of liquor, and how you run after the fair !

Shun playing at *shorts*—avoid quarrels and jars—
And don't take to smoking those nasty cigars !
—Let no run of bad luck, or despair for some Jewess-eyed
Damsel, induce you to contemplate suicide !
Don't sit up much later than ten or eleven !—
Be up in the morning by half after seven !
Keep from flirting—nor risk, warned by Rupert's miscarriage,
An action for breach of a promise of marriage ;—
    Don't fancy old fishes !   Don't prig silver dishes !
And to sum up the whole, in the shortest phrase I know,
BEWARE OF THE RHINE, AND TAKE CARE OF THE RHINO !

And now for " Sunny Italy,"—the " Land of the unforgotten brave,"—the land of blue skies and black-eyed Signoras.—I cannot discover from any recorded memoranda that " Uncle Perry " was ever in Venice, even in Carnival time—that he ever saw Garrick in Shylock I do not believe, and am satisfied that he knew nothing of Shakspeare, a circumstance that would by no means disqualify him from publishing an edition of that Poet's works.   I can only conclude that, in the course of his Continental wanderings, Sir Peregrine had either read, or heard of, the following history, especially as he furnishes us with some particulars of the eventual destination of his *dramatis personæ* which the Bard of Avon has omitted.   If this solution be not accepted, I can only say, with Mr. Puff, that probably " two men hit upon the same idea, and Shakspeare made use of it first."

The Merchant of Venice

A Legend of Italy

. . . Of the Merchant of Venice there are two 4to editions in 1600, one by Heyes and the other by Roberts.   The Duke of Devonshire and Lord Francis Egerton have copies of the edition by Heyes, and *they vary importantly.*

. . . It must be acknowledged that *this* is a very easy and happy emendation, which does not admit of a moment's doubt or dispute.

. . . Readers in general are not all aware of the *nonsense* they have in many cases been accustomed to receive as the genuine text of Shakspeare !

Reasons for a new edition of Shakspeare's Works, by J. Payne Collier.

I BELIEVE there are few   But have heard of a Jew,
Named Shylock, of Venice, as arrant a " Screw "
In money transactions, as ever you knew ;
An exorbitant miser, who never yet lent
A ducat at less than three hundred per cent.,
Insomuch that the veriest spendthrift in Venice,
Who'd take no more care of his pounds than his pennies,
When press'd for a loan, at the very first sight
Of his terms, would back out, and take refuge in *Flight.*
It is not my purpose to pause and inquire
If he might not, in managing thus to retire,
Jump out of the frying-pan into the fire ;
Suffice it, that folks would have nothing to do,
Who could possibly help it, with Shylock the Jew.

But, however discreetly one cuts and contrives,
We've been most of us taught, in the course of our lives,
That " Needs must when the Elderly Gentleman drives ! "

In proof of this rule,   A thoughtless young fool,
Bassanio, a Lord of the Tom-noddy school,
Who, by showing at Operas, Balls, Plays, and Court,
A " swelling " (Payne Collier would read " swilling ") " port,"
And inviting his friends to dine, breakfast, and sup,
Had shrunk his " weak means," and was "stump'd" and " hard-up,"
   Took occasion to send   To his very good friend
Antonio, a merchant whose wealth had no end,
And who'd often before had the kindness to lend
Him large sums, on his note, which he'd managed to spend.

" Antonio," said he,   " Now listen to me :
I've just hit on a scheme which, I think, you'll agree,
All matters considered, is no bad design,
And which, if it succeeds, will suit your book and mine.

In the first place, you know all the money I've got,
Time and often, from you has been long gone to pot,
And in making those loans you have made a bad shot ;
Now do as the boys do when, shooting at sparrows
And tom-tits, they chance to lose one of their arrows,
—Shoot another the same way—I'll watch well its track,
And, turtle to tripe, I'll bring both of them back !—
   So list to my plan,   And do what you can
To attend to and second it, that's a good man !

" There's a Lady, young, handsome beyond all compare, at
A place they call Belmont, whom, when I was there, at
The suppers and parties my friend Lord Mountferrat
Was giving last season, we all used to stare at.
Then, as to her wealth, her Solicitor told mine,
Besides vast estates, a pearl-fishery, and gold mine,
   Her iron strong box   Seems bursting its locks,
It's stuffed so with shares in ' Grand Junctions ' and ' Docks,'
Not to speak of the money she's got in the Stocks,
   French, Dutch, and Brazilian,
   Columbian, and Chilian,
In English Exchequer-bills full half a million,
Not ' kites,' manufactured to cheat and inveigle,
But the right sort of ' flimsy,' all sign'd by Monteagle.

Then I know not how much in Canal-shares and Railways,
And more speculations I need not detail, ways
Of vesting which, if not so safe as some think 'em,
Contribute a deal to improving one's income ;
   In short, she's a Mint :— Now I say, deuce is in't
If, with all my experience, I can't take a hint,
And her ' eye's speechless messages,' plainer than print
At the time that I told you of, know from a squint.
   In short, my dear Tony, My crusty old crony,
Do stump up three thousand once more as a loan—I
Am sure of my game—though, of course, there are brutes,
Of all sorts and sizes, preferring their suits
To her you may call the Italian Miss Coutts,
Yet Portia—she's named from that daughter of Cato's—
Is not to be snapp'd up like little potatoes,
   And I have not a doubt I shall rout every lout
Ere you'll whisper Jack Robinson—cut them all out—
   Surmount every barrier, Carry her, marry her !
—Then hey ! my old Tony, when once fairly noosed,
For her Three-and-a-half per Cents—New and Reduced !

With a wink of his eye His friend made reply
In his jocular manner, sly, caustic, and dry,
" Still the same boy, Bassanio,—never say ' die ' !
—Well—I hardly know how I shall do't, but I'll try,—
Don't suppose my affairs are at all in a hash,
But the fact is, at present I'm quite out of cash ;
The bulk of my property, merged in rich cargoes, is
Tossing about, as you know, in my Argosies,
Tending, of course, my resources to cripple,—I
've one bound to England,—another to Tripoli—
Cyprus—Masulipatam—and Bombay ;
   A sixth, by the way, I consign'd t'other day,
To Sir Richard M'Gregor, Cacique of Poyais,
A country where silver's as common as clay.
   Meanwhile, till they tack,
   And come, some of them, back,
What with Custom-house duties, and bills falling due,
My account with Jones Loyd and Co. looks rather blue ;
While, as for the ' ready,' I'm like a Church mouse,—
I really don't think there's five pounds in the house,

But, no matter for that,
Let me just get my hat,
And my new silk umbrella that stands on the mat,
And we'll go forth at once to the market—we two,—
And try what my credit in Venice can do ;
I stand well on 'Change, and when
    all's said and done, I
Don't doubt I shall get it for love
    or for money."

They were going to go,   When,
    lo ! down below,
In the street, they heard somebody
    crying, " Old Clo' ! "
—" By the Pope, there's the man
    for our purpose !—I knew
We should not have to search long.
    Salanio, run you,
—Salarino,—quick !—haste ! ere he
    get out of view,
And call in that scoundrel, old
    Shylock, the Jew ! "

With a pack,   Like a sack
    Of old clothes, at his back,
And three hats on his head, Shylock
    came in a crack,
Saying, Rest   you   fair,   Signior
    Antonio ! vat, pray,
Might your worship be pleashed
    for to vant in ma vay ? "

—" Why, Shylock, although,   As
    you very well know,
I am what they call ' warm,'—pay
    my way as I go,
And, as to myself, neither borrow nor lend,
I can break through a rule, to oblige an old friend ;
And that's the case now—Lord Bassanio would raise
Some three thousand ducats—well, knowing your ways,
And that nought's to be got from you, say what one will,
Unless you've a couple of names to the bill,

Why, for once, I'll put mine to it,
  Yea, seal and sign to it—
Now, then, old Sinner, let's hear what you'll say
As to ' doing ' a bill at three months from to-day ?
Three thousand gold ducats, mind—all in good bags
Of hard money—no sealing-wax, slippers, or rags ? "

   " —Vell, ma tear," says the Jew,
   " I'll see vat I can do !
But Mishter Antonio, hark you, 'tish funny
You say to me, ' Shylock, ma tear, ve'd have money ! '
   Ven you very vell knows
   How you shpit on ma clothes,
And use naughty vords—call me Dog—and avouch
Dat I put too much int'resht py half in ma pouch,
And vhile I, like de resht of ma tribe, shrug and crouch,
You find fault mit ma pargains, and say I'm a Smouch.
   —Vell !—no matters, ma tear,—   Von vord in your ear !
I'd be friends mit you bote—and to make dat appear,
Vy, I'll find you de monies as soon as you vill,
Only von littel joke musht be put in de pill ;—
   Ma tear, you musht say,   If on such and such day
Such sum, or such sums, you shall fail to repay,
I shall cut vere I like, as de pargain is proke,
A fair pound of your flesh—chest by vay of a joke."

   So novel a clause   Caused Bassanio to pause ;
But Antonio, like most of those sage " Johnny Raws "
   Who care not three straws   About Lawyers or Laws,
And think cheaply of " Old Father Antic," because
They have never experienced a gripe from his claws,
" Pooh, pooh'd " the whole thing.—" Let the Smouch have his
    way
   Why, what care I, pray,   For his penalty ?—Nay,
It's a forfeit he'd never expect me to pay ;
   And, come what come may,   I hardly need say
My ships will be back a full month ere the day."
So, anxious to see his friend off on his journey,
And thinking the whole but a paltry concern, he
   Affixed with all speed   His name to a deed,
Duly stamp'd and drawn up by a sharp Jew attorney.

Thus again furnished forth, Lord Bassanio, instead
Of squandering the cash, after giving one spread,
With fiddling and masques at the Saracen's Head,
   In the morning " made play,"
   And, without more delay,
Started off in the steam-boat for Belmont next day.
   But scarcely had he   From the harbour got free,
And left the Lagunes for the broad open sea, ·
Ere the 'Change and Rialto both rung with the news
That he'd carried off more than mere cash from the Jew's.

   Though Shylock was old,   And, if rolling in gold,
Was as ugly a dog as you'd wish to behold,
For few in his tribe 'mongst their Levis and Moseses,
Sported so Jewish an eye, beard, and nose as his,
Still, whate'er the opinions of Horace and some be,
Your *aquilæ* generate *some*times *Columbæ.**
Like Jephthah, as Hamlet says, he'd " one fair daughter,"
And every gallant, who caught sight of her, thought her
A jewel—a gem of the very first water ;
   A great many sought her,   Till one at last caught her,
And, upsetting all that the Rabbis had taught her,
To feelings so truly reciprocal brought her,
   That the very same night   Bassanio thought right
To give all his old friends that farewell " invite,"
And while Shylock was gone there to feed out of spite,
On " wings made by a tailor " the damsel took flight.

   By these " wings " I'd express   A grey duffle dress,
With brass badge and muffin cap, made, as by rule,
For an upper class boy in the National School.
Jessy ransack'd the house, popped her breeks on, and when so
Disguised, bolted off with her beau—one Lorenzo,
An " Unthrift," who lost not a moment in whisking
   Her into the boat,   And was fairly afloat
Ere her Pa had got rid of the smell of the griskin.

Next day, while old Shylock was making a racket,
And threatening how well he'd dust every man's jacket
Who'd helped her in getting aboard of the packet,

       * Nec imbellem feroces
         Progenerant aquilæ columbam.—Hor.

Bassanio at Belmont was capering and prancing,
And bowing, and scraping, and singing, and dancing,
Making eyes at Miss Portia, and doing his best
To perform the polite, and to cut out the rest ;
And, if left to herself, he, no doubt, had succeeded,
For none of them waltz'd so genteelly as he did ;
  But an obstacle lay,   Of some weight, in his way,
The defunct Mr. P., who was now turned to clay,
Had been an odd man, and, though all for the best he meant,
Left but a queer sort of " Last will and testament,"—
  Bequeathing her hand,   With her houses and land,
&c., from motives one don't understand,
As she rev'renced his memory, and valued his blessing,
To him who should turn out the best hand at guessing !

  Like a good girl, she did   Just what she was bid ;
In one of three caskets her picture she hid,
And clapped a conundrum a-top of each lid.

A couple of Princes, a black and a white one,
Tried first, but they both failed in choosing the right one ;
Another from Naples, who shoed his own horses ;
A French Lord, whose graces might vie with Count D'Orsay's ;—
A young English Baron ;—a Scotch Peer his neighbour :—
A dull drunken Saxon, all mustache and sabre ;—
As followed, and all had their pains for their labour.
Bassanio came last—happy man be his dole !
Put his conjuring cap on,—considered the whole,—
  The gold put aside as   Mere " hard food for Midas,"
  The silver bade trudge   As a " pale common drudge,"
Then choosing the little lead box in the middle,
Came plump on the picture, and found out the riddle.

Now you're not such a goose as to think, I dare say,
Gentle Reader, that all this was done in a day,
Any more than the dome   Of St. Peter's at Rome
Was built in the same space of time ; and, in fact,
  Whilst Bassanio was doing   His billing and cooing,
Three months had gone by ere he reach'd the fifth act ;
Meanwhile, that unfortunate bill became due,
Which his Lordship had almost forgot, to the Jew,

And Antonio grew   In a deuce of a stew,
For he could not cash up, spite of all he could do ;
(The bitter old Israelite would not renew,)
What with contrary winds, storms, and wrecks, and embargoes, his
Funds were all stopped, or gone down in his argosies,
None of the set having come into port,
And Shylock's attorney was moving the Court
For the forfeit supposed to be set down in sport.

The serious news   Of this step of the Jew's,
And his fix'd resolution all terms to refuse,
Gave the newly-made Bridegroom a fit of " the Blues,"
Especially, too, as it came from the pen
Of his poor friend himself on the wedding-day,—then,
When the Parson had scarce shut his book up, and when
The Clerk was yet uttering the final Amen.

" Dear friend," it continued, " all's up with me—I
Have nothing on earth now to do but to die !
And, as death clears all scores, you're no longer my debtor ;
    I should take it as kind
    Could you come—never mind—
If your love don't persuade you, why—don't let this letter ! "

I hardly need say this was scarcely read o'er
    Ere a post-chaise and four
    Was brought round to the door,
And Bassanio, though, doubtless, he thought it a bore,
Gave his Lady one kiss, and then started at score.
    But scarce in his flight   Had he got out of sight,
Ere Portia, addressing a groom, said, " My lad, you a
Journey must take on the instant to Padua ;
Find out there Bellario, a Doctor of Laws,
Who, like Follett, is never left out of a cause,
    And give him this note,   Which I've hastily wrote,
Take the papers he'll give you—then push for the ferry
Below, where I'll meet you—you'll do't in a wherry,
If you can't find a boat on the Brenta with sails to it—
—Stay !—bring his gown too, and wig with three tails to it."

    Giovanni (that's Jack)   Brought out his hack,
Made a bow to his mistress, then jump'd on its back,
Put his hand to his hat, and was off in a crack.

The Signora soon follow'd herself, taking as her
Own escort Nerissa her maid, and Balthazar.

*   *   *   *   *

" The Court is prepared, the Lawyers are met,
    The Judges all ranged, a terrible show ! "
As Captain Macheath says,—and when one's in debt,
    The sight's as unpleasant a one as I know,
Yet still not so bad after all, I suppose,
As if, when one cannot discharge, what one owes,
They should bid people cut off one's toes or one's nose ;
    Yet here, a worse fate,   Stands Antonio, of late
A Merchant, might vie e'en with Princes in state,
With his waistcoat unbotton'd, prepared for the knife,
Which, in taking a pound of flesh must take his life ;
—On the other side Shylock, his bag on the floor,
And three shocking bad hats on his head, as before,
    Imperturbable stands,   As he waits their commands,
With his scales and his great *sniker-snee* in his hands ;
—Between them, equipt in a wig, gown, and bands,
With a very smooth face, a young dandified Lawyer,
Whose air, ne'ertheless, speaks him quite a top-sawyer,
    Though his hopes are but feeble,   Does his *possible*
To make the hard Hebrew to mercy incline,
And in lieu of his three thousand ducats take nine,
Which Bassanio, for reasons we well may divine,
Shows in so many bags all drawn up in a line.
But vain are all efforts to soften him—still
    He points to the bond   He so often has conn'd,
And says in plain terms he'll be shot if he will.

So the dandified Lawyer, with talking grown hoarse,
Says, " I *can* say no more—let the law take its course."

Just fancy the gleam of the eye of the Jew,
As he sharpen'd his knife on the sole of his shoe
    From the toe to the heel,   And grasping the steel,
With a business-like air was beginning to feel
Whereabouts he should cut, as a butcher would veal,
When the dandified Judge puts a spoke in his wheel.
    " Stay, Shylock," says he,
    " Here's one thing—you see

This bond of yours gives you here no jot of blood !
—The words are ' A pound of flesh,'—that's clear as mud—
Slice away, then, old fellow—but mind !—if you spill
One drop of his claret that's not in your bill,
I'll hang you like Haman !—by Jingo I will ! "

When apprized of this flaw,   You never yet saw
Such an awfully marked elongation of jaw
As in Shylock, who cried, " Plesh ma heart ! ish dat law ? "—
   —Off went his three hats,
   And he look'd as the cats
Do, whenever a mouse has escaped from their claw.
—" Ish't the law ? "—why the thing won't admit of a query—
   " No doubt of the fact,   Only look at the act ;
Acto quinto, cap : tertio, Dogi Falieri—
Nay, if, rather than cut, you'd relinquish the debt,
The Law, Master Shy, has a hold on you yet.
See Foscari's ' Statutes at large '—' If a Stranger
A Citizen's life shall, with malice, endanger,
The whole of his property, little or great,
Shall go, on conviction, one half to the State,
And one to the person pursued by his hate ;
   And not to create   Any further debate,
The Doge, if he pleases, may cut off his pate.'
So down on your marrowbones, Jew, and ask mercy !
Defendant and Plaintiff are now *wisy wersy*."

What need to declare   How pleased they all were
At so joyful an end to so sad an affair ?
Or Bassanio's delight at the turn things had taken,
His friend having saved, to the letter, his bacon ?
How Shylock got shaved, and turn'd Christian, though late,
To save a life-int'rest in half his estate ?—
How the dandified Lawyer, who'd managed the thing,
Would not take any fee for his pains but a ring
Which Mrs. Bassanio had giv'n to her spouse,
With injunctions to keep it, on leaving the house ?—
   How when he, and the spark
   Who appeared as his clerk,
Had thrown off their wigs, and their gowns and their jetty coats,
There stood Nerissa and Portia in petticoats ?—

How they pouted and flouted, and acted the cruel,
Because Lord Bassanio had not kept his jewel ?—
　How they scolded and broke out,
　Till, having their joke out,
They kiss'd, and were friends, and, all blessing and blessed,
　Drove home by the light　Of a moonshiny night,
Like the one in which Troilus, the brave Trojan knight,
Sat astride on a wall, and sigh'd after his Cressid ?—

　All this, if 'twere meet,　I'd go on to repeat,
But a story spun out so's by no means a treat,
So, I'll merely relate what, in spite of the pains
I have taken to rummage among his remains,
No edition of Shakspeare, I've met with, contains :
But, if the account which I've heard be the true one,
We shall have it, no doubt, before long, in a new one.

　In an MS., then, sold　For its full weight in gold,
And knock'd down to my friend, Lord Tomnoddy, I'm told
It's recorded that Jessy, coquettish and vain,
Gave her husband, Lorenzo, a good deal of pain ;
Being mildly rebuked, she levanted again,
Ran away with a Scotchman, and, crossing the main,
Became known by the name of the " Flower of Dumblane."

That Antonio, whose piety caused, as we've seen,
Him to spit upon every old Jew's gaberdine,
　And whose goodness to paint　All colours were faint,
Acquired the well-merited prefix of " Saint,"
And the Doge, his admirer, of honour the fount,
Having given him a patent, and made him a Count,
He went over to England, got nat'ralis'd there,
And espous'd a rich heiress in Hanover Square.
That Shylock came with him, no longer a Jew,
But converted, I think may be possibly true,
But that Walpole, as these self-same papers aver,
By changing the y in his name into er,
Should allow him a fictitious surname to dish up,
And in Seventeen-twenty-eight made him a Bishop,
I cannot believe—but shall still think them two men
Till some Sage proves the fact " with his usual *acumen*."

MORAL.

From this tale of the Bard   It's uncommonly hard
If an Editor can't draw a moral—'Tis clear,
Then,—In ev'ry young wife-seeking Bachelor's ear
A maxim, 'bove all other stories, this one drums,
" PITCH GREEK TO OLD HARRY, AND STICK TO CONUNDRUMS ! ! "

To new-married Ladies this lesson it teaches,
" You're ' no that far wrong ' in assuming the breeches ! "

Monied men upon 'Change, and rich Merchants in schools
To look well to assets—nor play with edge-tools !
Last of all, this remarkable History shows men,
What caution they need when they deal with old-clothesmen !
    So bid John and Mary   To mind and be wary,
And never let one of them come down the are' !

From St. Mark to St. Lawrence—from the Rialto to the Escurial—from one Peninsula to another !—it is but a hop, step, and jump—your toe at Genoa, your heel at Marseilles, and a good hearty spring pops you down at once in the very heart of Old Castille. That Sir Peregrine Ingoldsby, then a young man, was at Madrid soon after the peace of Ryswick, there is extant a long correspondence of his to prove. Various passages in it countenance the supposition that his tour was partly undertaken for political purposes ; and this opinion is much strengthened by certain allusions in several of his letters, addressed, in after life, to his friend Sir Horace Mann, then acting in the capacity of Envoy to the Court of Tuscany. Although the Knight spent several months in Spain, and visited many of her principal cities, there is no proof of his having actually " seen Seville," beyond the internal evidence incidentally supplied by the following legend. The events to which it alludes were, of course, of a much earlier date, though the genealogical records of the " Kings of both the Indies " have been in vain consulted for the purpose of fixing their precise date, and even Mr. Simpkinson's research has failed to determine which of the royal stock rejoicing in the name of Ferdinand is the hero of the legend. The conglomeration of Christian names usual in the families of the *haute noblesse* of Spain adds to the difficulty ; not that this inconvenient accumulation of prefixes is peculiar to the country in question, witness my excellent friend Field-Marshal Count Herman Karl Heinrich Socrates von der Nodgerrie zü Pfefferkorn, whose appellations puzzled the recording clerk of one of our Courts lately,—and that not a little.

That a splendid specimen of the *genus Homo, species Monk,* flourished in the earlier moiety of the 15th century, under the appellation of Torquemada, is notorious,—and this fact might seem to establish the era of the story ; but then *his* name was John—not Dominic—though he was a *Dominican,* and hence the mistake, if any, may perhaps have originated—but then again the Spanish Queen to whom he was Confessor was called Isabella, and not Blanche—it is a puzzling affair altogether.

From his own silence on the subject, it may well be doubted whether the worthy transcriber knew, himself, the date of the transactions he has recorded ; the authenticity of the details, however, cannot be well called in question.—Be this as it may, I shall make no further question, but at once introduce my " pensive public " to

The Auto-da-fé

A Legend of Spain

With a moody air, from morn till noon,
King Ferdinand paces the royal saloon ;
    From morn till eve   He does nothing but grieve ;
Sighings and sobbings his midriff heave,
And he wipes his eyes with his ermined sleeve,
And he presses his feverish hand to his brow,
And he frowns, and he looks I can't tell you how :
    And the Spanish Grandees   In their degrees,
Are whispering about in twos and in threes,
And there is not a man of them seems at his ease,
But they gaze on the monarch, as watching what he does,
With their very long whiskers, and longer Toledos.
Don Gaspar, Don Gusman, Don Juan, Don Diego,
Don Gomez, Don Pedro, Don Blas, Don Rodrigo,
Don Jerome, Don Giacomo join Don Alphonso
    In making inquiries   Of grave Don Ramirez,
The Chamberlain, what it is makes him take on so ;
A Monarch so great that the soundest opinions
Maintain the sun can't set throughout his dominions ;
    But grave Don Ramirez   In guessing no nigher is
Than the other grave Dons who propound these inquiries ;
When, pausing at length, as beginning to tire, his
Majesty beckons, with stately civility,
    To Señor Don Lewis   Condé d'Aranjuez,
Who in birth, wealth, and consequence second to few is,
And Señor Don Manuel, Count de Pacheco,
A lineal descendant from King Pharaoh Neco,
Both Knights of the Golden Freece, highborn Hidalgos,
With whom e'en the King himself quite as a " pal " goes.

"Don Lewis," says he, "Just listen to me;
And you, Count Pacheco,—I think that we three
On matters of state, for the most part agree,—
   Now you both of you know That some six years ago,
Being then, for a King, no indifferent Beau,
At the altar I stood, like my forbears of old,
   The Peninsula's paragon, Fair Blanche of Aragon,
For better, for worse, and to have and to hold—
   And you're fully aware, When the matter took air,
How they shouted, and fired the great guns in the Square,
Cried '*Viva!*' and rung all the bells in the steeple,
   And all that sort of thing The mob do when a King
Brings a Queen-Consort home for the good of his people.

   "Well!—six years and a day Have flitted away
Since that blessed event, yet I'm sorry to say—
In fact it's the principal cause of my pain—
I don't see any signs of an Infant of Spain!—
   Now I want to ask you, Cavaliers true,
And Counsellors sage—what the deuce shall I do?—
The State—don't you see?—hey?—an heir to the throne—
Every monarch—you know—should have one of his own—
Disputed succession—hey—terrible Go!—
Hum!—hey?—Old fellows—you see!—don't you know?"—

   Now, Reader, dear, If you've ever been near
Enough to a Court to encounter a Peer
When his principal tenant's gone off in arrear,
And his brewer has sent in a long bill for beer,
And his butcher and baker, with faces austere,
   Ask him to clear Off, for furnish'd good cheer,
Bills, they say, "have been standing for more than a year,"
And the tailor and shoemaker also appear
   With their "little account" Of "trifling amount,"
For Wellingtons, waistcoats, pea-jackets, and—gear
Which to name in society's thought rather queer,—
While Drummond's chief clerk, with his pen in his ear,
And a kind of a sneer, says, "We've no effects here!"
   —Or if ever you've seen An Alderman, keen
After turtle, peep into a silver tureen,

In search for the fat call'd *par excellence* " green,"
When there's none of the meat left—not even the lean !—
—Or if ever you've witnessed the face of a sailor
Return'd from a voyage, and escaped from a gale, or
Poeticè " Boreas," that " blustering railer,"
To find that his wife, when he hastens to " hail " her,
Has just run away with his cash—and a tailor—
If one of these cases you've ever survey'd,
   You'll, without my aid,   To yourself have pourtray'd
The beautiful mystification display'd,
And the puzzled expression of manner and air
Exhibited now by the dignified pair,
When thus unexpectedly ask'd to declare
Their opinions as Counsellors, several and joint,
On so delicate, grave, and important a point.

   Señor Don Lewis   Condé d'Aranjuez
At length forced a smile 'twixt the prim and the grim,
And look'd at Pacheco—Pacheco at him—
Then, making a rev'rence, and dropping his eyes,
Cough'd, hemm'd, and deliver'd himself in this wise :

" My Liege !—unaccustom'd as I am to speaking
In public—an art I'm remarkably weak in—
I feel I should be—quite unworthy the name
Of a man and a Spaniard—and highly to blame,
   Were there not in my breast
   What—can't be exprest,—
And can therefore,—your Majesty—only be guess'd—
—What I mean to say is—since your Majesty deigns
To ask my advice on your welfare—and Spain's,—
And on that of your Majesty's Bride—that is, Wife—
It's the—as I may say—proudest day of my life !
But as to the point—on a subject so nice
It's a delicate matter to give one's advice,
   Especially too,   When one don't clearly view
The best mode of proceeding,—or know what to do ;
My decided opinion, however is this,
And I fearlessly say that you can't do amiss,
   If with all that fine tact   Both to think and to act,
In which all know your Majesty so much excels—
You are graciously pleased to—ask somebody else ! "

Here the noble Grandee   Made that sort of congée,
Which, as Hill used to say, " I once *happen'd to see* "
The great Indian conjuror, Ramo Samee,
Make, while swallowing what all thought a regular choker,
Viz., a small sword as long and as stiff as a poker.
    Then the Count de Pacheco,
    Whose turn 'twas to speak, o-
mitting all preface, exclaim'd with devotion,
" Sire, I beg leave to second Don Lewis's motion ! "

Now a Monarch of Spain   Of course could not deign
To expostulate, argue, or, much less, complain
Of an answer thus giv'n, or to ask them again ;
So he merely observ'd, with an air of disdain,
" Well, Gentlemen,—since you both shrink from the task
Of advising your Sovereign—pray, whom shall I ask ? "

Each felt the rub,   And in Spain not a Sub,
Much less than Hidalgo, can stomach a snub,
    So the noses of these   Castilian Grandees
Rise at once in an angle of several degrees,
Till the under-lip's almost becoming the upper,
Each perceptibly grows, too, more stiff in the crupper,
    Their right hands rest   On the left side the breast,
While the hilts of their swords, by their left hands deprest,
Make the ends of their scabbards to cock up behind,
Till they're quite horizontal instead of inclined,
And Don Lewis, with scarce an attempt to disguise
The disgust he experiences, gravely replies,
" Sire, ask the Archbishop—his Grace of Toledo !—
He understands these things much better than we do ! "
    —*Pauca Verba !*—enough,
    Each turns off in a huff,
This twirling his mustache, that fingering his ruff,
Like a blue-bottle fly on a rather large scale,
With a rather large corking-pin stuck through his tail.

            *   *   *   *   *

King Ferdinand paces the royal saloon,
With a moody brow, and he looks like a " Spoon,"
And all the Court Nobles who form the ring,
Have a spoony appearance, of course, like the King,

All of them eyeing King Ferdinand
As he goes up and down, with his watch in his hand,
Which he claps to his ear as he walks to and fro,—
" What is it can make the Archbishop so slow ? "
Hark !—at last there's a sound in the courtyard below,
Where the Beefeaters all are drawn up in a row,—
I would say the " Guards," for in Spain they're in chief eaters
Of *omelettes* and garlick, and can't be called Beefeaters ;
   In fact, of the few   Individuals I knew
Who ever had happened to travel in Spain
There has scarce been a person who did not complain
Of their cookery and dishes as all bad in grain,
And no one I'm sure will deny it who's tried a
Vile compound they have that's called *Olla podrida.*
. (This, by the bye,   's a mere rhyme to the eye,
For in Spanish the *i* is pronounced like an *e*,
And they've not quite our mode of pronouncing the *d*.
In Castille, for instance, it's giv'n through the teeth,
And what we call Ma*drid* they sound more like Mad*reeth*,)
Of course you will see in a moment they've no men
That at all corresponds with our Beefeating Yeomen ;
So call them " Walloons," or whatever you please,
By their rattles and slaps they're not " standing at ease,"
   But beyond all disputing,   Engaged in saluting
Some very great person among the Grandees ;—
Here a Gentleman Usher walks in and declares,
" His Grace the Archbishop's a-coming up-stairs ! "

The Most Reverend Don Garcilasso Quevedo
   Was just at this time, as he   Now held the Primacy,
(Always attached to the See of Toledo,)
A man of great worship *Officii virtute*
Versed in all that pertains to a Counsellor's duty,
   Well skill'd to combine   Civil law with divine ;
As a statesman, inferior to none in that line ;
   As an orator, too,   He was equalled by few ;
Uniting, in short, in tongue, head-piece, and pen,
The very great powers of three very great men,
Talleyrand,—who will never drive down Piccadilly more
To the Traveller's Club-House !—Charles Phillips—and Phillimore.
   Not only at home   But even at Rome

There was not a Prelate among them could cope
With the Primate of Spain in the eyes of the Pope.
(The Conclave was full, and they'd not a spare hat, or he
'd long since been Cardinal, Legate *à latere*,
A dignity fairly his due, without flattery,
So much he excited among all beholders
   Their marvel to see At his age—thirty-three
Such a very old head on such very young shoulders,)
No wonder the King, then, in this his distress,
Should send for so sage an adviser express,
   Who, you'll readily guess Could not do less
Than start off at once, without stopping to dress,
In his haste to get Majesty out of a mess.

His grace the Archbishop comes up the back way—
Set apart for such Nobles as have the *entrée*,
Viz., Grandees of the first class, both cleric and lay ;
Walks up to the monarch, and makes him a bow,
As a dignified clergyman always knows how,
Then replaces the mitre at once on his brow ;
   For, in Spain, recollect, As a mark of respect
To the Crown, if a Grandee uncovers, it's quite
As a matter of option, and not one of right ;
A thing not conceded by *our* Royal Masters,
Who always make noblemen take off their " castors,"
   Except the heirs male Of John Lord Kinsale,
A stalwart old Baron, who, acting as Henchman
To one of our early Kings, kill'd a big Frenchman ;
A feat which his Majesty deigning to smile on,
Allow'd him thenceforward to stand with his " tile " on ;
And all his successors have kept the same privilege
Down from those barbarous times to our civil age.

Returning his bow with a slight demi-bob,
And replacing the watch in his hand in his fob,
" My Lord," said the King, " here's a rather tough job,
   Which it seems, of a sort is To puzzle our *Cortes*.
And since it has quite flabbergasted that Diet, I
Look to your Grace with no little anxiety
   Concerning a point Which has quite out of joint
Put us all with respect to the good of society :—

Your Grace is aware
That we've not got an Heir ;
Now, it seems, one and all, they don't stick to declare
That of all our advisers there is not in Spain one
Can tell, like your Grace, the best way to obtain one ;
So put your considering cap on—we're curious
To learn your receipt for a Prince of Asturias."

One without the nice tact
Of his Grace would have backt
Out at once, as the Noblemen did,—and, in fact,
He was, at the first, rather pozed how to act—
One moment—no more !— Bowing then, as before,
He said, " Sire, 'twere superfluous for me to acquaint
The ' Most Catholic King ' in the world, that a Saint
Is the usual resource
In these cases,—of course
Of their influence your Majesty well knows the force ;
If I may be, therefore, allow'd to suggest
The plan which occurs to my mind as the best,
Your Majesty may go
At once to St. Jago,
Whom, as Spain's patron Saint, I pick out from the rest ;
If your Majesty looks
Into Guthrie, or Brooks,
In all the approved Geographical books,
You will find Compostella laid down in the maps
Some two hundred and sev'nty miles off ; and, perhaps,
In a case so important, you may not decline
A pedestrian excursion to visit his shrine ;
And, Sire, should you choose
To put peas in your shoes,
The Saint, as a Gentleman, can't well refuse
So distinguish'd a Pilgrim,—especially when he
Considers the boon will not cost him one penny ! "

His speech ended, his Grace bow'd, and put on his mitre
As tight as before, and perhaps a thought tighter.
" Pooh ! pooh ! " says the King,
" I shall do no such thing !

It's nonsense,—Old fellow—you see—no use talking—
The peas set apart, I abominate walking—
Such a deuced way off, too—hey ?—walk there—what me ?
Pooh !—it's no Go, Old fellow !—you know—don't you see ? "
" Well, Sire," with much sweetness the Prelate replied,
" If your Majesty don't like to walk—you can ride !
   And then, if you please,   In lieu of the peas,
A small portion of horse-hair, cut fine, we'll insert,
As a substitute, under your Majesty's shirt ;
Then a rope round your collar instead of a laced band,—
A few nettles tuck'd into your Majesty's waistband,—
Asafœtida mix'd with your *bouquet* and civet,
I'll warrant you'll find yourself right as a trivet ! "

   " Pooh ! pooh ! I tell you,"
   Quoth the King, " it won't do ! "
A cold perspiration began to bedew
His Majesty's cheek, and he grew in a stew,
When Jozé de Humez, the King's privy-purse-keeper,
(Many folks thought it could scarce have a worse keeper,)
Came to the rescue, and said with a smile,
" Sire, your Majesty *can't* go—'twould take a long while,
And you won't post it under TWO SHILLINGS A MILE ! !
   Twenty-seven pounds ten
   To get there—and then
Twenty-seven pounds ten more to get back agen ! !
Sire, the *tottle's* enormous—you ought to be King
Of Golconda as well as the Indies, to fling
Such a vast sum away upon any such thing ! "

   At this second rebuff
   The Archbishop look'd gruff,
And his eye glanced on Humez as if he'd say " Stuff ! "
But seeing the King seem'd himself in a huff,
He changed his demeanour, and grew smooth enough ;
Then taking his chin 'twixt his finger and thumb,
As a help to reflection, gave vent to a " Hum ! "
'Twas the pause of an instant—his eye assumed fast
That expression which says, " Come, I've got it at last ! "

" There's one plan," he resumed, " which, with all due respect to
Your Majesty, no one, I think, can object to—

—Since your Majesty don't like the peas in the shoe—or to
Travel—what say you to burning a Jew or two ?—
   Of all cookeries, most
   The Saints love a roast !
And a Jew's, of all others, the best dish to toast ;
   And then for a Cook
   We have not far to look—
Father Dominic's self, Sire, your own Grand Inquisitor,
Luckily now at your Court is a visitor ;
Of his Rev'rence's functions there is not one weightier
Than Heretic-burning—in fact, 'tis his *métier*,
   Besides Alguazils
   Who still follow his heels,
He has always Familiars enough at his beck at home,
To pick you up Hebrews enough for a hecatomb !
And depend on it, Sire, such a glorious specific
Would make every Queen throughout Europe prolific ! "

   Says the King, " That'll do !
   Pooh ! pooh !—burn a Jew ?
Burn half a score Jews—burn a dozen—burn two—
   Your Grace, it's a match
   Burn all you can catch,
Men, women, and children—Pooh ! pooh ! great and small—
Old clothes—slippers—sealing-wax—Pooh ! burn them all.
   For once we'll be gay,   A Grand *Auto-da-fé*
Is much better fun than a ball or a play ! "

So the warrant was made out without more delay,
Drawn, seal'd, and deliver'd, and
             (Signed)
                YO EL RE !

CANTO II.

THERE is not a nation in Europe but labours
To toady itself, and to humbug its neighbours—
" Earth has no such folks—no folks such a city,
So great, or so grand, or so fine, or so pretty,"
   Said Louis Quatorze, " As this Paris of ours ! "
—Mr. Daniel O'Connell exclaims, " By the Pow'rs

Ould Ireland's on all hands admitted to be
The first flow'r of the earth, and first *Gim* of the sea ! "—
—Mr. Bull will inform you that Neptune,—a lad he,
With more of affection than rev'rence styles " Daddy,"—
   Did not scruple to " say
   To Freedom one day,"
That if ever he changed his aquatics for dry land,
His home should be Mr. B.'s " Tight little Island."—
He adds, too, that he,   The said Mr. B.,
Of all possible Frenchmen can fight any three ;
That, with no greater odds, he knows well how to treat them,
To meet them, defeat them, and beat them, and eat them,—
—In Italy, too, 'tis the same to the letter ;
   There each Lazzarone
   Will cry to his crony,
" See Naples, then die* and the sooner the better ! "
The Portuguese say, as a well understood thing,
" Who has not seen Lisbon† has not seen a good thing ! "—
While an old Spanish proverb runs glibly as under,
   " Quien no ha visto Sevilla
   No ha visto Maravilla ! "
" He who ne'er has viewed Seville has ne'er viewed a Wonder ! "
And from all I can learn this is no such great blunder.
   In fact, from the river,   The famed Guadalquiver,
Where many a knight's had cold steel through his liver,‡
The prospect *is* grand.   The *Iglesia Mayor*
Has a splendid effect on the opposite shore,
With its lofty *Giralda*, while two or three score
Of magnificent structures around, perhaps more,
As our Irish friends have it, are there " to the fore ; "
   Then the old Alcazar,   More ancient by far,
As some say, while some call it one of the palaces
Built in twelve hundred and odd by Abdalasis,

* " Vedi Napoli e poi mori ! "
† " Quem naõ tem visto Lisboa
   Naõ tem visto cousa boa."
‡ " Rio verde, Rio verde," &c.
" Glassy water, glassy water,
   Down whose current clear and strong,
   Chiefs, confused in mutual slaughter,
   Moor and Christian, roll along."
          Old Spanish Romance.

With its horse-shoe shaped arches of Arabesque tracery,
Which the architect seems to have studied to place awry,
　　Saracenic and rich ;
　　And more buildings, " the which,"
As old Lilly, in whom I've been looking a bit o' late,
Says, " You'd be bored should I now recapitulate ; " *
　　In brief, then, the view　Is so fine and so new,
It would make you exclaim, 'twould so forcibly strike ye,
If a Frenchman, " *Superbe !* "—If an Englishman " Crikey !! "

Yes ! thou *art* " WONDERFUL ! "—but oh,
　　'Tis sad to think, 'mid scenes so bright
As thine, fair Seville, sounds of woe,
　　And shrieks of pain, and wild affright,
And soul-wrung groans of deep despair,
And blood, and death should mingle there !

Yes ! thou art " WONDERFUL ! "—the flames
　　That on thy towers reflected shine,
While earth's proud Lords and high-born Dames
　　Descendants of a mighty line,
With cold unalter'd looks are by
To gaze, with an unpitying eye,
On wretches in their agony.

All speak thee " WONDERFUL "—the phrase
Befits thee well—the fearful blaze
Of yon piled faggots' lurid light,
Where writhing victims mock the sight,—
The scorch'd limb shrivelling in its chains,—
The hot blood parch'd in *living* veins,—
The crackling nerve—the fearful knell
Rung out by that remorseless bell,—
Those shouts from human fiends that swell,—
That withering scream—that frantic yell,—
All Seville,—all too truly tell
Thou *art* a " MARVEL "—and a Hell !
God !—that the worm whom thou hast made
Should thus his brother worm invade !

* Cum multis aliis quæ nunc perscribere longum est.
　　　　　　　Propria quæ maribus.

Count deeds like these good service done,
And deem THINE eye looks smiling on ! !

Yet there at his ease, with his whole Court around him,
King Ferdinand sits " in his GLORY "—confound him !—
   Leaning back in his chair,
   With a satisfied air,
And enjoying the bother, the smoke, and the smother,
With one knee cocked carelessly over the other ;
   His pouncet-box goes
   To and fro at his nose,
As somewhat misliking the smell of old clothes,
And seeming to hint, by this action emphatic,
That Jews, e'en when roasted, are not aromatic ;
   There, too, fair Ladies
   From Xeres, and Cadiz,
Catalinas, and Julias, and fair Iñesillas.
In splendid lace-veils and becoming mantillas ;
Elviras, Antonias, and Cláras, and Floras,
And dark-eyed Jacinthas, and soft Isidoras,
Are crowding the " boxes," and looking on coolly as
Though 'twas but one of their common *tertulias,*
Partaking, as usual, of wafers and ices,
Snow-water, and melons cut out into slices,
And chocolate,—furnished at coffee-house prices ;
   While many a suitor, And gay coadjutor
In the eating-and-drinking line, scorns to be neuter ;
One, being perhaps just return'd with his tutor
From travel in England, is tempting his " *future* "
With a luxury neat as imported, " The Pewter,"
And charming the dear Violantes and Iñeses
With a three-corner'd Sandwich, and *soupçon* of Guinness's ; "
While another, from Paris but newly come back,
Hints " the least taste in life " of the best cogniac.
   Such ogling and eyeing, In short, and such sighing,
And such complimenting (one must not say l—g),
Of smart Cavaliers with each other still vying,
   Mix'd up with the crying, And groans of the dying,
All hissing, and spitting, and broiling and frying,
Form a scene, which, although there can be no denying
To a *bon Catholique* it may prove edifying,

I doubt if a Protestant, smart Beau, or merry Belle
Might not shrink from it as somewhat too terrible.
It's a question with me if you ever survey'd a
More stern-looking mortal than old Torquemada,
Renown'd Father Dominic, famous for twisting dom-
estic and foreign necks all over Christendom ;
 Morescoes or Jews, Not a penny to choose,
If a dog of a heretic dared to refuse
A glass of old port, or a slice from a griskin,
The good Padre soon would so set him a frisking,
That I would not, for—more than I'll say—be in his skin.

'Twas just the same thing with his own race and nation,
And Christian Dissenters of every persuasion,
 Muggletonian, or Quaker, Or Jumper, or Shaker,
No matter with whom in opinion partaker,
George Whitfield, John Bunyan, or Thomas Gat-acre,
They'd no better chance than a Bonze or a Fakir ;
If a woman, it skill'd not—if she did not deem as he
Bade her to deem touching Papal supremacy,
 By the Pope, but he'd make her !
 From error awake her,
Or else—pop her into an oven and bake her !
No one, in short, ever came half so near as he
Did, to the full extirpation of heresy ;
And if, in the times of which now I am treating,
There had been such a thing as a " Manchester Meeting,"
" Pretty pork " he'd have made " Moderator " and " Minister,"
Had he but caught them on his side Cape Finisterre ;—
Pye Smith, and the rest of them once to his bonfire, hence-
forth you'd have heard little more of the " CONFERENCE."
And—there on the opposite side of the ring,
He, too, sits " in his GLORY," confronting the King,
With his cast-iron countenance frowning austerely,
That matched with his *en bon point* body but queerly,
For, though grim his visage, his person was pursy,
 Belying the rumour Of fat folks' good-humour ;
Above waves his banner of " Justice and Mercy,"
Below and around stand a terrible band ad-
ding much to the scene,—*viz.*, The " Holy *Hermandad,*"
That's " Brotherhood,"—each looking grave as a Grand-dad.

Within the arena
Before them is seen a
Strange, odd-looking group, each one dress'd in a garment
Not " dandified " clearly, as certainly " varment,"
Being all over vipers and snakes, and stuck thick
With multiplied *silhouette* profiles of NICK ;
   And a cap of the same,
   All devils and flame,
Extinguisher-shaped, much like Salisbury Spire,
Except that the latter's of course somewhat higher ;
   A long yellow pin-a-fore
   Hangs down, each chin afore,
On which, ere the wearer had donn'd it, a man drew
The Scotch badge, a *Saltire*, or Cross of St. Andrew ;
Though I fairly confess I am quite at a loss
To guess why they should choose that particular cross,
   Or to make clear to you
   What the Scotch had to do
At all with the business in hand,—though it's true
That the vestment aforesaid, perhaps, from its hue,
Viz., yellow, in juxta-position with *blue*,
(A tinge of which latter tint could but accrue
On the faces of wretches, of course, in a stew
As to what their tormentors were going to do,)
Might make people fancy, who no better knew,
They were somehow connected with Jeffrey's Review ;
   Especially too
   As it's certain that few
Things would make Father Dominic blither or happier
Than to catch hold of *it*, or its *Chef*, Macvey Napier.—
No matter for that—my description to crown,
All the flames and the devils were turn'd upside down
On this habit, facetiously term'd *San Benito*,
   Much like the dress suit
   Of some nondescript brute
From the show-van of Wombwell, (not George,) or Polito.

   And thrice happy they,*   Dress'd out in this way
To appear with *éclat* at the *Auto-da-fé*,

       * O fortunati nimium sua si bona nôrint !

Thrice happy indeed whom the good luck might fall to
Of devils tail upward, and " *Fuego revolto*,"
   For, only see there,   In the midst of the Square,
Where, perch'd up on poles six feet high in the air,
Sit, chained to the stake, some two, three, or four pair
Of wretches, whose eyes, nose, complexion, and hair
Their Jewish descent but too plainly declare,
Each clothed in a garment more frightful by far, a
Smock-frock sort of gaberdine, call'd a *Samarra*,
With three times the number of devils upon it,—
A proportion observed on the sugar-loaf'd bonnet,
With this further distinction—of mischief a proof—
That every fiend Jack stands upright on his hoof !
   While the pictured flames, spread
   Over body and head,
Are three times as crooked, and three times as red !
All, too, pointing upwards, as much as to say,
" Here's the real *bonne bouche* of the Auto-da-fé ! "

   Torquemada, meanwhile,   With his cold, cruel smile,
Sits looking on calmly, and watching the pile,
As his hooded " Familiars " (their names, as some tell, come
From their being so much more " familiar " than " welcome,")
   Have, by this time, begun   To be " poking their fun,"
And their firebrands, as if they were so many posies
   Of lilies and roses,   Up to the noses
Of Lazarus Levi, and Money Ben Moses ;
While similar treatment is forcing out hollow moans
From Aby Ben Lasco, and Ikey Ben Solomons,
Whose beards—this a black, that inclining to grizzle—
Are smoking, and curling, and all in a fizzle ;
The King, at the same time, his Dons and his visitors,
Sit, sporting smiles, like the Holy Inquisitors,——

   Enough !—no more !—   Thank Heaven, 'tis o'er !
The tragedy's done ! and we now draw a veil
O'er a scene which makes outraged humanity quail ;
The last fire's exhausted, and spent like a rocket,
The last wretched Hebrew's burnt down in his socket ;
The Barriers are open, and all, saints and sinners,
King, Court, Lords, and Commons, gone home to their dinners,

With a pleasing emotion
Produced by the notion
Of having exhibited so much devotion,
All chuckling to think how the Saints are delighted
At having seen so many " *Smouches* " ignited :—
   All, save Privy-purse Humez,   Who sconced in his room is,
And, Cocker in hand, in his leather-back'd chair,
Is puzzling to find out how much the " affair "
(By deep calculations, the which I can't follow,) cost,—
The *tottle*, in short, *of the whole* of the Holocaust.

Perhaps you may think it a rather odd thing,
That, while talking so much of the Court and the King,
   In describing the scene
   Through which we've just been,
I've not said one syllable as to the Queen ;
Especially, too, as her Majesty's " Whereabouts,"
All things considered, might well be thought thereabouts ;
The fact was, however, although little known,
Sa Magestad had hit on a plan of her own,
And suspecting, perhaps, than an *Auto* alone
Might fail in securing this " Heir to the throne,"
   Had made up her mind,   Although well inclined
Towards *galas* and shows of no matter what kind,
For once to retire,   And bribe the Saints higher
Than merely by sitting and seeing a fire,—
A sight, after all, she did not much admire ;
   So she locked herself up,   Without platter or cup,
In her Oriel, resolv'd not to take bite or sup,
Not so much as her matin-draught (our "early purl "),
Nor put on her jewels, nor e'en let the girl,
Who help'd her to dress, take her hair out of curl,
But to pass the whole morning in telling her beads,
And in reading the lives of the Saints, and their deeds,
And in vowing to visit, without shoes or sandals,
Their shrines, with unlimited orders for candles,
Holy water, and Masses of Mozart's, and Handel's.*

* " That is, She *would* have order'd them—but none are known, I fear, as his,
    For Handel never wrote a Mass—and so She'd David Perez's—
       Bow ! wow ! wow ?   Fol, lol," &c. &c.
                    (*Posthumous Note by the Ghost of James Smith, Esq.*)

And many a *Pater*, and *Ave*, and *Credo*
Did She, and her Father Confessor, Quevedo,
(The clever Archbishop, you know, of Toledo,)
Who came, as before, at a very short warning,
Get through, without doubt, in the course of that morning ;
   Shut up, as they were,   With nobody there
To at all interfere with so pious a pair ;
And the Saints must have been stony-hearted indeed,
If they have not allow'd all these pains to succeed.
Nay, it's not clear to me but their very ability
   Might, Spain throughout,   Have been brought into doubt,
Had the Royal bed still remain'd curs'd with sterility ;
St. Jago, however, who always is jealous
In Spanish affairs, as their best authors tell us,
   And who, if he saw   Anything like a flaw
In Spain's welfare, would soon sing " Old Rose, burn the bellows ! "
Set matters to rights like a King of good fellows ;
   By his interference,   Three-fourths of a year hence,
There was nothing but capering, dancing, and singing,
Cachucas, Boleros, and bells set a-ringing,
   In both the Castilles,   Triple-bob-major peals,
Rope-dancing, and tumbling, and somerset-flinging,
   Seguidillas, Fandangos,   While ev'ry gun bang goes ;
And all the way through, from Gibraltar to Biscay,
Figueras and Sherry made all the Dons frisky,
(Save Moore's " Blakes and O'Donnells," who stick to the whisky ;)
   All the day long   The dance and the song
Continue the general joy to prolong ;
And even long after the close of the day
You can hear little else but " Hip ! hip ! hip ! hurray ! "
The Escurial, however, is not quite so gay,
For, whether the Saint had not perfectly heard
The petition the Queen and Archbishop preferr'd,—
Or whether his head, from his not being used
To an *Auto-da-fé*, was a little confused,—
Or whether the King, in the smoke and the smother,
Got bother'd, and so made some blunder or other,
   I am sure I can't say ;   All I know is, that day
There must have been *some* mistake !—that I'm afraid, is
   Only too clear,   Inasmuch as the dear
Royal Twins—though fine babies,—proved both little Ladies ! !

MORAL.

Reader !—Not knowing what your " persuasion " may be,
Mahometan, Jewish, or even Parsee,
Take a little advice which may serve for all three !

First—" When you're at *Rome*, do as Rome does ! " and note all her
Ways—drink what She drinks ! and don't turn Tea-totaler !
  In Spain, *raison de plus*,   You must do as they do,
Inasmuch as they're all there " at sixes or sevens,"
  Just, as you know,   They were, some years ago,
In the days of Don Carlos and Brigadier Evans ;
Don't be nice, then—but take what they've got in their shops,
Whether griskins, or sausages, ham, or pork-chops !

Next—Avoid Fancy-trousers !—their colours and shapes
Sometimes, as you see, may lead folks into scrapes !
  For myself, I confess   I've but small taste in dress,
My opinion is, therefore, worth nothing—or less—
But some friends I've consulted,—much given to watch one's
  Apparel—do say   It's by far the best way,
And the safest, to do as Lord Brougham does—buy Scotch ones !

I might now volunteer some advice to a King,—
Let Whigs say what they will, I shall do no such thing,
But copy my betters, and never begin
Until, like Sir Robert, " I'm duly CALLED IN ! "

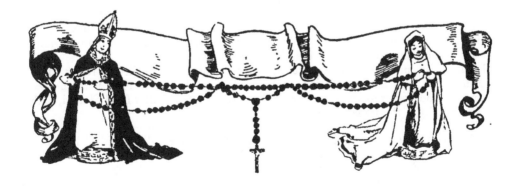

T

In the windows of the great Hall, as well as in those of the long Gallery, and the Library at Tappington, are, and have been, many of them from a very early period, various " storied panes " of stained glass, which, as Blue Dick's * exploits did not extend beyond the neighbouring city, have remained unfractured down to the present time.   Among the numerous escutcheons there displayed, charged with armorial bearings of the family and its connections, is one in which a *chevron between three eagles' cuisses, sable,* is blazoned quarterly with the *engrailed saltire* of the Ingoldsbys.   Mr. Simpkinson from Bath—whose merits as an antiquary are so well known and appreciated as to make eulogy superfluous, not to say impertinent—has been for some time bringing his heraldic lore to bear on those *monumenta vetusta.*   He pronounces the coat in question to be that of a certain Sir Ingoldsby Bray who flourished *temp. Ric. I.,* and founded the Abbey of Ingoldsby, in the county of Kent and diocese of Rochester, early in the reign of that monarch's successor.   The history of the origin of that pious establishment has been rescued from the dirt and mildew in which its chartularies have been slumbering for centuries, and is here given.   The link of connection between the two families is shown by the accompanying extract from our genealogical tree.

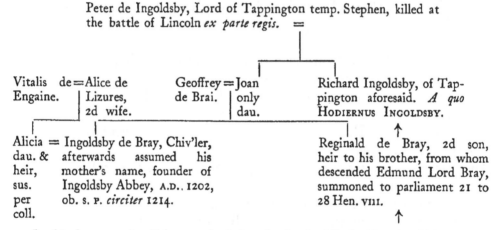

Peter de Ingoldsby, Lord of Tappington temp. Stephen, killed at the battle of Lincoln *ex parte regis.* =

Vitalis de = Alice de   Geoffrey = Joan   Richard Ingoldsby, of Tap-
Engaine. | Lizures,   de Brai. | only   pington aforesaid. *A quo*
            | 2d wife. | dau.   HODIERNUS INGOLDSBY.

Alicia = Ingoldsby de Bray, Chiv'ler,   Reginald de Bray, 2d son,
dau. &   afterwards   assumed   his   heir to his brother, from whom
heir,   mother's name, founder of   descended Edmund Lord Bray,
sus.   Ingoldsby Abbey, A.D.. 1202,   summoned to parliament 21 to
per   ob. s. p. *circiter* 1214.   28 Hen. VIII.
coll.

In this document it will be perceived that the death of Lady Alice Ingoldsby is attributed to strangulation superinduced by suspension, whereas in the veritable legend annexed no allusion is made to the intervention of a halter.   Unluckily, Sir Ingoldsby left no issue, or we might now be " calling Cousins " with (*ci devant*) Mrs. Otway Cave, in whose favour the abeyance of the old Barony of Bray has recently been determined by the Crown.   To this same Barony we ourselves were not without our pretensions, and, *teste Simpkinson,* had " as good a right to it as anybody else."   The " Collective wisdom of the Country " has, however, decided the point, and placed us among that very numerous class of claimants who are " wrongfully kept out of their property and dignities—by the right owners."

I seize with pleasure this opportunity of contradicting a malicious report that Mr. Simpkinson has, in a late publication, confounded King Henry the Fifth with the *Duke* of Monmouth, and positively deny that he has ever represented Walter Lord Clifford, (father to fair Rosamond,) as the leader of the O. P. row.

* Richard Culmer, parson of Chartham, commonly so called, distinguished himself, while Laud was in the Tower, by breaking the beautiful windows in Canterbury Cathedral, " standing on the top of the city ladder, near sixty steps high, with a whole pike in his hand, when others would not venture so high."   This feat of Vandalism the cærulean worthy called " rattling down proud Becket's glassie bones."

The Ingoldsby Penance !

A Legend of Palestine—and West Kent

I'll devise thee brave punishments for him !
SHAKSPEARE.

Out and spake Sir Ingoldsby Bray,
A stalwart knight, I ween, was he,
   " Come east, come west,   Come lance in rest,
Come falchion in hand, I'll tickle the best
Of all the Soldan's Chivalrie ! "

Oh, they came west, and they came east,
Twenty-four Emirs and Sheiks at the least,
   And they hammer'd away   At Sir Ingoldsby Bray,
Fall back, fall edge, cut, thrust, and point,—
But he topp'd off head, and he lopp'd off joint ;
   Twenty and three,   Of high degree,
Lay stark and stiff on the crimson'd lea,
All—all save one—and he ran up a tree !
" Now count them, my Squire, now count them and see ! "
   " Twenty and three !   Twenty and three !—
All of them Nobles of high degree :
There they be lying on Ascalon lea ! "

Out and spake Sir Ingoldsby Bray,
" What news ? what news ? come, tell to me !

What news ? what news, thou little Foot-page ?—
I've been whacking the foe till it seems an age
   Since I was in Ingoldsby Hall so free !
What news ? what news from Ingoldsby Hall ?
Come tell me now, thou Page so small ! "

" Oh, Hawk and Hound   Are safe and sound,
Beast in byre, and Steed in stall ;
   And the Watch-dog's bark,   As soon as it's dark,
Bays wakeful guard around Ingoldsby Hall ! "

—" I care not a pound   For Hawk or for Hound,
For Steed in stall, or for Watch-dog's bay :
   Fain would I hear   Of my dainty dear ;
How fares Dame Alice, my Lady gay ? "—
Sir Ingoldsby Bray, he said in his rage,
" What news ? what news ? thou naughty Foot-page ! "—

That little Foot-page full low crouch'd he,
And he doff'd his cap, and he bended his knee,
" Now lithe and listen, Sir Bray, to me :
Lady Alice sits lonely in bower and hall,
Her sighs they rise, and her tears they fall :
   She sits alone,   And she makes her moan ;
   Dance and song   She considers quite wrong ;
   Feast and revel   Mere snares of the devil ;
She mendeth her hose, and she crieth ' Alack !
When will Sir Ingoldsby Bray come back ? ' "

" Thou liest ! thou liest, thou naughty Foot-page,
Full loud dost thou lie, false Page, to me !
   There, in thy breast,   'Neath thy silken vest,
What scroll is that, false Page, I see ? "

Sir Ingoldsby Bray in his rage drew near,
That little Foot-page he blench'd with fear ;

" Now where may the Prior of Abingdon lie ?
King Richard's confessor, I ween, is he,
   And tidings rare   To him do I bear,
And news of price from his rich Ab-bee ! "

" Now nay, now nay, thou naughty Page
No learned clerk, I trow, am I,
   But well, I ween,   May there be seen
Dame Alice's hand with half an eye ;
Now nay, now nay, thou naughty Page,
From Abingdon Abbey comes not thy news ;
   Although no clerk,   Well may I mark
The particular turn of her P's and her Q's ! "

Sir Ingoldsby Bray, in his fury and rage,
By the back of the neck takes that little Foot-page ;
   The scroll he seizes,   The Page he squeezes,
And buffets,—and pinches his nose till he sneezes ;—
Then he cuts with his dagger the silken threads
Which they used in those days 'stead of little Queen's-heads.

When the contents of the scroll met his view,
Sir Ingoldsby Bray in a passion grew,
   Backward he drew   His mailed shoe,
And he kicked that naughty Foot-page, that he flew
Like a cloth-yard shaft from a bended yew,
I may not say whither—I never knew.

  " Now count the slain   Upon Ascalon plain,—
Go count them, my Squire, go count them again ! "

  " Twenty and three !   There they be,
Stiff and stark on that crimson'd lea !—
   Twenty and three ?—   —Stay—let me see !
   Stretched in his gore   There lieth one more !
By the Pope's triple crown there are twenty and *four !*
Twenty-four trunks, I ween, are there,
But their heads and their limbs are no-body knows where !
Ay, twenty-four corses, I rede, there be,
Though one got away, and ran up a tree ! "

  " Look nigher, look nigher,   My trusty Squire ! "—
" One is the corse of a barefooted Friar ! ! "

Out and spake Sir Ingoldsby Bray,
" A boon, a boon, King Richard," quoth he,

" Now Heav'n thee save,　A boon I crave,
A boon, Sir King, on my bended knee ;
　A year and a day　Have I been away,
King Richard, from Ingoldsby Hall so free ;
Dame Alice, she sits there in lonely guise,
And she makes her moan, and she sobs and she sighs,
And tears like rain-drops fall from her eyes,
And she darneth her hose, and she crieth, ' Alack !
Oh, when will Sir Ingoldsby Bray come back ? '
A boon, a boon, my Liege," quoth he,
" Fair Ingoldsby Hall I fain would see ! "

" Rise up, rise up, Sir Ingoldsby Bray,"
King Richard said right graciously,
　" Of all in my host　That I love the most,
I love none better, Sir Bray, than thee !
Rise up, rise up, thou hast thy boon ;
But—mind you make haste, and come back again soon ! "

FYTTE II.

Pope Gregory sits in St. Peter's chair,
Pontiff proud, I ween, is he,
　And a belted Knight　In armour dight,
Is begging a boon on his bended knee,
With signs of grief and sounds of woe,
Featly he kisseth his Holiness' toe.
" Now pardon, Holy Father, I crave,
O Holy Father, pardon and grace !
　In my fury and rage　A little Foot-page
I have left, I fear me, in evil case :
　A scroll of shame　From a faithless dame
Did that naughty Foot-page to a paramour bear ;
　I gave him a ' lick '　With a stick,　And a kick,
That sent him—I can't tell your Holiness where !
Had he as many necks as hairs,
He had broken them all down those perilous stairs ! "

" Rise up, rise up, Sir Ingoldsby Bray,
Rise up, rise up, I say to thee ;

A soldier, I trow,   Of the Cross art thou ;
Rise up, rise up from thy bended knee !
Ill it beseems that soldier true
Of Holy Church should vainly sue :—
—Foot-pages, they are by no means rare,
A thriftless crew, I ween, be they,
   Well mote we spare   A Page—or a pair,
For the matter of that—Sir Ingoldsby Bray,
   But stout and true   Soldiers, like you,
Grow scarcer and scarcer every day !—
   Be prayers for the dead   Duly read,
Let a mass be sung, and a *pater* be said ;
So may your qualms of conscience cease,
And the little Foot-page shall rest in peace ! "

—" Now pardon, Holy Father, I crave,
O Holy Father, pardon and grace !
   Dame Alice, my wife,   The bane of my life,
I have left, I fear me, in evil case !
A scroll of shame in my rage I tore,
Which that caitiff Page to a paramour bore ;
'Twere bootless to tell how I storm'd and swore ;
Alack ! alack ! too surely I knew
The turn of each P, and the tail of each Q,
And away to Ingoldsby Hall I flew !
   Dame Alice I found,—   She sank on the ground,
I twisted her neck till I twisted it round !
With jibe and jeer, and mock, and scoff,
I twisted it on—till I twisted it off !—
All the King's Doctors and all the King's Men
Can't put fair Alice's head on again ! "

" Well-a-day ! well-a-day !   Sir Ingoldsby Bray,
Why really—I hardly know what to say :—
Foul sin, I trow, a fair Ladye to slay,
Because she's perhaps been a little too gay.—
—Monk must chaunt and Nun must pray ;
For each mass they sing, and each pray'r they say,
   For a year, and a day,   Sir Ingoldsby Bray
A fair rose-noble must duly pay !
So may his qualms of conscience cease,
And the soul of Dame Alice may rest in peace ! "

"Now pardon, Holy Father, I crave,
O Holy Father, pardon and grace !
No power could save   That paramour knave,
I left him, I wot, in evil case !
　　There, 'midst the slain   Upon Ascalon plain,
Unburied, I trow, doth his body remain,
His legs lie here, and his arms lie there,
And his head lies—I can't tell your Holiness where ! "

"Now out and alas ! Sir Ingoldsby Bray,
Foul sin it were, thou doughty Knight,
　　To hack and to hew   A champion true
Of holy Church in such pitiful plight !
Foul sin her warriors so to slay,
When they're scarcer and scarcer every day !—
　　—A chauntry fair,   And of Monks a pair,
To pray for his soul for ever and aye,
Thou must duly endow, Sir Ingoldsby Bray,
And fourteen marks by the year must thou pay
　　For plenty of lights   To burn there o' nights—
None of your rascally ' *dips* '—but sound,
Round, ten-penny moulds of four to the pound ;—
And a shirt of the roughest and coarsest hair
For a year and a day, Sir Ingoldsby, wear !—
So may your qualms of conscience cease,
And the soul of the Soldier shall rest in peace ! "

"Now nay, Holy Father, now nay, now nay !
Less penance may serve ! " quoth Sir Ingoldsby Bray.
" No champion free of the Cross was he ;
No belted Baron of high degree ;
　　No Knight nor Squire   Did there expire ;
He was, I trow, but a bare-footed Friar !
And the Abbot of Abingdon long may wait
With his monks around him, and early and late
May look from loop-hole, and turret, and gate,
—He hath lost his Prior—his Prior his pate ! "

"Now Thunder and turf ! " Pope Gregory said,
And his hair raised his triple crown right off his head—

" Now Thunder and turf ! and out and alas !
A horrible thing has come to pass !
What ! cut off the head of a reverend Prior,
And say he was ' *only* (! ! !) a bare-footed Friar ! '—
  ' What Baron or Squire, ' Or Knight of the shire
Is half so good as a holy Friar ? '
  O, *turpissime ! Vir nequissime !*
Sceleratissime !—quissime !—issime !
Never, I trow, have the *Servi servorum*
  Had before 'em Such a breach of decorum,
Such a gross violation of *morum bonorum*,
And won't have again *sæcula sæculorum !*—
  Come hither to me, My Cardinals three,
  My Bishops *in partibus*, Masters *in Artibus*,
Hither to me, A.B. and D.D.
Doctors and Proctors of every degree !
Go fetch me a book !—go fetch me a bell
As big as a dustman's !—and a candle as well—
I'll send him—*where* good manners won't let me tell ! "

—" Pardon and grace !—now pardon and grace ! "
—Sir Ingoldsby Bray fell flat on his face—
" *Meâ culpâ !*—in sooth I'm in pitiful case.
Peccavi ! peccavi !—I've done very wrong !
But my heart it is stout, and my arm it is strong,
And I'll fight for Holy Church all the day long ;
And the Ingoldsby lands are broad and fair,
And they're here, and they're there, and I can't tell you where,
And Holy Church shall come in for her share ! "

Pope Gregory paused, and he sat himself down,
And he somewhat relaxed his terrible frown,
And his Cardinals three they pick'd up his crown.

" Now, if it be so that you own you've been wrong,
And your heart is so stout, and your arm is so strong,
And you really will fight like a trump all day long ;—
If the Ingoldsby lands do lie here and there,
And Holy Church shall come in for her share,—

Why, my Cardinals three,　You'll agree　With me,
That it gives a new turn to the whole affair,
And I think that the Penitent need not despair !
—If it be so, as you seem to say,
Rise up, rise up, Sir Ingoldsby Bray !

" An Abbey so fair Sir Bray shall found,
Whose innermost wall's encircling bound
Shall take in a couple of acres of ground ;
And there in that Abbey all the year round,
A full choir of monks, and a full choir of nuns,
Shall live upon cabbage and hot-cross-buns ;
　And Sir Ingoldsby Bray,　Without delay,
　Shall hie him again　To Ascalon plain,
And gather the bones of the foully slain :
And shall place said bones, with all possible care,
In an elegant shrine in his abbey so fair ;
　And plenty of lights　Shall be there o' nights ;
None of your rascally ' *dips*,' but sound,
Best superfine wax-wicks, four to the pound ;
　And Monk and Nun　Shall pray, each one,
For the soul of the Prior of Abingdon !
And Sir Ingoldsby Bray, so bold and so brave,
Never shall wash himself, comb, or shave,
　Nor adorn his body,　Nor drink gin-toddy,
　Nor indulge in a pipe,—　But shall dine upon tripe
And blackberries gather before they are ripe.
And for ever abhor, renounce, and abjure
Rum, hollands, and brandy, wine, punch, and *liqueur !* "
　(Sir Ingoldsby Bray　Here gave way
To a feeling which prompted a word profane,
But he swallow'd it down, by an effort, again,
And his Holiness luckily fancied his gulp a
Mere repetition of O, *meâ culpâ !*)

" Thrice three times upon Candlemas-day,
Between Vespers and Compline, Sir Ingoldsby Bray
Shall run round the Abbey, as best he may,
　Subjecting his back　To thump and to thwack,

Well and truly laid on by a bare-footed Friar,
With a stout cat o' ninetails of whip-cord and wire ;
    And nor he, nor his heir *   Shall take, use, or bear
    Any more from this day,   The surname of Bray,

SUBJECTING HIS BACK TO THUMP AND TO THWACK,
WELL AND TRULY LAID ON BY A BARE-FOOTED FRIAR

As being dishonour'd, but all issue male he has
Shall, with himself, go henceforth by an *alias !*
So his qualms of conscience at length may cease,
And Page, Dame, and Prior shall rest in peace ! "

Sir Ingoldsby (now no longer Bray)
Is off like a shot away and away,
    Over the brine   To far Palestine,

* His brother Reginald, it would seem by the pedigree, disregarded this prohibition.

To rummage and hunt over Ascalon plain
For the unburied bones of his victim slain.

" Look out, my Squire,   Look higher and nigher,
Look out for the corpse of a bare-footed Friar !
And pick up the arms, and the legs, of the dead,
And pick up his body, and pick up his head ! "

FYTTE III.

Ingoldsby Abbey is fair to see,
It hath manors a dozen, and royalties three,
With right of free-warren (whatever that be) ;
Rich pastures in front, and green woods in the rear,
All in full leaf at the right time of year ;
About Christmas or so, they fall into the sear,
And the prospect, of course, becomes rather more drear :
But it's really delightful in spring-time,—and near
The great gate Father Thames rolls sun-bright and clear.
Cobham woods to the right,—on the opposite shore
Laindon Hills in the distance, ten miles off or more ;
Then you've Milton and Gravesend behind,—and before
You can see almost all the way down to the Nore.*
   So charming a spot,   It's rarely one's lot
To see, and when seen it's as rarely forgot.

Yes, Ingoldsby Abbey is fair to see,
And its Monks and its Nuns are fifty and three,
And there they all stand each in their degree,
Drawn up in the front of their sacred abode,
Two by two, in their regular mode,
While a funeral comes down the Rochester road.

Palmers twelve, from a foreign strand,
Cockle in hat, and staff in hand,
Come marching in pairs, a holy band !

---

* Alas ! one might almost say that of this sacred, and once splendid, edifice, *periêrunt etiam ruinæ*. An elderly gentleman, however, of ecclesiastical cut, who oscillates between the Garrick Club and the Falcon in Gravesend, and is said by the host to be a " foreigneering Bishop," does not scruple to identify the ruins still to be seen by the side of the high Dover road, about a mile and a half below the town, with those of the haunted *Sa·ellum*. The general features of the landscape certainly correspond, and tradition, as certainly, countenances his conjecture.

Little boys twelve, dressed all in white,
Each with his brazen censer bright,
And singing away with all their might,
Follow the Palmers—a goodly sight ;
   Next high in air   Twelve Yeomen bear
On their sturdy necks, with a good deal of care,
A patent sarcophagus firmly rear'd,
Of Spanish mahogany (not veneer'd),
And behind walks a Knight with a very long beard.
   Close by his side   Is a Friar, supplied
With a stout cat o' ninetails of tough cow-hide,
   While all sorts of queer men
   Bring up the rear—Men-
at-arms, Nigger captives, and Bow-men, and Spear-men.

It boots not to tell   What you'll guess very well,
How some sang the *requiem*, some toll'd the bell ;
   Suffice it to say,   'Twas on Candlemas-day
The procession I speak about reached the *Sacellum ;*
   And in lieu of a supper   The Knight on his crupper
Received the first taste of the Father's *flagellum ;*—
   That, as chronicles tell,   He continued to dwell
All the rest of his days in the Abbey he'd founded,
By the pious of both sexes ever surrounded,
And, partaking the fare of the Monks and the Nuns,
Ate the cabbage alone, without touching the buns ;
—That year after year, having run round the *Quad*
With his back, as enjoin'd him, exposed to the rod,
Having not only kiss'd it, but bless'd it, and thank'd it, he
Died, as all thought, in the odour of sanctity,
When,—strange to relate ! and you'll hardly believe
What I'm going to tell you,—next Candlemas Eve
The Monks and the Nuns in the dead of the night
Tumble, all of them, out of their beds in affright,
   Alarm'd by the bawls,   And the calls, and the squalls
Of some one who seem'd running all round the walls !

   Looking out, soon   By the light of the moon
There appears most distinctly to ev'ry one's view,
And making, as seems to them, all this ado,
The form of a Knight with a beard like a Jew,

As black as if steep'd in that " Matchless ! " of Hunt's,
And so bushy, it would not disgrace Mr. Muntz ;
A bare-footed Friar stands behind him, and shakes
A *flagellum*, whose lashes appear to be snakes ;
While, more terrible still, the astounded beholders
Perceive the said Friar has NO HEAD ON HIS SHOULDERS,
 But is holding his pate. In his left hand, out straight,
As if by a closer inspection to find
Where to get the best cut at his victim behind,
With the aid of a small " bull's-eye lantern,"—as placed
By our own New Police,—in a belt round his waist.
 All gaze with surprise, Scarce believing their eyes,
When the Knight makes a start like a race-horse, and flies
From his headless tormentor, repeating his cries,—
In vain,—for the Friar to his skirts closely sticks,
" Running after him,"—so said the Abbot,—" like Bricks ! "

Thrice three times did the Phantom Knight
Course round the Abbey as best he might
Be-thwack'd and be-smack'd by the headless Sprite,
While his shrieks so piercing made all hearts thrill,—
Then a whoop and a halloo,—and all was still !

Ingoldsby Abbey has passed away,
 And at this time of day One can hardly survey
Any traces or track, save a few ruins, grey
With age, and fast mouldering into decay,
Of the structure once built by Sir Ingoldsby Bray ;
But still there are many folks living who say
That on every Candlemas eve, the Knight,
 Accoutred, and dight In his armour bright,
With his thick black beard,—and the clerical Sprite,
With his head in his hand, and his lantern alight,
Run round the spot where the old Abbey stood,
And are seen in the neighbouring glebe-land and wood ;
More especially still, if it's stormy and windy,
You may hear them for miles kicking up their wild shindy ;
 And that once in a gale Of wind, sleet, and hail,
They frighten'd the horses, and upset the mail.

Tumble out of their beds in affright

What 'tis breaks the rest   Of these souls unblest
Would now be a thing rather hard to be guess'd,
Though some say the Squire, on his death-bed, confess'd
That on Ascalon plain,   When the bones of the slain
Were collected that day, and pack'd up in a chest,
   Caulk'd, and made water-tight,
   By command of the Knight,
Though the legs and the arms they'd got all pretty right,
And the body itself in a decentish plight,
Yet the Friar's *Pericranium* was nowhere in sight;
So, to save themselves trouble, they pick'd up instead,
And popp'd on the shoulders a Saracen's Head!
Thus the Knight in the terms of his penance had fail'd,
And the Pope's absolution, of course, nought avail'd.

   Now, though this might be,   It don't seem to agree
With one thing which, I own, is a poser to me,—
I mean, as the miracles wrought at the shrine
Containing the bones brought from far Palestine
Were so great and notorious, 'tis hard to combine
This *fact* with the reason these people assign,
Or suppose that the head of the murder'd Divine
Could be aught but what Yankees would call " genu-*ine.*"
'Tis a very nice question—but be't as it may,
The Ghost of Sir Ingoldsby (*ci-devant* Bray),
It is boldly affirm'd, by the folks great and small
About Milton, and Chalk, and around Cobham Hall,
Still on Candlemas-day haunts the old ruin'd wall,
And that many have seen him, and more heard him squall.
So I think, when the facts of the case you recall,
My inference, reader, you'll fairly forestall,
   Viz. : that, spite of the hope   Held out by the Pope,
Sir Ingoldsby Bray was d—d after all!

MORAL.

Foot-pages, and Servants of ev'ry degree,
In livery or out of it, listen to me!
See what comes of lying!—don't join in a league
To humbug your master, or aid an intrigue!

Ladies !—married and single, from this understand
How foolish it is to send letters by hand !
Don't stand for the sake of a penny,—but when you
    've a *billet* to send   To a lover or friend,
Put it into the post, and don't cheat the revenue !

Reverend gentlemen !—you who are given to roam,
Don't keep up a soft correspondence at home !
But while you're abroad lead respectable lives ;
Love your neighbours, and welcome,—but don't love their wives !
And, as bricklayers cry from the tiles and the leads
When they're shovelling the snow off, " TAKE CARE OF YOUR HEADS ! "

Knights !—whose hearts are so stout, and whose arms are so strong,
Learn,—to twist a wife's neck is decidedly wrong !
If your servants offend you, or give themselves airs,
Rebuke them—but mildly—don't kick them down stairs !
To " Poor Richard's " homely old proverb attend,
" If you want matters well managed, *Go !*—if not, *Send !* "
A servant's too often a negligent elf ;
—If it's business of consequence, Do IT YOURSELF !

The state of society seldom requires
People now to bring home with them unburied Friars,
But they sometimes *do* bring home an inmate for life ;
Now—don't do that by proxy !—but choose your own wife !
For think how annoying 'twould be, when you're wed,
    To find in your bed,   On the pillow, instead
Of the sweet face you look for—A SARACEN'S HEAD !

Alas, for Ingoldsby Abbey !—Alas that one *should* have to say

Periêrunt etiam Ruinæ !
Its very Ruins now are tiny.

There is something in the very sight of an old Abbey—family associations apart—as Ossian says (or MacPherson for him), " pleasing yet mournful to the soul ! " nor could I ever yet gaze on the roofless walls and ivy-clad towers of one of these venerable monuments of the piety of bygone days, without something very like an unbidden tear rising to dim the prospect. Something of this, I think, I have already hinted in, recording our pic-nic with the Seaforths at Bolsover. Since then I have paid a visit to the beautiful remains of what once was Netley, and never experienced the sensation to which I have alluded in a stronger degree ;—if its character was somewhat changed before we parted—it is not my fault. Still, be the drawbacks what they may, I shall ever mark with a white stone the day on which I for the first time beheld the time-worn cloisters of

Netley Abbey

A Legend of Hampshire

I saw thee, Netley, as the sun
Across the western wave
  Was sinking slow, And a golden glow
To thy roofless towers he gave ;
  And the ivy sheen, With its mantle of green,
That wrapt thy walls around,
  Shone lovelily bright In that glorious light,
And I felt 'twas holy ground.

Then I thought of the ancient time—
The days of thy Monks of old,—
When to Matin, and Vesper, and Compline chime,
  The loud Hosanna roll'd,
  And, thy courts and " long-drawn aisles " among,
Swell'd the full tide of sacred song.

  And then a vision pass'd
  Across my mental eye ; *
And silver shrines, and shaven crowns,
And delicate Ladies, in bombazeen gowns,
  And long white veils, went by,
  Stiff, and staid, and solemn, and sad,—
—But one, methought, wink'd at the Gardener-lad !

Then came the Abbot, with mitre and ring,
And pastoral staff, and all that sort of thing,
And a Monk with a book, and a Monk with a bell,
  And " dear little souls," In clean linen stoles,
Swinging their censers, and making a smell.—

      * In my mind's eye, Horatio !—*Hamlet.*

U

And see where the Choir-master walks in the rear,
      With front severe,   And brow austere,
Now and then pinching a little boy's ear
When he chaunts the responses too late, or too soon,
Or his *Do, Re, Mi, Fa, Sol, La's* not quite in tune.
      (Then, you know,   They'd a " moveable *Do*,"
Not a fixed one as now—and of course never knew
How to set up a musical Hullah-baloo.)
It was, in sooth, a comely sight,
And I welcom'd the vision with pure delight.

      But then " a change came o'er "
      My spirit—a change of fear—
   That gorgeous scene I beheld no more,
   But deep beneath the basement floor
      A dungeon dark and drear !
And there was an ugly hole in the wall—
For an oven too big,—for a cellar too small !
      And mortar and bricks   All ready to fix,
And I said, " Here's a Nun has been playing some tricks !—
That horrible hole !—it seems to say,
' I'm a grave that gapes for a living prey ! ' "
And my heart grew sick, and my brow grew sad—
And I thought of that wink at the Gardener-lad.
   Ah me ! ah me ! 'tis sad to think
   That Maiden's eye, which was made to wink,
   Should here be compelled to grow blear, and blink,
      Or be closed for aye   In this kind of way,
   Shut out for ever from wholesome day,
   Wall'd up in a hole with never a chink,
   No light,—no air,—no victuals,—no drink !—
      And that Maiden's lip,   Which was made to sip,
   Should here grow wither'd and dry as a chip !
   —That wandering glance and furtive kiss
   Exceedingly naughty, and wrong, I wis,
   Should yet be considered so much amiss
   As to call for a sentence severe as this !
   And I said to myself, as I heard with a sigh
   The poor lone victim's stifled cry,*

* About the middle of the last century a human skeleton was discovered in a recess in the
wall among the ruins of Netley. On examination the bones were pronounced to be those

" Well ! I can't understand   How any man's hand
Could wall up that hole in a Christian land !
    Why, a Mussulman Turk   Would recoil from the work,
And though, when his Ladies run after the fellows, he
Stands not on trifles, if madden'd by jealousy,
Its objects, I'm sure, would declare, could they speak,
In their Georgian, Circassian, or Turkish, or Greek,
' When all's said and done, far better it was for us,
    Tied back to back,   And sewn up in a sack,
To be pitched neck-and-heels from a boat in the Bosphorus ! '
    —Oh ! a Saint 'twould vex   To think that the sex
Should be treated no better than Combe's double X !
Sure some one might run to the Abbess, and tell her
A much better method of stocking her cellar."

    If ever on polluted walls
    Heaven's·red right arm in vengeance falls,—
    If e'er its justice wraps in flame
    The black abodes of sin and shame,
    That justice, in its own good time,
    Shall visit for so foul a crime,
    Ope desolation's floodgate wide,
    And blast thee, Netley, in thy pride !

    Lo where it comes ! the tempest lours,—
    It bursts on thy devoted towers ;
    Ruthless Tudor's bloated form
    Rides on the blast, and guides the storm ;
    I hear the sacrilegious cry,
    " Down with the nests, and the rooks will fly ! "

    Down ! down they come—a fearful fall—
    Arch, and pillar, and roof-tree and all,
    Stained pane, and sculptured stone,
    There they lie on the greensward strown—
    Mouldering walls remain alone !
        Shaven crown,   Bombazeen gown,
    Mitre, and Crozier, and all are flown.

of a female. *Teste* James Harrison, a youthful but intelligent cab-driver of Southampton,
who " well remembers to have heard his grandmother say that ' Somebody told her so.' "

And yet, fair Netley, as I gaze
  Upon that grey and mouldering wall,
The glories of thy palmy days
  Its very stones recall !—
They " come like shadows, so depart "—
I saw thee as thou wert—and art—

Sublime in ruin !—grand in woe !
  Lone refuge of the owl and bat ;
No voice awakes thine echoes now !
    No sound—Good Gracious !—what was that ?
      Was it the moan,   The parting groan
Of her who died forlorn and alone,
Embedded in mortar, and bricks, and stone ?—
      Full and clear   On my listening ear
It comes—again—near, and more near—
Why 'zooks ! it's the popping of Ginger Beer !
    I rush to the door—   I tread the floor,
By Abbots and Abbesses trodden before, .
    In the good old chivalric days of yore,
    And what see I there ?—   In a rush-bottom'd chair
A hag, surrounded by crockery-ware,
Vending, in cups, to the credulous throng,
A nasty decoction miscall'd " Souchong,"—
And a squeaking fiddle and " wry-necked fife "
Are screeching away, for the life !—for the life !—
Danced to by " All the World and his Wife."
Tag, Rag, and Bobtail are capering there,
Worse scene, I ween, than Bartlemy Fair !—
Two or three Chimney-sweeps, two or three Clowns,
Playing at " pitch and toss," sport their " Browns,"
Two or three damsels, frank and free,
Are ogling, and smiling, and sipping Bohea.
Parties below, and parties above,
Some making tea, and some making love.
   Then the " toot—toot—toot "
   Of that vile demi-flute,—
    The detestable din   Of that cracked violin;
And the odours of " Stout," and tobacco, and gin !
"—Dear me ! " I exclaimed, " what a place to be in ! "

And I said to the person who drove my " shay,"
(A very intelligent man, by the way,)
" This, all things considered, is rather too gay !
It don't suit my humour,—so take me away !
Dancing ! and drinking ! cigar and song !
If not profanation, it's ' coming it strong,'
And I really consider it all very wrong.—
—Pray, to whom does this property now belong ? "—
   —He paused, and said, Scratching his head,
" Why, I really *do* think he's a little to blame,
But I can't say I knows the Gentleman's name ! "

   " Well—well ! " quoth I, As I heaved a sigh,
And a tear-drop fell from my twinkling eye,
" My vastly good man, as I scarcely doubt
That some day or other you'll find it out,
   Should he come in your way, Or ride in your ' shay,'
   (As perhaps he may,) Be so good as to say
That a Visitor, whom you drove over one day,
Was exceedingly angry, and very much scandalized,
Finding these beautiful ruins so Vandalized,
And thus of their owner to speak began,
   As he ordered you home in haste,
" No DOUBT HE'S A VERY RESPECTABLE MAN,
   But—*I can't say much for his taste.*" *

* Adieu, Monsieur Gil Blas ; je vous souhaite toutes sortes de prospérités, avec un peu plus de goût !—*Gil Blas.*

My very excellent brother-in-law, Seaforth, late of the Bombay Fencibles (lucky dog to have quitted the service before this shocking Afghan business !), seems to have been even more forcibly affected on the evening when he so narrowly escaped being locked in Westminster Abbey, and when—but let him describe his own feelings, as he has done, indeed, in the subjoined

Fragment

*　　*　　*　　*　　*

A FEELING sad came o'er me as I trod the sacred ground
Where Tudors and Plantagenets were lying all around :
I stepp'd with noiseless foot, as though the sound of mortal tread
Might burst the bands of the dreamless sleep that wraps the mighty
　　dead !

The slanting ray of the evening sun shone through those cloisters pale,
With fitful light on regal vest, and warrior's sculptured mail,
As from the stained and storied pane it danced with quivering gleam,
Each cold and prostrate form below seem'd quickening in the beam.

Now, sinking low, no more was heard the organ's solemn swell,
And faint upon the listening ear the last Hosanna fell :
It died—and not a breath did stir ;—above each knightly stall,
Unmoved, the banner'd blazonry hung waveless as a pall.

I stood alone !—a living thing 'midst those that were no more—
I thought on ages past and gone—the glorious deeds of yore—
On Edward's sable panoply, on Cressy's tented plain,
The fatal roses twined at length—on great Eliza's reign.

I thought on Naseby—Marston Moor—on Worc'ster's " crowning
　　fight " ;
When on mine ear a sound there fell—it chill'd me with affright,
As thus in low, unearthly tones I heard a voice begin,
—" This here's the Cap of Giniral Monk !—Sir ! please put summat
　　in ! "

*　　*　　*　　*　　*

Cætera desiderantur.

That Seaforth's nervous system was powerfully acted upon on this occasion I can well believe. The circumstance brings to my recollection a fearful adventure—or what might perhaps have proved one—of my own in early life while grinding Gerunds at Canterbury. A sharp touch of the gout, and the reputed sanatory qualities of a certain spring in St. Peter's Street, then in much repute, had induced my Uncle to take up a temporary abode within the Cathedral "Precinct." It was on one of those temporary visits which I was sometimes permitted to pay on half-holidays that, in self-defence, I had to recount the following true narrative. I may add, that this tradition is not yet worn out: a small maimed figure of a female in a sitting position, and holding something like a frying-pan in her hand, may still be seen on the covered passage which crosses the Brick Walk, and adjoins the house belonging to the sixth prebendal stall.—There are those, whom I know, who would, even yet, hesitate at threading the Dark Entry on a Friday—" not," *of course*, " that they believe one word about "

Nell Cook ! !

A Legend of the " Dark Entry "

THE KING'S SCHOLAR'S STORY

" From the ' Brick Walk ' branches off to the right a long narrow vaulted passage, paved with flagstones, vulgarly known by the name of the ' Dark Entry.' Its eastern extremity communicates with the cloisters, crypt, and, by a private staircase, with the interior of the Cathedral. On the west it opens into the ' Green-court,' forming a communication between it and the portion of the ' Precinct ' called the ' Oaks.' "—*A Walk round Canterbury*, &c.

Scene—A back parlour in Mr. John Ingoldsby's house in the Precinct.—A blazing fire.—Mine Uncle is seated in a high-backed easy-chair, twirling his thumbs, and contemplating his list shoe.—Little Tom, the " King's Scholar," on a stool opposite.—Mrs. John Ingoldsby at the table, busily employed in manufacturing a cabbage-rose (cauliflower ?) in many-coloured worsteds.—Mine Uncle's meditations are interrupted by the French clock on the mantelpiece.—He prologizeth with vivacity.

" HARK ! listen, Mrs. Ingoldsby,—the clock is striking nine !
Give Master Tom another cake, and half a glass of wine,
And ring the bell for Jenny Smith, and bid her bring his coat,
And a warm bandana handkerchief to tie about his throat.

" And bid them go the nearest way, for Mr. Birch has said
That nine o'clock's the hour he'll have his boarders all in bed ;
And well we know when little boys their coming home delay,
They often seem to walk and sit uneasily next day ! "

—" Nay, nay, dear Uncle Ingoldsby, now send me not, I pray,
Back by that Entry dark, for that you know's the nearest way ;

I dread that Entry dark with Jane alone at such an hour,
It fears me quite—it's Friday night !—and then Nell Cook hath pow'r ! "

" And who's Nell Cook, thou silly child ?—and what's Nell Cook to
        thee ?
That thou shouldst dread at night to tread with Jane that dark entrée. ? "
—" Nay, list and hear, mine Uncle dear ! such fearsome things they
        tell
Of Nelly Cook, that few may brook at night to meet with Nell ! "

" It was in bluff King Harry's days,—and Monks and Friars were then,
You know, dear Uncle Ingoldsby, a sort of Clergymen.
They'd coarse stuff gowns, and shaven crowns,—no shirts,—and no
        cravats ;
And a cord was placed about their waist—they had no shovel hats !

" It was in bluff King Harry's days, while yet he went to shrift,
And long before he stamped and swore, and cut the Pope adrift ;
There lived a portly Canon then, a sage and learned clerk ;
He had, I trow, a goodly house, fast by that Entry dark !

" The Canon was a portly man—of Latin and of Greek,
And learned lore, he had good store,—yet health was on his cheek.
The Priory fare was scant and spare, the bread was made of rye,
The beer was weak, yet he was sleek—he had a merry eye.

" For though within the Priory the fare was scant and thin,
The Canon's house it stood without ;—he kept good cheer within ;
Unto the best he prest each guest with free and jovial look,
And Ellen Bean ruled his *cuisine*.—He called her ' Nelly Cook.'

" For soups and stews, and choice *ragoûts*, Nell Cook was famous still ;
She'd make them even of old shoes, she had such wond'rous skill :
Her manchets fine were quite divine, her cakes were nicely brown'd,
Her boil'd and roast, they were the boast of all the ' Precinct ' round ;

" And Nelly was a comely lass, but calm and staid her air,
And earthward bent her modest look—yet she was passing fair ;
And though her gown was russet brown, their heads grave people
        shook :
—They all agreed no Clerk had need of such a pretty Cook.

" One day—'twas on a Whitsun-Eve—there came a coach and four ;—
It pass'd the ' Green-Court ' gate, and stopp'd before the Canon's
     door ;
The travel-stain on wheel and rein bespoke a weary way,—
Each panting steed relax'd its speed—out stept a Lady gay.

" ' Now welcome ! welcome ! dearest Niece,'—the Canon then did
     cry,
And to his breast the Lady prest—he had a merry eye,—
' Now, welcome ! welcome ! dearest Niece ! in sooth thou'rt welcome
     here,
'Tis many a day since we have met—how fares my Brother dear ? ' —

" ' Now, thanks, my loving Uncle,' that Lady gay replied ;
' Gramercy for thy benison ! '—then ' Out, alas ! ' she sighed ;
' My father dear he is not near ; he seeks the Spanish Main ;
He prays thee give me shelter here till he return again ! ' —

" ' Now, welcome ! welcome ; dearest Niece ; come lay thy mantle
     by ! '
The Canon kissed her ruby lip—he had a merry eye,—
But Nelly Cook askew did look,—it came into her mind
They were a little less than ' kin,' and rather more than ' kind.'

     *   *   *   *   *

" Three weeks are gone and over—full three weeks and a day,
Yet still within the Canon's house doth dwell that Lady gay ;
On capons fine they daily dine, rich cates and sauces rare ;
And they quaff good store of Bordeaux wine,—so dainty is their fare.

" And fine upon the virginals is that gay Lady's touch,
And sweet her voice unto the lute, you'll scarce hear any such ;
But is it ' *O Sanctissima !* ' she sings in dulcet tone ?
Or ' *Angels ever bright and fair ?* '—Ah, no !—it's ' *Bobbing Joan !* '

     *   *   *   *   *

" The Canon's house is lofty, and spacious to the view ;
The Canon's cell is ordered well—yet Nelly looks askew ;
The Lady's bower is in the tower,—yet Nelly shakes her head—
She hides the poker and the tongs in that gay Lady's bed !

     *   *   *   *   *

" Six weeks were gone and over—full six weeks and a day,
Yet in that bed the poker and the tongs unheeded lay !
From which, I fear, it's pretty clear that Lady rest had none ?
Or, if she slept in any bed—it was not in her own.

" But where that Lady pass'd her nights, I may not well divine,
Perhaps in pious oraisons at good St. Thomas' Shrine,
And for her father far away breath'd tender vows and true—
It may be so—I cannot say—but Nelly look'd askew.

" And still at night, by fair
moonlight, when all were
lock'd in sleep,
She'd listen at the Canon's
door,—she'd through the
keyhole peep—
I know not what she heard or
saw, but fury filled her eye—
—She bought some nasty Doctor's-stuff, and she put it in
a pie !
     *   *   *

" It was a glorious summer's-
eve—with beams of rosy red
The Sun went down—all
Nature smiled—but Nelly
shook her head !
Full softly to the balmy breeze
rang out the Vesper bell—
—Upon the Canon's startled
ear it sounded like a knell !

" ' Now here's to thee, mine Uncle ! a health I drink to thee !
Now pledge me back in Sherris sack, or a cup of Malvoisie ! '—
The Canon sigh'd—but rousing, cried, ' I answer to thy call,
And a Warden-pie's a dainty dish to mortify withal ! '

" 'Tis early dawn—the matin chime rings out for morning pray'r—
And Prior and Friar is in his stall—the Canon is not there !
Nor in the small Refect'ry hall, nor cloister'd walk is he—
All wonder—and the Sacristan says, ' Lauk-a-daisey-me ! '

" They've searched the aisles and Baptistry—they've searched above—
    around—
The ' Sermon House '—the ' Audit Room '—the Canon is not found.
They only find that pretty Cook concocting a *ragoût*,
They ask her where her master is—but Nelly looks askew ! ·

" They call for crow-bars—' jemmies ' is the modern name they bear—
They burst through lock, and bolt, and bar—but what a sight is there !—
The Canon's head lies on the bed—his Niece lies on the floor !
—They are as dead as any nail that is in any door !

" The livid spot is on his breast, the spot is on his back !
His portly form, no longer warm with life, is swoln and black !—
The livid spot is on her cheek, it's on her neck of snow,
And the Prior sighs, and sadly cries, ' Well ! here's a pretty Go ! '

       *   *   *   *   *

" All at the silent hour of night a bell is heard to toll,
A knell is rung, a *requiem's* sung as for a sinful soul,
And there's a grave within the Nave, it's dark, and deep, and wide,
And they bury there a Lady fair, and a Canon by her side !

" An Uncle—so 'tis whisper'd now throughout the sacred fane,—
And a Niece—whose father's far away upon the Spanish Main—
The Sacristan, he says no word that indicates a doubt,
But he puts his thumb unto his nose, and he spreads his fingers out !

" And where doth tarry Nelly Cook, that staid and comely lass ?
Ay, where ?—for ne'er from forth that door was Nelly known to pass.
Her coif, and gown of russet brown were lost unto the view,
And if you mention'd Nelly's name—the Monks all looked askew !

       *   *   *   *   *

" There is a heavy paving-stone fast by the Canon's door,
Of granite grey, and it may weigh some half a ton or more,
And it is laid deep in the shade within that Entry dark,
Where sun or moonbeam never play'd, or e'en one starry spark.

" That heavy granite stone was moved that night, 'twas darkly said,
And the mortar round its sides next morn seem'd fresh and newly laid ;

But what within the narrow vault beneath that stone doth lie,
Or if that there be vault, or no—I cannot tell—not I !

" But I've been told that moan and groan, and fearful wail and shriek
Came from beneath that paving-stone for nearly half a week—

For three long days and three long nights came forth those sounds of
       fear ;
Then all was o'er—they never more fell on the listening ear.

            *   *   *   *   *

    A hundred years were gone and past since last Nell Cook was seen,
When, worn by use, that stone got loose, and they went and told the
       Dean.—
—Says the Dean, says he, ' My Masons three ! now haste and fix it
       tight ; '
And the Masons three peep'd down to see, and they saw a fearsome
       sight.

" Beneath that heavy paving-stone a shocking hole they found—
It was not more than twelve feet deep, and barely twelve feet round ;
—A fleshless, sapless skeleton lay in that horrid well !
But who the deuce 'twas put it there those Masons could not tell.

" And near this fleshless skeleton a pitcher small did lie,
And a mouldy piece of ' kissing crust,' as from a warden-pie !
And Doctor Jones declared the bones were female bones and, ' Zooks !
I should not be surprised,' said he, ' if these were Nelly Cook's.'

' It was in good Dean Bargrave's days, if I remember right,
Those fleshless bones beneath the stones these Masons brought to light ;
And you may well in the ' Dean's Chapelle ' Dean Bargrave's portrait
        view,
' Who died one night,' says old Tom Wright, ' in sixteen forty-two ! '

" And so two hundred years have passed since that these Masons three,
With curious looks, did set Nell Cook's unquiet spirit free ;
That granite stone had kept her down till then—so some suppose,—
—Some spread their fingers out, and put their thumb unto their nose.

" But one thing's clear—that all the year on every Friday night,
Throughout that Entry dark doth roam Nell Cook's unquiet Sprite :
On Friday was that Warden-pie all by that Canon tried ;
On Friday died he, and that tidy Lady by his side !

" And though two hundred years have flown, Nell Cook doth still
        pursue
Her weary walk, and they who cross her path the deed may rue ;
Her fatal breath is fell as death ! the Simoom's blast is not
More dire—(a wind in Africa that blows uncommon hot).

" But all unlike the Simoom's blast, her breath is deadly cold,
Delivering quivering, shivering shocks unto both young and old,
And whoso in that Entry dark doth feel that fatal breath,
He ever dies within the year some dire, untimely death !

" No matter who—no matter what condition, age, or sex,
But some ' get shot,' and some ' get drown'd,' and some ' get ' broken
        necks ;

Some ' get run over ' by a coach ;—and one beyond the seas
' Got ' scraped to death with oyster-shells among the Caribbees

" Those Masons three, who set her free, fell first !—it is averred
That two were hang'd on Tyburn tree for murdering of the third :
Charles Storey,* too, his friend who slew, had ne'er, if truth they tell
Been gibbeted on Chartham Downs, had they not met with Nell !

" Then send me not, mine Uncle dear, oh ! send me not, I pray,
Back through that Entry dark to-night, but round some other way !
I will not be a truant boy, but good, and mind my book,
For Heaven forfend that ever I foregather with Nell Cook ! "

    *   *   *   *   *

The class was call'd at morning tide, and Master Tom was there ;
He look'd askew, and did eschew both stool, and bench, and chair.
He did not talk, he did not walk, the tear was in his eye,—
He had not e'en that sad resource, to sit him down and cry.

Hence little boys may learn, when they from school go out to dine,
They should not deal in rigmarole, but still be back by nine ;
For if when they've their great-coat on, they pause before they part
To tell a long and prosy tale,—perchance their own may smart !

---

* In or about the year 1780, a worthy of this name cut the throat of a journeyman paper-maker, was executed on Oaten Hill, and afterwards hung in chains near the scene of his crime. It was to this place, as being the extreme boundary of the City's jurisdiction, that the worthy Mayor with so much *naïveté* wished to escort Archbishop M—— on one of his progresses, when he begged to have the honour of " attending his Grace *as far as the Gallows*."

MORAL.

—A few remarks to learned Clerks in country and in town—
Don't keep a pretty serving-maid, though clad in russet brown !—
Don't let your Niece sing " Bobbing Joan ! "—don't with a merry eye,
Hob-nob in Sack and Malvoisie,—and don't eat too much piė ! !

And oh ! beware that Entry dark,—especially at night,—
And don't go there with Jenny Smith all by the pale moonlight !—
So bless the Queen and her Royal Weans,—and the Prince whose hand
　　she took,—
And bless us all, both great and small,—and keep us from Nell Cook !

Kind, good-hearted, gouty Uncle John ! how well I remember all the kindness and affection which my mischievous propensities so ill repaid—his bright blue coat and resplendent gilt buttons—his " frosty pow " *si bien poudré*—his little quill-like pigtail !—Of all my praiseworthy actions—they were " like angels' visits, few and far between "—the never-failing and munificent rewarder ; of my naughty deeds—they were multitudinous as the sands on the sea-shore —the ever-ready palliator ; my intercessor, and sometimes even my defender against punishment, " staying harsh justice in its mid career ! "—Poor Uncle John ! he will ever rank among the dearest of my

Nursery Reminiscences

I REMEMBER, I remember,
　　When I was a little Boy,
One fine morning in September
　　Uncle brought me home a toy.

I remember how he patted
　　Both my cheeks in kindliest mood ;
" Then," said he, " you little Fat-head,
　　There's a top because you're good ! "

Grandmama—a shrewd observer—
　　I remember gazed upon
My new top, and said with fervour,
　　" Oh ! how kind of Uncle John ! "

While Mama, my form caressing,—
  In her eye the tear-drop stood,
Read me this fine moral lesson,
  " See what comes of being good ! "

*   *   *

I remember, I remember,
  On a wet and windy day,
One cold morning in December,
  I stole out and went to play ;

I remember Billy Hawkins
  Came, and with his pewter squirt
Squibb'd my pantaloons and stockings
  Till they were all over dirt !

To my mother for protection
  I ran, quaking every limb :
—She exclaimed, with fond affection,
  " Gracious Goodness ! loo kat *him !* "—

Pa cried, when he saw my garment,
  —'Twas a newly-purchased dress—
" Oh ! you nasty little *Warment*,
  How came you in such a mess ? "

Then he caught me by the collar,
  —Cruel only to be kind—
And to my exceeding dolour,
  Gave me—several slaps behind.

Grandmama, while yet I smarted,
  As she saw my evil plight,
Said—'twas rather stony-hearted—
  " Little rascal ! *sarve* him right ! "

I remember, I remember,
  From that sad and solemn day,
Never more in dark December
  Did I venture out to play.

And the moral, which they taught, I
  Well remember ; thus they said—
" Little Boys, when they are naughty,
  Must be whipped and sent to bed ! "

Poor Uncle John !

" After life's fitful fever he sleeps well,"

in the old family vault in Denton Chancel—and dear Aunt Fanny too !—the latter also
" loo'd me weel," as the Scotch song has it,—and since, at this moment, I am in a most soft
and sentimental humour—(—whisky toddy should ever be made by pouring the *boiling* fluid
—*hotter* if possible—upon the thinnest lemon-peel,—and then—but every one knows " what
then—") I dedicate the following " True History " to my beloved

Aunt Fanny

A Legend of a Shirt

Virginibus, Puerisque canto.—Hor.

Old Maids, and Bachelors I chaunt to!—T. I.

I SING of a Shirt that *never was* new !
In the course of the year Eighteen hundred and two,
  Aunt Fanny began,   Upon Grandmama's plan,
To make one for me, then her " dear little man."—
—At the epoch I speak about, I was between
  A man and a boy,   A hobble-de-hoy,
A fat, little, punchy concern of sixteen,—
  Just beginning to flirt,   And ogle,—so pert,
I'd been whipt every day had I had my desert,
And Aunt Fan volunteer'd to make me a shirt !

  I've said she *began* it,—   Some unlucky planet
No doubt interfered,—for, before she, and Janet
Completed the " cutting-out," " hemming," and " stitching,"
A tall Irish footman appear'd in the kitchen ;—
  —This took off the maid,—   And, I'm sadly afraid,
My respected Aunt Fanny's attention, too, stray'd ;
For, about the same period, a gay son of Mars,
Cornet Jones of the Tenth (then the Prince's) Hussars,
  With his fine dark eyelashes,   And finer mustaches,
And the ostrich plume work'd on the corps' sabre-taches,
(I say nought of the gold-and-red cord of the sashes,
Or the boots far above the Guards' vile spatterdashes,)—
So eyed, and so sigh'd, and so lovingly tried
To engage her whole ear as he lounged by her side,
Looking down on the rest with such dignified pride,
  That she made up her mind
  She should certainly find
Cornet Jones at her feet, whisp'ring, " Fan, be my bride ! "—
—She had even resolved to say " Yes " should he ask it,
—And I—and my Shirt—were both left in the basket.

322

To her grief and dismay
She discover'd one day
Cornet Jones of the tenth was a little too gay ;
For, besides that she saw him—he could not say nay—
Wink at one of the actresses capering away
In a Spanish *bolero*, one night at the play,
She found he'd already a wife at Cambray ;—
One at Paris,—a nymph of the *corps de ballet ;*—
And a third down in Kent, at a place call'd Foot's Cray.—
    He was " viler than dirt ! "— Fanny vow'd to exert
All her powers to forget him,—and finish my Shirt.
    But, oh ! lack-a-day ! How time slips away !—
Who'd have thought that while Cupid was playing these tricks,
Ten years had elapsed, and I'd turn'd twenty-six ?—

    " I care not a whit, —He's not
        grown a bit,"
Says my Aunt, "it will still be a
        very good fit."
    So Janet, and She, Now about
        thirty-three,
(The maid had been jilted by Mr.
        Magee,)
Each taking one end of " the Shirt "
        on her knee,
Again began working with hearty
        good will,
" Felling the Seams," and " whipping
        the Frill,"—
For, twenty years since, though the
        Ruffle had vanish'd,
A Frill like a fan had by no means
        been banish'd ;
People wore them at playhouses, parties, and churches,
Like overgrown fins of overgrown perches.—

Now, then, by these two thus laying their caps
Together, my " Shirt " had been finish'd, perhaps,
But for one of those queer little three-corner'd straps,
Which the ladies call " Side-bits," that sever the " Flaps ; "
    —Here unlucky Janet Took her needle, and ran it

Right into her thumb, and cried loudly, " Ads cuss it !
I've spoiled myself now by that 'ere nasty Gusset ! "

For a month to come   Poor dear Janet's thumb
Was in that sort of state vulgar people call " Rum."
   At the end of that time,   A youth, still in his prime,
The Doctor's fat Errand-boy,—just such a dolt as is
Kept to mix draughts, and spread plaisters and poultices,—
Who a bread-cataplasm each morning had carried her,
Sigh'd,—ogled,—proposed,—was accepted,—and married her !

   Much did Aunt Fan   Disapprove of the plan ;—
She turn'd up her dear little snub at " the Man."
   She " could not believe it "—
   " Could scarcely conceive it
Was possible—What ! *such* a place !—and then leave it !—
And all for a ' Shrimp ' not as high as my hat—
A little contemptible ' Shaver ' like that ! !
With a broad pancake face, and eyes buried in fat ! "
   —For her part, " She was sure
   She could never endure
A lad with a lisp, and a leg like a skewer.—
Such a name too !—('twas Potts !)—and so nasty a trade—
No, no,—she would much rather die an old maid !—
He a husband, indeed !—Well—mine, come what may come,
Shan't look like a blister, or smell of Guaiacum ! "—
   But there ! She'd " declare,   It was Janet's affair—
—*Chacun à son goût*—   As she baked she might brew ;
She could not prevent her—'twas no use in trying it—
Oh, no—she had made her own bed, and might lie in it.—
They ' repent at leisure who marry at random.'
No matter—*De gustibus non disputandum !* "

Consoling herself with this choice bit of Latin,
Aunt Fanny resignedly bought some white satin,
   And, as the Soubrette   Was a very great pet
After all,—she resolved to forgive and forget,
And sat down to make her a bridal rosette,
With magnificent bits of some white-looking metal
Stuck in, here and there, each forming a petal.—
—On such an occasion one couldn't feel hurt,
Of course, that she ceased to remember—my Shirt !

"Ads cuss it! I've spoiled myself now by that 'ere nasty gusset!"

Ten years,—or nigh,—   Had again gone by,
When Fan, accidentally casting her eye
On a dirty old work-basket, hung up on high
In the store-closet where herbs were put by to dry,
Took it down to explore it—she didn't know why.—

Within, a pea-soup colour'd fragment she spied,
Of the hue of a November fog in Cheapside,
Or a bad piece of gingerbread spoilt in the baking.—
  —I still hear her cry,—   " I wish I may die
If here isn't Tom's Shirt, that's been so long a-making !
  My gracious me !   Well,—only to see !
I declare it's as yellow as yellow can be !
Why, it looks just as though't had been soak'd in green tea !
  Dear me !   *Did* you *ever ?*—
  But come—'twill be clever
To bring matters round !   so I'll do my endeavour
' Better Late,' says an excellent proverb, ' than Never ! '—
It *is* stain'd to be sure ;   but ' grass-bleaching ' will bring it
To rights ' in a jiffy,'—We'll wash it, and wring it ;
  Or stay,—' Hudson's Liquor '   Will do it still quicker,
And—" Here the new maid chimed in, " Ma'am, Salt of Lemon
Will make it, in no time, quite fit for the Gemman ! "—
So they " set in the gathers,"—the large round the collar,
While those at the wrist-bands of course were much smaller,—
The button-holes now were at length " overcast ; "
Then a button itself was sewn on—'twas the last !

  All's done !   All's won !   Never under the sun
Was Shirt so late finish'd—so early begun !—
  —The work would defy   The most critical eye
It was " bleach'd,"—it was wash'd,—it was hung out to dry,—
It was mark'd on the tail with a T, and an I !
  On the back of a chair it   Was placed, just to air it,
In front of the fire.—" Tom to-morrow shall wear it ! "—

—*O cæca mens hominum !*—Fanny good soul,
Left her charge for one moment—but one—a vile coal
Bounced out from the grate, and set fire to the whole !

          *   *   *   *   *

Had it been Doctor Arnott's new stove—not a grate ;—
Had the coal been a " Lord Mayor's coal,"—viz. : a slate ;—
What a diff'rent tale had I had to relate !
And Aunt Fan—and my Shirt—been superior to Fate !—
    One moment—no more !   —Fan open'd the door !
The draught made the blaze ten times worse than before ;
And Aunt Fanny sank down—in despair—on the floor !

You may fancy perhaps Agrippina's amazement,
When, looking one fine moonlight night from her casement,
    She saw, while thus gazing,   All Rome a-blazing,
And, losing at once all restraint on her temper, or
Feelings, exclaimed, " Hang that Scamp of an Emperor,
    Although he's my son !—   —He thinks it prime fun,
No doubt !—While the flames are demolishing Rome,
There's my Nero a-fiddling, and singing ' Sweet Home ! ' "
—Stay—I'm really not sure 'twas that lady who said
The words I've put down, as she stepp'd into bed,—
On reflection, I rather believe *she* was dead ;
    But e'en when at College, I   Fairly acknowledge, I
Never was very precise in Chronology ;
So, if there's an error, pray set down as mine a
Mistake of no very great moment—in fine, a
Mere slip—'twas some Pleb's wife, if not Agrippina.

You may fancy that warrior, so stern and so stony,
Whom thirty years since we all used to call BONEY,
When engaged in what he styled " fulfilling his destinies,"
He led his rapscallions across the Borysthenes,
    And had made up his mind   Snug quarters to find
In Moscow, against the catarrhs and the coughs
Which are apt to prevail 'mongst the " Owskis " and " Offs,"
    At a time of the year   When your nose and your ear
Are by no means so safe there as people's are here,
Inasmuch as " Jack Frost," that most fearful of Bogles,
Makes folks leave their cartilage oft in their " fogles."
    You may fancy I say,   That same BONEY's dismay,
When Count Rostopchin
At once made him drop chin,

And turn up his eyes, as his rapee he took,
With a sort of a *mort-de-ma-vie* kind of look,
   On perceiving that " Swing,"
   And " all that sort of thing,"
Was at work,—that he'd just lost the game without knowing it—
That the Kremlin was blazing—the Russians " a-going it,"—
Every plug in the place frozen hard as the ground,
And never a Turn-cock at all to be found !

You may fancy King Charles at some Court Fancy-Ball,
   (The date we may fix   In Sixteen sixty-six,)
In the room built by Inigo Jones at Whitehall,
Whence his father, the Martyr,—(as such mourn'd by all
Who, in *his*, wept the Law's and the Monarchy's fall,)—
Stept out to exchange regal robes for a pall—
You may fancy King Charles, I say, stopping the brawl,*
As bursts on his sight the old church of St. Paul,
By the light of its flames, now beginning to crawl
From basement to buttress, and topping its wall—
—You may fancy old Clarendon making a call,
And stating in cold, slow, monotonous drawl,
" Sire, from Pudding Lane's End, close by Fishmongers' Hall,
To Pye Corner, in Smithfield, there is not a stall
There, in market, or street,—not a house, great or small,
In which Knight wields his faulchion, or Cobbler his awl,
But's on fire ! ! "—You may fancy the general squall,
And bawl as they all call for wimple and shawl !—
—You may fancy all this—but I boldly assert
You *can't* fancy Aunt Fan—as she looked on MY SHIRT ! ! !

Was't Apelles ? or Zeuxis ?—I think 'twas Apelles,
That artist of old—I declare I can't tell his
Exact patronymic—I write and pronounce ill
These Classical names—whom some Grecian Town-Council
Employ'd—I believe, by command of the Oracle,—
To produce them a splendid piece, purely historical,
   For adorning the wall   Of some fane, or Guildhall,

---

* Not a " row," but a dance—
   " The brave Lord Keeper led the *brawls*,
     The seals and maces danced before him."—GRAY.
And truly Sir Christopher danced to some tune.

And who for his subject determined to try a
Large painting in oils of Miss Iphigenia
　　At the moment her Sire,　By especial desire
Of " that Spalpeen, O'Dysseus " (see Barney Maguire),
　　Has resolved to devote　Her beautiful throat
To old Chalcas's knife, and her limbs to the fire ;
—An act which we moderns by no means admire—
An off'ring, 'tis true, to Jove, Mars, or Apollo cost
No trifling sum in those days, if a holocaust,—
Still, although for economy we should condemn none,
In an αναξ ανδρων, like the great Agamemnon,
　　To give up to slaughter　An elegant daughter,
After all the French, Music, and Dancing they'd taught her,
And Singing,—at Heaven knows how much a quarter,—
　　In lieu of a Calf !—　It was too bad by half !
At a " nigger " * so pitiful who would not laugh,
And turn up their noses at one who could find
No decenter method of " Raising the Wind " ?
　　No doubt but he might,　Without any great *Flight*,
　　Have obtain'd it by what we call " flying a kite."
Or on mortgage—or sure, if he couldn't so do it, he
Must have succeeded " by way of annuity."
　　But there—it appears,　His crocodile tears,
His " Oh ! s " and his " Ah ! s " his " Oh Law ! s " and " Oh dear ! s "
　　Were all thought sincere,—so in painting his Victim
The Artist was splendid—but could not depict *Him*.
　　His features, and phiz awry　Show'd so much misery,
　　And so like a dragon he　Look'd in his agony,
　　That the foil'd Painter buried—despairing to gain a
Good likeness—his face in a printed Bandana.
—Such a veil is best thrown o'er one's face when one's hurt
By some grief which no power can repair or avert !—
—Such a veil I shall throw o'er Aunt Fan—and My Shirt !

MORAL.

And now for some practical hints from the story
Of Aunt Fan's mishap, which I've thus laid before ye ;
　　For, if rather too gay,　I can venture to say

* Hibernicè " nigger," *quasi* " niggard." *Vide* B. Maguire *passim.*

A fine vein of morality is, in each lay
Of my primitive Muse, the distinguishing *trait !*—

First of all—Don't put off till to-morrow what may,
Without inconvenience, be managed to-day !
That golden occasion we call " Opportunity "
Rarely's neglected by man with impunity !
And the " Future," how brightly soe'er by Hope's dupe colour'd,
     Ne'er may afford   You a lost chance restored,
Till both you, and YOUR SHIRT, are grown old and pea-soup-
     colour'd !

     I would also desire   You to guard your attire,
Young Ladies,—and never go too near the fire !—
—Depend on't there's many a dear little Soul
Has found that a Spark is as bad as a coal,—
And " in her best petticoat burnt a great hole ! "

Last of all, gentle Reader, don't be too secure !—
Let seeming success never make you " cock-sure ! "
     But beware !—and take care,
     When all things look fair,
How you hang your Shirt over the back of your chair !—
     —" There's many a slip   'Twixt the cup and the lip ! "
Be this excellent proverb, then, well understood,
And DON'T HALLOO BEFORE YOU'RE QUITE OUT OF THE WOOD ! ! !

It is to my excellent and erudite friend, Simpkinson, that I am indebted for his graphic description of the well-known chalk-pit, between Acol and Minster, in the Isle of Thanet, known by the name of the " Smuggler's Leap." The substance of the true history attached to it he picked up while visiting that admirable institution, the " Sea-Bathing Infirmary," of which he is a " Life Governor," and enjoying his *osium cum dignitate* last summer at the least aristocratic of all possible watering-places.

Before I proceed to detail it, however, I cannot, in conscience, fail to bespeak for him the reader's sympathy in one of his own

Misadventures at Margate

A Legend of Jarvis's Jetty

Mr. Simpkinson *loquitur*

'Twas in Margate last July, I walk'd upon the
    pier,
I saw a little vulgar Boy—I said, "What make
    you here ?—
The gloom upon your youthful cheek speaks
    anything but joy ; "
Again I said, " What make you here, you little
    vulgar Boy ? "

He frowned, that little vulgar Boy,—he deem'd
    I meant to scoff—
And when the little heart is big, a little " sets it
    off ; "
He put his finger in his mouth, his little bosom
    rose,—
He had no little handkerchief to wipe his little
    nose !

"Hark ! don't you hear, my little man ?—it's striking Nine," I said,
" An hour when all good little boys and girls should be in bed.
Run home and get your supper, else your Ma' will scold—Oh ! fie !—
It's very wrong indeed for little boys to stand and cry ! "

The tear-drop in his little eye again began to spring,
His bosom throbb'd with agony,—he cried like anything !
I stoop'd, and thus amidst his sobs I heard him murmur—" Ah !
I haven't got no supper ! and I haven't got no Ma' ! !—

" My father, he is on the seas,—my mother's dead and gone !
And I am here, on this here pier, to roam the world alone ;
I have not had this live-long day, one drop to cheer my heart,
Nor ' *brown* ' to buy a bit of bread with—let alone a tart !

331

" If there's a soul will give me food, or find me in employ,
By day or night, then blow me tight ! " (he was a vulgar Boy ;)
" And, now I'm here, from this here pier it is my fixed intent
To jump, as Master Levi did from off the Monu-ment ! "

" Cheer up ! cheer up ! my little man—cheer up ! " I kindly said,
" You are a naughty boy to take such things into your head :
If you should jump from off the pier, you'd surely break your legs,
Perhaps your neck—then Bogey'd have you, sure as eggs are eggs !

" Come home with me, my little man, come home with me and sup ;
My landlady is Mrs. Jones—we must not keep her up—
There's roast potatoes at the fire,—enough for me and you—
Come home, you little vulgar Boy—I lodge at Number 2."

I took him home to Number 2, the house beside "The Foy,"
I bade him wipe his dirty shoes,—that little vulgar Boy,—
And then I said to Mistress Jones, the kindest of her sex,
" Pray be so good as go and fetch a pint of double X ! "

But Mrs. Jones was rather cross, she made a little noise,
She said she " did not like to wait on little vulgar Boys."
She with her apron wiped the plates, and, as she rubb'd the delf,
Said I might " go to Jericho, and fetch my beer myself ! "

I did not go to Jericho—I went to Mr. Cobb—*
I changed a shilling—(which in town the people call " a Bob ")—
It was not so much for myself as for that vulgar child—
And I said, " A pint of double X, and please to draw it mild ! "

When I came back I gazed about—I gazed on stool and chair—
I could not see my little friend—because he was not there !
I peep'd beneath the table-cloth—beneath the sofa too—
I said, " You little vulgar Boy ! why, what's become of you ? "

I could not see my table-spoons—I look'd, but could not see
The little fiddle-pattern'd ones I use when I'm at tea ;
—I could not see my sugar-tongs—my silver watch—oh, dear !
I know 'twas on the mantel-piece when I went out for beer.

---

* Qui facit per alium facit per se—Deem not, gentle stranger, that Mr. Cobb is a petty dealer and chapman, as Mr. Simpkinson would here seem to imply. He is a *maker*, not a retailer of stingo,—and mighty pretty tipple he *makes*.

I could not see my Macintosh—it was not to be seen !—
Nor yet my best white beaver hat, broad-brimm'd and lined with green ;
My carpet-bag—my cruet-stand, that holds my sauce and soy,—
My roast potatoes !—all are gone !—and so's that vulgar Boy !

I rang the bell for Mrs. Jones, for she was down below,
—" Oh, Mrs. Jones ! what *do* you think ?—ain't this a pretty go ?—
—That horrid little vulgar Boy whom I brought here to-night,
—He's stolen my things and run away ! ! "—Says she, " And sarve you
    right ! ! "

     *   *   *   *   *

Next morning I was up betimes—I sent the Crier round,
All with his bell and gold-laced hat, to say I'd give a pound
To find that little vulgar Boy, who'd gone and used me so ;
But when the Crier cried, " O Yes ! " the people cried, " O No ! "

I went to " Jarvis' Landing-place," the glory of the town,
There was a common sailor-man a-walking up and down,
I told my tale—he seem'd to think I'd not been treated well,
And call'd me " Poor old Buffer ! "—what that means I cannot tell

That Sailor-man, he said he'd seen that morning on the shore,
A son of—something—'twas a name I'd never heard before,

A little " gallows-looking chap "—dear me ! what could he mean ?
With a " carpet-swab " and " muckingtogs," and a hat turned up with
  green.

He spoke about his " precious eyes," and said he'd seen him " sheer,"
—It's very odd that Sailor-men should talk so very queer—
And then he hitched his trousers up, as is, I'm told, their use,
—It's very odd that Sailor-men should wear those things so loose.

I did not understand him well, but think he meant to say
He'd seen that little vulgar Boy, that morning, swim away
In Captain Large's Royal George, about an hour before,
And they were now, as he supposed, " some*wheres* " about the Nore.

A landsman said, " I *twig* the chap—he's been upon the Mill—
And 'cause he *gammons* so the *flats*, ve calls him Veeping Bill ! "
He said he'd " done me wery brown," and nicely " *stow'd the swag*,"
—That's French, I fancy, for a hat—or else a carpet-bag.

I went and told the constable my property to track ;
He asked me if " I did not wish that I might get it back ? "
I answered, " To be sure I do !—it's what I'm come about."
He smiled and said, " Sir, does your mother know that you are out ? "

Not knowing what to do, I thought I'd hasten back to town,
And beg our own Lord Mayor to catch the Boy who'd " done me brown."
His Lordship very kindly said he'd try and find him out,
But he " rather thought that there were several vulgar boys about."

He sent for Mr. Whithair then, and I described " the swag,"
My Mactinosh, my sugar-tongs, my spoons, and carpet-bag ;
He promised that the New Police should all their powers employ ;
But never to this hour have I beheld that vulgar Boy !

MORAL.

Remember, then, what when a boy I've heard my Grandma' tell,
" BE WARN'D IN TIME BY OTHERS' HARM, AND YOU SHALL DO FULL WELL ! "
Don't link yourself with vulgar folks, who've got no fixed abode,
Tell lies, use naughty words, and say they " wish they may be blow'd ! "

Don't take too much of double X !—and don't at night go out
To fetch your beer yourself, but make the pot-boy bring your stout !
And when you go to Margate next, just stop, and ring the bell,
Give my respects to Mrs. Jones, and say I'm pretty well !

And now for his Legend, which, if the facts took place rather beyond the " memory of
the oldest inhabitant," are yet well known to have occurred in the neighbourhood " once
on a time ; " and the scene of them will be readily pointed out by any one of the fifty
intelligent fly-drivers who ply upon the pier, and who will convey you safely to the spot for
a guerdon which they term " three bob."

The Smuggler's Leap

A Legend of Thanet

" Near this hamlet (Acol) is a long-disused chalk-pit of formidable depth, known by the
name of 'The Smuggler's Leap.' The tradition of the parish runs, that a riding-officer from
Sandwich, called Anthony Gill, lost his life here in the early part of the present (last) century,
while in pursuit of a smuggler. A fog coming on, both parties went over the precipice. The
smuggler's horse *only*, it is said, was found crushed beneath its rider. The spot has, of course,
been haunted ever since."

See " *Supplement to Lewis's History of Thanet, by the Rev. Samuel Pegge, A.M., Vicar of
Gomersham.*" *W. Bristow, Canterbury*, 1796, *p.* 127.

THE fire-flash shines from Reculver cliff,
And the answering light burns blue in the skiff,
    And there they stand   That smuggling band,
Some in the water, and some on the sand,
Ready those contraband goods to land ;
The night is dark, they are silent and still,
—At the head of the party is Smuggler Bill !

" Now lower away ! come, lower away !
We must be far ere the dawn of the day.
If Exciseman Gill should get scent of the prey,
And should come, and should catch us here, what would he say ?
Come, lower away, lads—once on the hill,
We'll laugh, ho ! ho ! at Exciseman Gill ! "

The cargo's lower'd from the dark skiff's side,
And the tow-line drags the tubs through the tide,
    No flick nor flam,   But your real Schiedam.
" Now mount, my merry men, mount and ride ! "
Three on the crupper and one before,
And the led-horse laden with five tubs more ;
    But the rich point-lace,   In the oil-skin case
Of proof to guard its contents from ill,
" The prime of the swag," is with Smuggler Bill !

Merrily now, in a goodly row,
Away, and away, those smugglers go,
And they laugh at Exciseman Gill, ho ! ho !
    When out from the turn   Of the road to Herne,
Comes Gill, wide awake to the whole concern !
Exciseman Gill, in all his pride,
With his Custom-house officers all at his side ;
—They were called Custom-house officers then ;
There were no such things as " Preventive men."

    Sauve qui peut !   That lawless crew,
Away, and away, and away they flew !
Some dropping one tub, some dropping two ;—
Some gallop this way, and some gallop that,
Through Fordwich Level—o'er Sandwich Flat,
Some fly that way, and some fly this,
Like a covey of birds when the sportsmen miss ;
    These in their hurry   Make for Sturry,
With Custom-house officers close in their rear,
Down Rushbourne Lane, and so by Westbere,
    None of them stopping,   But shooting and popping,
And many a Custom-house bullet goes slap
Through many a three-gallon tub like a tap,
    And the gin spurts out,   And squirts all about,
And many a heart grew sad that day
That so much good liquor was thrown away.

    Sauve qui peut !   That lawless crew,
Away, and away, and away they flew !
Some seek Whitstable—some Grove Ferry,
Spurring and whipping, like madmen—very—

For the life ! for the life ! they ride ! they ride !
And the Custom-house officers all divide,
And they gallop on after them far and wide !
All, all, save one—Exciseman Gill,—
He sticks to the skirts of Smuggler Bill !

Smuggler Bill is six feet high,
He has curling locks, and a roving eye,
He has a tongue, and he has a smile
Train'd the female heart to beguile,
And there is not a farmer's wife in the Isle,
 From St. Nicholas quite To the Foreland Light,
But that eye, and that tongue, and that smile will wheedle her
To have done with the Grocer, and make *him* her Tea-dealer ·
There is not a farmer there but he still
Buys gin and tobacco from Smuggler Bill.

Smuggler Bill rides gallant and gay
On his dapple-grey mare, away, and away
And he pats her neck, and he seems to say
" Follow who will, ride after who may,
 In sooth he had need Fodder his steed,
In Lieu of Lent-corn, with a Quicksilver feed ;
—Nor oats, nor beans, nor the best of old hay,
Will make him a match for my own dapple-grey !
Ho ! ho !—ho ! ho ! " says Smuggler Bill—
He draws out his flask, and he sips his fill,
And he laughs " Ho ! ho ! " at Exciseman Gill.

Down Chistlett Lane, so free and so fleet]
Rides Smuggler Bill, and away to Up-street ;
 Sarre Bridge is won— Bill thinks it fun ;
" Ho ! ho ! the old tub-gauging son of a gun—
His wind will be thick, and his breeks be thin,
Ere a race like this he may hope to win ! "

 Away, away Goes the fleet dapple-grey,
Fresh as the breeze, and free as the wind,
And Exciseman Gill lags far behind.
" *I would give my soul*," quoth Exciseman Gill,
" For a nag that would catch that Smuggler Bill !—

Y

No matter for blood, no matter for bone,
No matter for colour, bay, brown, or roan,
  So I had but one ! "—   A voice cried " Done ! "
" Ay, dun," said Exciseman Gill, and he spied
A Custom-house officer close by his side,
On a high-trotting horse with a dun-coloured hide.—

A CUSTOM-HOUSE OFFICER CLOSE BY HIS SIDE,
ON A HIGH-TROTTING HORSE WITH A DUN-COLOURED HIDE

" *Devil take me*," again quoth Exciseman Gill,
" If I had but that horse, I'd have Smuggler Bill ! "

From his using such shocking expressions, it's plain
That Exciseman Gill was rather profane.
  He was, it is true,   As bad as a Jew,
A sad old scoundrel as ever you knew,

And he rode in his stirrups sixteen stone two.
—He'd just utter'd the words which I've mentioned to you,
When his horse, coming slap on his knees with him, threw
Him head over heels, and away he flew,
And Exciseman Gill was bruised black and blue.

When he arose,   His hands and his clothes
Were as filthy as could be,—he'd pitch'd on his nose,
And roll'd over and over again in the mud,
And his nose and his chin were all covered with blood ;
Yet he scream'd with passion, " I'd rather *grill*
Than not come up with that Smuggler Bill ! "
—" Mount ! Mount ! " quoth the Custom-house officer, " get
On the back of my Dun, you'll bother him yet.
Your words are plain, though they're somewhat rough
' Done and Done ' between gentlemen's always enough !—
I'll lend you a lift—there—you're up on him—so,—
He's a rum one to look at—*a devil to go !* "
   Exciseman Gill   Dash'd up the hill,
And mark'd not, so eager was he in pursuit,
The queer Custom-house officer's queer-looking boot.

Smuggler Bill rides on amain,
He slacks not girth—and he draws not rein,
Yet the dapple-grey mare bounds on in vain,
For nearer now—and he hears it plain—
Sounds the tramp of a horse—" 'Tis the Gauger again ! "
   Smuggler Bill   Dashes round by the mill
That stands near the road upon Monkton Hill,—
   " Now speed,—now speed,   My dapple-grey steed,
Thou ever, my dapple, wert good at need !
O'er Monkton Mead, and through Minster Level,
We'll baffle him yet, be he gauger or devil !
   For Manston Cave, away ! away !
Now speed thee, now speed thee, my good dapple-grey !
It shall never be said that Smuggler Bill
Was run down like a hare by Exciseman Gill ! "

Manston Cave was Bill's abode ;
A mile to the north of the Ramsgate Road,

(Of late they say　It's been taken away,
That is, levell'd, and filled up with chalk and clay,
By a gentleman there of the name of Day,)
Thither he urges his good dapple-grey ;
　And the dapple-grey steed,　Still good at need,
Though her chest it pants, and her flanks they bleed,
Dashes along at the top of her speed ;

But nearer and nearer Exciseman Gill
Cries, " Yield thee ! now yield thee, thou Smuggler Bill ! "

Smuggler Bill, he looks behind,
And he sees a Dun horse come swift as the wind,
And his nostrils smoke, and his eyes they blaze
Like a couple of lamps on a yellow post-chaise !
　Every shoe he has got　Appears red-hot !
And sparks, round his ears snap, crackle, and play,
And his tail cocks up in a very odd way,
Every hair in his mane seems a porcupine's quill,
And there on his back sits Exciseman Gill,
Crying " Yield thee ! now yield thee, thou Smuggler Bill ! "

Smuggler Bill from his holster drew
A large horse-pistol, of which he had two,
   Made by Nock; He pull'd back the cock
As far as he could to the back of the lock;
The trigger he touch'd, and the welkin rang
To the sound of the weapon, it made such a bang;
Smuggler Bill he ne'er miss'd his aim,
The shot told true on the Dun—but there came
From the hole where it enter'd,—not blood,—but flame!
   —He changed his plan, And fired at the man;
But his second horse-pistol flashed in the pan!
And Exciseman Gill, with a hearty good will,
Made a grab at the collar of Smuggler Bill.

The dapple-grey mare made a desperate bound
When that queer Dun horse on her flank she found,
Alack! and alas! on what dangerous ground!
It's enough to make one's flesh to creep
To stand on that fearful verge, and peep
Down the rugged sides so dreadfully steep,
Where the chalk-hole yawns full sixty feet deep,
O'er which that steed took that desperate leap!
It was so dark then under the trees,
No horse in the world could tell chalk from cheese—
Down they went—o'er that terrible fall,—
Horses, Exciseman, Smuggler, and all!!

   Below were found Next day on the ground,
By an elderly Gentleman walking his round,
(I wouldn't have seen such a sight for a pound,)
All smash'd and dash'd, three mangled corses,
Two of them human,—the third was a horse's,—
That good dapple-grey,—and Exciseman Gill
Yet grasping the collar of Smuggler Bill!

But where was the Dun? that terrible Dun?—
From that terrible night he was seen by none!—
There are some people think, though I am not one,
That part of the story all nonsense and fun,
   But the country-folks there, One and all, declare,
When the " Crowner's 'Quest " came to sit on the pair,

They heard a loud Horse-laugh up in the air !—
—If in one of the trips　Of the steamboat Eclipse
You should go down to Margate to look at the ships,
Or to take what the bathing-room people call " Dips,"
　　You may hear old folks talk　　　　.
　　Of that quarry of chalk ;
Or go over—it's rather too far for a walk,
But a three shilling drive will give you a peep
At that fearful chalk-pit—so awfully deep,
Which is call'd to this moment " The Smuggler's Leap !"
Nay more, I am told, on a moonshiny night,
If you're " plucky," and not over-subject to fright,
And go and look over that chalk-pit white,
　　You may see, if you will,　The Ghost of Old Gill
Grappling the Ghost of Smuggler Bill,
And the Ghost of the dapple-grey lying between 'em.—
I'm told so—I can't say I know one who's seen 'em !

Moral.

And now, gentle Reader, one word ere we part,
Just take a friend's counsel, and lay it to heart.
Imprimis, don't smuggle !—if, bent to please Beauty,
You *must* buy French lace,—purchase what has paid duty !
Don't use naughty words, in the next place,—and ne'er in
Your language adopt a bad habit of swearing !
　　Never say " Devil take me ! "—
　　Or, " shake me ! "—or, " bake me ! "
Or such-like expressions.—Remember Old Nick
To take folks at their word is remarkably quick.
Another sound maxim I'd wish you to keep,
Is, " Mind what you're after, and—Look ere you Leap ! "

Above all, to my last gravest caution attend—
NEVER BORROW A HORSE YOU DON'T KNOW OF A FRIEND ! ! !

For the story which succeeds I am indebted to Mrs. Botherby. She is a Shropshire Lady by birth, and I overheard her, a few weeks since, in the nursery, chaunting the following, one of the Legends peculiar to her native County, for the amusement and information of Seaforth's little boy, who was indeed " all ears." As Ralph de Diceto, who alludes to the main facts, was Dean of St. Paul's in 1183, about the time that the Temple Church was consecrated, the history is evidently as ancient as it is authentic, though the author of the present paraphrase has introduced many unauthorized, as well as "anachronismatical interpolations."— For the interesting note on the ancient family of Ketch, I need scarcely say, I am obliged to *the* Simpkinson.

Bloudie Jacke of Shrewsberrie

The Shropshire Bluebeard

A LEGEND OF "THE PROUD SALOPIANS"

Hisce ferè temporibus, in agro Salopiensi, Quidam cui nomen Johannes, Le Sanglaunt deinde nuncupatus, uxores quamplurimas ducit, enecat et (ita referunt) manducat ; ossa solùm cani miræ magnitudinis relinquens. Tùm demùm in flagrante delicto, vel "manu rubrâ," ut dicunt Jurisconsulti, deprensus, carnifice vix opprimitur.—RADULPHUS DE DICETO.

OH ! why doth thine eye gleam so bright,
                                    Bloudie Jacke !
Oh ! why doth thine eye gleam so bright ?—
    The Mother's at home,   The Maid may not roam,
She never will meet thee to-night !
                              By the light
Of the moon—it's impossible—quite !

Yet thine eye is still brilliant and bright,
                                    Bloudie Jacke !
It gleams with a fiendish delight—
    " 'Tis done—   She is won ! Nothing under the sun
Can loose the charm'd ring, though it's slight !
                              Ho ! ho !
It fits so remarkably tight ! "

The wire is as thin as a thread,
                                    Bloudie Jacke !
The wire is as thin as a thread !—
    " Though slight be the chain,   Again might and main
Cannot rend it in twain—She is wed !
                              She is wed !
She is mine, be she living or dead !
                              Haw ! haw ! ! "

Nay, laugh not, I pray thee, so loud,
                        𝔅𝔩𝔬𝔲𝔡𝔦𝔢 𝔍𝔞𝔠𝔨𝔢!
Oh! laugh not so loud and so clear!
    Though sweet is thy smile   The heart to beguile,
Yet thy laugh is quite shocking to hear,
                        O dear!
It makes the blood curdle with fear!

The Maiden is gone by the glen,
                        𝔅𝔩𝔬𝔲𝔡𝔦𝔢 𝔍𝔞𝔠𝔨𝔢!
She is gone by the glen and the wood—
    It's a very odd thing   She should wear such a ring,
While her tresses are bound with a snood.
                        By the rood!
It's a thing that's not well understood!

The Maiden is stately and tall,
                        𝔅𝔩𝔬𝔲𝔡𝔦𝔢 𝔍𝔞𝔠𝔨𝔢!
And stately she walks in her pride;
    But the Young Mary-Anne   Runs as fast as she can,
To o'ertake her, and walk by her side:
                        Though she chide—
She deems not her sister a bride!

But the Maiden is gone by the glen,
                        𝔅𝔩𝔬𝔲𝔡𝔦𝔢 𝔍𝔞𝔠𝔨𝔢!
Mary-Anne she is gone by the lea;
    She o'ertakes not her sister,
    It's clear she has miss'd her,
And cannot think where she can be!
                        Dear me!
" Ho! ho!—We shall see—we shall see! "

Mary-Anne is gone over the lea,
                        𝔅𝔩𝔬𝔲𝔡𝔦𝔢 𝔍𝔞𝔠𝔨𝔢!
Mary-Anne, she is come to the Tower;
    But it makes her heart quail,   For it looks like a jail,
A deal more than a fair Lady's bower,
                        So sour
Its ugly grey walls seem to lour.

For the Barbican's massy and high,
𝔅𝔩𝔬𝔲𝔡𝔦𝔢 𝔍𝔞𝔠𝔨𝔢 !
And the oak-door is heavy and brown,
   And with iron it's plated   And machecollated,
To pour boiling oil and lead down ;
How you'd frown
Should a ladle-full fall on your crown !

The rock that it stands on is steep,
𝔅𝔩𝔬𝔲𝔡𝔦𝔢 𝔍𝔞𝔠𝔨𝔢 !
To gain it one's forced for to creep ;
   The Portcullis is strong,   And the Drawbridge is long,
And the water runs all round the Keep ;
At a peep
You can see that the Moat's very deep !

The Drawbridge is long, but it's down,
𝔅𝔩𝔬𝔲𝔡𝔦𝔢 𝔍𝔞𝔠𝔨𝔢 !
And the Portcullis hangs in the air ;
   And no Warder is near   With his horn and his spear,
To give notice when people come there,—
I declare
Mary-Anne has run into the Square !

The oak-door is heavy and brown,
𝔅𝔩𝔬𝔲𝔡𝔦𝔢 𝔍𝔞𝔠𝔨𝔢 !
But the oak-door is standing ajar,
   And no one is there   To say, " Pray take a chair,
You seem tired, Miss, with running so far—
So you are—
With grown people you're scarce on a par ! "

But the young Mary-Anne is *not* tired,
𝔅𝔩𝔬𝔲𝔡𝔦𝔢 𝔍𝔞𝔠𝔨𝔢 !
She roams o'er your Tower by herself ;
   She runs through, very soon,   Each boudoir and saloon,
And examines each closet and shelf,
Your pelf,
All your plate, and your china—and delf.

She looks at your Arras so fine,
                        Bloudie Jacke!
So rich, all description it mocks ;
    And she now and then pauses   To gaze at the vases,
Your pictures, and or-molu clocks ;
                        Every box,
Every cupboard, and drawer she unlocks.

She looks at the paintings so rare,
                        Bloudie Jacke!
That adorn every wall in your house ;
    Your *impayable* pieces,   Your Paul Veroneses,
Your Rembrandts, your Guidos, and Dows,
                        Moreland's Cows,
Claude's Landscapes,—and Landseer's Bow-wows.

She looks at your Statues so fine,
                        Bloudie Jacke!
And mighty great notice she takes
    Of your Niobe crying,   Your Mirmillo dying,
Your Hercules strangling the snakes,—
                        How he shakes
The nasty great things as he wakes !

Your Laocoön, his serpents and boys,
                        Bloudie Jacke!
She views with some little dismay ;
    A copy of that I can   See in the Vatican
Unless the Pope's sent it away,
                        As they say,
In the Globe, he intended last May.*

There's your Belvidere Phœbus, with which,
                        Bloudie Jacke!
Mr. Milman says none other vies.
    (His lines on Apollo   Beat all the rest hollow,
And gained him the Newdigate prize.)
                        How the eyes
Seem watching the shaft as it flies !

* " The Pope is said—this fact is hardly credible—to have sold the Laocoon and the Apollo Belvidere to the Emperor of Russia for nine million of francs."—*Globe and Traveller.*

How you'd frown   Should a ladle-full fall on your crown

There's a room full of satins and silks,
                    Bloudie Jacke!
There's a room full of velvets and lace,
    There are drawers full of rings,
    And a thousand fine things,
And a splendid gold watch with a case
                    O'er its face,
Is in every room in the place.

There are forty fine rooms on a floor,
                    Bloudie Jacke!
And every room fit for a Ball,
    It's so gorgeous and rich,   With so lofty a pitch,
And so long, and so broad, and so tall;
                    Yes, all,
Save the last one—and that's very small!

It boasts not stool, table, or chair,
                    Bloudie Jacke!
But *one* Cabinet, costly and grand,
    Which has little gold figures   Of little gold Niggers,
With fishing-rods stuck in each hand.—
                    It's japann'd,
And it's placed on a splendid buhl stand.

Its hinges and clasps are of gold,
                    Bloudie Jacke!
And of gold are its key-hole and key,
    And the drawers within   Have each a gold pin,
And they're numbered with 1, 2, and 3,
                    You may see
All the figures in gold filigree!

Number 1's full of emeralds green,
                    Bloudie Jacke!
Number 2's full of diamonds and pearl;
    But what does she see   In drawer Number 3
That makes all her senses to whirl,
                    Poor Girl!
And each lock of her hair to uncurl?—

Wedding fingers are sweet pretty things,
                                        Bloudie Jacke!
To salute them one eagerly strives,
    When one kneels to " propose "—
    It's another *quelque chose*
When cut off at the knuckles with knives
                                        From our wives,
They are tied up in bunches of fives.

Yet there they lie, one, two, three, four !
                                        Bloudie Jacke!
There lie they, five, six, seven, eight !
    And by them in rows   Lie eight little Great-Toes,
To match in size, colour, and weight !
                                        From their state,
It would seem they'd been sever'd of late.

Beside them are eight Wedding-rings,
                                        Bloudie Jacke!
And the gold is as thin as a thread—
    " Ho ! ho !—She is mine—
    This will make up the Nine ! '—
Dear me ! who those shocking words said ?—
                                        —She fled
To hide herself under the bed.

But, alas ! there's no bed in the room,
                                        Bloudie Jacke!
And she peeps from the window on high ;
    Only fancy her fright   And the terrible sight
Down below, which at once meets her eye !
                                        " Oh My ! ! "
She half utter'd,—but stifled her cry.

For she saw it was You and your Man,
                                        Bloudie Jacke!
And she heard your unpleasant " Haw ! haw ! "
    While her sister stone dead,   By the hair of her head,
O'er the bridge you were trying to draw,
                                        As she saw—
A thing quite contra-ry to law !

Your man has got hold of her heels,
                    𝕭𝖑𝖔𝖚𝖉𝖎𝖊 𝕵𝖆𝖈𝖐𝖊!
𝕭𝖑𝖔𝖚𝖉𝖎𝖊 𝕵𝖆𝖈𝖐𝖊! you've got hold of her hair!
   But nor 𝕵𝖆𝖈𝖐𝖊 nor his Man
   Can see young Mary-Anne,
She has hid herself under the stair,
                    And there
Is a horrid great Dog, I declare!

His eyeballs are bloodshot and blear,
                    𝕭𝖑𝖔𝖚𝖉𝖎𝖊 𝕵𝖆𝖈𝖐𝖊!
He's a sad ugly cur for a pet;
   He seems of the breed   Of that " Billy," indeed,
Who used to kill rats for a bet;
                    —I forget
How many one morning he ate.

He has skulls, ribs, and vertebræ there,
                    𝕭𝖑𝖔𝖚𝖉𝖎𝖊 𝕵𝖆𝖈𝖐𝖊!
And thigh-bones;—and, though it's so dim,
   Yet it's plain to be seen
   He has pick'd them quite clean,—
She expects to be torn limb from limb,
                    So grim
He looks at her—and she looks at him!

She has given him a bun and a roll,
                    𝕭𝖑𝖔𝖚𝖉𝖎𝖊 𝕵𝖆𝖈𝖐𝖊!
She has given him a roll and a bun,
   And a Shrewsbury cake,   Of 𝕻𝖆𝖎𝖑𝖎𝖓'𝖘 * own make,
Which she happened to take ere her run
                    She begun—
She'd been used to a luncheon at One.

It's " a pretty particular Fix,"
                    𝕭𝖑𝖔𝖚𝖉𝖎𝖊 𝕵𝖆𝖈𝖐𝖊!
—Above,—there's the Maiden that's dead;
   Below—growling at her—
   There's that Cannibal Cur,

---

* Oh, Pailin! Prince of cake-compounders! the mouth liquefies at thy very name—but there!

Who at present is munching her bread,
$$\text{Instead}$$
Of her leg,—or her arm,—or her head.

It's " a pretty particular Fix,"
$$\text{Bloudie Jacke !}$$
She is caught like a mouse in a trap ;—
    Stay !—there's something, I think,
    That has slipp'd through a chink,
And fall'n, by a singular hap,
$$\text{Slap,}$$
Into poor little Mary-Anne's lap !

It's a very fine little gold ring,
$$\text{Bloudie Jacke !}$$
Yet, though slight, it's remarkably stout,
   But it's made a sad stain,   Which will always remain
On her frock—for Blood will not wash out ;
$$\text{I doubt}$$
Salts of Lemon won't bring it about !

She has grasp'd that gold ring in her hand,
$$\text{Bloudie Jacke !}$$
In an instant she stands on the floor,
   She makes but one bound   O'er the back of the hound,
And a hop, skip, and jump to the door,
$$\text{And she's o'er}$$
The drawbridge she traversed before !

Her hair's floating loose in the breeze,
$$\text{Bloudie Jacke !}$$
For gone is her " bonnet of blue."
   —Now the Barbican's past !—   Her legs " go it " as fast
As two drumsticks a-beating tattoo,
$$\text{As they do}$$
At Réveille, Parade, or Review !

She has run into Shrewsbury town,
$$\text{Bloudie Jacke !}$$
She has called out the Beadle and May'r,

And the Justice of Peace, And the Rural Police,
Till " Battle Field " swarms like a Fair,—
And see there !—
E'en the Parson's beginning to swear ! !

There's a pretty to-do in your Tower,
𝔅𝔩𝔬𝔲𝔡𝔦𝔢 𝔍𝔞𝔠𝔨𝔢 !
In your Tower there's a pretty to-do !
   All the people of Shrewsbury
   Playing old gooseberry
With you choice bits of taste and *virtù ;*
Each bijou
Is upset in their search after you !

They are playing the deuce with your things,
𝔅𝔩𝔬𝔲𝔡𝔦𝔢 𝔍𝔞𝔠𝔨𝔢 !
There's your Cupid is broken in two,

And so to, between us, is   Each of your Venuses,
The " Antique " ones you bought of the Jew,
                              And the new
One, George Robins swears came from St. Cloud.

The CALLIPYGE 's injured behind,
                              𝔅loubie 𝔍acke !
The DE MEDICI 's injured before ;
    And the ANADYOMENE   's injured in so many
Places, I think there's a score,
                              If not more,
Of her fingers and toes on the floor.

They are hunting you up stairs and down,
                              𝔅loubie 𝔍acke !
Every person to pass is forbid,
    While they turn out the closets
    And all their deposits—
" There's the dust-hole—come lift up the lid ! "—
                              So they did—
But they could not find where you were hid !

Ah ! Ah !—they will have you at last,
                              𝔅loubie 𝔍acke !
The chimneys to search they begin ;—
    They have found you at last !—
    There you are sticking fast,
With you knees doubled up to your chin,
                              Though you're thin !
—Dear me ! what a mess you are in !—

What a terrible pickle you're in,
                              𝔅loubie 𝔍acke !
Why, your face is as black as your hat !
    Your fine Holland shirt   Is all over dirt !
And so is your point-lace cravat !
                              What a Flat
To seek such an asylum as that !

They can scarcely help laughing, I vow,
                              𝔅loubie 𝔍acke !

In the midst of their turmoil and strife ;
   You're not fit to be seen ! —You look like Mr. Kean
In the play, where he murders his wife !—
              On my life
You ought to be scraped with a knife !

They have pull'd you down flat on your back,
            𝔅𝔩𝔬𝔲𝔡𝔦𝔢 𝔍𝔞𝔠𝔨𝔢!
They have pull'd you down flat on your back !
   And they smack, and they thwack,
    Till your " funny bones " crack,
As if you were stretched on the rack,
             At each thwack !—
Good lack ! what a savage attack !

They call for the Parliament Man,
            𝔅𝔩𝔬𝔲𝔡𝔦𝔢 𝔍𝔞𝔠𝔨𝔢!
And the Hangman, the matter to clinch,
   And they call for the Judge,
    But others cry " Fudge ! —
Don't budge Mr. Calcraft,* an inch !
            Mr. Lynch ! †
Will do very well at a pinch ! "

It is useless to scuffle and cuff,
            𝔅𝔩𝔬𝔲𝔡𝔦𝔢 𝔍𝔞𝔠𝔨𝔢!

* Jehan de Ketche acted as Provost Marshal to the army of William the Conqueror, and received from that monarch a grant of the dignity of Hereditary Grand Functionary of England, together with a croft or " parcel of land," known by the name of the 𝔒𝔩𝔡 𝔅𝔞𝔦𝔩𝔦𝔢, co. Middx., to be held by him, and the heirs general of his body, in Grand Serjeantry, by the yearly presentation of " ane hempen cravatte." After remaining for several generations in the same name, the office passed, by marriage of the heiress, into the ancient family of the Kirbys, and thence again to that of Callcraft (1st Eliz. 1558).—Abhorson Callcraft,' Esq. of Saffron Hill, co. Middx., the present representative of the Ketches, exercised his "function" on a very recent occasion, and claimed and was allowed the fee of 13½d. under the ancient grant as 𝔥𝔞𝔫𝔤𝔪𝔞𝔫'𝔰 𝔚𝔞𝔤𝔢𝔰.

ARMS.—1st and 4th, Quarterly, Argent and Sable ; in the first quarter a Gibbet of the second, noosed proper, *Callcraft.* 2nd, Sable, three Nightcaps Argent, tufted Gules, 2 and 1, *Ketche.* 3rd, Or, a Nosegay *fleurant, Kirby.*

SUPPORTERS.—*Dexter :* a Sheriff in his pride, robed Gules, chained and collared Or.— *Sinister :* An Ordinary displayed proper, wigged and banded Argent, nosed Gules.

MOTTO.—SIC ITUR AD ASTRA !

† The American Justinian, Compiler of the " Yankee Pandects."

It is useless to struggle and bite !
  And to kick and to scratch
  You have met with your match,
And the Shrewsbury Boys hold you tight,
          Despite
Your determined attempts " to show fight."

They are pulling you all sorts of ways,
          𝔅𝔩𝔬𝔲𝔡𝔦𝔢 𝔍𝔞𝔠𝔨𝔢!
They are twisting your right leg Nor-West,
  And your left leg due South,
  And your knees in your mouth,
And your head is poked down on your breast,
         And it's prest,
I protest, almost into your chest !

They have pulled off your arms and your legs,
          𝔅𝔩𝔬𝔲𝔡𝔦𝔢 𝔍𝔞𝔠𝔨𝔢!
As the naughty boys serve the blue flies ;
  And they've torn from their sockets,
  And put in their pockets
Your fingers and thumbs for a prize !
         And your eyes
A Doctor has bottled—from Guy's.*

Your trunk, thus dismember'd and torn,
          𝔅𝔩𝔬𝔲𝔡𝔦𝔢 𝔍𝔞𝔠𝔨𝔢!
They hew, and they hack, and they chop ;
  And, to finish the whole,   They stick up a pole
In the place that's still called the " 𝔚𝔶𝔩𝔡𝔢 ℭ𝔬𝔭𝔭𝔢."
         And they pop
Your grim gory head on the top !

They have buried the fingers and toes,
          𝔅𝔩𝔬𝔲𝔡𝔦𝔢 𝔍𝔞𝔠𝔨𝔢!
Of the victims so lately your prey.
  From those fingers and eight toes   Sprang early potatoes
" 𝔏𝔞𝔡𝔶𝔢𝔰' 𝔉𝔶𝔫𝔤𝔢𝔯𝔰 " they're called to this day ;
         —So they say,—
And you usually dig them in May.

---

* A similar appropriation is said to have been made, by an eminent practitioner, of those
of the late Monsieur Courvoisier.

What became of the dear little girl ?
>Bloudie Jacke!

What became of the young Mary-Anne ?
  Why, I'm sadly afraid   That she died an Old Maid,
For she fancied that every Young Man
>Had a plan

To trepan her like " poor Sister Fan ! "

So they say she is now leading apes,
>Bloudie Jacke!

And mends Bachelors' small-clothes below ;
  The story is old,   And has often been told,
But I cannot believe it is so—
>No ! No !

Depend on't the tale is " No Go ! "

Moral.

And now for the moral I'd fain,
>Bloudie Jacke!

That young Ladies should draw from my pen,—
  It's " Don't take these flights   Upon moon-shiny nights,
With gay, *harum-scarum* young men,
>Down a glen !—

You really can't trust one in ten ! "

Let them think of your terrible Tower,
>Bloudie Jacke!

And don't let them liberties take,
  Whether Maidens or Spouses, In Bachelors' houses ;
Or, some time or another, they'll make
>A Mistake !

And lose—more than a Shrewsberrie Cake !!

Her niece, of whom I have before made honourable mention, is not a whit behind Mrs. Botherby in furnishing entertainment for the young folks. If little Charles has the aunt to *sol fa* him into slumber, Miss Jenny is equally fortunate in the possession of a Sappho of her own.   It is to the air of " Drops of Brandy " that Patty has adapted her version of a venerable ditty, which we have all listened to with respect and affection under its old title of

The Babes in the Wood ; or, the Norfolk Tragedy

An Old Song to a New Tune

WHEN we were all little and good,—
  A long time ago, I'm afraid, Miss—
We were told of the Babes in the Wood
  By their false, cruel Uncle betray'd, Miss ;
Their Pa was a Squire, or a Knight ;
  In Norfolk I think his estate lay—
That is, if I recollect right,
  For I've not read the history lately.*

Rum ti, &c.

Their Pa and their Ma being seized
  With a tiresome complaint, which in some seasons,
People are apt to be seized
  With, who're not on their guard against plum-seasons,
Their medical man shook his head
  As he could not get well to the root of it ;
And the Babes stood on each side the bed,
  While their Uncle, he stood at the foot of it.

" Oh, Brother ! " their Ma whisper'd, faint
  And low, for breath seeming to labour, " Who'd
Think that this horrid complaint,
  That's been going about in the neighbourhood,
Thus should attack me,—nay, more,
  My poor husband besides,—and so fall on him !
Bringing us so near to Death's door
  That we can't avoid making a call on him !

" Now think, 'tis your Sister invokes
  Your aid, and the last word she says is,
Be kind to those dear little folks
  When our toes are turned up to the daisies !—

---

* See Bloomfield's History of the County of Norfolk, in which all the particulars of this lamentable history are (or ought to be) fully detailed, together with the names of the parties, and an elaborate pedigree of the family.

By the servants don't let them be snubb'd,—
—Let Jane have her fruit and her custard,
And mind Johnny's chilblains are rubb'd
Well with Whitehead's best essence of mustard.

" You know they'll be pretty well off in
Respect to what's called ' worldly gear,'
For John, when his Pa's in his coffin,
Comes in to three hundred a year ;
And Jane's to have five hundred pound
On her marriage paid down, ev'ry penny,
So you'll own a worse match might be found,
Any day in the week, than our Jenny ! "

Here the Uncle pretended to cry,
And, like an old thorough-paced rogue, he
Put his handkerchief up to his eye,
And devoted himself to Old Bogey
If he did not make matters all right,
And said, should he covet their riches,
He " wished the old Gentleman might
Fly away with him, body and breeches ! "

No sooner, however, were they
Put to bed with a spade by the sexton,
Than he carried the darlings away
Out of that parish into the next one,
Giving out he should take them to town,
And select the best school in the nation,
That John might not grow up a clown,
But receive a genteel education.

" Greek and Latin old twaddle I call ! "
  Says he, " While his mind's ductile and plastic,
I'll place him at Dotheboys Hall,
  Where he'll learn all that's new and gymnastic.
While Jane, as, when girls have the dumps,
  Fortune-hunters, by scores, to entrap 'em rise,
Shall go to those worthy old frumps,
  The two Misses Tickler of Clapham Rise ! "

Having thought on the How and the When
  To get rid of his nephew and niece,
He sent for two ill-looking men,
  And he gave them five guineas a-piece.—
Says he, " Each of you take up a child
  On the crupper, and when you have trotted
Some miles through that wood lone and wild,
  Take your knife out, and cut its carotid ! "—

" Done " and " done " is pronounced on each side,
  While the poor little dears are delighted
To think they a-cock-horse shall ride,
  And are not in the least degree frighted ;
They say their " Ta ! Ta ! " as they start,
  And they prattle so nice on their journey,
That the rogues themselves wish to their heart
  They could finish the job by attorney.

Nay, one was so taken aback
  By seeing such spirit and life in them,
That he fairly exclaim'd, " I say, Jack,
  I'm blowed if I *can* put a knife in them ! "—
" Pooh ! " says his pal, " you great dunce !
  You've pouched the good gentleman's money,
So out with your whinger at once,
  And scrag Jane, while I spiflicate Johnny ! "

He refused, and harsh language ensued,
  Which ended at length in a duel.
When he that was mildest in mood
  Gave the truculent rascal his gruel ;

Wandering about and "Boo-hoo"-ing

The Babes quake with hunger and fear,
  While the ruffian his dead comrade, Jack, buries ;
Then he cries, " Loves, amuse yourselves here
  With the hips, and the haws, and the blackberries !

" I'll be back in a couple of shakes ;
  So don't, dears, be quivering and quaking :
I'm going to get you some cakes,
  And a nice butter'd roll that's a-baking ! "
He rode off with a tear in his eye,
  Which ran down his rough cheek, and wet it,
As he said to himself with a sigh,
  " Pretty souls !—don't they wish they may get it ! ! "

From that moment the Babes ne'er caught sight
  Of the wretch who thus wrought their undoing,
But passed all that day and that night
  In wandering about and " boo-hoo "-ing.
The night proved cold, dreary, and dark,
  So that, worn out with sighings and sobbings,
Next morn they were found stiff and stark,
  And stone-dead, by two little Cock-Robins.

These two little birds it sore grieves
  To see what so cruel a dodge I call,—
They cover the bodies with leaves,
  An interment quite ornithological ;
It might more expensive have been,
  But I doubt, though I've not been to see 'em,
If among those in all Kensal Green
  You could find a more neat Mausoleum.

Now, whatever your rogues may suppose,
  Conscience always makes restless their pillows,
And Justice, though blind, has a nose
  That sniffs out all conceal'd peccadilloes.
The wicked old Uncle, they say,
  In spite of his riot and revel,
Was hippish and qualmish all day,
  And dreamt all night long of the d—l.

He grew gouty, dyspeptic, and sour,
　　And his brow, once so smooth and so placid,
Fresh wrinkles acquired every hour,
　　And whatever he swallow'd turn'd acid.
The neighbours thought all was not right,
　　Scarcely one with him ventured to parley,
And Captain Swing came in the night,
　　And burnt all his beans and his barley.

There was hardly a day but some fox
　　Ran away with his geese and his ganders ;
His wheat had the mildew, his flocks
　　Took the rot, and his horses the glanders ;
His daughters drank rum in their tea,
　　His son, who had gone for a sailor,
Went down in a steamer at sea,
　　And his wife ran away with a tailor !

It was clear he lay under a curse,
　　None would hold with him any communion ;
Every day matters grew worse and worse,
　　Till they ended at length in the Union ;
While his man being caught in some fact,
　　(The particular crime I've forgotten,)
When he came to be hanged for the act,
　　Split, and told the whole story to Cotton.

Understanding the matter was blown,
　　His employer became apprehensive
Of what, when 'twas more fully known,
　　Might ensue—he grew thoughtful and pensive ;
He purchased some sugar-of-lead,
　　Took it home, popp'd it into his porridge,
Ate it up, and then took to his bed,
　　And so died in the workhouse at Norwich.

MORAL.

Ponder well now, dear Parents, each word
　　That I've wrote, and when Sirius rages
In the dog-days, don't be so absurd
　　As to blow yourself out with Green-gages !

Of stone-fruits in general be shy,
   And reflect it's a fact beyond question
That Grapes, when they're spelt with an *i*,
   Promote anything else but digestion.—

—When you set about making your will,
   Which is commonly done when a body's ill,
Mind, and word it with caution and skill,
   And avoid, if you can, any codicil !
When once you've appointed an heir
   To the fortune you've made, or obtained, ere
You leave a reversion, beware
   Whom you place in contingent remainder !

Executors, Guardians, and all
   Who have children to mind, don't ill treat them,
Nor think that, because they are small
   And weak, you may beat them, and cheat them !
Remember that " ill-gotten goods
   Never thrive ; " their possession's but cursory ;
So never turn out in the woods
   Little folks you should keep in the nursery.

Be sure he who does such base things
   Will ne'er stifle Conscience's clamour ;
His " riches will make themselves wings,"
   And his property come to the hammer !
Then He,—and not those he bereaves,—
   Will have most cause for sighings and sobbings,
When he finds *himself* smother'd with leaves
   (Of fat catalogues) heaped up by Robins !

The incidents recorded in the succeeding Legend were communicated to a dear friend of our family by the late lamented Sir Walter Scott. The names and localities have been scrupulously retained, as she is ready to testify. The proceedings in this case are, I believe, recorded in some of our law reports, though I have never been able to lay my hand upon them.

The Dead Drummer

A Legend of Salisbury Plain

Oh, Salisbury Plain is bleak and bare,—
At least so I've heard many people declare,
For I fairly confess I never was there ;—
  Not a shrub nor a tree,   Nor a bush can you see ;
No hedges, no ditches, no gates, no stiles,
Much less a house, or a cottage for miles ;—
—It's a very sad thing to be caught in the rain
When night's coming on upon Salisbury Plain.

  Now, I'd have you to know   That, a great while ago,
The best part of a century, may be, or so,
Across this same plain, so dull and so dreary,
A couple of Travellers, wayworn and weary,
  Were making their way ;
  Their profession, you'd say,
At a single glance did not admit of a query ;
The pump-handled pig-tail, and whiskers, worn then,
With scarce an exception by sea-faring men,
The jacket,—the loose trousers " bows'd up together "—all
Guiltless of braces, as those of Charles Wetherall,—
The pigeon-toed step, and the rollicking motion,
Bespoke them two genuine sons of the Ocean,
And show'd in a moment their real charácters,
(The accent's so placed on this word by our Jack Tars.)

362

The one in advance was sturdy and strong,
With arms uncommonly bony and long,
  And his Guernsey shirt
  Was all pitch and dirt,
Which sailors don't think inconvenient or wrong.
  He was very broad-breasted, And very deep-chested ;
His sinewy frame correspond with the rest did,
Except as to height, for he could not be more
At the most, you would say, than some five feet four,
And if measured, perhaps had been found a thought lower.
Dame Nature, in fact,—whom some person or other,
—A Poet,—has call'd " a capricious step-mother,"—
  You saw, when beside him,
  Had somehow denied him
In longitude what she had granted in latitude,
  A trifling defect
  You'd the sooner detect
From his having constructed a stoop in his attitude.
Square-built and broad-shoulder'd, good-humoured and gay,
With his collar and countenance open as day,
The latter—'twas mark'd with small-pox, by the way,—
Had a sort of expression good will to bespeak ;
He'd a smile in his eye, and a quid in his cheek !
And, in short, notwithstanding his failure in height,
He was just such a man as you'd say, at first sight,
You would much rather dine, or shake hands, with than fight !

The other, his friend and companion, was taller
By five or six inches, at least, than the smaller ;—
  From his air and his mien It was plain to be seen,
  That he was, or had been, A something between
The real " Jack Tar " and the " Jolly Marine."
For, though he would give an occasional hitch,
Sailor-like to his " slops," there was something the which,
On the whole savoured more of the pipe-clay than pitch.—
Such were now the two men who appeared on the hill,
Harry Waters the tall one, the short " Spanking Bill."
  To be caught in the rain, I repeat it again,
Is extremely unpleasant on Salisbury Plain ;
And when with a good-soaking shower there are blended
Blue lightnings and thunder, the matter's not mended ;

Such was the case   In this wild dreary place,
On the day that I'm speaking of now, when the brace
Of trav'llers alluded to, quickened their pace,
Till a good steady walk became more like a race,
To get quit of the tempest which held them in chase.

   Louder, and louder   Than mortal gunpowder,
The heav'nly artill'ry kept crashing and roaring,
The lightning kept flashing, the rain too kept pouring,
   While they, helter-skelter,   In vain sought for shelter
From, what I have heard term'd, " a regular pelter ; "
   But the deuce of a screen   Could be anywhere seen,
Or an object except that on one of the rises,
   An old way-post show'd   Where the Lavington road
Branch'd off to the left from the one to Devizes ;
And thither the footsteps of Waters seem'd tending,
Though a doubt might exist of the course he was bending,
To a landsman, at least, who, wherever he goes,
Is content, for the most part, to follow his nose ;—
   While Harry kept " backing,
   And filling "—and " tacking,"—
Two nautical terms which, I'll wager a guinea, are
   Meant to imply   What you, Reader, and I
Would call going zig-zag, and not rectilinear.

But here, once for all, let me beg you'll excuse
All mistakes I may make in the words sailors use
   'Mongst themselves, on a cruise,
   Or ashore with the Jews,
Or in making their court to their Polls and their Sues,
Or addressing those shop-selling females afloat—women
Known in our navy as oddly-named boat-women.
The fact is, I can't say I'm vers'd in the school
So ably conducted by Marryat and Poole ;
(See the last-mentioned gentleman's " Admiral's Daughter.")
   The grand *vade mecum*   For all who to sea come,
And get, the first time in their lives, in blue water ;
Of course in the use of sea terms you'll not wonder
If I now and then should fall into some blunder,
For which Captain Chamier, or Mr. T. P. Cooke
Would call me a " Lubber," and " Son of a Sea-cook."

Or making their court to their Polls and their Sues

To return to our muttons—This mode of progression
At length, upon Spanking Bill made some impression.
    —" Hillo, messmate, what cheer ?
    How queer you *do* steer ! "
Cried Bill, whose short legs kept him still in the rear.
" Why, what's in the wind, Bo ?—what is it you fear ? "
For he saw in a moment that something was frightening
His shipmate much more than the thunder and lightning.

—" Fear ? " stammer'd out Waters, " why, HIM !—don't you see
What faces that Drummer-boy's making at me !—
    —How he dodges me so   Wherever I go ?—
What is it he wants with me, Bill,—do you know ? "
—" What Drummer-boy, Harry ? " cries Bill, in surprise,
(With a brief exclamation, that ended in " eyes,")
" What Drummer-boy, Waters ?—the coast is all clear,
We haven't got never no Drummer-boy here ! "

—" Why, there !—don't you see   How he's following me ?
Now this way, now that way, and won't let me be !
    Keep him off, Bill—look here—
    Don't let him come near !
Only see how the blood-drops his features besmear !
What, the dead come to life again !—Bless me !—Oh dear ! "

Bill remarked in reply, " This is all very queer—
What, a Drummer-boy—bloody, too—eh !—well, I never—
I can't see no Drummer-boy here whatsumdever ! "
" Not see him !—why there ;—look !—he's close by the post—
Hark !—hark !—how he drums at me now !—he's a Ghost ! "

" A what ? " return'd Bill,—at that moment a flash
More than commonly awful preceded a crash
Like what's call'd in Kentucky " an Almighty Smash."—
And down Harry Waters went plump on his knees,
While the sound, though prolong'd, died away by degrees ;
In its last sinking echoes, however, were some
Which Bill could not help thinking, resembled a drum !

" Hollo ! Waters !—I says,"   Quoth he in amaze,
" Why, I never see'd *nuffin* in all my born days
    Half so queer   As this here,
    And I'm not very clear
But that one of us two has good reason for fear—
You to jaw about drummers, with nobody near us !—
I must say as how that I thinks it's mysterus."

" Oh, mercy ! " roared Waters, " do keep him off, Bill,
And, Andrew, forgive !—I'll confess all !—I will !
    I'll make a clean breast,   And as for the rest,
You may do with me just what the lawyers think best ;
But haunt me not thus !—let these visitings cease,
And, your vengeance accomplish'd, Boy, leave me in peace ! "
—Harry paused for a moment,—then turning to Bill,
Who stood with his mouth open, steady and still,
Began " spinning " what nauticals term " a tough yarn,"
Viz. : his tale of what Bill call'd " this precious *consarn*."

        *   *   *   *   *

" It was in such an hour as this,
    On such a wild and wintry day,
The forked lightning seemed to hiss,
    As now, athwart our lonely way,
When first these dubious paths I tried—
Yon livid form was by my side !—

" Not livid then—the ruddy glow
    Of life, and youth, and health it bore !
And bloodless was that gory brow,
    And cheerful was the smile it wore,
And mildly then those eyes did shine—
—Those eyes which now are blasting mine ! !

" They beamed with confidence and love
    Upon my face,—and Andrew Brand
Had sooner fear'd yon frighten'd dove
    Than harm from Gervase Matcham's hand !
—I am no Harry Waters—men
Did call me Gervase Matcham then.

" And Matcham, though a humble name,
  Was stainless as the feathery flake
From Heaven, whose virgin whiteness came
  Upon the newly-frozen lake ;
Commander, comrade, all began
To laud the Soldier,—like the Man.

" Nay, muse not, William, I have said
  I was a soldier—staunch and true
As any he above whose head
  Old England's lion banner flew ;
And, duty done,—her claims apart,—
'Twas said I had a kindly heart.

" And years roll'd on,—and with them came
  Promotion—Corporal—Sergeant—all
In turn—I kept mine honest fame—
  Our Colonel's self,—whom men did call
The veriest Martinet—ev'n he,
Though cold to most, was kind to me !—

" One morn—oh ! may that morning stand
  Accursed in the rolls of fate
Till latest time !—there came command
  To carry forth a charge of weight
To a detachment far away,—
—It was their regimental pay !—

" And who so fit for such a task
  As trusty Matcham, true and tried,
Who spurn'd the inebriating flask,
  With honour for his constant guide ?—
On Matcham fell their choice—and HE,—
' Young Drum,'—should bear him company !

" And grateful was that sound to hear,
  For he was full of life and joy,
The mess-room pet—to each one dear,
  Was that kind, gay, light-hearted boy.
—The veriest churl in all our band
Had aye a smile for Andrew Brand.—

—" Nay, glare not as I name thy name !
　　That threat'ning hand, that fearful brow
Relax—avert that glance of flame !
　　Thou seest I do thy bidding now !
Vex'd Spirit, rest !—'twill soon be o'er,—
Thy blood shall cry to Heav'n no more !

" Enough—we journey'd on—the walk
　　Was long,—and dull and dark the day,—
And still young Andrew's cheerful talk
　　And merry laugh beguiled the way ;
Noon came—a sheltering bank was there,—
We paused our frugal meal to share.

" Then 'twas, with cautious hand, I sought
　　To prove my charge secure,—and drew
The packet from my vest, and brought
　　The glittering mischief forth to view,
And Andrew cried,—No ! 'twas not He !—
It was THE TEMPTER spoke to me !

" But it was Andrew's laughing voice
　　That sounded in my tingling ear,
—' Now, Gervase Matcham, at thy choice,'
　　It seem'd to say, ' are gawds and gear,
And all that wealth can buy or bring,
Ease,—wassail,—worship,—every thing !

" ' No tedious drill, no long parade,
　　No bugle call at early dawn ;—
For guard-room bench, or barrack bed,
　　The downy couch, the sheets of lawn,
And I thy Page,—thy steps to tend,
Thy sworn companion,—servant,—friend ! '

—" He ceased—that is, I heard no more,
　　Though other words pass'd idly by,
And Andrew chatter'd as before,
　　And laugh'd—I mark'd him not—not I.
' 'Tis at thy choice ! ' that sound alone
Rang in mine ear—voice else was none.

" I could not eat—the untasted flask
  Mock'd my parch'd lip,—I passed it by.
' What ails thee, man ? ' he seem'd to ask.—
  I *felt*, but could not *meet* his eye,—
' *'Tis at thy choice !* '—it sounded yet,—
A sound I never may forget.

—" ' Haste ! haste ! the day draws on,' I cried,
  ' And, Andrew, thou hast far to go ! '—
' *Hast far to go !* ' the Fiend replied
  Within me,—'twas *not* Andrew—no !
'Twas Andrew's voice no more—'twas HE
Whose then I was, and aye must be !

—" On, on we went ;—the dreary plain
  Was all around us—we were *Here !*
Then came the storm,—the lightning,—rain,—
  No earthly living thing was near,
Save one wild Raven on the wing,
—If that, indeed, were earthly thing !

" I heard its hoarse and screaming voice
  High hovering o'er my frenzied head,
' *'Tis, Gervase Matcham, at thy choice !*
  But he—the Boy ! ' methought it said.
—Nay, Andrew, check that vengeful frown,—
I lov'd thee when I struck thee down !

     *   *   *   *   *

" 'Twas done !—the deed that damns me—done
  I know not how—I never knew ;—
And *Here* I stood—but not alone,—
  The prostrate Boy my madness slew,
Was by my side—limb, feature, name,
'Twas HE ! !—another—yet the same !

     *   *   *   *   *

" Away ! away ! in frantic haste
  Throughout that live-long night I flew—
Away ! away !—across the waste,—
  I know not how—I never knew,—
My mind was one wild blank—and I
Had but one thought,—one hope—to fly !

" And still the lightning ploughed the ground,
　The thunder roared—and there would come
Amidst its loudest bursts a sound,
　Familiar once—it was—A DRUM !—
Then came the morn,—and light,—and then
Streets,—houses,—spires,—the hum of men.

" And Ocean roll'd before me—fain
　Would I have whelm'd me in its tide,
At once beneath the billowy main
　My shame, my guilt, my crime to hide ;
But HE was there !—HE cross'd my track,—
I dared not pass—HE waved me back !

" And then rude hands detained me—sure
　Justice had grasp'd her victim—no !
Though powerless, hopeless, bound, secure,
　A captive thrall, it was not so ;
They cry, ' The Frenchman's on the wave ! '
The press was hot—and I a slave.

" They dragg'd me o'er the vessel's side ;
　The world of waters roll'd below ;
The gallant ship, in all her pride
　Of dreadful beauty, sought her foe ;
—Thou saw'st me, William, in the strife—
　Alack ! I bore a charmed life ;

" In vain the bullets round me fly,
　In vain mine eager breast I bare ;
Death shuns the wretch who longs to die,
　And every sword falls edgeless there !
Still HE is near !—and seems to cry,
' Not *here*, nor *thus*, may Matcham die ! '—

" Thou saw'st me, on that fearful day,
　When, fruitless all attempts to save,
Our pinnace foundering in the bay,
　The boat's-crew met a watery grave,—
All, all—save ONE—the ravenous sea
　That swallow'd all—rejected ME !

" And now, when fifteen suns have each
    Fulfilled in turn its circling year,
Thrown back again on England's beach,
    Our bark paid off—HE drives me *Here !*
I could not die in flood or fight—
    HE drives me HERE ! ! "—
                " And sarve you right !

" What ! bilk your Commander !—desart—and then rob !
And go scuttling a poor little Drummer's-boy's nob !
Why, my precious eyes ! what a bloodthirsty swab !
    There's old Davy Jones,   Who cracks Sailor's bones
For his jaw-work would never, I'm sure, s'elp me Bob,
Have come for to go for to do sich a job !
Hark ye, Waters,—or Matcham—whichever's your purser-name,
—T'other, your own, is, I'm sartain, the worser name,—
Twelve years have we lived on like brother and brother !—
Now—your course lays one way, and mine lays another ! "

      " No, William, it may not be so ;
        Blood calls for blood !—'tis Heaven's decree !
      And thou with me this night must go,
        And give me to the gallows-tree !
      Ha !—see—HE smiles—HE points the way !
      On, William on ! no more delay ! "

Now Bill,—so the story, as told to me, goes,
And who, as his last speech sufficiently shows,
Was a " regular trump,"—did not like to " turn Nose " ;
But then came a thunder-clap louder than any
Of those that preceded, though they were so many ;
And hark !—as its rumblings subside in a hum
What sound mingles too ?—" By the hokey—A DRUM ! ! "

      *   *   *   *   *

I remember I once heard my Grandfather say,
That some sixty years since he was going that way,
    When they show'd him the spot
    Where the gibbet—was not—
On which Matcham's corse had been hung up to rot ;
It had fall'n down—but how long before, he'd forgot ;

And they told him, I think, at the Bear in Devizes,
The town where the Sessions are held—or the 'Sizes,
   That Matcham confess'd,   And made a clean breast
To the May'r ; but that, after he'd had a night's rest,
And the storm had subsided, he " pooh-pooh'd " his friend,
Swearing all was a lie from beginning to end ;
   Said " he'd only been drunk—
   That his spirits had sunk
At the thunder—the storm put him into a funk,—
That, in fact, he had nothing at all on his conscience,
And found out, in short, he'd been talking great nonsense."—

   But now one Mr. Jones   Comes forth and depones
That, fifteen years since, he had heard certain groans
On his way to Stone Henge (to examine the stones
Described in a work of the late Sir John Soane's,)
   That he'd followed the moans,
   And led by their tones,
Found a Raven a-picking a Drummer-boy's bones !—
   —Then the Colonel wrote word
   From the King's Forty-third,
That the story was certainly true which they heard,
For, that one of their drummers, and one Sergeant Matcham,
Had " brushed with the dibs," and they never could catch 'em.

So Justice was sure, though a long time she'd lagg'd,
And the Sergeant, in spite of his " Gammon," got " scragg'd ; "
  And people averr'd   That an ugly black bird,
The Raven, 'twas hinted, of whom we have heard,
Though the story, I own, appears rather absurd,
  Was seen (Gervase Matcham not being interr'd),
To roost all that night on the murderer's gibbet ;
An odd thing, if so, and it may be a fib—it,
However, 's a thing Nature's laws don't prohibit.
—Next morning, they add, that " black gentleman " flies out,
Having picked Matcham's nose off, and gobbled his eyes out !

Moral.

Avis au Voyageur.

Imprimis.

  If you contemplate walking o'er Salisbury Plain,
  Consult Mr. Murphy, or Moore, and refrain
  From selecting a day when it's likely to rain !

2°.

   When trav'lling, don't " flash "
   Your notes or your cash
  Before other people—it's foolish and rash !

3°.

  At dinner be cautious, and note well your party ;—
  There's little to dread where the appetite's hearty,—
  But mind and look well to your purse and your throttle
  When you see a man shirking, and passing his bottle !

4°.

   If you chance to be needy,
   Your coat and hat seedy,
  In war-time especially, never go out
  When you've reason to think there's a press-gang about !

5°.

  Don't chatter, nor tell people all that you think,
  Nor blab secrets,—especially when you're in drink,—
  But keep your own counsel in all that you do !
  —Or a Counsel may, some day or other, keep you.

6°.

Discard superstition !—and don't take a post,
If you happen to see one at night, for a Ghost !
—Last of all, if by choice, or convenience, you're led,
To cut a man's throat, or demolish his head,
Don't do't in a thunderstorm—wait for the summer !
And mind, above all things, the MAN's NOT A DRUMMER ! !

Among a bundle of letters I find one from Sucklethumbkin, dated from London, and containing his version of perhaps the greatest theatrical Civil War since the celebrated " O. P.
row." As the circumstances are now become matter of history, and poor Doldrum himself
has been, alas ! for some time the denizen of a far different " House," I have ventured to
preserve it. Perhaps it may be unnecessary to add, that my Honourable friend has of late
taken to Poetry, and goes without his cravat.

A Row in an Omnibus (Box)

A Legend of the Haymarket

Omnibus hoc vitium cantoribus.—Hor.

DOL-DRUM the Manager sits in his chair,
With a gloomy brow and dissatisfied air,
And he says as he slaps his hands on his knee,
" I'll have nothing to do with Fiddle-de-dee ! "

—" But Fiddle-de-dee sings clear and loud,
And his trills and his quavers astonish the crowd ;
    Such a singer as he   You'll nowhere see ;
They'll all be screaming for Fiddle-de-dee ! "

—" Though Fiddle-de-dee sings loud and clear,
And his tones are sweet, yet his terms are dear !
    The ' glove won't fit ! '   The deuce a bit.
I shall give an engagement to Fal-de-ral-tit ! "

The Prompter bow'd, and he went to his stall,
And the green-baize rose at the Prompter's call,
And Fal-de-ral-tit sang fol-de-rol-lol ;
   But, scarce had he done   When a " row " begun,
Such a noise was never heard under the sun.
   " Fiddle-de-dee !—   —Where is he ?
He's the *Artiste* whom we all want to see !
   Dol-drum !—Dol-drum !   —Bid the manager come !
It's a scandalous thing to exact such a sum
For boxes and gallery, stalls and pit,
And then fob us off with a Fal-de-ral-tit !—
   Deuce a bit ! We'll never submit !
Vive Fiddle-de-dee ! *à bas* Fal-de-ral-tit ! "

Dol-drum the Manager rose from his chair,
With a gloomy brow and dissatisfied air ;
   But he smooth'd his brow,   As he well knew how,
And he walk'd on, and made a most elegant bow,
And he paused, and he smiled, and advanced to the lights,
In his opera-hat, and his opera-tights ;
" Ladies and Gentlemen," then said he,
" Pray what may you please to want with me ? "

   " Fiddle-de-dee !—   Fiddle-de-dee ! "
Folks of all sorts and of every degree,
Snob, and Snip, and haughty Grandee,
Duchesses, Countesses, fresh from their tea,
And Shopmen, who'd only come there for a spree,
Halloo'd, and hooted, and roar'd with glee
   " Fiddle-de-dee !—   —None but He !—
Subscribe to his terms, whatever they be !—
Agree, agree, or you'll very soon see
In a brace of shakes we'll get up an O.P. ! "

Dol-drum the Manager, full of care,
With a gloomy brow and dissatisfied air,
   Looks distrest,   And he bows his best,
And he puts his right hand on the side of his breast,
   And he says,—says he,   " We *can't* agree ;
His terms are a vast deal too high for me.—

There's the rent, and the rates, and the sesses, and taxes—
I can't afford Fiddle-de-dee what he *axes*.
    If you'll only permit   Fal-de-ral-tit——"

The " Generous Public " cried, " Deuce a bit !
    Dol-drum !—Dol-drum !—   We'll none of us come.
It's ' No Go ! '—it's ' Gammon ! '—it's ' all a Hum : '—
    You're a miserly Jew !—   ' Cock-a-doodle-do ! '
He *don't* ask too much, as you know—so you do—
It's a shame—it's a sin—it's really too bad—
You ought to be 'shamed of yourself—so you had ! "

Dol-drum the Manager never before
In his life-time had heard such a wild uproar.
Dol-drum the Manager turn'd to flee ;
    But he says—says he,   " *Mort de ma vie !*
I shall *nevare* engage vid dat Fiddle-de-dee ! "
Then all the gentlefolks flew in a rage,
And they jump'd from the Omnibus on to the Stage,
Lords, Squires, and Knights, they came down to the lights,
In their opera-hats, and their opera-tights.
    Ma'am'selle Cherrytoes   Shook to her very toes,
She couldn't hop on, so hopped off on her merry toes.
And the " evening concluded " with " Three times three ! "
" Hip !—hip !—hurrah ! for Fiddle-de-dee ! "

Dol-drum the Manager, full of care,
With a troubled brow and dissatisfied air,
    Saddest of men,   Sat down, and then
Took from his table a Perryan pen,
And he wrote to the " News,"
How MacFuze, and Tregooze,
Lord Tomnoddy, Sir Carnaby Jenks of the Blues,
And the whole of their tail, and the separate crews
Of the Tags and the Rags, and the No-one-knows-whos,
Had combined Monsieur Fal-de-ral-tit to abuse,
    And make Dol-drum agree   With Fiddle-de-dee,
Who was not a bit better singer than he.
—Dol-drum declared " he never could see,
For the life of him, yet, why Fiddle-de-dee,

Who, in B flat, or C,—Or whatever the key,
Could never at any time get below G,
Should expect a fee the same in degree
As the great Burlybumbo who sings double D."
Then slily he added a little N.B.
" If they'd have him in Paris he'd not come to me ! "

The Manager rings,   And the Prompter springs
To his side in a jiffy, and with him he brings
A set of those odd-looking envelope things,
Where Britannia (who seems to be crucified), flings
To her right and her left funny people with wings,
Amongst Elephants, Quakers, and Catabaw Kings ;
   And a taper and wax,
   And small Queen's heads in packs,
Which, when notes are too big, you're to stick on their backs.
Dol-drum the Manager sealed with care
The letter and copies he'd written so fair,
And sat himself down with a satisfied air ;
   Without delay   He sent them away,
In time to appear in " our columns " next day !

Dol-drum the Manager, full of care,
Walk'd on to the stage with an anxious air,
And peep'd through the curtain to see who were there.
   There was MacFuze,   And Lieutenant Tregooze,
And there was Sir Carnaby Jenks of the Blues,
And the Tags, and the Rags, and the No-one-knows-whos ;
And the green-baize rose at the Prompter's call,
And they all began to hoot, bellow, and bawl,
And cry " Cock-a-doodle," and scream, and squall
   " Dol-drum !—Dol-drum !   Bid the Manager come ! "
   You'd have thought from the tones
   Of their hisses and groans,
They were bent upon breaking his (Opera) bones.
And Dol-drum comes, and he says—says he,
" Pray what may you please to want with me ? "—
   " Fiddle-de-dee !—   Fiddle-de-dee !—
We'll have nobody give us *sol fa* but He !
For he's the *Artiste* whom we all want to see."

—Manager Dol-drum says—says he—
(And he looks like an Owl in " a hollow beech-tree,")
  " Well, since I see The thing must be,
I'll sign an agreement with Fiddle-de-dee ! "
  Then MacFuze, and Tregooze, And Jenks of the Blues,
And the Tags, and the Rags, and the No-one-knows-whos,
Extremely delighted to hear such good news,
Desist from their shrill " Cock-a-doodle-doos."
  " *Vive* Fiddle-de-dee ! Dol-drum and He !
They are jolly good fellows as ever need be !
And so's Burlybumbo, who sings double D !
And whenever they sing, why, we'll all come and see ! "

  So, after all This terrible squall,
  Fiddle-de-dee 's at the top of the tree,
And Dol-drum and Fal-de-ral-tit sing small !
Now Fiddle-de-dee sings loud and clear
At I can't tell you how many thousands a year,
And Fal-de-ral-tit is considered " Small Beer ; "
  And Ma'am'selle Cherrytoes Sports her merry toes.
Dancing away to the fiddles and flutes,
In what the folks call a " Lithuanian " in boots.

So here's an end to my one, two, and three ;
And bless the Queen—and long live She !
And grant that there never again may be
Such a halliballoo as we've happened to see
About nothing on earth but " Fiddle-de-dee ! "

We come now to the rummaging of Father John's stores. The extracts which I shall submit from them are of the same character as those formerly derived from the same source, and may be considered as theologico-historical, or Tracts for his times.

With respect to the first legend on this list, I have to remark that, though the good Father is silent on the subject, there is every reason to believe that the " little curly-wigged " gentleman, who plays, though passively, so prominent a part in it, had Ingoldsby blood in his veins. This conjecture is supported by the fact of the arms of Scroope, impaling Ingoldsby, being found, as in the Bray case, in one of the windows, and by a very old marriage-settlement, nearly, or quite, illegible, a facsimile of the seal affixed to which is appended to this true history.

The Lay of St. Cuthbert; or, the Devil's Dinner-Party

A Legend of the North Countree

Nobilis quidam, cui nomen *Monsr. Lescrop, Chivaler*, cum invitasset convivas, et, hora convivii jam instante et apparatu facto, spe frustratus esset, excusantibus se convivis cur non compararent, prorupit iratus in hæc verba : " *Veniant igitur omnes dæmones, si nullus hominum mecum esse potest !* "

     *   *   *   *   *   *   *

Quod cum fieret, et Dominus, et famuli, et ancillæ, a domo properantes, forte obliti, infantem in cunis jacentem secum non auferunt. Dæmones incipiunt comessari et vociferari, prospicereque per fenestras formis ursorum, luporum, felium, et monstrare pocula vino repleta. *Ah*, inquit pater, *ubi infans meus?* Vix cum hæc dixisset, unus ex Dæmonibus ulnis suis infantem ad fenestram gestat, &c.—*Chronicon de Bolton.*

It's in Bolton Hall, and the Clock strikes One,
And the roast meat's brown, and the boil'd meat's done,
And the barbecu'd sucking-pig's crisp'd to a turn,
And the pancakes are fried, and beginning to burn ;
   The fat stubble-goose   Swims in gravy and juice
With the mustard and apple-sauce ready for use ;
Fish, flesh, and fowl, and all of the best,
Want nothing but eating—they're all ready drest.
But where is the Host, and where is the Guest ?

Pantler and serving-man, henchman and page,
Stand sniffing the duck-stuffing (onion and sage),
   And the scullions and cooks,   With fidgety looks,
Are grumbling, and mutt'ring, and scowling as black
As cooks always do when the dinner's put back ;
For though the board's deckt, and the napery, fair
As the unsunn'd snow-flake, is spread out with care,
And the Daïs is furnish'd with stool and with chair,
And plate of *orfèvrerie* costly and rare,
Apostle-spoons, salt-cellar, all are there,
   And Mess John in his place,   With his rubicund face,
And his hands ready folded, prepared to say Grace,
Yet where is the Host ?—and his convives—where ?

The Scroope sits lonely in Bolton Hall,
And he watches the dial that hangs by the wall,
He watches the large hand, he watches the small,
    And he fidgets, and looks   As cross as the cooks,
And he utters—a word which we'll soften to " Zooks ! "
As he cries, " What on earth has become of them all ?—
    What can delay   De Vaux and De Saye ?
What makes Sir Gilbert de Umfraville stay ?
What's gone with Poyntz, and Sir Reginald Braye ?
Why are Ralph Ufford and Marny away ?
And De Nokes, and De Stiles, and Lord Marmaduke Grey ?
    And De Roe ?   And De Doe ?—
Poynings, and Vavasour—where be they ?
Fitz-Walter, Fitz-Osbert, Fitz-Hugh, and Fitz-John,
And the Mandevilles, *père et filz* (father and son) ?
Their cards said ' Dinner precisely at One ! '
    There's nothing I hate, in   The world, like waiting !
It's a monstrous great bore, when a Gentleman feels
A good appetite, thus to be kept from his meals ! "

It's in Bolton Hall, and the clock strikes Two !
And the scullions and cooks are themselves in " a stew,"
And the kitchen-maids stand, and don't know what to do,
For the rich plum-puddings are bursting their bags,
And the mutton and turnips are boiling to rags,
    And the fish is all spoil'd   And the butter's all oil'd,
And the soup's got cold in the silver tureen,
And there's nothing, in short, that is fit to be seen !
While Sir Guy Le Scroope continues to fume,
And to fret by himself in the tapestried room,
    And still fidgets, and looks   More cross than the cooks,
And repeats that bad word, which we've softened to " Zooks ! "

Two o'clock's come, and Two o'clock's gone,
And the large and the small hands move steadily on,
    Still nobody's there,   No De Roos, or De Clare,
To taste of the Scroope's most delicate fare,
Or to quaff off a health unto Bolton's Heir,
That nice little boy who sits there in his chair,
Some four years old, and a few months to spare,
With his laughing blue eyes, and his long curly hair,
Now sucking his thumb, and now munching his pear.

Again, Sir Guy the silence broke,
" It's hard upon Three !—it's just on the stroke !
Come, serve up the dinner !—A joke is a joke ! "—
Little he deems that Stephen de Hoaques,*
Who " his fun," as the Yankees say, everywhere " pokes,"
And is always a great deal too fond of his jokes,
Has written a circular note to De Nokes,
And De Stiles, and De Roe, and the rest of the folks,
    One and all,   Great and small,
Who were asked to the Hall,
To dine there, and sup, and wind up with a ball,
And had told all the party a great bouncing lie he
Cook'd up, that " the *fête* was postponed *sine die,*
The dear little curly-wig'd heir of Le Scroope
Being taken alarmingly ill with the croup ! "

    When the clock struck Three,
    And the Page on his knee
Said, " An't please you, Sir Guy Le Scroope, *On a servi !* "
And the Knight found the banquet-hall empty and clear,
    With nobody near   To partake of his cheer,
He stamp'd, and he storm'd—then his language !—Oh dear !
'Twas awful to see, and 'twas awful to hear !
And he cried to the button-deck'd Page at his knee,
Who had told him so civilly " *On a servi,*"
" Ten thousand fiends seize them, wherever they be !
—The Devil take *them !* and the Devil take *thee !*
And the DEVIL MAY EAT UP THE DINNER FOR ME ! ! "

    In a terrible fume   He bounced out of the room,
He bounced out of the house—and page, footman, and groom
Bounced after their master ; for scarce had they heard
Of this left-handed Grace the last finishing word,
Ere the horn, at the gate of the Barbican tower,
Was blown with a loud twenty-trumpeter power,

* For a full account of this facetious " *Chivaler,*" see the late (oh ! that we should have
to say " late " !) Theodore Hook's " History of the illustrious Commoners of Great Britain,"
as quoted in the Memoirs of John Bragg, Esq., page 344 of the 75th volume of the Standard
Novels. In the third volume of Sir Harris Nicholas's elaborate account of the Scrope and
Grosvenor controversy, commonly called the " Scrope Roll," a Stephen de Hoques, Écuyer,
is described as giving his testimony on the Grosvenor side.—*Vide* page 247.

And in rush'd a troop
Of strange guests !—such a group
As had ne'er before darkened the doors of the Scroope !

This looks like De Saye—yet—it is not De Saye—
And this is—no, 'tis not—Sir Reginald Braye—
This has somewhat the favour of Marmaduke Grey—
But stay !—*Where on earth did he get those long nails ?*
Why, they're *claws !*—then, Good Gracious !—they've all of
    them *tails !*
That can't be De Vaux—why, his nose is a bill,
Or, I would say, a beak !—and he can't keep it still !—
Is that Poynings ?—Oh Gemini !—look at his feet ! !
Why, they're absolute *hoofs !*—is it gout or his corns
That have crumpled them up so ?—by Jingo, he's *horns !*
Run ! run !—There's Fitz-Walter, Fitz-Hugh, and Fitz-John,
And the Mandevilles, *père et filz* (father and son),
And Fitz-Osbert, and Ufford—*they've all got them on !*
    Then their great saucer eyes—   It's the Father of lies
And his Imps—run ! run ! run !—they're all fiends in disguise,
Who've partly assumed, with more sombre complexions,
The forms of Sir Guy Le Scroope's friends and connexions,
And He—at the top there—that grim-looking elf—
Run ! run !—that's the " muckle-horned Clootie " himself !

    And now what a din   Without and within !
For the court-yard is full of them.—How they begin
To mop, and to mowe, and make faces, and grin !
    Cock their tails up together,
    Like cows in hot weather,
And butt at each other, all eating and drinking,
The viands and wine disappearing like winking.
    And then such a lot   As together had got !
Master Cabbage, the steward, who'd made a machine
To calculate with, and count noses,—I ween
The cleverest thing of the kind ever seen,—
    Declared, when he'd made,
    By the said machine's aid,
Up, what's now called, the " tottle " of those he survey'd,
There were just—how he proved it I cannot divine,—
Nine thousand, nine hundred, and ninety, and nine,

The horn . . . Was blown with a loud twenty-trumpeter power

Exclusive of Him,   Who, giant in limb,
And black as the crow they denominate *Jim*,
With a tail like a bull, and a head like a bear,
Stands forth at the window,—and what holds he there,
　Which he hugs with such care,
　And pokes out in the air,
And grasps as its limbs from each other he'd tear ?
　Oh ! grief and despair ! I vow and declare
It's Le Scroope's poor, dear, sweet, little, curly-wig'd Heir !
Whom the nurse had forgot, and left there in his chair,
Alternately sucking his thumb and his pear !

What words can express   The dismay and distress
Sir Guy, when he found what a terrible mess
His cursing and banning had now got him into ?
That words, which to use are a shame and a sin too,
Had thus on their speaker recoiled, and his malison
Placed in the hands of the Devil's own " pal " his son !—
　He sobb'd, and he sigh'd,
　And he scream'd and he cried,
And behaved like a man that is mad, or in liquor,—he
Tore his peaked beard, and he dashed off his " Vicary," *
　Stamped on the jasey   As though he were crazy,
And staggering about just as if he were " hazy,"
Exclaimed, " Fifty pounds ! " (a large sum in those times,)
" To the person, whoever he may be, that climbs
To that window above there, *en ogive*, and painted,
And brings down my curly-wi'——" here Sir Guy fainted !

---

* A peruke so named from its inventor. Robert de Ros and Eudo Fitz-Vicari were celebrated *perruquiers*, who flourished in the eleventh century. The latter is noticed in the Battle-
Abbey roll, and is said to have curled William the Conqueror's hair when dressing for the
battle of Hastings. Dugdale makes no mention of him, but Camden says that Humfrey, one
of his descendants, was summoned to Parliament, 26 Jan. 25 Edw. I. (1297). It is doubtful,
however, whether that writ can be deemed a regular writ of Summons to Parliament, for
reasons amply detailed in the " Synopsis of the British Peerage."—(Art. Fitz-John.) A writ
was subsequently addressed to him as " *Humfry Fitz-Vicari, Chivr.*" 8 Jan. 6 Edw. II. (1313),
and his descendants appear to have been regularly summoned as late as 5 and 6 of Philip and
Mary, 1557-8. Soon after which Peter Fitz-Vicari dying, s. p. m. this Barony went into abeyance between his two daughters, Joan, married to Henry de Truefit, of Fullbottom, and Alice,
wife of Roger Wigram, of Caxton Hall, in Wigton, co. Cumb. Esq., among whose representatives
it is presumed to be still in abeyance.

With many a moan   And many a groan,
What with tweaks of the nose, and some *eau de Cologne*,
He revived,—Reason once more remounted her throne,
Or rather the instinct of Nature,—'twere treason
To Her, in the Scroope's case, perhaps, to say Reason,—
But what saw he then ?—Oh ! my goodness ! a sight
Enough to have banished his reason outright !—
In that broad banquet hall   The fiends, one and all,
Regardless of shriek, and of squeak, and of squall,
From one to another were tossing that small,
Pretty, curly-wig'd boy, as if playing at ball :
Yet none of his friends or his vassals might dare
To fly to the rescue, or rush up the stair,
And bring down in safety his curly-wig'd Heir ! .

Well a day ! Well a day ! All he can say
Is but just so much trouble and time thrown away ;
Not a man can be tempted to join the *mêlée*,
E'en those words cabalistic, " I promise to pay
Fifty pounds on demand," have, for once, lost their sway,
    And there the Knight stands,   Wringing his hands
In his agony—when, on a sudden, one ray
Of hope darts through his midriff !—His Saint !—Oh, it's funny,
    And almost absurd,   That it never occurr'd !—
" Ay ! the Scroope's Patron Saint !—he's the man for my money !
Saint—who is it ?—really I'm sadly to blame,—
On my word I'm afraid,—I confess it with shame,—
That I've almost forgot the good Gentleman's name,—
Cut—let me see—Cutbeard ?—no !—Cuthbert !—egad
St. Cuthbert of Bolton !—I'm right—he's the lad !
Oh ! holy St. Cuthbert, if forbears of mine—
Of myself I say little,—have knelt at your shrine,
And have lash'd their bare backs, and—no matter—with twine,
    Oh ! list to the vow   Which I make to you now,
Only snatch my poor little boy out of the row
Which that Imp's kicking up with his fiendish bow-wow
And his head like a bear, and his tail like a cow !
Bring him back here in safety !—perform but this task,
And I'll give !—Oh !—I'll give you whatever you ask !—
    There is not a shrine   In the County shall shine
With a brilliancy half so resplendent as thine,
Or have so many candles, or look half so fine !—

Haste, holy St. Cuthbert, then—hasten in pity!"—
—Conceive his surprise   When a strange voice replies,
"It's a bargain!—but, mind, sir, THE BEST SPERMACETI!"—
Say, whose that voice?—whose that form by his side,
That old, old grey man, with his beard long and wide,
   In his coarse Palmer's weeds,
   And his cockle and beads?—
And, how did he come?—did he walk?—did he ride?
Oh! none could determine,—oh! none could decide,—
The fact is, I don't believe any one tried,
For while ev'ry one stared, with a dignified stride,
   And without a word more,   He march'd on before,
Up a flight of stone steps, and so through the front door,
To the banqueting-hall, that was on the first floor,
While the fiendish assembly were making a rare
Little shuttlecock there of the curly-wig'd Heir.—
—I wish, gentle Reader, that you could have seen
The pause that ensued when he stepp'd in between,
With his resolute air, and his dignified mien,
And said, in a tone most decided, though mild,
"Come!—I'll trouble you just to hand over that child!"

The Demoniac crowd   In an instant seem'd cowed;
Not one of the crew volunteer'd a reply,
All shrunk from the glance of that keen-flashing eye,
Save one horried Humgruffin, who seem'd by his talk,
And the airs he assumed, to be Cock of the walk,
He quailed not before it, but saucily met it,
And as saucily said, "Don't you wish you may get it?"

My goodness!—the look that the old Palmer gave!
And his frown!—'twas quite dreadful to witness—"Why, slave!
   You rascal!" quoth he, "This language to ME!!
—At once, Mr. Nicholas! down on your knee,
And hand me that curly-wig'd boy!—I command it—
Come!—none of your nonsense!—you know I won't stand it."

Old Nicholas trembled,—he shook in his shoes,
And seem'd half inclined, but afraid, to refuse.
   "Well, Cuthbert," said he,   "If so it must be,

—For you've had your own way from the first time I knew ye ;—
Take your curly-wig'd brat, and much good may he do ye !
But I'll have in exchange—" —here his eye flash'd with rage—
" That chap with the buttons—he *gave me* the Page ! "

" Come, come," the Saint answer'd, " you very well know
The young man's no more his than your own to bestow—
Touch one button of his if you dare, Nick—no ! no !
Cut your stick, sir—come, mizzle !—be off with you !—go ! "—
    The Devil grew hot—" If I do I'll be shot !
An you come to that, Cuthbert, I'll tell you what's what ;
He has *asked* us to *dine here*, and go we will not !
    Why, you Skinflint,—at least
    You may leave us the feast !
Here we've come all that way from our brimstone abode,
Ten million good leagues, Sir, as ever you strode,
And the deuce of a luncheon we've had on the road—
—' Go ! '—' Mizzle ! ' indeed—Mr. Saint, who are you,
I should like to know ?—' Go ! '—I'll be hang'd if I do !
He invited us all—we've a right here—it's known
That a Baron may do what he likes with his own—
Here, Asmodeus—a slice of that beef !—now the mustard !—
What have *you* got ?—oh, apple-pie—try it with custard ! "

    The Saint made a pause As uncertain, because
He knew Nick is pretty well " up " in the laws,
And they *might* be on *his* side—and then, he'd such claws !
On the whole, it was better, he thought, to retire
With the curly-wig'd boy he'd pick'd out of the fire,
And give up the victuals—to retrace his path,
And to compromise—(spite of the Member for Bath).
    So to Old Nick's appeal, As he turn'd on his heel,
He replied, " Well, I'll leave you the mutton and veal,
And the soup *à la Reine*, and the sauce *Bechamel*.
As The Scroope *did* invite you to dinner, I feel
I can't well turn you out—'twould be hardly genteel—
But be moderate, pray,—and remember thus much,
Since you're treated as Gentlemen, show yourselves such,
    And don't make it late, But mind and go straight
Home to bed when you've finish'd—and don't steal the plate !
Nor wrench off the knocker—or bell from the gate.

Walk away, like respectable Devils, in peace,
And don't ' lark ' with the watch, or annoy the police ! "

    Having thus said his say,   That Palmer grey
Took up little Le Scroope, and walk'd coolly away,
While the Demons all set up a " Hip ! hip ! hurray ! "
Then fell, tooth and claw, on the victuals, as they
Had been guests at Guildhall upon Lord Mayor's day,
All scrambling and scuffling for what was before 'em, .
No care for precedence or common decorum.
    Few ate more hearty   Than Madame Astarte,
And Hecate,—considered the Belles of the party,
Between them was seated Leviathan, eager
To " do the polite," and take wine with Belphegor ;
Here was *Morbleu* (a French devil), supping soup-meagre,
And there, munching leeks, Davy Jones of Tredegar
(A Welsh one), who'd left the domains of Ap Morgan,
To " follow the sea,"—and next him Demorgorgon,—
Then Pan with his pipes, and Fauns grinding the organ
To Mammon and Belial, and half a score dancers,
Who'd joined with Medusa to get up " the Lancers ; "
—Here's Lucifer lying blind drunk with Scotch ale,
While Beelzebub's tying huge knots in his tail.
There's Setebos, storming because Mephistopheles
    Gave him the lie,   Said he'd " blacken his eye,"
And dash'd in his face a whole cup of hot coffee-lees ;—
    Ramping, and roaring,   Hiccoughing, snoring,
Never was seen such a riot before in
A gentleman's house, or such profligate revelling
At any *soirée*—where they don't let the Devil in.

    Hark !—as sure as fate   The clock's striking Eight !
(An hour which our ancestors called " getting late,")
When Nick, who by this time was rather elate,
Rose up and addressed them.

                   " 'Tis full time," he said,
" For all elderly Devils to be in their bed ;
For my own part I mean to be jogging, because
I don't find myself now quite so young as I was ;
But, Gentlemen, ere I depart from my post,
I must call on you all for one bumper—the toast
Which I have to propose is,—OUR EXCELLENT HOST !

—Many thanks for his kind hospitality—may
   We also be able   To see at *our* table
Himself, and enjoy, in a family way,
His good company *down stairs* at no distant day !
   You'd, I'm sure, think me rude
   If I did not include
In the toast my young friend there, the curly-wig'd Heir.
He's in very good hands, for you're all well aware
That St. Cuthbert has taken him under his care ;
   Though I must not say ' bless,'—
   —Why, you'll easily guess,—
May our Curly-wig'd Friend's shadow never be less ! "
Nick took off his heel-taps—bow'd—smiled—with an air
Most graciously grim,—and vacated the chair,—
   Of course the *élite*   Rose at once on their feet,
And followed their leader, and beat a retreat ;
When a sky-larking imp took the President's seat,
And, requesting that each would replenish his cup,
Said, " Where we have dined, my boys, there let us sup ! "—
—It was three in the morning before they broke up ! ! !

      *   *   *   *   *

   I scarcely need say   Sir Guy didn't delay
To fulfil his vow made to St. Cuthbert, or pay
For the candles he'd promised, or make light as day
The shrine he assured him he'd render so gay.
In fact, when the votaries came there to pray,
All said there was nought to compare with it—nay,
   For fear that the Abbey   Might think he was shabby,
Four Brethren thenceforward, two cleric, two lay,
He ordained should take charge of a new-founded chantry,
With six marks apiece, and some claims on the pantry ;
   In short, the whole County
   Declared, through his bounty,
The Abbey of Bolton exhibited fresh scenes
From any displayed since Sir William de Meschines,*
And Cecily Roumeli came to this nation
With William the Norman, and laid its foundation.

   For the rest, it is said,   And I know I have read
In some Chronicle—whose, has gone out of my head—

* *Vide* Dugdale's Monasticon, Art. *Prioratus de Bolton, in agro Eboracensi.*

That, what with these candles, and other expenses,
Which no man would go to if quite in his senses,
　　He reduced, and brought low　His property so,
That, at last, he'd not much of it left to bestow ;
And that, many years after that terrible feast,
Sir Guy in the Abbey was living a Priest ;
And there, in one thousand and—something,—deceased.
　　(It's supposed by this trick
　　He bamboozled Old Nick,
And slipped through his fingers remarkably " slick "),
While, as to young Curly-wig,—dear little Soul,
Would you know more of him, you must look at " The Roll,"
　　Which records the dispute,　And the subsequent suit,
Commenced in " Thirteen sev'nty-five,"—which took root
In Le Grosvenor's assuming the arms Le Scroope swore
That none but *his* ancestors, ever before,
In foray, joust, battle, or tournament wore,
To wit, " *On a Prussian-blue field, a Bend Or ;* "—
While the Grosvenor averred that *his* ancestors bore
The same, and Scroope lied like a—somebody tore
Off the simile,—so I can tell you no more,
Till some A double S shall the fragment restore.*

MORAL.

This Legend sound maxims exemplifies—*e.g.*—

1*mo*.　　Should anything tease you,
　　Annoy, or displease you,
Remember what Lilly says, " *Animum rege !* " †
And as for that shocking bad habit of swearing,—
In all good society voted past bearing,—
Eschew it !—and leave it to dust-men and mobs,
Nor commit yourself much beyond " Zooks ! " or " Odsbobs ! "

2*do*.　　When asked out to dine by a Person of Quality,
Mind, and observe the most strict punctuality !—

* It is with the greatest satisfaction that I learn from Mr. Simpkinson this consummation, so devoutly to be wished, is about to be realized, and that the remainder of this most interesting document, containing the whole of the defendant's evidence, will appear in the course of the ensuing summer, under the same auspices as the former portion.　We shall look with eagerness for the identification of " Curly-wig."

† Animum rege ! qui nisi paret, imperat.—LILLY's *Grammar*.

For should you come late,
  And make dinner wait,
And the victuals get cold, you'll incur, sure as fate,
The Master's displeasure, the Mistress's hate—
And—though both may, perhaps, be too well bred to swear,
They heartily *wish* you—I need not say *Where.*

3*tio.*   Look well to your Maid-servants !—say you expect them
To see to the children, and not to neglect them !—
And if you're a widower, just throw a cursory
Glance in, at times, when you go near the Nursery !—
—Perhaps it's as well to keep children from plums
And from pears in the season,—and sucking their thumbs !

4*to.*   To sum up the whole with a " Saw " of much use,
Be *just*, and be *generous*—don't be *profuse !*—
Pay the debts that you owe,—keep your word to your friends,
But—DON'T SET YOUR CANDLES ALIGHT AT BOTH ENDS ! !—
For of this be assured, if you " go it " too fast,
  You'll be " dish'd " like Sir Guy,
  And like him, perhaps, die
A poor, old, half-starved Country Parson at last.

From a seal attached to an ancient deed penes Thomas Ingoldsby, Esq. preserved in the archives at Tappington Everard.

For the Legend that follows Father John has, it will be seen, the grave authority of a Romish Prelate. The good Father, who, as I have before had occasion to remark, received his education at Douai, spent several years, in the earlier part of his life, upon the Continent. I have no doubt but that during this period he visited Blois; and there, in all probability, picked up, in the very scene of its locality, the history which he has thus recorded.

The Lay of St. Aloys

A Legend of Blois

S. Heloïus in hâc urbe fuit episcopus, qui, defunctus, sepulturus est a fidelibus. Nocte autem sequenti, veniens quidam paganus lapidem, qui sarcophagum tegebat, revolvit, erectumque contra se corpus Sancti spoliare conatur. At ille, lacertis constrictum, ad se hominem fortiter amplexatur, et usque mane, populis spectantibus, tanquam constipatum loris, ita miserum brachiis detinebat. . . . Judex loci sepulchri violatorem jubet abstrahi, et legali pœnae sententiâ condemnari; sed non laxabatur a Sancto. Tunc intelligens voluntatem defuncti, Judex, factâ de vitâ promissione, absolvit, deinde laxatur, et sic incolumis redditur : non vero fur demissus quin se vitam monastericam amplexurum spopondisset.

Greg : Turonens : de Gloriâ Confessorum.

SAINT·ALOYS
 Was the Bishop of Blois,
And a pitiful man was he,
 He grieved and he pined
 For the woes of mankind,
And of brutes in their degree —
 He would rescue the rat
 From the claws of the cat,
And set the poor captive free ;
 Though his cassock was swarming
 With all sorts of vermin,
He'd not take the life of a flea !—
 Kind, tender, forgiving
 To all things living
From injury still he'd endeavour to screen 'em,
Fish, flesh, or fowl,—no difference between 'em—
 NIHIL PUTAVIT A SE ALIENUM.

 The Bishop of Blois was a holy man,—
 A holy man was he !
For Holy Church
He'd seek and he'd search

As a Bishop in his degree
From foe and from friend
He'd " rap and he'd rend,"
To augment her treasurie.
Nought would he give, and little he'd lend,
That Holy Church might have more to spend.—
" Count Stephen * (of Blois) " was a worthy Peer,
His breeches cost him but a crown,
He held them sixpence all too dear.
And so he call'd the Tailor lown."—
Had it been the Bishop instead of the Count,
And he'd overcharged him to half the amount,
He had knock'd that Tailor down !—
Not for himself !— He despised the pelf ;
He dressed in sackcloth, he dined off delf ;
And, when it was cold, in lieu of a *surtout*,
The good man would wrap himself up in his virtue.†
Alack ! that a man so holy as he,
So frank and free in his degree,
And so good and so kind, should mortal be !

Yet so it is—for loud and clear
From St. Nicholas' tower, on the listening ear,
With solemn swell,   The deep-toned bell
Flings to the gale a funeral knell ;
And hark !—at its sound,   As a cunning old hound,
When he opens, at once causes all the young whelps
Of the cry to put in their less dignified yelps,
So—the little bells all,   No matter how small,
From the steeples both inside and outside the wall,
With bell-metal throat   Respond to the note,
And join the lament that a prelate so pious is
Forced thus to leave his disconsolate diocese,
Or, as Blois' Lord May'r   Is heard to declare,
" Should leave this here world for to go to that there."

---

* *Teste* Messire Iago, a distinguished subaltern in the Venetian service, *circiter* A.D. 1580.
His Biographer, Mr. William Shakspeare, a contemporary writer of some note, makes him say
" *King* Stephen," inasmuch as the " worthy peer " subsequently usurped the crown of England.
The anachronism is a pardonable one.—*Mr. Simpkinson of Bath*.

†   ————————·Meâ
                            Virtute me involvo.—Hor.

And see, the portals opening wide,
From the Abbey flows the living tide ;
   Forth from the doors   The torrent pours,
Acolytes, Monks, and Friars in scores,
This with his chasuble, that with his rosary,
This from his incense-pot turning his nose awry,
   Holy Father, and Holy Mother,
   Holy Sister, and Holy Brother,
   Holy Son, and Holy Daughter,
   Holy Wafer, and Holy Water ;
      Every one drest   Like a guest in his best.
In the smartest of clothes they're permitted to wear,
Serge, sackcloth, and shirts of the same sort of hair
As now we make use of to stuff an arm-chair,
Or weave into gloves at three shillings a pair,
And employ for shampooing in cases rheumatic,—a
Special specific, I'm told, for Sciatica.

Through groined arch, and by cloister'd stone,
With mosses and ivy long o'ergrown,
   Slowly the throng   Come passing along,
With many a chaunt and solemn song,
Adapted for holidays, high-days, and Sundays,—
   Dies iræ, and *De profundis*,
   Miserere, and *Domine dirige nos*,—
Such as, I hear, to a very slow tune are all,
Commonly chaunted by Monks at a funeral,
   To secure the defunct's repose,
And to give a broad hint to Old Nick, should the news
Of a prelate's decease bring him there on a cruise,
That he'd better be minding his P's and his Q's,
And not come too near,—since they can, if they choose,
Make him shake in his hoofs—as he does not wear shoes.

   Still on they go,   A goodly show,
With footsteps sure, though certainly slow,
Two by two, in a very long row ;
   With feathers, and Mutes,   In mourning suits,
Undertaker's men walking in hat-bands and boots,—

Then comes the Crosier, all jewels and gold,
Borne by a lad about eighteen years old ;
Next, on a black velvet cushion, the Mitre,
Borne by a younger boy, 'cause it is lighter.
　　Eight Franciscans, sturdy and strong,
　　Bear, in the midst, the good Bishop along ;
　　Eight Franciscans, stout and tall,
　　Walk at the corners, and hold up the pall ;
　　Eight more hold a canopy high over all,
With eight Trumpeters tooting the Dead March in Saul.—
Behind, as Chief Mourner, the Lord Abbot goes, his
Monks coming after him, all with posies,
And white pocket-handkerchiefs up at their noses,
Which they blow whenever his Lordship blows his—
　　And oh ! 'tis a comely sight to see
　　How Lords and Ladies, of high degree,
　　Vail, as they pass, upon bended knee,
While quite as polite are the Squires and the Knights,
In their helmets, and hauberks, and cast-iron tights.

　　Ay, 'tis a comely sight to behold,
　　　As the company march
　　　Through the rounded arch
　　　　Of that Cathedral old !—
Singers behind 'em, and singers before 'em,
All of them ranging in due decorum,
Around the inside of the *Sanctum Sanctorum*,
　　While, brilliant and bright,　An unwonted light
(I forgot to premise this was all done at night)
The links, and the torches, and flambeaux shed
On the sculptured forms of the Mighty Dead,
That rest below, mostly buried in lead,
And above, recumbent in grim repose.
　　With their mailed hose,
　　And their dogs at their toes,
And little boys kneeling beneath them in rows,
Their hands join'd in pray'r, all in very long clothes,
With inscriptions on brass, begging each who survives,
As they some of them seem to have led so-so lives,
To 𝔓𝔯𝔞𝔦𝔢 𝔣𝔬𝔯 𝔱𝔥𝔢 𝔖𝔬𝔴𝔩𝔢𝔰 of themselves and their wives.—

—The effect of the music, too, really was fine,
When they let the good prelate down into his shrine,
   And by old and young, The " *Requiem* " was sung ;
Not vernacular French, but a classical tongue,
That is—Latin—I don't think they meddled with Greek—
In short, the whole thing produced—so to speak—
What in Blois they would call a *Coup d'œil magnifique !*

     Yet, surely, when the level ray
       Of some mild eve's descending sun
     Lights on the village pastor, grey
       In years ere ours had well begun—

     As there—in simplest vestment clad,
       He speaks, beneath the churchyard tree,
     In solemn tones—but yet not sad,—
       Of what Man is—what Man shall be !

     And clustering round the grave, half hid
       By that same quiet churchyard yew,
     The rustic mourners bend, to bid
       The dust they loved a last adieu—

     —That ray, methinks, that rests so sheen
     Upon each briar-bound hillock green,
     So calm, so tranquil, so serene,
     Gives to the eye a fairer scene,—
     Speaks to the heart with holier breath
     Than all this pageantry of Death.—

But *chacun à son goût*—this is talking at random—
We all know " *De gustibus non disputandum !* "
So canter back, Muse, to the scene of your story,
   The Cathedral of Blois— Where the Sainted Aloys
Is by this time, you'll find, " left alone in his glory,"
" In the dead of the night," though with labour opprest,
Some " mortals " disdain " the calm blessings of rest ; "
Your cracksman, for instance, thinks night-time the best
To break open a door, or the lid of a chest ;
And the gipsy who close round your premises prowls,
To ransack your hen-roost, and steal all your fowls,

Always sneaks out at night with the bats and the owls,
—So do Witches and Warlocks, Ghosts, Goblins, and Ghouls,
To say nothing at all of these troublesome " Swells "
Who come from the playhouses, " flash-kens," and " hells,"
To pull off people's knockers, and ring people's bells.

Well—'tis now the hour   Ill things have power !
And all who, in Blois, entertain honest views,
Have long been in bed, and enjoying a snooze,—
   Nought is waking   Save Mischief and Faking,*
And a few who are sitting up brewing or baking,
When an ill-looking Infidel, sallow of hue,
Who stands in his slippers some six feet two
(A rather remarkable height for a Jew),
Creeps cautiously out of the churchwarden's pew,
Into which, during service, he'd managed to slide himself—
While all were intent on the anthem, and hide himself.

From his lurking place,   With stealthy pace,
Through the " long-drawn aisle " he begins to crawl,
As you see a cat walk on the top of a wall,
When it's stuck full of glass, and she thinks she shall fall.
  —He proceeds to feel   For his flint and his steel,
(An invention on which we've improved a great deal
Of late years—the substitute best to rely on
's what Jones of the Strand calls his *Pyrogeneion*,)
   He strikes with despatch !—his   Tinder catches !—
Now where is his candle ?—and where are his matches ?—
   'Tis done !—they are found !—
   He stands up, and looks round
By the light of a " dip " of sixteen to the pound !
—What is it now that makes his nerves to quiver ?—
His hand to shake—and his limbs to shiver ?—
Fear ?—Pooh !—it is only a touch of the liver,—
   All is silent—all is still—
Its " gammon "—its " stuff ! "—he may do what he will !

* " Nix my dolly, pals, *Fake* away ! "—words of deep and mysterious import in the ancient language of Upper Egypt, and recently inscribed on the sacred standard of Mehemet Ali. They are supposed to intimate, to the initiated in the art of Abstraction, the absence of all human observation, and to suggest the propriety of making the best use of their time—and fingers.

Witches and warlocks, ghosts, goblins and ghouls

Carefully now he approaches the shrine,
In which, as I've mentioned before, about nine,
They had placed in such state the lamented Divine !
But not to worship—No !—No such thing !—
His aim is—to " PRIG " THE PASTORAL RING ! !

   Fancy his fright   When, with all his might
Having forced up the lid, which they'd not fastened quite,
Of the marble sarcophagus—" All in white "
The dead Bishop started up, bolt upright
On his hinder end,—and grasped him so tight,
   That the clutch of a kite,   Or a bull-dog's bite
When he's most provoked and in bitterest spite,
May well be conceived in comparison slight,
And having thus " tackled " him—blew out his light ! !

   Oh, dear ! Oh ! dear ! The fright and the fear !—
      No one to hear !—nobody near !
In the dead of the night !—at a bad time of year !—
A defunct Bishop squatting upright on his bier,
And shouting so loud, that the drum of his ear
He thought would have split as these awful words met it—
" AH, HA ! MY GOOD FRIEND !—DON'T YOU WISH YOU MAY GET
      IT ? "—
   Oh, dear ! Oh, dear ! *'Twas* a night of fear !
—I should just like to know, if the boldest man here,
In his situation, would not have felt queer ?

   The wretched man bawls,
     And he yells, and he squalls,
But there's nothing responds to his shrieks save the walls,
And the desk, and the pulpit, the pews, and the stalls.
   Held firmly at bay,   Kick and plunge as he may,
His struggles are fruitless—he can't get away,
He really can't tell what to do or to say,
And being a Pagan, don't know how to pray ;
Till, through the east window, a few streaks of grey
Announce the approach of the dawn of the day !

   Oh, a welcome sight   Is the rosy light,
Which lovelily heralds a morning bright,

Above all to a wretch
  kept in durance all
  night
By a horrid dead gentle-
  man holding him
  tight,—
Of all sorts of gins that a
  trespasser can trap,
The most disagreeable kind of a man
  trap !
—Oh ! welcome that bell's
  Matin chime, which tells
To one caught in this worst of all
  possible snares,
That the hour is arrived to begin
  Morning Prayers,
And the monks and the friars are coming down
  stairs !

Conceive the surprise
  Of the Choir—how their eyes
Are distended to twice their original size,—
How some begin bless—some anathematize,—
And all look on the thief as old Nick in dis-
  guise.
While the mystified Abbot cries, " Well !—I declare !—
—This is really a very mysterious affair !—
Bid the bandy-legg'd sexton go run for the May'r ! "

The May'r and his *suite*
  Are soon on their feet,—
(His worship kept house in the very same street,—)
  At once he awakes,
  " His compliments " makes,
" He'll be up at the Church in a couple of shakes ! "
Meanwhile the whole Convent is pulling and hauling,
  And bawling and squalling, And terribly mauling
The thief whose endeavour to follow his calling
Had thus brought him into a grasp so enthralling.—
  Now high, now low, They drag " to and fro,"—
Now this way, now that way they twist him—but—No !—

The glazed eye of St. Aloys distinctly says " Poh !
You may pull as you please, I shall *not* let him go ! "
Nay, more ;—when his Worship at length came to say
He was perfectly ready to take him away,
And fat him to grace the next *Auto-da-fé*,
   Still closer he prest   The poor wretch to his breast,
While a voice—though his jaws still together were jamm'd—
Was heard from his chest, " If you do, I'll——" here slamm'd
The great door of the Church,—with so awful a sound
That the close of the good Bishop's sentence was drown'd !

         Out spake *Frère Jehan*,   A pitiful man,
            Oh ! a pitiful man was he !
         And he wept, and he pined
         For the sins of mankind,
            As a Friar in his degree.
" Remember, good gentlefolks," so he began,
" Dear Aloys was always a pitiful man !—
   That voice from his chest   Has clearly exprest
He has pardoned the culprit—and as for the rest,
Before you shall burn him—he'll see you all blest ! "

The Monks, and the Abbot, the Sexton, and Clerk
Were exceedingly struck with the Friar's remark,
And the Judge, who himself was by no means a shark
Of a Lawyer, and who did not do things in the dark,
But still leaned (having once been himself a gay spark,)
To the merciful side,—like the late Alan Park,—
   Agreed that, indeed,   The best way to succeed,
And by which this poor caitiff alone could be freed,
Would be to absolve him, and grant a free pardon,
On a certain condition, and that not a hard one,
Viz.: " That he, the said Infidel, straightway should ope
His mind to conviction, and worship the Pope,
And ' ev'ry man Jack ' in an amice or cope ;—
   And that, to do so,   He should forthwith go
To Rome, and salute there His Holiness' toe ;—
   And never again   Read Voltaire, or Tom Paine,
Or Percy Bysshe Shelley, or Lord Byron's Cain :—
His pilgrimage o'er, take St. Francis's habit ;—
If anything lay about, never to ' nab ' it ;—

Or, at worst, if he *should* light on articles gone astray,
To be sure and deposit them safe in the Monast'ry!"

The oath he took— —As he kiss'd the book,
Nave, transept, and aisle with a thunder-clap shook!
The Bishop sank down with a satisfied look,
    And the Thief, releas'd   By the Saint deceas'd,
Fell into the arms of a neighbouring Priest!

It skills not now   To tell you how
The transmogrified Pagan perform'd his vow;
    How he quitted his home,   Travell'd to Rome,
And went to St. Peter's, and look'd at the Dome,
And obtain'd from the Pope an assurance of bliss,
And kiss'd—whatever he gave him to kiss—
Toe, relic, embroidery, naught came amiss;
    And how Pope Urban   Had the man's turban
Hung up in the Sistine chapel, by way
Of a relic—and how it hangs there to this day.—
    Suffice it to tell,   Which will do quite as well,
That the whole of the Convent the miracle saw,
And the Abbot's report was sufficient to draw
Ev'ry *bon Catholique* in *la belle France* to Blois,
Among others, the Monarch himself, François,
The Archbishop of Rheims, and his " Pious Jack-daw " *
And there was not a man in Church, Chapel, or Meeting-house,
Still less in *Cabaret*, Hotel, or Eating-house,
    But made an oration,   And said, " In the nation
If ever a man deserved canonization,
It was the kind, pitiful, pious Aloys."—
    So the Pope says,—says he, " Then a Saint he shall be!"
So he made him a Saint,—and remitted the fee.

What became of the Pagan I really can't say;
    But I think I've been told,   When he'd enter'd their fold
And was now a Franciscan some twenty days old,
He got up one fine morning before break of day,
Put the *Pyx* in his pocket—and then ran away.

* *Vide* Ingoldsby Legends (First Series), page 140.

Moral.

I think we may coax out a moral or two
From the facts which have lately·come under our view.
First—Don't meddle with Saints !—for you'll find if you do,
They're what Scotch people call, " kittle cattle to shoe ! "
And when once they have managed to take you in tow,
It's a deuced hard matter to make them let go !

Now to you, wicked Pagans !—who wander about,
Up and down Regent Street every night, " on the scout,"—
Recollect the Police keep a sharpish look-out,
And, if once you're suspected, your skirts they will stick to,
Till they catch you at last *in flagrante delicto !*—
    Don't the inference draw   That because he of Blois
Suffer'd *one* to bilk " Old father Antic the Law,"
That *our* May'rs and *our* Aldermen—and we've a City full—
Show themselves, at *our* Guildhall, quite so pitiful !

Lastly, as to the Pagan who play'd such a trick,
First assuming the tonsure, then cutting his stick,
There is but one thing which occurs to me—that
Is,—Don't give too much credit to people who " rat ! "
    —Never forget   Early habit's a net
Which entangles us all, more or less, in its mesh ;
And " What's bred in the bone won't come out of the flesh ! "
We must all be aware Nature's prone to rebel, as
Old Juvenal tells us, *Naturam expellas*,
    Tamen usque recurret !   There's no making Her rat !
So that all that I have on this head to advance
Is,—whatever they think of these matters in France,
There's a proverb, the truth of which each one allows here,
" You never can make a silk purse of a sow's ear ! "

In the succeeding Legend we come nearer home.—Father Ingoldsby is particular in describing its locality, situate some eight miles from the Hall—less, if you take the bridle-road by the Church-yard, and so along the valley by Mr. Fector's Abbey.—In the enumeration of the various attempts to appropriate the treasure (drawn from a later source) is omitted one, said to have been undertaken by the worthy ecclesiastic himself, who, as Mrs. Botherby insinuates, is reported to have started for Dover, one fine morning, duly furnished with all the means and appliances of Exorcism.—I cannot learn, however, that the family was ever enriched by his expedition.

The Lay of the Old Woman Clothed in Grey

A Legend of Dover

ONCE there lived, as I've heard people say,
An " Old Woman clothed in grey,"
  So furrow'd with care,   So haggard her air,
In her eye such a wild supernatural stare,
    That all who espied her   Immediately shied her,
And strove to get out of her way.

This fearsome Old Woman was taken ill :
—She sent for the Doctor—he sent her a pill,
  And by way of a trial,   A two-shilling phial
Of green-looking fluid, like lava diluted,
To which I've profess'd an abhorrence most rooted,*
One of those draughts they so commonly send us,
Labell'd " *Haustus catharticus mane sumendus ; "*—
  She made a wry face,   And, without saying Grace,
Toss'd it off like a dram—it improv'd not her case.
  —The Leech came again ;   He now open'd a vein,
Still the little Old Woman continued in pain
So her " Medical Man," although loth to distress her,
Conceived it high time that her Father Confessor
Should be sent for to shrive, and assoilzie, and bless her,
That she might not slip out of these troublesome scenes
" Unanneal'd and Unhouseled,"—whatever that means.†
  Growing afraid,   He calls to his aid
A bandy-legg'd neighbour, a " *Tailor by trade,*" ‡

---

* *Vide* page 236.

  † Alack for poor William Linley to settle the point ! His elucidation of Macbeth's " Hurly-burly " casts a halo around his memory. In him the world lost one of its kindliest Spirits, and the Garrick Club its acutest commentator.

  ‡ All who are familiar with the Police Reports, and other Records of our Courts of Justice, will recollect that every gentleman of this particular profession invariably thus describes himself, in contradistinction to the Bricklayer, whom he probably presumes to be indigenous, and to the Shoemaker, *born* a Snob.

Tells him his fears,
Bids him lay by his
shears,
His thimble, his goose,
and his needle, and
hie
With all possible speed
to the Convent hard
by,
Requests him to say
That he begs they'll
all pray
Viz.: The whole pious
brotherhood, Cleric
and Lay,
For the soul of an Old
Woman clothed in
grey,
Who was just at that time in a
very bad way,
And he really believed couldn't
last out the day ;—
And to state his desire
That some erudite Friar
Would run over at once, and ex-
amine, and try her ;
For he thought he would find
There was " something behind,"
A something that weigh'd on the Old
Woman's mind,—
" In fact he was sure, from what fell
from her tongue,
That this little Old Woman had done something wrong."
—Then he wound up the whole with this hint to the man,
" Mind and pick out as holy a friar as you can ! "

Now I'd have you to know   That this story of woe,
Which I'm telling you, happen'd a long time ago ;
I can't say exactly *how* long, nor, I own,
What particular monarch was then on the throne,

But 'twas here in Old England : and all that one knows is,
It must have preceded the Wars of the Roses.*
 Inasmuch as the times Described in these rhymes
Were as fruitful in virtues as ours are in crimes ;
 And if 'mongst the Laity Unseemly gaiety
Sometimes betray'd an occasional taint or two,
 At once all the Clerics Went into hysterics,
While scarcely a convent but boasted its Saint or two ;
So it must have been long ere the line of the Tudors,
 As since then the breed Of Saints rarely indeed
With their dignified presence have darken'd our pew doors.
—Hence the late Mr. Froude, and the live Dr. Pusey
We moderns consider as each worth a Jew's eye ;
Though Wiseman, and Dullman † combine against Newman,
With Doctors and Proctors, and say he's no true man.
—But this by the way.—The Convent I speak about
Had Saints in scores—they said Mass week and week about ;
And the two now on duty were each, for their piety,
" Second to none " in that holy society,
 And well might have borne
 Those words which are worn
By our " *Nulli Secundus* " Club—poor dear lost muttons—
Of Guardsmen—on Club days, inscribed on their buttons.—
 They would read, write, and speak
 Latin, Hebrew, and Greek,
A radish-bunch munch for a lunch,—or a leek ;
 Though scoffers and boobies Ascribe certain rubies
That garnished the nose of the good Father Hilary
To the overmuch use of Canary and Sillery,
—Some said spirituous compounds of viler distillery—
 Ah ! little reck'd they That with Friars, who say
Fifty *Paters* a night, and a hundred a day,
A very slight sustenance goes a great way—
Thus the consequence was that his colleague, Basilius
Won golden opinions, by looking more bilious,

---

* " An antient and most pugnacious family," says our Bath friend. " One of their descendants, George Rose, Esq., late M.P. for Christchurch (an elderly gentleman now defunct), was equally celebrated for his vocal abilities and his wanton destruction of furniture when in a state of excitement.—" Sing. old Rose, and burn the bellows ! " has grown into a proverb.

 † The worthy Jesuit's polemical publisher.—I am not quite sure as to the orthography ;— it's *idem sonans,* at all events.

From all who conceived strict monastical duty
By no means conducive to personal beauty ;
And being more meagre, and thinner, and paler,
He was snapt up at once by the bandy-legg'd Tailor.

The latter's concern   For a speedy return
Scarce left the Monk time to put on stouter sandals,
Or go round to his shrines, and snuff all his Saint's candles ;
Still less had he leisure to change the hair-shirt he
Had worn the last twenty years—probably thirty,—
Which, not being wash'd all that time, had grown dirty.
    —It seems there's a sin in
    The wearing clean linen,
Which Friars must eschew at the very beginning,
Though it makes them look frowsy, and drowsy, and blowsy,
And—a rhyme modern etiquette never allows ye.—
    As for the rest   E'en if time had not prest,
It didn't much matter how Basil was drest,
Nor could there be any great need for adorning,
The Night being almost at odds with the Morning.

> Oh ! sweet and beautiful is Night,
>   When the silver Moon is high,
> And countless Stars, like clustering gems,
>   Hang sparkling in the sky,
> While the balmy breath of the summer breeze
>   Comes whispering down the glen,
> And one fond voice alone is heard—
>   Oh ! Night is lovely then !
> But when that voice, in feeble moans
>   Of sickness and of pain,
> But mocks the anxious ear that strives
>   To catch its sounds in vain,—
> When silently we watch the bed,
>   By the taper's flickering light,
> Where all we love is fading fast—
>   How terrible is Night ! !

More terrible yet,   If you happen to get
By an old woman's bedside, who, all her life long,

Has been what the vulgar call, " coming it strong "
In all sorts of ways that are naughty and wrong —

As Confessions are sacred, it's not very facile
To ascertain what the old hag said to Basil;
    But whatever she said,   It fill'd him with dread,
And made all his hair stand on end on his head,—
No great feat to perform, inasmuch as said hair
Being clipp'd by the tonsure, his crown was left bare,
So of course Father Basil had little to spare;
    But the little he had
    Seem'd as though't had gone mad,
Each lock, as by action galvanic, uprears
In the two little tufts on the tops of his ears.—
    What the old woman said
    That so " fill'd him with dread,"
We should never have known any more than the dead,
If the bandy-legg'd Tailor, his errand thus sped,
Had gone quietly back to his needle and thread,
    As he ought; but instead,   Curiosity led,—
A feeling we all deem extremely ill-bred,—
He contrived to secrete himself under the bed !
    —Not that he heard   One half, or a third
Of what past as the Monk and the Patient conferred,
But he here and there managed to pick up a word,
    Such as " Knife,"   And " Life,"
And he thought she said " Wife,"
And " Money," that source of all evil and strife; *
Then he plainly distinguished the words " Gore," and " Gash,"
Whence he deem'd—and I don't think this inference rash—
She had cut some one's throat for the sake of his cash !

    Intermix'd with her moans,
    And her sighs, and her groans,
Enough to have melted the hearts of the stones,
Came at intervals Basil's sweet, soft silver tones,
For somehow it happened—I can't tell you why—
The good Friar's indignation,—at first rather high,—

---

* Effodiuntur Opes Irritamenta Malorum.—LILLY's *Grammar.*

To judge from the language he used in reply,
Ere the Old Woman ceased, had a good deal gone by ;
And he gently addressed her in accents of honey,
" Daughter, don't you despair !—WHAT'S BECOME OF THE
    MONEY ? "

In one just at Death's door it was really absurd
To see how her eye lighted up at that word—
Indeed there's not one in the language that I know,
(Save its synonyms " Spanish," " Blunt," " Stumpy," and " Rhino,")
    Which acts so direct,   And with so much effect
On the human *sensorium,* or makes one erect
One's ears so, as soon as the sound we detect—
    It's a question with me   Which of the three,
Father Basil himself, though a grave S.T.P.
(Such as he have, you see, the degree of D.D.)
Or the eaves-dropping, bandy-legg'd Tailor,—or She
Caught it quickest—however, traditions agree
That the Old Woman perked up as brisk as a bee,—

'Twas the last quivering flare of the taper,—the fire
It so often emits when about to expire !
Her excitement began the same instant to flag,
She sank back, and whisper'd " Safe !—Safe ! in the Bag ! ! "

Now I would not by any means have you suppose
That the good Father Basil was just one of those
    Who entertain views   We're so apt to abuse,
As neither befitting Turks, Christians, nor Jews,
    Who haunt death-bed scenes,   By underhand means
To toady or teaze people out of a legacy,—
For few folk, indeed, had such good right to beg as he,
Since Rome, in her pure Apostolical beauty,
Not only permits, but enjoins, as a duty,
    Her sons to take care That, let who will be heir,
The Pontiff shall not be chous'd out of his share,
Nor stand any such mangling of chattels and goods,
As, they say, was the case with the late Jemmy Wood's ;
Her Conclaves, and Councils, and Synods, in short, main-
tain principles adverse to statutes of *Mortmain ;*
    Besides, you'll discern   It at once, when you learn

That Basil had something to give in return,
Since it rested with him to say how she would burn,
Nay, as to her ill-gotten wealth, should she turn it all
To uses he named, he could say, " You shan't burn at all,
    Or nothing to signify,   Not what you'd dignify
So much as even to call it a roast,
But a mere little singeing, or scorching at most,—
What many would think not unpleasantly warm,—
Just to keep up appearance—mere matter of form."
    All this in her ear—He declared, but I fear
That her senses were wand'ring—she seem'd not to hear,
Or, at least understand,—for mere unmeaning talk her
Parch'd lips babbled now,—such as " Hookey ! "—and " Walker ! "
—She expired, with her last breath expressing a doubt
If " his Mother were fully aware he was out ? "

Now it seems there's a place they call Purgat'ry—so
I must write it, my verse not admitting the O—
But as for the *venue*, I vow I'm perplext
To say if it's in this world, or if in the next—
Or whether in both—for 'tis very well known
That St. Patrick, at least, has got one of his own,
In a " tight little Island " that stands in a Lake
Call'd " Lough-dearg "—that's " The Red Lake," unless I mistake,—
In Fermanagh—or Antrim—or Donegal—which
    I declare I can't tell,   But I know very well
It's in latitude 54, nearly their pitch
(At Tappington, now, I could look in the Gazetteer,
But I'm out on a visit, and nobody has it here).
There are some, I'm aware   Who don't stick to declare
There's " no differ " at all 'twixt " this here " and " that there,"
That it's all the same place, but the Saint reserves his entry
From the separate use of the " finest of pisentry,"
    And that his is no more   Than a mere private door
For the *rez-de-chaussée*,—as some call the ground floor,—
To the one which the Pope had found out long before.

    But no matter—lay   The *locale* where you may ;
—And where it is no one exactly can say—
There's one thing, at least, which is known very well,
That it acts as a Tap-room to Satan's Hotel.

" Entertainment " there's worse
Both for " Man and for Horse ; "
For broiling the souls   They use Lord Mayor's coals ;—
Then the sulphur's inferior, and boils up much slower
Than the fine fruity brimstone they give you down lower,
     It's by no means so strong—
     Mere sloe-leaves to Souchong ;
The " prokers " are not half so hot, or so long,
By an inch or two, either in handle or prong ;
The Vipers and Snakes are less sharp in the tooth,
And the Nondescript Monsters not near so uncouth ;—
In short, it's a place the good Pope, its creator,
Made for what's called by Cockneys a " Minor The-átre."
Better suited, of course, for a " minor performer,"
Than the " House," that's so much better lighted and warmer,
Below, in that queer place which nobody mentions,—
     —You understand where,
     I don't question—down there,
Where, in lieu of wood blocks, and such modern inventions,
The Paving Commissioners use " Good Intentions,"
Materials which here would be thought on by few men,
With so many founts of Asphaltic bitumen
At hand, at the same time to pave and illumine.

     To go on with my story,   This same Purga-tory,
(There ! I've got in the O, to my Muse's great glory),
Is close lock'd, and the Pope keeps the keys of it—that I can
Boldly affirm—in his desk in the Vatican ;
     —Not those of St. Peter—
     Those of which I now treat, are
A bunch by themselves, and much smaller and neater—
And so cleverly made, Mr. Chubb could not frame a
Key better contrived for its purpose—nor Bramah.
     Now it seems that by these   Most miraculous keys
Not only the Pope, but his " clargy," with ease
Can let people in and out, just as they please ;
And—provided you " make it all right " about fees,
There is not a friar, Dr. Wiseman will own, of them,
But can always contrive to obtain a short loan of them ;
     And Basil, no doubt,   Had brought matters about,
If the little old woman would but have " spoke out,"

So far as to get for her one of those tickets,
Or passes, which clear both the great gates and wickets ;
   So that after a grill,   Or short turn on the Mill,
And with no worse a singeing, to purge her iniquity,
Than a Freemason gets in the " Lodge of Antiquity,"
   She'd have rubb'd off old scores,
   Popp'd out of doors,
And sheer'd off at once for a happier port,
Like a white-wash'd Insolvent that's " gone through the Court."

   But Basil was one   Who was not to be *done*
By any one, either in earnest or fun ;—
The cunning old beads-telling son of a gun,
In all bargains, unless he'd his *quid* for his *quo*,
Would shake his bald pate, and pronounce it " No Go."
   So, unless you're a dunce,   You'll see clearly, at once,
When you come to consider the facts of the case, he
Of course never gave her his *Vade in pace ;*
And the consequence was, when the last mortal throe
Released her pale Ghost from these regions of woe,
The little Old Woman had nowhere to go !

   For, what could she do ?   She very well knew
If she went to the gates I have mention'd to you,
Without Basil's, or some other passport to show,
The Cheque-takers never would let her go through ;
While, as to *the other place*, e'en had she tried it,
And really had wished it, as much as she shied it,
(For no one who knows what it is can abide it),
Had she knock'd at the portal with ne'er so much din,
Though she died in, what folks at Rome call, " Mortal sin,"
Yet Old Nick, for the life of him, daren't take her in,
As she'd not been turn'd formally out of " the pale ; "—
So much the bare name of the Pope made him quail,
In the times that I speak of, his courage would fail
Of Rome's vassals the lowest and worst to assail,
Or e'en touch with so much as the end of his tail ;
   Though, now he's grown older,
   They say he's much bolder,
And his Holiness not only gets the " cold shoulder,"

But Nick rumps him completely, and don't seem to care a
Dump—that's the word—for his triple tiara.

    Well—what shall she do ?—
    What's the course to pursue ?—
" Try St. Peter ?—the step is a bold one to take ;
For the Saint is, there can't be a doubt, ' wide awake ;
    But then there's a quaint   Old Proverb says, ' Faint
Heart ne'er won fair Lady,' then how win a Saint ?—
    I've a great mind to try—   One can but apply ;
If things come to the worst, why he can but deny—
    The sky's rather high   To be sure—but, now I
That cumbersome carcass of clay have laid by,
I am just in the ' order ' which some folks—though why
I am sure I can't tell you—would call ' Apple-pie.'
    Then ' never say die ! '   It won't do to be shy,
So I'll tuck up my shroud, and—here goes for a fly ! "
—So said and so done—she was off like a shot,
And kept on the whole way at a pretty smart trot.

    When she drew so near   That the Saint could see her,
In a moment he frown'd, and began to look queer,
And scarce would allow her to make her case clear,
Ere he pursed up his mouth 'twixt a sneer and a jeer,
With " It's all very well—but you do not lodge here ! "—
Then, calling her everything but " My dear ! "
He applied his great toe with some force *au derrière*,
And dismissed her at once with a flea in her ear.

    " Alas ! poor Ghost ! "   It's a doubt which is most
To be pitied—one doom'd to fry, broil, boil, and roast,—
Or one bandied about thus from pillar to post,—
To be " all abroad "—to be " stump'd " not to know where
    To go—so disgraced   As not to be " placed,"
Or, as Crocky would say to Jem Bland, " To be Nowhere."—
    However that be,   The *affaire* was *finie*,
And the poor wretch rejected by all, as you see !

Mr. Oliver Goldsmith observes—not the Jew—
That the " Hare whom the hounds and the huntsmen pursue,"

Having no other sort of asylum in view,
" Returns back again to the place whence she flew,"—
A fact which experience has proved to be true.—
Mr. Gray,—in opinion with whom Johnson clashes,—
Declares that our " wonted fires live in our ashes."— *
These motives combined, perhaps, brought back the hag,
The first to her mansion, the last to her bag,
When only conceive her dismay and surprise,
As a Ghost how she open'd her cold stony eyes,
When there,—on the spot where she'd hid her " supplies,"—
In an underground cellar of very small size,
    Working hard with a spade,   All at once she survey'd
That confounded old bandy-legged " Tailor by trade."

    Fancy the tone   Of the half moan, half groan,
Which burst from the breast of the Ghost of the crone !
As she stood there,—a figure 'twixt moonshine and stone,—
Only fancy the glare in her eyeballs that shone !
Although, as Macbeth says, " they'd no speculation,"
    While she uttered that word,   Which American Bird
Or James Fenimore Cooper, would render " Tarnation ! ! "
    At the noise which she made
    Down went the spade !—
And up jump'd the bandy-legg'd " Tailor by trade,"
(Who had shrewdly conjectured, from something that fell, her
Deposit was somewhere concealed in the cellar ;)
    Turning round at a sound   So extremely profound,
The moment her shadowy form met his view
He gave vent to a sort of a lengthen'd   Bo-o—ho-o ! "—
With a countenance Keeley alone could put on,
Made one grasshopper spring to the door—and was gone !
    Erupit ! Evasit !
    As at Rome they would phrase it—
His flight was so swift, the eye scarcely could trace it,
Though elderly, bandy-legg'd, meagre, and sickly,
I doubt if the Ghost could have vanish'd more quickly ;—
He reach'd his own shop, and then fell into fits,
And it's said never rightly recover'd his wits,
While the chuckling old Hag takes his place, and there sits !

*   " E'en in our ashes live their wonted fires ! "—GRAY.
" A position at which Experience revolts, Credulity hesitates, and even Fancy stares ! "—
JOHNSON.

Made one grasshopper spring to the door—and was gone!

I'll venture to say,   She'd sat there to this day,
Brooding over what Cobbett calls " vile yellow clay,"
Like a Vulture, or other obscene bird of prey,
O'er the nest-full of eggs she has managed to lay,
If, as legends relate, and I think we may trust 'em, her
Stars had not brought her another guess customer—

   'Twas Basil himself !—   Come to look for her pelf :
But not, like the tailor, to dig, delve, and grovel,
And grub in the cellar with pickaxe and shovel ;
   Full well he knew   Such tools would not do —
Far other the weapons he brought into play,
Viz., a Wax-taper " hallow'd on Candlemas-day,"

   To light to her ducats,—   Holy water, two buckets,
(Made with salt—half a peck to four gallons—which brews a
Strong triple X " strike,"—see Jacobus de Chusa.)
   With these, too, he took   His bell and his book—
Not a nerve ever trembled,—his hand never shook
As he boldly march'd up where she sat in her nook,
Glow'ring round with that wild indescribable look,
Which *Some* may have read of, perchance, in " Nell Cook," *
All, in " Martha the Gipsy " by Theodore Hook.

And now, for the reason I gave you before,
Of what passed then and there I can tell you no more.
As no Tailor was near with his ear at the door ;
   But I've always been told,   With respect to the gold,
For which she her " jewel eternal " had sold,
   That the old Harridan,   Who, no doubt, knew her man,
Made some compromise—hit upon some sort of plan,
By which Friar and Ghost were both equally pinn'd—
Heaven only knows how the " Agreement " got wind ;—
   But its purport was this,   That the things done amiss
By the Hag should not hinder her ultimate bliss ;
   Provided—" *Imprimis*,   The cash from this time is
The Church's—impounded for good pious uses—
—Father B. shall dispose of it just as he chooses,
   And act as trustee—   In the meantime, that She,
The said Ghostess,—or Ghost,—as the matter may be,
From ' impediment,' ' hindrance,' and ' let ' shall be free,
To sleep in her grave, or wander, as he,
The said Friar, with said Ghost may hereafter agree.—

            * See page 311.

Moreover—The whole   Of the said cash, or ' cole,'
Shall be spent for the good of said Old Woman's soul !

" It is farther agreed—while said cash is so spending,
Said Ghost shall be fully absolv'd from attending,
    And shall quiet remain   In the grave, her domain,
To have, and enjoy, and uphold, and maintain,
Without molestation, or trouble, or pain,
Hindrance, let, or impediment, (over again)
From Old Nick, or from any one else of his train,
Whether Pow'r,—Domination, or Princedom,—or Throne,*
Or by what name soever the same may be known,
Howsoe'er called by Poets, or styled by Divines,—
Himself,—his executors, heirs, and assigns.

" Provided that,—nevertheless,—notwithstanding
All herein contained,—if whoever's a hand in
Dispensing said cash,—or said ' cole,'—shall dare venture
To misapply money, note, bill, or debenture
To uses not named in this present Indenture,
Then that such sum, or sums, shall revert, and come home again
Back to said Ghost,—who thenceforward shall roam again
Until such time, or times, as the said Ghost produces
Some good man and true, who no longer refuses
To put sum, or sums, aforesaid, to said uses ;
Which duly performed, the said Ghost shall have rest,
The full term of her natural death, of the best,
In full consideration of this, her bequest,
In manner and form aforesaid,—as exprest :—
In witness whereof, we, the parties aforesaid,
Hereunto set our hands and our seals—and no more said
Being all that these presents intend to express,
Whereas—notwithstanding—and nevertheless.

" Sign'd, sealed, and deliver'd, this 20th of May,
Anno Domini, blank, (though I've mentioned the day,)
(Signed)
          BASIL.
              OLD WOMAN (late) CLOTHED IN GREY."

* Thrones ! Dominations ! Princedoms ! Virtues ! Powers !

Basil now, I am told,   Walking off with the gold,
Went and straight got the document duly enroll'd,
And left the testatrix to mildew and mould
In her sepulchre, cosey, cool,—not to say cold.
But somehow—though how I can hardly divine,—
   A runlet of fine   Rich Malvoisie wine
Found its way to the Convent that night before nine,
With custards, and " flawns " and a " fayre florentine,"
Peach, apricot, nectarine, melon, and pine ;—
And some half a score Nuns of the rule Bridgetine,
Abbess and all, were invited to dine
At a very late hour,—that is after Compline.—
—Father Hilary's rubies began soon to shine
With fresh lustre, as though newly dug from
     the mine ;
   Through all the next year,
   Indeed, 'twould appear
That the Convent was much better off, as
     to cheer,
Even Basil himself, as I very much fear,
No longer addicted himself to small beer ;
   His complexion grew clear,
   While in front and in rear
He enlarged so, his shape seem'd approach-
     ing a sphere.

No wonder at all, then, one cold winter's night,
That a servant girl going down stairs with a light
To the cellar we've spoken of, saw, with affright,
An Old Woman, astride on a barrel, invite
Her to take, in a manner extremely polite,
With her left hand, a bag, she had got in her right ;—
For tradition asserts that the Old Woman's purse
Had come back to her *scarcely one penny the worse !*

   The girl, as they say,   Ran screaming away,
Quite scared by the Old Woman clothed in grey ;
But there came down a Knight, at no distant a day,
   Sprightly and gay   As the bird on the spray,
One Sir Rufus Mountfardington, Lord of Foot's-cray,

Whose estate, not unlike those of most of our " Swell " beaux,
Was, what's, by a metaphor, term'd " out at elbows ; "
And the fact was, said Knight was now merely delay'd
From crossing the water to join the Crusade
For converting the Pagans with bill, bow, and blade,
By the want of a little pecuniary aid
To buy arms and horses, the tools of his trade,
And enable his troop to appear on parade ;—
    The unquiet Shade   Thought Sir Rufus, 'tis said,
Just the man for her money,—she readily paid
For the articles named, and with pleasure convey'd
To his hands every farthing she ever had made ;
    But alas ! I'm afraid   Most unwisely she laid
Out her cash—the *beaux yeux* of a Saracen maid
(Truth compels me to say a most pestilent jade)
Converted the gallant converter—betray'd
Him to do everything which a Knight could degrade,
—E'en to worship Mahound !—She required—He obey'd,—
The consequence was, all the money was wasted
On Infidel pleasures he should not have tasted ;
So that, after a very short respite, the Hag
Was seen down in her cellar again with her bag.

Don't fancy, dear Reader, I mean to go on
Seriatim through so many ages by-gone,
    And to bore you with names
    Of the Squires, and the Dames,
Who have managed, at times, to get hold of the sack,
But spent the cash so that it always came back ;
    The list is too long   To be giv'n in my song,—
There are reasons beside would perhaps make it wrong ;
I shall merely observe, in those orthodox days,
When Mary set Smithfield all o'er in a blaze,
    And show'd herself very se-   -vere against heresy,
While many a wretch scorned to flinch, or to scream, as he
Burnt for denying the Papal supremacy,
    Bishop Bonner the bag got,
    And all thought the Hag got
Releas'd, as he spent all in fuel and faggot.—
    But somehow—though how   I can't tell you, I vow—

I suppose by mismanagement—ere the next reign
The Spectre had got all her money again.

The last time, I'm told,   That the Old Woman's gold
Was obtained,—as before,—for the asking,—'twas had
By a Mr. O—Something—from Ballinafad ;
And the whole of it, so 'tis reported, was sent
To John Wright's, in account for the Catholic Rent,
And thus—like a great deal more money—" it went ! "
   So 'tis said at Maynooth,   But I can't think it's truth ;
Though I know it was boldly asserted last season,
Still I can *not* believe it ; and that for this reason,
It's certain *the cash has got back to its owner !*—
—Now no part of the Rent to do *so* e'er was known,—or,
In any shape, ever come home to the donor.   .

GENTLE READER !—you must know the proverb, I think—
" To a blind horse a Nod is as good as a Wink ! "
   Which some learned Chap,   In a square College cap,
Perhaps would translate by the words " *Verbum Sap !* "

   —Now, should it so chance
   That you're going to France
In the course of next Spring, as you probably may,
   Do pull up, and stay,   Pray,   If but for a day,
At Dover, through which you must pass on your way,
At the York,—or the Ship,—where, as all people say,
You'll get good wine yourself, and your horses good hay,
Perhaps, my good friend, you may find it will *pay*,
And you cannot lose much by so short a delay.

   First DINE !—you can do   That on joint or *ragoût*—
Then say to the waiter,—" I'm just passing through,—
Pray,—where can I find out the old *Maison Dieu ?* "—
He'll show you the street—(the French call it a *Rue*,
But you won't have to give here a *petit écu*).

Well,—when you've got there,—never mind how you're taunted,---
Ask boldly, " Pray, which is the house here that's haunted ? "
—I'd tell you myself, but I can't recollect
The proprietor's name ; but he's one of that sect

2 D

Who call themselves " Friends," and whom others call " Quakers,"---
You'll be sure to find out if you ask at the Baker's.—
    Then go down, with a light,   To the cellar at night !
And as soon as you see her don't be in a fright !
    But ask the old Hag,   At once, for the bag !—
If you find that she's shy, or your senses would dazzle,
Say, " Ma'am, I insist !—in the name of St. Basil ! "
    If she gives it you, seize   It, and—do as you please—
But there is not a person I've ask'd but agrees,
You should spend—part at least—for the Old Woman's ease !
—For the rest—if it *must* go back some day—why—let it !—
Meanwhile, if you're poor, and in love, or in debt, it
May do you some good, and—
                I WISH YOU MAY GET IT ! ! !

To whom is the name of Cornelius Agrippa otherwise than familiar, since " a Magician,"
of renown not inferior to his own, has brought him and his terrible " Black Book " again before
the world ?—That he was celebrated, among other exploits, for raising the Devil, we are all
well aware ;—how he performed this feat—at least one, and that, perhaps, the most certain
method, by which he did it—is thus described.

Raising the Devil

A Legend of Cornelius Agrippa

" AND hast thou nerve enough ? " he said,
That grey Old Man above whose head
    Unnumber'd years had roll'd,—
" And hast thou nerve to view," he cried,
" The incarnate Fiend that Heaven defied !—
    —Art thou indeed so bold ?

" Say, canst Thou, with unshrinking gaze,
Sustain, rash youth, the withering blaze
    Of that unearthly eye,
That blasts where'er it lights,—the breath
That, like the Simoom, scatters death
    On all that yet *can* die !

—" Darest thou confront that fearful form,
That rides the whirlwind, and the storm,
   In wild unholy revel !—
The terrors of that blasted brow,
Archangel's once,—though ruin'd now—
   Ay,—dar'st thou face THE DEVIL ? "—

" I dare ! " the desperate Youth replied,
And placed him by that Old Man's side,
   In fierce and frantic glee,
Unblenched his cheek, and firm his limb ;
—" No paltry juggling Fiend, but HIM !
   —THE DEVIL !—I fain would see !—

" In all his Gorgon terrors clad,
His worst, his fellest shape ! " the Lad
   Rejoined in reckless tone.—
—" Have then thy wish ! " Agrippa said,
And sigh'd, and shook his hoary head,
   With many a bitter groan.

He drew the mystic circle's bound,
With skull and cross-bones fenc'd around ;
He traced full many a sigil there ;
He mutter'd many a backward pray'r,
   That sounded like a curse—
" He comes ! " he cried, with wild grimace,
" The fellest of Apollyon's race ! "—
—Then in his startled pupil's face
   He dash'd—an EMPTY PURSE ! !

One more legend, and then, gentle Reader, " A Merry Christmas to you and a Happy New Year ! "—We have travelled over many lands together, and had many a good-humoured laugh by the way ;—if we have, occasionally, been " more merry than wise," at least we have not jostled our neighbours on the road,—much less have we kicked any one into a ditch.

So wishing you heartily all the compliments of the season,—and thanking you cordially for your good company, I, Thomas Ingoldsby, bid you heartily farewell, and leave you in that of

Saint Medard

A Legend of Afric

"Heus tu! inquit Diabolus, hei mihi! fessis insuper humeris reponenda est sarcina; fer opem, quæso!"

"Le Diable a des vices;—c'est là ce qui le perd.—Il est gourmand. Il eut dans cette minute-là l'idée de joindre l'âme de Medard aux autres âmes qu'il allait emporter.—Se rejeter en arrière, saisir de sa main droite son poignard, et en percer l'outre avec une violence, et une rapidité formidable,—c'est ce que fit Medard.—Le Diable poussa un grand cri. Les âmes délivrés s'enfuirent par l'issue que le poignard venait de leur ouvrir, laissant dans l'outre leurs noirceurs, leurs crimes, et leurs méchancetés," &c. &c.

In good King Dagobert's palmy days,
 When Saints were many, and sins were few,
  Old Nick, 'tis said, Was sore bested
One evening,—and could not tell what to do.—

He had been East, and he had been West,
 And far had he journey'd o'er land and sea;
  For women and men Were warier then,
And he could not catch one where now he'd catch three.

He had been north, and he had been South,
 From Zembla's shores unto far Peru,
  Ere he fill'd the sack Which he bore on his back—
Saints were so many, and sins so few!

The way was long, and the day was hot;
 His wings were weary; his hoofs were sore;
  And scarce could he trail His nerveless tail,
As it furrowed the sand on the Red-Sea shore!

The day had been hot, and the way was long;
 —Hoof-sore, and weary, and faint was he;
  He lower'd his sack, And the *heat of his back*,
As he leaned on a palm-trunk, blasted the tree!

420

He sat himself down in the palm-tree's shade,
  And he gaz'd, and he grinn'd in pure delight,
    As he peep'd inside The buffalo's hide
He had sewn for a sack, and had cramm'd so tight.

For, though he'd " gone over a good deal of ground,"
  And game had been scarce, he might well report
    That still he had got A decentish lot,
And had had, on the whole, not a bad day's sport.

He had pick'd up in France a *Maître de Danse,*—
  A Maîtresse en titre,—two smart *Grisettes,*
    A Courtier at play,— And an English *Roué*—
Who had bolted from home without paying his debts.—

—He had caught in Great Britain a Scrivener's clerk,
  A Quaker,—a Baker,—a Doctor of Laws,—
    And a Jockey of York—But Paddy from Cork
" Desaved the ould divil," and slipp'd through his claws !

In Moscow, a Boyar knouting his wife
  —A Corsair's crew, in the Isles of Greece—
    And, under the dome Of St. Peter's, at Rome,
He had snapp'd up a nice little Cardinal's Niece.—

He had bagg'd an Inquisitor fresh from Spain—
  A mendicant Friar—of Monks a score ;
    A grave Don or two, And a Portuguese Jew,
Whom he nabb'd while clipping a new Moidore.

And he said to himself, as he lick'd his lips,
  " Those nice little Dears ! what a delicate roast !—
    —Then, that fine fat Friar, At a very quick fire,
Dress'd like a Woodcock, and serv'd on toast ! "

—At the sight of tit-bits so toothsome and choice
  Never did mouth water more than Nick's ;
    But,—alas ! and alack !— He had stuff'd his sack
So full that he found himself quite " in a fix : "

For, all he could do, or all he could say,
  When, a little recruited, he rose to go,
    Alas! and alack! he could *not* get the sack
Up again on his shoulders " whether or no ! "

Old Nick look'd East, old Nick look'd West,
  With many a stretch, and with many a strain,
    He bent till his back   Was ready to crack,
And he pull'd and he tugg'd,—but he tugg'd in vain.

Old Nick look'd North, old Nick look'd South ;
  —Weary was Nicholas, weak, and faint,—
    And he was aware   Of an old man there,
In Palmer's weeds, who look'd much like a Saint.

Nick eyed the Saint,—then he eyed the Sack—
  The greedy old glutton !—And thought, with a grin,
    " Dear heart alive !   If I could but contrive
To pop that elderly gentleman in !—

" For, were I to choose among all the *ragoûts*
  The *cuisine* can exhibit—flesh, fowl, or fish,—
    To myself I can paint,   That a barbecued Saint ·
Would be for my palate the best side-dish ! "

Now St. Medard dwelt on the banks of the Nile,
  —In a Pyramis fast by the lone Red Sea.
    (We call it " Semiramis,"   Why not say Pyramis ?—
Why should we change the S into a D ?)

St. Medard, he was a holy man,
  A holy man I ween was he,
    And even by day,   When he went to pray,
He would light up a candle, that all might see !

He *salaam'd* to the East, he *salaam'd* to the West ;—
  —Of the gravest cut, and the holiest brown
    Were his Palmer's weeds,—And he finger'd his beads
With the right side up, and the wrong side down.—

     *   *   *   *   *

    (*Hiatus in MSS. valde deflendus.*)

St. Medard dwelt on the banks of the Nile ;—
  He had been living there years fourscore,—
    And now, " taking the air, And saying a pray'r,"
  He was walking at eve on the Red-Sea shore.

Little he deem'd—that Holy man !—
  Of old Nick's wiles, and his fraudful tricks,—
    When he was aware Of a Stranger there,
  Who seem'd to have got himself into a fix.

Deeply that Stranger groan'd and sigh'd,
  That wayfaring Stranger, grisly and grey :—
    " I can't raise my sack On my poor old back !—
  Oh ! lend me a lift, kind Gentleman, pray !—

" For I have been East, and I have been West,
  Foot-sore, weary, and faint am I,
    And, unless I get home Ere the Curfew bome,
  Here in this desert I well may die ! "

" Now Heav'n thee save ! "—Nick winced at the words,
  As ever he winces at words divine—
    " Now Heav'n thee save !—
    What strength I have,—
  It's little, I wis,—shall be freely thine !

" For foul befall that Christian man
  Who shall fail, in a fix—woe worth the while !—
    His hand to lend To foe, or to friend,
  Or to help a lame dog over a stile ! "—

—St. Medard hath boon'd himself for the task :
  To hoist up the sack he doth well begin ;
    But the fardel feels Like a bag full of eels,
  For the folks are all curling, and kicking within.—

St. Medard paused—he began to " smoke "—
  For a Saint—if he isn't exactly a cat,—
    Has a very good nose, As this world goes,
  And not worse than his neighbour's for " smelling a rat."

The Saint look'd up, and the Saint look'd down ;
  He " *smelt* the rat," and he " *smoked* " the trick ;
    —When he came to view   His comical shoe,
He saw in a moment his friend was Nick !

He whipp'd out his oyster-knife, broad and keen—
  A Brummagem blade which he always bore,
    To aid him to eat,   By way of a treat,
The " natives " he found on the Red-Sea shore ;—

He whipp'd out his Brummagem blade so keen,
  And he made three slits in the Buffalo's hide,
    And all its contents,
      Through the rents, and the vents,
Came tumbling out,—and away they all hied !

Away went the Quaker,—away went the Baker,
  Away went the Friar—that fine fat Ghost,
    Whose marrow Old Nick   Had intended to pick,
Dress'd like a Woodcock, and served on toast !

—Away went the nice little Cardinal's Niece,—
   And the pretty *Grisettes*,—and the Dons from Spain,—
     And the Corsair's Crew,
     And the coin-clipping Jew,—
And they scamper'd, like lamplighters, over the plain.—

—Old Nick is a black-looking fellow at best,
   Ay, e'en when he's pleased ; but never before
     Had he look'd *so* black As on seeing his sack
Thus cut into slits on the Red-Sea shore.

You may fancy his rage, and his deep despair,
   When he saw himself thus befool'd by one
     Whom, in anger wild He profanely styled
" A stupid old snuff-colour'd Son of a gun ! "

Then his supper—so nice !—that had cost him such pains—
   —Such a hard day's work—now " all on the go ! "
     —'Twas beyond a joke, And enough to provoke
The mildest and best-temper'd Fiend below !

Nick snatch'd up one of those great big stones,
   Found in such numbers on Egypt's plains,
     And he hurl'd it straight At the Saint's bald pate,
To knock out " the gruel he call'd his brains."

Straight at his pate he hurl'd the weight,
   The crushing weight of that great big stone ;—
     But Saint Medard Was remarkably hard
And solid about the parietal bone.

And though the whole weight of that great big stone
   Came straight on his pate, with a great big thump,
     It fail'd to graze The skin,—or to raise
On the tough epidermis a lump, or bump !—

As the hail bounds off from the pent-house slope,—
   As the cannon recoils when it sends its shot,—
     As the finger and thumb Of an old woman come
From the kettle she handles, and finds too hot ;—

—Or, as you may see, in the Fleet, or the Bench,—
　—Many folks do in the course of their lives,—
　　The well-struck ball　Rebound from the wall,
When the Gentlemen jail-birds are playing at " fives : "

All these,—and a thousand fine similes more,—
　Such as all have heard of, or seen, or read
　　Recorded in print,　May give you a hint
How the stone bounced off from St. Medard's head !

—And it curl'd, and it twirl'd, and it whirl'd in air,
　As this great, big stone at a tangent flew !—
　　—Just missing his crown,　It at last came down
Plump upon Nick's Orthopedical shoe !

Oh ! what a yell and a screech were there !—
　How did he hop, skip, bellow, and roar !
　　—" Oh dear ! oh dear ! "—
　You might hear him here,
Though we're such a way off from the Red-Sea shore !

It smash'd his shin, and it smash'd his hoof,
　Notwithstanding his stout Orthopedical shoe ;
　　And this is the way　That, from that same day,
Old Nick became what the French call *Boiteux !*

Quakers, and Bakers, *Grisettes*, and Friars,
　And Cardinal's Nieces,—wherever ye be,
　　St. Medard bless !　You can scarcely do less
If you of your *corps* possess any *esprit.*—

And, mind and take care, yourselves,—and beware
　How you get in Nick's buffalo bag !—if you do,
　　I very much doubt　If you'll ever get out,
Now sins are so many, and Saints so few ! !

MORAL.

Gentle reader, attend To the voice of a friend !
And if ever you go to Herne Bay or Southend,
Or any gay Wat'ring-place outside the Nore,
Don't walk out at eve on the lone sea-shore ;
—Unless you're too Saintly to care about Nick,
And are sure that your head is sufficiently thick !—

Learn not to be greedy !—and, when you've enough,
Don't be anxious your bags any tighter to stuff—
Recollect that good fortune too far you may push,
And, " A BIRD IN THE HAND IS WORTH TWO IN THE BUSH ! "
Then turn not each thought to increasing your store,
Nor look always like " Oliver asking for more ! "

Gourmandise is a vice—a sad failing, at least ;—
So remember " Enough is as good as a feast ! "—
And don't set your heart on " stew'd," " fried," " boil'd," or
      " roast,"
Nor on delicate " Woodcocks served up upon toast ! "

Don't give people nick-names !—don't, even in fun,
Call any one " snuff-coloured son of a gun ! "
Nor fancy, because a man *nous* seems to lack,
That, whenever you please, you can " give him the sack ! "

Last of all, as you'd thrive, and still sleep in whole bones,
IF YOU'VE ANY GLASS WINDOWS, NEVER THROW STONES ! ! !

Third Series

The Lord of Thoulouse

A Legend of Languedoc

Veluti in speculum.
Theatre Royal, Cov. Gard.

COUNT RAYMOND rules in Languedoc,
  O'er the champaign fair and wide,
With town and stronghold many a one,
Wash'd by the wave of the blue Garonne,
And from far Auvergne to Rousillon,
  And away to Narbonne,
  And the mouths of the Rhone ;
And his Lyonnois silks and his Narbonne honey,
Bring in his lordship a great deal of money.

A thousand lances, stout and true,
Attend Count Raymond's call ;
And Knights and Nobles, of high degree,
From Guienne, Provence, and Burgundy,
Before Count Raymond bend the knee,
  And vail to him one and all.

And Isabel of Arragon
  He weds, the Pride of Spain,
You might not find so rich a prize,
A Dame so " healthy, wealthy, and wise ; "
So pious withal—with such beautiful eyes—
So exactly the Venus de Medicis' size
  In all that wide domain.

Then his cellar is stored   As well as his board,
With the choicest of all *La Belle France* can afford ;

428

Chambertin, Château Margaux, La Rose, and Lafitte,
With Moet's Champagne, " of the Comet year," " neat
As imported,"—" fine sparkling,"—and not over sweet ;
While his Chaplain, good man, when call'd in to say grace,
Would groan, and put on an elongated face
At such turtle, such turbot, John Dory, and plaice ;
Not without blushing, pronouncing a benison,
Worthy old soul ! on such *very* fat venison,
Sighing to think   Such victuals and drink
Are precisely the traps by which Satan makes men his own,
And grieving o'er scores   Of huge barbecued Boars,
Which he thinks should not darken a Christian man's doors,
Though 'twas all very well Pagan Poets should rate 'em
As "*Animal propter convivia natum.*"

He was right, I must say,   For at this time of day,
When we're not so precise, whether cleric or lay,
With respect to our food, as in time so *passé*,
We still find our Boars, whether grave ones or gay,
After dinner, at least, very much in the way,
(We spell the word now with an E, not an A ;)
And as honest *Père Jacques* was inclined to spare diet, he
Gave this advice to all grades of society,
" Think less of pudding—and think more of piety."

As to his clothes,   Oh ! nobody knows
What lots the Count had of cloaks, doublets, and hose,
Pantoufles, with bows   Each as big as a rose,
And such shirts, with lace ruffles, such waistcoats, and those
Indescribable garments it is not thought right
To do more than whisper to *oreilles* polite.

Still, in spite of his power, and in spite of his riches,
In spite of his dinners, his dress, and his——which is
The strangest of all things—in spite of his Wife,
The Count led a rather hum-drum sort of life.
He grew tired, in fact, of mere eating and drinking,
Grew tired of flirting, and ogling, and winking
At nursery maids   As they walk'd the Parades,
The Crescents, the Squares, and the fine Colonnades,
And the other gay places, which young ladies use
As their *promenade* through the good town of Thoulouse.

He was tired of hawking, and fishing, and hunting,
Of billiards, short-whist, chicken-hazard, and punting ;
   Of popping at pheasants,   Quails, woodcocks, and—peasants :
   Of smoking, and joking,   And soaking, provoking
   Such headaches next day   As his fine St. Peray,
Though the best of all Rhone wines can never repay,
Till weary of war, women, roast-goose, and glory,
With no great desire to be " famous in story,"
   All the day long,   This was his song,
     " Oh, dear ! what will become of us ?
      Oh, dear ! what shall we do ?
   We shall die of blue devils if some of us
     Can't hit on something that's new ! "

Meanwhile his sweet Countess, so pious and good,
Such pomps and such vanities stoutly eschew'd,
With all fermented liquors and high-seasoned food,
Deviled kidneys, and sweetbreads, and ducks and green peas ;
Baked sucking-pig, goose, and all viands like these,
Hash'd calf's-head included, no longer could please,
A curry was sure to elicit a breeze,
So was ale, or a glass of port-wine after cheese,
   Indeed, anything strong,
   As to tipple, was wrong ;
She stuck to " fine Hyson," " Bohea," and " Souchong,"
And similar imports direct from Hong Kong.
In vain does the family doctor exhort her
To take with her chop one poor half-pint of porter ;
   No !—she alleges   She's taken the pledges !
   Determined to aid   In a gen'ral Crusade
Against publicans, vintners, and all of that trade
And to bring in sherbet, ginger-pop, lemonade,
Eau sucrée, and drinkables mild and home-made ;
So she claims her friends' efforts, and vows to devote all hers
Solely to found " The Thoulousian Teetotalers."
   Large sums she employs
   In dressing small boys
In long duffle jackets, and short corduroys,
And she boxes their ears when they make too much noise ;
In short, she turns out a complete Lady Bountiful,
Filling with drugs and brown Holland the county full.

Now just at the time when our story commences,
   It seems that a case   Past the common took place,
To entail on her ladyship further expenses,
In greeting with honour befitting his station
The Prior of Arles, with a Temperance Legation,
Despatched by Pope Urban, who seized this occasion
To aid in diluting that part of the nation,
   An excellent man,   One who stuck to his can
Of cold water " without "—and he'd take such a lot of it ;
   None of your sips   That just moisten the lips ;
At one single draught he'd toss off a whole pot of it,
   No such bad thing
   By the way, if they bring
It you iced, as at Verrey's, or fresh from the spring,
When the Dog Star compels folks in town to take wing,
Though I own even then I should see no great sin in it,
Were there three drops of Sir Felix's gin in it.

Well, leaving the lady to follow her pleasure,
And finish the pump with the Prior at leisure,
Let's go back to Raymond, still bored beyond measure,
   And harping away   On the same dismal lay,
     " Oh, dear ! what will become of us ?
     Oh, dear ! what can we do ?
    We shall die of blue devils if some of us
     Can't find out something that's new ! "
At length in despair of obtaining his ends
By his own mother wit, he takes courage, and sends,
Like a sensible man as he is, for his friends,
Not his Lyndhursts or Eldons, or any such high sirs,
But only a few of his " backstairs " advisers ;
   " Come hither," says he, " My gallants so free,
My bold Rigmarole, and my brave Rigmaree,
And my grave Baron Proser, now listen to me !
You three can't but see I'm half dead with *ennui*.
   What's to be done ?   I *must* have some fun,
And I will too, that's flat—ay, as sure as a gun.
So find me out ' something new under the sun,'
Or I'll knock your three jobbernowls all into one !—
   You three   Agree !   Come, what shall it be ?
   Resolve me—propound in three skips of a flea ! "

Rigmarole gave a " Ha ! " Rigmaree gave a " Hem ! "
They look'd at Count Raymond—Count Raymond at them,
As much as to say, " Have you *nihil ad rem ?* "
   At length Baron Proser
   Responded, " You know, sir,
That question's some time been a regular poser ;
   Dear me !—Let me see,—   In the way of a ' spree '
Something new ?—Eh !—No !—Yes !——*No !*—'tis really no go, sir."
   Says the Count, " Rigmarole,
   You're as jolly a soul,
On the whole, as King Cole, with his pipe and his bowl ;
Come, I'm sure you'll devise something novel and droll."—
In vain—Rigmarole with a look most profound,
With his hand to his heart and his eye to the ground,
Shakes his head as if nothing was there to be found.
   " I can only remark,   That as touching a ' lark '
I'm as much as your Highness can be, in the dark ;
I can hit on no novelty—none, on my life,
Unless, peradventure, you'd ' tea ' with your wife ! "
   Quoth Raymond, " Enough !
   Nonsense !—humbug !—fudge !—stuff !
Rigmarole, you're an ass,—you're a regular Muff !
Drink tea with her ladyship ?—I ?—not a bit of it !
Call you that fun ?—faith I can't see the wit of it ;
   Mort de ma vie !   My dear Rigmaree,
You're the man, after all,—come, by way of a fee,
If you will but be bright, from the simple degree
Of a knight I'll create you at once a *Mar-quis !*
Put your conjuring cap on—consider and see,
If you can't beat that stupid old ' Sumph ' with his ' tea ! ' "

   " That's the thing ! that will do !
   Ay, marry, that's new ! "
Cries Rigmaree, rubbing his hands, " that will please—
My ' *Conjuring cap* '—it's the thing ;—it's ' the cheese ! '
It was only this morning I picked up the news ;
Please your Highness a *Conjuror's* come to Thoulouse ;
   I'll defy you to name us   A man half so famous
For devildoms,—Sir, it's the great Nostradamus !
Cornelius Agrippa 'tis said went to school to him
Gyngell's an ass, and old Faustus a fool to him,

Talk of Lilly, Albertus, Jack Dee !—pooh ! all six
He'd soon put in a pretty particular fix ;
Why, he'd beat at digesting a sword, or ' Gun tricks '
The great Northern Wizard himself all to sticks !
    I should like to see you Try to *sauter le coup*
With this chap at short whist, or unlimited loo,
By the Pope you'd soon find it a regular ' Do : '
Why, he does as he likes with the cards,—when he's got 'em,
There's always an Ace or a King at the bottom ;
Then for casting Nativities !—only you look
At the volume he's published,—that wonderful book !
In all France not another, to swear I dare venture, is
Like, by long chalks, his ' Prophetical Centuries '—
Don't you remember how, early last summer, he
Warned the late King 'gainst the Tournament mummery ?
Didn't his Majesty call it all flummery,
    Scorning The warning, And get the next morning
His poke in the eye from that clumsy Montgomery ?
    Why, he'll tell you before You're well inside his door,
All you're Highness may wish to be up to, and more ! "

" Bravo !—capital !—come, let's disguise ourselves—quick !
—Fortune's sent him on purpose here, just in the nick ;
We'll see if old Hocus will smell out the trick ;
Let's start off at once—Rigmaree, you're a Brick ! "

    The moon in gentle radiance shone
      O'er lowly roof and lordly bower,
      O'er holy pile and armed tower,
    And danced upon the blue Garonne :
    Through all that silver'd city fair,
    No sound disturbed the calm, cool air,
      Save the lover's sigh alone !
    Or where, perchance, some slumberer's nose
    Proclaim'd the depth of his repose,
    Provoking from connubial toes
      A hint—or elbow bone ;
It might, with such trifling exceptions, be said,
That Thoulouse was as still as if Thoulouse were dead,
And her " oldest inhabitant " buried in lead.

        2 E

But hark ! a sound invades the ear,
Of horses' hoofs advancing near !
They gain the bridge—they pass—they're here !
   Side by side   Two strangers ride,
For the streets in Thoulouse are sufficiently wide,
That is I'm assured they are—not having tried.
   —See, now they stop   Near an odd looking shop,
And they knock, and they ring, and they won't be denied.
   At length the command   Of some unseen hand
     Chains, and bolts, and bars obey,
     And the thick-ribbed oaken door, old and grey,
     In the pale moonlight gives, slowly, way.

They leave their steeds to a page's care,
Who comes mounted behind on a Flanders mare,
And they enter the house, that resolute pair,
With a blundering step but a dare-devil air,
And ascend a long, darksome, and rickety stair ;
While, armed with a lamp that just helps you to see
How uncommonly dark a place can be,
The grimmest of lads with the grimmest of grins,
Says, " Gentlemen, please to take care of your shins !
Who ventures this road need be firm on his pins !
Now turn to the left—now turn to the right—
Now a step—now stoop—now again upright—
Now turn once again, and directly before ye
's the door of the great Doctor's Labora-tory."

   A word ! a blow !   And in they go !
No time to prepare, or to get up a show,
Yet everything there they find quite *comme il faut :*—
Such as queer-looking bottles and jars in a row,
Retorts, crucibles, such as all conjurors stow
In the rooms they inhabit, huge bellows to blow
The fire burning blue with its sulphur and tow ;
From the roof a huge crocodile hangs rather low,
With a tail such as that which, we all of us know,
Mr. Waterton managed to tie in a bow ;
Pickled snakes, potted lizards, in bottles and basins,
Like those at Morel's, or at Fortnum and Mason's,
All articles found, you're aware without telling,
In every respectable conjuror's dwelling.

Looking solemn and wise,   Without turning his eyes,
Or betraying the slightest degree of surprise,
In the midst sits the doctor—his hair is white,
And his cheek is wan—but his glance is bright,
And his long black roquelaure, not over-tight,
Is marked with strange characters much, if not quite,
Like those on the bottles of green and blue light
Which you see in a chymist's shop-window at night.
His figure is tall and erect—rather spare about
Ribs,—and no wonder—such folks never care about
  Eating or drinking,   While reading and thinking,
Don't fatten—his age might be sixty or thereabout.

Raising his eye so grave and so sage,
From some manuscript work of a bygone age,
The seer very composedly turns down the page
  Then shading his sight,   With his hand from the light,
Says, " Well, Sirs, what would you at this time of night ?
What brings you abroad these lone chambers to tread,
When all sober folks are at home and abed ? "
  " Trav'lers we,   In our degree,
  All strange sights we fain would see,
  And hither we come in company ;
We have far to go, and we come from far,
Through Spain and Portingale, France and Navarre ;
  We have heard of your name,
  And your fame, and our aim,
Great Sir, is to witness, ere yet we depart
From Thoulouse,—and to-morrow at cock-crow we start—
Your skill—we would fain crave a touch of your art ! "

" Now naye, now naye—no trav'lers ye !
     Nobles ye be   Of high degree !
With half an eye that one may easily see,—
Count Raymond, your servant !—Yours, Lord Rigmaree !
I must call you so now since you're made a *Mar-quis ;*
Faith, clever boys both, but you can't humbug me !
     No matter for that !   I see what you'd be at—
     Well—pray no delay,   For it's late, and ere dav
I myself must be hundreds of miles on my way ;
So tell me at once what you want with me—say !
     Shall I call up the dead
     From their mouldering bed ?—
Shall I send you yourselves down to Hades instead ?—
Shall I summon old Harry himself to this spot ? "
—" Ten thousand thanks, No ! we had much rather not.
     We really can't say   That we're curious that way ;
But, in brief, if you'll pardon the trouble we're giving,
We'd much rather take a sly peep at the living ?
     Rigmaree, what say you, in   This case, as to viewing
Our spouses, and just ascertain what they're doing ? "
" Just what pleases your Highness—I don't care a *sous* in
The matter—but don't let old Nick and his crew in ! "
—" Agreed !—pray proceed then, most sage Nostradamus,
And show us our *Wives*—I dare swear they won't shame us ! "

A change comes o'er the wizard's face,
And his solemn look by degrees gives place
To a half grave, half comical, kind of grimace
     " For good or for ill, I work your will !
     Yours be the risk, and mine the skill ;
     Blame not my art if unpleasant the pill ! "

He takes from a shelf, and he pops on his head,
A square sort of cap, black, and turned up with red,
And desires not a syllable more may be said ;
     He goes on to mutter,   And stutter, and sputter
Hard words, such as no men but wizards dare utter.
     " Dies mies !—Hocus pocus—
     Adsis Demon ! non est jokus !
     Hi Cocolorum—don't provoke us !—
          Adesto !   Presto !   Put forth your best toe ! "
And many more words, to repeat which would choke us,—

Such a sniff then of brimstone !—it did not last long,
Or they could not have borne it, the smell was so strong.

A mirror is near,   So large and so clear,
If you priced such a one in a drawing-room here,
And was ask'd fifty pounds, you'd not say it was dear ;
But a mist gather'd round at the words of the Seer,
   Till at length, as the gloom,   Was subsiding, a room
On its broad polish'd surface began to appear,
And the Count and his comrade saw plainly before 'em
The room Lady Isabel called her " *Sanctorum.*"
   They start, well they might,   With surprise at the sight,
Methinks I hear some lady say, " Serve 'em right ! "
   For on one side the fire   Is seated the Prior,
   At the opposite corner a fat little Friar ;
By the side of each gentleman, easy and free,
Sits a lady, as close as close well may be,
She might almost as well have been perch'd on his knee.
   Dear me ! dear me !   Why, one's Isabel—she
On the opposite side's *La Marquise Rigmaree !*—
   To judge from the spread
   On the board, you'd have said
That the *partie quarrée* had like aldermen fed,
And now from long flasks, with necks cover'd with lead,
They were helping themselves to champagne, white and red,
   Hobbing and nobbing,   And nodding and bobbing,
   With many a sip   Both from cup and from lip,
And with many a toast followed up by a " Hip !—
   Hip !—hip !—huzzay ! "   —The Count, by the way
Though he sees all they're doing, can't hear what they say,
   Notwithstanding both he   And *Mar-quis Rigmaree*
Are so vex'd and excited at what they can *see*,
That each utters a sad word beginning with D.

   That word once spoke,   The silence broke,
In an instant the vision is cover'd with smoke !
But enough has been seen.   " Horse ! horse ! and away ! "
They have, neither, the least inclination to stay,
E'en to thank Nostradamus, or ask what's to pay.—
   They rush down the stair,
   How, they know not, nor care,

The next moment the Count is astride on his bay
And my Lord Rigmaree on his mettlesome grey;
  They dash through the town,.
  Now up, and now down,
And the stones rattle under their hoofs as they ride,
As if poor Thoulouse were as mad as Cheapside; *
  Through lane, alley, and street,
  Over all that they meet;
The Count leads the way on his courser so fleet,
My Lord Rigmaree close pursuing his beat.
With the page in the rear to protect the retreat.
Where the bridge spans the river, so wide and so deep,
Their headlong career o'er the causeway they keep,
Upsetting the watchman, two dogs, and a sweep,
All the town population that was not asleep.
They at length reached the castle, just outside the town,
Where—in peace it was usual with Knights of renown—
The portcullis was up, and the drawbridge was down.
They dash by the sentinels—" *France et Thoulouse !* "
Ev'ry soldier (—they then wore cock'd hats and long *queues*,
Appendages banish'd from modern reviews),
His arquebus lower'd, and bow'd to his shoes;
While Count Raymond pushed on to his lady's *boudoir*—he
Had made up his mind to make one at her *soirée.*
  He rush'd to that door, Where ever before
He had rapped with his knuckles, and " tirl'd at the pin."
Till he heard the soft sound of his Lady's " Come in ! "
But now, with a kick from his iron-heel'd boot,
Which, applied to a brick wall, at once had gone through't,
  He dash'd open the lock; It gave way at the shock !
(—Dear ladies, don't think, in recording the fact,
That your bard's for one moment defending the act,
No—it is not a gentleman's—none but a low body—
No—could perform it)—and there he saw—NOBODY ! !
  Nobody ? —No ! ! Oh, ho !—Oh, ho !
There was not a table, there was not a chair
Of all that Count Raymond had ever seen there
(They'd maroon-leather bottoms well stuff'd with horse hair)

* " The stones did rattle underneath
   As if Cheapside were mad."
          Gilpin's Tour in Middlesex and Herts.

That was out of its place !—There was not a trace
Of a party—there was not a dish or a plate—
No sign of a tablecloth—nothing to prate
Of a supper, *symposium*, or sitting up late ;
There was not a spark of fire left in the grate,
It had all been poked out, and remained in that state.
  If there was not a fire, Still less was there Friar,
Marquise, or long glasses, or Countess, or Prior,
And the Count, who rush'd in open-mouth'd, was struck dumb,
And could only ejaculate, " Well !—this *is* rum ! "

He rang for the maids—had them into the room,
With the butler, the footman, the coachman, the groom.
He examined them all very strictly—but no !
Notwithstanding he cross- and re-questioned them so,
'Twas in vain—it was clearly a case of " No go ! "
  " Their Lady," they said, " Had gone early to bed,
Having rather complain'd of a cold in her head—
The stout little Friar, as round as an apple,
Had pass'd the whole night in a vigil in chapel,
While the Prior himself, as he'd usually done,
Had rung in the morning, at half after one,
For his jug of cold water and twopenny bun,
And been visible, since they were brought him, to none.
  But," the servants averr'd,
  " From the sounds that were heard
To proceed now and then from the father's *sacellum*,
  They thought he was purging
  His sins with a scourging,
And making good use of his knotted *flagellum*."
  For Madame Rigmaree, They all testified, she
Had gone up to her bed-chamber soon after tea,
And they really supposed that there still she must be,
  Which her spouse, the *Mar-quis*,
  Found at once to agree
With the rest of their tale, when he ran up to see.

Alack for Count Raymond ! he could not conceive
How the case really stood, or know *what* to believe ;
Nor could Rigmaree settle to laugh or to grieve.

There was clearly a hoax,
But which of the folks
Had managed to make them the butt of their jokes,
Wife or wizard, they both knew no more than Jack Nokes ;
That glass of the wizard's
Stuck much in their gizzards,
His cap, and his queer cloak all X's and Izzards ;
Then they found, when they came to examine again,
Some slight falling off in the stock of champagne,
Small, but more than the butler could fairly explain.
However, since nothing could make the truth known,
Why,—they thought it was best to let matters alone.
The Count in the garden　Begg'd Isabel's pardon
Next morning for waking her up in a fright,
By the racket he'd kicked up at that time of night ;
And gave her his word he had ne'er misbehaved so,
Had he not come home as tipsy as David's sow.
Still, to give no occasion for family snarls,
The Friar was pack'd back to his convent at Arles,
While as for the Prior,　At Raymond's desire,
The Pope raised his rev'rence a step or two higher,
And made him a Bishop *in partibus*—where
His see was I cannot exactly declare,
Or describe his cathedral, not having been there,
But I dare say you'll all be prepared for the news,
When I say 'twas a good many miles from Thoulouse,
Where the prelate, in order to set a good precedent,
Was enjoined, as a *sine quâ non*, to be resident.
You will fancy with me,
That Count Raymond was free,
For the rest of his life, from his former *ennui ;*
Still it somehow occurr'd that as often as he
Chanced to look in the face of my Lord Rigmaree,
There was something or other—a trifling degree
Of constraint—or embarrassment—easy to see,
And which seem'd to be shared by the noble *Mar-quis,*
While the ladies—the queerest of all things by half in
My tale, never met from that hour without laughing !

MORAL.

Good gentlemen all, who are subjects of Hymen,
Don't make new acquaintances rashly, but try men,
Avoid above all things your cunning (that's sly) men !
 Don't go out o' nights To see conjuring sleights,
But shun all such people, delusion whose trade is ;
Be wise !—stay at home and take tea with the ladies.

 If you *chance* to be out, At a " regular bout,"
And get too much of " Abbot's Pale Ale " or " Brown Stout,"
Don't be cross when you come home at night to your spouse,
Nor be noisy, nor kick up a dust in the house !

Be careful yourself, and admonish your sons,
To beware of all folks who love twopenny buns !
And don't introduce to your wife or your daughter
A sleek, meek, weak gent—who subsists on cold water !

The main incident recorded in the following *excerpta* from our family papers has but too solid a foundation. The portrait of Roger Ingoldsby is not among those in the gallery, but I have some recollection of having seen, when a boy, a picture answering the description here given of him, much injured, and lying without a frame in one of the attics.

The Wedding-Day

Or, The Buccaneer's Curse

A Family Legend

IT has a jocund sound
That gleeful marriage chime,
 As from the old and ivied tower,
 It peals, at the early Matin hour,
  Its merry, merry round ;

And the Spring is in its prime,
  And the song-bird, on the spray,
  Trills from his throat, in varied note,
    An emulative lay—
      It has a joyous sound ! !
And the Vicar is there with his wig and his book,
And the Clerk with his grave, *quasi*-sanctified look,
And there stand the Village maids all with their posies,
Their lilies, and daffy-down-dillies, and roses,
  Dight in white,   A comely sight,
Fringing the path to the left and the right ;
—From our nursery days we all of us know
Ne'er doth " Our Ladye's garden grow "
So fair for a " Grand Horticultural Show "
As when border'd with " pretty maids all on a row."
And the urchins are there, escaped from the rule
Of that " Limbo of Infants," the National School,
  Whooping, and bawling,   And squalling, and calling,
  And crawling, and creeping,
  And jumping, and leaping,
Bo-peeping 'midst " many a mouldering heap " in
Whose bosom their own " rude forefathers " are sleeping ;
—Young rascals !—instead of lamenting and weeping,
  Laughing and gay,   *A gorge deployée*—
Only now and then pausing—and checking their play,
To " wonder what 'tis makes the gentlefolks stay,"
  Ah, well-a-day !   Little deem they,
Poor ignorant dears ! the bells ringing away,
  Are anything else   Than mere parish bells,
Or that each of them, should we go into its history,
Is but a " Symbol " of some deeper mystery—
  That the clappers and ropes
  Are mere practical tropes
Of " trumpets " and "tongues," and of " preachers," and
  popes,
Unless Clement the Fourth's worthy Chaplain, *Durand*, err,
See the " *Rationale*," of that goosey-gander.

  Gently ! gently, Miss Muse !
  Mind your P's and your Q's !
Don't be malapert—laugh, Miss, but never abuse !

Calling names, whether done to attack or to back a schism,
Is, Miss, believe me, a great piece of Jack-ass-ism,
    And as, on the whole,   You're a good-natured soul,
    You must never enact such a pitiful *rôle*.
No, no, Miss, pull up, and go back to your boys
In the churchyard, who're making this hubbub and noise—
But hush ! there's an end to their romping and mumming,
For voices are heard—here's the company coming !

    And see !—the avenue gates unfold,
      And forth they pace, that bridal train,
    The grave, the gay, the young, the old,
      They cross the green and grassy lane,
Bridesman, Bridesmaid, Bridegroom, Bride,
Two and two, and side by side,
Uncles, and aunts, friends tried and proved,
And cousins, a great many times removed.
    A fairer or a gentler she,
    A lovelier maid, in her degree,
    Man's eye might never hope to see,
Than darling, bonnie Maud Ingoldsby,
The flow'r of that goodly company ;
While whispering low, with bated voice,
Close by her side, her heart's dear choice,
Walks Fredville's hope, young Valentine Boys.
    —But where, oh where,—   Is Ingoldsby's heir ?
Little Jack Ingoldsby ?—where, oh where ?
    Why, he's here,—and he's there,
    And he's every where—
    He's there, and he's here ;
    In the front—in the rear,—
Now this side, now that side,—now far, and now near—
The Puck of the party, the darling " pet " boy,
Full of mischief, and fun, and good-humour and joy ;
With his laughing blue eye, and his cheek like a rose,
And his long curly locks, and his little snub nose ;
In his tunic, and trousers, and cap—there he goes !
Now pinching the bridesmen,—now teasing his sister,
And telling the bridesmaids how " Valentine kiss'd her ; "
The torment, the plague, the delight of them all,
See he's into the churchyard !—he's over the wall—

Gambolling, frolicking, capering away,
He's the first in the church, be the second who may !

*   *   *   *   *

'Tis o'er ;—the holy rite is done,
The rite that " incorporates two in one,"
—And now for the feasting, and frolic, and fun !
Spare we to tell of the smiling and sighing,
The shaking of hands, the embracing, and crying,
   The " toot—toot—toot " Of the tabour and flute
Of the white wigg'd Vicar's prolonged salute,
Or of how the blithe " College *Youths*," rather old stagers,
Accustom'd, for years, to pull bell ropes for wagers—
Rang, faster than ever, their " triple-bob-MAJORS ; "
   (So loud as to charm ye, At once and alarm ye ;
—" *Smybolic,*" of course, of that rank in the army.)

Spare we to tell of the fees and the dues
To the " little old woman that open'd the pews,"
Of the largesse bestow'd on the Sexton and Clerk,
Of the four-year-old sheep roasted whole in the park,
   Of the laughing and joking,
   The quaffing and smoking,
And chaffing, and broaching—that is to say, poking
A hole in a mighty magnificent tub
Of what men, in our hemisphere, term " Humming Bub,"
But which gods,—who, it seems, use a different lingo
From mortals,—are wont to denominate " Stingo."

Spare we to tell of the horse-collar grinning ;
The cheese ! the reward of the ugly one winning ;
Of the young ladies racing for Dutch body-linen,—
—The soapy-tail'd sow,—a rich prize when you've caught her,—
Of little boys bobbing for pippins in water ;
   The smacks and the whacks,
   And the jumpers in sacks,
These down on their noses and those on their backs ;—
Nor skills it to speak of those darling old ditties,
Sung rarely in hamlets now—never in cities,
The " *King and the Miller,*" the " *Bold Robin Hood,*"
" *Chevy Chase,*" " *Gilderoy,*" and the " *Babes in the Wood !* "
   —You'll say that my taste Is sadly misplaced,

But I can't help confessing those simple old tunes,
The " *Auld Robin Grays*," and the " *Aileen Aroons*,"
The " *Gramachree Mollys*," and the " *Sweet Bonny Doons*,"
    Are dearer to me,   In a tenfold degree,
Than a fine *fantasia* from over the sea ;
And, for sweetness, compared with a Beethoven fugue, are
As " best-refined loaf " to the coarsest " brown sugar ; " *
—Alack, for the Bard's want of Science ! to which he owes
All this misliking of foreign *capricios !*—

    Not that he'd say   One word, by the way,
To disparage our new Idol, Monsieur Duprez—
But he grudges, he owns, his departed half guinea,
Each Saturday night when, devoured by chagrin, he
Sits listening to singers whose names end in *ini.*

But enough of the rustics—let's leave them pursuing
Their out-of-door gambols, and just take a view in
The inside the hall, and see what *they* are doing ;
    And first there's the Squire,   The hale, hearty sire
Of the bride,—with his coat-tails subducted and higher,
A thought, than they're commonly wont to aspire ;
His back and his buckskins exposed to the fire ;—

    * *Ad Amicum, Servientem ad legem*—
        This rhyme, if, when scann'd by your critical ear, it
        Is not *quite* legitimate, comes pretty near it.—T. I.

—Bright, bright are his buttons,—and bright is the hue
Of his squarely cut coat of fine Saxony blue ;
And bright the shalloon of his little quilled *queue* ;
—White, white as " Young England's," the dimity vest
Which descends like an *avalanche* o'er his broad breast,
Till its further progression is put in arrest
By the portly projection that springs from his chest,
Overhanging the garment—that can't be exprest ;
—White, white are his locks,—which, had Nature fair
    play,
Had appeared a clear brown, slightly sprinkled with
    grey ;
But they're white as the peaks of Plinlimmon to-day,
Or Ben Nevis, his pate is *si bien poudré* !
Bright, bright are the boots that envelop his heels,
—Bright, bright is the gold chain suspending his seals,
And still brighter yet may the gazer descry
The tear-drop that spangles the fond Father's eye
    As it lights on the bride—
    His belov'd one—the pride
And delight of his heart,—sever'd now from his side ;—
    But brighter than all   Arresting its fall,
Is the smile, that rebukes it for spangling at all,
—A clear case, in short, of what old poets tell, as
Blind Homer for instance, εν δακρυσι γελως.

Then, there are the Bride and the Bridegroom, withdrawn
To the deep Gothic window that looks on the lawn.
Ensconced on a squab of maroon-coloured leather,
And talking—and *thinking*, no doubt—of the weather.

But here comes the party—Room ! room for the guests !
In their Pompadour coats, and laced ruffles, and vests,
    —First, Sir Charles Grandison,   Baronet, and his son,
Charles, the mamma does not venture to " show "—
    —Miss Byron, you know,   She was call'd long ago—
For that Lady, 'twas *said*, had been playing the d—l.
Last season, in town, with her old beau, Squire Greville,
Which very much shock'd, and chagrin'd, as may well be
    upposed, " Doctor Bartlett," and " Good Uncle Selby."

—Sir Charles, of course, could not give Greville his gruel, in
Order to prove his abhorrence of duelling,
Nor try for, deterr'd by the serious expense, a
Complete separation *a thoro et mensá*,
So he " kept a calm sough," and, when asked to a party,
A dance, or a dinner, or tea and *écarté*,
He went with his son, and said, looking demurely,
He'd " left her at home, as she found herself poorly."
   Two foreigners near, " Of distinction," appear ;
A pair more illustrious you ne'er heard of, or saw,
Count Ferdinand Fathom,—Count Thaddeus of Warsaw,
All cover'd with glitt'ring *bijouterie* and hair—Poles,
Whom Lord Dudley Stuart calls " Patriot,"—Hook " Bare
    Poles ; "
Such rings, and such brooches, such studs, and such pins !
   'Twere hard to say which
    Were more gorgeous and rich,
Or more truly Mosaic, their chains or their chins !
Next Sir Roger de Coverley,—Mr. Will Ramble,
With Dame Lismahago (*née* Tabitha Bramble),—
Mr. Random and Spouse—Mrs. Pamela Booby,
(Whose nose was acquiring a tinge of the ruby,
And " people *did say* "—but no matter for that . . .
Folks were not then enlighten'd by good Father Mat.)—
—Three friends from " the Colonies " near them were seen,
The great Massachusetts man, General Muff Green,—
Mr. Jonathan W. Doubikins,—men
" Influential *some*,"—and their " smart " Uncle Ben ;—
Rev. Abraham Adams (preferr'd to a stall),—
—Mr. Jones and his Lady, from Allworthy Hall ;
   —Our friend Tom, by the way,
   Had turn'd out rather gay
For a married man—certainly " people *did say*,"
He was shrewdly suspected of using his wife ill,
And being as sly as his half-brother Blifil.—
(Miss Seagrim, 'tis well known, was now in high feather,
And " people *did say*," they'd been seen out together,—
A fact, the " Boy Jones," who, in our days, with malice
Aforethought, so often got into the Palace,
Would seem to confirm, as, 'tis whispered he owns, he's
The son of a natural son of Tom Jones's.)

Lady Bellaston, (*mem.* she had not been invited !)
Sir Peregrine Pickle, now recently knighted,—
All joyous, all happy, all looking delighted !
—It would bore you to death should I pause to describe,
Or enumerate, half of the elegant tribe
   Who filled the back ground,
   And among whom were found
The *élite* of the old country families round,
Such as Honeywood, Oxenden, Knatchbull, and Norton,
Matthew Robinson,* too, with his beard from Monk's Horton,
The Faggs, and Finch-Hattons, Tokes, Derings, and Deedses,
And Fairfax, (who then called the castle of Leeds his ;)
   Esquires, Knights, and Lords,
   In bag-wigs and swords ;
   And the troops, and the groups
   Of fine Ladies in hoops ;
The *pompons*, the *toupées*, and the diamonds and feathers,
   The flowered-silk *sacques*
   Which they wore on their backs,—
—How ?—*sacques* and *pompoons*, with the Squire's boots and
    leathers ?—
   Stay ! stay !—I suspect,   Here's a trifling neglect
On your part, Madame Muse—though your commonly accurate
As to costume, as brown Quaker, or black Curate,
   For once, I confess,   Here you're out as to dress ;—
You've been fairly caught napping, which gives me distress,
For I can't but acknowledge it is not the thing,
Sir Roger de Coverley's laced suit to bring
Into contact with square-cut coats,—such as George Byng,
And poor dear Sir Francis appeared in, last spring.—
So, having for once been compelled to acknowledge, I
've made a small hole in our mutual chronology,
Canter on, Miss, without further apology,—
   Only don't make   Such another mistake,
Or you'll get in a scrape, of which I shall partake ;—
Enough !—you are sorry for what you have done,
So dry your eyes, Miss, blow your nose, and go on !

---

* A worthy and eccentric country gentleman, afterwards the second Lord Rokeby, being cousin (" a great many times removed ") and successor in the barony to Richard, Archbishop of Armagh, who first bore that title.—His beard was truly patriarchal.—Mr. Muntz's—pooh !—

Well—the party are met, all radiant and gay,
And how ev'ry person is dress'd—we won't say ;
Suffice it, they all come glad homage to pay
To our dear " bonnie Maud," on her own wedding-day,
To dance at her bridal, and help " throw the stocking,"
—A practice that's now discontinued as shocking.

There's a breakfast, they know— There always is so
On occasions like these, wheresoever you go.
Of course there are " lots " of beef, potted and hung,
Prawns, lobsters, cold fowl, and cold ham, and cold tongue,
Hot tea, and hot coffee, hot rolls, and hot toast,
Cold pigeon-pie (rook ?), and cold boil'd and cold roast,
Scotch marmalade, jellies, cold creams, colder ices—
Blancmange, which young ladies say, so very nice is,—
Rock-melons in thick, pines in much thinner slices,—
Char, potted with clarified butter and spices,
Renewing an appetite long past its crisis—
Refined barley-sugar, in various devices,
Such as bridges, and baskets, and temples, and grottoes—
And nasty French lucifer snappers with mottoes.
—In short, all these gimcracks together were met
Which people of fashion tell Gunter to get
When they give a *grand déjeuner à la fourchette*—
(A phrase which, though French, in our language still lingers,
Intending a breakfast with forks and not fingers.)
And see ! what a mountainous bridecake !—a thing
By itself—with small pieces to pass through the ring !

Now as to the wines !—" Ay, the wine ? " cries the Squire,
Letting fall both his coat-tails,—which nearly take fire,—
  Rubbing his hands,   He calls out, as he stands,
To the serving-men waiting " his Honour's " commands,
" The wine !—to be sure—here you, Harry—Bob—Dick—
The wine, don't you hear ?—bring us lights—come, be quick !—
And a crow-bar to knock down the mortar and brick—
  Say what they may,   'Fore George, we'll make way
Into old Roger Ingoldsby's cellar to-day ;
And let loose his captives, imprison'd so long,
His flasks, and his casks, that he bricked up so strong ! "—

2 F

—" Oh dear ! oh dear ! Squire Ingoldsby, bethink you what you
    do ! "
Exclaims old Mrs. Botherby,*—she is in *such* a stew !—
" Oh dear ! oh dear ! what do I hear ?—full oft you've heard me
    tell
Of the curse ' Wild Roger ' left upon whoe'er should break his cell !

" Full five-and-twenty years are gone since Roger went away,
As I bethink me, too, it was upon this very day !
And I was then a comely dame, and you, a springald gay,
Were up and down to London town, at opera, ball, and play ;
Your locks were nut-brown then, Squire—you grow a little grey !—

" ' Wild Roger,' so we call'd him then, your grandsire's youngest son,
    He was in truth   A wayward youth,
      We fear'd him, every one.
In ev'ry thing he had his will, he would be stayed by none,
And when he did a naughty thing, he laugh'd and call'd it fun !
—One day his father chid him sore—I know not what he'd done,
    But he scorn'd reproof ;   And from this roof
      Away that night he run !

" Seven years were gone and over—' Wild Roger ' came again,
He spoke of forays and of frays upon the Spanish Main ;
And he had store of gold galore, and silks, and satins fine,
And flasks and casks of Malvoisie, and precious Gascon wine !
Rich booties he had brought, he said, across the western wave,
And came, in penitence and shame, now of his sire to crave
Forgiveness and a welcome home—his sire was in his grave !

" Your Father was a kindly man—he played a brother's part,
He press'd his brother to his breast—he had a kindly heart.
Fain would he have him tarry here, their common hearth to share,
But Roger was the same man still,—he scorn'd his brother's pray'r !
He call'd his crew,—away he flew, and on those foreign shores
Got kill'd in some outlandish place—they call it the Eyesores ; †

   * Great grandmamma, by the father's side, to the excellent lady of the same name who yet
" keeps the keys " at Tappington.
   † Azores ?—Mrs. Botherby's orthography, like that of her distinguished contemporary
Baron Duberly, was a " little loose."

But ere he went, And quitted Kent,
    —I well recall the day,—
His flasks and casks of Gascon wine he safely ' stow'd away ; '
Within the cellar's deepest nook, he safely stow'd them all,
And Mason Jones brought bricks and stones, and they built up the
    wall.

" Oh ! then it was a fearful thing to hear ' Wild Roger's ' ban !
Good gracious me ! I never heard the like from mortal man ;
' Here's that,' quoth he, ' shall serve me well when I return at last,
A batter'd hulk, to quaff and laugh at toils and dangers past ;
Accurst be he, whoe'er he be, lays hand on gear of mine,
Till I come back again from sea, to broach my Gascon wine ! '
And more he said, which filled with dread all those who listen'd
    there ;
In sooth my very blood ran cold, it lifted up my hair
With very fear, to stand and hear ' Wild Roger ' curse and
    swear ! !
He saw my fright, as well he might, but still he made his game,
He called me ' Mother Bounce-about,' my Gracious, what a name !
Nay more, ' an old '—some ' boat-woman '—I may not say .for
    shame !—
Then, gentle Master, pause awhile, give heed to what I tell,
Nor break, on such a day as this, ' Wild Roger's ' secret cell ! "

" Pooh ! pooh ! " quoth the Squire,
    As he mov'd from the fire,
And bade the old Housekeeper quickly retire,
    " Pooh !—never tell me ! Nonsense—fiddle-de-dee !
What ?—wait Uncle Roger's return back from sea ?—
    Why he may, as you say,
    Have been somewhat too gay,
And, no doubt, was a broth of a boy in his way ;
But what's that to us, now, at this time of day ?
    What if some quarrel With Dering or Darrell—
—I hardly know which, but I think it was Dering,—
Sent him back in a huff to his old privateering,
Or what his unfriends chose to call Buccaneering,
It's twenty years since, as we very well know,
He was knock'd on the head in a skirmish, and so
Why rake up ' auld warld ' tales of deeds long ago ?—

—Foul befall him who would touch the deposit
Of living man, whether in cellar or closet !
   But since, as I've said,   Knock'd on the head,
Uncle Roger has now been some twenty years dead.
   As for his wine,   I'm his heir, and it's mine !
And I'd long ago work'd it well, but that I tarried
   For this very day—
   And I'm sure you'll all say
I was right—when my own darling Maud should get married !
So lights and a crow-bar !—the only thing lies
On my conscience, at all, with respect to this prize,
Is some little compunction anent the Excise—
   Come—you, Master Jack,
   Be the first, and bring back
Whate'er comes to hand—Claret, Burgundy, Sack—
Head the party, and mind that you're back in a crack ! "

   Away go the clan,   With cup and with can,
Little Jack Ingoldsby leading the van ;
Little reck they of the Buccaneer's ban :
Hope whispers, " Perchance we'll fall in with strong beer too
    here ! "
Blest thought ! which sets them all grinning from ear to ear !

Through cellar one, through cellars two,
Through cellars three they pass'd !
   And their way they took   To the farthest nook
Of cellar four—the last !—
Blithe and gay, they batter away,
   On this wedding-day of Maud's,
With all their might, to bring to light
   " Wild Roger's " " Custom-house frauds ! "
   And though stone and brick   Be never so thick,
When stoutly assailed, they are no bar
   To the powerful charm   Of a Yeoman's arm
When wielding a decentish crow-bar !
Down comes brick, and down comes stone,
   One by one—   The job's half done !—
" Where is he ?—now come—where's Master John ? "—
—There's a breach in the wall three feet by two,
And little Jack Ingoldsby soon pops through !

Hark !—what sound's that ?—a sob ?—a sigh ?—
The choking gasp of a stifled cry ?—
   —" What can it be ?—
   Let's see !—let's see !—
It *can't* be little Jack Ingoldsby ?
   The candle—quick ! "—
   Through stone and through brick
They poke in the light on a long split stick ;
But ere he who holds it can wave it about,
He gasps, and he sneezes—the LIGHT GOES OUT !

Yet were there those, in after days,
Who said that pale light's flickering blaze,
For a moment, gleam'd on a dark Form there,
Seem'd as bodied of foul black air !—
—In Mariner's dress,—with cutlass braced
By buckle and broad black belt, to its waist,—
   —On a cock'd-hat, laced   With gold, and placed
With a *degagée*, devil-may-care, kind of taste,
O'er a *balafré* brow by a scar defaced !—
That Form, they said, so foul and so black,
Grinn'd as it pointed at poor little Jack.—
—I know not, I, how the truth may be,
But the pent-up vapour, at length set free,
   Set them all sneezing,   And coughing, and wheezing,
   As, working its way   To the regions of day,
It, at last, let a purer and healthier breeze in !

   Of their senses bereft,   To the right and the left,
Those varlets so lately courageous and stout,
There they lay kicking and sprawling about,
Like Billingsgate fresh fish, unconscious of ice,
Or those which, the newspapers give us advice,
Mr. Taylor, of Lombard-street, sells at half-price ;
—Nearer the door, some half dozen or more !
   Scramble away   To the *rez de chaussée*,
(As our Frenchified friend always calls his ground-floor,)
And they call, and they bawl, and they bellow and roar
For lights, vinegar, brandy, and fifty things more.
At length, after no little clamour and din,
The foul air let out, and the fresh air let in,

They drag one and all   Up into the hall,
Where a medical Quaker, the great Dr. Lettsom,
Who's one of the party, " bleeds, physics, and sweats 'em."
    All ?—all—save One—   —" But He !—my Son ?—
Merciful Heaven !—where—WHERE IS JOHN ? "

    *   *   *   *   *

Within that cell, so dark and deep,
Lies One, as in a tranquil sleep,
A sight to make the sternest weep !—
—That little heart is pulseless now,
And cold that fair and open brow,
And closed that eye that beam'd with joy
And hope—" Oh, God !—my Boy !—my Boy ! "

Enough !—I may not,—dare not,—show
The wretched Father's frantic woe,
The Mother's tearless, speechless—No !
I may not such a theme essay—
Too bitter thoughts crowd in and stay
My pen—sad memory will have way !
Enough !—at once I close the lay,
Of fair Maud's fatal Wedding-day !

It has a mournful sound,
    That single, solemn Bell !
As to the hills and woods around
    It flings its deep-toned knell !
That measured toll !—alone—apart,
It strikes upon the human heart !
—It has a mournful sound !—

MORAL.

Come, come, Mrs. Muse, we can't part in this way,
Or you'll leave me as dull as ditch-water all day.
Try and squeeze out a Moral or two from your lay !
And let us part cheerful, at least, if not gay !

First and foremost then, Gentlefolks, learn from my song,
Not to lock up your wine, or malt-liquor, too long !

Though Port should have age,
  Yet I don't think it sage
To entomb it, as some of your *connoisseurs* do,
Till it's losing in flavour, and body, and hue ;
—I question if keeping it does it much good
After ten years in bottle and three in the wood.

If any young man, though a snubb'd younger brother,
When told of his faults by his father and mother,
Runs restive, and goes off to sea in a huff,
Depend on't, my friends, that young man is a Muff !

Next—ill-gotten gains   Are not worth the pains !—
They prosper with no one !—so whether cheroots,
Or Havanna cigars,—or French gloves, or French boots,—
Whatever you want, pay the duty ! nor when you
Buy any such articles, cheat the revenue !

And " now to conclude,"—
  For it's high time I should,—
When you *do* rejoice, mind,—whatsoever you do,
That the hearts of the lowly rejoice with you too !—
  Don't grudge them their jigs,
  And their frolics and " rigs,"
And don't interfere with their soapy-tail'd pigs ;
Nor " because thou art virtuous," rail, and exhale
An *anathema*, breathing of vengeance and wail,
Upon every complexion less pale than sea-kale !
Nor dismiss the poor man to his pump and his pail,
With " Drink *there* !—we'll have henceforth no more cakes
  and ale ! ! "

Mox Regina filium peperit a multis optatum et a Deo sanctificatum. Cumque Infans natus fuisset, statim clarâ voce, omnibus audientibus, clamavit " *Christianus sum! Christianus sum! Christianus sum!*" Ad hanc vocem Presbyteri duo, Widerinus et Edwoldus, dicentes *Deo Gratias*, et omnes qui aderant mirantes, cœperunt cantare *Te Deum laudamus.* Quo facto rogabat Infans cathecumenum a Widerino sacerdote fieri, et ab Edwoldo teneri ad præsignaculum fidei et Romwoldum vocari.—Nov. Legend. Angl in Vita Scti. Romualdi.

The Blasphemer's Warning

A Lay of St. Romwold

In Kent, we are told, There was seated of old,
A handsome young gentleman, courteous and bold,
He'd an oaken strong-box, well-replenish'd with gold,
With broad lands, pasture, arable, woodland, and wold,
Not an acre of which had been mortgaged or sold ;
He'd a Pleasaunce and Hall passing fair to behold,
He had beeves in the byre, he had flocks in the fold,
And was somewhere about five-and-twenty years old.
His figure and face, For beauty and grace,
To the best in the county had scorn'd to give place.
Small marvel, then, If, of women and men
Whom he chanced to foregather with, nine out of ten
Express'd themselves charm'd with Sir Alured Denne.

From my earliest youth,
I've been taught, as a truth,
A maxim which most will consider as sooth,
Though a few, peradventure, may think it uncouth ;
There are three social duties, the whole of the swarm
In this great human hive of ours, ought to perform,
And that too as soon as conveniently may be ;
The first of the three— Is, the planting a Tree !
The next, the producing a Book—then, a Baby !
(For my part, dear Reader, without any jesting, I
So far at least, have accomplished my destiny.)

From the foremost, *i.e.*, The " planting the Tree,"
The Knight may, perchance, have conceiv'd himself free,
Inasmuch as that, which way soever he looks,
Over park, mead, or upland, by streamlets and brooks,
His fine beeches and elms shelter thousands of rooks ;
In twelve eighty-two, There would also accrue
Much latitude as to the article, Books ;
But, if those we've disposed of, and need not recall,
Might, as duties, appear in comparison small,

One remain'd, there was no getting over at all,
—The providing a male Heir for Bonnington Hall;
Which, doubtless, induced the good Knight to decide,
As a matter of conscience, on taking a Bride.

It's a very fine thing, and delightful to see
Inclination and duty unite and agree,
   Because it's a case   That so rarely takes place;
In the instance before us, then, Alured Denne
Might well be esteem'd the most lucky of men,
   Inasmuch as hard by,   Indeed so very nigh,
That her chimneys, from his, you might almost descry,
Dwelt a Lady at whom he'd long cast a sheep's eye,
One whose character scandal itself could defy,
While her charms and accomplishments rank'd very high,
   And who would not deny   A propitious reply,
But reflect back his blushes, and gave sigh for sigh.
(A line that's not mine, but Tom Moore's, by-the-bye.)

There was many a gay and trim bachelor near,
Who felt sick at heart when the news met his ear,
That fair Edith Ingoldsby, she whom they all
The " Rosebud of Tappington " ceas'd not to call,
   Was going to say,   " Honour, love and obey "
To Sir Alured Denne, Knight, of Bonnington Hall,
That all other suitors were left in the lurch,
And the parties had even been " out-asked " in church.
   For every one says,   In those primitive days,
And I must own I think it redounds to their praise,
None dream'd of transferring a daughter or niece,
As a bride, by an " unstamp'd agreement " or lease,
'Fore a Register's Clerk, or a Justice of Peace,
   While young ladies had fain   Single women remain,
And unwedded maids to the last " crack of doom " stick
Ere marry, by taking a jump o'er a broomstick.

So our bride and bridegroom agreed to appear
At holy St. Romwold's, a Priory near,
Which a long while before, I can't say in what year,
Their forebears had join'd with the neighbours to rear,

And endow'd, some with bucks, some with beef, some with beer,
To comfort the friars, and make them good cheer.
   Adorning the building,   With carving and gilding,
And stone altars, fix'd to the chantries and fill'd in ;
(Papistic in substance and form, and on this count
With Judge Herbert Jenner Fust justly at discount.
See *Cambridge Societas Camdeniensis*
V. *Faulkner, tert. prim. Januarii mensis,*
With " Judgment reversed, costs of suit, and expenses ; ")
All raised to St. Romwold, with some reason styled
By Duke Humphrey's confessor,* " a Wonderful Child,"
For ne'er yet was Saint, except him, upon earth
Who made his " profession of faith " at his birth,
And when scarce a foot high, or six inches in girth,
Converted his " Ma," and contrived to amend a
Sad hole in the creed of his grandsire, King Penda

   Of course to the shrine   Of so young a divine
Flow'd much holy water, and some little wine,
And when any young folks did to marriage incline,
The good friars were much in request, and not one
Was more " sought unto " than the Sub-Prior, Mess John ;
   To him, there and then,   Sir Alured Denne
Wrote a three-corner'd note with a small crow-quill pen,
To say what he wanted, and fix " the time when,"
And, as it's well known that your people of quality
Pique themselves justly on strict punctuality,
Just as the clock struck the hour he'd nam'd in it,
The whole bridal party rode up to the minute.

Now whether it was that some rapturous dream,
Comprehending " fat pullets and clouted cream,"
Had borne the good man, in his vision of bliss,
Far off to some happier region than this—
Or whether his beads, 'gainst the fingers rebelling,
Took longer than usual that morning in telling ;
Or whether, his conscience with knotted cord purging,
Mess John was indulging himself with a scourging,

---

* Honest John Capgrave, the veracious biographer of " English Saints," author, or rather compiler of the " Nova Legenda Angliæ," was chaplain to Humphrey, " the Good Duke " of Gloucester.   A beautiful edition of his work was printed by Wynkyn de Worde.

In penance for killing some score of the fleas,
Which, infesting his hair-shirt, deprived him of ease,
Or whether a barrel of Faversham oysters,
Brought in, on the evening before, to the cloisters,
   Produced indigestion,   Continues a question,
The particular case is not worth a debate ;
For my purpose it's clearly sufficient to state
That whatever the reason, his rev'rence *was* late.
   And Sir Alured Denne,   Not the meekest of men,
Began banning away at a deuce of a rate.

Now here, though I do it with infinite pain,
Gentle reader, I find I must pause to explain
   That there was—what, I own,
   I grieve to make known—
On the worthy Knight's character one single stain,
But for which, all his friends had borne witness, I'm sure,
He had been *sans reproche*, as he still was *sans peur.*
The fact is, that many distinguish'd commanders
" Swore terribly " (*teste* T. Shandy) " in Flanders."
Now into these parts our Knight chancing to go, countries
Named from this sad, vulgar custom, " The *Low* Countries,"
Though on common occasions as courteous as daring,
Had pick'd up this shocking bad habit of swearing.
And if anything vex'd him, or matters went wrong,
Was given to what low folks call " Coming it strong."
Good, bad, or indifferent then, young or old,
He'd consign them, when once in a humour to scold,
To a place where they certainly would not take cold.
—Now if there are those, and I've some in my eye,
Who'd esteem this a crime of no very deep dye,
Let them read on—they'll find their mistake by-and-bye.

   Near or far,   Few people there are
But have heard, read, or sung about Young Lochinvar,
How in Netherby Chapel, " at morning tide,"
The Priest and the Bridegroom stood waiting the Bride ;
   How they waited, " but ne'er   A Bride was there."
Still I don't find, on reading the ballad with care,
The bereaved Mr. Graham proceeded to swear,

And yet to experience so serious a blight in
One's dearest affections, is somewhat exciting.
    'Tis manifest then   That Sir Alured Denne
Had far less excuse for such bad language, when
It was only the Priest not the Bride who was missing—
He had fill'd up the interval better with kissing,
    And 'twas really surprising,   And not very wise in
A Knight to go on so anathematising,
When the head and the front of the Clergyman's crime
Was but being a little behind as to time :—
    Be that as it may,   He swore so that day
At the reverend gentleman's ill-judged delay,
That not a bystander who heard what he said,
But listen'd to all his expressions with dread,
And felt all his hair stand on end on his head ;
    Nay, many folks there   Did not stick to declare
The phenomenon was not confined to the hair,
For the little stone Saint who sat perched o'er the door,
St. Romwold himself, as I told you before,
    What will scarce be believed,   Was plainly perceived
To shrug up his shoulders, as very much grieved,
    And look down with a frown   So remarkably brown,
That all saw he'd now quite a different face on
From that he received at the hands of the mason ;
Nay, many averr'd he half rose in his niche,
When Sir Alured, always in metaphor rich,
Call'd his priest an " old son of—" some animal—which,
Is not worth the inquiry—a hint's quite enough on
The subject—for more I refer you to Buffon.

    It's supposed that the Knight
    Himself saw the sight,
And it's likely he did, as he easily might,
For 'tis certain he paused in his wordy attack,
And, in nautical language, seem'd " taken aback."
    In so much that when now
    The " prime cause of the row,"
Father John, in the chapel at last made his bow,
The Bridegroom elect was so mild and subdued,
None could ever suppose he'd been noisy and rude,
Or made use of the language to which I allude ;

Fair Edith herself, while the knot was a-tying,
Her bridesmaids around her, some sobbing, some sighing,
Some smiling, some blushing, half-laughing, half-crying,
Scarce made her responses in tones more complying
Then he who'd been raging and storming so recently,
All softness now, and behaving quite decently.
Many folks thought too the cold stony frown
Of the Saint up aloft from his niche looking down,
Brought the sexton and clerk each an extra half-crown,
When, the rite being over, the fees were all paid,
And the party remounting, the whole cavalcade
Prepared to ride home with no little parade.

In a climate so very unsettled as ours
It's as well to be cautious and guard against showers,
    For though, about One,   You've a fine brilliant sun,
When your walk or your ride is but barely begun,
Yet long ere the hour-hand approaches the Two,
There is not in the whole sky one atom of blue,
But it " rains cats and dogs," and you're fairly wet through
Ere you know where to turn, what to say, or to do ;
For which reason I've bought, to protect myself well, a
Good stout *Taglioni* and gingham umbrella.
But in Edward the First's days I very much fear,
    Had a gay cavalier   Thought fit to appear
In any such " toggery "—then 'twas term'd " gear "—
He'd have met with a highly significant sneer,
Or a broad grin extending from ear unto ear
On the features of every soul he came near ;
There was no taking refuge too then, as with us,
On a slip-sloppy day, in a cab or a *'bus ;*
    As they rode through the woods
    In their wimples and hoods,
Their only resource against sleet, hail, or rain
Was, as Spenser describes it, to " pryck o'er the plaine,"
That is to clap spurs on, and ride helter-skelter
In search of some building or other for shelter.

    Now it seems that the sky,   Which had been of a dye
As bright and as blue as your lady-love's eye,
The season in fact being genial and dry,

Began to assume   An appearance of gloom
From the moment the Knight began fidget and fume,
Which deepen'd and deepen'd till all the horizon
Grew blacker than aught they had ever set eyes on,
And soon, from the far west the elements' rumbling
Increased, and kept pace with Sir Alured's grumbling,
  Bright flashes between,   Blue, red, and green,
All livid and lurid began to be seen ;

At length down it came—a whole deluge of rain,
A perfect Niagara, drenching the plain,
  And up came the reek,   And down came the shriek
Of the winds like a steam-whistle starting a train ;
And the tempest began so to roar and to pour,
That the Dennes and the Ingoldsbys, starting at score,
As they did from the porch of St. Romwold's church door,
Had scarce gain'd a mile, or a mere trifle more,
  Ere the whole of the crew
  Were completely wet through.
They dash'd o'er the downs, and they dash'd through the vales,
They dash'd up the hills, and they dash'd down the dales,
As if elderly Nick was himself at their tails ;

The Bridegroom in vain   Attempts to restrain
The Bride's frighten'd palfrey by seizing the rein,
     When a flash and a crash,
     Which produced such a splash,
That a Yankee had called it " an Almighty Smash,"
     Came down so complete   At his own courser's feet,
That the rider, though famous for keeping his seat,
From its kickings and plungings, now under, now upper,
Slipp'd out of his demi-pique over the crupper,
And fell from the back of his terrified cob
On what bards less refined than myself term his " Nob."
(To obtain a *genteel* rhyme's sometimes a tough job).

Just so—for the nonce to enliven my song
With a classical simile cannot be wrong—
Just so—in such roads and in similar weather,
Tydides and Nestor were riding together,
When, so says old Homer, the King of the Sky,
The great " Cloud-compeller," his lightnings let fly,
And their horses both made such a desperate shy
     At this freak of old Zeus,
     That at once they broke loose,
Reins, traces, bits, breechings were all of no use ;
If the Pylian Sage, without any delay,
Had not whipp'd them sharp round and away from the fray,
They'd have certainly upset his *cabriolet*,
And there'd been the—a name I won't mention—to pay.

Well, the Knight in a moment recover'd his seat,
Mr. Widdicombe's mode of performing that feat
At Astley's could not be more neat or complete,
—It's recorded, indeed, by an eminent pen
Of our own days, that this *our* great Widdicombe, then
In the heydey of life, had afforded some ten
Or twelve lessons in riding to Alured Denne,—
     It is certain the Knight   Was so agile and light
That an instant sufficed him to set matters right,
Yet the Bride was by this time almost out of sight ;
For her palfrey, a rare bit of blood, who could trace
Her descent from the " pure old Caucasian race,"
     Sleek, slim, and bony, as   Mr. Sidonia's

Fine " Arab Steed "   Of the very same breed,
Which that elegant gentleman rode so genteelly
—See " Coningsby " written by " B. Disraeli "—
   That palfrey, I say,   From this trifling delay
Had made what at sea's call'd a " great deal of way."
" More fleet than the roe-buck," and free as the wind,
She had left the good company rather behind ;
They whipp'd and they spurr'd, and they after her press'd,
Still Sir Alured's steed was " by long chalks " the best
Of the party, and very soon distanced the rest ;
But long ere e'en he had the fugitive near'd,
She dashed into the wood and at once disappear'd !
It's a " fashious " affair when you're out on a ride,
—Ev'n supposing you're *not* in pursuit of a bride,
If you are it's more fashious, which can't be denied,—
And you come to a place where three cross-roads divide
Without any way-post, stuck up by the side
Of the road, to direct you and act as a guide,
With a road leading here, and a road leading there,
And a road leading no one exactly knows where.
   When Sir Alured came   In pursuit of the dame
To a fork of this kind,—a three-prong'd one—small blame
To his scholarship if in selecting his way
His respect for the Classics now led him astray ;
But the rule, in a work I won't stop to describe is,
In medio semper tutissimus ibis,
So the Knight being forced of the three paths to enter one,
Dash'd, with these words on his lips, down the centre one.

   Up and down hill,   Up and down hill,
Through brake and o'er briar he gallops on still
Aye banning, blaspheming, and cursing his fill
At his courser because he had given him a " spill ; "
   Yet he did not gain ground
   On the palfrey, the sound,
On the contrary, made by the hoofs of the beast
Grew fainter, and fainter,—and fainter,—and—ceased !
Sir Alured burst through the dingle at last,
To a sort of a clearing, and there—he stuck fast ;
For his steed, though a freer one ne'er had a shoe on,
Stood fix'd as the Governor's nag in " Don Juan,"

Or much like the statue that stands, cast in copper, a
Few yards south-east of the door of the Opera,
Save that Alured's horse had not got such a big tail,
While Alured wanted the cock'd hat and pig-tail.

Before him is seen   A diminutive Green
Scoop'd out from the covert—a thick leafy screen
Of wild foliage, trunks with broad branches between
Encircle it wholly, all radiant and sheen,
For the weather at once appear'd clear and serene,
And the sky up above was a bright mazarine,
Just as though no such thing as a tempest had been,
In short it was one of those sweet little places
In Egypt and Araby known as " oases."
   There, under the shade   That was made by the glade,
The astonish'd Sir Alured sat and survey'd
A little low building of Bethersden stone,
With ivy and parasite creepers o'ergrown,
   A *Sacellum*, or cell   In which Chronicles tell
Saints and anchorites erst were accustomed to dwell ;
A little round arch, on which, deeply indented,
The zig-zaggy pattern by Saxons invented
Was cleverly chisell'd, and well represented,
   Surmounted a door   Some five feet by four
It might have been less or it might have been more,
In the primitive ages they made these things lower
Than we do in buildings that had but one floor.
   And these Chronicles say   When an anchorite gray
Wish'd to shut himself up and keep out of the way,
He was commonly wont in such low cells to stay,
And pray night and day on the *rez de chaussée*.

There, under the arch I've endeavoured to paint,
   With no little surprise,   And scarce trusting his eyes,
The Knight now saw standing that little Boy Saint !
   The one whom before   He'd seen over the door
Of the Priory shaking his head as he swore—
With mitre, and crozier, and rochet, and stole on,
The very self-same—or at least his Eidolon !
With a voice all unlike to the infantine squeak
You'd expect, that small Saint now address'd him to speak ;

In a bold, manly tone, he　Began, while his stony
Cold lips breath'd an odour quite *Eau-de-Cologne-y* ;
In fact, from his christening, according to rumour, he
Beat Mr. Brummell to sticks, in perfumery.*

" Sir Alured Denne ! "　Said the Saint, " be atten-
tive !　Your ancestors, all most respectable men,
Have for some generations been vot'ries of mine ;
They have bought me mould candles, and bow'd at my shrine,
They have made my monks presents of ven'son and wine,
With a right of free pasturage, too, for their swine,
　And, though you in this　Have been rather remiss,
Still I owe you a turn for the sake of ' Lang Syne.'
And I now come to tell you, your cursing and swearing
Have reach'd to a pitch that is really past bearing.
　'Twere a positive scandal.　In even a Vandal,
It ne'er should be done, save with bell, book, and candle :
And though I've now learn'd, as I've always suspected,
Your own education's been somewhat neglected ;
Still, you're not such an uninform'd pagan, I hope,
As not to know cursing belongs to the Pope !
And his Holiness feels, very properly, jealous
Of all such encroachments by paltry lay fellows.
　Now, take my advice,　Saints never speak twice,
So take it at once, as I once for all give it ;
Go home !　you'll find there all as right as a trivet,
But mind, and remember, if once you give way
To that shocking bad habit, I'm sorry to say,
I have heard you so sadly indulge in to-day,
As sure as you're born, on the very first trip　　　.
That you make—the first oath that proceeds from your lip,
　I'll soon make you rue it !—　I've said it—I'll do it !
' Forewarned is forearmed,' you shan't say but you knew it ;
Whate'er you hold dearest or nearest your heart,
I'll take it away, if I come in a cart !
I will, on my honour !　you know it's absurd
To suppose that a Saint ever forfeits his word

　* In eodem autem prato in quo baptizatus Sanctus Romualdus nunquam gratissimus odor deficit ; neque ibi herbæ pallescunt, sed semper in viriditate permanentes magna nectaris suavitate redolent.—*Nov, Legend Angl.*

For a pitiful Knight, or to please any such man—
I've said it ! I'll do't—if I don't, I'm a Dutchman ! "—

He ceased—he was gone as he closed his harangue,
And some one inside shut the door with a bang !
   Sparkling with dew,   Each green herb anew
Its profusion of sweets round Sir Alured threw,
As pensive and thoughtful he slowly withdrew,
(For the hoofs of his horse had got rid of their glue,)
And the cud of reflection continued to chew
Till the gables of Bonnington Hall rose in view.
Little reck'd he what he smelt, what he saw,
   Brilliance of scenery,   Fragrance of greenery,
Fail'd in impressing his mental machinery ;
Many an hour had elapsed, well I ween, ere he
Fairly was able distinction to draw
'Twixt the odour of garlic and *bouquet du Roi.*

   Merrily, merrily sounds the horn,
     And cheerily ring the bells ;
       For the race is run,   The goal is won,
The little lost mutton is happily found,
The Lady of Bonnington's safe and sound
     In the Hall where her new Lord dwells '
Hard had they ridden, that company gay,
After fair Edith, away and away :
This had slipp'd back o'er his courser's rump,
That had gone over his ears with a plump,
But the lady herself had stuck on like a trump,
   Till her panting steed   Relax'd her speed,
And feeling, no doubt, as a gentleman feels
When he's once shown a bailiff a fair pair of heels,
Stopp'd of herself, as it's very well known
Horses will do, when they're thoroughly blown,
And thus the whole group had foregathered again,
Just as the sunshine succeeded the rain.

Oh, now the joy, and the frolicking, rollicking
   Doings indulged in by one and by all !
Gaiety seized on the most melancholic in
   All the broad lands around Bonnington Hall.

All sorts of revelry,   All sorts of devilry,
All play at " High Jinks " and keep up the ball.
Days, weeks, and months, it is really astonishing,
    When one's so happy, how Time flies away ;
Meanwhile the Bridegroom requires no admonishing
    As to what pass'd on his own wedding day ;
        Never since then   Had Sir Alured Denne
Let a word fall from his lip or his pen
That began with a D, or left off with an N !

Once, and once only, when put in a rage,
By a careless young rascal he'd hired as a Page,
    All buttons and brass,   Who in handling a glass
    Of spiced hippocras, throws   It all over his clothes,
And spoils his best pourpoint, and smartest trunk hose,
While stretching his hand out to take it and quaff it (he
'd given a rose noble a yard for the taffety),
Then, and then only, came into his head
A very sad word that began with a Z,
    But he check'd his complaint,
    He remember'd the Saint,
In the nick—Lady Denne was beginning to faint.
That sight on his mouth acted quite as a bung,
Like Mahomet's coffin, the shocking word hung
Half-way 'twixt the root and the tip of his tongue.

    Many a year   Of mirth and good cheer
Flew over their heads, to each other more dear
Every day, they were quoted by peasant and peer
As the rarest examples of love ever known,
Since the days of *Le Chivaler D'Arbie* and *Joanne*,
Who in Bonnington chancel lie sculptured in stone.
    Well—it happen'd at last,   After certain years past,
That an embassy came to our court from afar—
From the Grand-duke of Muscovy—now call'd the Czar,
And the Spindleshank'd Monarch, determined to do
All the grace that he could to a Nobleman, who
Had sail'd all that way from a country which few
In our England had heard of, and nobody knew,

With a hat like a muff, and a beard like a Jew,
Our arsenals, buildings, and dock-yards to view,
  And to say how desirous His Prince Wladimirus
Had long been with mutual regard to inspire us,
And how he regretted he was not much nigher us,
  With other fine things, Such as Kings say to Kings
When each tries to humbug his dear Royal Brother, in
Hopes by such " gammon " to take one another in—
  King Longshanks, I say, Being now on his way
Bound for France, where the rebels had kept him at bay
  Was living in clover At this time at Dover
I' the castle there, waiting a tide to go over.

He had summon'd, I can't tell you how many men,
Knights, nobles, and squires to the wars of Guienne,
And among these of course was Sir Alured Denne,
  Who, acting like most Of the knights in the host,
Whose residence was not too far from the coast,
Had brought his wife with him, delaying their parting,
Fond souls, till the very last moment of starting.

Of course, with such lots of lords, ladies, and knights,
In their *Saracenettes*,* and their bright chain-mail tights
All accustom'd to galas, grand doings, and sights,
A matter like this was at once put to rights ;
  'Twould have been a strange thing,
  If so polish'd a king,
With his board of Green Cloth, and Lord Steward's department,
Couldn't teach an Ambassador what the word " smart " meant.
A banquet was order'd at once for a score,
Or more, of the *corps* that had just come on shore,
And the King, though he thought it " a bit of a bore,"
  Ask'd all the *élite* Of his *levée* to meet
The illustrious Strangers and share in the treat ;
For the Boyar himself, the Queen graciously made him her
Beau for the day, from respect to Duke Wladimir.
(Queer as this name may appear in the spelling,
  You won't find it trouble you, Sound but the W
Like the first L in Llan, Lloyd, and Llewellyn !)

---

* This silk, of great repute among our ancestors, had been brought home, a few years before, by Edward, from the Holy Land.

Fancy the fuss and the fidgety looks
Of Robert de Burghersh, the constables, cooks ;
　For of course the *cuisine*　Of the King and the Queen
Was behind them at London, or Windsor, or Sheen,
Or wherever the Court ere it started had been,
　And it's really no jest,　When a troublesome guest
Looks in at a time when you're busy and prest,
Just going to fight, or to ride, or to rest,
And expects a good lunch when you've none ready drest.
　The servants no doubt　Were much put to the rout
By this very *extempore* sort of set out.

But they wisely fell back upon Poor Richard's plan,
" When you can't what you would, you must do what you can ! "
So they ransack'd the country, folds, pig-styes, and pens,
For the sheep and the porkers, the cocks and the hens ;
'Twas said a Tom-cat of Sir Alured Denne's,
　A fine tabby-gray,　Disappear'd on that day,
And whatever became of him no one could say ;
　They brought all the food　That ever they cou'd,
Fish, flesh, and fowl, with sea-coal and dry wood,
To his Majesty's *Dapifer*, Eudo (or Ude),
They lighted the town up, set ringing the bells,
And borrow'd the waiters from all the hotels.
A bright thought, moreover, came into the head
Of *Dapifer* Eudo, who'd some little dread,
As he said, for the thorough success of his spread.
So he said to himself, " What a thing it would be
　Could I have here with me　Some one, two, or three
Of their outlandish scullions from over the sea !
It's a hundred to one if the *Suite* or their Chief
Understand our plum-puddings, and barons of beef ;
But with five minutes' chat with their cooks or their valets
We'd soon dish up something to tickle their palates ! "
With this happy conceit for improving the mess,
Pooh-poohing expense, he dispatch'd an express
In a waggon and four on the instant to Deal,
Who dash'd down the hill without locking the wheel,
And, by means which I guess but decline to reveal,
Seduced from the Downs, where at anchor their vessel rode,
Lumpoff Icywitz, serf to a former Count Nesselrode,

A cook of some fame,   Who invented the same
Cold pudding that still bears the family name.
This accomplish'd, the *Chef's* peace of mind was restor'd,
And in due time a banquet was placed on the board
" In the very best style," which implies in a word
" All the dainties the season " (and king) " could afford."
  There were snipes, there were rails,
  There were woodcocks and quails,
There were peacocks served up in their pride (that is tails),
  Fricandeau, fricassees,   Ducks and green peas,
Cotelettes à l'Indienne, and chops *à la Soubise*
(Which last you may call " onion sauce " if you please),
There were barbecu'd pigs
Stuff'd with raisins and figs,
Omelettes and *haricots,* stews and *ragoûts,*
And pork griskins, which Jews still refuse and abuse.
Then the wines,—round the circle how swiftly they went !
Canary, Sack, Malaga, Malvoisie, Tent ;
Old Hock from the Rhine, wine remarkably fine,
Of the Charlemagne vintage of seven ninety-nine,—
Five cent'ries in bottle had made it divine !
The rich juice of Rousillon, Gascoygne, Bordeaux,
  Marasquin, Curaçoa,   Kirschen Wasser, Noyeau,
And gin which the company voted " No Go ; "
  The guests all hob-nobbing,   And bowing and bobbing ;
Some prefer white wine, while others more value red,
  Few, a choice few,   Of more orthodox *goût,*
Stick to " old crusted port," among whom was Sir Alured ;
Never indeed at a banquet before
Had that gallant commander enjoy'd himself more.

Then came " sweets "—served in silver were tartlets and pies—
    in glass
Jellies composed of punch, calves' feet, and isinglass,
Creams, and whipt-syllabubs, some hot, some cool,
Blancmange, and quince-custards, and gooseberry fool.
And now from the good taste which reigns it's confest
In a gentleman's, that is an Englishman's, breast,
And makes him polite to a stranger and guest,
  They soon play'd the deuce
  With a large *Charlotte Russe ;*

More than one of the party dispatch'd his plate twice
With " I'm really ashamed, but—another small slice !
Your dishes from Russia are really *so* nice ! "
Then the prime dish of all !   " There was nothing so good in
    The whole of the Feed "   One and all were agreed,
" As the great Lumpoff Icywitz' Nesselrode pudding ! "
Sir Alured Denne, who'd all day, to say sooth,
Like Iago, been " plagued with a sad raging tooth,"
Which had nevertheless interfered very little
With his—what for my rhyme I'm obliged to spell—vittle,
    Requested a friend   Who sat near him to send
Him a spoonful of what he heard all so commend,
And begg'd to take wine with him afterwards, grateful
Because for a spoonful he'd sent him a plateful.
Having emptied his glass—he ne'er balk'd it or spill'd it—
The gallant Knight open'd his mouth—and then fill'd it !

You must really excuse me—there's nothing could bribe
Me at all to go on and attempt to describe
    The fearsome look then   Of Sir Alured Denne !
—Astonishment, horror, distraction of mind,
Rage, misery, fear, and iced pudding—combined !
Lip, forehead, and cheek—how these mingle and meet ;
All colours, all hues, now advance, now retreat,
Now pale as a turnip, now crimson as beet !
How he grasps his arm-chair in attempting to rise,
See his veins how they swell ! mark the roll of his eyes !
Now east and now west, now north and now south,
Till at once he contrives to eject from his mouth
    That vile " spoonful " —what
    He has got he knows not,
He isn't quite sure if it's cold or it's hot ;
At last he exclaims, as he starts from his seat,
" A SNOWBALL by —— ! " what I decline to repeat,—
'Twas the name of a bad place, for mention unmeet.

Then oh what a volley !—a great many heard
What flow'd from his lips, and 'twere really absurd
To suppose that each man was not shock'd by each word ;
A great many heard too, with mix'd fear and wonder,
The terrible crash of the terrible thunder,
That broke as if bursting the building asunder ;

But very few heard, although every one might,
The short, half-stifled shriek from the chair on the right,
Where the Lady of Bonnington sat by her Knight;
And very few saw—some—the number was small,
In the large ogive window that lighted the hall,
A small stony Saint in a small stony pall,
With a small stony mitre, and small stony crosier,
And small stony toes that owed nought to the hosier,
Beckon stonily downward to *some one* below,
As Merryman says, " for to come for to go ! "
While every one smelt a delicious perfume
That seem'd to pervade every part of the room !

Fair Edith Denne, The *bonne et belle* then,
Never again was beheld among men !
But there was the *fauteuil* on which she was placed,
And there was the girdle that graced her small waist,
And there was her stomacher brilliant with gems,
And the mantle she wore, edged with lace at the hems,
Her rich brocade gown sat upright in its place,
And her wimple was there—but where—WHERE WAS HER FACE ?
'Twas gone with her body—and nobody knows,
Nor could any one present so much as suppose
How that Lady contrived to slip out of her clothes !

But 'twas done—she was quite gone—the how and the where
No mortal was ever yet found to declare;
Though inquiries were made, and some writers record
That Sir Alured offer'd a handsome reward.

    *   *   *   *   *

King Edward went o'er to his wars in Guienne,
Taking with him his barons, his knights, and his men.
   You may look through the whole
   Of that King's muster-roll,
And you won't find the name of Sir Alured Denne ;
But Chronicles tell that there formerly stood
A little old chapel in Bilsington Wood ;
   The remains to this day,   Archæologists say,
May be seen, and I'd go there and look if I could.
There long dwelt a hermit remarkably good,
   Who lived all alone,   And never was known
To use bed or bolster, except the cold stone ;

But would groan and would moan in so piteous a tone,
A wild Irishman's heart had responded " Och hone ! "
As the fashion with hermits of old was to keep skins
To wear with the wool on—most commonly sheep-skins—
He, too, like the rest was accustom'd to do so ;
His beard, as no barber came near him, too, grew so,
He bore some resemblance to Robinson Crusoe,
In Houndsditch, I'm told, you'll sometimes see a Jew so.

He lived on the roots,   And the cob-nuts and fruits,
Which the kind-hearted rustics, who rarely are churls
In such matters, would send by their boys and their girls ;
  They'd not get him to speak,
  If they'd tried for a week,
But the colour would always mount up in his cheek,
And he'd look like a dragon if ever he heard
His young friends use a naughty expression or word.
How long he lived, or at what time he died,
'Twere hard, after so many years to decide,
But there's one point on which all traditions agree,
That he *did* die at last, leaving no legatee,
And his linen was marked with an A and a D.

Alas ! for the glories of Bonnington Hall !
Alas, for its splendour ! alas for its fall !
  Long years have gone by
  Since the trav'ler might spy
Any decentish house in the parish at all.
For very soon after the awful event
I've related, 'twas said through all that part of Kent
That the maids of a morning, when putting the chairs
And the tables to rights, would oft pop unawares
In one of the parlours, or galleries, or stairs,
On a tall female figure, or find her, far horrider,
Slowly o' nights promenading the corridor ;
But whatever the hour, or wherever the place,
No one could ever get sight of her face !
  Nor could they perceive   Any arm in her sleeve,
While her legs and her feet too, seem'd mere " make-believe,"
For she glided along with that shadow-like motion
  Which gives one the notion
Of clouds on a zephyr, or ships on the ocean ;

And though of her gown they could *hear* the silk rustle,
They saw but that side on't *ornée* with the bustle.
The servants, of course, though the house they were born in,
Soon " wanted to better themselves," and gave warning,
While even the new Knight grew tired of a guest
Who would not let himself or his family rest ;
    So he pack'd up his all,   And made a bare wall
Of each well-furnish'd room in his ancestors' Hall,
Then left the old Mansion to stand or to fall,
Having previously barr'd up the windows and gates,
To avoid paying sesses and taxes and rates,
And settled on one of his other estates,
Where he built a new mansion, and called it Denne Hill,
And there his descendants reside, I think, still.

Poor Bonnington, empty, or left, at the most,
To the joint occupation of rooks and a Ghost,
    Soon went to decay,   And moulder'd away,
But whether it dropp'd down at last I can't say,
Or whether the jackdaws produced, by degrees, a
Spontaneous combustion like that one at Pisa
    Some cent'ries ago,   I'm sure I don't know,
But you can't find a vestige now ever so tiny,
" *Perierunt,*" as some one says, " *etiam ruinæ.*"

MORAL.

The first maxim a couple of lines may be said in,
If you *are* in a passion, don't swear at a wedding !

Whenever you chance to be ask'd out to dine,
Be exceedingly cautious—don't take too much wine !
In your eating remember one principal point,
Whatever you do, have your eye on the joint !
Keep clear of side dishes, don't meddle with those
Which the servants in livery, or those in plain clothes,
Poke over your shoulders and under your nose ;
Or, if you *must* live on the fat of the land,
And feed on fine dishes you don't understand,
Buy a good book of cookery !   I've a compact one,
First rate of the kind, just brought out by Miss Acton,

This will teach you their names, the ingredients they're made of,
And which to indulge in, and which be afraid of,
Or else, ten to one, between ice and cayenne,
You'll commit yourself some day, like Alured Denne.

" To persons about to be married," I'd say
Don't exhibit ill-humour, at least on The Day !
And should there perchance be a trifling delay
On the part of officials, extend them your pardon,
And don't snub the parson, the clerk, or churchwarden !

To married men this—For the rest of your lives,
Think how your misconduct may act on your wives !
Don't swear then before them, lest haply they faint,
Or what sometimes occurs—run away with a Saint !

A serious error, similar to that which forms the subject of the following legend, is said to have occurred in the case of one, or rather two gentlemen named Curina, who dwelt near Hippo in the days of St. Augustine. The matter was set right, and a friendly hint at the same time conveyed to the ill-used individual, that it would be advisable for him to apply to the above-mentioned Father, and be baptized with as little delay as possible. The story is quoted in " The Doctor," together with another of the same kind, which is given on no less authority than that of Gregory the Great.

The Brothers of Birchington

A Lay of St. Thomas à Becket

You are all aware that   On our throne there once sat
A very great King who'd an Angevin hat,
With a great sprig of broom, which he wore as a badge in it,
Named from this circumstance, Henry Plantagenet.

Pray don't suppose   That I'm going to prose
O'er Queen Eleanor's wrongs, or Miss Rosamond's woes,
With the dagger and bowl, and all that sort of thing,
Not much to the credit of Miss, Queen, or King.

The tale may be true,   But between me and you,
With the King's *escapade* I'll have nothing to do ;
But shall merely select, as a theme for my rhymes,
A fact, which occurr'd to some folks in his times.

If for health, or a " lark,"   You should ever embark
In that best of improvements on boats since the Ark,
The steam-vessel call'd the " Red Rover," the barge
Of an excellent officer, named Captain Large,

You may see, some half way   'Twixt the pier at Herne Bay
And Margate, the place where you're going to stay,
A village called Birchington, fam'd for its " Rolls,"
As the fishing-bank, just in its front, is for Soles.

Well,—there stood a fane   In this Harry Broom's reign,
On the edge of the cliff, overhanging the main,
Renown'd for its sanctity all through the nation,
And orthodox friars of the Austin persuasion.

Among them there was one,   Whom if once I begun
To describe as I ought I should never have done,
Father Richard of Birchington, so was the Friar
Yclept, whom the rest had elected their Prior.

He was tall and upright,   About six feet in height,
His complexion was what you'd denominate light,
And the tonsure had left, 'mid his ringlets of brown,
A little bald patch on the top of his crown.

His bright sparkling eye   Was of hazel, and nigh
Rose a finely arch'd eyebrow of similar dye
He'd a small, well-form'd mouth with the *Cupidon* lip
And an aquiline nose, somewhat red at the tip.

In doors and out   He was very devout,
With his *Aves* and *Paters*—and oh, such a knout ! !
For his self flagellations ! the Monks used to say
He would wear out two penn'orth of whip-cord a day !

Then how his piety   Shows in his diet, he
Dines upon pulse, or, by way of variety,
Sand-eels or dabs ; or his appetite mocks
With those small periwinkles that crawl on the rocks.

In brief, I don't stick   To declare Father Dick—
So they call'd him, " for short "—was a " Regular Brick,"
A metaphor taken—I have not the page aright—
Out of an ethical work by the Stagyrite.

Now Nature, 'tis said,   Is a comical jade,
And among the fantastical tricks she has play'd,
Was the making our good Father Richard a Brother,
As like him in form as one pea's like another ;

He was tall and upright,   About six feet in height,
His complexion was what you'd denominate light,
And, though he had not shorn his ringlets of brown,
He'd a little bald patch on the top of his crown.

He'd a bright sparkling eye   Of the hazel, hard by
Rose a finely-arch'd sourcil of similar dye ;
He'd a small, well-shaped mouth, with a *Cupidon* lip,
And a good Roman nose, rather red at the tip.

But here, it's pretended,   The parallel ended ;
In fact, there's no doubt his life might have been mended,
And people who spoke of the Prior with delight,
Shook their heads if you mentioned his brother, the Knight.

If you'd credit report   There was nothing but sport,
And High Jinks going on night and day at " the court,"
Where Sir Robert, instead of devotion and charity,
Spent all his time in unseemly hilarity.

He drinks and he eats   Of choice liquors and meats,
And he goes out on We'n'sdays and Fridays to treats,
Gets tipsy whenever he dines or he sups,
And is wont to come quarrelsome home in his cups.

No *Paters*, no *Aves ;*   An absolute slave he's
To tarts, pickled salmon, and sauces, and gravies ;
While as to his beads—what a shame in a Knight !—
He really don't know the wrong end from the right !

So, though 'twas own'd then   By nine people in ten,
That " Robert and Richard were two pretty men,"
Yet, there the praise ceased, or, at least the good Priest
Was consider'd the " Beauty," Sir Robert the " Beast."

Indeed, I'm afraid   More might have been laid
To the charge of the Knight than was openly said,
For then we'd no " Phiz's," no " H. B.'s," nor " Leeches,"
To call Roberts " Bobs," and illustrate their speeches.

'Twas whisper'd he'd rob,   Nay, murder ! a job
Which would stamp him no " brick," but a " regular snob,"
(An obsolete term, which, at this time of day,
We should probably render by *mauvais sujet.*)

Now if *here* such affairs   Get wind unawares,
They are bruited about, doubtless, much more " down stairs,"
Where Old Nick has a register-office, they say,
With commissioners quite of such matters *au fait.*

Of course when he heard   What his people averr'd
Of Sir Robert's proceedings in deed and in word,
He asked for the ledger, and hasten'd to look
At the leaves on the creditor side of this book.

'Twas with more than surprise   That he now ran his eyes
O'er the numberless items,·oaths, curses, and lies,
Et cetera, set down in Sir Robert's account,
He was quite " flabbergasted " to see the amount.

" Dear me ! this is wrong !   It's a great deal too strong,
I'd no notion this bill had been standing so long—
Send Levybub here ! " and he filled up a writ
Of " *Ça sa*," duly prefaced with " Limbo to wit."

"Here, Levybub, quick!"   To his bailiff, said Nick,
"I'm 'ryled,' and 'my dander's up,' 'Go a-head slick'
Up to Kent—not Kentuck—and at once fetch away
A snob there—I guess that's a *mauvais sujet*.

"One De Birchington, knight—'Tis not clear quite
What his t'other name is—they've not enter'd it right,
Ralph, Robert, or Richard? they've not gone so far,
Our critturs have put it down merely as 'R.'

"But he's tall and upright,   About six feet in height,
His complexion, I reckon, you'd calculate light,
And he's farther 'set down' having ringlets of brown,
With a little bald patch on the top of his crown.

"Then his eye and his lip,   Hook-nose, red at tip
Are marks your attention can't easily slip;
Take Slomanoch with you, he's got a good knack
Of soon grabbing his man, and be back in a crack!"

That same afternoon,   Father Dick, who as soon
Would "knock in" or "cut chapel" as jump o'er the moon,
Was missing at vespers—at compline—all night!
And his monks were, of course, in a deuce of a fright.

Morning dawn'd—'twas broad day,   Still no Prior! the tray
With his muffins and eggs went untasted away;—
He came not to luncheon—all said, "it was rum of him!"
—None could conceive what on earth had become of him.

They examined his cell,   They peep'd down the well;
They went up the tow'r and looked into the bell,
They dragg'd the great fish-pond, the little one tried,
But found nothing at all, save some carp—which they fried.

"Dear me! Dear me!   Why, where can he be?
He's fall'n over the cliff?—tumbled into the sea?"
"Stay—he talk'd," exclaimed one, "if I recollect right,
Of making a call on his brother, the Knight!"

But found nothing at all, save some carp—which they fried

He turns as he speaks,   The " Court Lodge " he seeks,
Which was known then, as now, by the queer name of Quekes,
But scarce half a mile on his way had he sped,
When he spied the good Prior in the paddock—stone dead !

Alas ! 'twas too true !   And I need not tell you
In the convent his news made a pretty to do ;
Through all its wide precincts so roomy and spacious,
Nothing was heard but " Bless *me !* " and " Good Gracious ! ! "

They sent for the May'r   And the Doctor, a pair
Of grave men, who began to discuss the affair,
When in bounced the Coroner, foaming with fury,
" Because," as he said, " 'twas pooh ! pooh ! ing his jury."

Then commenced a dispute,   And so hot they went to't,
That things seem'd to threaten a serious *émeute*,
When, just in the midst of the uproar and racket,
Who should walk in but St. Thomas à Becket.

Quoth his saintship, " How now ?   Here's a fine coil, I trow !
I should like to know, gentlemen, what's all this row ?
Mr. Wickliffe—or Wackliffe—whatever your name is—
And you, Mr. May'r, don't you know, Sirs, what shame is ?

" Pray, what's all this clatter   About ?—what's the matter ? "
Here a monk, whose teeth funk and concern made to chatter,
Sobs out, as he points to the corpse on the floor,
" 'Tis all dickey with poor Father Dick—he's no more ! "

" How !—what ? " says the saint,   " Yes he is—no he ain't,*
He can't be deceased—pooh ! it's merely a faint,
Or some foolish mistake which may serve for our laughter,
' He *should* have died,' like the old Scotch Queen, ' hereafter.

" His time is not out ;   Some blunder, no doubt,
It shall go hard but what I'll know what it's about—
I sha'n't be surprised if that scurvy Old Nick's
Had a hand in't ; it savours of one of his tricks."

---

* *Cantise*, for " is not ; " St. Thomas, it seems, had lived long enough in the country to pick up a few of its provincialisms.

When a crafty old hound   Claps his nose to the ground,
Then throws it up boldly, and bays out, " I've found ! "
And the pack catch the note, I'd as soon think to check it,
As dream of bamboozling St. Thomas à Becket.

Once on the scent,   To business he went,
" You Scoundrel, come here, Sir," ('twas Nick that he meant,)
" Bring your books here this instant—bestir yourself—do,
I've no time to waste on such fellows as you."

Every corner and nook   In all Erebus shook,
As he struck on the pavement his pastoral crook,
All its tenements trembled from basement to roofs,
And their *nigger* inhabitants shook in their hoofs.

Hanging his ears,   Yet dissembling his fears,
Ledger in hand, straight " Auld Hornie " appears,
With that sort of half-sneaking, half-impudent look,
Bankrupts sport when cross-question'd by Cresswell
    or Cooke.

" So, Sir-r-r ! you are here,"
    Said the Saint with a sneer,
" My summons, I trust, did not much interfere
With your morning engagements—I merely desire,
At your leisure, to know what you've done with my Prior ?

" Now, none of your lies,   Mr. Nick ! I'd advise
You to tell me the truth without any disguise,
Or-r-r ! " The Saint, while his rosy gills seem'd to grow rosier,
Here gave another great thump with his crosier.

Like a small boy at Eton,   Who's not quite a Crichton,
And don't know his task but expects to be beaten,
Nick stammer'd, scarce knowing what answer to make,
" Sir, I'm sadly afraid there has been a mistake.

" These things will occur,   We are all apt to err,
The most cautious sometimes as you know, holy Sir ;
For my own part—I'm sure I do all that I can—
But—the fact is—I fear—we have got the wrong man."

"Wrong man!" roar'd the Saint— But the scene I can't paint,
The best colours I have are a great deal too faint—
Nick afterwards own'd that he ne'er knew what fright meant,
Before he saw Saint under so much excitement.

"Wrong man! don't tell me— Pooh!—fiddle-de-dee!
What's your right, Scamp, to *any* man!—come, let me see;
I'll teach you, you thorough-paced rascal, to meddle
With church matters, come, Sirrah, out with your schedule!"

In support of his claim   The fiend turns to the name
Of "De Birchington" written in letters of flame,
Below which long items stand, column on column,
Enough to have eked out a decent-sized volume!

Sins of all sorts and shapes   From small practical japes,
Up to dicings, and drinkings, and murders, and rapes,
And then of such standing!—a merciless tick,
From an Oxford tobacconist,—let alone Nick.

The Saint in surprise,   Scarce believed his own eyes,
Still he knew he'd to deal with the father of lies,
And "So *this!*—you call *this!*" he exclaimed in a searching tone,
"This!!! the account of my friend Dick de Birchington!"

"Why," said Nick, with an air   Of great candour, "it's there
Lies the awkwardest part of this awkward affair—
I thought all was right—see the height tallies quite,
The complexion's what all must consider as light;
There's the nose, and the lip, and the ringlets of brown,
And the little bald patch on the top of the crown.

"And then the surname,   So exactly the same—
I don't know—I can't tell how the accident came,
But *some* how—I own it's a very sad job,
But—my bailiff grabb'd Dick when he *should* have nabb'd Bob.

"I am vex'd beyond bounds   You should have such good grounds
For complaint; I would rather have given five pounds,
And any apology, sir, you may choose,
I'll make with much pleasure, and put in the *News*."

" An apology !—pooh !   Much good that will do !
An ' *apology* ' quotha !—and that too from you !—
Before any proposal is made of the sort,
Bring back your stol'n goods, thief !—produce them in Court ! "

In a moment so small   It seem'd no time at all,
Father Richard sat up on his what-do-ye-call—
Sur son séant—and, what was as wondrous as pleasing,
At once began coughing, and sniffing, and sneezing.

While, strange to relate,   The Knight, whom the fate
Of his brother had reach'd, and who'd knocked at the gate,
To make further inquiries, had scarce made his bow
To the Saint, ere he vanish'd and no one knew how !

Erupit—evasit,   As Tully would phrase it,
And none could have known where to find his *Hic jacet*—
That sentence which man his mortality teaches—
Sir Robert had disappear'd, body and breeches !

" Heyday ! Sir, heyday !   What's the matter now—eh ? "
Quoth à Becket, observing the gen'ral dismay,·
" How, again !—'pon my word this is really too bad !
It would drive *any* saint in the calendar mad.

" What, still at your tricking ?   You *will* have a kicking ?
I see you won't rest till you've got a good licking—
Your claim, friend ?—what claim ?—why you show'd me before
That your *old* claim was cancell'd—you've crossed out the score !

" Is it that way you'd Jew one ?   You've settled the true one ?
Do you mean to tell me he has run up a new one ?
Of the thousands you've cheated   And scurvily treated,
Name one you've dared charge with a bill once receipted !
In the Bankruptcy Court should you dare to presume
To attempt it, they'd soon kick you out of the room,
—Ask Commissioner Fonblanque, or ask my Lord Brougham.

" And then to make under   So barefaced a blunder
Your caption !—why, what's the world come to, I wonder ?

My patience ! it's just like his impudence, rat him !
—Stand out of the way there, and let me get at him ! "

The Saint raised his arm   But Old Nick, in alarm,
Dash'd up through the skylight, not doing much harm,
While, *quitte pour la peur*, the Knight, sound on the whole,
Down the chimney came tumbling as black as a coal !

Spare we to tell   Of what after befell !
How the Saint lectured Robert de Birchington well,
Bade him alter his life, and held out as a warning
The narrow escape he'd made on't that morning.

Nor need we declare   How, then and there,
The Jury and Coroner blew up the May'r
For his breach of decorum as one of the *Quorum*,
In not having Levybub brought up before 'em.

Nor will you require   Me to state how the Prior
Could never thenceforth bear the sight of a fire,
Nor ever was heard to express a desire
In cold weather to see the thermometer higher.

Nor shall I relate   The subsequent fate
Of St. Thomas à Becket, whose reverend pate
Fitzurse and De Morville, and Brito and Tracy
Shaved off, as his crown had been merely a jasey.*

Suffice it to say   From that notable day
The " Twin Birchington Brothers " together grew grey :
In the same holy convent continued to dwell,
Same food and same fastings, same habit, same cell.

No more the Knight rattles   In broils and in battles,
But sells, by De Robins, his goods and his chattels,
And counting all wealth a mere Will-o'-the-Wisp,
Disposes of Quekes to Sir Nicholas Crispe.

* Nec satis fuit eis sanguine sacerdotis et nece ecclesiam prophanare, nisi, coronâ capitis amputatâ, funestis gladiis jam defuncti ejicerent cerebrum.—*Matt. Paris.*

One spot alone   Of all he had known
Of his spacious domain he retain'd as his own,
In a neighbouring parish, whose name, I may say
Scarce any two people pronounce the same way.

Re-*cul*-ver some style it,   While others revile it
As bad, and say *Re*-culver—'tisn't worth while, it
Would seem, to dispute, when we know the result immat-
erial—I accent, myself, the penultimate.·

Sages, with brains   Full of " Saxon remains,"
May call me a booby, perhaps, for my pains,
Still I hold, at the hazard of being thought dull by 'em,
Fast by the quantity mark'd for *Regulbium*.·

Call't as you will,   The traveller still,
In the voyage that we talk'd about, marks on the hill
Overhanging the sea,·the " twin towers " raised then
By " Robert and Richard, those two pretty men."

Both tall and upright,   And just equal in height ;
The Trinity House talked of painting them white,
And the thing was much spoken off some time ago,
When the Duke, I believe—but I really don't know.·

Well—there the " Twins " stand   On the verge of the land,
To warn mariners off from the Columbine sand,
And many a poor man have Robert and Dick
By their vow caused to 'scape, like themselves, from Old Nick.

So whether you're sailors   Or Tooley-street Tailors
Broke loose from your masters, those sternest of jailers,
And, bent upon pleasure, are taking your trip
In a craft which you fondly conceive is a ship,
    When you've passed by the Nore,   And you hear the winds roar
In a manner you scarce could have fancied before,
    When the cordage and tackling   Are flapping and crackling,
    And the boy with the bell   Thinks it useless to tell
You that's " dinner on table," because you're unwell ;

When above you all's " scud,"   And below you the flood
Looks a horrible picture of soap-suds and mud,
    When the timbers are straining,   And folks are complaining,
The dead-lights are letting the spray and the rain in,
    When the helm's-man looks blue,   And Captain Large too,
And you really don't know what on earth you shall do.

    In this hubbub and row,   Think where you'd be now
Except for the Birchington boys and their vow !
And while o'er the wide wave you feel the craft pitch hard,
𝔓raie for 𝔶e ſo𝔴les of 𝔕obertte anꝺ 𝔕𝔶𝔠𝔥arꝺ.

                    MORAL.·

It's a subject of serious complaint in some houses,
With young married men who have elderly spouses,
That persons are seen in their figures and faces,
With very queer people in very queer places,
So like them that one for the other's oft taken,
And conjugal confidence thereby much shaken :
Explanations too often are thought mere pretences,
And Richard gets scolded for Robert's offences.

    In a matter so nice,   If I'm ask'd my advice,
I say copy King Henry to obviate that,
And stick something remarkable up in your hat !

Next, observe, in this world where we've so many cheats,
How useful it is to preserve your receipts !
If you deal with a person whose truth you don't doubt,
Be particular, still, that your bill is cross'd out ;
But, with any inducement to think him a scamp,
Have a formal receipt on a regular stamp !

Let every gay gallant my story who notes,
Take warning, and not go on " sowing wild oats ! "
    Nor depend that some friend   Will always attend,
And by " making all right " bring him off in the end :
He may be mistaken, so let him beware,
St. Thomas à Beckets are now rather rare.

Last of all, may'rs and magistrates, never be rude
To juries ! they are people who *won't* be pooh-pooh'd !
Especially Sandwich ones—no one can say
But himself may come under their clutches one day ;
  They then may pay off   In kind any scoff,
And, turning, their late verdict quite " *wisey wersey,*"
" *Acquit* you, and *not* recommend you to mercy." *

The Knight and the Lady

A Domestic Legend of the Reign of Queen Anne

" Hail wedded love ! mysterious tie ! "

Thomson—or Somebody.

THE Lady Jane was tall and slim,
  The Lady Jane was fair,
And Sir Thomas, her Lord, was stout of limb,
But his cough was short, and his eyes were dim,
And he wore green " specs," with a tortoiseshell rim,
And his hat was remarkably broad in the brim,
And she was uncommonly fond of him,—
  And they were a loving pair !—
    And the name and the fame
    Of the Knight and his Dame
Were ev'rywhere hail'd with the loudest acclaim ;
And wherever they went, or wherever they came,
Far and wide,   The people cried,
Huzza ! for the Lord of this noble domain,—
Huzza ! Huzza ! Huzza !—once again !—
    Encore !—Encore !—   One cheer more !—
—All sorts of pleasure, and no sort of pain
  To Sir Thomas the Good, and the Fair Lady Jane ! !

* At a Quarter Sessions held at Sandwich (some six miles from Birchington), on Tuesday the 8th of April last, before W. F. Boteler, Esq., the recorder, Thomas Jones, mariner, aged 17, was tried for stealing a jacket, value ten shillings. The jury, after a patient hearing, found him " not guilty," and " recommended him to mercy."—See the whole case reported in the " Kentish Observer," April 10, 1845.

Sir Thomas, her Lord, was stout of limb

Now Sir Thomas the Good,   Be it well understood,
Was a man of a very contemplative mood,—
  He would pore by the hour,   O'er a weed, or a flower,
Or the slugs that come crawling out after a shower ;
Black-beetles, and Bumble-Bees,—Blue-bottle flies,
And Moths were of no small account in his eyes ;
An " Industrious Flea " he'd by no means despise,
While an " Old Daddy-long-legs," whose " long legs " and
    thighs
Pass'd the common in shape, or in colour, or size,
He was wont to consider an absolute prize.
Nay, a hornet or wasp he could scarce " keep his paws off "—he
  Gave up, in short,   Both business and sport,
And abandon'd himself, *tout entier*, to Philosophy.

Now, as Lady Jane was tall and slim,
  And Lady Jane was fair,
And a good many years the junior of him,—
  And as he,   All agree,
    Look'd less like her *Mari*,
As he walk'd by her side than her *Père*,*
There are some might be found entertaining a notion
That such an entire and exclusive devotion
To that part of science, folks style Entomology,
  Was a positive shame,   And, to such a fair Dame,
Really demanded some sort of apology ;
  —No doubt, it *would* vex   One half of the sex
To see their own husband, in horrid green " specs,"
Instead of enjoying a sociable chat,
Still poking his nose into this and to that,
At a gnat, or a bat, or a cat, or a rat,
  Or great ugly things,   All legs and wings,
With nasty long tails arm'd with nasty long stings ;
And they'd join such a log of a spouse to condemn,
—One eternally thinking,   And blinking, and winking
At grubs,—when he ought to be winking at them.—
  But no !—oh no !   'Twas by no means so

* My friend, Mr. Hood,
In his comical mood,
Would have probably styled the good Knight and his Lady—
Him—" Stern-old and Hopkins," and her " Tête and Braidy."

With the Lady Jane Ingoldsby—she, far discreeter,
And, having a temper more even and sweeter,
 Would never object to *Her* spouse, in respect to
 His poking and peeping After " things creeping ; "
Much less be still keeping lamenting, and weeping,
Or scolding at what she perceived him so deep in.

 Tout au contraire, No lady so fair
Was e'er known to wear more contented an air ;
And,—let who would call,—every day she was there
Propounding receipts for some delicate fare,
Some toothsome conserve, of quince, apple, or pear,
Or distilling strong waters,—or potting a hare,—
Or counting her spoons and her crockery-ware ;—
Or else, her tambour-frame before her, with care
Embroidering a stool or a back for a chair,
With needle-work roses, most cunning and rare,
Enough to make less-gifted visitors stare,
 And declare, where'er
 They had been, that, " they ne'er
In their lives had seen aught that at all could compare
With dear Lady Jane's housewifery—that they would swear."

 Nay more ; don't suppose With such doings as those
This account of her merits must come to a close ;
No ;—examine her conduct more closely, you'll find
She by no means neglected improving her mind ;
For there, all the while, with air quite bewitching,
She sat herring-boning, tambouring, or stitching,
Or having an eye to affairs of the kitchen,
 Close by her side, Sat her kinsman, MacBride,
Her cousin, fourteen-times removed,—as you'll see
If you look at the Ingoldsby family tree,
In " Burke's Commoners," vol. xx. page 53.
 All the papers I've read agree, Too, with the pedigree,
Where, among the collateral branches, appears
" Captain Dugald MacBride, Royal Scots Fusileers ; "
And I doubt if you'd find in the whole of his clan
A more highly intelligent, worthy young man ;—
 And there he'd be sitting, While she was a-knitting,
Or hemming, or stitching, or darning and fitting.
 Or putting a " gore," or a " gusset," or " bit " in,

Reading aloud, with a very grave look,
Some very "wise saw" from some very good book,—
  Some such pious divine as St. Thomas Aquinas :
  Or, equally charming, The works of Bellarmine ;
  Or else he unravels The "voyages and travels"
Of Hackluytz—(how sadly these Dutch names *do* sully verse !)—
Purchas's, Hawksworth's, or Lemuel Gulliver's,—
Not to name others, 'mongst whom there are few so
Admired as John Bunyan, and Robinson Crusoe.—
  No matter who came, It was always the same,
The Captain was reading aloud to the Dame,
Till, from having gone through half the books on the shelf,
They were almost as wise as Sir Thomas himself.

  Well,—it happened one day, —I really can't say
The particular month ;—but I *think* 'twas in May,—
'Twas, I *know*, in the Spring-time,—when "Nature looks gay,"
As the Poet observes,—and on tree-top and spray
The dear little dickey-birds carol away ;
When the grass is so green, and the sun is so bright,
And all things are teeming with life and with light,—.
That the whole of the house was thrown into affright,
For no soul could conceive what was gone with the Knight !

  It seems he had taken A light breakfast—bacon,
An egg—with a little broil'd haddock—at most
A round and a half of some hot butter'd toast,
With a slice of cold sirloin from yesterday's roast.
  And then—let me see !— He had two—perhaps three
Cups (with sugar and cream) of strong gunpowder tea,
With a spoonful in each of some choice *eau de vie*,
—Which with nine out of ten would perhaps disagree.—
  —In fact, I and my son Mix "black" with our "Hyson,"
Neither having the nerves of a bull, or a bison,
And both hating brandy like what some call "pison,"
  No matter for that— He had call'd for his hat,
With the brim that I've said was so broad and so flat,
And his "specs" with the tortoiseshell rim, and his cane
With the crutch-handled top, which he used to sustain
His steps in his walks, and to poke in the shrubs
And the grass, when unearthing his worms and his grubs—

Thus arm'd, he set out on a ramble—alack !
He *set out*, poor dear Soul !—but he never came back !

" First dinner-bell " rang   Out its euphonous clang
At five—folks kept early hours then—and the " Last "
Ding-dong'd, as it ever was wont, at half-past,
    While Betsey, and Sally,   And Thompson, the *Valet*,
And every one else was beginning to bless himself,
Wondering the Knight had not come in to dress himself.—
—Quoth Betsey, " Dear me ! why, the fish will be cold ! "—
Quoth Sally, " Good gracious ! how ' Missis ' *will* scold ! "—
    Thompson, the *Valet*,   Look'd gravely at Sally,
As who should say, " Truth must not always be told ! "
Then, expressing a fear lest the Knight might take cold,
    Thus exposed to the dews,
    Lambs'-wool stockings, and shoes,
    Of each a fresh pair,   He put down to air,
And hung a clean shirt to the fire on a chair.—

Still the Master was absent—the Cook came and said, " he
Much fear'd, as the dinner had been so long ready,
    The roast and the boil'd   Would be all of it spoil'd,
And the puddings, her Ladyship thought such a treat,
He was morally sure, would be scarce fit to eat ! "
    This closed the debate—   " 'Twould be folly to wait,"
Said the Lady.   " Dish up !—Let the meal be served straight ;
And let two or three slices be put on a plate,
And kept hot for Sir Thomas.—He's lost, sure as fate !
And, a hundred to one, won't be home till it's late ! "
—Captain Dugald MacBride then proceeded to face
The Lady at table,—stood up, and said grace,—
Then set himself down in Sir Thomas's place.

    Wearily, wearily, all that night,
      That live-long night, did the hours go by ;
    And the Lady Jane,   In grief and in pain,
      She sat herself down to cry !—
    And Captain MacBride,   Who sat by her side,
Though I really can't say that he actually cried,
      At least had a tear in his eye !—

As much as can well be expected, perhaps,
From very " young fellows," for very " old chaps ; "
  And if he had said   What he'd got in his head,

'Twould have been, " Poor old Buffer ! he's certainly dead ! "
The morning dawn'd,—and the next,—and the next
And all in the mansion were still perplex'd ;
No watch-dog " bay'd a welcome home," as
A watch-dog should, to the " Good Sir Thomas ; "
  No knocker fell   His approach to tell
Not so much as a runaway ring at the bell—
The Hall was silent as Hermit's cell.

Yet the sun shone bright upon tower and tree,
And the meads smiled green as green may be,
And the dear little dickey-birds caroll'd with glee,
And the lambs in the park skipp'd merry and free—
—Without, all was joy and harmony !
" And thus 'twill be,—nor long the day,—
  Ere we, like him, shall pass away !
  Yon Sun, that now *our* bosoms warms,
  Shall shine,—but shine on other forms ;—
  Yon Grove, whose choir so sweetly cheers
  Us now, shall sound on other ears,—
  The joyous Lamb, as now, shall play,
  But other eyes its sports survey,—
  The Stream we loved shall roll as fair,
  The flowery sweets, the trim Parterre
  Shall scent, as now, the ambient air,—
  The Tree, whose bending branches bear
  The One loved name—shall yet be there ;—
  But where the hand that carved it ?—Where ? "

These were hinted to me as   The very ideas
Which passed through the mind of the fair Lady Jane,
Her thoughts having taken a sombre-ish train,
As she walk'd on the esplanade, to and again,
  With Captain MacBride   Of course, at her side,
Who could not look quite so forlorn,—though he tried,
—An " idea," in fact, had got into *his* head,
That if " poor dear Sir Thomas " should really be dead,

It might be no bad " spec." to be there in his stead,
And, by simply contriving, in due time, to wed
   A Lady who was young and fair,
     A Lady slim and tall,
   To set himself down in comfort there
     The Lord of Tapton * Hall.—

Thinks he, " We have sent   Half over Kent,
And nobody knows how much money's been spent,
Yet no one's been found to say which way he went !—
   The groom, who's been over
   To Folkestone and Dover,
Can't get any tidings at all of the rover !
—Here's a fortnight and more has gone by, and we've tried
Every plan we could hit on—the whole country-side,
   Upon all its dead walls, with placards we've supplied,—
And we've sent out the Crier, and had him well cried—
   ' Missing ! ! Stolen, or stray'd, Lost, or mislaid,
A Gentleman ;—middle-aged, sober, and staid ;—
Stoops slightly ;—and when he left home was array'd
In a sad-coloured suit, somewhat dingy and fray'd ;—
Had spectacles on with a tortoiseshell rim,
And a hat rather low-crown'd, and broad in the brim.—
   Whoe'er Shall bear, Or shall send him with care,
(Right side uppermost) home ;—or shall give notice where
The said middle-aged Gentleman is ; or shall state
Any fact, that may tend to throw light on his fate,
To the man at the turnpike, called Tappington Gate,
Shall receive a Reward of Five Pounds for his trouble,—
(☞ N.B.—If defunct the Reward will be double ! ! ☜) '

   " Had he been above ground
   He *must* have been found.—
No ; doubtless he's shot,—or he's hang'd,—or he's drown'd !—
   Then his Widow—ay ! ay !—But, what will folk say !—
To address her at once—at so early a day !
Well—what then ?—who cares ?—let 'em say what they may—
A fig for their nonsense and chatter !—suffice it, her
Charms will excuse one for casting sheep's eyes at her ! "

* The familiar abbreviation for Tappington Everard still in use among the tenantry.—*Vide
Prefatory Introduction to the Ingoldsby Legends.*

When a man has decided   As Captain MacBride did,
And once fully made up his mind on the matter, he
Can't be too prompt in unmasking his battery.
He began on the instant, and vow'd that " her eyes
Far exceeded in brilliance the stars in the skies,—
That her lips were like roses—her cheeks were like lilies—
Her breath had the odour of daffy-down-dillies ! "—
With a thousand more compliments equally true,
And expressed in similitudes equally new !
  —Then his left arm he placed
  Round her jimp, taper waist—
—Ere she'd fix'd to repulse, or return, his embrace,
Up came running a man, at a deuce of a pace,
With that very peculiar expression of face
Which always betokens dismay or disaster,
Crying out,—'twas the Gardener,—" Oh, Ma'am ! we've found
    Master ! "—
—" Where ? where ? " scream'd the lady ; and Echo scream'd—
    " Where ? "
  —The man couldn't say " There ! "
  He had no breath to spare,
But, gasping for air, he could only respond
By pointing—he pointed, alas !—TO THE POND.

—'Twas e'en so—poor dear Knight !—with his " specs " and his hat
He'd gone poking his nose into this and to that ;
  When, close to the side   Of the bank, he espied
An " uncommon fine " Tadpole, remarkably fat !
  He stooped ;—and he thought her
  His own ;—he had caught her !
Got hold of her tail,—and to land almost brought her,
When—he plump'd head and heels into fifteen feet water !

  The Lady Jane was tall and slim,
    The Lady Jane was fair,
  Alas, for Sir Thomas !—she grieved for him,
  As she saw two serving-men, sturdy of limb,
    His body between them bear.
She sobb'd, and she sigh'd ; she lamented, and cried,
  For of sorrow brimful was her cup ;
She swoon'd, and I think she'd have fall'n down and died,

If Captain MacBride   Had not been by her side,
With the Gardener ; they both their assistance supplied,
    And managed to hold her up.—
      But, when she " comes to,"
      Oh ! 'tis shocking to view
    The sight which the corpse reveals !
      Sir Thomas's body,   It look'd so odd—he
    Was half eaten up by the eels !
His waistcoat and hose, and the rest of his clothes
    Were all gnawed through and through ;
      And out of each shoe   An eel they drew ;
And from each of his pockets they pull'd out two
And the Gardener himself had secreted a few,
      As well we may suppose ;
For, when he came running to give the alarm,
He had six in the basket that hung on his arm.

    Good Father John *   Was summon'd anon ;
    Holy water was sprinkled,   And little bells tinkled,
    And tapers were lighted,   And incense ignited,
And masses were sung, and masses were said,
All day, for the quiet repose of the dead,
And all night no one thought about going to bed.

    But Lady Jane was tall and slim,
      And Lady Jane was fair,—
And, ere morning came, that winsome dame
Had made up her mind—or, what's much the same,
Had *thought about*—once more " changing her name,"
      And she said, with a pensive air,
To Thompson, the valet, while taking away,
When supper was over, the cloth and the tray,—
      " Eels a many   I've ate ; but any
    So good ne'er tasted before !—
They're a fish, too, of which I'm remarkably fond.—
Go—pop Sir Thomas again in the Pond—
      Poor dear !—HE'LL CATCH US SOME MORE ! ! "

* For some account of Father John Ingoldsby, to whose papers I am so much beholden, see
p. 135. This was the last ecclesiastical act of his long and valuable life.

MORAL.

All middle-aged Gentlemen let me advise,
If you're married, and have not got very good eyes,
Don't go poking about after blue-bottle flies !—
If you've spectacles, don't have a tortoiseshell rim,
And don't go near the water,—unless you can swim !

Married Ladies, especially such as are fair,
Tall, and slim, I would next recommend to beware
How, on losing *one* spouse, they give way to despair ;
But let them reflect, " There are fish, and no doubt on't—
As good *in* the river as ever came *out* on't ! "

Should they light on a spouse who is given to roaming
In solitude—*raison de plus*, in the " gloaming,"—
Let them have a fix'd time for said spouse to come home in !
And if, when " last dinner-bell " 's rung, he is late,
To insure better manners in future—Don't wait !—

If of husband or children they chance to be fond,
Have a stout iron-wire fence put all round the pond !

One more piece of advice, and I close my appeals—
That is—if you chance to be partial to eels,
Then—*Crede experto*—trust one who has tried—
Have them spitch-cock'd,—or stew'd—they're too oily when fried !

The House-Warming ! !

A Legend of Bleeding-Heart Yard

Did you ever see the Devil dance ?—OLD QUERY.

SIR CHRISTOPHER HATTON he danced
    with grace,
He'd a very fine form and a very fine
    face,
And his cloak and his doublet were
    guarded with lace,
    And the rest of his clothes,
    As you well may suppose,
In taste were by no means inferior
    to those ;
    He'd a yellow-starch'd ruff,
    And his gloves were of buff,
On each of his shoes a red heel and
    a rose,
And nice little moustaches under his
    nose ;
    Then every one knows
    How he turn'd out his toes,

And a very great way that accomplishment goes,
In a Court where it's thought, in a lord or a duke, a
Disgrace to fall short in " the Brawls "—(their Cachouca).
So what with his form, and what with his face,
And what with his velvet cloak guarded with lace,
And what with his elegant dancing and grace,
    His dress and address   So tickled Queen Bess
That her Majesty gave him a very snug place ;
And seeing, moreover, at one single peep, her
Advisers were, few of them, sharper or deeper
(Old Burleigh excepted), she made him Lord Keeper !

I've heard, I confess, with no little surprise,
English history called a farrago of lies ;
    And a certain Divine,   A connexion of mine,
Who ought to know better, as some folks opine,

498

Is apt to declare,   Leaning back in his chair,
With a sort of a smirking, self-satisfied air,
That " all that's recorded in Hume, and elsewhere,
    " Of our early ' *Annales* '   A trumpery tale is,
" Like the ' bold Captain Smith's,' and the ' Luckless Miss
        Bayley's '—
" That old Roger Hoveden, and Ralph de Diceto,
" And others (whose names should I try to repeat o-
" ver, well I'm assured you would put in your veto),
    " Though all holy friars,   Were very great liars,
" And raised stories faster than Grissel and Peto—
" That Harold escaped with the loss of a ' glim '—
" —That the shaft which killed Rufus ne'er glanced from a limb
" Of a tree, as they say, but was aimed slap at *him*,—
" That Fair Rosamond never was poison'd or spitted,
" But outlived Queen Nell, who was much to be pitied ;—
" That Nelly her namesake, Ned Longshanks's wife,
" Ne'er went crusading at all in her life,
" Nor suck'd the wound made by the poison-tipp'd knife !
    " For as she,   O'er the sea,
    " Towards far Galilee,
" Never, even in fancy, march'd carcass or shook shanks,
" Of course she could no more suck Longshanks than Cruick-
        shanks,
" But, leaving her spindle-legged liege lord to roam,
" Stayed behind, and suck'd something much better at home,—
    " That it's quite as absurd
    " To say Edward the Third,
" In reviving the Garter, afforded a handle
" For any Court-gossip, detraction, or scandal,
    " As 'twould be to say   That at Court t'other day
" At the fête which the newspapers say was so gay,
" His Great Representative then stole away
" Lady Salisbury's garters as part of the play,—
" —That as to Prince Hal's being taken to jail,
" By the London Police, without mainprize or bail,
    " For cuffing a judge,   It's a regular fudge ;
" And that Chief-Justice Gascoigne, it's very well known,
" Was kicked out the moment he came to the throne,—
" —Then that Richard the Third was a ' marvellous proper man '—
" Never killed, injur'd, or wrong'd of a copper, man.—

" Ne'er wished to smother   The sons of his brother,—
" Nor ever stuck Harry the Sixth, who, instead
" Of being squabash'd, as in Shakspeare we've read,
" Caught a bad influenza, and died in his bed,
" In the Tower, not far from the room where the Guard is
" (The octagon one that adjoins Duffus Hardy's) ;
" —That, in short, all the ' facts ' in the *Decem Scriptores*,
" Are nothing at all but sheer humbugging stories."

Then if, as he vows, both this country and France in,
Historians thus gave themselves up to romancing,
Notwithstanding what most of them join in advancing
Respecting Sir Christopher's capering and prancing,
　'Twill cause no surprise   If we find that his rise
Is *not* to be solely ascribed to his dancing !
The fact is, Sir Christopher, early in life,
As all bachelors should do, had taken a wife,
A Fanshawe by family,—one of a house
Well descended, but boasting less " nobles " than *nous ;*
Though e'en as to purse   He might have done worse,
For I find, on perusing her Grandfather's will, it is
Clear she had " good gifts beside possibilities," *
　Owches and rings,   And such sort of things,
Orellana shares (then the American Stocks),
Jewell'd stomachers, coifs, ruffs, silk-stockings with clocks,
Point-lace, cambric handkerchiefs, nightcaps, and—socks—
(Recondite apparel contained in her box),
　—Then the height of her breeding
　And depth of her reading
Might captivate any gay youth, and, in leading
Him on to " propose," well, excuse the proceeding :
Truth to tell, as to " reading," the Lady was thought to do
More than she should, and know more than she ought to do ;
　Her maid, it was said,   Declared that she read
(A custom all staid folks discourage) in bed ;
　And that often o' nights   Odd noises and sights
In her mistress's chamber had giv'n her sad frights,
After all in the mansion had put out their lights,

---

* " Seven hundred pounds and possibilities is good gifts.
　　　　　　　　　　　　　　　　SIR HUGH EVANS.

And she verily thought that hobgoblins and sprites
Were there, kicking up all sorts of devil's delights ;—
Miss Alice, in short, was supposed to " collogue "—I
Don't much like the word—with the subtle old rogue, I
've heard call'd by so many names—one of them's " Bogy "—
 Indeed 'twas conceived, And by most folks believed,
—A thing at which all of her well-wishers griev'd,—
That should she incline to play such a vagary,
Like sage Lady Branxholm, her contempo-rary,
(Excuse the false quantity, reader, I pray),
She could turn a knight into a wagon of hay,
Or two nice little boys into puppies at play,
Raison de plus, not a doubt could exist of her
Pow'r to turn " Kit Hatton " into " Sir Christopher ; "
But what " mighty magic," or strong " conjuration,"
Whether love-powder, philtre, or other potation
 She used, I confess, I'm unable to guess,—
 Much less to express By what skill and address
She ." cut and contrived " with such signal success,
As we Londoners say, to " inwiggle " Queen Bess,
 Inasmuch as I lack heart To study the Black Art ;
Be that as it may,—it's as clear as the sun,
That, however she did it, 'twas certainly done !

Now, they're all very well, titles, honour, and rank,
Still, we can't but admit, if we choose to be frank,
There's no harm in a snug little sum in the Bank !
 An old proverb says, " Pudding still before praise ! "
An adage well known I've no doubt in those days,
And George Colman the Younger, in one of his plays,
Makes one of his characters loudly declare
That " a Lord without money,"—I quote from his " Heir-
At-Law "—" 's but a poor wishy-washy affair ! "—
In her subsequent conduct I think we can see a
Strong proof the Dame entertained some such idea,
 For, once in the palace, We find Lady Alice
Again playing tricks with her Majesty's chalice
 In the way that the jocose, in
 Our days, term " hocussing : "
The liquor she used, as I've said, she kept close,
But, whatever it was, she now doubled the dose !

(So true is the saying　"We never can stay, in
Our progress, when once with the foul fiend we league us.")
—She "doctor'd" the punch, and she "doctor'd" the negus,
Taking care not to put in sufficient to flavour it,
　Till, at every fresh sip　That moisten'd her lip
The Virgin Queen grew more attach'd to her Favourite.
　"No end" now he commands　Of money and lands,
And as George Robins says, when he's writing about houses,
"Messuages, tenements, crofts, tofts, and outhouses,"
Parks, manors, chases, She "gives and she grants,
To him and his heirs, and his uncles and aunts;"
Whatever he wants, he has only to ask it,
And all other suitors are "left in the basket,"
　Till Dudley and Rawleigh　Began to look squally,
While even grave Cecil, the famous Lord Burleigh,
Himself, "shook his head," and grew snappish and surly.
　All this was fine sport,　As our authors report,
To Dame Alice, become a great Lady at Court,
Where none than her Ladyship's husband look'd bigger, •
Who "led the brawls" * still with the same grace and vigour,
Though losing a little in slimness and figure;
For eating and drinking all day of the best
　Of viands well drest,　With "Burgess's Zest,"
Is apt, by degrees, to enlarge a man's vest;
And, what in Sir Christopher went to increase it, he
'd always been rather inclined to obesity;
—Few men in those times were found to grow thinner
With beefsteaks for breakfast and pork-pie for dinner.

Now it's really a difficult problem to say
How long matters might have gone on in this way.
If it had not unluckily happen'd one day
　That NICK,—who, because
　He'd the gout in his claws,
And his hoofs—(he's by no means so young as he was,
And is subject of late to a sort of rheumatic a-
ttack that partakes both of gout and sciatica,)—

* The grave Lord Keeper led the brawls,
　　The seals and maces danced before him.—GRAY.

All the night long had twisted and grinn'd,
His pains much increased by an easterly wind,
Which always compels him to hobble and limp,
Was strongly advised by his Medical Imp
To lie by a little and give over work,
For he'd lately been slaving away like a Turk,
On the Guinea-coast, helping to open a brave trade
In Niggers, with Hawkins * who founded the slave-trade,
So he call'd for his ledger, the constant resource
Of your Mercantile folk, when they're " not in full force ; "
—If a cold or catarrh makes them husky and hoarse,
Or a touch of gout keeps them away from " the Bourse,"
They look over their books as a matter of course.
Now scarce had Nick turn'd over one page, or two,
Ere a prominent *item* attracted his view,
A Bill !—that had now been some days overdue,
From one Alice Hatton, *née* Fanshawe—a name
Which you'll recognise, reader, at once as the same
With that borne by Sir Christopher's erudite dame !
The signature—much more *prononcée* than pink,
Seem'd written in *blood*—but it might be red ink—
   While the rest of the deed He proceeded to read,
Like ev'ry " bill, bond, or acquittance " whose date is
Three hundred years old, ran in Latin.—" *Sciatis*
(*Diaboli ?*) *omnes ad quos hæc pervenient* "—
—But courage, dear Reader, I mean to be lenient,
And scorn to inflict on you half the " Law-reading "
I picked up " umquhile " in three days' Special pleading
Which cost me—a theme I'll not pause to digress on—
Just thirty-three pounds six-and-eightpence a lesson—
" As I'm stout, I'll be merciful," therefore, and sparing
All these technicalities, end by declaring
   The deed so correct As to make one suspect,
(Were it possible any such person could go there)
Old Nick had a Special Attorney below there :
'Twas so fram'd and express'd no tribunal could shake it,
And firm as red wax and *black* ferret could make it.

---

* Sir John Hawkins for " his *worthye* attempts and services," and because " in the same he had dyvers conflights with the Moryans and slew and toke dyvers of the same Moryans " received from Elizabeth an *honourable* augmentation to his coat armour, including, for his crest, " *A Demi-Moor sable, with two manacles on each arm, or.*"

By the roll of his eye   As Old Nick put it by,
It was clear he had made up his mind what to do
In respect to the course he should have to pursue
When his hoof would allow him to put on a shoe ! !

No, although the Lord Keeper held under the Crown, house
And land in the country—he'd never a Town-house.
    And, as we have seen,   His course always had been,
When he wanted a thing, to solicit the Queen,
So now, in the hope of a fresh acquisition,
He danced off to Court with his " Humble Petition."

" Please your Majesty's Grace,   I have not a place
" I can well put my head in, to dine, sup, or sleep !
" Your Grace's Lord Keeper has nowhere to *keep*,
    " So I beg and intreat,   At your Majesty's feet,
" That your Grace will be graciously pleas'd for to say,
    " With as little delay   As your Majesty may,
" Where your Majesty's Grace's Lord Keeper's to stay—
" —And your Grace's Petitioner ever will pray ! "

    The Queen, when she heard   This petition preferr'd,
Gave ear to Sir Christopher's suit at a word ;—
" Odds Bobs, my good Lord ! " was her gracious reply,
    " I don't know, not I,   Any good reason why
" A Lord Keeper, like you, should not always be nigh
" To advise—and devise—and revise—our supply—
" A House ! we're surprised that the thing did not strike
" Us before—Yes !—of course !—Pray, whose House would you
    like ?
" When I *do* things of this kind, I do them genteelly,
" A House ?—let me see ! there's the Bishop of Ely !
" A capital mansion, I'm told, the proud knave is in,
" Up there in Holborn, just opposite Thavies' Inn—
" Where the Strawberries grow so fine and so big,
" Which our Grandmother's Uncle tucked in like a pig,
" King Richard the Third, which you all must have read of—
" The day,—don't you know ?—he cut Hastings' head off—
" And mark me, proud Prelate !—I'm speaking to you,
" Bishop Heaton !—you need not, my lord, look so blue—

" Give it up on the instant ! I don't mean to shock you,
" Or else by—— !—(The Bishop *was* shocked !)—I'll unfrock you ! ! "

The Queen turns abruptly her back on the group,
The Courtiers all bow as she passes, and stoop
To kiss, as she goes, the hind flounce of her hoop,
And Sir Christopher, having thus danced to some tune,
Skips away with much glee in his best rigadoon !
 While poor Bishop Heaton,
 Who found himself beaten,
In serious alarm at the Queen's contumelious
And menacing tone, at once gave him up Ely House,
With every appurtenance thereto belonging,
Including the strawberry beds 'twas so strong in ;
Politely he bow'd to the gratified minion,
And said, " There can be, my good lord, in opinion
 No difference betwixt yours And mine as to fixtures
 And tables, and chairs— We need no survey'rs—
Take them just as you find them, without reservation,
Grates, coppers, and all, at your own valuation ! "

 Well ! the object is gained !
 A good town-house obtained !
The next thing to be thought of, is now
The " house-warming " party—the *when* and the *how*—
 The Court ladies call, One and all, great and small,
For an elegant " Spread," and more elegant Ball,
So, Sir Christopher, vain as we know, of his capering,
No sooner had finished his painting and papering,
 Than he sat down and wrote A nice little pink note
To every great Lord whom he knew, and his spouse,
" From our poor place on Holborn-hill (late Ely House),
" Lord Keeper and Dame Alice Hatton request
" Lord So-and-so's (name, style, or title exprest)
 " Good company on The next Eve of St. John,
" Viz. : Friday week, June 24th, as their guest,
 " To partake of pot-luck, And taste a fat buck.
" N.B. Venison on table exactly at 3,
" Quadrilles in the afternoon. R. S. V. P.
" For my good Lord of So-and-so these, and his wife ;
" Ride ! Ride ! for thy life ! for thy life ! for thy life ! "

Thus courtiers were wont to indorse their expresses
In Harry the VIIIth's time, and also Queen Bess's.
The Dame, for her part, too, took order that cards
Should be sent to the mess-rooms of all the Hussards,
The Household troops, Train-bands, and horse and foot Guards.

Well, the day for the rout　　At length came about,
And the bells of St. Andrew's rang merrily out,
As horse-litter, coach, and pad-nag, with its pillion,
(The mode of conveyance then used by the " Million,")
　　All gallant and grand,　　Defiled from the Strand,
Some through Chancery (then an unpaved and much wetter) Lane,
Others through Shoe (which was not a whit better) Lane ;
Others through Fewtar's (corrupted to Fetter) Lane ;
Some from Cheapside, and St. Mary-le-Bow,
From Bishopsgate Street, Dowgate Hill,* and Budge Row.
　　They come and they go,
　　Squire and Dame, Belle and Beau,
Down Snore Hill (which we have since whitewash'd to Snow),
All eager to see the magnificent show,
And sport what some call " a fantastical toe ; "
　　In silk and in satin,　　To batten and fatten
Upon the good cheer of Sir Christopher Hatton.

A flourish, trumpets !—sound again !—
　　He comes, bold Drake, the chief who made a
Fine hash of all the pow'rs of Spain,
　　And so serv'd out their Grand Armada :
With him come Frobisher and Hawkins,
In yellow ruffs, rosettes, and stockings.

Room for my Lord !—proud Leicester's Earl
　　Retires awhile from courtly cares,
Who took his wife, poor hapless girl !
　　And pitch'd her neck and heel down stairs ;
Proving, in hopes to wed a richer,
If not her ".friend," at least her " pitcher."

A flourish, trumpets ! strike the drums !
　　Will Shakspeare, never of his pen sick,

* Sir Francis Drake's house, " the Arbour," stood here.

Is here—next Doctor Masters comes,
   Renown'd afar for curing men sick,—
Queen's Serjeant Barham * with his bums
   And tipstaves, coif, and wig forensic ;
(He lost, unless Sir Richard lies, his
Life at the famous " Black Assizes.")

Room ! Room ! for great Cecil !—place, place, for his Dame !—
Room ! Room ! for Southampton—for Sidney, whose name
As a *Preux Chevalier*, in the records of Fame,
" Beats Banagher "—e'en now his praises, we all sing 'em,
Knight, Poet, Gentleman !—Room ! for sage Walsingham !—

Room ! for Lord Hunsdon !—for Sussex !—for Rawleigh !—
For INGOLDSBY ! ! Oh ! it's enough to appal ye !
   Dear me ! how they call !
   How they squall ! how they bawl !
This dame has lost her shoe—that one her shawl—
My lord's got a tumble—my lady a fall !—
   Now a Hall ! a Hall ! A Brawl ! a Brawl !
Here's my Lord Keeper Hatton, so stately and tall !
Has led out Lady Hunsdon to open the Ball !

Fiddlers ! Fiddlers ! fiddle away !
Resin your catgut ! fiddle and play !
   A roundelay ! Fiddle away !
Obey ! obey !—hear what they all say !
Hip !—Music !—Nosey ! !—play up there !—play !
Never was anything half so gay
As Sir Christopher Hatton's grand holiday !

The clock strikes twelve !—Who cares for the clock ?
Who cares for—Hark !—What a loud Single-knock !
   Dear me ! dear me ! Who can it be ?—
Why, who can be coming at this time of night,
With a knock *like that* honest folk to affright !—
" Affright ? "—yes *affright !*—there are many who mock
At fear, and in danger stand firm as a rock,
Whom the roar of the battle-field never could shock,
Yet quail at the sound of a vile " Single-knock ! "

Called by Sir Richard Baker " The famous Lawyer."—*See his Chronicle.*

Hark !—what can the Porter be thinking of ?—What !—
If the booby has not let him in I'll be shot !—
 Dear me ! how hot The room's all at once got !—
  And what rings through the roof ?—
  It's the sound of a *hoof !*
It's some donkey a-coming upstairs at full trot !
Stay !—the folding-doors open ! the leaves are thrown back,
And in dances a tall *Figurant*—ALL IN BLACK ! !

Gracious me what an *entrechat !* Oh, what a bound !
Then with what an *a-plomb* he comes down to the ground !
 Look there ! look there ! Now he's up in the air !
Now he's here !—now he's there—now he's no one knows where !—
See ! see !—he's kicked over a table and chair !
There they go !—all the strawberries, flowers, and sweet herbs,
 Turn'd o'er and o'er, Down on the floor,
Ev'ry caper he cuts oversets or disturbs
All the " Keen's Seedlings " and " Wilmot's Superbs ! "
 There's a *pirouette !*—we're All a great deal too near !
A ring !—give him room or he'll " shin " you—stand clear !
There's a spring again !—oh ! 'tis quite frightful !—oh dear !
His toe's broke the top of the glass chandelier ! !
Now he's down again !—look at the *congées* and bows
And *salaams* which he makes to the Dame of the House,
Lady Alice, the noble Lord Treasurer's spouse !
 Come, now we shall view A grand *pas de deux*
Perform'd in the very first style by these two.
—But no !—she recoils—she could scarce look more pale if
Instead of a Beau's 'twas the bow of a Bailiff !—
He holds out his hand—she declines it, and draws
Back her own—see !—he grasps it with horrid black claws,
Like the short, sharp, strong nails of a Polar Bear's paws ! !

 Then she " scream'd such a scream ! "
 Such another, I deem,
As, long after, Miss Mary Brown * scream'd in her dream.
Well she might ! for 'twas shrewdly remark'd by her Page,
A sharp little boy about twelve years of age,
 Who was standing close by When she utter'd her cry,
That the whole of her arm shrivell'd up and grew dry,

* *Vide* the celebrated ballad of " Giles Scroggins."—*Catnach's ed. Seven Dials, Lond.* 1841.

A grand *pas de deux* Performed in the very first style by these two

While the fingers and thumb of the hand he had got
In his clutches became on the instant RED HOT ! !

   Now he whirls and he twirls
   Through the girls in their curls,
And their rouge, and their feathers, and diamonds, and pearls ;
   Now high,—now low,— Now fast, and now slow,
In terrible circumgyration they go,
The flame-coloured Belle and her coffee-faced Beau !
Up they go once ! and up they go twice !—
Round the hall !—round the hall !—and now up they go thrice !
Now one grand *pirouette*, the performance to crown !
Now again they go UP ! !—and they NEVER COME DOWN ! ! !

    *   *   *   *   *

   The thunder roars ! And the rain it pours !
And the lightning comes in through the windows and doors !
   Then more calling, and bawling,
   And squalling, and falling,
Oh ! what a fearful " stramash " they are all in !
   Out they all sally, The whole *corps de ballet*—
Some dash down Holborn-hill into the valley,
Where stagnates Fleet Ditch at the end of Harp Alley,
Some t'other way, with a speed quite amazing,
Nor pause to take breath till they get beyond Gray's Inn.
In every sense of the word, such a *rout* of it,
Never was made in London, or out of it !

When they came the next day to examine the scene,
There was scarcely a vestige of all that had been ;
The beautiful tapestry, blue, red, and green,
Was all blacken'd and scorch'd, and look'd dirty and mean,
All the crockery broken, dish, plate, and tureen !
While those who look'd up could perceive in the roof
One very large hole in the shape of a *hoof !*

Of poor Lady Hatton, it's needless to say
No traces have ever been found to this day,
Or the terrible dancer who whisk'd her away ;
But out in the court-yard—and just in that part
Where the pump stands—lay bleeding a LARGE HUMAN HEART !

And sundry large stains   Of blood and of brains,
Which had not been wash'd off notwithstanding the rains,
Appear'd on the wood, and the handle and chains,
As if somebody's head with a very hard thump,
Had been recently knock'd on the top of the pump.
That pump is no more !—that of which you've just read,—
But they've put a new iron one up in its stead,
    And still, it is said,   At that " small hour " so dread,
When all sober people are cosey in bed,
There may sometimes be seen on a moonshiny night.
Standing close by the new pump, a Lady in White,
Who keeps pumping away with, 'twould seem, all her might,
Though never a drop comes her pains to requite !
And hence many passengers now are debarr'd
From proceeding at nightfall through Bleeding-Heart Yard !

MORAL.

    Fair ladies, attend !   And if you've a " friend
At Court," don't attempt to bamboozle or trick her !
—Don't meddle with negus, or any mix'd liquor !—
Don't dabble in " Magic ! " my story has shown
How wrong 'tis to use any charms but your own !

Young Gentlemen, too, may, I think, take a hint
Of the same kind, from what I've here ventured to print,
All Conjuring's bad ! they may get in a scrape
Before they're aware, and whatever its shape,
They may find it no easy affair to escape.
It's not everybody that comes off so well
From *leger-de-main* tricks as Mr. Brunel.

Don't dance with a Stranger who looks like a Guy,
And *when* dancing don't cut your capers too high !
    Depend on't the fault's in   Your method of waltzing,
If ever you kick out the candles—don't try !

    At a ball or a play,   Or any *soirée*,
When a *petit souper* constitutes the " *Après*,"
If strawb'ries and cream with CHAMPAGNE form a part,
Take care of your HEAD !—and take care of your HEART !

If you want a new house
  For yourself and your spouse,
Buy, or build one,—and honestly pay, every brick, for it !
Don't be so green as to go to Old Nick for it—
—Go to George Robins—he'll find you " a perch,"
(*Dulce domum*'s his word,) without robbing the Church !

The last piece of advice which I'd have you regard
Is, " don't go of a night into Bleeding-Heart Yard,"
It's a dark, little, dirty, black, ill-looking square,
With queer people about, and unless you take care,
You may find, when your pocket's clean'd out and left bare,
That the *iron* one is not the *only* " PUMP " there !

The Forlorn One

AH ! why those piteous sounds of woe,
  Lone wanderer of the dreary night ?
Thy gushing tears in torrents flow,
  Thy bosom pants in wild affright !

And thou, within whose iron breast
  Those frowns austere too truly tell,
Mild pity, heaven-descended guest,
  Hath never, never deign'd to dwell.

" That rude, uncivil touch forego,"
  Stern despot of a fleeting hour !
Nor " make the angels weep " to know
  The fond " fantastic tricks " of power !

Know'st thou not " mercy is not strain'd,
  But droppeth as the gentle dew,"
And while it blesseth him who gain'd,
  It blesseth him who gave it too ?

Say, what art thou ? and what is he,
  Pale victim of despair and pain,
Whose streaming eyes and bended knee
  Sue to thee thus—and sue in vain ?

Cold, callous man !—he scorns to yield,
    Or aught relax his felon gripe,
But answers, " I'm Inspector Field !
    And this here Warment's prigg'd your wipe ! "

Jerry Jarvis's Wig

A Legend of the Weald of Kent

" The wig's the thing ! the wig ! the wig."—*Old Song.*

" Joe," said old Jarvis, looking out of his window,—it was his ground-floor back,—" Joe, you seem to be very hot, Joe,—and you have got no wig ! "

" Yes, sir," quoth Joseph, pausing, and resting upon his spade, " it's as hot a day as ever I *see ;* but the celery must be got in, or there'll be no autumn crop, and——"

" Well, but, Joe, the sun's so hot, and it shines so on your bald head, it makes one wink to look at it. You'll have a *coup de soleil,* Joe."

" A *what,* sir ? "

" No matter ; it's very hot working ; and if you'll step indoors, I'll give you——"

" Thank ye, your honour, a drop of beer will be very acceptable."

Joe's countenance brightened amazingly.

" Joe, I'll give you—my old wig ! "

The countenance of Joseph fell, his grey eye had glistened as a blest vision of double X flitted athwart his fancy ; its glance faded again into the old, filmy, gooseberry-coloured hue, as he growled in a minor key, " A wig, sir ! "

" Yes, Joe, a wig ! The man who does not study the comfort of his dependants is an unfeeling scoundrel. You shall have my old worn-out wig."

" I hope, sir, you'll give me a drop o' beer to drink your honour's health in,—it *is* very hot, and——"

" Come in, Joe, and Mrs. Witherspoon shall give it you."

" Heaven bless your honour ! " said honest Joe, striking his spade perpendicularly into the earth, and walking with more than usual alacrity towards the close-cut, quick-set hedge which separated Mr. Jarvis's garden from the high road.

From the quickset hedge aforesaid he now raised, with all due delicacy, a well-worn and somewhat dilapidated jacket, of a stuff by drapers most pseudonymously termed "everlasting." Alack! alack! what is there to which *tempus edax rerum* will accord that epithet? In its high and palmy days it had been all of a piece; but as its master's eye now fell upon it, the expression of his countenance seemed to say with Octavian,

> "Those days are gone, Floranthe!"

It was now, from frequent patching, a coat not unlike that of the patriarch, one of many colours.

Joseph Washford inserted his wrists into the corresponding orifices of the tattered garment, and with a steadiness of circumgyration, to be acquired only by long and sufficient practice, swung it horizontally over his ears, and settled himself into it.

"Confound your old jacket!" cried a voice from the other side the hedge, "keep it down you rascal! don't you see my horse is frightened at it?"

"Sensible beast!" apostrophized Joseph, "I've been frighten'd at it myself every day for the last two years!"

The gardener cast a rueful glance at its sleeve, and pursued his way to the door of the back kitchen.

"Joe," said Mrs. Witherspoon, a fat, comely dame, of about five-and-forty, "Joe, your master is but too good to you; he is always kind and considerate. Joe, he has desired me to give you his old wig."

"And the beer, Ma'am Witherspoon?" said Washford, taking the proffered caxon, and looking at it with an expression somewhat short of rapture;—"and the beer, ma'am?"

"The beer, you guzzling wretch! what beer? Master said nothing about no beer. You ungrateful fellow, has not he given you a wig?"

"Why, yes, Madam Witherspoon; but then, you see, his honour said it was very hot, and I'm very dry, and——"

"Go to the pump, sot!" said Mrs. Witherspoon, as she slammed the back-door in the face of the petitioner.

Mrs. Witherspoon was "of the Lady Huntingdon persuasion," and Honorary Assistant Secretary to the Appledore branch of the "Ladies' Grand Junction Water-working Temperance Society."

Joe remained for a few moments lost in mental abstraction; he looked at the door, he looked at the wig; his first thought was to throw it into the pig-stye,—his corruption rose, but he resisted the impulse;

he got the better of Satan; the half-formed imprecation died before it reached his lips. He looked disdainfully at the wig; it had once been a comely jasey enough, of the colour of over-baked ginger-bread, one of the description commonly known during the latter half of the last century by the name of a "brown George." The species, it is to be feared, is now extinct, but a few, a very few of the same description, might, till very lately, be occasionally seen,—*rari nantes in gurgite vasto*, —the glorious relics of a by-gone day, crowning the *cerebellum* of some venerated and venerable provost, or judge of assize; but Mr. Jarvis's wig had one peculiarity; unlike most of its fellows, it had a tail!— "cribbed and confined," indeed, by a shabby piece of faded shalloon.

Washford looked at it again; he shook his bald head; the wig had certainly seen its best days; still, it had about it something of an air of faded gentility,—it was "like ancient Rome, majestic in decay," —and as the small ale was not to be forthcoming, why—after all, an old wig was better than nothing!

Mr. Jeremiah Jarvis, of Appledore, in the Weald of Kent, was a gentleman by act of parliament; one of that class of gentlemen who, disdaining the *bourgeois*-sounding name of "attorney-at-law," are, by a legal fiction, denominated solicitors. I say by a legal fiction, for surely the general tenor of the intimation received by such as enjoy the advantage of their correspondence, has little in common with the idea usually attached to the term "solicitation." "If you don't pay my bill, and costs, I'll send you to jail," is a very energetic *entreaty*. There are, it is true, etymologists who derive their style and title from the Latin infinitive "*solicitare*," to "make anxious,"—in all probability they are right.

If this be the true etymology of his title, as it was the main end of his calling, then was Jeremiah Jarvis a worthy exemplar of the *genus* to which he belonged. Few persons in his time had created greater solicitude among his Majesty's lieges within the "Weald." He was rich, of course. The best house in the country-town is always the lawyer's, and it generally boasts a green door, stone steps, and a brass knocker. In neither of these appendages to opulence was Jeremiah deficient; but then, he was so *very* rich; his reputed wealth, indeed, passed all the common modes of accounting for its increase. True, he was so universal a favourite that every man whose will he made was sure to leave him a legacy; that he was a sort of general assignee to all the bankruptcies within twenty miles of Appledore; was clerk to half the "trusts;" and treasurer to most of the "rates," "funds," and "subscriptions," in that part of the country; that he was land-agent

His first thought was to throw it into the pig-stye

to Lord Mountrhino, and steward to the rich Miss Tabbytale of Smerri-diddle Hall! that he had been guardian (?) to three young profligates, who all ran through their property, which, somehow or another, came at last into his hands, " at an equitable valuation." Still his possessions were so considerable, as not to be altogether accounted for, in vulgar esteem, even by these and other honourable modes of accumulation; nor were there wanting those who conscientiously entertained a belief that a certain dark-coloured gentleman, of indifferent character, known principally by his predilection for appearing in perpetual mourning, had been through life his great friend and counsellor, and had mainly assisted in the acquirement of his revenues. That " old Jerry Jarvis had sold himself to the devil " was, indeed, a dogma which it were heresy to doubt in Appledore;—on this head, at least, there were few schismatics in the parish.

When the worthy " Solicitor " next looked out of his ground-floor back, he smiled with much complacency at beholding Joe Washford again hard at work—in his wig—the little tail aforesaid oscillating like a pendulum in the breeze. If it be asked what could induce a gentle-man, whose leading principle seems to have been self-appropriation, to make so magnificent a present, the answer is, that Mr. Jarvis might, perhaps, have thought an occasional act of benevolence necessary or politic; he is not the only person, who, having stolen a quantity of leather, has given away a pair of shoes, *pour l'amour de Dieu,*—perhaps he had other motives.

Joe, meanwhile, worked away at the celery bed; but truth obliges us to say, neither with the same degree of vigour or perseverance as had marked the earlier efforts of the morning. His pauses were more frequent; he rested longer on the handle of his spade; while ever and anon his eye would wander from the trench beneath him to an object not unworthy the contemplation of a natural philosopher. This was an apple-tree.

Fairer fruit never tempted Eve, or any of her daughters; the bending branches groaned beneath their luxuriant freight, and, drooping to earth, seemed to ask the protecting aid of man either to support or to relieve them. The fine, rich glow of their sun-streaked clusters derived additional loveliness from the level beams of the descending day-star. An anchorite's mouth had watered at the pippins.

On the precise graft of the espalier of Eden " Sanchoniathon, Manetho, and Berosus " are undecided; the best-informed Talmudists, however, have, if we are to believe Dr. Pinner's German Version, pronounced it a Ribstone pippin, and a Ribstone pippin-tree it was that now attracted the optics, and discomposed the inner man of the thirsty, patient, but perspiring gardener. The heat was still oppressive; no beer had moistened his lip, though its very name, uttered as it was in the ungracious tones of a Witherspoon, had left behind a longing as intense as fruitless. His thirst seemed supernatural, when at this moment his left ear experienced " a slight and tickling sensation," such as we are assured is occasionally produced by an infinitesimal dose in homœopathy; a still, small *voice*—it was as though a daddy-long-legs were whispering in his *tympanum*—a small *voice* seemed to say, " Joe!—take an apple, Joe!!"

Honest Joseph started at the suggestion; the rich crimson of his jolly nose deepened to a purple tint in the beams of the setting sun; his very forehead was incarnadine. He raised his hand to scratch his ear,—the little tortuous tail had worked its way into it,—he pulled it out by the bit of shalloon, and allayed the itching, then cast his eye wistfully towards the mansion where his master was sitting by the open window. Joe pursed up his parched lips into an arid whistle, and with a desperate energy struck his spade once more into the celery-bed.

Alack! alack! what a piece of work is man!—how short his triumphs! —how frail his resolutions!

From this fine and very original moral reflection we turn reluctantly to record the sequel. The celery-bed, alluded to as the main scene of Mr. Washford's operations, was drawn in a rectilinear direction, nearly across the whole breadth of the parallelogram that comprised the " kitchen garden." Its northern extremity abutted to the hedge before mentioned, its southern one—woe is me that it should have been so!—was in fearful vicinity to the Ribstone pippin-tree. One branch, low bowed to earth, seemed ready to discharge its precious burden into the very trench. As Joseph stooped to insert the last plant with his dibble, an apple of more than ordinary beauty bobbed against his knuckles.—" He's taking snuff, Joe," whispered the same small *voice;*—the tail had twisted itself into its old position. " He is sneezing!—now, Joe!—now!" And, ere the agitated horticulturist could recover from his surprise and alarm, the fruit was severed, and— in his hand!

" He! he! he!" shrilly laughed, or seemed to laugh, that accursed little pigtail.—Washford started at once to the perpendicular;—with an enfrenzied grasp he tore the jasey from his head, and, with that in one hand, and his ill-acquired spoil in the other, he rushed distractedly from the garden!

*   *   *   *   *   *   *

All that night was the humble couch of the once happy gardener haunted with the most fearful visions. He was stealing apples,—he was robbing hen-roosts,—he was altering the chalks upon the milk-score,—he had purloined three *chemises* from a hedge, and he awoke in the very act of cutting the throat of one of Squire Hodge's sheep! A clammy dew stood upon his temples,—the cold perspiration burst from every pore,—he sprang in terror from the bed.

"Why, Joe, what ails thee, man?" cried the usually incurious Mrs. Washford; "what be the matter with thee? Thee hast done nothing but grunt and growl all t' night long, and now thee dost stare as if thee saw summut. What bees it, Joe?"

A long-drawn sigh was her husband's only answer; his eye fell upon the bed. "How the devil came *that* here?" quoth Joseph, with a sudden recoil: "who put that thing on my pillow?"

"Why, I did, Joseph. Th' ould night-cap is in the wash, and thee didst toss and tumble so, and kick the clothes off, I thought thee mightest catch cowld, so I clapt t' wig atop o' thee head."

And there it lay,—the little sinister-looking tail impudently perked up, like an infernal gnomon on a Satanic dial-plate—Larceny and Ovicide shone in every hair of it!

> "The dawn was overcast, the morning lower'd,
> And heavily in clouds brought on the day,"

when Joseph Washford once more repaired to the scene of his daily labours; a sort of unpleasant consciousness flushed his countenance, and gave him an uneasy feeling as he opened the garden gate; for Joe, generally speaking, was honest as the skin between his eye-brows; his hand faltered as it pressed the latch. "Pooh, pooh! 'twas but an apple, after all!" said Joseph. He pushed open the wicket, and found himself beneath the tempting tree.

But vain now were all its fascinations; like fairy gold seen by the morning light, its charms had faded into very nothingness. Worlds, to say nothing of apples, which in shape resemble them, would not have bought him to stretch forth an unhallowed hand again. He went steadily to his work.

The day continued cloudy, huge drops of rain fell at intervals, stamping his bald pate with spots as big as half-pence; but Joseph worked on. As the day advanced, showers fell thick and frequent; the fresh-turned earth was itself fragrant as a *bouquet.*—Joseph worked on—and when at last *Jupiter Pluvius* descended in all his majesty, soaking the ground into the consistency of a dingy pudding, he put on his party-coloured jacket, and strode towards his humble home, rejoicing in his renewed integrity. " 'Twas but an apple, after all! Had it been an apple-pie, indeed! "—

"An apple-pie!" the thought was a dangerous one—too dangerous to dwell on. But Joseph's better Genius was at this time lord of the ascendant;—he dismissed it, and passed on.

On arriving at his cottage, an air of bustle and confusion prevailed within, much at variance with the peaceful serenity usually observable in its economy. Mrs. Washford was in high dudgeon; her heels clattered on the red-tiled floor; and she whisked about the house like a parched pea upon a drum-head; her voice, generally small and low, —"an excellent thing in woman,"—was pitched at least an octave above its ordinary level; she was talking fast and furious. Something had evidently gone wrong. The mystery was soon explained. The " *cussed ould twoad* of a cat " had got into the dairy, and licked off the cream from the only pan their single cow had filled that morning! And there she now lay,—purring as in scorn, Tib, heretofore the meekest of mousers, the honestest, the least " *scaddle* " of the feline race,—a cat that one would have sworn might have been trusted with untold fish,—yes, there was no denying it,—proofs were too strong against her,—yet there she lay, hardened in her iniquity, coolly licking her whiskers, and reposing quietly upon—what ?—Jerry Jarvis's old wig ! !

The patience of a Stoic must have yielded;—it had been too much for the temperament of the Man of Uz. Joseph Washford lifted his hand —that hand which had never yet been raised on Tibby, save to fondle and caress—it now descended on her devoted head in one tremendous " dowse." Never was cat so astonished,—so enraged—all the tiger portion of her nature rose in her soul. Instead of galloping off, hissing and sputtering, with arched back and tail erected, as any ordinary Grimalkin would unquestionably have done under similar circumstances, she paused a moment,—drew back on her haunches,—all her energies seemed concentrated for one prodigious spring ; a demoniac fire gleamed in her green and yellow eyeballs, as, bounding upwards, she fixed her talons firmly in each of her assailant's cheeks !—many and many a day after were sadly visible the marks of those envenomed claws,—then, dashing over his shoulder with an unearthly mew, she leaped through the open casement, and—was seen no more.

" The Devil's in the cat ! " was the apostrophe of Mrs. Margaret Washford. Her husband said nothing, but thrust the old wig into his pocket, and went to bathe his scratches at the pump.

Day after day, night after night, 'twas all the same—Joe Washford's life became a burden to him; his natural upright and honest mind struggled hard against the frailty of human nature. He was ever restless and uneasy; his frank, open, manly look, that blenched not from the gaze of the spectator, was no more; a sly and sinister expression had usurped the place of it.

Mr. Jeremiah Jarvis had little of what the world calls "Taste," still less of Science—Ackerman would have called him a "Snob," and Buckland a "Nincompoop." Of the Horticultural Society, its *fêtes*, its fruits, and its fiddlings, he knew nothing. Little recked he of flowers—save cauliflowers—in these, indeed, he was a *connoisseur*: to their cultivation and cookery the respective talents of Joe and Madam Witherspoon had long been dedicated; but as for a *bouquet!*—Hardham's 37 was "the only one fit for a gentleman's nose." And yet, after all, Jerry Jarvis had a good-looking tulip-bed. A female friend of his had married a Dutch merchant; Jerry drew the settlements; the lady paid him by a cheque on "Child's," the gentleman by a present of a "box of roots." Jerry put the latter in his garden—he had rather they had been schalots.

Not so his neighbour, Jenkinson; he *was* a man of "Taste" and of "Science;" he was an F.R.C.E.B.S., which, as he told the vicar, implied "Fellow of the Royal Cathartico-Emetico-Botanical Society," and his autograph in Sir John Frostyface's album stood next to that of the Emperor of all the Russias. Neighbour Jenkinson fell in love with the pips and petals of "neighbour Jarvis's" tulips. There were one or two among them of such brilliant, such surpassing beauty,—the "cups" so well formed,—the colours so defined. To be sure, Mr. Jenkinson had enough in his own garden; but then "Enough," says the philosopher, "always means a little more than a man has got." —Alas! alas! Jerry Jarvis was never known to *bestow*,—his neighbour dared not offer to *purchase* from so wealthy a man; and, worse than all, Joe, the gardener was incorruptible—ay, but the Wig?

Joseph Washford was working away again in the blaze of the midday sun; his head looked like a copper saucepan fresh from the brazier's.

"Why, where's your wig, Joseph?" said the voice of his master from the well-known window; "what have you done with your wig?" The question was embarrassing,—its tail had tickled his ear till it had made it sore; Joseph had put the wig in his pocket.

Mr. Jeremiah Jarvis was indignant; he liked not that his benefits should be ill appreciated by the recipient.—"Hark ye, Joseph Washford," said he, "either wear my wig, or let me have it again!"

There was no mistaking the meaning of his tones; they were

resonant of indignation and disgust, of mingled grief and anger, the amalgamation of sentiment naturally produced by

> " Friendship unreturn'd,
> And unrequited Love."

Washford's heart smote him : he felt all that was implied in his master's appeal. " It's here, your Honour," said he ; " I had only taken it off because we have had a smartish shower ; but the sky is brightening now." The wig was replaced, and the little tortuous pigtail wriggled itself into its accustomed position.

At this moment neighbour Jenkinson peeped over the hedge.

" Joe Washford ! " said neighbour Jenkinson.

" Sir, to you," was the reply.

" How beautiful your tulips look after the rain ! "

" Ah, sir, master sets no great store by them flowers," returned the gardener.

" Indeed ! Then perhaps he would have no objection to part with a few ? "

" Why, no !—I don't think master would like to *give* them,—or anything else,—away, sir ; "—and Washford scratched his ear.

" Joe ! ! "—said Mr. Jenkinson—" Joe ! ! "

The Sublime, observes Longinus, is often embodied in a mono-syllable—" Joe ! ! ! "—Mr. Jenkinson said no more ; but a half-crown shone from between his upraised fingers, and its " poor, poor dumb mouth " spoke for him.

How Joe Washford's left ear *did* itch !—He looked to the ground-floor back—Mr. Jarvis had left the window.

Mr. Jenkinson's ground-plot boasted, at daybreak next morning, a splendid *Semper Augustus*, " which was not so before," and Joseph Washford was led home, much about the same time, in a most extra-ordinary state of " civilation," from " The Three Jolly Potboys."

From that hour he was the Fiend's ! !

*　　　*　　　*　　　*　　　*　　　*　　　*

" *Facilis descensus Averni !* " says Virgil. " It is only the first step that is attended with any difficulty," says—somebody else,—when speaking of the decollated martyr, St. Denis's walk with his head under his arm. " The First Step ! "—Joseph Washford had taken that step ! —he had taken two—three—four steps ; and now, from a hesitating, creeping, cat-like mode of progression, he had got into a firmer tread— an amble—a positive trot !—He took the family linen " to the wash : "

—one of Madam Witherspoon's best Holland *chemises* was never seen after.

"Lost ?—impossible ! How *could* it be lost ?—where *could* it be gone to ?—who *could* have got it ? It was her best—her *very* best !—she should know it among a hundred—among a thousand—it was marked with a great W in the corner !—Lost ?—impossible ?—She would *see !*"—Alas ! she never *did* see—the chemise—*abit,—erupit,—evasit,* — it was

"Like the lost Pleiad, seen on earth no more ! "

—but Joseph Washford's Sunday shirt *was* seen, finer and fairer than ever, the pride and *dulce decus* of the Meeting.

The Meeting ?—ay, the Meeting. Joe Washford never missed the Appledore Independent Meeting House, whether the service were in the morning or afternoon,—whether the Rev. Mr. Slyandry exhorted or made way for the Rev. Mr. Tearbrain. Let who would officiate, there was Joe. As I have said before, he never missed ;—but other people missed—one missed an umbrella,—one a pair of clogs. Farmer Johnson missed his tobacco-box,—Farmer Jackson his greatcoat ;— Miss Jackson missed her hymn-book,—a diamond edition, bound in maroon-coloured velvet, with gilt corners and clasps. Everything, in short, was missed—but Joe Washford ; there *he* sat, grave, sedate, and motionless—all save that restless, troublesome, fidgety little Pigtail attached to his wig, which nothing *could* keep quiet, or prevent from tickling and interfering with Miss Thompson's curls, as she sat, back to back with Joe, in the adjoining pew. After the third Sunday, Nancy Thompson eloped with the tall recruiting sergeant of the Connaught Rangers.

The summer passed away,—autumn came and went,—and Christmas, jolly Christmas, that period of which we are accustomed to utter the mournful truism, it " comes but *once* a-year," was at hand. It was a fine bracing morning ; the sun was just beginning to throw a brighter tint upon the Quaker-coloured ravine of Orlestone Hill, when a medical gentleman, returning to the quiet little village of Ham Street, that lies at its foot, from a farmhouse at Kingsnorth, rode briskly down the declivity.

After several hours of patient attention, Mr. Moneypenny had succeeded in introducing to the notice of seven little expectant brothers and sisters a " remarkably fine child," and was now hurrying home in the sweet hope of a comfortable " snooze " for a couple of hours before the announcement of tea and muffins should arouse him to fresh

exertion.   The road at this particular spot had, even then, been cut deep
below the surface of the soil, for the purpose of diminishing the abruptness of the descent, and, as either side of the superincumbent banks
was clothed with a thick mantle of tangled copsewood, the passage,
even by day, was sufficiently obscure, the level beams of the rising or
setting sun, as they happened to enfilade the gorge, alone illuminating
its recesses.   A long stream of rosy light was just beginning to make
its way through the vista, and Mr. Moneypenny's nose had scarcely
caught and reflected its kindred ray, when the sturdiest and most active
cob that ever rejoiced in the appellation of a " Suffolk punch," brought
herself up in mid career upon her haunches, and that with a suddenness which had almost induced her rider to describe that beautiful
mathematical figure, the *parabola*, between her ears.   Peggy—her name
was Peggy—stood stock-still, snorting like a stranded grampus, and
alike insensible to the gentle hints afforded her by hand and heel.

"Tch!—tch!—get along, Peggy!" half exclaimed, half whistled
the equestrian.   If ever steed said in its heart, "I'll be shot if I do!"
it was Peggy at that moment.   She planted her forelegs deep in the
sandy soil, raised her stump of a tail to an elevation approaching the
horizontal, protruded her nose like a pointer at a covey, and with
expanded nostril continued to snuffle most egregiously.

Mr. Geoffrey Gambado, the illustrious " Master of the Horse to
the Doge of Venice," tells us, in his far-famed treatise on the Art
Equestrian, that the most embarrassing position in which a rider can
be placed is, when *he* wishes to go one way, and his horse is determined
to go another.   There is, to be sure, a *tertium quid*, which, though it
"splits the difference," scarcely obviates the inconvenience;   this is
when the parties compromise the matter by not going any way at all—
to this compromise Peggy, and her (*soi-disant*) master were now reduced;
they had fairly joined issue.   "Budge!" quoth the doctor.—"Budge
not!" quoth the fiend,—for nothing short of a fiend could, of a surety,
inspire Peggy at such a time with such unwonted obstinacy.—Moneypenny whipped and spurred—Peggy plunged and reared, and kicked,
and for several minutes to a superficial observer the termination of the
contest might have appeared uncertain;   but your profound thinker
sees at a glance that, however the scales may appear to vibrate, when the
question between the sexes is one of perseverance, it is quite a lost
case for the masculine gender.   Peggy beat the doctor, " all to sticks,"
and when he was fairly tired of goading and thumping, maintained her
position as firmly as ever.

It is of no great use, and not particularly agreeable, to sit still, on a cold frosty morning in January, upon the outside of a brute that will neither go forwards nor backwards—so Mr. Moneypenny got off, and muttering curses *both* "loud" *and* "deep" between his chattering teeth, "progressed," as near as the utmost extremity of the extended bridle would allow him, to peep among the weeds and brushwood that flanked the road, in order to discover, if possible, what it was that so exclusively attracted the instinctive attention of his Bucephalus.

His curiosity was not long at fault; the sunbeam glanced partially upon some object ruddier even than itself—it was a scarlet waistcoat, the wearer of which, overcome perchance by Christmas compotation, seemed to have selected for his "thrice driven bed of down," the thickest clump of the tallest and most imposing nettles, thereon to doze away the narcotic effects of the superabundant juniper.

This, at least, was Mr. Moneypenny's belief, or he would scarcely have uttered, at the highest pitch of his *contralto*, "What are you doing there, you drunken rascal? frightening my horse!"—We have already hinted, if not absolutely asserted, that Peggy was a mare; but this was no time for verbal criticism.—"Get up, I say,—get up, and go home, you scoundrel!"—But the "scoundrel" and "drunken rascal" answered not; he moved not, nor could the prolonged shouting of the appellant, aided by significant explosions from a double-thonged whip, succeed in eliciting a reply. No motion indicated that the recumbent figure, whose outline alone was visible, was a living and a breathing man!

The clear, shrill tones of a ploughboy's whistle sounded at this moment from the bottom of the hill, where the broad and green expanse of Romney Marsh stretches away from its foot for many a mile, and now gleamed through the mists of morning, dotted and enamelled with its thousand flocks. In a few minutes his tiny figure was seen "slouching" up the ascent, casting a most disproportionate and ogre-like shadow before him.

"Come here, Jack," quoth the doctor,—"come here, boy, lay hold of this bridle, and mind that my horse does not run away."

Peggy threw up her head, and snorted disdain of the insinuation,— she had not the slightest intention of doing any such thing.

Mr. Moneypenny meanwhile, disencumbered of his restive nag, proceeded by manual application to arouse the sleeper. Alas! the Seven of Ephesus might sooner have been awakened from their century of somnolency. His was that "dreamless sleep that knows no waking;" his cares in this world were over. Vainly did Moneypenny practise his own constant precept, "To be well shaken!"—there lay before him the lifeless body of a MURDERED MAN!

The corpse lay stretched upon its back, partially concealed, as we have before said, by the nettles which had sprung up among the stumps of the half-grubbed underwood; the throat was fearfully lacerated, and the dark, deep, arterial dye of the coagulated blood showed that the carotid had been severed. There was little to denote the existence of any struggle; but as the day brightened, the sandy soil of the road exhibited an impression as of a body that had fallen on its plastic surface, and had been dragged to its present position, while fresh horse-shoe prints seemed to intimate that either the assassin or his victim had been mounted. The pockets of the deceased were turned out, and empty; a hat and heavy-loaded whip lay at no great distance from the body.

"But what have we here?" quoth Doctor Moneypenny; "what is it that the poor fellow holds so tightly in his hand?"

That hand had manifestly clutched some article with all the spasmodic energy of a dying grasp—IT WAS AN OLD WIG!!

* * * * * * *

Those who are fortunate enough to have seen a Cinque Port Court-house may possibly divine what that useful and most necessary edifice was some eighty years ago. Many of them seem to have undergone little alteration, and are in general of a composite order of architecture, a fanciful arrangement of brick and timber, with what Johnson would have styled "interstices, reticulated, and decussated between inter-sections" of lath and plaster. Its less euphonious designation in the "Weald" is a "noggin." One half the basement story is usually of the more solid material, the other, open to the street,—from which it is separated only by a row of dingy columns, supporting a portion of the superstructure,—is paved with tiles, and sometimes does duty as a market-place, while, in its centre, flanking the broad staircase that leads to the sessions-house above, stands an ominous-looking machine, of heavy perforated wood, clasped within whose stern embrace "the rude forefathers of the hamlet sleep" off occasionally the drowsiness produced by convivial excess, in a most undignified position, an inconvenience much increased at times by some mischievous urchin, who, after abstracting the shoes of the helpless *détenu*, amuses himself by tickling the soles of his feet.

It was in such a place, or rather in the Court-room above, that in the year 1761 a hale, robust man, somewhat past the middle age, with a very bald pate, save where a continued tuft of coarse, wiry hair, stretching from above each ear, swelled out into a greyish-looking bush upon the occiput, held up his hand before a grave and enlightened assemblage of Dymchurch jurymen. He stood arraigned for that offence most heinous in the sight of God and man, the deliberate and cold-blooded butchery of an unoffending, unprepared fellow creature, —*homicidium quod nullo vidente, nullo auscultante clam perpetratur.*

The victim was one Humphry Bourne, a reputable grazier of Ivy-church, worthy and well to do, though, perchance, a thought too apt to indulge on a market-day, when " a score of ewes " had brought in a reasonable profit. Some such cause had detained him longer than usual at an Ashford cattle-show ; he had left the town late and alone ; early in the following morning his horse was found standing at his own stable-door, the saddle turned round beneath its belly, and much about the time that the corpse of its unfortunate master was discovered some four miles off, by our friend the pharmacopolist.

That poor Bourne had been robbed and murdered there could be no question.

Who, then, was the perpetrator of the atrocious deed ?—The unwilling hand almost refuses to trace the name of—Joseph Washford.

Yet so it was. Mr. Jeremiah Jarvis was himself the coroner for that division of the county of Kent known by the name of " The Lath of Scraye." He had not sat two minutes on the body before he recognised his *quondam* property, and started at beholding in the grasp of the victim, as torn in the death-struggle from the murderer's head, his own OLD WIG,—his own perky little pigtail, tied up with a piece of shabby shalloon, now wriggling and quivering, as in salutation of its ancient master. The silver buckles of the murdered man were found in Joe Washford's shoes,—broad pieces were found in Joe Washford's pockets,—Joe Washford had himself been found, when the hue-and-cry was up, hid in a corn-rig at no great distance from the scene of slaughter, his pruning-knife red with the evidence of his crime—" the grey hairs yet stuck to the heft ! "

For their humane administration of the laws, the lieges of this portion of the realm have long been celebrated. Here it was that merciful verdict was recorded in the case of the old lady accused of larceny, " We find her Not Guilty, and hope she will never do so any more ! " Here it was that the more experienced culprit, when called upon to plead with the customary, though somewhat superfluous, inquiry, as to " how he would be tried ? " substituted for the usual reply, " By God and my country," that of " By your worship and a Dymchurch Jury." Here it was—but enough !—not even a

Dymchurch jury could resist such evidence, even though the gallows (*i.e.*, the expense of erecting one) stared them, as well as the criminal, in the face. The very pig-tail alone !—ever at his ear !—a clearer case of *suadente Diabolo* never was made out. Had there been a doubt, its very conduct in the Court-house would have settled the question. The Rev. Joel Ingoldsby, umquhile chaplain to the Romney Bench, has left upon record that, when exhibited in evidence, together with the blood-stained knife, its twistings, its caperings, its gleeful evolutions, quite " flabbergasted " the jury, and threw all beholders into a consternation. It was remarked, too, by many in the Court, that the Forensic Wig of the Recorder himself was, on that trying occasion, palpably agitated, and that its three depending, learned-looking tails lost curl at once, and slunk beneath the obscurity of the powdered collar, just as the boldest dog recoils from a rabid animal of its own species, however small and insignificant.

Why prolong the painful scene ?—Joe Washford was tried—Joe Washford was convicted—Joe Washford was hanged ! !

The fearful black gibbet, on which his body clanked in its chains to the midnight winds, frowns no more upon Orlestone Hill ; it has sunk beneath the encroaching hand of civilization ; but there it might be seen late in the last century, an awful warning to all bald-pated gentlemen how they wear, or accept, the old wig of a Special Attorney.

Timeo Danaos et dona ferentes !

Such gifts, as we have seen, may lead to a " Morbid Delusion, the climax of which is Murder ! "

The fate of the Wig itself is somewhat doubtful : nobody seems to have recollected, with any degree of precision, what became of it. Mr. Ingoldsby " had heard " that, when thrown in the fire by the Court-keeper, after whizzing, and fizzling, and performing all sorts of supernatural antics and contortions, it at length whirled up the chimney with a bang that was taken for the explosion of one of the Feversham powder-mills, twenty miles off ; while others insinuate that in the " Great Storm " which took place on the night when Mr. Jeremiah Jarvis went to his " long home,"—wherever that may happen to be,— and the whole of " The Marsh " appeared as one broad sheet of flame, something that looked very like a Fiery Wig—perhaps a miniature Comet—it had unquestionably a tail—was seen careering in the blaze, —and seeming to " ride on the whirlwind and direct the storm."

When a score of ewes had brought in a reasonable profit

Unsophisticated Wishes

By Miss Jemima Ingoldsby, aged 15

(*Communicated by her Cousin Tom*)

Oh! how I should like in a Coach to ride,
  Like the Sheriffs I saw upon Lord Mayor's day,
With a Coachman and little Postillion astride
  On the back of the leader, a prancing bay.

And then behind it, oh! I should glory
  To see the tall serving men standing upright,
Like the two who attend Mister Montefiore,
  (Sir Moses I should say) for now he's a Knight.

And then the liveries, I know it is rude to
  Find fault—but I'll hint as he can't see me blush,
That I'd not have the things I can only allude to
  Either orange in hue or constructed of plush ;

But their coats and their waistcoats and hats are delightful,
  Their charming silk stockings—I vow and declare
Our John's ginger gaiters so wrinkled and frightful,
  I never again shall be able to bear.

Oh! how I should like to have diamonds and rubies,
  And large plume of feathers and flowers in my hair,
My gracious! to think how our Tom and those boobies,
  Jack Smith and his friend Mister Thompson, would stare.

Then how I should like to drive to Guildhall,
  And to see the nobility flocking in shoals,
With their two guinea tickets to dance at the ball
  Which the Lord Mayor gives for relief of the Poles

And to look at the gas so uncommonly pretty,
   And the stars and the armour all just as they were,
The day that the Queen came in state to the city
   To dine with the whole Corporation and Mayor.

Oh ! how I should like to see Jane and Letitia,
   Miss Jones and the two Misses Frump sitting still,
While dear Ensign Brown, of the West Kent Militia,
   Solicits my hand for the " Supper " Quadrille.

With his fine white teeth and his cheek like a rose,
   And his black cravat and his diamond pin,
And the nice little mustache under his nose,
   And the dear *little* tuft on the tip of his chin.

And how I should like some fine morning to ride
   In my coach, and my white satin shoes and gown,
To St. James's Church, with a Beau by my side,
   And I shouldn't much care if his name was Brown.

𝔐iscellaneous 𝔓oems

Hermann ; or, The Broken Spear

An Emperor famous in council and camp,
Has a son who turns out a remarkable scamp ;
. Takes to dicing and drinking
' And d—mning and sinking,
And carries off maids, wives, and widows, like winking !
Since the days of Arminius, his namesake, than Hermann
There never was seen a more profligate German.

He escapes from the City ;   And joins some banditti
Insensible quite to remorse, fear, and pity ;
Joins in all their carousals, and revels, and robberies,
And in kicking up all sorts of shindies and bobberies.

Well, hearing one day   His associates say
That a bridal procession was coming their way,
   Inflamed with desire, he   Breaks into a Priory,
And kicking out every man Jack of a friar, he
Upsets in a twinkling the mass-books and hassocks,
And dresses his rogues in the clergymen's cassocks.

The new married folks   Taken in by this hoax,
Mister Hermann grows frisky and full of his jokes :
To the serious chagrin of her late happy suitor,
Catching hold of the Bride, he attempts to salute her.

Now Heaven knows what   Had become of the lot,
It's Turtle to Tripe they'd have all gone to pot—
   If a dumb Lady, one   Of her friends, had not run
To her aid, and, quite scandalized, stopp'd all his fun !
   Just conceive what a caper   He cut, when her taper
Long fingers scrawled this upon whitey-brown paper,
(At the instant he seized, and before he had kissed her)—
" Ha' done, Mister Hermann ! for shame ! it's your sister ! "
His hair stands on end,—He desists from his tricks,
And remains in " a pretty particular fix."

As he knows Sir John Nicholl
Still keeps rods in pickle,
Offences of this kind severely to tickle,
At so near an escape from his court and its sentence
His eyes fill with tears, and his breast with repentance :
    So, picking and stealing,   And unrighteous dealing,
Of all sorts, he cuts, from this laudable feeling :
    Of wickedness weary,   With many a tear, he
Now takes a French leave of the vile *Condottieri* :
And the next thing we hear of this penitent villain,
He is begging in rags in the suburbs of Milan.

    Half starv'd, meagre, and pale,   His energies fail,
When his sister comes in with a pot of mild ale ;
    But though tatter'd his jerkins,
    His heart is whole,—workings
Of conscience debar him from " Barclay and Perkins."
    " I'll drink," exclaims he,
    " Nothing stronger than tea,
And that but the worst and the weakest Bohea,
Till I've done—from my past scenes of folly a far actor—
Some feat shall redeem both my wardrobe and character."
At signs of remorse so decided and visible
Nought can equal the joy of his fair sister Isabel,
    And the Dumb Lady too,
    Who runs off to a Jew,
And buys him a coat of mail spick and span new,
In the hope that his prowess and deeds as a Knight
Will keep his late larcenies quite out of sight.
By the greatest good luck, his old friends the banditti
Choose this moment to make an attack on the city !
    Now you all know the way
    Heroes hack, hew, and slay,
When once they get fairly mixed up in a fray :
    Hermann joins in the *mêlée*,   Pounds this to a jelly,
Runs that through the back, and a third through the belly.
Till many a broken bone, bruised rib, and flat head,
Make his *ci-devant* friends curse the hour that he ratted.
    Amid so many blows,   Of course you'll suppose
He must get a black eye, or, at least, bloody nose :

"Take that !" cried a bandit, and struck, while he spoke it,
His spear in his breast, and, in pulling out, broke it.
  Hermann fainted away   When, as breathless he lay,
A rascal claimed all the renown of the day ;
A recreant, cowardly, white-liver'd knight,
Who had skulked in a furze-bush the whole of the fight.
  But the Dumb Lady soon   Put some gin in a spoon,
And half strangles poor Hermann, who wakes from his swoon,
And exhibits his wound, when the head of the spear
Fits its handle, and makes its identity clear.
The murder thus out, Hermann's *fêted* and thankèd,
While his rascally rival gets tossed in a blanket :
  And to finish the play—
  As reformed rakes, they say,
Make the best of all husbands—the very same day
Hermann sends for a priest, as he must wed with some—lady,
Buys a ring and a licence, and marries the Dumb Lady.

Moral.

Take warning, young people of every degree,
From Hermann's example, and don't live too free !
If you get in bad company, fly from it soon !
If you chance to get thrash'd, take some gin in a spoon ;
And remember, since wedlock's not *all* sugar-candy,
If you wish to 'scape " wigging," a dumb wife's the dandy !

Hints for an Historical Play

To be Called

William Rufus ; or, The Red Rover

Act i.

Walter Tyrrel, the son of a Norman Papa,
Has, somehow or other, a Saxon Mama :
Though humble, yet far above mere vulgar loons,
He's a sort of a sub in the Rufus dragoons ;
Has travelled, but comes home abruptly, the rather
That some unknown rascal has murder'd his father ;

And scarce has he pick'd out, and stuck in his quiver,
The arrow that pierced the old gentleman's liver,
When he finds, as misfortunes come rarely alone,
That his sweetheart has bolted,—with whom is not known.
But, as murder will out, he at last finds the lady
At court with her character grown rather shady :
This gives him the " blues," and impairs the delight
He'd have otherwise felt when they dub him a Knight,
For giving a runaway stallion a check,
And preventing his breaking King Rufus's neck.

Act 2.

Sir Walter has dress'd himself up like a Ghost,
And frightens a soldier away from his post ;
Then, discarding his helmet, he pulls his cloak higher,
Draws it over his ears, and pretends he's a Friar.
This gains him access to his sweetheart, Miss Faucit ;
But, the King coming in, he hides up in her closet,
Where oddly enough, among some of her things,
He discovers some arrows he's sure are the King's,
Of the very same pattern with that which he found
Sticking into his father when dead on the ground !
Forgetting his funk, he bursts open the door,
Bounces into the Drawing-room, stamps on the floor,
With an oath on his tongue, and revenge in his eye,
And blows up King William the Second, sky-high ;
Swears, storms, shakes his fist, and exhibits such airs,
That his Majesty bids his men kick him down stairs.

Act 3.

King Rufus is cross when he comes to reflect,
That as King, he's been treated with gross disrespect ;
So he pens a short note to a holy physician,
And gives him a rather unholy commission,
Viz. : to mix up some arsenic and ale in a cup,
Which the chances are Tyrrel may find and drink up.
Sure enough, on the very next morning, Sir Walter
Perceives in his walks, this same cup on the altar.
As he feels rather thirsty, he's just about drinking,
When Miss Faucit in tears, comes in running like winking ;

He pauses, of course, and as she's thirsty too,
Says, very politely, " Miss, I after you ! "
The young lady curtsies, and being so dry,
Raises somehow her fair little finger so high,
That there's not a drop left him to " wet t'other eye ; "
While the dose is so strong, to his grief and surprise,
She merely says, " Thankee, Sir Walter," and dies.
At that moment the King, who is riding to cover,
Pops in *en passant* on the desperate lover,
Who has vow'd, not five minutes before, to transfix him,
—So he does,—he just pulls out his arrow and sticks him.
From the strength of his arm, and the force of his blows,
The Red-bearded Rover falls flat on his nose ;
And Sir Walter, thus having concluded his quarrel,
Walks down to the footlights, and draws this fine moral :
   " Ladies and Gentlemen,
       Lead sober lives :—
Don't meddle with other folks' Sweethearts or Wives !—
When you go out a-sporting, take care of your gun,
And—never shoot elderly people in fun ! "

Marie Mignot

Miss MARIE MIGNOT was a nice little Maid,
Her Uncle a Cook, and a Laundress her trade,
And she loved as dearly as any one can
Mister Lagardie, a nice little man.
  But Oh ! But Oh ! Story of woe !
A sad interloper, one Monsieur Modeau,
  Ugly and old,   With plenty of gold,
    Made his approach   In an elegant coach,
Her fancy was charm'd with the splendour and show
And he bore off the false-hearted Molly Mignot.

Monsieur Modeau was crazy and old,
And Monsieur Modeau caught a terrible cold,
His nose was stuffed, and his throat was sore,
He had physic by the quart and Doctors by the score.

They sent squills   And pills,   And very long bills
And all they could do did not make him get well,
He sounded his M's and his N's like an L.
   A shocking bad cough   At last took him off,
And Mister Lagardie her former young beau,
Came a-courting again to the Widow Modeau.

Mister Lagardie, to gain him *éclat*,
Had cut the Cook's shop and follow'd the law ;
And when Monsieur Modeau set out on his journey,
Was an Articled Clerk to a Special Attorney.
   He gave her a call   On the day of a ball,
To which she'd invited the court, camp and all ;
   But " poor dear Lagardie "   Again was too tardy,
For a Marshal of France   Had just asked her to dance ;
In a twinkling, the *ci-devant* Madame Modeau
Was wife of the Marshal Lord Marquis Dinot.
Mister Lagardie was shock'd at the news,
And went and enlisted at once in the Blues.
   The Marquis Dinot   Felt a little so so—
Took physic, grew worse, and had *notice to go*—
He died, and was shelved, and his Lady so gay
Smiled again on Lagardie now placed on full pay,
A Swedish Field-Marshal with a guinea a day ;
   When an old Ex-King   Just show'd her the ring :
To be Queen, she conceived was a very fine thing ;
   But the King turned a Monk,
   And Lagardie got drunk,
And said to the Lady with a deal of ill-breeding,
" You may go to the d—l and I'll go to Sweden."
   Thus between the two stools,   Like some other fools,
   Her Ladyship found   Herself plump on the ground ;
So she cried, and she stamped, and she sent for a hack,
And she drove to a convent and never came back.

MORAL.

Wives, Maidens, and Widows, attend to my lay—
If a fine moral lesson you'd draw from a play,
   To the Haymarket go   And see *Marie Mignot*.
Miss Kelly plays Marie, and Williams Modeau ;

Mrs. Glover and Vining   Are really quite shining,
 And though Thompson for a Marquis
 Has almost too much carcass,
 Yet it's not fair to pass him or
 John Cooper's Cassimir,
 And the piece would be barren
 Without Mr. Farren;
No matter, go there, and they'll teach you the guilt
Of coquetting and ogling, and playing the jilt.
Such folks gallop awhile, but at last they get spilt;
 Had Molly Mignot   Behaved *comme il faut,*
Nor married the Lawyer nor Marquis Dinot,
She had ne'er been a nun, whose fare very hard is,
But the mother of half-a-score little Lagardies.

The Truants

 THREE little Demons have broken loose
  From the National School below!
 They are resolved to play truant to-day,
 Their primer and slate they have cast away,
  And away, away they go!
   " Hey boys! hey boys! up go we!
   Who so merry as we three ? "

 The reek of that most infernal pit,
  Where sinful souls are stewing,
 Rises so black, that in viewing it,
 A thousand to one but you'd ask with surprise
 As its murky columns meet your eyes,
  " Pray is Old Nick a-brewing ? "
 Thither these three little Devils repair,
 And mount by steam to the uppermost air.

 They have got hold of a wandering star,
 That happen'd to come within hail.
  O swiftly they glide!   As they merrily ride
  All a cock-stride   Of that Comet's tail.

Oh the pranks !   Oh the pranks,
The merry pranks, the mad pranks,
 These wicked urchins play !
They kissed the *Virgin* and fill'd her with dread,
They popp'd the *Scorpion* into her bed ;
They broke the pitcher of poor *Aquarius*,
They stole the arrows of *Sagittarius*,
And they skimm'd the *Milky Way*.
They filled the *Scales* with sulphur full,
They halloed the *Dog-star* on at the *Bull*,
 And pleased themselves with the noise.
  They set the *Lion*   On poor *Orion* ;
  They shaved all the hair   Off the *Lesser Bear* !
  They kicked the shins   Of the *Gemini Twins*—
Those heavenly Siamese Boys !—
Never was such confusion and wrack,
As they produced in the Zodiac !—

" Huzza !   Huzza !   Away !   Away !
Let us go down to the earth and play !
 Now we go up, up, up,
 Now we go down, down, down,
 Now we go backwards and forwards,
 Now we go round, round, round ! "
Thus they gambol, and scramble, and tear,
Till at last they arrive at the nethermost air.

And pray now what were these Devilets call'd ?
These three little Fiends so gay !
 One was *Cob !*   Another was *Mob !*
The last and the least was young *Chittabob !*
Queer little Devils were they !
 Cob was the strongest.   *Mob* was the wrongest,
Chittabob's tail was the finest and longest !
Three more frolicsome Imps, I ween,
Beelzebub's self hath seldom seen.

 Over Mountain, over Fell,
 Glassy Fountain, mossy Dell,
 Rocky Island, barren Strand,
 Over Ocean, over Land ;

With frisk and bound, and squeaks and squalls,
Heels over head, and head over heels ;
With curlings and twistings, and twirls and wheeleries,
Down they drop at the gate of the *Tuileries*.

Courtiers were bowing and making legs,
While Charley *le Roi* was bolting eggs ;
  " *Mob*," says *Cob*,   " *Chittabob*," says *Mob*,
" Come here, you young Devil, *we're in for a job !* "
Up jumps *Cob* to the Monarch's ear,
" Charley, my jolly boy, never fear ;
  If you mind all their jaw   About Charter and Law,
You might just as well still be the *Count d'Artois !*
  No such thing,   Show 'em you're King,
Tip 'em an Ordinance, that's the thing ! "
  Charley dined,   Took his pen and sign'd ;
Then *Mob* kicked over his throne from behind !
" Huzza !   Huzza ! we may scamper now !
For here we have kicked up a jolly good row ! "

" Over the water, and over the Sea,
  And over the water with Charlie ; "
Now they came skipping and grinning with glee,
  Not pausing to *chaff* or to parley.
    Over, over,   On to Dover ;
    On fun intent,   All through Kent
These mischievous devils so merrily went.

Over hill and over dale,
Sunken hollow, lofty ridge,
Frowning cliff, and smiling vale,
Down to the foot of Westminster-bridge.
  " Hollo," says *Cob*,   " There's the Duke and Sir Bob !
After 'em *Chittabob*, after 'em *Mob*."
Mob flung gravel, and *Chittabob* pebbles,
His Grace c——'d them both for a couple of rebels ;
  His feelings were hurt   By the stones and the dirt—
  In went he,   In an ecstasy,
And *blew up* the nobles of high degree.

  " Mr. Brougham, Mr. Hume,   May fret and may fume—
And so may all you whom I see in this room ;

Come weal, come woe, come calm, come storm—
I'll see you all—*blessed*—ere I give you reform ; "
  " Bravo," says *Chittabob*, " That's your sort,
Come along, schoolfellows, here's more sport.
    Look there ! look there !
    There's the great Lord May'r !
With the gravest of Deputies close to his chair ;
  With Hobler, his Clerk ! Just the thing for *a lark ;*
Huzza ! huzza ! boys, follow me now ;
Here we may *kick* up another good row."
    Here they are, Swift as a star,
They shoot in mid air, over Temple Bar !
    Zach. Macaulay beheld the flight
Of these three little dusky sons of night,
And his heart swell'd with joy and elation—
  " Oh, see ! " quoth he, " Those *Niggerlings* three,
Who have just got *emancipation !* "

Lord Key took fright : At the very first sight,
The whole Court of Aldermen wheel'd to the right ;
Some ran from *Chittabob*—more from *Mob*,
The great *locum tenens* jump'd up upon *Cob*,
  Who roar'd and ran, With the Alderman
To the Home Office, pick-a-back—catch 'em who can !
  " Stay at home—here's a plot,
  And I can't tell you what,
If you don't I'll be shot, But you'll all go to pot."
Ah, little he ween'd while the ground he thus ran over,
'Twas a *Cob* he bestrode—not his white horse from Hanover.

Back they came galloping through the Strand,
When Joseph Lancaster, stick in hand,
Popp'd up his head before 'em.
  Well we know That honest old Joe
Is a sort of High Master down below,
And teaches the imps decorum.
Satan had started him off in a crack,
To flog those three little runaways back.

  Fear each assails ; Every one quails ;
" Oh dear ! how he'll tickle our little black tails !

We carved her initials

Have done, have done, Here's that son of a gun,
Old Joe, come after us,—run, boys, run."
  Off ran *Cob*, Off ran *Mob*,
And off in a fright ran young *Chittabob*.
Joe caught *Chittabob* just by the tail,
  And *Cob* by his crumpled horn ;
Bitterly then did these Imps bewail
    That ever they were born !
    Mob got away, But none to this day
Know exactly whither he went ;
Some say he's been seen about Blackfriars-bridge,
  And some say he's down in Kent.

But where'er he may roam,
He has not ventured home
Since the day the three took wing,
  And many suppose He has changed his clothes,
And now goes by the name of " *Swing*."

The Poplar

Ay, here stands the Poplar, so tall and so stately,
  On whose tender rind—'twas a little one then—
We carved *her* initials ; though not very lately
  We think in the year eighteen hundred and ten.

Yes, here is the G which proclaimed Georgiana ;
  Our heart's empress then ; see, 'tis grown all askew ;
And it's not without grief we perforce entertain a
  Conviction, it now looks much more like a Q.

This should be the great D too, that once stood for Dobbin,
  Her lov'd patronymic—ah ! can it be so ?
Its once fair proportions, time too has been robbing ;
  A D ?—we'll be *Deed* if it isn't an O !

Alas ! how the soul sentimental it vexes,
  That thus on our labours stern *Chronos* should frown ;
Should change our soft liquids to izzards and Xes,
  And turn true-love's alphabet all upside down !

New-Made Honour

(Imitated from Martial)

A FRIEND I met, some half-hour since—
  " *Good-morrow, Jack !* " quoth I ;
The new-made Knight, like any Prince,
  Frowned, nodded, and passed by ;
When up came Jem—" *Sir John, your Slave !* "
  " Ah, James ; we dine at eight—
Fail not—(low bows the supple knave)
  Don't make my lady wait."
The King can do no wrong ? As I'm a sinner,
He's spoilt an honest tradesman and my dinner.

My Letters

"Litera scripta manet."—OLD SAW.

ANOTHER mizzling, drizzling day !
  Of clearing up there's no appearance ;
So I'll sit down without delay,
  And here, at least, I'll make a clearance !

Oh, ne'er " on such a day as this "
  Would Dido, with her woes oppressèd,
Have woo'd Æneas back to bliss,
  Or Troilus gone to hunt for Cressid !

No, they'd have stayed at home, like me,
  And popped their toes upon the fender,
And drank a quiet cup of tea :—
  On days like this one can't be tender.

So, Molly, draw that basket nigher,
  And put my desk upon the table—
Bring that Portfolio—stir the fire—
  Now off as fast as you are able !

540

First here's a card from Mrs. Grimes,
    " A Ball ! "—she knows that I'm no dancer—
That woman's asked me fifty times,
    And yet I never send an answer.

" DEAR JACK,—
          Just lend me twenty pounds,
  Till Monday next, when I'll return it.
     Yours truly,
         HENRY GIBBS,"
                  Why, Z—ds !
  I've seen the man but twice—here, burn it.

One from my Cousin Sophy Daw—
  Full of Aunt Margery's distresses ;
" The cat has kittened in ' the *draw*,'
  And ruined two bran-new silk dresses."

From Sam, " The Chancellor's motto,"—nay,
  Confound his puns, he knows I hate 'em ;
" Pro Rege, Lege, Grege,"—Ay,
  " For King read Mob ! " Brougham's old *erratum*.

From Seraphina Price—" At two "—
  " Till then I can't, my dearest John, stir ; "
Two more because I did not go,
  Beginning " Wretch " and " Faithless Monster ! "

" DEAR SIR,—
        " This morning Mrs. P——
  Who's doing quite as well as may be
Presented me, at half-past three
  Precisely, with another baby.

" We'll name it John, and know with pleasure
  You'll stand "—Five guineas more, confound it !—
I wish they'd call'd it Nebuchadnezzar,
  Or thrown it in the Thames and drown'd it.

What have we next ?　A cival Dun :
　　" John Brown would take it as a favour "—
Another, and a surlier one,
　　" I can't put up with *sich* behaviour."

" Bill so long standing,"—" quite tired out,"—
　　" Must sit down to insist on payment,"
" Called ten times,"—Here's a fuss about
　　A few coats, waistcoats, and small raiment !

For once I'll send an answer, and in-
　　form Mr. Snip he needn't " call " so ;
But when his bill's as " tired of standing "
　　As he is, beg 'twill " sit down also."

This from my rich old Uncle Ned,
　　Thanking me for my annual present ;
And saying he last Tuesday wed
　　His cook-maid, Molly—vastly pleasant !

An ill-spelt note from Tom at school,
　　Begging I'll let him learn the fiddle ;
Another from that precious fool,
　　Miss Pyefinch, with a stupid riddle.

" D'ye give it up ? " indeed I do :
　　Confound these antiquated minxes ;
I won't play " *Billy Black* " to a " *Blue*,"
　　Or Œdipus to such old sphinxes.

A note sent up from Kent to show me,
　　Left with my bailiff, Peter King :
" I'll burn them precious stacks down, blow me !
　　" Yours most sincerely,
　　　　　　　　　　" CAPTAIN SWING."

Four begging letters with petitions,
　　One from my sister Jane, to pray
I'll " execute a few commissions "
　　In Bond Street, " when I go that way ; "

" And buy at Pearsal's in the City
 Twelve skeins of silk for netting purses :
Colour no matter, so it's pretty ;—
 Two hundred pens—" two hundred curses !

From Mistress Jones : " My little Billy
 Goes up his schooling to begin,
Will you just step to Piccadilly,
 And meet him when the coach comes in ?

" And then, perhaps, you will, as well, see
 The poor dear fellow safe to school
At Dr. Smith's in Little Chelsea ! "
 Heaven send he flog the little fool !

From Lady Snooks : " Dear Sir, you know
 You promised me last week a Rebus ;
A something smart and *apropos*,
 For my new Album ? "—Aid me, Phœbus !

" My first is follow'd by my second ;
 Yet should my first my second see,
A dire mishap it would be reckon'd,
 And sadly shocked my first would be,

" Were I but what my whole implies,
 And pass'd by chance across your portal ;
You'd cry, ' Can I believe my eyes ?
 I never saw so queer a mortal ! '

" For then my head would not be on,
 My arms their shoulders must abandon ;
My very body would be gone,
 I should not have a leg to stand on."

Come, that's dispatch'd—what follows ?—Stay,
 " Reform demanded by the nation ;
Vote for Tagrag and Bobtail ! " Ay,
 By Jove, a blessed *Reformation !*

Jack, clap the saddle upon Rose—
  Or no !—the filly—she's the fleeter ;
The devil take the rain—here goes,
  I'm off—a plumper for Sir Peter !

The Confession

THERE'S somewhat on my breast, father,
  There's somewhat on my breast !
The livelong day I sigh, father,
  And at night I cannot rest.
I cannot take my rest, father,
  Though I would fain do so ;
A weary weight oppresseth me—
  This weary weight of woe !

'Tis not the lack of gold, father,
  Nor want of worldly gear ;
My lands are broad, and fair to see,
  My friends are kind and dear.
My kin are leal and true, father,
  They mourn to see my grief ;
But oh ! 'tis not a kinsman's hand
  Can give my heart relief !

'Tis not that Janet's false, father,
  'Tis not that she's unkind ;
Tho' busy flatterers swarm around—
  I know her constant mind.
Tis not *her* coldness, father,
  That chills my labouring breast,
It's that confounded cucumber
  I've eat and can't digest.

Epigram

BRAVE L——, so says a knight of the pen,
" Has exposed himself much at the head of his men,"
As his men ran away without waiting to fight,
To expose himself there's to be first in the flight.
Had it not been as well, when he saw his men quail,
To have stay'd and exposed himself more at their tail ?
Or say, is it fair, in this noblest of quarrels,
To suffer the chief to engross all the laurels ?
No ! his men, so the muse to all Europe shall sing,
Have exposed themselves fully as much as their king.

Song

I

THERE sits a bird on yonder tree,
  More fond than Cushat Dove ;
There sits a bird on yonder tree,
  And sings to me of love.
Oh ! stoop thee from thine eyrie down !
  And nestle thee near my heart,
    For the moments fly, And the hour is nigh,
When thou and I must part,
      My love !
When thou and I must part.

II

In yonder covert lurks a Fawn,
  The pride of the sylvan scene ;
In yonder covert lurks a Fawn,
  And I am his only Queen ;
Oh ! bound from thy secret lair,

545

For the sun is below the west ;
    No mortal eye   May our meeting spy,
For all are closed in rest,
                My love !
Each eye is closed in rest.

III

Oh ! sweet is the breath of morn !
    When the sun's first beams appear ;
Oh ! sweet is the shepherd's strain,
    When it dies on the listening ear ;
And sweet the soft voice which speaks
    The Wanderer's welcome home ;
      But sweeter far   By yon pale mild star,
With our true Love thus to roam,
              My dear !
With our own true Love to roam !

Epigram

Eheu Fugaces

WHAT Horace says is, *Eheu fugaces*
Anni labuntur, Postume, Postume !
Years glide away, and are lost to me, lost to me !
Now, when the folks in the dance sport their merry toes,
Taglionis and Ellslers, Duvernays and Ceritos,
Sighing I murmur, " *O mihi præteritos !* "

Song

’Tis sweet to think the pure ethereal being,
　Whose mortal form reposes with the dead,
Still hovers round unseen, yet not unseeing,
　Benignly smiling o’er the mourner’s bed !

She comes in dreams, a thing of light and lightness.
　I hear her voice in still small accents tell
Of realms of bliss, and never-fading brightness,
　Where those who lov’d on earth, together dwell.

Ah ! yet a while, blest shade, thy flight delaying,
　The kindred soul with mystic converse cheer ;
To her rapt gaze, in visions bland displaying
　The unearthly glories of thy happier sphere !

Yet, yet remain ! till freed like thee, delighted,
　She spurns the thraldom of encumbering clay ;
Then, as on earth, in tenderest love united,
　Together seek the realms of endless day !

As I Laye A-Thynkynge

THE LAST LINES OF THOMAS INGOLDSBY

As I laye a-thynkynge, a-thynkynge, a-thynkynge,
Merrie sang the Birde as she sat upon the spraye !
　　There came a noble Knyghte,
　　With his hauberke shynynge brighte,
　　And his gallant heart was lyghte,
　　　　Free and gaye ;
As I laye a-thynkynge, he rode upon his waye.

As I laye a-thynkynge, a-thynkynge, a-thynkynge,
Sadly sang the Birde as she sat upon the tree !
   There seem'd a crimson plain,
   Where a gallant Knyghte laye slayne,
   And a steed with broken rein
      Ran free,
As I laye a-thynkynge, most pitiful to see !

As I laye a-thynkynge, a-thynkynge, a-thynkynge,
Merrie sang the Birde as she sat upon the boughe ;
   A lovely Mayde came bye,
   And a gentil youth was nyghe,
   And he breathed many a syghe
      And a vowe ;
As I laye a-thynkynge, her hearte was gladsome now.

As I laye a-thynkynge, a-thynkynge, a-thynkynge,
Sadly sang the Birde as she sat upon the thorne ;
   No more a youth was there,
   But a Maiden rent her haire,
   And cried in sad despaire,
      " That I was borne ! "
As I laye a-thynkynge, she perished forlorne.

As I laye a-thynkynge, a-thynkynge, a-thynkynge,
Sweetly sang the Birde as she sat upon the briar ;
   There came a lovely childe,
   And his face was meek and mild
   Yet joyously he smiled
      On his sire ;
As I laye a-thynkynge, a Cherub mote admire.

As I laye a-thynkynge, a-thynkynge, a-thynkynge,
And sadly sang the Birde as it perch'd upon a bier ;
   That joyous smile was gone,
   And the face was white and wan,
   As the downe upon the Swan
      Doth appear,
As I laye a-thynkynge—oh ! bitter flow'd the tear !

As I lay a-thynkynge, he rode upon his way

As I laye a-thynkynge, the golden sun was sinking,
O merrie sang that Birde as it glitter'd on her breast
    With a thousand gorgeous dyes,
    While soaring to the skies,
      'Mid the stars she seem'd to rise,
        As to her nest ;
As I laye a-thynkynge, her meaning was exprest :—
    " Follow, follow me away,
    It boots not to delay,"—
    'Twas so she seem'd to saye,
      " Here is rest ! "   T. I.

THE END

CPSIA information can be obtained at www.ICGtesting.com
Printed in the USA
LVOW02*1148201014

408843LV00003BA/3/P